Thomas Wright

Caricature history of the Georges, or annals of the house of

Hanover

comp. from squibs, broadsides, window pictures, lampoons, and pictorial

caricatures of the time

Thomas Wright

Caricature history of the Georges, or annals of the house of Hanover
comp. from squibs, broadsides, window pictures, lampoons, and pictorial caricatures of the time

ISBN/EAN: 9783741193248

Manufactured in Europe, USA, Canada, Australia, Japa

Cover: Foto ©Andreas Hilbeck / pixelio.de

Manufactured and distributed by brebook publishing software (www.brebook.com)

Thomas Wright

Caricature history of the Georges, or annals of the house of

Hanover

PREFACE.

The application of song, and satire, and picture to politics, is a thing of no modern date; for we trace it more or less among every people with whose history we have much acquaintance. Caricatures have been found in Egyptian tombs. The song and the lampoon were the constant attendants on, and incentives in, those incessant political struggles which, during the middle ages, were preparing for the formation of modern society; and many an old manuscript and sculptured block, whether of wood or stone, show that our forefathers in those times understood well the permanent force of pictorial satire. But it is more especially in religious matters that the middle ages, like antiquity, have shown a full perception of the importance of appealing through the eye to the hearts of the masses. In the rapid and temporary movements of political strife, this weapon could not be adopted with much effect until after the invention of printing, when, by a quick process, pictures engraved could be multiplied indefinitely. It was in the latter part of the sixteenth, and especially during the seventeenth century, that engraved caricatures became a very formidable instrument in working upon the feelings of the populace. Songs and lampoons, which every tongue could assist in circulating, have never ceased to show themselves in great abundance during every political movement since the period when the small amount of historical information which time has left us, allows us first to trace them; and they, as well as caricatures, have been by far too much neglected as historical documents,—for in them, perhaps, alone can we hope to trace many of the real motives which caused or exerted an influence over all the great popular revolutions of the past.

In the wish to show the utility of such records, by illustrating a given period of modern history from materials entirely derived from these sources, originated the following picture of the reigns of the first three Georges. It is to us an interesting period, because in it arose all those distinctions of political parties, and that peculiar spirit of constitutional antagonism, which exist at the present day. With it most of the political questions now in dispute took their rise. It consists in itself of two periods; the first, that in which the House of Brunswick was established on the throne of England upon the ruin of Jacobitism, and by the overthrow of the political creed of despotism; the second, that in which the same dynasty and its throne were defended against the encroachments of that fearful flood of republicanism which burst out from a neighbouring kingdom, and when they thus gained a victory over democracy. During these periods both the great political parties in this country came into play; in the first, the constitution owed its salvation to the Whigs; in the second, it was in all probability saved, perhaps not altogether designedly, by the Tories. It may be necessary to state that in the present work the political colour of the history has been generally given more or less as represented in the class of materials on which it is founded.

This was the period during which political caricatures flourished in England—when they were not mere pictures to amuse and excite a laugh, but when they were made extensively subservient to the political warfare that was going on. This use of them seems to have been imported from Holland, and to have first come into extensive practice after the revolution of 1688. Before that time, the art of engraving had not made sufficient progress in this country to allow them to be produced with much effect. The older caricatures, those, for instance, upon Cromwell, were chiefly executed by Dutch artists; and even in the great inundation of caricatures occasioned by the South-Sea bubble, the majority of them came from Holland. It was a defect of the earlier productions of this class, that they partook more of an emblematical character than of what we now understand by the term caricature. Even Hogarth, when he turned his hand to politics, could not shake off the old prejudice on this subject, and it would be difficult to point out worse examples than the two celebrated publications which drew upon him so much popular odium, "The Times." Modern caricature took its form from the pencils of a number of clever amateur artists, who were actively engaged in the political intrigues of the reign of George II.; it became a rage during the first years of his successor; and then seemed to be dying away, to revive suddenly in the splendid conceptions of Gillray. This able artist was certainly the first caricaturist of our country; during his long career, he produced a series of prints which form a complete history of the age.

The Work now laid before the public is necessarily but a sketch; only the more prominent points of the history of a hundred years are seized upon, and put forward in relief. The plan adopted has been to use caricatures and satires in the same manner that other historical illustrations are commonly used, by extracting from them the point, or at least a point, which bears more particularly or directly on the subject under consideration; thus a few figures are taken from a caricature, or a few lines from a song. Some of the more remarkable caricatures have been given entire, on separate plates. The idea, it is believed, is new, and I had to contend with the difficulties of labouring in so extensive a field, where nobody had previously cleared the way. These difficulties were, indeed, much greater than I foresaw, for no public collections of caricatures, or of political tracts or papers, exist. The poverty of our great national establishment, the British Museum, in works of this class, is deplorable. As far as regards caricatures, I had fortunately obtained access to several very extensive private collections. Unfortunately, no one, as far as I have been able to discover, has made any considerable collection of political songs, satires, and other such tracts, published during the last century and the present. This is a circumstance much to be regretted, for it is a class of popular literature which is rapidly perishing.

although the time is not yet past when such a collection might
be made with considerable success.

In conclusion, I will merely add, that I have had to deal with
a class of literature which is always more coarse than any other,
and during a period which was celebrated for anything rather
than for delicacy. I have steered clear of this evil as carefully
as I could without infringing on the truth of the picture of
manners and sentiments which this book is intended to represent. For a similar reason I have avoided entering upon the
religious disputes, which were productive of much caricature
and satire; but when caricature is applied to such subjects, it
seldom escapes the blot of being more or less profane.

So far I had written as a preface to the first edition of this
book, which appeared in 1848. I have only to add that, for
this new edition, I have carefully revised the whole, and that
I have made corrections where they seemed to be called for. It
is further to be remarked that the title of this book having been
originally " England under the House of Hanover," it has been
judged desirable, for several reasons, to change it in the second
edition to that which it now bears—which, in fact, describes it
to the general reader more intelligibly, as well as more correctly ;
for it is, strictly speaking, the History, by Caricature and Political Satire, of the Reigns of the Three Georges.

THOMAS WRIGHT.

Sydney-street, Brompton,
Dec. 1867.

CONTENTS.

CHAPTER IV.

GEORGE II.

CHAPTER V.

GEORGE II.

CHAPTER VI.

GEORGE II.

CHAPTER VII.

GEORGE II. AND III.

CONTENTS.

CONTENTS.

LIST OF FULL PAGE ENGRAVINGS.

———

CARICATURE HISTORY

OF

THE GEORGES.

CHAPTER I.

GEORGE I.

State of Parties at the end of Queen Anne's Reign—High-Church and
Dr. Sacheverell—Accession of George I.—Political Squibs that followed
—Attacks upon the ex-Ministers—Robert, the Political Juggler—
Agitation at the Elections—Jacobitish Popularity of the Duke of
Ormond—Caricatures of the Pretender—Jacobite Riots and the Riot
Act—Failure of the Rebellion and Exultation of the Whigs—History of
the London Jacobite Mob—The King's Departure for Hanover.

IT was the 30th July, 1714, when a queen of England had
just sunk upon her death-bed; and, perhaps, no monarch ever
left the world in the midst of more critical circumstances. Not
that the loss of the Queen herself was the object of any especial
regret; for we are informed in the papers of the time, that, on
the morning of the 31st, when it was reported in London that
Anne was dead, the public funds immediately rose three or four
per cent., and that in the afternoon, when it was known that
she was still alive, they fell at once to their former value.

We must review briefly the politics of the years which had
immediately preceded, to understand this singular position of
affairs. Two opposing parties had arisen out of the revolution
of '88. The Whigs, as the natural and staunch supporters of the
new state of things, had continued, with but slight interruptions,
to hold the reins of government, when they were at length
thrown out of power by the intrigues of the Bed-chamber in
1710, at a moment when they had every reason to suppose
themselves strong in the confidence and sympathies of their
countrymen. The Tories, even when most moderate, were

B

secret well-wishers to the exiled family; and this feeling, cherished more or less strongly, produced various shades or gradations of party, until it expressed itself in a form little short of open treason in the non-jurors and Jacobites. There can be little doubt that the whole Tory party of the reign of Queen Anne would have ultimately declared in favour of the Pretender, had he once obtained any certain prospect of success.

The antipathy between the two great political parties was of the bitterest description; and each endeavoured to render its opponents odious to the public by personal abuse and calumny, which were scattered abroad with the scurrilous licence of the press that had been handed down from the times of the Commonwealth and Charles the Second. It is hardly possible to conceive anything more abhorrent to good feeling than the virulent language of the political pamphlets of the age of which we are speaking, which crept even into the more respectable literature of the day. A Tory newspaper, the *Post-Boy* of March 30, 1714. observes seriously, that "To desire the Whigs to forbear lying, we are sensible would be a most unreasonable request; because it is their nature, and their faction could not subsist without it." Their enemies endeavoured to throw upon the Whigs, as a body, the imputation with which the Commonwealth men had been stigmatized in the previous century : they were a hypocritical set of schismatics and republicans, worthy only to figure on the gallows or the pillory. A song, circulated in 1712, describes them as a pack of ill-grained dogs.

> "There's atheists and deists, and fawning Dissenter ;
> There's republican sly, and long-winded canter ;
> There's heresy, schism, and mild moderation,
> That's still in the wrong for the good of the nation ;
> There's Baptist, Socinian, and Quakers with scruples,
> Till kind toleration links 'em all in church-couples.

> "Some were bred in the army, some dropt from the fleet ;
> Under bulks some were litter'd, and some in the street ;
> Some are good harmless curs, without teeth or claws ;
> Some were whelp'd in a shop, and some runners at laws ;
> Some were wretched poor curs, mongrel starvers and setters,
> Till, dividing the spoil, they put in with their betters."

The Whigs were by no means backward in throwing similar dirt in the faces of the Tories, whom they looked upon in the light of traitors and rebels. Among the clergy, unfortunately, these political animosities were more acrimonious than among the laity, and the pulpit everywhere teemed with seditious and libellous sermons. A considerable portion of the clergy had refused to acknowledge King William, and were strongly tainted with Jacobitism; and a still greater number had only conformed to the circumstances of the times, reluctantly and with mental reservations, in order to preserve the temporal advantages they derived from the Church. Although several of the bishops, such as Burnet and Hoadly, with a number of the lower clergy, were distinguished by their liberal and tolerant feelings, a very large party, who claimed the lofty-sounding title of the High-Church, hated everything like a Dissenter with an intense spirit of persecution, and detested the Whigs as much for the protection they afforded them, as for their political creed. The Tory papers could hardly allude to a misfortune which had occurred to a Dissenter without a sneer or a joke. The *Weekly Packet* of November 12, 1715, has the following article:—"On Monday last, the Presbyterian minister at Epsom broke his leg, which was so miserably shattered, that it was cut off the next day. This is a great token, that those pretenders to sanctity do not walk so circumspectly as they give out." The other party was by no means slow in retaliating on the Church, which lost its dignity and its sacred character in these unseemly disputes. The Whig pamphlets and songs pictured in broad colours the unsanctified lives of many of the Church clergy, their venality and greediness; and one song ends with the taunt, that

> "They swallow all up
> Without e'en a gulp:
> There's nought chokes a priest but a halter."

Unfortunately, too, many of the leading men on both sides sullied their great talents by dishonesty and profligacy, and gave a handle for the malice of their opponents.

The Revolution had been essentially aristocratic in character, and no appeal had then been made to the passions of the multitude. Hence arose the great strength of the Whigs in the House of Lords. The first regular political mob was a High-Church mob, stirred up for the purpose of raising a clamour against the Whigs, and to influence the elections for Parliament. This appeal to the lower orders was made through a divine of very little moral character and no great abilities, the notorious Dr. Henry Sacheverell, who, a renegade from Whiggism which had not been profitable to him, was now a violent Tory with a better prospect of gain; and, after two or three attacks on the Government, which had been passed over with contempt, preached a sermon at St. Paul's before the Lord Mayor and

Corporation on the 5th of November, 1709; in which, taking
for his text the words of St. Paul, " Perils from false brethren,"
he held up the Whig Lord Treasurer Godolphin to the hatred
of his countrymen under the title of Volpone, attacked in a
scurrilous manner the bishops who were against persecuting the
Dissenters, condemned the Revolution, and asserted in the
broadest sense the doctrine of passive obedience to arbitrary
power. Such of the congregation as listened to the sermon
were offended at the language of the preacher; and the matter
was brought before the Privy Council, which determined upon
an impeachment, and thus fell into a snare that had perhaps
been laid for them. The seditious sermon was printed, and the
Tories exerted themselves with so much activity in dispersing it
abroad, that no less than forty thousand copies are said to have
been sold. A tedious trial, ill-conducted, ended in the condemnation of the sermon (which was burnt by the hangman),
and in the Doctor being inhibited from preaching during three
years. The trial was the making of Sacheverell; he was now
held forth by the High-Church party as a martyr for the good
cause; and it was darkly intimated that the Queen (who had a
strong leaning towards the High Church) secretly approved of
his conduct. Every kind of means was employed to provoke
people to join in the cry, that the Church and the Crown were
in danger from those who now ruled the country, and that
Sacheverell was persecuted because he had stood up in their
defence. Incendiary sermons were preached from the pulpit;
money is said to have been freely distributed among the mob,
and songs were written to keep up the excitement; even caricatures, which at this time were not so much in use as half a
century later, were made in considerable numbers on this occasion. In fact, it was the first event of English history in the
eighteenth century which furnished a subject for caricatures.
Dean Kennett, in a pamphlet published in 1714,* tells us, that,
" For distinguishing the friends of Dr. Sacheverell as the only
true churchmen, and representing his enemies as betrayers of
the Church, there were several cuts and pictures designed for
the mob; among others a copper-plate, with a crown, mitre,
bible, and common prayer, as supported by the truly evangelical
and apostolical, truly monarchical and episcopal, truly legal and
canonical, or truly Church of England fourteen," who had sup-

* *The Wisdom of looking backwards*, p. 13. Several of the prints here
alluded to are in the collection of Mr. Hawkins. In general, they are
equally poor in design and execution. I have not met with a copy of the
"copper-plate" described by Kennett.

ported Sacheverell through his trial. A verse or two will be
quite sufficient as a sample of the Sacheverell songs. One of
them, entitled "The Doctor Militant; or, Church Triumphant,"
to be sung to the tune of "Pakington's Pound," begins with the
following attack upon the Whigs:—

> "Bold Whigs and fanatics now strive to pull down
> The true Church of England, both mitre and crown;
> To introduce anarchy into the nation,
> As they did in Oliver's late usurpation.
>   In Queen Anne's happy reign
>   They attempt it again,
> Who burn the text, and the preacher arraign.
> Sachev'rell, Sachev'rell, thou art a brave man,
> To stand for the Church and our gracious Queen Anne."

It must be confessed that there was little in the doings of the
Whigs of Queen Anne's reign to justify the fear that they were
introducing anarchy. After a few more verses in this strain,
and some allusions to the turbulence under the Commonwealth,
the song ends with a lamentation for the loss of the "*golden
days*" of King Charles the Second:—

> "While knaves thus contended to sit on the throne,
> The owner had hopes to recover his own;
> And so it fell out in the midst of their jars,
> The King's restoration did finish the wars;
>   In whose golden days
>   The Church held the keys,
> And kept in subjection such rebels as these.
> For there were Sachev'rells, whom God did inspire
> To rescue the Church from fanatical fire."

But the allusions of the time show us that there were many
songs of a far more violent, and even treasonable character,
which were sung about the streets, and only printed clandestinely.
Few or none of these have been preserved, but they probably
pointed much more distinctly to the real aim of the party, the
introduction of the Pretender, to the exclusion of the House of
Hanover, which was the covert design of all this abuse of the
Cromwellian period and lavish praise of the reign of the restored
Charles. This design we shall very soon see carried out more
openly. Another song, entitled "High-Church Loyalty," goes
on in the same tone as the one quoted above:—

> "Ye Whigs and Dissenters, what would ye have done!
> Ne'er think of restoring your old '41.
>   Then fill up a bowl, fill it up to the brim;
>   Here's a health to all those whom the Church do esteem!

We know the pretence, you for liberty bawl;
But had you your will, you'd destroy Church and all.
    Then fill, &c.
      *   *   *   *

While the Phœnix stands up, and the Bow bells do ring,
Here's a health to Sachev'rell, and God bless the Queen !'

This song was answered and parodied in doggrel about as good
as that in which it was itself written :—

"You pinnacle-flyers, where would you advance !
What, would ye be bringing of Perkin from France ?
Instead of a bowl fill'd up to the brim,
A halter for those that would bring Perkin in !"

The Whigs not only wrote and sung against Sacheverell, but
they caricatured him, and that very severely. In an engraving

THE THREE FALSE BRETHREN.

of this time the Doctor is represented in the act of writing his
sermon, prompted on one side by the Pope and on the other by
the Devil, these three being the "false brethren" from whom
the Church was really in danger. The other party, in revenge,
caricatured Bishop Hoadly, the friend of the Dissenters, and one
of the most able of the Low-Church party, in a number of
prints, in which the evil one was pictured as closeted with that
prelate, whose bodily infirmities were turned to ridicule. Moreover, they made a nearly exact copy of the caricature of
Sacheverell, with a bishop mitred in the place of the Pope, and
the Devil flying away in terror at the Doctor's sermon, thus
insinuating that this miserable tool was the great defence of the
Church of Christ against the attacks of Satan. A remarkable
instance of this adaptation of one design to the two sides of the

question is furnished by the medal, which must have been distributed in large quantities, having on one side the head of the preacher surrounded by the words H. SACH. D.D., while the inscription on the reverse, IS FIRM TO THEE, surrounded on some copies of the medal a mitre, and on others the head of the Pope, thus being calculated to suit purchasers of all parties.* The Whigs looked upon him as the trumpeter of the Pope, while with the Tories he was the champion of the Church of England. For the Whigs and Dissenters had raised the cry of "No Popery!" in answer to the Tory outcry of the danger of the Church; and every sensible man saw that the contest between High Church and Low Church was in reality a struggle for the succession to the crown between the House of Stuart and the House of Hanover. A large portion of the nation looked forwards, with a variety of different feelings, to the possibility of Queen Anne being succeeded on the throne by the Pretender.

It was clearly with this object that a cabal sought to displace the Whig ministry. Plunder and mischief were a much greater incitement than any abstract principles to the class of persons who composed the mob; and the Dissenters, who were not persecuted for any crimes of their own, but for the pretended offences of the older age of Presbyterian rule (for under the tolerant governments of King William and Queen Anne they had become a quiet and harmless portion of the community), were deliberately pointed out as objects of attacks. On the second day of Sacheverell's trial, the mob which had followed him to Westminster Hall was assembled in the evening; and, being joined by a multitude of persons of the very lowest class of society, proceeded to Lincoln's-Inn Fields, where was the meeting-house of a celebrated Dissenting preacher, Mr. Burgess, now known by the name of Gate-street Chapel. The mob burst into this chapel; and, amid ferocious shouts of "High Church and Sacheverell!" tore out the pulpit, pews, and everything combustible, and with these and the cushions and bibles made a large bonfire in the middle of Lincoln's-Inn Fields. They

* The caricatures here alluded to will all be found in the collection of Mr. Hawkins. The figure of Dr. Sacheverell was placed on a multitude of different articles of ornament or use. Mr. C. Roach Smith possesses a tobacco-stopper, with a medal-formed extremity, bearing the head of Sacheverell, and the reverse of the mitre, with the same inscription as the medal described in the text. Amid the virulent partyism of this age, all kinds of ornamented articles were made the means of conveying caricatures, and we even find them on seals for letters, and on buttons for people's coats, as somewhat later they appear on playing-cards and on ladies' fans.

treated in the same manner other well-known meeting-houses in Long Acre, in New Street, Shoe Lane, in Leather Lane, in Blackfriars, and in Clerkenwell. In the latter neighbourhood they mistook an episcopal chapel for a Dissenter's meeting-house, because it had no steeple, and would have destroyed the house of Bishop Burnet, had they not met with a vigorous resistance. No stop was put to their proceedings until it was reported that they were going to attack the Bank, when they were dispersed by a detachment of the Queen's guards. It was commonly stated that persons of a higher class of society in hackney-coaches directed the movements of this mob, and distributed money. In fact, the High-Church party approved of these proceedings, and justified them by referring to the attacks on Popish chapels at the period of the Revolution. The writer of a poem "Upon the Burning of Mr. Burgess's Pulpit" exclaims,

> "Invidious Whigs, since you have made your boast,
> That you a Church of England priest would roast,
> Blame not the mob for having a desire,
> With Presbyterian tubs to light the fire."

The success which had so far attended this plan encouraged Sacheverell's patrons to carry it further, and to try its effects on the mobs of other parts of the kingdom. The Doctor made a progress through various parts of England, marching in a sort of triumphal procession, and was received in cities and towns as though he had been some great dignitary.

> "Good folks, I pray, have you not heard
> Of a criminal of late,
> Who has rode through town and country too
> In a most pompous state?
> In a most pompous state indeed,
> In a train of brainless fools,
> All managed by some knaves above,
> And made their easy tools."

So says one of the Whig ballads of the day; and the object of Sacheverell's progress was apparent to all. Robert Harley and Henry St. John, who were shortly afterwards raised to the peerage by the titles of Lords Oxford and Bolingbroke, had obtained the ear of the Queen, and thrown out the Whigs without possessing the confidence of the nation; and they seized the moment of excitement thus raised by Sacheverell for the election of a new Parliament, and succeeded in obtaining a large Tory majority. It is hardly necessary to describe the reckless manner in which the new ministry sacrificed the honour and interests of the

country at Utrecht, or the succession of intrigues which ended
in the disgrace of the Earl of Oxford only three days before the
period mentioned at the beginning of this chapter. Bolingbroke, now at the height of his ambition, and less scrupulous
even than his former colleague, formed a ministry which could
be designed for no other purpose than to sacrifice this country
to France and introduce the Pretender,—a ministry of which
more than one-half were subsequently attainted of high treason.

On the 1st of August, 1714, Queen Anne died. The plans of
the Jacobite ministry had, in the meantime, been entirely defeated by the energetic activity of the Whig nobles, and George I.
was proclaimed King of England without opposition. As
might naturally be expected, the new monarch threw himself
entirely into the hands of the Whigs. To them in a great
measure he owed his throne; and he could not help looking
upon the Tories as the personal enemies of his family. This
treatment probably drove the latter to unite in stronger
measures of opposition than many of them would, in other
circumstances, have approved.

The exultation of the party now restored to power was soon
visible in a number of lampoons and satirical writings. On the
7th of August, the *Flying Post*, one of the most violent organs
of the Whigs, gave, instead of its usual proportion of intelligence
and political observations, three songs, under the title of "A
Hanover Garland," the third of which concludes with the
lines,—

> "Keep out, keep out Han—'s [*Hanover's*] line,
> 'Tis only J—s [*James*] has right divine,
> As Romish parsons cant and whine,
>   And sure we must believe them:
> But if their Prince can't come in peace,
> Their stock will every day decrease,
> And they will ne'er see Perkin's face,
>   So their false hopes deceive them."

The same journal, on the 10th of August, gives a burlesque list
of articles for public sale, among which are, "The Art of
Billingsgate; or, infallible rules to rail and talk nonsense. In
10 volumes. By Harry Sacheverell. They will be sold cheap
because they are lately damag'd with mum;" and "Rules for
making a bad peace when an enemy is under one's power; or,
the way to part with all rather than ask anything. Wrote by
a minister of state to Queen Dido, and dedicated to all fools and
ninnyhammers." Both these sarcastic allusions contained intimations of the desire, if not the design, of revenge.

In the moment of his success, Sacheverell is said to have

been flattered with the prospect of a bishopric; but the only preferment he eventually obtained was the good living of St. Andrew's, Holborn, and he had long been looked upon with the personal contempt he deserved by those whose tool he had been, when the accession of the House of Hanover came to excite his apprehensions. We learn from the newspapers of the day, that in the first week after the death of Queen Anne, there was some talk of ejecting the Doctor from his living; and his name was brought forward on one or two other occasions. But he seems to have been cautious of provoking too far a party in power, when he had evidently much to lose and nothing to gain; and, as his own party had soon more illustrious martyrs to cry up, in the persons of Lord Bolingbroke and the Duke of Ormond, he was regarded as an object too mean even for persecution, and he was allowed to enjoy what he had until his death.

It was, however, soon evident that the late ministers were not likely to escape with the same ease. The cabal by which they had risen first to power had been peculiarly undignified; not only the mode in which they had concluded the war, but the whole of their administration had been anti-national in the extreme; and the persecutions to which they had subjected many of the distinguished Whigs now led to recrimination and passions which were not to be pacified without vengeance. The *Flying Post* of the 10th of August, the same in which occurs the burlesque just mentioned, contained also the following advertisement:—" The traytor's coat of arms, curiously engraved on a copper-plate: the crest a Welshman strip'd of his grandeur, playing upon a hornpipe, to lull his senses under his misfortunes; an Earl's coronet, filled with French flower-de-luces, and tipt with French gold; the Pretender's head in the middle. The coat, three toads in a black field; the three toads are the old French coat of arms,—being in reverse denotes treason in perfection. The supporters are, a French Popish priest in his habit, with a warming-pan upon his shoulder, and a penknife in his left hand, ready to execute what the Popish religion dictates upon Protestants: on the other side a Scots Highlander, some call him Gregg; a pack upon his back, and a letter in his hand, betraying the kingdom's safety; for his encouragement and protection, he has his master's magic wand and borrowed golden angel. The motto, *Pour la veuve et l'orphelin*, i. e. For the widow and orphan. Sold by A. Doulter, without Temple Bar." This was apparently the first English caricature published during the reign of George I.; a *second*

edition was advertised shortly after its appearance, and it therefore probably enjoyed considerable popularity, yet I have not
been able to ascertain that a single copy is now in existence.
It was of course aimed at the ex-Lord Treasurer, Robert
Harley, Earl of Oxford, one of whose creatures, a Scot named
Gregg, had been engaged in some unpatriotic intrigues during
the late ministry. The "widow and orphan" were Mary
of Modena and the Pretender. The warming-pan will be
explained a little farther on.

The conduct of Anne's Tory ministry began now also to
be arraigned in political romances and tales, a style of writing
which had been imported from France, and had become
popular since the Restoration. About the end of August
appeared the "History of the Crown Inn, with the death of the
widow, and what happened thereon," dedicated to the Lord
John Bull. The "Secret History of the White Staff" (by De
Foe), and the different pamphlets in answer to it and in defence
of it, in which the character of the Lord Treasurer Oxford
(who, having been the principal mover in the Bed-chamber
plots by which Marlborough and Godolphin had been overthrown, was an object of especial odium among the Whigs) was
very freely discussed, also made con-
siderable noise. At the beginning
of the year 1715 was published "A
Second Tale of a Tub; or, the History of Robert Powel, the Puppet-
showman," written by Thomas Burnet, a son of the Bishop of Salisbury;
in which the various intrigues by
which Harley and his colleagues had
attained to power are told under
fictitious characters, in a manner
well calculated to take hold upon
the sentiments of an ordinary class
of readers. A second edition of this
book was published within a few
weeks. In the frontispiece, the Earl
of Oxford, the great political juggler
of the time, is caricatured under the
figure of Powel (a man immortalized
in the *Spectator* as the keeper of a
puppet-show in the Piazza of Covent

ROBERT, THE POLITICAL JUGGLER.

Garden) exhibiting his puppets to
the world. "Well, gentlemen, you shan't be baulk'd. I'll hang

ou. ..ny canvas too, and like my brother monster-mongers, well daub'd into the bargain. Stare then—and behold—the novel figure. You see what is written over his head, *This is Mr. Powel*—that's he—the little crooked gentleman, that holds a *staff* in his hand, without which he must fall. The sight is well worth your money, for you may not see such another these seven years, nay, perhaps not this age." In one part of this book we have a rather ingenious story or vision of au island of noses, in which the dreamer meets with a large hooked nose (Marlborough), covered with rags and dirt, the reward he had received for beating the enemies of his country. Suddenly a procession of flat-noses is seen approaching; "for a distemper lately come from France [an allusion to the intrigues of Anne's last ministry with the French court] has swept away most of our palates, and sunk our noses in the manner that you will see, and that is one reason why the high hook-noses have of late been so much out of fashion." "My friend was going on, when, at the end of the aforesaid cavalcade, a parcel of rabble flat Frenchify'd bridgeless noses came and set upon him in a most base and barbarous manner, and with a snuffling broken tone, call'd him 'Traytor!' Upon which my friendly Mucterian took to his heels, and by that escap'd their fury. I could not but ask in a fret why they dealt with him in that inhuman manner; which I no sooner had said, when up comes a nose quite black and rotten, and in pieces of words tells me that I am a sawcy fellow to question a thing so well known. 'As what?' quoth I. 'As what?' says he; why, that fellow you was in company with is a traytor, for 'tis plain he beat our enemies, and so prolonged an offensive war. Besides he's a high hooked nose, and is a traytor of course!' Indeed, I observed my friend's nose was something high and crooked; but, in all my life, I never heard the shape of a nose urged as treason before. In short, these vile flat-noses [the Tories] did not stay for my answer; but one of the most stinking among them blew himself out upon me, and then called me 'Nasty fellow!' and so left me to wipe up the affront."

The discomfited Tories, who were not generally backward in taking up the pen, or deficient in able men to use it, were at first entirely confounded by the sudden and unexpected course of events. One of the first lampoons upon the Whigs came from the pen of the scurrilous publican-poet, Ned Ward. Marlborough, who had sought quiet in voluntary exile,—the high hooked-nose escaped from the flat-noses, as Thomas Burnett has it,—returned immediately on the death of the Queen, landed at Dover, and was conducted in triumph to London by a long train of gentlemen in carriages and on horseback, on the 4th of August. The Hanoverian envoy, Bothmar, writes, that the Duke " came to town amidst the acclamations of the people, as if he had gained another battle of Hochstet." Ned Ward gave vent to the spleen of his party by ridiculing this procession in Hudibrastic doggrel, under the title of " The Republican Procession ; or, the tumultuous Cavalcade." Ward describes the Duke's escort as

> " Consisting of a factious crew,
> Of all the sects in Ross's "View,"*
> From Calvin's Anti-Babylonians,
> Down to the frantick Muggletonians ;
> Mounted on founder'd skins and bones,
> That scarce could crawl along the stones,
> As if the Roundheads had been robbing
> The higglers' inns of Ball and Dobbin,
> And all their skeletonian tits
> That could but halt along the streets :
> The frightful troops of thin-jaw'd zealots,
> Curs'd enemies to kings and prelates.
> Those champions of religious errors,
> Looking as if the prince of terrors
> Was coming with his dismal train
> To *plague* the city once again."

The Tories of that age affected to look with contempt on the commercial interests of the country, and on the moneyed houses of the City, for the merchants had placed their confidence in the foreign policy of the Whigs. Ward, after speaking of the " Low-Church city elders," says :—

> " Next these, who, like to blazing stars,
> Portend domestic feuds and wars,
> Camp managers and bank-directors,
> King-killers, monarchy-electors,
> And votaries for lord-protectors ;
> That, had old subtle Satan spread
> His net o'er all the cavalcade,
> He might at one surprizing pull
> Have fill'd his low'r dominion full
> Of atheists, rebels, Whigs, and traytors,
> Reforming knaves and regulators ;
> And sav'd at once this land of more
> And greater plagues than Egypt bore."

Under the circumstances of the times, the Tories did not

* Alexander Ross was the author of a book, rather well known at that time, entitled, " View of all Religions, with a Discovery of all known Heresies, and Lives of Notorious Hereticks," published in 1696.

venture, except in rare instances, to exhibit the extent of their exasperation by the ordinary way of publicity. They reckoned again upon the mob to embarrass the Government, and a multitude of low libels and seditious papers were hawked and distributed about the streets for halfpence and pence, which kept the populace in a perpetual state of excitement. Few of these papers are now preserved. There is one, in a broadside, "price one penny," in the British Museum, which, under the title of "A Dialogue between my Lord B——ke and my Lord W——n," (Bolingbroke and Wharton,) contains a satirical attack on the Duke of Marlborough, when he was returning to England. Before the end of August a multitude of such penny and halfpenny libels were spread over the country, in which the Whigs were compared to the levellers of the days of Charles I.; and attacks, as scurrilous and indecent as they were unprovoked, were heaped upon the Dissenters. "The Tories," says a newspaper of the date just mentioned, "who have the *black* mob on their side, cry, 'No calves' heads !' 'No king-killers !'" In November, the political hawkers and ballad-singers had become extremely troublesome about the streets of London, and the Lord Mayor was compelled to seize upon many of them, and throw them into the House of Correction. On the 16th of November, an Order of Council appeared for the suppression and punishment of "false and scandalous libels" hawked about the streets; and on the 24th of the same month another proclamation to the same purpose was made; but the object of these measures appears to have been but partially effected. The *Political State* (November, 1714, p. 446) gives the titles of some of the seditious pamphlets sent abroad in this manner; among which appears "The Duke of Marlborough's Cavalcade," probably the poem of Ned Ward described above. Some of these papers and ballads appear to have been of a treasonable description. To give instances from a little later date, out of a great number which might be collected together, we may mention, that, in the *Weekly Packet* of January 7, 1716, we are informed, "Last Monday the Lord Mayor committed a woman to Newgate for singing a seditious ballad in Gracechurch Street;" and it is stated in the *Flying Post* of the 27th of May immediately following, that "last Saturday" the grand jury of the City of London "presented a seditious and scandalous paper, called 'Robin's last Shift, or Shift Shifted,' and the singing of scandalous ballads about the streets, as a common nuisance, tending to alienate the minds of the people; and we hear an order will be published to apprehend those who cry about or sing such scandalous papers. They have also presented such as go about with wheelbarrows and dice, and make it their practice to cheat people; and such as go about streets to clean shoes on the Sabbath day." Scraps of information like this give us a curious view of the streets of London nearly a hundred and fifty years ago.

The prejudices against Dissenters were inflamed in every possible manner, for the hardly concealed purpose of raising a new High-Church mob, and exerting through it the same violent influence over the elections which had been so successful in bringing together the Parliament that was now separating. Two agents, opposite enough in their characters, were actively employed in this work—the pulpit and the stage. Before the end of December it was found necessary, by a royal proclamation, to order the clergy to avoid entering upon state affairs in their sermons. At the theatre, the plays or the prologues often contained political sentiments or allusions which led at times to serious riots. Farces were brought out in which the Dissenters were exhibited in an odious or degrading light. To quote from the journals of the period at which the consequent excitement was pushed up to its highest point, and when mobs were perpetrating mischief and destruction in many parts of the kingdom, we find advertised, in the beginning of June, 1715, "The City Ramble; or, the Humours of the Compter. As it is now acted with universal applause at the theatre in Lincoln's Inn Fields. By Captain Knipe." It is added, that the book was "adorned with a curious frontispiece, respecting a Presbyterian teacher and his doxy as committed to the Compter." I have not been able to meet with the book, or the "curious frontispiece," which was what may be looked upon legitimately as a caricature; but it had no doubt an immediate aim, for the theatre in Lincoln's Inn Fields was in close proximity to the same celebrated Dissenters' meeting-house which had been so rudely treated by the Sacheverell mob. Even at Oxford, after a High-Church riot about this time, a member of the University, in an anonymous tract in justification of it, stated that an anabaptist preacher of that town had baptized two young women in the morning, and been found in bed between them at night,—one of those slanderous stories which had been borrowed from the days of the Cavaliers. .

The effect of this incessant agitation was not long in showing itself; for the first outbreak took place on the day of the King's coronation, the 20th of October, 1714. On the evening of that day, the citizens of Bristol illuminated their windows, and made bonfires in the streets, and the corporation gave a ball. The first signal for the riot which followed is said to have been a report that the Whigs were going to burn the effigy of Sacheverell; upon which a mob suddenly collected together and rushed through the streets, breaking the windows that were illuminated, and putting out the bonfires, at the same time raising ferocious shouts of "Down with the Roundheads! God bless Dr. Sacheverell!" They repaired to the town-hall, and threw large stones through the windows of the ball-room, to the great danger of the persons assembled there. The attacks of the mob were now more especially directed against the Dissenters; they entirely gutted the house of one of them, a baker named Stevens, who was killed by the assailants in an attempt to expostulate with them. This fatal catastrophe appears to have arrested the mob, and no further mischief was done; but several of the rioters were tried and severely punished. The town of Chippenham, in Wiltshire, continued in an uproar during several nights, and houses were attacked and their inmates ill-treated. Other riots, equally alarming, occurred at the same time at Norwich, Reading, Birmingham, and Bedford. At Birmingham the mob was very violent, and their shout was, "Sacheverell for ever! Down with the Whigs!" At Bedford, where the proceedings of the mob seem to have been countenanced by the magistrates, the public May-pole was dressed in mourning. In spite of a proclamation against riots, issued on the 2nd of November, the mobs in many places continued to create disturbances. At Axminster, in Devonshire, on the 5th of November, the "High-Church rabble," as the newspapers call them, shouted for the Pretender, and drank his health as King of England.

The elections which came on in January were carried on even with more violence than those of 1710; * but times were altered, and the Whigs obtained an overpowering majority. It was on these two occasions that English elections of members for Parliament first took that character of turbulence and acrimony which for more than a century destroyed the peace and tranquillity of our country towns, and from which they have only been relieved within the last few years. The *Flying Post* of January 27, 1715, gives the following burlesque "bill of costs

---

* Many seditious and treasonable writings were spread about in January, one of which made much noise, and was vigorously prosecuted. Under the title of "English Advice to the Freeholders of England," it was a violent attack upon the Whigs, both personally and collectively, and was particularly rancorous against the Duke of Marlborough; it pointed out the pretended dangers of the Church from the principles of the House of Hanover, and exhorted the electors to fly to its aid.

for a late Tory election in the West," in which part of the country the Tory interest was strongest:—

	£	s.	d.
Imprimis, for bespeaking and collecting a mob .	10	0	0
Item, for many suits of knots for their heads	30	0	0
For scores of huzza-men	40	0	0
For roarers of the word "Church" . . .	40	0	0
For a set of "No Roundhead" roarers . .	40	0	0
For several gallons of Tory punch on church tomb-stones	30	0	0
For a majority of clubs and brandy-bottles .	20	0	0
For bell-ringers, fiddlers, and porters . .	10	0	0
For a set of coffee-house praters . . .	40	0	0
For extraordinary expense for cloths and lac'd hats on show days, to dazzle the mob . . .	50	0	0
For Dissenters' damners	40	0	0
For demolishing two houses . . .	200	0	0
For committing two riots	200	0	0
For secret encouragement to the rioters .	40	0	0
For a dozen of perjury men	100	0	0
For packing and carriage paid to Gloucester .	50	0	0
For breaking windows	20	0	0
For a gang of alderman-abusers . . .	40	0	0
For a set of notorious liars . . .	50	0	0
For pot-ale	100	0	0
For law, and charges in the King's Bench .	300	0	0
	1460	0	0

It will be observed in this "bill" that bribery is not put down as one of the prominent features of an election at this period; violence was, as yet, found to be more effective than corruption.

The new Parliament met towards the end of March. The following statement in the *Weekly Packet* (a Tory paper) of April 2, 1715, will furnish an amusing picture, not only of parliamentary manners *outside* the house at this date, but of the wild spirit of party :—" Last week the footmen belonging to the members of the House of Commons, according to the custom of their masters, (which they had strictly imitated for more than thirty years,) proceeded to the choice of a Speaker; when those that espouse the cause of the Whigs chose Mr. Strickland's man, and the Tory livery gentry the servant of Sir Thomas Morgan. Hence a battle ensued between the two contending parties, wherein several broken heads discovered the resolution of each to abide by its respective choice, though the combatants were at that time forced to leave the victory undecided (the House rising). But on Monday last they returned to their former trial of skill; and the Tories, after an obstinate resistance from the

c

Whigs, who would by no means show themselves passive, but disputed their ground inch by inch, had the better of their adversaries, and carried their mock Speaker three times round Westminster Hall. After which, he that was chosen to fill their chair, as well as his predecessor, according to ancient usage, spent their crowns apiece in drink at a dinner, which an adjacent alehouse entertained them with gratis."

No sooner had the Parliament assembled, than the Tories were alarmed by the threatened impeachment of the late ministers. This gave rise to a fierce controversy with the pen, before it became a matter of debate in the senate: for two or three weeks, pamphlet upon pamphlet, on both sides of the question, issued daily from the press, some written calmly and moderately, while others were characterized by all the bitterness and scurrility of the party spirit of those days. Among the Whig writers, who made the greatest noise in their different circles, were Thomas Burnett, already mentioned, whose father the Bishop was now dead, and the more prolific party-writer John Dunton, whose pamphlets were calculated for wider distribution among a somewhat lower class of readers. Burnett was rather rudely handled in this controversy, and was made the butt of several satirical tracts, the writer of one of which undertook to prove that he was asleep when he wrote his pamphlet in defence of the impeachment. Dunton was a scheming needy writer; he was a broken bookseller, and now, as old age approached, sought to gain a support from Government by the zeal and number of his political writings; he was withal somewhat of a wag. A few months after the date of which we are speaking, on the 1st of May, 1716, we learn from the *Flying Post* that John Dunton and "a devil" ("*i. e.* a printer's boy:" this appears to be an early instance of the use of the term) were seen marching through the streets of London, and distributing a book entitled "Seeing's believing; or, King George proved a Usurper." The citizens, astonished that any one should possess the impudence to sell such a book openly, probably thought he was mad; but he was without delay arrested and carried first before the Lord Mayor, and subsequently before one of the Secretaries of State. A rumour was soon spread abroad that Dunton had become a convert to Jacobitism; and, while the Whigs were scandalised at his defection, the Tories rejoiced loudly at having gained so popular a champion. But their joy was changed into vexation, when it was made known that the tract in question, instead of being a treasonable libel, was a bitter lampoon on their own party; and Dunton and his friends went to a noted Whig tavern in St. John's Lane, to laugh in their sleeves and to drink loyal toasts.

The history of the impeachments is well known: Bolingbroke and Ormond fled to France, and openly joined the Pretender, and they were accordingly attainted. Oxford was thrown into the Tower; but, after a wearisome imprisonment, he escaped without further hurt. The result was advantageous, as far as it secured the principle that ministers of the Crown are personally responsible for the acts of their administration; and it forced secret enemies, who were plotting against the Government, to show themselves openly. Indeed, this measure, probably more than anything else, led to the premature outbreak of the Jacobite rebellion towards the end of the year.

Ormond was the only one of the late ministers who enjoyed much popularity, and his name was now substituted for that of Sacheverell in the cries of the mob. From this moment the Doctor lost his importance; and within a few years, at the time when Hogarth drew his series of the "Harlot's Progress," Sacheverell's portrait was looked upon as a fit companion for that of the no less notorious Captain Mackheath in the vilest dens of profligacy. The head of "Duke Ormond" now figured as an ornament on articles of common use, as Dr. Sacheverell's had done before; and a very remarkable proof of the length of time which it requires to eradicate feelings and prejudices impressed on the popular mind in times of great political excitement, is furnished by the following rather droll song upon the Duke of Ormond, preserved traditionally in the Isle of Wight and in Kent. The copy I give here, which is the best I have been able to obtain,* was still sung, some thirty or forty years ago, by several old men in the neighbourhood of Maidstone in Kent.

"SONG OF ORMOND AND MARLBOROUGH.

"I am Ormond the Brave, did you ever hear of me,
A man lately forced from his own country,
They sought for my life, and they plundered my estate,
All for being so loyal to Queen Anne the great.
    Chorus—And sing, Hey, ho, ho,
        I am Ormond, you know,
        I am Ormond, you know,
        Though they call me Jemmy Butler,
        I am Ormond you know.

* It was communicated to me by a gentleman of Mereworth, near Maidstone. In the first edition of this book I printed a much more corrupt and imperfect text, communicated to me by Mr. C. Roach Smith, who had taken it down, in 1841, from the mouth of an itinerant fishmonger in the Isle of Wight, who knew no more about it than that it had been sung by his father

c 2

"Betwixt Ormond and Marlborough arose a great dispute ;
Says Ormond to Marlborough, 'I was born a duke,
And you but a footboy to wait upon a lady ;
You may thank your kind fortune and the wars which have made ye.'
    And sing, Hey, ho, ho, &c.

"'I never was a traitor, like you, thou false knave,
Nor ever cursed Queen Anne when she lay in her grave ;
But I was Queen Anne's darling, and my country's delight,
And for the crown of England so boldly I did fight.'
    And sing, Hey, ho, ho, &c.

"'Begone, then,' says Ormond, 'you cowardly creature,
To rob my poor soldiers, it never was my nature,
Which you have done before, as we well understand ;
You have filled your own purse, and impoverished the land.'
    And sing, 'Hey, ho, ho, &c.

"Says Marlborough to Ormond, 'Now do not say so,
Or from the Court I will force you to go.'
Says Ormond to Marlborough, 'Now do not be so cruel,
But draw forth your sword, and we'll end it in a duel.'
    And sing, Hey, ho, ho, &c.

"Says Marlborough to Ormond, 'I'll go and ask my lady,
And, if she is willing, to fight you I'm ready.'
But Marlborough went away, and he came no more there,
So this noble Duke of Ormond threw his sword in the air.
    And sing, Hey, ho, ho, &c."

It was by songs of this character that the minds of the lower classes in England were to have been prepared, it was hoped, to join in a general rising in favour of the exiled house of Stuart. The Jacobite minstrelsy of Scotland had, no doubt, its counterpart in this country ; but its effects were much less considerable, and it was soon forgotten, with the exception of scattered scraps like that given above. The name of the Pretender was sometimes uttered by the disorderly rabble amid the election riots at the beginning of the year ; but after the flight of Bolingbroke and Ormond it was heard much more frequently, and songs and satires against the Hanoverian family were sought and listened to with avidity. The Whigs replied to these with a shoal of pamphlets and papers, reproducing all the old tales of the Revolution, and casting ridicule and contempt upon the son of James II., whom they insisted on looking upon as a mere impostor. The common story was, that the Pretender was the child of a miller, and that, when newly born, he had been con-

and grandfather before him. I look upon this song as one of the most curious relics of English Jacobite literature I have yet met with. It was no doubt one of those sung about the country on the eve of the Rebellion of 1715. I am told that a few years ago this song was commonly sung at the harvest-homes in the Isle of Wight.

veyed into the Queen's bed by means of a warming-pan; and this contrivance having been ascribed to the ingenuity of Father Petre, the Whigs always spoke of the Pretender by the name of *Perkin*, or little Peter. The *warming-pan* figures repeatedly in the satirical literature of the day. The birth of the Pretender had been the subject of a number of caricatures, chiefly of foreign growth, in the reign of King William, which were now as suitable as when first published. In one of these the Queen

THE CATHOLIC FAMILY.

is represented sitting by the cradle, while her Jesuit adviser whispers her in the ear, with his hand over her neck in a familiar manner, which might at least be designated as *un peu leste*. It is a complete Catholic family. The infant has a child's windmill on its bed, to mark the trade of its real parents; and a bowl of milk and an orange are on the table below. A much larger caricature, executed in Holland, represents the child in its cradle as here, with the windmill also, but accompanied by its two mothers and the Jesuit, while the picture is filled with a host of princes, diplomatists, ecclesiastics, &c., looking on with astonishment. It bears the title "L'Europe allarmée pour la

TRUTH EXPOSING THE SECRET.

Fils d'un Meunier." Many satirical medals were also distributed abroad.   One of these, a large silver medal of fine execution, bears on one side a group representing a child on a cushion, crowned and carrying the pax (as the symbol of Romanism) in his right hand ; but Truth, crushing a serpent with her foot, opens the door of a cupboard or chest under the cushion, in which we see Father Petre pushing the child up through the roof.[*]

Tho disaffected party now prepared for the dangerous game they were resolved to play by incessant agitation; for the political maxim, " Agitate, agitate," was known and practised long before the reigns of King William and Queen Victoria.   The mob was, as usual, soon urged into open violence by the old cry of " The Church !" while the Dissenters underwent a much fiercer persecution than that with which they had been visited in 1710, and they bore it in general with exemplary moderation. On the 23rd of April, 1715, the anniversary of the birthday of Queen Anne, the London mob began to assemble towards evening at the conduit on Snow Hill, where they hung up a flag and a hoop, and money having been given them to purchase wine, they collected round a large bonfire.   From thence they moved off in parties in different directions, patrolling the streets during the whole night, shouting " God bless the Queen and High-Church I Bolingbroke and Sacheverell !" and attacking houses, breaking windows, insulting and robbing passengers, and levying contributions everywhere.   Many of the mob were armed with dangerous weapons, and several persons were severely wounded. It was at one time proposed to pull down the Dissenters' meeting-houses, but this project was for some reason or other abandoned.   The streets continued to be more or less infested in this manner night after night for some time.   The 29th of April was the Duke of Ormond's birthday, and that night the streets of London were the scene of new riots and outrages. On the night of Saturday, May 28 (the King's birthday), and on the Sunday night, the 29th (the anniversary of the Restoration), the mob committed great outrages in different parts of London, and dangerously wounded some of the constables and watch.   They burnt the effigies of the chief Dissenting ministers, shouted ' High Church and Ormond !" and publicly drunk the Pretender's health in Ludgate Street and other places.   A riot

* This medal is still not very uncommon.   Copies of it will be found in the collections of Mr. Haggard and Mr. W. H. Diamond.   The caricatures alluded to, with others on the same subject, are in the collections of Mr. Hawkins and Mr. Burke.

of a similar character occurred at Oxford on the King's birth-day, and the Quakers' chapel was attacked and stript by the mob. Within a few days of this time the same riotous spirit had carried itself into several of the largest provincial towns. At Manchester, early in June, the mob had become absolutely master of the town for several days; they destroyed all the Dissenters' chapels, threw open the prison, drunk the Pretenders' health, and committed many outrages. There was near the same time a Jacobite riot at Leeds in Yorkshire. A troop of soldiers were sent to Manchester, and the Mayor of Leeds, who was accused of connivance, was brought to London in the custody of a king's messenger. Yet in July this spirit had become still more general, and had spread especially through Staffordshire, Shropshire, and Cheshire. Very serious tumults occurred at Wolverhampton, Warrington, Shrewsbury, Stafford, Newcastle-under-Line, Litchfield, West-Bromwich, and many other places. The meeting-houses of the Dissenters were everywhere destroyed; cowardly outrages were committed, and in some places sanguinary combats ended in loss of life. When the mob was pulling down the meeting-house at Wolverhampton, one of their leaders mounted on the roof, flourished his hat round his head, and shouted, "—— King George and the Duke of Marlborough!" At Shrewsbury, where the old cry of "High Church and Dr. Sacheverell!" was raised, a justice of the peace and a substantial tradesman were convicted of being ringleaders of the mob. At the end of July there was a serious riot at Leek, in Staffordshire, where much mischief was done; and there was another at Oxford as late as the 1st of September, when the mob shouted, "Ormond!" and "No George!" and the Pretender's health was said to have been drunk in some of the colleges.

These tumults called forth the Riot Act, still in force, which was passed in the month of June, and which, by making the offence felony, and obliging the city or hundred to make good the damages committed, did much towards restoring order; but more, perhaps, was done by the wholesale severity shewn towards the rioters in the trials that followed shortly after. A newspaper of the 2nd of September tells us, that "the judges have behaved very bravely." With a view to other events, which were now literally casting their shadow before them, troops of horse were quartered in several of the towns which had shewn themselves most disaffected.

We cannot at the present day feel otherwise than astonished at the facility with which these riots were carried on, and the regular communication which must have existed between the leaders of the mobs in different parts of the country. It would appear as though there had been no laws to provide against such emergencies, and no police or military force distributed through the country to hinder or suppress outbreaks of popular turbulence. It is true that, in London at least, the pillory and the whipping-cart were in daily use; but these instruments of punishment were robbed of the greater portion of their terrors when a sympathising crowd (paid, as it is said, by richer men of the party) escorted the sufferer, cheered him by their shouts, and carried him away in triumph when it was over. The *Flying Post*, a violent Whig paper, in its intelligence from Coventry of the date of September 10, gives rather an amusing anecdote of the preventive effect of the new Riot Act, and of the methods sometimes taken to evade it for the perpetration of mischief. On the Sunday preceding, a mob had been collected at Burton-upon-Trent, with the desire at least of pulling down a Dissenters' meeting-house there at the time of divine service; but, informed of the consequences, they procured a young bull, cut off its ears and tail, tied squibs and crackers to it, and thus goaded it forwards towards the meeting-house door. The Whig writer exultingly tells us how the tortured animal suddenly turned round, and rushed through the mob, knocking down and trampling upon all who stood in its way; and how it then ran nearly two miles and furiously threw itself into the parish church, where it killed and severely injured several of the congregation.

These systematic riots were intimately connected with plots of a more serious character, with which the Government became gradually acquainted during the summer months; and these discoveries upon which many persons of distinction were placed in custody, had a further effect in hastening the commencement of the rebellion, while they destroyed the prospects of the Jacobites in England. The prisons throughout the country were soon filled with political offenders, many of whom were Church of England clergymen. Among other persons whom it was thought necessary to place under arrest was Sir William Wyndham, member for Somersetshire (where the Jacobites were strong), and one of the leaders of the Tory party in the House of Commons. A song called "The Vagabond Tories," published on the 20th of August, intimates the suspicion, that he was preparing to fly into France to join the Pretender.

> "The knight of such fire
> From S—tshire,
> Who for High Church is always so hearty,
> Tho' in England he tarries,
> Is equipping for Paris,
> To *prevent any schism* in the party."

Sir Constantine Phipps, the Jacobite ex-Chancellor of Ireland, who had been Sacheverell's advocate at his trial, and to whom the University of Oxford had given a degree in a markedly factious manner on the King's coronation day, is also pointed out as a conspirator :—

> "The impudent P—pps
> Must come in for snips,
> Who at Oxford so lately was dubb'd ;
> Tho' instead of degree,
> Such a bawler as he
> Deserv'd to be heartily drubb'd.

> "Young Perkin, poor elf,
> May promise himself
> Two things from the face of that man ;
> There's brass within reach
> To furnish a speech
> And *the lid of a warming-pan.*"

The taunts on those who had not fled are followed by sneers on those who had :—

> "What Ormond, with fraud,
> Long ago did abroad,
> With fear he does over again ;
> 'Tis but an old dance
> To leave England for France,
> He played the same trick at Denain." *

While the ministry of King George was successfully pursuing measures of security, the exultation of the Whig party sought an outlet in multitudes of songs like the foregoing ; and their newspapers and pamphlets became more numerous and more exciting. Most of these songs are set to the tunes of popular ballads ; one, to the tune of "A begging we will go," thus speaks of the "High-Church rebels :"—

> "See how they pull down meetings,
> To plunder, rob, and steal ;
> To raise the mob in riots,
> And teach them to rebel.
>   Oh ! to Tyburn let them go !

An allusion to the desertion of the allies by the English army, under the Duke of Ormond, in the year 1712.

> "At Oxford, Bath, and Bristol,
> The rogues design'd to rise ;
> But George's care and vigilance
> There's nothing can surprize.
> So to Tyburn let them go !
>
> "Their plot is all discover'd now,
> Their treason nought avails ;
> The Tow'r and Newgate quite are full,
> And all our county jails.
> So to Tyburn let them go !"

In another, which was a parody upon a Jacobite song, the Tories are made to call upon the Pretender in despair :—

> "To you, dear Jemmy, at Lorrain,
> We mournful Tories send,
> Unless you'll venture one campaign,
> Our cause is at an end :
> We've nothing left but to be stout,
> For all our plots are now found out.
> With a fa la la la," &c.
>
> "We sent you first Lord Bolingbroke,
> In hopes to bring you over ;
> And then we sent wise Ormond's duke,
> That rival of Hanover :
> You need not fear if you are beat,
> Since he's so good at a retreat !
> With a fal la la la, &c."

When the rebellion was entirely suppressed, and the Scottish minstrels were lamenting pathetically the departure of their prince, their brethren in England were indulging in parodies like the following :—

> "'Twas when the seas were roaring
> With blasts of northern wind,
> Young Perkin lay deploring
> On warming-pan reclin'd :
> Wide o'er t e roaring billows
> He cast a dismal look,
> And shiver'd like the willows
> That tremble o'er the brook."

The Tories at the same time appeared discomfited even in their writings. The newspapers give no intelligence, and make no remarks, until, as soon as the rebellion lost all appearance of success, they begin to talk of the "rebels" as if they were themselves staunch supporters of the Hanoverian succession. John Dunton in a pamphlet entitled "Mob War," published at this time, says, "Even Abel Roper* now

---

* The *Post Boy*, a Tory newspaper.

grows modest and tender-conscienced. Drunken P——tin is
wretchedly dull in his Jacobite *Packet*,* and there are thoughts
of dismissing him from the service. Whig papers and
pamphlets are only in demand, and the booksellers who engaged
in hereditary right are just a breaking. The *Examiner*† has
spent himself quite, and would give five shillings apiece for
political lyes, and three shillings for a probable reflection upon
the present ministry." The Tories in general made their peace
with the powers that were, by taking the oath of allegiance;
and the *Daily Courant* of November 30, 1715, contains the
following advertisement of a caricature on this subject, of which
no copy, as far as I can learn, is now preserved :—"This day is
published, 'A Call to the Unconverted; being an emblem
of the Tories' manner of taking the oaths.' Price sixpence."
A week after this, the *St. James's Post* of December 7 contains
the following advertisement:—"This day is published, 'An
Argument proving all the Tories in Great Britain to be Fools.'
Price Fourpence."

Amid the uneasiness and alarm which prevailed throughout the country, the metropolis was the continual scene of riot
and agitation. There appears to have been no efficient police
in London to keep order in the streets, along which it was
unsafe to pass after dusk. We have already seen the ascen-
dancy which the Jacobite mob had gained there in the spring,
and which they seem to have kept undisturbed during the
summer, waiting for the numerous anniversary days in the
autumn to begin again their riotous proceedings. But a
new power was rising up, which though it did not prevent the
riots, prevented some of the mischief to which they might
have led.

Amid the political excitement of the preceding year, which
pervaded every class of society, and seemed to have estranged
people's minds from every other subject, even the taverns and
public-houses of the metropolis had been gradually taking a
political character to such a degree, that about this time a
guide-book was published, under the title of the " Vade-mecum
of Malt-worms," containing a list of all the ale-houses in London, with an account of the persons who held them, and the
political principles of each. Some of these, under the name of
mug-houses, became the resort of small societies or clubs of
political partisans, who met there on certain occasions to celebrate memorable anniversaries. Two of the oldest Whig houses

* The *Weekly Packet*, a newspaper we have quoted more than once.
† A violent Jacobite paper, at one period chiefly conducted by Swift.

were the Roebuck, in Cheapside, (opposite Bow Church,) and a
mug-house in Long Acre. A society calling itself the Loyal
Society, held its meetings at the Roebuck, after the Accession of
George I.; and in the history of the London riots in 1715 and
1716 this house obtained an especial celebrity. Next in fame
to these were the Magpie, without Newgate (the Magpie and
Stump still standing in the Old Bailey) ; a mug-house in St.
John's Lane, Clerkenwell ; another in Tavistock Street, Covent
Garden ; one in Salisbury Court, near Fleet Street ; and one in
Southwark Park. The two last became eventually objects of
great hostility with the mob. The Tory ale-houses, which were
less numerous, appear to have stood chiefly about Holborn Hill
(Dr. Sacheverell's parish) and Ludgate Street. The Whig
societies who frequented the mug-houses began in the autumn
of 1715 to unite in parties to fight the Jacobite mob which
had so long tyrannised over the streets, and they were probably
joined on such occasions by a number of others, who, like the
London apprentices of old, looked upon the whole only as a
rough kind of diversion.

At the end of October and beginning of November, a number of political anniversaries crowded together. The Prince of
Wales's birthday, the 30th of October, was celebrated on
Monday the 31st. The *Flying Post*, the chief chronicler of
the tumults, informs us that " A parcel of the Jacobite rabble,
such as Bridewell boys, &c., committed outrages on Ludgate
Hill, broke the windows that were illuminated, scattered a bonfire, and cried out ' An Ormond !' &c. ; but they were dispersed
and soundly thrashed by a party of the Loyal Society, who had
lately burnt the Pretender in effigy." From this time we shall
find the new self-constituted police constantly at war with the
mob. The latter had prepared an effigy of King William to be
burnt on the anniversary of that monarch's birth, Friday, November 4, and on the approach of night they assembled round
a large bonfire in the Old Jewry for that purpose. But information of their design having been carried to a party of the
Loyal Society, who were met at the Roebuck to celebrate King
William's birthday, and who were therefore close at hand, these
gentlemen hastened to the spot, and "gave the Jacks* due
chastisement with oaken plants, demolished their bonfire, and
brought off the effigies in triumph to the Roebuck." On the
morrow, the 5th of November, the Whig mob had their cele-
bration. They had prepared caricature effigies of the Pope, the

* This was the term popularly given to the Jacobites.

Pretender, Ormond, Bolingbroke, and the Earl of Marr, which were carried in the following order;—"First, two men bearing each a *warming-pan*, with the representation of the infant Pretender, a nurse attending him with a sucking-bottle, and another playing with him by beating the warming-pan." These were followed by three trumpeters, playing *Lilliburlero* and other Whig tunes. Then came a cart, with Ormond and Marr, appropriately dressed." This was followed by another cart, containing the Pope and Pretender seated together, and Bolingbroke as the secretary of the latter. They were all drawn backwards, with halters round their necks. The procession, thus arranged, passed from the Roebuck along Cheapside, through Newgate Street and up Holborn Hill, where the Jacobite bells of St. Andrew's Church were made to ring a merry peal. From thence they passed through Lincoln's-Inn Fields and Covent Garden to St. James's, where they made a stand before the palace; and so went back by Pall Mall and the Strand, through St. Paul's Churchyard, into Cheapside; but here they found that the "Jacks" had been beforehand with them, and stolen the faggots which had been piled up for their bonfire. They therefore made a circuit of the city whilst a new bonfire was prepared, and on their return burnt all the effigies amid the shouts of the crowd.

The enmity between the mob and the Loyal Society was embittered by these first encounters, and it soon came to a fierce issue. On the 17th of November the Loyal Society met at the Roebuck, to celebrate the anniversary of Queen Elizabeth. The mob had also met to celebrate it, but in a different manner; and towards seven o'clock in the evening intelligence reached the Roebuck that they had assembled at St. Martin-le-Grand, and were preparing, amid shouts of "High Church, and Ormond, and King James!" to burn the effigies of King William, King George, and the Duke of Marlborough, in Smithfield. The "Loyal" gentlemen immediately marched out, and overtook them in Newgate Street, where a desperate fight took place, and, after twenty or thirty of them had been "knocked down," the mob was dispersed. They had concealed their effigies; but a boy who had been captured pointed them out to the victors, who marched back in triumph to the Roebuck. There they had hardly arrived, when a much greater mob began to assemble, and, after breaking the windows of the Roebuck, as well as those of the adjacent houses, and pulling down the sign, proceeded to burst open the door, and threatened summary vengeance upon the inmates. In this extremity, a member of the

Loyal Society fired with a loaded gun down the passage, and killed one of the assailants, and the Lord Mayor and city officers coming up at the same time, the mob took to their heels. The inquest on the body of the man who was killed returned a verdict that he was slain, while in open riot and rebellion, by some one who had fired in self-defence. On subsequent nights the Roebuck appears to have been exposed to renewed, but less serious attacks, and the mob war was carried on at least less ostentatiously during the winter.

In February we hear again of the riotous conduct of the Jacobite mob, and the mug-houses appear to have been actively refitting and preparing for a new campaign. New songs were compiled and printed for the use of the loyal gentry who frequented them, and well suited to keep up the popular excitement. One of these gives the following description of the mob, and shows that these faction fights were very serious things.

> "Since the Tories could not fight
> And their master took his flight,
> They labour to keep up their faction ;
> With a bough and a stick,
> And a stone and a brick,
> They equip their roaring crew for action.
>
> "Thus in battle array,
> At the close of the day,
> After wisely debating their deep plot,
> Upon windows and stall
> They courageously fall,
> And boast a great victory they have got.
>
> "But, alas ! silly boys !
> For all the mighty noise
> Of their ' High Church and Ormond for ever !'
> A brave Whig with one hand,
> At George's command,
> Can make their mightiest hero to quiver."

Towards spring festive entertainments were given at most of the mug-houses—a sort of house-warming or introduction to the season, at which the proprietors delivered formal addresses, often in verse, stating their sentiments and intentions, and boasted of their former feats against the "Jacks." One of these, the keeper of the mug-house in St. John's Lane, speaks of his frequent encounters with the mob, and after threatening what he will do himself, proceeds :—

> "Nor is it for myself I speak alone :
> There is my wife,—'tis true, she is but one,
> But, fegs ! she'll play her part against the ty'er's son."

Several of these addresses will be found in the mug-house song-books. One of these festivals is thus announced in the *Flying Post* of April 12, 1716 :—" This is to give notice to all gentlemen who are *well affected to the present establishment*, and lovers of good home-brew'd ale, that this present Thursday, being the 12th of April, Mrs. Smyth's mug-house in St. John's Lane, near Smithfield, will be opened ; when there will be a prologue spoke, suitable to the occasion." And on the 21st of April the same paper prints this "prologue," with the following *editorial* remark :—" The following is inserted at the request of several honest gentlemen, who are hearty well-wishers to those *useful societys* that are carry'd on in Long Acre and St. John's Lane, for *the reformation of Toryism* and the propagation of loyalty to the present happy government." The same newspaper had shortly before given a new mug-house song, commencing,—

> "We friends of the mug are met here to discover
> Our zeal to the Protestant house of Hanover,
> Against the attempts of a bigotted rover.
> Which nobody can deny.
>
> "Prepare then in bumpers confusion to drink
> To their cursed devices who otherwise think ;
> For now that vile int'rest must certainly sink.
> Which nobody can deny.
>
> "The Tories, 'tis true, are yet skulking in shoals,
> To show their affection to Perkin in bowls ;
> But in time we will ferret them out of their holes.
> Which nobody can deny."

From this period the members of the Loyal Society send to the newspapers regular reports of their night's campaign, duly dated from the head-quarters at the Roebuck. On the night of the 8th of March, the anniversary of the death of King William, a considerable mob assembled, to the old cry of " High Church and Ormond !" and marched along Cheapside to the well-known mug-house, where a party of the Loyal Society were met " for the defence of the house ;" but when these issued forth, to the numb.. of "about forty," the mob ran away, leaving many of their sticks behind them. The Loyalists then marched in procession through Newgate Street, paid their respects to the Magpie, where another party was met, and proceeded to Ludgate Hill in bravado of the "Jacks," who were strong there, but on their return they found that the mob had been collecting in greater strength in their rear in Newgate Street, where a great fight took place, in which the Whigs were again victorious, after having, to use the words of the newspaper account, " made rare work for the surgeons." The conquerors returned direct to the Roebuck, shouting " King George!" as they went, and there spent the greater part of the night in drinking loyal toasts.

The next very serious tumult occurred on the 23rd of April (the anniversary of the birth of Queen Anne). In the evening of that day the marrow bones and cleavers, the usual signal of gathering for the mob, were heard rattling along the streets; and, towards seven o'clock, parties were to be seen forming in Smithfield, the Old Bailey, Ludgate Hill, and Fleet Street, to shouts of " High Church and Ormond!" " No Rump Parliament!" and other similar cries. The Loyalists began to assemble at the Roebuck about the same time, and by nine o'clock had become tolerably numerous ; upon which they marched forth in procession to the Magpie, and thence to Ludgate Hill, where the mob showed themselves, but would not stand. The Loyal Society then returned to the Roebuck, from whence they made a circuit into the city and returned again to the Roebuck without meeting with any opponents. But they had hardly settled themselves down to their mugs, when news arrived that the mob was coming up in great force. They then lost no time in gaining the street, and found the mob already in Cheapside at the end of Wood Street, where there was a fierce battle, ending as usual in the discomfiture of the "Jacks." The heroes of the Roebuck now marched towards the Magpie ; but at the end of Giltspur Street they again found the mob, and had a more obstinate fight than before, but with the same result, and they returned to their quarters with a pile of captured hats and sticks as trophies.

An anniversary was now approaching which had always been celebrated with tumults, and such preparations appear to have been made for the present occasion, as shewed that the mob did not act solely by their own impulse. On the 29th of May, the anniversary of the Restoration of Charles II., green boughs were carried about the streets and worn on the person ; and there were large meetings at St. Andrew's (to hear Dr. Sacheverell), and at the "Jacobites' conventicle in Scroops' Court, over against it." Towards night the mob became very riotous, and threatened to pull down the Roebuck and the mug-house in St. John's Lane. One of the lookers-on says, " There never was seen such a crew of tatterdemalions, for they looked as if hell had broke loose. They had gathered together all the blackguard boys, wheelbarrow-men, and ballad-singers, and knocked down people that did not carry their badges." They were, however, "soundly thresh'd " by the societies which met at the two mug-houses they had threatened; and a party of horse guards, which just then arrived and patrolled the streets during the night, put an end to the disturbance. Yet on the 10th of June, the birth-day of the Pretender, there were greater riots than ever, and the Loyal Society had to bring their whole force to the struggle. A Roebuck correspondent of the *Flying Post* writes some days after, " You omitted to take notice, that, on the 10th of June, several Whigs of the Loyal Society at the Roebuck, having fur-nish'd themselves with little *warming-pans* fit for the pocket, did ring such a dismal peal with them in the ears of the white-rose mob, that their flowers soon disappeared, and could not keep 'em from fainting." The white rose was the Pretender's badge, and had been worn on this occasion.

From this time we hear less of the Roebuck in the public prints, although it had hitherto eclipsed the fame of the other houses. But they also had been engaged with their respective mobs, especially the mug-house in Southwark, and that in Salis-bury Court. On the 12th of July following the last-mentioned exploit of the Roebuck heroes, a mob, armed with clubs, assembled in Southwark, with shouts of " High Church and Ormond!" " Down with the mug-houses!" and, attacking the mug-house there, broke the shutters and windows. The society within, however rushed out, and drove them away. A week after this, on Friday, the 20th of July, the London mob, which, we are told, had "strangely" increased since the King's de-parture for Hanover, made a desperate attack on a mug-house in Salisbury Court. The society then assembled there sent for assistance to their allies in the mug-house in Tavistock Street; and, thus reinforced, they succeeded in driving away the assailants. A second attack was, however, made by a much stronger mob on the evening of Monday the 23rd; but the society held them successfully at bay till the following morning, when they had been so much increased that further resistance seemed vain. The proprietor of the house, named Read, then advanced to the door with a blunderbuss, and threatened any one who should attempt to enter the house. Instead of falling back, the mob rushed towards him with clubs and sticks, whereupon he fired and shot their ringleader dead. The mob, rendered still more furious, threw themselves upon Read, and left him to appearance lifeless: and then broke down the sign, entirely gutted the lower part of the house, drank as much ale in the cellar as they could, and let the rest run out. The magistrates and soldiers

D

arrived about mid-day, and dispersed the mob, though not till a soldier and some other persons had been severely injured in the fray. The Loyal Society, who had barricaded themselves in the upper part of the house, were thus relieved from their unpleasant position. The inquest gave a verdict of wilful murder against Read, and he was brought to trial, but acquitted, and the Government made good the damage he had sustained. Several of the rioters were also brought to their trial; and, convicted of being active in the work of destruction, they were hanged without mercy. This event appears to have thrown a final damp upon the spirits of the mob.

At the end of June, the King left England for Hanover. On his departure a treasonable libel was hawked about the streets, entitled " King G——'s farewell to England ; or, the Oxford Scholars in mourning." We know little of the contents of the libels against the King's person which were thus hawked about the streets ; but to judge from what is preserved in some of the early Scottish Jacobite songs, the scandals attached to George's wife and to his mistresses were plentifully raked up. The latter were often hooted by the mob as they passed through the streets. Horace Walpole, in his *Reminiscences*, assures us that nothing could be grosser than the ribaldry that was vomited out in lampoons, libels, and every channel of abuse, against the Sovereign and the new Court, and chaunted even in their hearing in the public streets.

CHAPTER II.

GEORGE I.

Party Feeling after the Rebellion—Prevalence of Highway Robbery—The Mob—Bishop Hoadly's Sermon, and Colley Cibber's "Non-Juror"—The French Mississippi Scheme—The South Sea Bubble—Sudden Multiplication of Stock Jobbing Bubbles—Fall of the "Paper King" Law—The South Sea Ballads—South Sea Caricatures—Bubble Cards, and Stock-Jobbing Cards—Knight and the "Screen"—Election for a New Parliament—New Efforts in favour of the Pretender—Bishop Atterbury's Plot.

THE hasty and ill-advised and ill-conducted Rebellion of 1715 had effectually strengthened the power of the Whig party, and had shewn to all reasonable and thinking persons how little was to be expected from a person deficient in courage and in capacity as the Pretender had shewn himself. After the excitement caused by trials and executions of rebels had subsided, the political strife of the day sank down into a dull and monotonous war of newspaper abuse and mob sedition, which lasted for several years, with no other variety than that occasioned by some accidental outburst of more than ordinary virulence. We read almost daily of the application of the pillory or the lash to punish seditious ballad singers and indiscreet individuals, generally of a low class in life, who had made too open an exhibition of hostility to the House of Hanover. Almost every newspaper or periodical, whether Tory or Whig, became in turn the object of prosecution for letting its party zeal go beyond the limits of moderation, although the Tory press came in for much more than an equal share of punishment. Restrained, indeed, from any more effectual method of showing their hostility, except in an occasional duel or riot, the language of the opposition became more violent and scurrilous; and the lowest and most trivial occurrences were greedily seized upon as an opportunity for insulting a political opponent. In the beginning of February, 1717, two street bullies had drawn their swords and killed a drunken man, and had been hanged for the murder. Some of the Tory papers stated that the offenders had been members of one of the Whig societies which met at the taverns, or, as they were now familiarly termed "Muggites." The Whig newswriters indignantly repelled this accusation, and, in revenge, declared that they were both known to be notorious Tories, or " Jacks." On the 4th of January, 1718, Read's *Weekly Journal* (a violent Whig paper) tells us, that, " Last Thursday morning, a woman *we suppose High Church*, coming out *of a Geneva shop* in Red-Cross Street, fell down, and within some few minutes departed this mortal life for another." The latter part of the phrase is an example of the loose style of writing which distinguishes the newspaper literature of the day. A paper of this period gravely tells us, that " Yesterday three ladies were brought to bed of *a male child*," and proceeds to give their names. About the same date last quoted, a Tory paper, describing the immodest behaviour of some young women in church, asserts that they belonged to a violent Whig family ; while the Whig journals made every unfortunate woman who was committed to Bridewell a Tory. A Whig clergyman was stated to have refused to bury a man who died an " *impenitent* Tory." This bitterness of party feeling was often shewn in practical jokes. Read's *Weekly Journal* of June 15, 1717, says, " Last Monday being suppos'd to be the birthday of the sovereign of the white rose, in respect to the anniversary an honest Whig went from the Roebuck to St. James's, with a jack-daw finely drest in white roses, and set on a warming-pan bedeckt with the same sweet-scented commodity, which caused abundance of laughter all the way, to the great mortification of the knights companions of that order, and all the other Jacks, to see their sovereign so maltreated in the person of his representative."

The feelings evinced in these few examples tainted and embittered every class of society, and were also attended by a general laxity of morals, and, compared with the present day (or even with almost any other period), an insecurity of property. Robbery was carried on on a fearful scale in the streets of London, even by daylight ; housebreaking was of frequent occurrence by night ; and every road leading to the metropolis was beset by bands of reckless highwaymen, who carried their depredations into the very heart of the town. Respectable women could not venture in the streets alone after nightfall, even in the city, without risk of being grossly outraged. In the beginning of 1720, we learn from the papers that ladies of condition, when they went out in their chairs at night at the Court end of the town, were often attended by servants with loaded blunderbusses " to shoot at the rogues." The best notion of the state of security of London at this time will be given by a chronicle of acts of robbery with violence, taken from the newspapers during three weeks at the end of January and beginning of February, 1720; premising, that it appears, from several circumstances, that the newspapers of that time give a very imperfect and incomplete report of such occurrences. We begin with—

Wednesday, January 20, on the night of which day five highwaymen robbed a man, coming to London, near Stratford.

Thursday, 21.—About five o'clock in the evening, the stage coach from London to Hampstead was attacked and robbed by highwaymen at the foot of the hill, and one of the passengers severely beaten for attempting to hide his money.

Friday, 22.—Either on this, or on one of the two preceding days, it is not very clearly specified, three highwaymen attacked a gentleman of the Prince's household in his coach near Poland Street, and obliged the watchman to throw away his lanthorn and stand quietly by, while they abused and robbed him. Other highwaymen attacked Colonel Montague as he was passing along Frith Street, Soho, between twelve and one at night, and fired at his coachman and wounded one of his horses because he refused to stand. The Duchess of Montrose, coming from Court in her chair, was stopped by three highwaymen well mounted between Bond Street and the New Building.

Saturday, 23.—A man was attacked at night by highwaymen in Chiswell Street. The same night a house near Bishopsgate was broken into, and a man murdered.

Sunday, 24.—At eight o'clock in the evening two highwaymen attacked a gentleman in a coach on the south side of St. Paul's Churchyard, and robbed him.

Monday, 25.—As the Duke of Chandos, a nobleman celebrated for his courage against this class of depredators, was coming into town at night from his house at Canons, he was attacked by five highwaymen, but his servants were too strong for them. They had already committed several robberies on the road.

Tuesday, 26.—The Chichester mail, going from London about three o'clock in the morning, was attacked by highwaymen in Battersea Bottom, and robbed of its letter-bags.

Wednesday, 27.—The Bristol mail was robbed on its way to London, and a considerable sum of money taken in bank bills inclosed in the letters. The same night an extensive robbery was perpetrated at Acton, and a booty of about two thousand pounds taken.

On one day of this week a lady was stopped in her chaise near

"Barclet" Street by highwaymen, and robbed of her money, jewels, and gold watch.

Saturday, 30.—A house in Bishopsgate Street was broken into.

Sunday, 31.—A gentleman was robbed and murdered in Bishopsgate Street.

Monday, February 1.—The Duke of Chandos, coming from Canons, had another encounter with highwaymen, whom he captured.

Tuesday, 2.—The post-boy was attacked by three highwaymen in Tyburn Road, but the Duke of Chandos happening to pass that way, came to his rescue.

Wednesday, 3.—The stage-coach going in the evening from London to Stoke Newington, was robbed by highwaymen near the Palatine Houses.

On one day of this week "all the stage-coaches coming from Surrey to London were robbed by highwaymen." And in the course of the week a gentleman in his coach was robbed near Chelsea; another was attacked and robbed at twelve o'clock at night at the upper end of Cheapside; a gang of highwaymen by open day robbed all passengers on the Croydon road for some hours together; and several robberies were committed on the Epping road.

Tuesday, 9.—A member of Parliament, with two ladies, returning in a coach from a party near Smithfield at eleven o'clock at night, was dogged by three highwaymen mounted and three on foot till they came to Denmark Street, St. Giles's, where their coach was stopped, and they were rifled of money and jewels to the value of about two hundred and fifty pounds. The robbers drove away the watch, and fired two pistols to frighten the ladies when they screamed for help.

Wednesday, 10.—A man was beaten and robbed in White Conduit Fields at four o'clock in the afternoon. At night a gentleman was attacked in St. George's Fields, robbed, and beat so severely that his life was despaired of. Three gentlemen in a hackney-coach were attacked in Denmark Street, St. Giles's, and robbed of everything but their clothes. A man was robbed in Cheapside of his coat and money.

This alarming increase of highwaymen about London struck every class of society with terror, for none were secure except those few who could go about strongly guarded. A poor man was stripped of his pence equally with a rich man of his gold. In one instance, close to London, after having robbed a labourer of one shilling and four-pence, the highwayman broke his arm with a pistol shot, as a warning of what he might expect if he ventured to go again abroad at night with so little money in his pocket. On the 23rd of January, a proclamation came out, offering a reward of a hundred pounds, in addition to the previous inducements, for the capture of any highwayman within five miles of London; the main effect of which was to place considerable sums of money in the pockets of the notorious Jonathan Wild, who secured several offenders in and about the metropolis within the space of two or three weeks. Of these, it was observed that several, on examination, proved to be persons moving in their class of society as honest and respectable men; among them are mentioned a tradesman of good repute in London, the valet of "a great duke," and the keeper of a boxing-school.

The affair in Salisbury Court, mentioned in our last chapter, damped considerably the spirits of the mob, although, for a time, the war between the gentlemen of the Roebuck and the "Jacks" continued to be carried on upon a less extensive scale. The Tories began to complain, and with some reason, that the mug-houses were themselves the chief provocations to these nightly tumults. It appears that in the beginning of November, 1717, the society of the Roebuck had fought with the butchers, who composed the most active part of the mobs of this period. On the 16th of November, the Whig *Weekly Journal* has the following paragraph:—"Whereas the author of the *St. James's Weekly Journal* has most grossly scandalized the gentlemen of the Roebuck Society in his paper of last Saturday; this is to satisfie the world, that, before the aforesaid loyal body beat the butchers of Newgate Market to their heart's content, they assaulted them first for expressing their joy for the birth of the young Prince, on the 2nd of November last, as will be prov'd by affidavits that are now making in order to punish the ringleaders of all Jacobite mobs." It is evident, however, that the proceedings of the mug-house societies began to be discountenanced by the less violent Whigs; and nothing could be more calculated to keep up the ill-feelings which were tearing society to pieces, than the satirical processions that were paraded through London-streets on every occasion that offered itself. Several of these processions were prepared on a very large scale in 1717 and 1718, but they were forbidden by the authorities, and the effigies were exhibited privately at the Roebuck, or were made public only in printed descriptions. The Tories called loudly for the suppression of the mug-houses themselves, and several pamphlets for and against them appeared in the earlier part of the year 1717.

In the mean time, High Church and Low Church continued
to wage unremitting warfare with each other. An unusually
violent controversy was raised in 1717, by two performances of
Bishop Hoadly of Bangor, a discourse and a sermon preached
before the King, in which he advocated tolerance and moderation towards those who differed in religious opinions, and condemned persecution. The convocation of the clergy, which, up
to this period, had met at the same time as the Parliament, took
up the matter with so much fury, that they were suddenly prorogued by the King, and have not since, until very recently,
been called together. The animosity to which this dispute gave
rise soon led to personal slander, in which Hoadly's chief opponents, Dr. Snape, master of Eton College, and the Bishop of
Carlisle, made certainly an undignified appearance. Perhaps no
one subject of dispute ever gave rise to so many controversial
pamphlets as were published during 1717 and 1718 for and
against Bishop Hoadly; the affair was made the burthen of
ballads and epigrams, and was taken up by those who of all
others were least able to understand the merits of the case—the
street mob, who only distinguished a Dissenters' chapel from a
church by the absence of the steeple. In the *Post-Boy* of the
6th of June, 1717, we find advertised, "The Inquisition: a
farce; as it was acted at Child's Coffee House, and the King's
Arms Tavern in St. Paul's Churchyard; wherein the controversy between the Bishop of Bangor and Dr. Snape is fairly
stated and set in a true light. By Mr. Philips." In the midst
of this controversy, which for nearly two years occupied the
minds of all classes in society, the Non-Jurors, or those who
avoided taking the oaths to the present dynasty, and who were
the extreme of the High-Church party, were unusually active,
and openly erected meeting-houses in different parts of London. The "farce" just mentioned was by no means a solitary instance of dragging the religious disputes on the stage.
In the midst of the Hoadly dispute, Colley Cibber brought
out the "Tartuffe" of Molière, a little changed, in an English clothing, under the title of "The Non-Juror," in which
the author acted with great effect the part of Dr. Wolf, a
Non-Juror and concealed Papist, who by his unprincipled intrigues nearly effects the ruin of a rich and respectable family,
and at last is discovered and given up to the punishment he
merits. Read's *Weekly Journal* of December 7, 1717, informs
us, that "Last night the comedy call'd the 'Non-Juror' was
acted at his Majesty's theatre in Drury Lane, which very naturally displaying *the villany of that most wicked and abominable
crew*, it gave great satisfaction to all the spectators." The

"Non-Juror" had in fact great success; and the anger of the extreme High-Church party was increased by the circumstances that the prologue had been written by the poet-laureat, Nicholas Rowe, that the King and Prince both went to see the play, and were said to have applauded it heartily, and that the King not only gave his permission for the printed edition to be dedicated to himself, but rewarded the author with a gratuity of two hundred pounds. Even this was enough to raise a war of pamphlets, and a storm of newspaper scurrility fell upon poor Cibber. In a pamphlet entitled "The Theatre Royal turn'd into a mountebank's stage; in some remarks upon Mr. Cibber's quack-dramatical performance, called the 'Non-Juror,'" the writer (it professes to be written "by a Non-Juror") complains bitterly that the stage should be permitted to make a clergyman the subject of ridicule, while the clergy were forbidden to preach politics from the pulpit. Another anonymous writer gave to the world a farce entitled "The Juror," in which were revived the old worn-out charges of fanaticism and hypocrisy. Other pamphleteers took part with Cibber: one published "A Complete Key to the Play;" and another gave "Some Cursory Remarks" upon it, which conclude with the hope that the writer would live "to see it as common in every house as a Prayer Book or Duty of Man!"

All these disputes were, however, shortly to be forgotten in an extraordinary social convulsion of a totally different kind.

For several years, since the conclusion of the war, there had appeared a growing taste for money speculations, not only in England, but throughout other parts of Europe. This was first taken advantage of for state purposes in France, where the national finances had been thrown into so hopeless a state, that the government was on the eve of bankruptcy. A Scottish gentleman of the name of Law, who had killed a man in a duel, in consequence of which he had retired to France, projected a company to have a monopoly of the trade of the country of the Mississippi in North America, on condition that they should undertake the payment of the state bills. The Regent established this company in 1717, and made Law principal director. The plan went on, without any extraordinary success, till 1719, when the French India and China Companies were incorporated with it; and then there was a sudden and immense rise in the value of the shares, or, as they were called, *actions*. Soon after the Midsummer of 1719, Mr. Law and the Regent formed the project of extending the company very largely, and then the shares rose still more rapidly, till, in a short time, they reached twelve hundred per cent. It may be

mentioned, as a proof of the wonderful confidence the French
placed in Law at this time, that the mere report of his being
seized with a slight indisposition caused a sudden fall in the
funds. The French government now found itself relieved from
all its pecuniary difficulties; the nobility and courtiers became
immensely rich, and Paris was so full of money, that people
scarcely knew how to employ it. Law was looked upon as the
great European financier; and, at the beginning of February,
he was admitted into the Privy Council, and was appointed
Comptroller-General of the finances of France.

The success of this scheme in France provoked imitation in
England, where a chartered trading company, called the South
Sea Company, had been established in 1711. The English
Ministry, in conjunction with Sir John Blunt, one of the leading South Sea directors, conceived the plan of making this company pay off the national debt, which had become burdensome
by the long war, in the same manner that the Mississippi Company had just relieved the government of France from its embarrassments. Aislabie (the Chancellor of the Exchequer),
Stanhope, and Sunderland were all equally sanguine of the result
of this plan, and it was brought before the House of Commons
in the month of February, 1720. It there met with considerable opposition, especially from Sir Robert Walpole, who was
the most profound financier in the House, and was now out of
the ministry; but the South Sea bill was eventually carried by
considerable majorities, and received the royal assent on the 7th
of April, 1720. The infatuation with which people entered
upon this rash project is perfectly astonishing. In Paris, Law
had already become embarrassed in his financial plans, and it
was evident that the reign of the "paper king" was approaching to a close. The Tory papers in England had already begun
to ridicule both the man and his projects. "If you are ambitious," says Mist's *Weekly Journal*, early in February, "you
must put on a sword, kill a beau or two, get into Newgate, be
condemned to be hanged, break prison, IF YOU CAN—*remember
that, by the way*—get over to some strange country, set up a
Mississippi stock, bubble a nation, and you may soon be a great
man." The same journal tells us, on the 20th of February,
"Last week, at the masquerade in the Haymarket, appeared a
fine lady in a very odd comical dress; she told the company
that she came from Mississippi, and was going to be married to
the South Sea." We shall see this disposition to caricature
soon carried to a much greater extent. A few days after the
act was passed, Walpole published a pamphlet, giving a strong

warning of the mischiefs which were to be expected from the South Sea project; yet, before the month of April, the rage for dealing in South Sea shares had become so great, that the dealers had already become an object of ridicule on the stage. Among the advertisements in the newspapers of this month appear a play, entitled "The Stock-Jobbers; or, Humours of Change Alley;" and "Exchange Alley; or, the Stock-Jobber turned Gentleman: a tragi-comical Farce." Within a few weeks South Sea stock rose to above a thousand per cent.

The town now presented an extraordinary appearance. Stock-jobbing seemed to be the sole business of all classes, and Whigs, and Tories, and Jacobites, High Church, and Low Church, and Dissenters, forgot their mutual animosity in the general infatuation. In spite of a proclamation, forbidding the formation of companies without legal authority, an immense number of stock-jobbing companies sprung up like mushrooms around the larger scheme. These soon became known by the popular title of *bubbles,* advertisements of which filled the newspapers during the months of June and July. Many of these were mere gambling, or, more properly speaking, swindling speculations; and there were instances in which a man took a room for the day, opened a subscription book in the morning, taking a very small deposit on the shares, and in the evening shut up both book and shop, decamping with a large sum of money. When a new company was announced, no one thought of inquiring if the project were a practical one or not: a company was even announced, and its shares bought, which was merely advertised as "for an undertaking which shall in due time be revealed." Square bits of card, with the impression in sealing-wax of the sign of the Globe Tavern, conveying to their possessors merely the permission to subscribe some time afterwards to a new sail-cloth company not yet formed, were actually sold in Exchange Alley, under the title of "Globe permits," for sixty guineas and upwards. The *Political State of Great Britain* gives a list of these bubbles in July, amounting to a hundred and four, among which are companies "for assurance of seamen's wages;" "for a wheel for perpetual motion;" "for improving gardens;" "for insuring and increasing children's fortunes;" "for making looking glasses;" "for improving malt liquors;" "for breeding and providing for bastard children," (the first idea of the foundling hospital;) and "for insuring against thefts and robberies." Among other odd projects were companies "for planting of mulberry trees and breeding of silkworms in Chelsea Park;" "for importing a number of large jackasses from Spain, in order

to propagate a larger breed of mules in England ;" " for fattening of hogs." A clergyman proposed a company to discover
the land of Ophir, and monopolise the gold and silver which
that country was believed still to produce. It would be almost
impossible here to carry the ridiculous beyond what was represented in matter of fact; but there were some burlesque lists,
containing companies " for curing the gout," " for insuring
marriages against divorce," and the like. Within two or three
days after they were subscribed for, the shares in these different
companies sold for amazing prices : those in the Water-Engine
Company, on which four pounds were paid, rose to fifty pounds;
the stocking company's shares, for which two pounds ten shillings were paid, sold for thirty pounds; the shares in a company " for manuring of land," subscribed at two shillings and
sixpence, sold for one pound ten shillings.

Among the previously existing companies which were dragged
in among the bubbles of this year, was the York Buildings Company, which had purchased the site of York House in the Strand,
to build works for the supplying of the West End with water
from the Thames. It is a remarkable fact, and one that appears
to be entirely forgotten, that, within two or three years of the
date of which we are speaking, a veritable steam-engine was constructed here, which is thus described in the *Foreigner's Guide
to London*, published in 1729 :—" Here you see a high wooden
tower and a water-engine of a new invention, that draws out of
the Thames above three tons of water in one minute, by means
of the steam arising from water boiling in a great copper, a continual fire being kept to that purpose; the steam being com-
pressed and condensed, moves by its evaporation and strikes a
counterpoise, which counterpoise striking another, at last moves
a great beam, which by its motion of going up and down, draws
the water from the river, which mounts through great iron pipes
to the height of the tower, discharging itself there into a deep
leaden cistern ; and thence falling down through other large iron
pipes, fills them that are laid along the streets, and so continuing
to run through wooden pipes,* as far as Mary-bone fields, falls
there into a large pond or reservoir, from whence the new buildings near Hanover Square, and many thousand houses, are supplied with water. This machine is certainly a great curiosity ;
and, though it be not so large as that of Marley in France, yet,
considering its smallness in comparison with that, and the little

---

* Many of the wooden pipes here alluded to were, just before the publication of the first edition of this book, taken up in excavations in Brook Street,
Grosvenor Square, and in some other places along the line here described.

charge it was built and is kept with, and the quantity of water it draws, its use and benefit is much beyond that."[*]

All other trade but that of stock-jobbing was now neglected; Exchange Alley was crowded from morning till night with persons of both sexes; and society seemed for a moment turned upside-down. In the course of a few days, a multitude of individuals were raised from indigence to a profusion of wealth, which many of them expended in luxurious living and in reckless profligacy. In the park these upstart gentlemen mixed in their carriages with the aristocracy of the land; but they were singled out as objects of insult and derision by the rabble, and at first the "stock-jobbers'" carriages seldom appeared in the

[*] As the York Buildings Company's steam-engine appears not to have attracted much notice in the works on the history of this invention, which has created so extraordinary a revolution in modern society, it may not be thought uninteresting to add here a curious burlesque announcement of its first erection, with one or two other notices of it, taken from the journals of the day.

In the autumn of 1731, the supply of water to Mary-le-bone was discontinued, and the use of the engine was consequently discontinued at the same time. *Read's Journal*, in September 1731, announces briefly that "The York Buildings Company have given over working their fire-engine."

The engine was, however, allowed to remain there for several years, though inactive, and seems to have been shewn as a curiosity. In an account of London published in *All Alive and Merry: or the London Daily Post*, of Saturday, April 18, 1741, we have the following notice of it: "There is a famous machine in York Buildings, which was erected to force water by the means of fire, thro' pipes laid for that purpose into several parts of the town, and it was carry'd on for some time to effect; but the charge of working it, and some other reasons concurring, made its proprietors, the York Buildings Company, lay aside the design; and no doubt but the inhabitants in its neighbourhood are very glad of it; for its working, which was by sea-coal, was attended with so much smoak, that it not only pollute the air thereabouts, but spoil the furniture."

These apprehensions, which are amusing when we compare them with the present state of the metropolis, appear to have existed previous to the erection of the engine, and form part of the foundation of the following *jeu d'esprit*. It is advertised as "published this day," price 6d., in the *Daily Courant* of December 14, 1725; but it is here reprinted from *Read's Weekly Journal*, of December 18, 1725.

"*The York Buildings Dragons; or, a full and true account of a most horrid and barbarous murder intended to be committed next Monday, on the bodies, goods, and name of the greatest part of his Majesty's liege subjects dwelling and inhabiting between Temple Bar in the East, and St. James's in the West, and between Hungerford Market in the South, and St. Mary-la-bone in the North, by a set of evil-minded persons, who do assemble twice a week, to carry on their wicked purposes, in a private room over a stable by the Thames side, in a remote corner of the town.*

"Now these conspirators have purchased two enormous dragons from the deserts of Lybia of such monstrous sizes that the tail of one of 'em is a mile

streets without being mobbed. A newspaper of the 9th of July says satirically, " We are informed that, since the late hurly-burly of stock-jobbing, there has appeared in London two hundred new coaches and chariots, besides as many more now on the stocks in the coachmakers' yards ; above four thousand embroidered coats ; about three thousand gold watches at the sides of their —— and their wives ; some few private acts of charity ; and about two thousand broken tradesmen." In the midst of

and a half long,) which they have brought into this metropolis *incognito*, by the assistance of a conjurer, whom they have employed in that matter.

" This conjurer, therefore, by the help of a hunting-whip that has a talisman in the handle of it, contrived a means to run these dragons without paying any duty to the government; for, by applying this talisman to the head of each dragon, he shut up all the life within one particular gland of the head, and then anatomically dissected the two monsters, so that they could be easily stowed in several ships, and be brought in as coming from different parts of the world. And accordingly most of the nerves and sinews came from Sweden ; the greatest part of the head from Norway, by the help of another conjurer who combined with the first ; the joints, and veins, and arteries were brought from Derbyshire ; the breast from Worcestershire ; and the back and wings from Kent, Berkshire, and Hertfordshire; the belly from Cornwall ; and the greatest part of the tail from the West country, except the thick end next to the body, which, together with the snout and teeth, came out of Sussex by sea, and passed at the Custom House for some outlandish curiosity, imported by some virtuosos of Great Britain. *And you know natural knowledge is so much encouraged, that such things never pay any duty, but pass unexamined ;—*witness Villette's great burning-glass, the Hugenian telescope, and the wax-work anatomies. Now, if there had been any astrologers among the Custom House officers, nothing of this would have happened ; for they are perfectly well acquainted with dragons' heads and dragons' tails. But what would you have men do that never saw a dragon in all their lives ? Since there never was any in this kingdom before, but one, and that was at Wantley, almost two hundred miles distant from London, who was killed by More, of More Hall, before he could come southward ; and he was but a little dragon in comparison, for he only devoured *three children*, whereas these dragons either have or will devour whole families.

" But to return to our account. The conjuror and his abettors have concealed under a large tract of ground, the dreadful tail * of one of these monsters, and are now vivifying the whole animal by the reunion of its parts ; and diffusing its life from the *glandula pinealis* to the very extremities of the nostrils, wings, and tail.

" On Monday, therefore, the 20th instant, at 14 minutes past 10 in the morning, a Lancashire wizard, with long black hair and grim visage, will for some hours feed the eldest dragon with live coals ; and a Wel-bman, bred on the top of Penmaenmaur, will lay hold of the bridle to direct the motion of the creature. Then on a sudden will the monster clap his

---

* This, of course, is an allusion to the wooden pipes, already mentioned, extending from the York Buildings to Mary-le-bone Fields, to convey the Thames water to the great reservoir there.

these doings, about the 20th of July, news arrived in London that, on the preceding Wednesday, the 17th, Law had been insulted by the populace of Paris, who were only hindered from destroying his house in the Rue Quinquenpoix by the timely arrival of the Swiss Guards; and that they had broken his coach, beaten his coachman, and obliged him to seek refuge in the Palais Royal. The great projector was now looked upon by the populace as the sole cause of the misery in which they found

wings several times successively with prodigious force, and so terrible will be the noise thereof, that it will be heard as far as Calais, if the wind set right. All those who have musical ears, within the hills of mortality, will be struck deaf; those who have no ear will become deaf; and all who were deaf before, will start up and run away.

"The next disaster will be occasioned by the Welshman, who will cry 'Bob!' to make the dragon drink, who immediately dipping his two heads into the Thames, will suck out thence such a prodigious quantity of water, that barges will never after be able to go through bridges; the wharfs will become useless from the Steel Yard to Millbank; and the tide will not rise high enough to fill the basin of a set of good-natured gentlemen who have been at immense pains to serve the new buildings with water.

"*The next calamity will be this,*—That, whereas, the dragon lives upon Newcastle and Scotch coal, (which, by the bye, will produce scarcity of coal, by reason of the great consumption,) and other bituminous substances, and is of himself of a *huffing, snuffing* temper, he will dart out of his nostrils perpendicularly up to the skies two such vast, dense, and opake columns of smoke, that those who live in the Borough will hardly see the sun at noon-day. Now this smoke being *ponderous*, will descend again upon all the neighbouring inhabitants; being *elastic*, will spread and fall upon all the evergreens within ten miles of London; and being *fuliginous*, will so discolor their hue, that it will puzzle a very nice botanist to determine concerning any leaf within that compass of ground whether it be of a *subfusc* or a downright *piceous* colour after this accident. *Happy* will then the ladies be who have papered up all their furniture before they went out of town! *Happy* the stationers who have timely shut up their shops to preserve their paper! And *thrice happy* the poor washer-women, who have closed up and pointed the garret-windows where they have hung up their linen clothes to dry. Besides all this, the sulphureous particles arising from the coals will be so pernicious to the lungs of all who suck them in, that they will break several blood-vessels with coughing. Add to all this, that upon the subsiding of this black pillar, the cities of London and Westminster will lose sight of one another, though in the clearest day; so that nobody can possibly receive any benefit by this contrivance, unless it be the link-boys, who will be absolutely necessary to conduct people through the smoke.

"*But the worst consequence* of all, and which I almost dread to relate, is, *this dragon's way of poisoning.* Through a long proboscis, something like an elephant's trunk, this creature can at pleasure filtrate and suck in all the venomous effluvia out of the air, water, and other fluids. And, therefore, to make up the desolation of this poor city, he will from the Thames in great abundance draw in all the fœtidocabbageous, deaddoggilious, deadcatitious, Fish-streethillious, Drurylanious, issueplaste-

themselves involved, and he was obliged to give way so far to the general clamour as to resign his office of Comptroller of Finances. In November he was entirely deserted by the Regent; and, after securing his great fortune, retired into Italy.

In August the stock of the various London companies was calculated to exceed the value of five hundred millions. The first great shock was given by the jealousy of the South Sea Company, who procured writs of *scire facias* to be issued against some of the unauthorised bodies. The destruction of these exposed the fallacy of the whole, and recoiled almost immediately on the larger company itself. By the end of September, South Sea stock had sunk in value from 850 to 175; and thousands of families were reduced at one blow to absolute beggary; "some of whom," to quote the words of a writer who lived at the time,

rious, excrementitious, and all common-shoreitions particles therein contained from time to time; and having therewith filled his stomach, this mixtgious compound will pass the pylorus, and being carried along the viscera by the peristaltic motion, will issue out at the anus, (which in this animal is in the last joint of the tail) with great stench, in vast quantities, into a large receptacle prepared by the aforesaid conjuror for receiving and containing this hellish liquor. Now, as this fluid is always to run in, and never to go out, it is evident to all chemists and naturalists, and several other ingenious gentlemen besides, that there must be an intestine motion, because the fluid stands still, and this intestine motion will cause a fermentation, which fermentation will cast out *androsuagus* such pestiferous streams and vapours, as will depopulate all the whole neighbourhood in such a manner that grass will grow in Queen Anne Street, Chandos Street, Mortimer Street, and all the adjacent streets, till the genius of architecture comes to the relief of the desolate place. And if it should so happen, that, by the violent motion of the beast, it should receive any wounds in its tail, from every wound will issue with impetuosity rivers of this abominable liquor, which will inundate and render impassable the streets, drown all those that come within its vortex, and such as venture to look out of their chamber-windows will be suffocated with the putrid vapour.

"To *conclude* my dismal story: I must let the world know that these conspirators are enemies to the souls as well as the bodies of all persons they can have any influence over, by setting up a new kind of *Popery*, and have already persuaded several families to worship these dragons. Among other things, they have a ceremony much like *Transubstantiation*; for, by the mixture of Ceres and Neptune, (*and what is the Popish Host but bread and water!*) they have contrived a *consigillated wafer*, which turns paper into money.

"Now to give my reader a little hope, before I quit this melancholy tale, I must acquaint him that a set of honest and brave gentlemen intend to prosecute these *vile men*, who will find themselves deceived in trusting to the *Toleration Act*; for that act allows of no *image-worship* within ten miles of London, except it be in a foreign amb——r's chapel.

"Written by a club of ingenious gentlemen.

"*Anodine Necklace*, Secretary."

"after so long living in splendour, were not able to stand the shock of poverty and contempt, and died of broken hearts; others withdrew to remote parts of the world, and never returned."

In the month of August, even before the issuing of the writs of *scire facias*, people began to foresee the catastrophe, and some prudent men withdrew, after having realized great fortunes. Towards the end of August "the bubbles" were turned to ridicule in a multitude of songs and satirical pieces. In the first days of September appeared the celebrated South Sea ballad, which was sung about the streets of London for months together, and helped not a little to bring stock-jobbing into discredit.

A SOUTH SEA BALLAD; OR, MERRY REMARKS UPON EXCHANGE ALLEY BUBBLES.

To a new tune called "The Grand Elixir; or, the Philosopher's Stone Discovered."

1.

"In London stands a famous pile
And near that pile an alley,
Where merry crowds for riches toil,
And Wisdom stoops to Folly.
Here sad and joyful, high and low,
Court Fortune for her graces;
And as she smiles or frowns, they show
Their gestures and grimaces.

2.

"Here stars and garters do appear,
Among our lords the rabble;
To buy and sell, to see and hear,
The Jews and Gentiles squabble.
Here crafty courtiers are too wise
For those who trust to Fortune;
They see the cheat with clearer eyes,
Who peep behind the curtain.

3.

"Our greatest ladies hither come,
And ply in chariots daily;
Oft pawn their jewels for a sum
To venture in the Alley.
Young harlots, too, from Drury Lane,
Approach the 'Change in coaches,
To fool away the gold they gain
By their impure debauches.

4.

"Longheads may thrive by sober rules,
Because they think, and drink not;

E

But headlong are our thriving fools,
  Who only drink and think not.
The lucky rogues, like spaniel dogs,
  Leap into South Sea Water,
And there they fish for golden frogs,
  Not caring what comes a'ter.

5.

"'Tis said that alchemists of old
  Could turn a brazen kettle,
Or leaden cistern, into gold,—
  That noble tempting metal;
But if i. here may be allow'd
  To bring in great and small things,
Our cunning South Sea, like the gods,
  Turns nothing into all things!

6.

"What need have we of Indian wealth,
  Or commerce with our neighbours?
Our constitution is in health,
  And riches crown our labours.
Our South Sea ships have golden shrouds,
  They bring us wealth, 'tis granted,
But lodge their treasure in the clouds,
  To hide it till it's wanted.

7.

"O Britain, bless thy present state,
  Thou only happy nation;
So oddly rich, so madly great,
  Since bubbles came in fashion!
Successful rakes exert their pride,
  And count their airy millions;
Whilst homely drabs in coaches ride,
  Brought up to town on pillions.

8.

"Few men, who follow reason's rules,
  Grow fat with South Sea diet;
Young rattles and unthinking fools,
  Are those that flourish by it.
Old musty jades, and pushing blades,
  Who've least consideration,
Grow rich apace; whilst wiser heads
  Are struck with admiration.

9.

"A race of men, who t' other day
  Lay crush'd beneath disasters,
And now by stock brought into play,
  And made our lords and masters.
But should our South Sea Babel fall,
  What numbers would be frowning!
The losers then must ease their gall
  By hanging or by drowning.

10.

" Five hundred millions, notes and bonds,
Our stocks are worth in value ;
But neither lie in goods or lands,
Or money, let me tell you.
Yet though our foreign trade is lost,
Of mighty wealth we vapour ;
When all the riches that we boast
Consists in scraps of paper ! "

From the month of October to the end of the year, songs,
and squibs, and pamphlets of all descriptions, on the misfortunes
occasioned by the explosion of the bubble system, became exceedingly numerous. Two dramatic pieces, " The Broken
Stock-Jobbers," a farce, " as lately acted by his Majesty's subjects in Exchange Alley," and " South-Sea ; or, The Biter Bit,"
a farce, are advertised in the mouth of October. The general
feeling against the directors was becoming so strong in the
mouth of November, that we are told it had become a practice
among the ladies, when in playing at cards they turned up a
knave, to cry, " There is a director for you !"

The period of the South Sea bubble is that in which political
caricatures began to be common in England ; for they had before been published at rare intervals, and partook so much of
the character of emblems, that they are not always very easy to
be understood. Read's *Weekly Journal* of November 1, 1718,
gives a caricature against the Tories, engraved on wood, which
is called " an hieroglyphic," so little was the real nature of a
caricature then appreciated. Another fault under which these
earlier caricatures labour is that of being extremely elaborate.
The earliest English caricature on the South Sea Company is
advertised in the *Post Boy* of June 21, 1720, under the title of
" The Bubblers bubbled ; or, The Devil take the Hindmost."
It no doubt related to the great rush which was made to subscribe to the numerous companies afloat in that month." I have
not met with a copy of it, but in the advertisement it is stated
to be represented " by a *great number of figures*. In the advertisement of another caricature, on the 29th of February in this
year, called " The World in Masquerade," it is set forth, as one
of its great recommendations, that it was " represented in nigh
eighty figures." In France and in Holland (where the bubble-
mania had thrown everything into the greatest confusion), the
number of caricatures published during the year 1720 was very
considerable. In the latter country, a large number of these
caricatures, as well as many satirical plays and songs, were
collected together and published in a folio volume, which is still

not uncommon, under the title, "Het groote Tafereel der Dwaasheid" (The great Picture of Folly). The greater portion of these foreign caricatures relate to Law and his Mississippi scheme. In one of these, a number of persons of both sexes, and of all ages and conditions in society, are represented acting the part of Atlas, each supporting a globe on his shoulders. Law, the Atlas who supported the world of paper, —*l'Atlas acticux de papier*, as he is termed in the French description of the plate,—bears his globe but unsteadily, and is obliged to call in Hercules to his aid.

A MODERN ATLAS.

> "Roi Atlas, hé! pourquoi te fatiguer ainsi?
> Permets qu'Hercule vienne, et te donne assistance,
> Et t'aide à soutenir ton charge d'importance.
> Quoi qu'on dit c'est papier ou du vent, aujourd'hui,
> Il n'y a en ce temps d'espèce si pesante ;
> Puis qu'en troc et trafic il pèse plus que d'or."

So little point is there often in these caricatures, and so great appears to have been the call for them in Holland, that people seemed to have looked up old engravings, designed originally for a totally different purpose, and, adding new inscriptions and new explanations, they were published as caricatures on the bubbles. These betray themselves sometimes by the costume. A large wood-cut which represents the meeting of a King and a nobleman in the court of a palace, attended by a crowd of courtiers in the costume of the days of Henry IV. or Louis XIII., is thus made to represent the crowding of the stock-jobbers to the Rue Quinquenpoix. In the same manner a large plate, which seems originally to have been an allegorical representation of the battle between Carnival and Lent (a rather popular subject at an earlier period), is here given under the new title of "The Battle between the good-living Bubble-lords and approaching Poverty," (*Stryd tuszen de smullende Bubbel-Heeren en de aanstaande Armoede.*)

The best of these caricatures is a large engraving by Picart, which appears in the Dutch volume, with explanations in French and Dutch, and which was re-engraved with English descriptions and applications in London. It is a general satire on the madness which characterized the memorable year 1720. "Qui," says the inscription,—

> "Qui le croira ? qui l'eût jamais pensé !
> Qu'en un siècle si sage un système insensé
> Fît du commerce un jeu de la Fortune !
> Et se jeu pernicieux,
> Euvorci lant Jeunes et vieux,
> Remplit tous les esprits d'une yvresse commune."

Fortune is here driven in her car by Folly, the car being drawn by the personifications of the principal companies who began the pernicious trade of stock-jobbing, as the Mississippi, represented with a wooden leg ; the South Sea, with a sore leg, and the other bound with a ligament ; the Bank, treading under foot a serpent, &c. The agents of some of the larger companies are turning the wheels of the car, and are represented with foxes' tails, "to show their policy and cunning." The spokes of the wheels are inscribed with the names of different companies, which, as the car moves forward, are alternately up and down ; while books of merchandise, crushed and torn beneath them, represent the destruction of trade and commerce. In the clouds the Devil appears making bubbles of soap, which mingle with the "actions" and other things (good and bad) that Fortune is distributing to the crowd. "Those," it is added, "that will give themselves the trouble of examining the print, may discover many things which are not here explained, in order that the curious may have the pleasure *of having some-*

DOUBLE ROBBERY.

thing to guess at!" In fact there are a number of different groups in the picture which are not described. On one side, one of the fox-tailed gentlemen is whispering into the ear of a simple buyer of actions, while a roguish lad is picking his pockets behind. Those who brought their money into Exchange Alley were exposed to every description of robbery. Near these, in the original print, a handsome young damsel is thrown by the sudden frown of Fortune into the longing arms of an old and ill-favoured but more fortunate worshipper of the capricious goddess.

> " Quand on est jeune et belle, et qu'on a le malheur
> D'avoir perdu son bien dans un jeu si funeste,
> Gare qu'un billet au porteur
> Ne fasse encore perdre le reste !"

TRANSFER.

We are well assured by the writers of the time, that the profligacy which followed this mad gambling was almost incredible. On the other side of the picture is a group occupied in buying and selling stock : the seller appears eager for the purchase-money, which the buyer is counting out upon a block, while a Jew broker transacts the affair. The word "transfer" is inscribed on the block in the English print. The car of Fortune proceeds from a large coffee-house, over the door of which, in the original plate, we read the word "Quinquenpoix;" in place of which the English copy has "Jonathan's," which was the great place of resort in London for bubblers and bubbled. At the other extremity of the picture, the infatuated crowd is hurrying forward to fill the three places of its final destination,—the mad-house, the poor-house, and the hospital. The latter is called, in the English print, "The House of Fools;" but, in several particulars of this kind, as well as in artistical execution, the original engraving of Picart is much superior to the English copy. Folly is represented with the spacious hoop-petticoat, patches, and other extravagant fashions of the day,—a true female exquisite of the year 1720.

The *Post-Boy* of October 20, 1720 contains an advertisement of the publication " this day " of " a pack of bubble cards," each containing an engraving relating to one of the numerous companies formed or projected during the summer, and accompanied with an appropriate epigram, "the lines by the author of the ' South Sea Ballad,' and the ' Tippling Philosopher.'" In the *Weekly Packet* and in Mist's *Weekly Journal* of December 10, " A new Pack of Stock-jobbing Cards" is announced as published that day, with lines

FOLLY IS THE GAME OF 1720.

by the same author. The price of each pack is stated to be two shillings and sixpence. The notion of political playing-cards was not altogether new ; one, at least, had appeared in the latter times of the Commonwealth, and in the reign of Charles II. a pack of such cards had been published on the celebrated Popish Plot, which had caused almost as great an excitement throughout the country as the bubbles of the year 1720. A set of bubble cards had also been published in this latter year in Holland ; but whether the Dutch took the hint from the English, or the English from the Dutch, it is not easy to determine.

These packs of South Sea cards are preserved in the collection of Mr. Burke. Each of the " bubble cards " contains an engraving representing the object of one of the numerous companies that grew up round the greater bubble of the South Sea scheme, with an epigram in four lines, which is frequently quaint and amusing. The ten of hearts has a ship freighting with timber, in allusion to the company for exporting timber from Germany, and the lines,

> " You that are rich, and hasty to be poor,
> Buy timber export from the German shore ;
> For gallowses, built up of foreign wood,
> If rightly us'd, may do 'Change Alley good."

The object of another company was the " curing tobacco for snuff ;" and the card represents two negroes and their overseer passing the snuff through a sieve, whilst their eyes very unequivocally suffer from the dust :—

> "Here slaves for snuff are sifting Indian weed,
> Whilst their o'erseer does the riddle feed ;
> The dust arising gives their eyes much trouble,
> To show their blindness that espouse the bubble."

The " stock-jobbing " cards are more decidedly caricatures than
the others, and they deal more especially with the doings of
the bubblers and their dupes, than with the bubbles themselves.
On the three of clubs we see two stock-jobbers inventing political news, and resolving to proclaim the birth of a young Pretender, or rather two, from the marriage of the old one with
the Polish Princess Sobieski, as the news most likely to affect
the value of the funds.

> "Two jobbers for the day invent a lie,
> And broach the same to low'r the stocks thereby.
> One says the Pole 's delivered ; t' other swears
> She's brought to bed of two pretending heirs."

The king of clubs gives a receipt against bankruptcy ; a tradesman in distress receives counsel from his friend : " I'd advise
you to buy stock, and take it up in fourteen days ; it may
chance to rise, but if it falls you can but then go off." The
tradesman takes the hint :—" 'Tis true, one breaking will serve
for all ; but if I succeed, 'twill make me a man ;" and it appears
he is successful.

> " A bending tradesman to retrieve his fortune,
> Buys stock to take it in a fortnight certain ;
> It rises greatly by the time of taking,
> And thus the buyer saves himself from breaking."

The nine of hearts tells a different story :—

> " A merchant liv'd of late in reputation,
> But bilk'd by stock, like thousands in the nation,
> Goes to the Mint, his bad success bemoaning,
> To shun his ruin, saves himself by breaking."

In another card, three bubble directors advise with their lawyer:
one says to his legal adviser, " Sir, if you can evade this act, you
and I may ride in our coaches." " My advice," answers the
lawyer, " is, get what money you can, give me some, and make
off with the rest." The other two bubblers are consulting in a
corner of the room on the most effectual way of securing the
zeal of the lawyer in their cause : " Tell him he shall be a
director," says the one. The verses on the card are not worth
quoting. On the three of diamonds—

> " A lady pawns her jewels by her maid,
> And in declining stock presumes to trade ;
> Till in South Sea she drowns her coin,
> And now in Bristol stones is glad to shine."

The greater number of the English caricatures on the follies of the year 1720 were published in the year following. The *London Journal*, April 22, 1721, announces, as "Just publish'd, six fine prints, representing the humours of the French, Dutch, and English bubblers and stock-jobbers; with variety of humours," &c. These probably included the two "Bubblers' Medleys;" and two equally well-known plates, entitled "The Bubbler's Mirrour," in one of which is represented a figure joyful for the rise of stock, and in the other a man in deep mourning lamenting its fall. Both of these latter prints are surrounded by lists of the bubbles, accompanied with the same epigrams which appear on the bubble cards. The English caricatures of this time are but poor imitations of the foreign ones; in fact, the taste for them seems to have been imported from abroad, and the South Sea disaster must be looked upon as the beginning of the rage for caricatures which appeared in this country a few years after. It must not be forgotten, that Hogarth's first political caricature related to the bubbles of 1720, and was published in 1721.

The misery produced by these bubbles in the winter of 1720, both in England and on the Continent, can with difficulty be conceived. Yet, after the space of a century, the same folly reappeared in the mania of 1825, and some of the same bubbles were revived; but their effects at the latter period were small in comparison to those of 1720. A German medal in the collection of Mr. Haggard, struck probably towards the end of the year last mentioned, represents on one side the momentary prosperity of the stock-jobbers, and on the reverse the frightful catastrophe. Suicide by hanging and drowning, hasty flight, and despair, as here represented, were the share of hundreds. The clamour of the sufferers overcame all other appeals to the Government during the year 1721. A searching examination by a committee of the House of Commons exposed to public view many iniquitous transactions; and the general dissatisfaction was increased by the belief that not only the ministers of the Crown, but more especially the King's mistresses and his greedy Ger-

THE END OF BUBBLING.

man followers, had received bribes in the first instance for
procuring the passing of the South Sea bill, and had afterwards
made great profits by stock-jobbing. The South Sea directors
became objects of hatred and persecution, and their property was
confiscated and themselves imprisoned. The ministry was
broken up; and, at the beginning of April, remodelled under the
guidance of Mr. Walpole, who, though accused of having pro-
fitted largely by trading in stock himself, was the only man
capable at this moment of bringing a remedy to the evil.
Robert Knight, the treasurer of the South Sea Company, after
undergoing a partial examination, fled (with the book which, it
was believed, contained the greatest secrets of the late transactions) to France, and thence to Brabant, where he was arrested
and confined in the castle at Antwerp. There he remained
during the greater part of the year, for the States of Brabant
refused to deliver him up to the English Government. It was
commonly believed that the flight of the South Sea treasurer
had been contrived by greater persons; that the attempts to
bring him back to England were not made in earnest; and that
his arrest in Brabant was a mere act of collusion, the whole
being a screen to hide the conduct of great persons about Court,
whom it was essential to keep from public view. This screen,
and Knight's escape from England, began to be the subject of a
variety of caricatures after the month of April, 1721. In one of
these the fugitive is represented as taking refuge in the infernal
regions, the fittest receptacle, as it was represented, for so detested an individual. In another, entitled "The Brabant Screen,"
Knight is figured in his travelling garb, receiving his de-

KNIGHT'S DEPARTURE.

spatches, which are given to
him from behind the screen by
the King's chief mistress, or
left-hand wife, the Duchess of
Kendal, who was said to have
received enormous sums from
the South Sea Company, and
who chiefly was supposed to
hinder Knight from being
delivered to justice. On the
other side of the screen, a
paper lying on a table bears
the words, " Patience, time,
and money set everything
to rights; " insinuating that
Knight had been designedly

rent out of the way until the public feeling could be appeased. Underneath the engraving are some verses, the spirit of which will be sufficiently shewn by the first half-dozen :—

> " In vain Great Britain sues for Knight's discharge,
> In vain we hope to see that wretch at large ;
> If traitors here the villain there secure,
> Our ills must all increase, our woes be sure.
> Should he return, the screen would unclose be,
> And all men then the mystery would see." *

The wise measures of Walpole gradually alleviated the evils which the South Sea affair had inflicted on society, although they were felt heavily for some time ; and the name of stock-jobber has never entirely thrown off the weight of popular odium which it contracted on this occasion. The effect upon politics was, however, much less than the opponents of King George's government hoped for and reckoned upon : but a new subject of agitation was now approaching, which helped in some measure to make people forget the former. The first Parliament of George I. would naturally have expired in 1717 ; but the ministers, who had already experienced on two memorable occasions the danger of general elections in a moment of excitement, and imagined that there was much then to be dreaded from the intrigues of the Jacobites, had obtained in 1716 an act of Parliament repealing the Triennial Act, and fixing the legal duration of a Parliament to seven years, and the bill was made to apply to the Parliament then in existence. By this alteration King George's first Parliament was to end with the year 1721 ; and the elections, to all appearance, would fall amid the still existing excitement of the misfortunes of the bubble explosion. We find, however, that this subject of complaint was very little agitated in the elections which took place in the spring of 1722. The chief attack upon the Court party was made by exciting the old mob-prejudices against the Commonwealth and Dissenters. The Tories accused the late Parliament of a design to constitute themselves another "Long" Parliament, published lists of those who voted for and against the repeal of the Triennial Act, and stigmatized the former by the old and unpopular title of the "Rump." Pamphlets on the

* The caricatures mentioned above, and one or two others on the same subject, are preserved in the collection of Mr. Burke and Mr. Hawkins. The print representing the entrance of Knight into the infernal regions was probably published later in the year, for a caricature entitled " Robin's Flight ; or, the ghost of the late S. S. treasurer ferry'd into hell," is advertised as just published in a newspaper of Sept. 23, 1721.

misdeeds of the Rump Parliament were diligently spread abroad; and in some places the old custom of burning rumps was again practised by the mob, whose usual cry was " Up with the Church, and down with the Rump !"

But Walpole brought now into action what would seem to have been a new system of electioneering, by which he gained a signal victory over his opponents, who still placed their dependence on the old plan of raising a popular excitement, which under other circumstances had proved so eminently successful in Queen Anne's time, and had embarrassed the Government even under the disadvantages to the Tories which accompanied the change of the reigning family. Long before the dissolution of the Parliament, the Government candidates declared themselves openly, and personally canvassed the electors ; and no expedient was left untried to secure their votes. The Tory papers complain bitterly, that, on this occasion, noblemen and gentlemen condescended to solicit votes with an undignified familiarity. We cannot now be otherwise than amused at complaints like the following, published in a Tory paper, Applebee's *Original Weekly Journal* of January 6, 1722 :—" Altho' we think the appointing general meetings of the gentlemen of counties, for making agreements for votes for the election of a new Parliament before the old Parliament is expir'd, is a most scandalous method and an evident token of corruption, yet we find it daily practic'd, and, which is worse, publickly own'd, particularly in the county of Surrey, where the very names of the candidates are publish'd, and the votes of the freeholders openly sollicited in the publick prints. The like is now doing, or preparing to be done, for Buckinghamshire ; and we are told, likewise, that it is doing for other counties also." In fact, this deliberate preparing of votes was eminently calculated to counteract the sudden influence of popular agitation and mob excitement throughout the country ; and aware, by what had so recently passed, of the power of money at that time, Walpole is said to have practised on the present occasion a very extensive system of bribery.

When the Parliament was dissolved in March, a host of pamphlets were sent into the world, as had been done before on similar occasions, to influence the votes of electors ; and the old system of getting up mobs was again resorted to. These mobs, in some instances, beat and kept away those who were on their way to vote for the opposite party : in some cases they carried them off, and locked them up till the election was over. In several places, especially at Coventry, fearful riots took place.

In London there was much agitation; and, on this occasion,
Westminster began those scenes of uproar which were afterwards
so often repeated. But the influence of the mob diminished
before Walpole's foresight and his gold, and in the new Parliament the Government obtained an overwhelming majority. The
opposition was reduced to a state of weakness, in which it could
only vent its spleen in political squibs and caricatures. In the
midst of the elections, but when the result was no longer
doubtful, on the 31st of March. an advertisement in the Tory
Post-Boy announces as just published, price sixpence each, two
prints, under the titles of " The Prevailing Candidate; or, the
election carried by bribery and the D——l;" and " Britannia
stript by a Villain ; to which is added, the true phiz of a late
member." The first of these only appears now to be known :*
the right-hand side is occupied by a screen of seven folds, which
are intended to represent the seven almost barren years of the
late Parliament; while on the left appears the group here repre-

AN ELECTION EPISODE.

sented, which is explained by the verses underneath. This is the
earliest caricature on elections with which I am acquainted.

> " Here's a minion sent down to a corporate town,
>   In hopes to be newly elected ;

* This rare print, which is one of the best of the caricatures of the reign
of George the First, is in the collection of Mr. Hawkins.

By his prodigal show, you may easily know
To the Court he is truly affected.

" He 'as a knave by the hand, who has power to command
All the votes in the corporation ;
Shoves a sum in his pocket, the D——l cries ' Take it,
'Tis all for the good of the nation !'

" The wife, standing by, looks a little awry
At the candidate's way of addressing ;
But a priest stepping in avers bribery no sin,
Since money 's a family blessing.

" Say the boys, ' Ye mad rogues, here are French wooden brogues,
To reward your vile treacherous knavery ;
For such traitors as you are the rascally crew
That betray the whole kingdom to slavery.' "

The more violent Tories, in their despair, seem to have been
thrown again upon dangerous undertakings. We have seen,
that, even in the midst of the bubble mania, the movements of
the Pretender were considered sufficient to affect the public
funds ; and the eyes of Englishmen were constantly fixed upon
him in his retreat at Rome. The joy of the Jacobites was great,
when they learnt, at the end of the year 1720, that his Polish
wife had given birth to a son, a young Pretender, destined to be
brought on the stage when the little energy over possessed by
his father was gone. They hoped much from the dissatisfaction
and sufferings caused by the disasters of the South Sea scheme,
and they had been signally disappointed in the result of the
elections. The excitement of these had scarcely subsided, when
the English Government received from France information of a
formidable conspiracy at home against King George ; and it was
discovered that the Pretender had left Rome, and that the
Duke of Ormond was on his way from Madrid to be prepared on
the coast of Biscay for a descent on that of England. A camp
was immediately formed in Hyde Park, to protect the King and
the metropolis, from which latter all Papists, or reputed Papists,
were warned to depart, by a royal proclamation issued on the
9th of May. At the same time we trace attempts to raise a
new feeling among the mob in favour of the exiled family ; and
it is announced, in Read's *Weekly Journal* of May 26, that
" The messenger of the press has caused fourteen persons to be
sent to the House of Correction, for crying about the city scandalous and traiterous songs." In perilous undertakings like
this, caricatures were circulated on medals, rather than in prints,
and we have such a medal struck at this time, with a head of
the Pretender on the obverse, and the legend UNICA SALUS, and
on the reverse, under the legend QUID GRAVIUS CAPTA, a distant

view of London, with Britannia
weeping in the foreground, and
before her face the horse of
Hanover trampling upon her
lion and unicorn. The Jacobites
pretended that the nation had
been enslaved by the Court influence in the elections; and on
the 20th of September, long
after the English conspirators
had been seized, the Pretender issued a mad declaration, which
was printed and industriously distributed in England, in which
he dwelt especially on the pretended violation of the freedom of
voting. The declaration was ordered by the British Parliament,
which was then assembled, to be burnt by the hands of the
hangman.

A bishop was the principal conspirator in the Jacobite plot of
1722. Atterbury, of Rochester, was a minister of the Crown
under the brief premiership of Bolingbroke in the few last days
of the reign of Queen Anne; on whose death he alone had been
bold enough to propose that they should proclaim the son, or
reputed son, of James II. as her successor to the throne. He
had been ever since noted for his disaffection to the Hanoverian
government; and now he seems to have rashly embraced the
hope that a few troops under the Duke of Ormond, landed on
the southern coast, would be enough to overthrow it. At the
end of May, several inferior, but active, conspirators, were taken
into custody; they were, a non-juring clergyman named Kelly,
an Irish Catholic priest of the name of Neynoe, Layer, (a young
barrister of the Temple,) and another Irishman, (a Jesuit named
Plunket.) Their examinations led to the arrest of Bishop
Atterbury, who was committed a close prisoner to the Tower on
the 24th of August. The High-Church party were furious at
what they considered the sacrilege of imprisoning a bishop; and
the Tories declared publicly that the whole plot was a fiction,
that the Pretender had never quitted Rome, and that his party
had no designs against King George's government. This was
soon contradicted by the Pretender's own declaration; and
documents which have of late years come to light destroy all
doubts that might have been entertained of the guilt of Atterbury. In the beginning of 1723 Layer was brought to his trial,
and was convicted of having enlisted men for the Pretender's
service, in order to raise a new rebellion; he was executed at
Tyburn. The Tories still ridiculed the plot, and as late as the

16th of April, 1723, we learn from the *Daily Journal*, that "diligent search is making after the contrivers and dispersers of a seditious copy of verses burlesquing the discovery of the late wicked conspiracy, and the methods taken for punishing the conspirators." In May, however, Atterbury was brought to trial before the House of Lords; a bill of pains and penalties was passed, by which he was deprived of his bishopric, and banished the kingdom; and on the 18th of June he was put on board a King's ship and conveyed to France, where he at once entered the service of the Pretender. A medal was now struck to commemorate the defeat of the design, which the Pretender's medal above mentioned was intended to forward. On the obverse, the conspirators are represented as seated round a table in deep consultation, the Bishop presiding and delivering a paper to them. Above is a legend intimating the determination to restore the exile to his lost crown—DECRETUM EST, REGNO DOITO RESTITUATUR ADACTUS—the numeral letters of which

make the date 1722, as that in which the plot was carried on. On the reverse of the medal, the eye of Providence never asleep, darts its lightnings among the conspirators, casting the Bishop's mitre from his head, and striking apparently with death another conspirator seated on the right, probably intended to represent the Templar, Layer. The inscription on this side is, CONSPIRATE, APEBIT DEUS, [oculum], ET VOS FULMINE PULSAT, the numeral letters of which make the date 1723, the year in which the plotters were convicted and punished. At the foot of the medal, obverse and reverse, is the inscription CONSPIRATIO BRITANNICA.*

* This medal as well as the Pretender's medal mentioned before, is in the collection of Mr. Haggard.

From this time the government of King George was relieved from most of its uneasiness. The ministers, strong in their parliamentary majorities, paid little heed to the clamours of the opposition ; trade went on flourishing, and the Pretender was no longer in a position to give alarm. The greatest subjects of political agitation were an Irish squabble about half-pence, or a Scottish riot against taxes. Even before the elections, the London newspapers had found leisure to dispute about the murder of Julius Cæsar and the patriotism of Brutus ; and for several years after the bitterness of party feeling appears to have cast itself chiefly into the ranks of literature and science.

CHAPTER III.

GEORGE I. AND II.

Literature Debased by the Rage for Politics—The Stage—Operas, Masquerades, and Pantomimes—Heidegger and his Singers—Orator Henley—The "Beggar's Opera"—"The Dunciad"—Continued Popularity of the Opera—Political use of the Stage—Act for Licensing Plays—Attacks upon Pope—New Edition of the "Dunciad."

THE agitation produced by the year of bubbles was followed by loud outcries against the alarming increase of immorality and profligacy, the debased character of the stage, and the low state of literature, all of which were made alternately the watchwords of political strife. A long-established opinion, perhaps not altogether just, has fixed upon the reign of Queen Anne as the Augustan age of English literature; but the few pure models of English composition which that age produced were scattered stars among a countless multitude of unworthy scribblers, whose fame was in subsequent times embodied in the name of Grubb Street, and who, from a variety of causes, were gradually driving the more classic writers out of the field. The first kings of the Hanoverian dynasty had no love for letters; and it happened that one or two of the most distinguished literary names belonged to the party in opposition to their government. Those only could live by their writings who would throw themselves into the troubled sea of party, or who would pander to the depraved taste of the mob of readers; or, in other words, who would be the slaves of the newspapers or of the booksellers. The party newspapers were increasing daily in scurrility as well as in number; but, instead of the wit and elegance of the *Spectators* and *Tattlers*, they were filled with calumny and defamation, or with wearisome tales of gallantry, varied only by occasional and not unfrequent patches of indecent ribaldry. It is clear, indeed, that the national taste had become as vulgar as the national manners, and as corrupt as the principles of a large majority of the public men of that period. The works which received the greatest encouragement were scandalous memoirs, secret history surreptitiously obtained and sent forth under fictitious names, (such as the books which came from the pens of Eliza Haywood, Mrs. Manley, and other equally shameless female writers, and from the press of Edmund Curll,) and ill-disguised obscenity.

A great number of the low political writers of the day were well paid with the government money. The secret committee appointed to inquire into the sins of Walpole's administration, after he had retired from office, reported that no less than fifty thousand and seventy-seven pounds eighteen shillings were paid to authors and printers of newspapers in the course of ten years, between February 10, 1731, and February 10, 1741. Of this, it appears, by the report just quoted, that William Arnall, a very active political writer, received in the course of four years, "for *Free Britons* and writing," eleven thousand pounds out of the Treasury.

After the employment of writing for Government, the most profitable was that of writing for the stage. The drama was suffering perhaps more than any other class of literature by the debasement of public taste, although it had certainly been raised in moral character since the days of Charles II. Under his reign there had been two sets of actors, known as "the King's" and "the Duke's;" but, in 1690, these were united in one company, who, under one patent, had their house in Drury Lane. Internal dissension, however, soon led to disunion in the company; and the seceders, under Betterton, obtained from King William a licence to act independently, and a theatre was built for them in Lincoln's Inn Fields. There was, of course, a zealous rivalry between the two parties, which in the opinion of Colley Cibber, led each to seek patronage by yielding to the taste of the mob, instead of being able to guide it; but after the experience of another century, we have every reason to disagree in the opinion formed by Cibber on this tendency. In 1706 a new and "stately" theatre was provided in the Haymarket for the Lincoln's Inn company, built under the direction of Sir John Vanbrugh; and an attempt was made to effect a reunion between the two companies, but without effect. The Haymarket theatre, known under Anne as the Queen's, and under her successors as the King's theatre, was found not to answer well its original intention, and it was afterwards appropriated to the Italian Opera; for, as Cibber tells us, "not long before this time the Italian Opera began first to steal into England, but in as rude a disguise and unlike itself as possible; in a lame, hobbling translation into our own language, with false quantities, or metre out of measure to its original notes, sung by our own unskilful voices, with graces misapplied to almost every sentiment, and with action lifeless and unmeaning through every character."

After a number of vicissitudes, the licensed companies of actors remained in nearly the same position towards each other under George the First. "His Majesty's company of comedians," under the joint management of Booth, Cibber, and Wilks, held Drury Lane; the theatre in Lincoln's Inn Fields had been rebuilt for the opposition company under Rich: and the King's theatre in the Haymarket was devoted exclusively to the Italian Opera, under the management of the celebrated John James Heidegger.* Not long before the rise of the South Sea scheme, masquerades were introduced at the Opera House as a new attraction to popularity; and in a short time they became, under Heidegger's management, the rage of the town. Every one seemed to relish the momentary saturnalia in which all ranks and classes, in outward disguise at least, mixed together in indiscriminate confusion; where, to use the words of a contemporary writer,

> "Fools, dukes, rakes, cardinals, fops, Indian queens,
> Belles in tye-wigs, and lords in Harlequins,
> Troops of right honourable porters come,
> And garter'd small coal-merchants crowd the room;
> Valets stuck o'er with coronets appear,
> Lacquey's of state, and footmen with a star;
> Sailors of quality with judges mix,
> And chimney-sweepers drive their coach and six:
> Statesmen, so used at Court the mask to wear,
> Now condescend again to use it here;
> Idiots turn conjurers, and courtiers clowns,
> And sultans drop their handkerchiefs to nuns."

The masquerade soon became more than a figurative leveller of society; for sharpers, and women of ill-repute, and others, gained admission, and the consequence was nightly scenes of robbery, and quarrels, and scandalous licentiousness. The general agreement of contemporary writers on this subject can leave no doubt on our minds of the evil effects of masquerades on the morality of the day. The South Sea convulsion had hardly subsided, when a general outcry was heard against the alarming increase of atheism, profaneness, and immorality, and an attempt was made to suppress them by Act of Parliament, but the bill for that purpose was not allowed to pass. The

---

* There was also a "new theatre over against the Opera, which, in the latter years of the reign of George I., was held by a party of French players; and an unlicensed company of English players acted in a theatre in Goodman's Fields.

dangerous effects of masquerades were particularly insisted upon; and they soon became the object of severe attacks in the newspapers, and in satirical as well as serious pamphlets. In spite, however, of all that could be done, these proscribed entertainments continued to flourish; and for successive years the most prominent advertisements in the daily papers were those announcing where masquerade dresses of every variety were to be lent for the night on reasonable terms. On Monday, January 6, 1726, the Bishop of London preached in Bow Church, Cheapside, before the Society for the Reformation of Manners, a sermon directed especially against masquerades, which made a considerable sensation, and so far drew the attention of Government to the subject, that it was followed by a royal proclamation against the favourite entertainments of the town, the only result of which was, that they were in future carried on under the Italian title of *ridottos*, or the English one of balls; and, in order to satisfy in some measure the scruples of the authorities, the public advertisements of each ball contained a paragraph stating that guards were stationed within and without to prevent "all disorders and indecencies." The Middlesex grand juries on several occasions presented these masquerades as public nuisances, and complained of the manner in which the King's orders had been evaded, but without any permanent effect. George the Second was warmly attached to masquerades, as well as to the Opera, and he not unfrequently honoured them with his presence, and showed great favour to Heidegger, whom, nevertheless, a grand jury in 1729, after describing the ill consequences of these Opera balls, presented, under his name, "as the principal promoter of vice and immorality, in defiance of the laws of this land, to the great scandal of religion, the disturbance of his Majesty's Government, and the damage of many of his good subjects."

The attempts at a reformation of manners were the less effectual, because they were too often mixed up with political partizanship, and were not always distinguished by the prudence and judicious moderation which ensure success. The Whig *Flying Post*, in the August of 1725, contains an attack on the writings of the poet Prior, for their presumed immoral tendency, complaining that the names of an archbishop, several bishops, and numerous other dignitaries of the Church, had appeared as subscribers to the new edition of his works on large paper, and adducing, as a remarkable proof of the degeneracy of public manners, that, while Prior's writings were printed elegantly on the finest paper, any sort of print or paper was considered good

enough for the editions of the Holy Scriptures! This pointed
attack upon the poet, then recently dead, is best explained by
the circumstance that he had been Harley's agent in the negotiations connected with the obnoxious peace of Utrecht, that he
had been a prisoner of state at the beginning of King George's
reign, and that up to the last he had been looked upon as a disaffected Tory. There was probably a satirical aim in a paragraph of the *London Journal* for February 11, 1724, which
stated, that, "At the last *ridotto* or ball at the Opera House in
the Haymarket, a daughter of his grace the Archbishop of
Canterbury won the highest prize."*

The operas had flourished equally with the masquerades, and
were looked upon with jealousy by those who advocated the
dignity of the legitimate English stage. Singers and dancers
from Italy, such as Cuzzoni, and Faustina, and Farinelli, obtained large sums of money, and returned to build themselves
palaces at home, while first-rate actors at Drury Lane or Lincoln's Inn Fields experienced a difficulty in obtaining respectable
audiences. The portraits of the former were engraved handsomely, and exhibited in every picture-shop. After a serious
dispute between Cuzzoni and Faustina for precedence, in the
summer of 1727, in which the latter appears to have been the
victor, an obscure satirist of the day says,—

> "Cuzzoni can no longer charm,
> Faustina now does all alarm;
> And we must buy her pipe so clear
> With hundreds twenty-five a year.
> Either we've money very plenty,
> Or else our skulls are wondrous empty."

The regular theatres were driven, in their own defence, to seek
some new method of attracting the patronage which seemed to
have been stolen from them by the Italian Opera, and they introduced that class of performances, also of foreign growth, which
has since become so well known under the title of Pantomime.
Cibber, in his autobiographical "Apology," laments the necessity
which obliged them to give way to a taste so contrary to the
interests of the drama, and his contemporaries in general bear
witness that the Drury Lane company opposed the innovation as
far as they could. It was Rich, with his Lincoln's Inn company, who first attempted to compete with the Opera by intro-

---

* It appears that gambling of various kinds, as well as lotteries, were
permitted at the masquerades. These, with the intrigues of another description, not unfrequently led to quarrels, which ended sometimes in duels,
with melancholy results.

ducing singing and dancing, and English operas and English pantomimes, and what were designated in the play-bills as " grotesque entertainments." In the winter of 1723 this house produced "The Necromancer; or, Harlequin Dr. Faustus," which had an extraordinary run; and the next season they brought out a " Harlequin Jack Shepherd." The latter was of course founded upon the exploits of the notorious character, whose history was then fresh in every one's memory, for it was the year of his execution. A rival " Dr. Faustus " was brought out at Drury Lane, and, as it appears, with equal success. This was not the only instance in which the two theatres performed at the same time pantomimes under the same title; in February, 1726, they were both exhibiting a pantomime of Apollo and Daphne, and other similar instances might be pointed out. In these fantastic pieces, wild beasts, and dragons, and other strange personages, made their appearance, such as had never before trodden upon the English stage; and the writers of the time tell us, with a scornful smile, that on one occasion a moveable windmill was introduced, and that it produced no small sensation among the astonished spectators. Nor did the innovations stop here, for in the winter of 1726 mountebanks, and tumblers, and rope-dancers were brought in as a novelty amongst the "grotesque entertainments" of the theatres.

The character of the stage, thus smothered under a complicated weight of operas, masquerades, pantomimes, and mountebank performances, became more and more an object of attack for the press; and the papers of the opposition took up the subject with the greater zeal, because the evil seemed to be encouraged by the patronage of the Court. The stage-managers themselves were not unfrequently made the objects of galling personalities, in pamphlets, as well as in the public newspapers. Caricatures exhibited to the eye in exaggerated drawing the shortness of Cuzzoni, the tall awkwardness of Farinelli, and the ugliness of Heidegger.* The manager of masquerades and operas, whom the King had appointed master of the revels, or, as he was termed by foreigners, *le surintendant des plaisirs de l'Angleterre,* sometimes made a joke of himself as being one of the ugliest men of his age, and it is not therefore to be wondered at if his deficiency in beauty was often a subject of ridicule to the satirist. Fielding, in a satirical poem of his younger days,

* The caricature represented on the next page is said to have been designed by the Countess of Burlington, and to have been etched by Goupy; at least, so we learn from a manuscript note on a copy in the possession of Mr. Burke.

"The Masquerade," thus passes a joke on Heidegger's face, which is represented by other writers as having been often mistaken for a monstrous mask.

CUZZONI, FARINELLI, AND HEIDEGGER.

" ' Hold, madam, pray what hideous figure
Advances!' 'Sir, that's Count H—d—g—r.'
' How could it come into his gizzard,
T' invent so horrible a vizzard !'
'How could it, sir!' says she, ' I'll tell you
It came into his mother's belly ;
For you must know that horrid phiz is
(*Paris naturalibus*) his visage.'
' Monstrous ! that human nature can
Have form'd so strange burlesque a man !' "

Heidegger, who was a native of Zurich, in Switzerland, and had come to England as a mere fortune-hunter, was much caressed by the Court and by the nobility, and was now gaining a large income, much of which he expended in charity. He lived profusely, and mixed with the highest society, where his oddness of character and appearance made him sometimes the subject of practical jokes. On one occasion the Duke of Montagu invited him to a tavern, where he was made drunk, and fell asleep. In that situation a mould of his face was taken, from which was made a mask, bearing the closest resemblance to the original, and the Duke provided a man of the same stature to appear in a similar dress, and thus to personate Heidegger, on the night of the next masquerade, when the King (who was apprised of the plot) was to be present. On his Majesty's entrance, Heidegger, as was usual, bade the music play "God save the King;" but no sooner was his back turned, than the impostor, assuming his voice and manner, ordered them to play "Charley over the water." On this Heidegger raged, stamped, and swore, and commanded them to re-commence the loyal tune of "God save the King." The instant he retired the impostor returned, and ordered them to resume the seditious air. The musicians thought their master was drunk, but durst not disobey. The house was now thrown into an uproar; "Shame! shame!" resounded from all parts; and some officers of the guards, who were in attendance upon the King, insisted upon kicking the musicians out, had not the Duke of Cumberland, who, as well as his father, was privy to the plot, restrained them. Heidegger now came forward and offered to discharge his band; when the impostor advanced, and cried in a plaintive tone, "Sire, the whole fault lies with that devil in my likeness." This was too much; poor Heidegger turned round, grew pale, but could not speak. The Duke of Montagu, seeing it take so serious a turn, ordered the fellow to unmask. Heidegger retired in great wrath, seated himself in an arm-chair, furiously commanded his attendants to extinguish the lights, and swore he would never again superintend the masquerade, unless the mask was defaced and the mould broken in his presence. A sketch by Hogarth has preserved and immortalised the face of Heidegger on this occasion, when it truly merited the description given in one of the satirical attacks on the manager of the Opera:—

HEIDEGGER IN A RAGE.

"With a hundred deep wrinkles impress'd on thy front,
Like a map with a great many rivers upon 't."

It was the degeneracy of the stage at this period which brought forward the satirical talents of Hogarth, then a young man. In 1723, immediately after the appearance of the pantomime of "Dr. Faustus" at Lincoln's Inn Fields, he published his plate of "Masquerades and Operas," with the gate of Burlington House in the background, as a lampoon upon the bad taste of the age in every branch of the art. On one side, Satan is represented as dragging a multitude of people through a gateway to the masquerade and opera, while Heidegger is looking down upon them from a window with an air of satisfaction. A large sign-board above has a representation of Cuzzoni on the stage, to whom the Earl of Peterborough is making an offer of eight thousand pounds. On the opposite side of the picture, a crowd rushes into the theatre to witness the pantomimes; and over this gateway appears the sign of Dr. Faustus, with a dragon and a windmill, explained by the lines under the picture,—

> "Long has the stage productive been
> Of offspring it could brag on;
> But never till this age was seen
> A windmill and a dragon."

In the front of the picture a barrow-woman is seen wheeling away, as "waste paper for shops," a load of books, which appear by the inscriptions to be the dramatic works of Shakespeare, Ben Jonson, Dryden, Congreve, and Otway.

In 1725 Hogarth published another caricature, entitled "A just View of the British Stage," more especially levelled at the pantomimic performances of the theatres of Drury Lane and Lincoln's Inn Fields, and suggesting a plan for combining in one piece "Dr. Faustus" and "Jack Shepherd," "with Scaramouch Jack Hall the chimney-sweeper's escape from Newgate through the privy." The three managers of Drury Lane are placed round a table in the centre of the picture. To the left Wilks, dangling the effigy of Punch, exclaims, in exultation at the expected superiority which this expedient is to give them over the rival theatre, "Poor Rich! faith, I pity thee!" Cibber, holding up Harlequin Jack Shepherd, invokes the Muses, who are painted somewhat grotesquely on the ceiling, "Assist, ye sacred nine!" Booth, at the other end of the table, is letting

RUBBISH.

the effigy of Hall down the passage by which he is said to have made his exit, and declaring his satisfaction at the new plan by

THEATRICAL CONTRIVANCES.

a coarse exclamation. The ghost of Ben Jonson rises from a trap-door, and shows his contempt for the new-fangled contrivances of the stage in a manner that cannot be misunderstood.

In 1727 Hogarth published a large "Masquerade Ticket," bitterly satirical on the immoral tendency of masquerades, as well as on their manager, Heidegger.

The eagerness with which the public at this period ran after every new sight, and listened to every new opinion, was an object of frequent ridicule to the satirical writers of the day, and this probably made it the age of deistical writers, such as Mandeville and Woolston, Toland, Tindal, and Collins. There were others also, who, without being deists, ventured to broach fantastic notions, which had followers for a time. In the summer of 1726 appeared, what the *Political State* for that year describes as "a blazing star, that seemed portentous to the Established Church." John Henley, a native of Leicestershire, had graduated at Cambridge, but, filled as it would appear with overweening vanity and assurance, he defied the authority of the Established Church, and not only set up a new religious scheme, which he called Primitive Christianity, but, with a mere smattering of knowledge, undertook to teach and lecture upon all sciences, all languages, and, in fact, all subjects whatever, on

which, to judge from all accounts, he must have talked a great
deal of unintelligible rigmarole. On the 14th of May, 1726,
Henley first advertised his scheme in the public newspapers, and
on the 10th of July, having taken a licence from a magistrate
to deliver public lectures, he established what he called his
"Oratory," in a sort of wooden booth, built over the shambles
in Newport Market, near Leicester Fields, which had formerly
been used for a temporary meeting-house by a congregation of
French refugees. Here, and in Lincoln's Inn Fields ("the
corner near Clare Market"), to which latter place he removed at
the end of February, 1729, Henley continued to hold forth for
some years, preaching on theological subjects on the Sunday,
and on all other subjects on the Wednesday evening, to which
sometimes he added a lecture on Monday and Friday. In spite
of his locality among the butchers,—to whom at times he gave
a lecture, which he called his "butchers' oration,"—the orator
exhibited himself in an ostentatious manner, clad in the full
robes of a priest, attended by his clerk or reader; and he employed a man to attend the door, whom he dignified with the
name of his "ostiary," and who took a shilling a head for
admission. On certain occasions he administered what he
termed the "primitive eucharist," and he performed other religious ceremonies. The clergy were highly indignant at this
man's proceedings, and he met with opposition from other
sources : on the 18th of January, 1729, he was presented by a
grand jury for profaning the character of a priest, by delivering
indecent discourses in clerical robes, which was probably the
cause of his removal to Lincoln's Inn Fields; but he braved all,
until he gradually lost the popularity which for a while filled
his Oratory with a numerous audience. This man continued
his performances in Clare Market till after the middle of the
century.

When we look over Henley's weekly advertisements in the
newspapers, we cannot but give him credit for singular ingenuity
in selecting subjects calculated to excite general curiosity, both
in his theological discourses on the Sunday, and in his miscellaneous lectures on the other days of the week. As he proceeded, he took up exciting political questions, discussed very
freely the character of the statesmen and the scholars of the
day, made historical parallels, and became abusive, scurrilous,
and licentious in his language, invoking the lowest passions
rather than the reasoning faculties of his hearers. This course
has been attempted in later times, but never with the extraordinary success which for a time attended the discourses of

"orator Henley." In one advertisement it is announced that "The Wednesday's oration will be on Westward Hoe ; or, a frolick on the water,—*fire*-new :" in another, "The Wednesday's subject will be 'Over the hills, and far away ; or, Prince Eugene's march.'" On one occasion he states merely that the subject will be "Something alive ;" on another it is "A merrythought ;" and, among the incredible variety of subjects which composed his long list, it will be quite enough to mention the following, taken at random :—"The world toss'd at tennis ; or, a lesson for a king ;" "Whether man or woman be the finer creature ;" "A-la-mode de France ; or, the art of rising ;" "The wedding lottery ;" "A Platonic chat on Box-hill, *de osculis et virginibus* ;" "The Cambridge jig ; or, the humours of a commencement ;" "The Doctors ogling the ladies through their spectacles ;" "A wonder at Windsor ; or, the dream of a dame of honour ;" "Jack at a pinch ; or, Sir Humphrey Haventall ;" "The triumphs of Tag, Rag, and Bobtail,—*spick-span new !*" The most common subjects were made seductive by some quaint and extraordinary title.

We are easily led to doubt the morality of a schemer like Henley, and the reports of his contemporaries seem to rank it

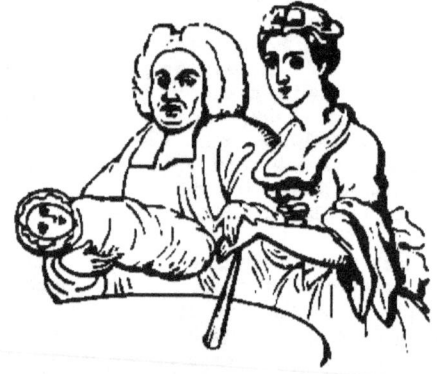

AN "ORATORY" BAPTISM.

rather low. Hogarth introduced him, according to common report, among the characters in his "Modern Midnight Conversation ;" and the same satirical artist represented him in another picture performing the rites of baptism, but evidently more attentive to the beauty of the mother than to the operation he is performing on the infant. Another rough sketch by Hogarth represents in burlesque the interior of the Oratory during service. The orator's fame was, however, so great, that several engravings were made of him, representing him holding forth from his pulpit, enriched with velvet and gold.

The dispute between Cuzzoni and Faustina, already mentioned, combined with some other circumstances of disagreement, had thrown the Opera management into confusion; and, in the earlier months of the year 1728, the newspapers contain repeated complaints of the neglect into which the Italian Opera had fallen. It was at this moment that an event occurred, which, for a time, threw both Italian Opera and pantomime into the shade. In February, 1728, appeared at the theatre in Lincoln's Inn Fields the celebrated "Beggar's Opera," by John Gay, with a tide of success never equalled by any other single piece. This success no doubt arose in a considerable measure from the attractive character of the music, and partly from its peculiar aptness to the moment at which it was published, when highway and street robberies had been increasing in an alarming degree, and the characters thus brought on the stage were those on whom people's attention was daily and painfully fixed. The "Beggar's Opera" became, in a few days, the universal talk of the town. Lavinia Fenton, formerly an obscure actress, to whom was given the part of Polly, became an object of general admiration, was celebrated in street-ballads, and her portrait exhibited in every shop, and within a short time she became Duchess of Bolton. The airs of the "Beggar's Opera" were adopted as the tunes of political ballads. The piece itself was even performed in a booth at Bartholomew Fair in the autumn following. It was also acted in various parts of England, Wales, Scotland, and Ireland, an unusual thing for a new piece in those days; the favourite songs were printed upon fans for the ladies; houses, as we learn from the notes to the "Dunciad," were furnished with it in screens; and, as usual, it became the origin of a number of inferior imitations which appeared in different theatres, under the titles of "The Lover's Opera," "The Gypsies' Opera," "The Beggar's Wedding," &c.

There were others who cried against the "Beggar's Opera" as loudly as the town cried it up. Many said, with some reason, that its extraordinary success was a proof of a degraded national taste; others, with much less cause, represented it as an attack upon public morals, and as having a dangerous tendency; and, as it happened that, during the period which followed its representation, street robberies in London were unusually frequent, they hesitated not to ascribe this circumstance to the influence of the "Beggar's Opera." Hogarth caricatured it in a print, representing the actors with the heads of animals, and Apollo and the Muses fast asleep under the stage. In another caricature Parnassus was turned into a bear-garden; Pegasus was drawing a dust-cart, and the Muses were employed in sifting cinders.

> "Parnassus now like a bear-garden appears,
> And Apollo there plays on his crowd to the bears:
> Poor Pegasus draws an old dust-cart along,
> And the Muses sift cinders, and hum an old song,
> With a fa, la, &c."

Among other prints, a medley was published in the style of those on the South Sea scheme, with the title, "The Stage Medley; representing the polite taste of the town, and the matchless merits of poet G——, Polly Peachum, and Captain Macheath." Other prints, of a similar tendency, were distributed about the town. At least one clergyman preached against it from the pulpit; and, even in the latter part of the century, Ireland, Hogarth's editor, repeats traditionary stories, that, after its appearance, young practisers in highway robbery were not unfrequently caught with the "Beggar's Opera" in their pocket. But there was also a political feeling on the subject, for the Lincoln's Inn theatre had the Tory partialities on its side; and Gay, slighted by the Whigs, had given dissatisfaction to the Court, and was looked upon as the friend of Pope, Swift, and Bolingbroke. The "Beggar's Opera" itself contained some satirical reflections on the Court; and the Tory press alone ventured to speak in its favour. Mist's *Journal* of the 2nd of March, 1728, observes, "Certain people, of an envious disposition, attribute the frequency of the late robberies to the success of the 'Beggar's Opera,' and the pleasure the town takes in the character of Captain Macheath; but others, less concern'd in that affair, and more for the publick, account for them by the general poverty and corruption of the times, and the prevalence of *some powerful examples.*"

For these or some other reasons the Court openly discountenanced the "Beggar's Opera;" and, when its author had composed for the following season a second part, under the title of "Polly," it was not allowed to be acted. The Duchess of Queensbury, who had advocated Gay's cause with the King and the royal family, was forbidden to appear at Court. But the town took vengeance for their disappointment upon a rival, though, as it would appear, an unoffending writer. Colley

Cibber had just completed a piece, also in imitation of the
"Beggar's Opera," entitled "Love in a Riddle," which he was
preparing to bring out at Drury Lane. A report was industriously spread abroad that Cibber had obtained the prohibition
against Gay's "Polly," in order that he might monopolise the
stage to himself; and, on the day of Cibber's representation, a
powerful cabal obtained possession of the theatre, and compelled
him to withdraw his performance. Gay published his "Polly"
soon after, with some prefatory remarks, in which he protested
against the injustice with which it had been treated.

By Pope and others Gay was looked upon only as a new
instance of the sacrifice of literary genius to party feelings, and
the treatment he experienced, perhaps, led in some measure to
the appearance of a much more remarkable literary production,
which agitated the world of letters for several years. Pope, and
his friend Swift, equally bitter in their sentiments, and who both
at this period of Whig supremacy lay under a kind of proscription, had, within a few months, taken an effective revenge by
the publication of several violent satires against the degeneracy
of their age. In 1727 Swift published the "Travels of Gulliver;" in which he went on ridiculing statesmen, and scholars,
and men of the world, and every other class of society, until he
ended in one universal libel upon the whole human race. In the
same year Pope gave to the world his "Treatise on the Bathos;
or, the Art of sinking in Poetry," under the name of Martinus
Scriblerus. These works and their authors were attacked with
almost every kind of weapon that the anger of the multitude of
inferior writers of the press could supply. Pope especially,
whose splenetic and sensitive temper had severed most of his
literary friendships, was subjected to every kind of annoyance,
and was driven to the highest degree of exasperation, for the
judicious but cutting satire of his remarks touched to the quick
almost every poetical scribbler of the day. The newspapers
were filled with attacks upon his writings, and with jests upon
his character, his religion (he had been educated a Roman Catholic), his politics (he was the friend of Atterbury and Bolingbroke), and even upon his personal deformity. Ambrose Phillips,
known chiefly by his Pastorals, is said to have proceeded so far
as to hang a rod up in Button's Coffee-house, with which he
threatened to chastise the poet of Twickenham the first time he
made his appearance there. These attacks were often galling,
especially when they came from a class of persons for whom the
poet professed extreme contempt; and it was under the irritation they caused that Pope formed the plan of one general

satire, in which he might give vent to all his resentments, just or unjust; and which soon afterwards gave birth to the "Dunciad," perhaps the most perfect and finished of his writings. The wholesale nature of the attack is only justified by our knowledge of the degraded state of our national literature at the time he wrote.

In this remarkable poem, which was dedicated to Swift, Pope celebrates the wide-extending empire of Dulness, and describes the goddess as holding her court in the neighbourhood of Moorfields, which then rivalled in celebrity the literary precincts of Grub Street.

> " Where wave the tatter'd ensigns of Rag-fair,
> A yawning ruin hangs and nods in air;
> Keen, hollow winds howl thro' the bleak recess,
> Emblem of music caused by emptiness.
> Here, in one bed, two shiv'ring sisters lie,
> The cave of Poverty and Poetry.
> This the great Mother, dearer held than all
> The clubs of Quidnuncs, or her own Guildhall.
> Here stood her opium, here she nursed her owls,
> And destin'd bards the imperial seat of fools.
> Hence springs each weekly muse, the living lumst
> Of Curll's chaste press, and Lintot's rubric post:
> Hence hymning Tyburn's elegiac lay;
> Hence the soft sing-song on Cecilia's day,
> Sepulchral lies, our holy walls to grace,
> And new-year odes, and all the Grub-street race.
> 'Twas here in clouded majesty she shone;
> Four guardian virtues, round, support her throne;
> Fierce champion Fortitude, that knows no fears
> Of hisses, blows, or want, or loss of ears;
> Calm Temperance, whose blessings those partake
> Who hunger and who thirst for scribbling sake;
> Prudence, whose glass presents th' approaching jail;
> Poetic Justice, with her lifted scale,
> Where, in nice balance, truth with gold she weighs,
> And solid pudding against empty praise."

The scene is laid at the moment when the poet Settle, the King of Dulness, was dying, and the goddess is introduced deliberating on the choice of a successor.

Lewis Theobald, or, as he was popularly called, Tib'ald, was then an active writer for the stage, but is now chiefly known by his edition of Shakespeare. Pope, also, had been induced, for what was then a handsome remuneration, to place his name to an edition of Shakespeare; and Theobald, who was far better versed in the literary antiquities necessary to explain and .illustrate the text of the great dramatist, pointed out the defects of Pope's edition and the errors of his notes in a number of arti-

G

clue in the weekly papers. Nettled beyond measure at these attacks, for the notes to Shakespeare were a sore place in the poet's reputation, Pope determined to make Theobald the hero of his poem, and him the goddess chooses as the successor to the throne of Dulness, after casting her eyes in vain on Eusden (who then held the place of poet-laureat), "slow" Phillips, and "mad" Dennis.

> "In each she marks her image full express'd,
> But chief in Tibbald's monster-breeding breast,
> Sees gods with demons in strange league engage,
> And earth, and heav'n, and hell her battles wage.
> She eyed the bard, where supperless he sate,
> And pined, unconscious of his rising fate:
> Studious he sate, with all his books around,
> Sinking from thought to thought, a vast profound !
> Plunged for his sense but found no bottom there ;
> Then writ, and flounder'd on in mere despair.
> He roll'd his eyes, that witness'd huge dismay,
> Where yet unpawn'd much learned lumber lay ;
> Volumes, whose size the space exactly fill'd,
> Or which fond authors were so good to gild,
> Or where, by sculpture made for ever known,
> The page admires new beauties, not its own."

The description of Theobald's library, and of his sacrifice to Dulness, is an unjust satire on the class of reading which had enabled him to detect the errors of Pope's Shakespearian criticism.

The goddess suddenly reveals herself to the fortunate aspirant, transports him to her temple, and initiates him into her mysteries. She finally announces the death of Settle, and anoints and proclaims him her successor.

> "Know, Settle, cloy'd with custard and
>   with praise,
> Is gather'd to the dull of ancient days,
> Safe where no critics damn, no duns
>   molest."

"HENLEY'S GILT-TUB."

The second book opens with Theobald's enthronement, in a position even more lofty than that occupied by the orator of Newport Market in his pulpit, or by the bookseller Curll, when he was condemned to the pillory for his licentious publications.

Among a number of prints and caricatures relating to Henley'
one in the collection of Mr. Hawkins represents him as a fox
seated upon his tub, with the words "The Orator" beneath.
A monkey peeps from within, with neck-bands (acting as clerk),
and pointing to money in his hand, the object of the orator's
worship: beneath him is written the word "Amen." Behind
the orator is a curtain, on which Henley is pictured addressing
a large audience, with the inscription INVENIAM AUT FACIAM,
the vain-glorious motto which he placed on medals struck for
distribution among his followers.

> "High on a gorgeous seat, that far outshone
> Henley's gilt tub, or Fleckno's Irish throne,
> Or that where on her Curlls the public pours
> All-bounteous, fragrant grains, and golden show'rs,
> Great Tibbald nods. The proud Parnassian sneer,
> The conscious simper, and the jealous leer,
> Mix in his look. All eyes direct their rays
> On him, and crowds grow foolish as they gaze.
> Not with more glee, by hands pontific crown'd,
> With scarlet hats, wide waving, circled round,
> Rome in her capitol saw Querno sit,
> Throned on seven hills, the Antichrist of wit."

This division of the poem is entirely occupied with a description of the games celebrated by the goddess in honour of "Tibbald's" elevation to the throne. The first prizes are contended
for by the booksellers, against whom Pope had proclaimed his
hostility in the preface to his and Swift's "Miscellanies,"
printed in 1727. Curll had provoked him by the surreptitious
publication of some of his letters; but what was Lintot's
offence, who had been the publisher of his Homer, is not so
clear. These games are described in a style of disgusting
coarseness, too characteristic of the satirical writings and caricatures of the period, and which makes it difficult to reproduce
them entire at the present day. When the various prizes of the
booksellers have been disposed of, others are proposed to be contended for by the poets, in tickling, vociferating, and diving:
"The first holds forth the arts and practices of dedicators, the
second of disputants and fustian poets, the third of profound,
dark and dirty authors." The operation of diving takes place
in the muddy waters of the Fleet Ditch, where it emptied itself
into the Thames. The last exercise is reserved for the critics,
who are to listen without sleeping to the dull nonsensical prose
of the orator Henley, and to the everlasting rhymes of Blackmore.

> "Her critics there she summons, and proclaims
> A gentler exercise to close the games.

> ' Here, you ! in whose grave heads or equal scales
> I weigh what author's heaviness prevails,—
> Which most conduce to soothe the soul in slumbers,
> My Henley's periods, or my Blackmore's numbers,—
> Attend the trial we propose to make :
> If there be man who o'er such works can wake,
> Sleep's all-subduing charms who dares defy,
> And busst Ulysses' ear with Argos' eye—
> To him we grant our amplest powers to sit
> Judge of all present, past, and future wit,
> To cavil, censure, dictate, right or wrong,
> Full and eternal privilege of tongue.''

This trial is too much for the critics, and the whole assembly
is soon buried in profound slumber, in the midst of which the
goddess transports the new king to her temple, whence he is
carried in a vision to the Elysian shades, and there meets the
ghost of his predecessor Settle, who takes him to the summit of
a mountain, whence he is shown the past history, the present
state, and the future prospects of the empire of Dulness.   In
the present he beholds the different worshippers of Dulness in
her various walks :—on the stage in Cibber; in the doggrel
minstrelsy of Ward ;—

> " From the strong fate of drama, if thou get free,
> Another Durfey, Ward, shall sing in thee.
> Then shall each ale-house, thee each gill-house mourn,
> And answering gin-shops sourer sighs return ;"—

in the more presuming writings of Haywood and Centlivre, of
Ralph, Welsted, Dennis, and Gildon ; in the party politics of
Thomas Burnet, who wrote in a weekly paper called *Pasquin*,
and was rewarded for his zeal with a consulship, and Ducket,
who wrote the " Grumbler," and also received an appointment
under Government ;—

> " Behold yon pair, in strict embraces join'd :
> How like in manners, and how like in mind !
> Famed for good-nature, Burnet, and for truth ;
> Ducket for pious passion to the youth.
> Equal in wit, and equally polite,
> Shall this a 'Pasquin,' that a 'Grumbler' write.
> Like are their merits, like rewards they share,
> That shines a consul, this commissioner ; "—

in the peculiar style of antiquarianism of Thomas Hearne ; and
in the divinity of Henley, who, the phenomenon of his day, as
an apt type of its intellectual character, is again brought forward in the full amplitude of his pretensions :—

> " But where each science lifts its modern type,
> History her pot, Divinity his pipe,

While proud Philosophy repines to show
(Dishonest sight !) his breeches rent below,
Imbrown'd with native bronze, lo ! Henley stands,
Tuning his voice, and balancing his hands.
How fluent nonsense trickles from his tongue!
How sweet the periods, neither said nor sung !
Still break the benches, Henley, with thy strain,
While Kennet, Hare, and Gibson preach in vain.
O great restorer of the good old stage,
Preacher, at once, and zany of thy age !
O worthy thou of Egypt's wise abo les,
A decent priest where monkeys were the gods !
But fate with butchers placed thy priestly stall,
Meek modern faith to murder, back, and maul ;
And bade thee live, to crown Britannia's praise,
In Toland's, Tindal's, and in Woolston's days."

From these spectacles the eye of the visionist is suddenly
turned to the modern vagaries of the stage, on which dragons
and other monsters were brought as actors, and heaven and hell
were made the scenery :—

" He look'd and saw a sable sorcerer rise,
Swift to whose hand a winged volume flies ;
All sudden, Gorgons hiss and dragons glare,
And ten-horned fiends and giants rush'd to war.
Hell rises, heaven descends, and dance on earth
Gods, imps, and monsters, music, rage, and mirth ;
A fire, a jig, a battle, and a ball,
Till one wide conflagration swallows all."

Greater wonders than these were now crowded into the
theatres ; and, to complete the absurdity, in one of the pantomimes Harlequin was hatched upon the stage out of a large
egg :—

" Thence a new world, to nature's laws unknown,
Breaks out refulgent, with a heav'n its own ;
Another Cynthia her new journey runs,
And other planets circle other suns :
The forests dance, the rivers upwards rise,
Whales sport in woods, and dolphins in the skies ;
And, last, to give the whole creation grace,
Lo ! one vast egg produces human race !"

These were the creations of Rich, in his empire in Lincoln's Inn
Fields :—

" A matchless youth ! his nod these worlds controls,
Wings the red lightning, and the thunder rolls :
Angel of Dulness, sent to scatter round
Her magic charms o'er all unclassic ground.
Yon stars, yon suns, he rears at pleasure higher,
Illumes their light, and sets their flames on fire.

> Immortal Rich! how calm he sits at ease
> Mid snows of paper and fierce hail of peas;
> And proud his mistress' orders to perform,
> Rides in the whirlwind, and directs the storm."

He, too, has his rivals :—

> " But lo! to dark encounter in mid-air
> New wizards rise: here Booth, and Cibber there.
> Booth in his cloudy tabernacle shrined,
> On grinning dragons Cibber mounts the wind:
> Dire is the conflict, dismal is the din,
> Here shouts all Drury, there all Lincoln's Inn."

These are pronounced to be the advanced guards of the host of Dulness, who is proceeding surely,

> " Till raised from booths to theatre, to court
> Her seat imperial Dulness shall transport:
> Already Opera prepares the way,
> The sure forerunner of her gentle sway."

The natural consequence of this general invasion of barbarism in public taste is, that talent is allowed to starve in the obscurity of neglect.

> " While Wren with sorrow to the grave descends;
> Gay dies unpension'd with a hundred friends;
> Hibernian politics, O Swift, thy fate;
> And Pope's whole years to comment and translate."

Upon the character of the stage Pope's verses had no more effect than Hogarth's prints; for masquerades continued to be

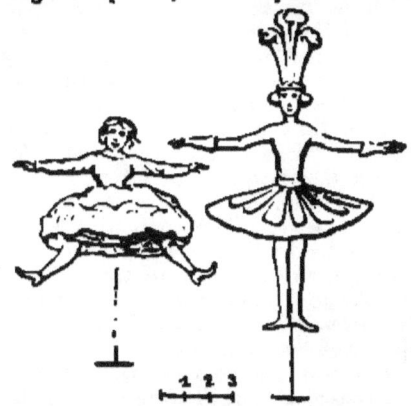

THE CHARMERS OF THE AGE, IN 1740

the favourite amusements of the town till late in the century, and pantomimes and operas have never altogether lost their popularity. The letters of Horace Walpole bear frequent testimony to the attention which the opera excited in fashionable society: yet satirists of every class continued to attack it, and among others Hogarth, who, in 1742, showed his inimitable skill, in giving the character of grotesque coarseness to what so large a portion of his contemporaries looked upon as attractive elegance, in a caricature entitled "The Charmers of the Age," representing the dancing attitudes of two popular *artistes* of the day, Monsieur Desnoyer and the Signora Barberina, who performed at Drury Lane. Underneath the plate Hogarth has added an observation, of which we hardly perceive the whole bearing : "The dotted lines show the rising heights."

At the same time the stage became every day, until 1737, more and more a political agent. The pantomimes, by a harmless tendency to satirise the follies of the day, which they have preserved to the present time, had perhaps some influence in producing this state of things. In October, 1728, a farce called "The Craftsman; or, the Weekly Journalist," alluding to the scurrilous paper, so celebrated for its attacks on the ministry of Sir Robert Walpole, was performed at the theatre in the Haymarket, "with several entertainments of singing and dancing." Farces, similar in character, appeared frequently during the following years.

In 1733 Rich and his company left Lincoln's Inn Fields to take possession of the new and handsome theatre which had been built for them in Covent Garden ; on which occasion Hogarth published a print, representing Rich's triumphal entry into the new house, with a long train of actors, authors, scenery, &c. Rich, clad in the skin of a dog, one of the personages in the harlequinade of "Perseus and Andromeda," is seated with his mistress in a chariot drawn by satyrs, with Harlequin for his driver. Before them, Gay is carried into the new theatre on the shoulders of a porter. The diminutive figure of Pope is seen in one corner, treating the "Beggar's Opera " in the most contemptuous manner; from which we are probably justified in supposing that the poet, jealous (as was usual with him) of the extraordinary success of his old friend, had expressed an unfavourable opinion of his production.

The year 1737 was one more eventful in the history of the stage. In the preceding year, Fielding (who had begun writing for the stage in 1727 as a young man) brought out at the Haymarket Theatre a farce styled "Pasquin," which was a direct

lampoon on the Government, and gave no little offence. It may
be observed that this was "the new theatre in the Haymarket,"
which has been already mentioned as occupied, under George I.,
by a company of French actors. Other such pieces attacked
different passing follies in a remarkable style. One, brought on
the stage in the beginning of 1737, under the title of "The
Worm-doctor, with Harlequin female Bonesetter," threw ridicule
upon two remarkable quacks, Dr. Taylor and Mrs. Mapp, who
were then practising upon the credulity of the public. Towards
May, several farces were acted at the Haymarket, which were
open pasquinades on the ministry, and which were universally
spoken of as such. The most remarkable of these was a drama-
tical satire, in three acts, entitled the "Historical Register for
the year 1736," by Fielding, which had a great run during the
month of April. Some say that Walpole was alarmed by the
effects of this piece; but, according to Smollett, the manager of
a play-house communicated to the minister a still more objectionable farce in manuscript, entitled "The Golden Rump,"
which was filled with treason and abuse upon the Government,
and had been offered for exhibition on the stage. Which of
these might be the real provocation is of little importance;
Walpole brought the matter before the House of Commons, and
descanted on the impudent sedition and immorality which had
been of late propagated in theatrical pieces. The result was
the passing of the Act "for restraining the licentiousness of the
stage;" by which it was ordered that no new play should in
future be brought on the stage without an express license, a
bill which has remained in force to the present time, and under
which was established the office of Licencer of Plays. A great
but ineffectual clamour was raised against this bill, both within
doors and without, particularly by the *Craftsman* and other
opposition papers, who represented it as a violent attempt upon
the liberty of the press.

Pope's satire upon the literature of his time was more effectual than that upon the stage ; because, though the "Dunciad"
was palpably a mere receptacle for all the poet's personal resentments (which were not always just in themselves), it contained more of absolute truth, and was therefore more generally
felt. English literature soon afterwards began to rise from the
low state to which it had fallen under George I. The "Dunciad " is stated to have been written in 1726; surreptitious
editions, perhaps with the author's connivance, appeared at
Dublin (and were reprinted almost immediately in London)
during 1727 ; but it was not publicly owned by Pope till the

next year, when he gave to the world an authorized and complete edition, with the notes, which conveyed more venom than the poem itself. The uproar among men of letters which this satire caused was almost beyond anything we can conceive. The attack was so general, that almost everybody was up in arms, and the newspapers brought, with provoking regularity, their weekly load of banter and insult. At first, Pope is said to have enjoyed the annoyance he had given to his enemies ; but, in a short time, his sensitive feelings gained the mastery, and, as the attacks upon him became more galling, he experienced more and more the inconveniences usually attendant upon a satirical disposition. The poet must have been suffering under an extraordinary attack of sensitiveness, when he condescended to answer a pretended account of his being horsewhipped as he was walking in Ham Walks, near Twickenham, by an advertisement like the following, which appeared in the *Daily Post* of June 14, 1728:— " Whereas there has been a scandalous paper cried about the streets, under the title of 'A Popp upon Pope,' insinuating that I was whipped in Ham Walks on Thursday last, this is to give notice that I did not stir out of my house at Twickenham all that day ; and the same is a malicious and ill-grounded report. —A. POPE."

Among the most determined of Pope's assailants at this time was the bookseller Curll, who was grossly attacked in the "Dunciad," and who had been the victim of the poet's practical resentment on a former occasion. From his shop issued, within two or three months, the "Popiad," the "Curliad," the "Female Dunciad," and several others, in which the private character of the poet was attacked as freely as his public doings. Pope's personal appearance, which was not prepossessing, was also made the subject of satire ; and a quarto pamphlet, entitled "Pope Alexander's Supremacy and Infallibility examined," is prefaced by an engraving in which his portrait is placed on the shoulders

POPE PUG.

of a monkey—the personality of Poet Pug, which was sometimes given to him. A poem called the "Martiniad," in allusion to the assumed title of Martinus Scriblerus, under which
Pope had ushered the "Treatise on Sinking in Poetry" into
the world, gives the following description of his person :—

> "At Twickenham, chronicles remark,
> There dwelt a little parish clerk,
> A peevish wight, full fond of fame,
> And Martin Scribbler was his name ;
> Meager and wan, and steeple-crown'd,
> His visage long and shoulders round.
> His crippled corpse two spindle legs
> Support, instead of human legs ;
> His shrivell'd skin, of dusky grain,—
> A cricket's voice, and monkey's brain."

We may give the following from *Brice's Weekly Journal* of
May 2, 1729, as an example of the epigrammatic squibs with
which Pope was constantly assailed in the newspapers.

> "*A Receipt against Pope-ish Poetry.*
>
> "Select a wreath of wither'd bays,
> And place it on the brow of P—— ;
> Then, as reward for stolen lays,
> His neck encircle with a rope.
> When this is done, his look will show it,
> Which he's most like,—a thief or poet."

Pope seems, indeed, to have found few partisans, either
among the writers or among the artists of his time. Hogarth

THE CLUMSY DAUBER.

has introduced him into several of his compositions. In his caricature of "The Man of Taste," published in 1732, Pope is introduced in all his diminutive deformity, in the character of a plasterer, bedaubing the gate of Burlington House with white-wash, while he is throwing, by his awkwardness, a shower of dirt on a coach below, which is understood to have been that of the Duke of Chandos. With his foot he is overturning a pail, and throwing a part of its contents on a man walking beneath, who is designated in the picture by the letter B, which is explained at the foot of the engraving as "anybody that comes in his way;" while the hero of the piece is described as "A. P—pe, a Plasterer, whitewashing and bespattering." The poet had indeed obtained the character of a bespatterer of everybody he met. A little before the appearance of Hogarth's caricature, he had, in his "Epistle on Taste," addressed to the Earl of Burlington, lauded that nobleman's taste in architecture and the other arts at the expense of that of his old patron, the Duke of Chandos, who had recently built himself a magnificent seat at Canons.

The satirist was tormented by the number, rather than by the strength, of his assailants, very few of whom were for their talent worthy of his notice, and those who did possess talent were in general the least deserving of his attacks. In 1730, when the uproar occasioned by the "Dunciad" was at its height, a ballad, entitled "The Beau Monde, or the Pleasures of St. James's," informs us,

> "There's Pope has made the willings mad,
>   Who labour all they can
> To pull his reputation down,
>   And maul the *little* man.
> But wit and he so close are link'd,
>   In vain is all their pother;
> They never can demolish one,
>   Without destroying t'other.*"

POPE AND CURLL.

In Hogarth's engraving of "The Distressed Poet," a picture attached to the wall of the Poet's room, in the first edition of the print, represents Pope triumphing over Curll. The contest between a poet of the rank of Pope, and a bookseller of the character of Curll, carried on in the way in which their quarrel had been conducted, had little of dignity; and Pope has

been often blamed for giving undue importance to his victims, by
the mode in which he treated them. But he was perhaps more to
be blamed for allowing himself, after the lapse of some years, to
republish the "Dunciad" in an altered form, for the purpose, as
it would seem, of making an unjust, and not very provoked,
attack on a man like Colley Cibber. Cibber's "Non-Juror"
had never been forgotten by either of the political parties whom
it concerned; he had been rewarded by the Court in 1730 with
the place of poet-laureate, and incurred, on the other hand,
during his life, the hatred of the Jacobites and the ill-will of
the Tories. He is said to have offended Pope by passing a joke
on the stage upon the ill-success of a dramatic piece by the
poet, who never forgave him. In 1742 appeared a fourth book
of the "Dunciad,"—which was already complete in three,—
and this fourth book contained a new attack upon Cibber, who
had been lampooned in the former part of the "Dunciad," and
in other satirical writings by the same author. Cibber now at
last winced, and published a violent pamphlet against Pope,
who was so incensed that he immediately revised the whole
"Dunciad," printed it anew, and substituted as its hero Cibber,
in the place of his old enemy "Tibbald."

Pope appears now to have made an entirely new set of antagonists, and in the fourth book of the "Dunciad," the goddess
of Dulness extends her empire over scholars, philosophers, and
statesmen. The satirist lampoons, with a mixture of justice
and injustice, the course of university education; the corrupting
system (then so generally prevalent) of sending youths of
family and rank to complete their education abroad, by making
themselves proficient in all the vices and follies of continental
society; and the pursuits at home of the naturalist, the philosopher, and the mathematician. The individual instances are
again selected according to the poet's personal resentments, and
it is enough to say, that among objects of attack with whom
we feel less sympathy, we meet with the names of Bentley,
Mead, Clarke, and Wollaston. The only object of attack in the
first "Dunciad," which reappears here, is the Opera, to which
Pope's hostility remained unabated. The goddess, in the new
book, holds a sort of levee, at which all classes of her worshippers attend. The legitimate theatre is present by means of
force only, for Pope was one of those who believed that the
licensing act was a death blow to the stage.

>   "But held in ten-fold bonds the Muses lie,
>   Watch'd both by Envy's and by Flatt'ry's eye:

There to her heart sad Tragedy address'd
The dagger wont to pierce the tyrant's breast ;
But sober History restrain'd her rage,
And promised vengeance on a barb'rous age.
There sunk Thalia, nerveless, cold, and dead,
Had not her sister Satire held her head."

While the new occupant of the stage enters partly as a willing attendant, supported by that class of society who had learnt to admire her by an early acquaintance in foreign climes :—

"When, lo ! a harlot form soft gliding by,
With mincing step, small voice, and languid eye ;
Foreign her air, her robe's discordant pride
In patchwork flutt'ring, and her head aside :
By singing peers upheld on either hand,
She tripp'd and laugh'd, too pretty much to stand ;
Cast on the prostrate Nine a scornful look,
And thus in quaint recitativo spoke."

CHAPTER IV.

GEORGE II.

Sir Robert Walpole's Administration—Pulteney, Bolingbroke, and the
"Patriots"—Accession of George II.—The Congress of Soissons—
Prosecution of the *Craftsman*—The Excise—Increasing Attacks upon
Walpole—Violence in the Elections—The Gin Act—The Prince of
Wales Leads the Opposition—Foreign Policy : Walpole and Cardinal
Fleury—Renewed Attacks upon Walpole, and Diminution of the
Ministerial Majorities—The "Motion," and its Consequences—The
Queen of Hungary—Walpole in the Minority, and Consequent Resig-
nation—The Committee of Inquiry.

THE misfortunes of the South Sea scheme had, as we have
already seen, placed Walpole at the head of the ministry,
upon which the Whigs, who had been divided since his retirement from office in 1717, became again united into one body,
with an overwhelming ministerial majority in Parliament, and
the hopes of the Tory and Jacobite opposition seemed to be
reduced to the lowest ebb. Under Walpole's rule, with comparative tranquillity at home and peace abroad, the country was
increasing rapidly in commercial prosperity, and consequently in
riches and strength. It can hardly be doubted by anybody,
that, to the firm and able government of Sir Robert Walpole,
more than to any other cause, the house of Brunswick owed its
permanent establishment in this country, while his pacific policy
counteracted the evils that might otherwise have arisen from
King George's continental partialities, which had been too
much encouraged by the previous ministry. Yet it was Walpole's foreign policy, and his alleged subservience to France,
which the opposition attacked with the greatest pertinacity,
until they drove the veteran from his post, after he had held
the reins of government during twenty-two years.

The bitterest and most galling attacks to which Walpole was
subsequently exposed arose from a new division among the
Whigs, the effects of personal pique and disappointed ambition.
William Pulteney, the friend and constant adherent of Walpole
for many years, and one of the most effective speakers in the
House of Commons, disappointed because his promotion, as he
thought, was not so rapid as his services merited, quarrelled
with his old colleague in 1724, resigned his office of cofferer to

the household, and placed himself at the head of a violent party
of discontented Whigs, who now took the title of "the Patriots."
In the meantime Walpole had been induced to act with leniency
towards the exiled Lord Bolingbroke, who had deceived, betrayed,
and quarrelled with the Pretender and the Jacobites, but had
become enriched, as was said, by a French marriage and by
speculations in the Mississippi scheme, and was now residing
near Paris. A bill was passed in 1724, restoring him to his
forfeited estates, though he was not allowed to recover his seat
in the House of Lords, in spite of the intrigues of the King's
mistress, the Duchess of Kendal, whose interest he had secured
by liberal bribes. Bolingbroke thus returned to England more
enraged on account of what had been withheld from him, than
grateful for what he had obtained, and he immediately made
common cause with the Tory opposition, and year after year his
talents and his skill in intriguing furnished the sharpest weapons,
and contrived the most dangerous plots, against the administration.

Pulteney, with the ultra-Whigs, or "Patriots," joined the
Tory opposition, whose leader in the House of Commons had
hitherto been that staunch old Jacobite, Sir William Wyndham,
who, in his personal resentment against Walpole, formed a close
alliance with Bolingbroke. By their means the country was
again filled with seditious attacks upon the Government, in
every variety of shape, and the mob was again raised into importance. In the December of 1726, Bolingbroke and Pulteney started a political paper under the title of the *Craftsman*,
which was at first issued daily in single leaves, but in 1727 it
was changed into a weekly newspaper, published under the title
of the *Country Journal, or Craftsman*, and seems in that form
to have had an extensive circulation. It was edited by Nicholas
Amhurst, under the fictitious name of Caleb d'Anvers. Bolingbroke was, at the same time, pursuing his intrigues with the
King's mistress, and it is impossible to say what might have
been the result of her determined endeavours to overthrow Sir
Robert Walpole, had not her power expired with the sudden
death of George I. in the June of 1727.

Bolingbroke's faction was doomed, on this occasion, to undergo a succession of disappointments and consequent mortifications.
When the hopes they had derived from the Duchess of Kendal
were overthrown, they hastened to pay their court to the mistress of the new monarch; but George II. was governed more
by his wife than by his mistress, and Queen Caroline was, to
the end of her life, Walpole's firmest friend. They next placed

their hopes in the elections; but in the Parliament chosen in 1727 the ministerial majority was greater than ever, and the Tories and Patriots were reduced to vent their harmless rage in new exclamations against bribery and corruption. One of the few caricatures of this period, but of which several copies are preserved, was entitled " Ready Money the prevailing Candidate; or, the humours of an election." The scene is laid in a country town, where a crowd of voters are receiving bribes in the most public manner. One allows the price of his vote to be deposited quietly in his coat pocket, while he is distinguishing himself by the loudness of his cries of " No bribery!" though he adds, in a diminished tone, " but pockets are free."

The voice of the opposition was now raised chiefly against the foreign policy of the ministry, who were accused of involving the country in continental quarrels, and of sacrificing the English interest abroad, to gratify the King's partiality for his Hanoverian dominions. With a perfect disregard for truth or honesty, (which appear indeed to have been in no great estimation with any party during this corrupt age,) and heedless of anything but personal interests and resentments, when the foreign measures of the Government took a bold and threatening character, the opposition cried out strenuously for peace; and when the ministers were bent upon securing peace, their opponents were equally clamorous for war. Peace was, however, established and preserved by the moderation and forbearance of the English and French courts, the councils of the latter being now ruled by Cardinal Fleury; and the threatening combinations which had clouded the foreign politics of the latter part of the reign of George I. were to a great measure dissipated in the Congress of Soissons, opened on the 10th of June, 1728.

Satisfied with the success of his policy abroad, the minister retired in the autumn, as usual, to seek a brief relaxation at his seat of Houghton Hall, in Norfolk, and indulge in his favourite pastime of hunting. But the *Craftsman* fell furiously on the proceedings at Soissons; and as winter and the consequent meeting of Parliament approached, ballads and papers were hawked about the streets, turning the foreign measures of the Court into ridicule, and holding up the minister to contempt as the dupe of French prejudices and partialities. In November, a squib in prose, with a fictitious imprint, was distributed abroad under the title of " The Norfolk Congress; or, a full and true account of the hunting, feasting, and merry-making: being singularly delightful, and likewise very instructive for the public." This was followed in December by a ballad version, under the title of " The Hunter hunted ; or, entertainment upon entertainment. A new ballad." The minister and his adherents, according to this squib, repair to the country for the purpose of a great hunting match :—

> " To Houghton Hall, some few days since,
>   All bonny, blithe, and gay,
> With menial nobles, like a prince,
>   Sir Blue-String took his way.
>
> " A mighty hunting was decreed
>   By this same noble crew ;
> The fox already donned to bleed,
>   Already in their view."

The fox, we are to suppose, represents the wily court of Spain. Before the guests depart for the chase their host gives them a breakfast, which consists of all kinds of foreign dishes. Their hunting is not very successful, for they only set up a vixen which they lost, for it was screened by an eagle (Austria), and they return disappointed to their dinner, where, instead of finding good English diet, they are again surprised with foreign dishes : ·

> " Westphalia bacon, many a slice ;
>   Of English beef a chine :
> Dutch pickled herrings, salted nice,
>   And truffles from the Seine.
>
> " 'Twas with great cost and charges made,
>   Yet none could eat a bit ;
> For 't would not easily, they said,
>   On English stomachs sit."

At the middle of the table sat the Cardinal. The taste of the host was singular :—

> " The master of the house was seen
>   *Plumb*-pudding to devour,
> And to regale with stomach keen
>   On *stock*-fish a good store."

Walpole was always looked upon as the great patron of the monied and funded interests. He is accused of having imbibed this taste for French dishes only recently :—

> " At ta' les once he said and swore,
>   With manly resolution,
> French kickshaws, bal as poison, tore
>   An English constitution.
>
> " But now French sauces all go down,
>   And things *garecca'd* all pass ;
> So much a Frenchman be is grown,
>   So changed from what he was

11

> " *Corrupted tongues* he daily em's ;
>   On these bestows his praises ;
>   With these his bosom friends he treats,
>   With these his own bulk raises."

At the same time appeared another metrical effusion of a similar stamp, entitled " Quadrille to Perfection, as played at Soissons ; or, the Norfolk Congress, pursu'd, versify'd, and enliven'd ; by the Hon. W. P., Esq.:" in which the various European powers were introduced playing at cards, and uttering sentiments expressive of the motives and designs which the opposition attributed to them. These and other similar productions were well calculated to excite the feelings of the populace.

With the opening of the year 1729, the prospects of peace were threatened by new misunderstandings with the Spaniards ; and then the opposition cried out that the Government was running the nation into a war ; yet, when these threats ended only in the treaty of Seville, altogether advantageous to England, that treaty was attacked in *Craftsman* after *Craftsman,* and the ministers were held up to hatred and ridicule in pamphlets and ballads, as base betrayers of the interests of their country to the greediness of Spain. On the 13th of September the Pulteney and Bolingbroke writers issued a tract of twenty pages of ballad verse, entitled " The Craftsman's Business," in which they lampooned the ministerial party under the character of birds, and described Walpole as " a large macaw," particoloured with red and blue.

As the interest of the foreign transactions died away, and occasions of attack on the Government measures became for a time less frequent, the satire of the opposition papers became more personal and more pointed ; and in 1730 and 1731 the country was literally deluged with political ballads, in which the prime minister was introduced under such names as Sir Blue-String (alluding to his blue ribbon as knight of the Garter), Sir Robert Brass, Sir Robert Lynn, and still plainer Robin and Bob ; and held forth as the betrayer and oppressor of his country, the selfish encourager of corruption in the nation,— one who fattened and grew rich upon the public money. Insinuations and rumours of all kinds relating to his domestic life, which were likely to render the minister unpopular with the unthinking part of the community, were industriously propagated. On the 7th of November, 1730, while he was enjoying the relaxation of his country-house, the *Craftsman* inserted a paragraph stating, that, " from Norfolk they write that Sir Robert Walpole keeps open house at Houghton ; and that so numerous are his attendants and dependants, that it is thought his household expenses cannot be less than 1500l. a week."

The effect of all this was to raise much political excitement among the middle and lower classes. A caricature, entitled "The Politicians," belonging to this period, represents the politics of the day and the conduct of the Government as the engrossing subject of conversation among tradesmen and labourers of every kind, each complaining of some imaginary grievance felt especially by those of his own calling. This caricature furnishes a figure of one of a class of persons whom we have had frequent occasion to mention,—the women who hawked seditious papers and political ballads about the streets. Among other personages, the proprietor of a newspaper ad-

THE POLITICAL BALLAD SINGER.

dresses a Scotchman (an intimation, probably, that his countrymen were among the most active of the mercenary writers for the press), "Mr. Macdonald will you undertake to write me a smart remonstrance against arbitrary power?"—and receives for answer from the wary northern, "By my saul, sir, I canna do it, for fear of offending his lairdship; for ye ken he's a mon o' muckle authority."

Towards the end of the year last mentioned, as the annual period of the meeting of Parliament approached, the writings of the opposition became more violent and more provokingly personal. The pens of Bolingbroke and Pulteney were unusually active. Caricatures and satires were handed about more frequently than ever. On the 2nd of January, 1731, the *Craftsman* contained a political letter dated from the Hague, but generally understood to be written by Bolingbroke, which was calculated seriously to embarrass the foreign relations of the country. This was followed by an anonymous pamphlet controversy, begun by Pulteney, in such a libellous tone, that it led, on the 25th, of January, to a duel between that gentleman and Lord Hervey, who was wrongly suspected of being the author of an attack upon Pulteney. "The duel" was the subject of

caricatures and ballads, and of satirical pieces of other kinds ;
and Pulteney's party sent out a pamphlet under the title of
"Iago display'd," which gave a pretended account of the
causes of the older quarrel between Walpole and Pulteney, and
a history of the duel, under the feigned names of Iago
(Walpole), Cassio (Pulteney), and Roderigo (Hervey), little to
the credit of the prime minister. The *Craftsman* continued to
pour on the ministry, and especially on their foreign policy, an
unceasing volley of essays and misrepresented statements, and
verses, and epigrams. They were accused of playing a confused and unintelligible game, which could only turn to the
advantage of foreign courts, and entailed upon England a waste-
ful expenditure of money in foreign subsidies and bribes,
without procuring any advantage. It was, in reality, a system
into which England was necessarily drawn by the uncertain
and unprincipled policy of the different European powers
during the greater part of the last century, and is not ill
described in the following epigram, which appeared in the
Craftsman of March, 13, 1731:—

> "Have you not seen at country wake,
> A crew of dancers merry-make !
> They figure in and figure out,
> Go back to back and turn about :
> They set, take hands ; they cross, change sides ;
> (Each movement a scrub minstrel guides ;)
> Around the measured labyrinth trace,
> Till each regains his former place.
> So certain potentates, (two couple,)
> Leagued in alliance light quadruple,
> Af er a maze of treaties run,
> Are e'en just where they first begun.
> I wont affirm who led the dance,
> (Yet, for the rhyme, suppose it France,)
> But this I dare at least to say,
> Old E——d must the piper pay."

These attacks in the press were accompanied by an unusually
violent opposition in Parliament to King George's foreign
policy, to his subsidies and the expense of supporting his
Hanoverian troops, in all which Pulteney took a very prominent part. In the course of the spring the political essays
which had appeared in the *Craftsman* since its commencement
were collected together, and published in seven volumes, with
as many engraved frontispieces, representing, in what were
termed "hieroglyphics," the pretended wickedness of the
premier's career, and his designs against the liberties of the
people. These seven plates were immediately reproduced in

the form of a broadside, with verses still more provoking than
the prints, under the title, " Robin's Reign ; or, Seven's the
Main : being an explanation of Caleb d'Anvers's seven Egyptian
hieroglyphics, prefixed to the seven volumes of the *Craftsman*."
The first of these plates represents John swearing obedience to
Magna Charta. In a second, the prime minister is pictured as
a harlequin, the minister of Satan, by whose counsel he
tramples upon the liberty of the press.

> " See here, good folks, a harlequin of state,
> Trembling with guilt, and yet with pride elate.
> To his great patron see the villain sue,
> And mark the mischief hell and he can do.
> Thus Satan speaks: ' Whole quires of w—ts [warrants] send,
> And for your messenger lo ! here a fiend !
> By arts like these you must your foes controul,
> Till Justice strike—and I receive your soul.' "

The third plate represents the art of printing as the great
support of the liberties and prosperity of the nation. In the
fourth, the courtiers are seen purchasing votes with money.
The fifth is a satire on the foreign policy which was intended to
keep the " balance of power " in Europe : Cardinal Fleury is
outwitting the minister, who is attempting in vain to weigh
down the scale with " whole reams of treaties," while the
Gallic cock is crowing proudly on the back of the sleeping lion.

THE BALANCE OF POWER.

In the sixth, Walpole is seen aspiring, by a dangerous path, to
a coronet ; and the seventh represent Caleb d'Anvers as the
oracle of political wisdom. Another version, apparently of

this series of caricatures, or probably only a different edition, was published under the title " Robin's Game ; or, Seven's the Main." Among the ballads of this period, the titles of which are preserved, we may mention, "Sir Robert Brass; or, the intrigues of the Knight of the Blazing Star," published in February ; and "The Knight and the Cardinal, a new ballad," published in June.

The King was so incensed at these virulent attacks, and at the quarter from whence they came, and especially at the pertinacious opposition to his foreign measures, that, on the 1st of July, he called for the council-book, and with his own hand struck the name of William Pulteney out of the list of privy councillors. Read's *Weekly Journal* of July 10, 1731, informs us that "three hawkers were on Monday last (July 5) committed to Tothill Fields Bridewell, for crying about the streets a printed paper, called ' Robin's Game ; or, Seven's the Main.' " Two days after, on Wednesday, July 7, the grand jury of Middlesex presented this same paper, with the seven plates of " Robin's Reign," described above, some numbers of the *Craftsman*, and several political ballads, as seditious libels. A prosecution was immediately commenced in accordance with this presentment. On the Saturday (10th July) one Collins was taken into custody on suspicion of being the author of "that scandalous libel" called " Robin's Game;" and Franklin, the publisher of the *Craftsman*, with other persons implicated, were subsequently arrested. The ministers now exerted themselves to crush the factious journal, and they obtained a severe verdict of a court of justice against Franklin, which obliged the writers in the *Craftsman* to be more cautious for some time. The newspapers and magazines during the summer were chiefly occupied in discussing the propriety of legal prosecutions against the press.

Bolingbroke and Pulteney, in a somewhat subdued tone, continued their personal attacks upon Walpole. On the 30th of March, 1732, the *Craftsman*, boldly insinuated, "that all the corruption of this age is owing to one great man now in the ministry;" and in May the same journal attempted to throw odium on the Whigs, by insinuating that they had a design to get all the lands in England into their own hands, and then destroy the British constitution. In the autumn a great outcry was raised in the same quarter, on the dangers to be apprehended from bad ministers. Towards the end of the year a new cause of alarm was started, which eventually raised the greatest storm to which Sir Robert Walpole's administration had yet been exposed,—the rumour already spread abroad of the minister's intention of proposing a new scheme of excise.

This scheme, which Pultney in the House of Commons stigmatized as "that *monster* the excise," had nothing very threatening *in itself*. The trade in wine, and especially tobacco, and the duties which those articles paid, had been liable to very extensive and shameful frauds, injurious alike to the planters, to the merchants, and to the Government: several articles of consumption had long been subject to excise duties, and Walpole's plan was to extend those duties to wine and tobacco, by which the frauds on the public would be in a great measure prevented, and the Government revenue would be considerably increased. But the name of excise had been unpopular in England ever since the days of the Commonwealth; and this circumstance was eagerly seized upon by the opposition, who, long before the ministerial plan was made public, spread abroad misrepresentations of the most extravagant kind, making people believe that every article of daily use was to be excised under the new plan, and that it was a base design to crush the people and establish tyranny. An incredible quantity of pamphlets and ballads, filled with misstatements, were industriously spread over the country as early as the months of January and February, although Walpole did not lay his plan before the House until the 14th of March. Among the caricatures issued at this period, one represents the lion and the unicorn, broken-spirited and harnessed, and march-

THE NEW MONSTER.

ing in wooden shoes, the usual symbol at this time of French influence. A soldier rides on the unicorn, and is supported by the standing army, one of the great objects of the attacks against the Government. The lion is drawing a barrel, on which sits Excise, in the form of a portly individual, intended apparently to represent Sir Robert Walpole. On one side trade leans sorrowfully over a hogshead of tobacco. The plate is entitled "The triumphant Exciseman." It was now common to mount caricatures upon fans; and among the few fan-caricatures still preserved, there are more than one against the excise, which, agreeably to the epithet bestowed upon it by Pulteney, is represented as a bloated monster, fattening itself upon the goods of the people. In another caricature, the monster appears in the form of a many-headed dragon, drawing the minister in his coach, and pouring into his lap, in the shape of gold, what it had eaten up in the forms of mutton, hams, cups, glasses, mugs, pipes, and any other articles that fall in its way, while people are flying from its ravages in every direction. A "new ballad," entitled "Britain Excised," one of the numerous effusions of a similar class which made their appearance early in the year, speaks of it as a mad project, which already excited the indignation of the *Craftsman* (Caleb) :—

> " Folks talk of supplies
> To be raised by excise,
> Old Caleb is horribly nettled ;
> Sure B——[*Bob*] has more sense
> Than to levy his pence,
> Or troops, when his peace is quite settled,
> Horse, foot, and dragoons,
> Battalions, platoons,
> Excise, wooden shoes, and no jury ;
> Then taxes increasing,
> While traffic is ceasing,
> Would put all the land in a fury."

The monster Excise was the most dangerous of them all :—

> " See this dragon, Excise,
> Has ten thousand eyes,
> And five thousand mouths to devour us ;
> A sting and sharp claws,
> With wide-gaping jaws,
> And a belly as big as a storehouse."

He begins, perhaps, with wine and liquors, but his greediness will not be appeased with these :—

> " Grant these, and the glutton
> Will roar out for mutton,
> Your beef, bread, and bacon to boot ;
> Your goose, pig, and pullet
> He'll thrust down his gullet,
> Whilst the labourer munches a root."

He will leave no corner unturned that is likely to conceal anything from his ravenous appetite, and threatens the same
tyranny which formerly provoked the rebellions of Jack Straw
and Wat Tyler:—

> " At first he'll begin ye
> With a pipe of Virginia,
> Then search ev'ry shop in his rambles ;
> If you force him to flee
> From the Custom-house key,
> The monster will lodge in your shambles.
>
> " Your cellars he'll range,
> Your pantry and grange,
> No barn can the monster restrain ;
> Wherever he comes,
> Swords, trumpets, and drums,
> And slavery march in his train.
>
> " Then sometimes he stoops
> To take up the hoops
> Of your daughters as well as your barrels :
> Tho' an army can awe
> A Tyler or Straw,
> Heav'n keep us from any such quarrels !"

Such arguments as these were well calculated to prevail with the
rabble ; and when the minister brought his plan before the House
of Commons, the voice of opposition within doors was nothing in
comparison with the mad clamour of the mob without. Walpole
calmly persisted in his project, and explained the absurdity and
wickedness of the misrepresentations which had gone abroad,
but to no purpose; the mob increased daily, and even the
minister's life was in danger. During the month of April,
ballad after ballad and pamphlet upon pamphlet deluged the
metropolis. The Lord Mayor, who happened to be a noted
Jacobite, persuaded the Common Council to draw up a violent
petition against the measure ; and several towns in different
parts of the country, such as Coventry, Nottingham, &c., followed the example. Awed by the increasing excitement, Walpole at length determined to relinquish his plan ; and, when its
fate was publicly known, the whole country was filled with
rejoicing, as if some extraordinary advantage had been gained.
Bonfires blazed in almost every town, and in London the mob
burnt the effigy of the minister in Fleet Street. In the University of Oxford, which still preserved its reputation for Jacobitism,
the joy at the defeat of the minister was unbounded, and was
openly exhibited in an unbecoming manner. In July, however,
after the close of the session, Walpole was received in Norfolk

(where the Excise madness appears to have prevailed least)
with unusual marks of respect, and his entry into Norwich
resembled a triumph. This, in London, was soon made the subject of satirical ballads, in which he was burlesqued under the
character of "Sir Sidrophel," and his reception by his constituents turned into ridicule.

The overstrained personalities of Bolingbroke and Pulteney
were now exciting indignation among reflecting people, who
began to question their motives and designs. Several biting
epigrams upon them and their *Craftsmen* appeared during the
month of May. Something like an intimation appears to have
been dropped, of a willingness, on the part of Pulteney, to listen
to conciliatory offers from Walpole; and the *Gentleman's
Magazine* for the month of May, 1733, contains the following
parody on the ninth ode of the third book of Horace :—

"A DIALOGUE BETWEEN THE RIGHT HON. SIR R——T
W——LE AND W——M P——Y, ESQ.

" *W.* While I and you were cordial friends,
Alike our interest and our ends,
I thought my character and place
Secure, and dreaded no disgrace.
No statesman, sure, was more carest,
Or more in his good fortune blest.

" *P.* While I your other self was deem'd,
And worthy such renown esteem'd,—
Ere great Newcastle won your heart,
And in your council took such part,—
I was the happiest man in life,
And, but with Tories, had no strife.

" *W.* Newcastle, noble and polite,
Whom George approves, is my delight;
His loyal merit is his claim,
For him I'd hazard life and fame.

" *P.* Me St. John now, whom every Muse
And every grace adorns, subdues.
Attached to him, I've learnt to hate
Your person, politics, and state.

" *W.* What if our former friendship should
Return, and you have what you would?
If, for your sake, the noble duke
Should be discarded and forsook?

" *P.* Though St. John now my fury warms,
And all his measures have such charms,—
Though he is fond, indifferent you,—
Our ancient league I'd yet renew;
For you I'd speech it in the house,
For you write *Craftsmen* and carouse;

> For you with all my soul I'd vote,
> For you make friends, impeach, and plot;
> For you I'd do—what would I not?"

Read's *Weekly Journal* of the 12th of the same month contains the following severe lines on the ingratitude of Bolingbroke:—

"AYE AND NO.

> "When from the axe good D'Anvers flew,
> And to his King for mercy cried;
> His generous King the axe withdrew,
> And *Yes* to all he ask'd replied.

> "His monarch's goodness to repay,
> When moved to act against the foes
> Of him who gave him life—'twas *Nay!*
> And all his voice could breathe were *No's.*

> "O George! hadst thou this *craftsman* known,
> The sentence had not seem'd amiss,
> For life when cringing to thy throne,
> Hadst thou said *No!* instead of *Yes!*

> "Yet though his pen so long has raved,
> Let him in time chastise his quill;
> That law whose *Aye!* has often saved,
> May one time have a *No!* to kill."

Every expedient, lawful or unlawful, was, however, now resorted to for the purpose of raising a mob excitement against the elections, for the ensuing session was the last of the present Parliament, and every nerve was strained to render the ministry unpopular with the electors. The excise agitation had not subsided with the year 1733, and to this was now added an outcry against the Riot Act, with exaggerated statements of the depredations which the Spaniards were suffered to commit upon our trade. Agents of the opposition were employed in various parts of the country in preparing for the approaching struggle, months before the dissolution of Parliament. On the 5th of January, 1734, the *Craftsman* says, "They write from Shropshire, that the disputes about the ensuing elections run so high there, that the dragoons are oftentimes called in to appease the disorders." The opposition candidates made progresses in some of the counties during January, which were attended with serious riots and outrages. It has been already observed that caricatures were now frequently mounted on fans: in January, 1734, the newspapers contain repeated advertisements of "a beautiful excise and election fan." Among the ballads was one in which the prime minister was satirized as "The Norfolk Gamester." The self-named Patriots began in return to be attacked se-

verely, and their patriotism was cried down as mere selfish ambition—the desire of place.   A rhymer in Read's *Weekly
Journal* of January 7th says—

> " You wish, my friend, I'd be so kind,
> Sincerely to declare my mind
> Of those who talk so loud and wise
> Against oppression and excise.
> Briefly, the case is now no more
> Than what it oft has been before.
> The quarrel, that has been so long,
> Is not in fact who's right or wrong ;
> But this, my friend, no longer doubt,
> 'Tis who is in, and who is out."

The same journal, on the 26th of January, publishes an attack
on the opposition under the title of " The Modern Patriots : a
proper new Ballad ;" in which the electors are warned against
the evil designs of a faction, the chief leaders of which are pictured in no very flattering colours.   Bolingbroke heads the
list :—

> " Of all these famed Patriots, so tight and so true,
> It would take too much time for a thorough review ;
> But a few of their worthies 'tis fit to record :
> And the first is a 'squire, that once was a lord.
> With a hey derry, &c."

After giving an account of the ex-peer's offences, the ballad
adds, with an allusion to his friend Pope, who had written a play
for the stage, which was unsuccessful—

> " Whate'er were his faults, they have taught him the wit
> The blots of his neighbours the better to hit ;
> As oftentimes poets, whose writings were damn'd,
> Have after for critics been notably famed.
> With a hey derry, &c."

Next comes Pulteney, who had drawn up the report of the
parliamentary committee against Bishop Atterbury, Bolingbroke's friend :—

> " The next is a 'squire, who once roasted a bishop,
> And an excellent feast to the courtiers did dish up ;
> But he turn'd cat in pan, as soon as debarr'd
> Of the perquisite sauce, which he thought his reward.
> With a hey derry, &c."

> " And now ever since he hath warm'y espoused
> The cause of his country, and liberty roused ;
> And he'll rouse it again, for he that's possess'd
> With the spirit of envy, can let nothing rest.
> With a hey derry, &c."

Wyndham, and one or two others, are described in a similar strain. The faction led by Bolingbroke and Pulteney seem now to have discarded their title of Patriots, and adopted that of the Country Interest, which was their watchword in the elections of 1734.

During the month of April a greater number of ballads and pamphlets were sent forth than had probably ever been issued before in the same space of time. An anniversary of the defeat of the excise scheme was celebrated by the populace early in the month. On the 16th the Parliament was dissolved, and the elections took place at the end of the month and at the beginning of May. The opponents of ministers never exerted themselves so much; and they practised bribery and corruption as unblushingly as their antagonists. In cases where the corporation of a town were in their interest, they endeavoured to make a majority by creating honorary freemen. Their anxiety about the result is shown strikingly in the following paragraph of the *Craftsman* of the 20th of April:—" We are credibly informed it will be so ordered that the elections of most counties and corporations, where the friends of *a certain great gentleman* are most likely to succeed, will be brought on first, by way of precedent and encouragement to the *others.* We don't mention this as any extraordinary piece of news, but only to prevent any surprise at the *first returns.*" The elections were in most cases hotly contested, and were unusually tumultuous. There was a riot even at Norwich; and the *Craftsman* states, that when Walpole mounted the hustings there, to give his vote as an honorary freeman, "the people called aloud to have the oath administered to him, *that he had received no money for that purpose.*" Pulteney's faction was again doomed to disappointment; for, although they had gained a few votes, the strength of the ministry remained unshaken; and they did not even attempt to conceal their mortification. On the 18th of May, a political pamphlet was advertised, under the title of "The City Garland," "with a curious copper-plate representing the humours of an election."

It was in the session of Parliament which had closed in April, that Sir William Wyndham made his famous personal attack on Walpole in the House of Commons, when the minister retorted with a no less violent, but truer, character of Bolingbroke. This is said to have contributed, with several other causes, to drive the latter from the arena of political strife; and he soon afterwards retired to the Continent, with the conviction that his party was carrying on a hopeless contest. A poet of the *Gentle-*

man's Magazine, in the month of June, compares their unwearied efforts to the labours of Sisyphus.

"Thus (as ancient stories tell)
Sisyphus, condemn'd in hell,
Up a hill, eternal, toils
To roll a stone, which back recoils.
Since the labour's much the same,
Sisyphus be P——y's name.

Ever may he toil in vain,
W——le's life or place to gain !
Still to aim, and still to fail,
Striving still, and ne'er prevail !
Its his hell in life—and can
Worse befall th' ambitious man !"

Pulteney was, indeed, discouraged and gloomy, and he showed now some inclination to seek a reconciliation with the minister. A calm, as usual, followed the political storm ; and during the rest of the year the only occurrences which made much noise were some religious disputes, arising chiefly from the ultra High Church zeal of one Dr. Codex, and the extraordinary celebrity of the pills of a quack named Ward.

While the opposition were exclaiming loudly against the dangers to be apprehended from a standing army, the provinces were suffering from riot and tumult which there was no efficient superior force to control. In the western counties, and more especially in Gloucestershire and Herefordshire, an active rebellion had for several years been carried on against turnpike-gates, in which, singularly enough, the insurgents disguised themselves in women's clothes, thus presenting a remarkable resemblance to those who, at a much more recent period, figured so prominently under the title of "Rebecca and her Daughters." We hear of the proceedings of these people as early as 1730 and 1731 ; and, as the excitement of political faction left a moment of leisure to the newspapers, they convey glimpses of their proceedings until 1735, when the turnpike destroyers in Herefordshire had carried their outrages to so extraordinary a height that they awed even the county magistrates.*

* The following particulars relating to these insurgents are taken from the *Daily Gazetter* of October 8 and December 9, 1735 :—

" *Hereford, October* 4.—There are now committed to the county gaol two, and more are daily expected, of the Ledbury rioters, who rather deserve the name of rebels, for they appeared a hundred in a gang, armed with guns and swords, as well as axes to hew down the turnpikes, and were dressed in women's apparel, with high-crown'd hats, and their faces blacken'd.   I suppose you have heard of the attack they made at Ledbury on the 21st of September, about nine o'clock at night, when in two hours' time they cut

With respect to Walpole's foreign policy, the factious character of the opposition was becoming so apparent, that it now caused little embarrassment or uneasiness to the Government, and exhibited itself publicly in a way not likely to produce much effect. At the beginning of 1734, when a peace seemed to be securely established, the "Patriots" had clamoured for war.

down five or six turnpikes to the ground; but, before they had gone through all their work, they were disturbed by a worthy magistrate in the neighbourhood, John Skipp, Esq.; who, being in the commission of the peace, caused the proclamation to be read against riots, and then the act of Parliament; but to no purpose; for this gentleman, with his servants and neighbours, going to defend the last turnpike, a skirmish ensued, in which he took two of those miscreants prisoners, whom he secured for that night in his own house; but the whole gang appeared soon after, who demanded the said prisoners, threatening, in case of refusal, to pull his house down, and burn his barns and stables, and immediately discharged several loaded pieces into the house, which happily did no damage. The justice finding himself and family beset in such a manner, discharged several blunderbusses and fowling-pieces at them, whereby one was shot dead on the spot, and several so wounded, that 'tis not believed they will recover. At this the rioters fled with precipitation, leaving their two companions behind them. But 'tis fear'd that more blood will yet be spilt, the country being in the greatest confusion, and I am informed that an attempt is designed upon the county gaol; but the quarter sessions being to be held next week, a petition will no doubt be presented to the justices for relief."

Hereford, December 6.—You have already heard that two men were committed to the keeper of the gaol of this county, for the riot at Ledbury. I am now to acquaint you, that on Sunday last above twenty of those turnpike cutters or levellers, as they call themselves, though that is a character by much too good for them, met with the said keeper at the King's Head Inn at Ross fair, and demanding his reasons for detaining those two men in custody, without giving him time to return an answer, dragged him out of the inn into the street, knocked him down several times, and almost murdered him, notwithstanding all that the innkeeper and his servants could do to prevent it, who were used in a very cruel manner for assisting him. The villains immediately carried the keeper to Wilton's Bridge, where at first they concluded to throw him into the river Wye; but at length they agreed to carry him to a place where they would secure him till they themselves had fetched the prisoners out of custody. The better to complete that design, they dragged him four miles in his boots and spurs, to a place called Honewithey, a public-house, where he was kept prisoner, treat in a shameful manner by those merciless wretches, and obliged to write a discharge to the turnkey, being threatened, in case of refusal, to be hanged up on the spot. Four gentlemen from Hereford, who followed them, and endeavoured to dissuade them from such wickedness and cruelty, were inhumanly beat, and obliged to ride off for their lives. After they had detained the keeper near six hours at the house aforesaid, they ferried him over the Wye, walked him about the country till near four o'clock in the morning, and then robbed him of his money. Those that robbed him made off, but left others to guard him, who, quarrelling and fighting about dividing the booty, it gave the keeper an opportunity to make his escape out of the villains' hands with his life, but not without bruises in abundance."

A few months after this a war appeared imminent, and then the same opposition cried out for peace, and complained that the Government was unnecessarily involving the nation in hostilities with its neighbours. Before the end of 1735 the danger had vanished, and then the opposition became as warlike as ever, and the English people was told daily and weekly of the pusillanimity of its rulers. The "balance of power," which was the watchword of Walpole's foreign politics and the object of his negotiations, was made the object of ridicule, and his brother Horace Walpole, who was his great negotiator, received the *sobriquet* of "the balancing master." When he returned from Holland to attend to his parliamentary duties, in the beginning of 1736, the *Craftsman* of Jan. 17 published the following satirical announcement :—

"Just arrived from Holland,

"THE GREATEST CURIOSITY IN EUROPE!

"Being a *fine large dove*, of the male kind, lineally descended from that of Mount Ararat; which both had the honour to be shewn in several courts, and given entire satisfaction.

"His feathers are formed exactly in the shape of olive leaves, with a little tuft just rising upon his head, somewhat like a *coronet*. He is of such a wonderful pacific nature, that, as soon as he begins to coo, the most inveterate enemies cannot help shaking hands and growing friends again. He hath not only reconciled several men and their wives, after all other remedies have proved ineffectual, but also divers *great princes*, who have had an hereditary hatred against each other for many generations.

"He likewise sings a variety of merry tunes and catches, to the admiration of all that have heard him.*

"To be seen every day, during the sitting of Parliament, in a room adjoining to the Court of Requests; where all gentlemen and ladies are desired to satisfy their curiosity, before he is *sent abroad again*."

People in general seem not to have partaken in the warlike propensities of the opposition papers at this time; and when the King went to open the Parliament in the middle of January, he was greeted by the mob with unusual acclamations. The next *Craftsman* let out its spleen in an intemperate article, in which it accused the mob of being bribed, spoke of "hired huzzas," and stigmatized those who uttered them as a "ragged rabble." On this occasion, the following spirited epigram went the round of the Whig journals :—

"Round Brunswic's coach the happy Britons throng,
And bear with grateful shouts their Prince along;

* Old Horace Walpole was an active speaker in the House of Commons, though he appears by no means to have possessed the eloquence of his brother. The opposition affected to laugh at his speeches, which are perhaps alluded to here as the "merry tunes and catches," that caused so much admiration.

Joy fills the skies, with intermingled prayers,
And Europe's general voice seems raised in theirs.
Caleb alone with grief surveys the crowd,
Nor can contain his rage, he vents aloud :
'Are these my toils repaid, ye witless herd !
Is Britain's peace at last to mine preferr'd !
Ye ragged rascals, ye are hired to this ;
Be incorrupt like me, and give a hiss.
Huzzah, ye *bribed !* but give me patriot strife,
And let me, *gratis,* hiss away my life.'"

The disappointed "Patriots" were now exposed to ridicule in
their turn, and the newspapers contained satirical allusions to
their eagerness to obtain the places held by their opponents.
The following is taken from the *Daily Gazetteer* of December
26, 1735:—

"AN ADVERTISEMENT.

"To be sold at a stationer's shop in *Covent Garden,* a neat and curious
collection of well-chosen *similes, allusions, metaphors, and allegories,* from
the best plays and romances, modern and ancient ; proper to adorn a poem
or a panegyric on the glorious patriots designed to succeed the present
ministry. The similes 5s., the metaphors ten, and the allegories a guinea
each.

"The author gives notice, that all sublunary metaphors, of a new minister
being a rock, a pillar, a bulwark, a strong tower, or a spire-steeple, will be
allowed very cheap ; celestial ones must be disposed of something dearer,
as they are fetched at a greater expense from another world. The new
treasurer (W. W.)* may be a *Phœbus,* the new secretary (W. S.)† a *Mercury,* the new general (D. of O——d) a *Mars,* for a moidore each ; and a
tip-top *Neptune,* to introduce the Chevalier, at the same price. A right
Jupiter, being a capital allusion, and fit only for a prime favourite, will be
rated at a ducatoon. Comets and blazing stars are reserved for privy-
councillors only ; twelve of which are already bespoke and paid for. Mr.
Fog and Mr. *A——rr‡* have desired to be each a satellite of *Jupiter,* at a
penny the satellite, which is granted. A vagrant, thin, whiffling meteor,
dark, yet easily seen thro', is set aside for *E. B——ll.§* Esq. ; and another
of the same odd qualities, for the author of the 'Persian Letters.' The
belt of Saturn, little worse for wearing, will be sold a pennyworth. The
North Star is bespoke for a hero in the South,‖ as soon as he arrives next
in Scotland to finish his conquests ; and the *Great Bear* for his first minister
and confessor.¶ All the signs in the zodiac, except *Scorpio,* will be sold in

* Sir William Wyndham.
† William Shippen, M.P.
‡ *Fog's Journal,* the successor to *Mist's,* was the chief organ of the
Tories after the *Craftsman.* The latter was, as has been already stated,
edited by Nicholas Amhurst, under the assumed name of *Caleb d'Anvers.*
§ Perhaps Eustace Budgell, Esq., a writer in the *Craftsman,* who com-
mitted suicide not long after this date. A series of attacks were made on
the English ministry at this period, under the fictitious character of
memoirs of *Persian* affairs.
‖ The Pretender.
¶ Probably Bishop Atterbury.

I

one lot; which, for its biting, stinging, scratching, poisonous quality, is set aside for a *Gray's-Inn* barrister. * For his steady, regular, uniform motion, W. P.,† Esq., may, with great propriety, be a *fixed star* of the first magnitude, for five guineas; and a certain viscount,‡ the *Syrius ardens* of *Horace*, or the incendiary enflaming light *in capite Leonis*, at the same price.

" *P.S.*—The same author has, with great pains and study, prepared a collection of state satires, enriched with the newest and most fashionable topics of defamation, which may serve, with a very little variation, to libel a judge, a bishop, or a prime minister. The maker of these satires, a great observer of decorums, begs leave to acquaint the public, that he thinks, a king, in respect to the dignity of his character, ought never to be abused but in folio, morocco leather, and the leaves gilt; a queen in quarto, neatly bound; a peer in octavo, letter'd on the back; and a commoner in 12mo., stitch'd only.

" *N.B.*—The same satirist has collections of reasons ready by him against the ensuing peace, though he has not yet read the preliminaries, or seen one article of the pacification."

While the violence of opposition appeared to be subsiding, a new subject of popular discontent suddenly arose in 1736. The depravity of the lower orders, and the debased state of public morals, had frequently been made a subject of declamation, and had been attributed to a variety of causes. Many persons of late had ascribed the worst disorders of the times to the increasing vice of drunkenness; and, in fact, the drinking of gin and other spirituous liquors appears to have prevailed among the lower classes of society to a degree at once alarming and revolting. A paragraph in the *Old Whig* of Feb. 26, 1736, informs us, "We hear that a strong-water shop was lately opened in Southwark, with this inscription on the sign :§—

" 'Drunk for 1d.
Dead drunk for 2d.
Clean straw for nothing.' "

The newspapers of the period contain frequent announcements of sudden deaths in the taverns from excessive drinking of gin. Some zealous reformers of public manners formed the project of putting a stop to this bane of society by prohibiting the sale of the article which fed it, or, which was the same thing, laying on it a heavy duty, which would make it too expensive to be purchased by the poor, and at the same time prohibiting the sale of

* Amhurst, the editor of the *Craftsman*, was of Gray's Inn.
† William Pulteney.
‡ 1 Lord Carteret.
§ This inscription was afterwards introduced by Hogarth into his caricature of Gin Lane, and was remembered at the time of the repeal of the Gin Act in 1743. See Smollett.

it in small quantities. A bill with this object was brought into
Parliament by Sir Joseph Jekyl, and although Walpole seems
not to have given it his entire approbation, was passed, after an
energetic opposition by the Patriots in the House, and by those
whose interests it affected out of the House. This bill was to
come into operation on the 29th of September following.
It appears to have caused no great excitement at first; but, as
the time approached when the populace was to be deprived of
their favourite gin, their discontent began to show itself in a
riotous shape, and the opponents of the ministry urged them on
in every possible manner. Ballads in lamentation of " Mother
Gin " were sung in the streets. As early as the 17th July, the
Craftsman announces the publication of a caricature, entitled
" The Funeral of Madam Geneva," with the addition, " who
died, Sept. 29, 1736." As the date last mentioned approached,
the excitement increased, and serious riots were prevented only
by the watchfulness of the authorities. The signs of the liquor-
shops were everywhere put in mourning; and some of the
dealers made a parade of mock ceremonies for " Madam Geneva's
lying in state," which was the occasion of mobs, and the justices
were obliged to commit "the chief mourners " to prison. The
Daily Gazetteer says, " Last Wednesday (Sept. 29), several
people made themselves very merry on the death of Madam Gin,
and some of both sexes got soundly drunk at her funeral, for
which the mob made a formal procession with torches, but committed no outrages." The same newspaper adds: " The exit of
Mother Gin in Bristol has been enough bewailed by the retailers
and drinkers of it; many of the latter, willing to have their fill,
and to take the last farewell in a respectful manner of their be-
loved dame, have not scrupled to pawn and sell their very
clothes, as the last devoir they can pay to her memory. It was
observed, Monday, Tuesday, and Wednesday, that several retailers' shops were well crowded, some tippling on the spot,
while others were carrying it off from a pint to a gallon; and
one of those shops had such a good trade, that it put every cask
they had upon the stoop; and the owner with sorrowful sighs
said, ' Is not this a barbarous and cruel thing, that I must not
be permitted to fill them again?' and pronounced a heavy woe
on the instruments of their drooping. Such has been the lamentation, that on Wednesday night her funeral obsequies were
performed with formality in several parishes, and some of the
votaries appeared in ragged clothes, some without gowns, and
others with one stocking; but among them all, we don't hear of
any that have carried their grief so far, as to hang or drown

themselves, rather choosing the drinking part to finish their sorrow ; and accordingly a few old women are pretty near tipping off the perch, by sipping too large a draught. We hear from Bath, that Mother Gin has been lamented in that city much after the same manner." Similar scenes were witnessed in other cities and towns. In reading accounts like these, we seem to have before our eyes the pictures of Hogarth.

The Gin Act did but little good; for while, on one hand, it encouraged a troop of common informers, who became the pest of the country, it was on the other hand evaded in every possible manner, and with great facility. Not only was gin publicly sold in shops, but hawkers carried it about the streets in flasks and bottles, under fictitious names. The titles thus adopted were in some cases amusing enough. Read's *Weekly Journal* of October 23rd tells us, " The following drams are sold at several brandy-shops in High Holborn, St. Giles's, Thieving Lane, Tothill Street, Rosemary Lane, Whitechapel, Shoreditch, Old Mint, Kent Street, &c. ; viz. *Sangree, Tom Roe, Cuckold's Comfort, Parliament Gin, Make Shift, the Last Shift, the Ladies' Delight, the Baulk, King Theodore or Corsica, Cholick* and *Grips Waters,* and several others, to evade the late Act of Parliament." Others coloured the liquor, and exposed it in bottles, labelled " Take two or three spoonfuls of this four or five times a day, or as often as the fit takes you." Some people set up as chemists, selling chiefly " cholick-water " and "gripe-water," with the further intimation that they gave " advice gratis " And when some of the evaders of the law were brought before the courts for examination, and it was observed that the chemists' shops were much more frequented than formerly, they are represented as giving for answer, " that the late act had given many people the cholic, and that was the reason they had so many patients."

The gin agitation continued unabated through the years 1737 and 1738, and gave rise to many a ballad and broadside. In the July of the former year appeared, among many other similar productions, " The Fall of Bob ; or, The Oracle of Gin : a tragedy ;" and " Desolation ; or, The Fall of Gin : a poem." It was not an unusual thing to hear of three or four hundred informations against people for the illegal sale of gin at one time. The informers were unprincipled people, who not only used all kinds of snares to decoy their victims, but sometimes laid false informations, to gratify private revenge. They thus became objects of extreme hatred to the mob ; and whenever they fell into the hands of the populace, they were treated in an unmerciful manner, beaten rudely, rolled in the dirt, pumped upon, and often carried to some horse-pond outside the town to be ducked. In some cases this last operation was performed in the Thames; and there were instances in which the offender was thrown into the river, and narrowly escaped drowning. This exercise of mob-justice had become so frequent in the autumn of 1737, that it was found necessary in September to issue a proclamation, offering a reward of £20 for the discovery of any person concerned in such outrages, a measure which had, however, a very limited effect in checking them.

In the course of 1737 Walpole lost his best supporter in Queen Caroline, who died on the 20th of November; and the opposition had already been strengthened by the accession to their ranks of Frederick Prince of Wales, who had first been led into a violent quarrel with his father, and then took the lead in all measures likely to embarrass his father's government. The Prince had taken up his residence at Norfolk House, where, from this time, all the movements of the opposition were discussed and resolved upon. Encouraged by this great addition to their strength, the allied " Patriots " and Tories roused themselves for the senatorial strife, and the session of 1738 was perhaps the most stormy one that Walpole had yet passed. The object of attack was the foreign policy ; for the opposition believed, that, if they could only push the country into a war, the present ministry would be obliged to go out of office. The English merchant-vessels had been long in the habit of carrying on an illicit commerce on the coast of the Spanish possessions in America, to hinder which the Spanish government had lately ordered its guarda-costas to be more watchful in their duties, and the Spanish commanders in carrying out these duties, seem often to have shown an unnecessary degree of insolence and severity. The right of search, which has usually been claimed under such circumstances, was always a tender question ; and the English merchants, on the present occasion, made loud complaints of the injuries they were daily suffering. One Captain Robert Jenkyns pretended, that, when his vessel had been searched, the Spaniards had, in an insolent and cruel manner, cut off one of his ears. It was insinuated by the ministerial supporters, that, if Jenkyns had lost his ear at all, it had been taken from him on the pillory. He was evidently the tool of a party. Nevertheless, this story, which Edmund Burke afterwards called " the fable of Jenkyns' ear," produced an extraordinary sensation, and the captain was brought forward to make a statement of his wrongs before the House of Commons. Walpole found himself, to a certain degree, obliged to give way to the popular clamour, and make a slight show of warlike demonstration. He felt, in fact, that the conduct of the Spaniards could not in all respects be defended; but he still clung to his pacific policy, and carried on negotiations with the court of Spain which led at the end of the year to a convention, stipulating for the release of some prizes and the payment of certain sums of money, but which convention was understood in the light of a preliminary to the arrangement of a subsequent treaty.

These negotiations were not what the opposition wanted, and they openly accused the minister of sacrificing the interests of his country, with no other object than that of keeping his place. In November, we find the *Craftsman* employing its pleasantry on Walpole's great belly and on his luxurious living, and accusing him of suppressing the truth, in order to conceal the real extent of the Spanish depredations. Among the most popular caricatures published at this time, was a series of prints (continued in the year following) under the title of "The European Races," which require, what was really printed, a pamphlet to explain them. Another caricature, entitled "In Place," represents the minister sitting at his official table, and refusing to

PARING THE NAILS OF THE BRITISH LION.

hear the numerous petitions and complaints, while a man with a candle is burning one of the numbers of the *Craftsman.* A print, entitled "Slavery," exhibits the well known story of Jenkyns' ear. Another, published in October, 1738, applies the fable of the lion in love, and represents Sir Robert Walpole keeping the lion of England tame, while the Spaniard cuts his nails. The character of the pamphlets on the same subject may be surmised from the title of one advertised in the mouth of September, " Ministerial Virtue; or, Long-suffering extolled in a great man." The negotiations of the minister were satirised bitterly in "The Negotiators; or, Don Diego brought to reason : an excellent new ballad ; " which may be cited as an example of the political ballads made on this occasion. Walpole's negotiations, according to this ballad, must silence the clamours of the injured merchants :—

> "Our merchants and tars a strange pother have made,
> With losses sustain'd in their ships and their trade ;
> But now they may laugh and quite banish their fears,
> Nor mourn for lost liberty, riches, or ears:
>   Since Blue-String the great,
>   To better their fate,
>   Once more has determined he'll *negotiate ;*
> And swears the proud Don, whom he dares not to fight,
> Shall submit to his logic, and do 'em all right.
>
> "No sooner the knight had declared his intent,
> But straight to the Irish Don Diego he went ;
> And lest, if alone, of success he might fail,
> Took with him his brother to balance the scale.
>   For long he had known,
>   What all men must own,
>   That two heads were ever deem'd better than one :
> And sure in Great Britain no two heads there are
> That can with the knight's and his brother's compare."

The Don will not receive them on their first call, but he admits them on the second day, and the knight (Walpole) states their business, and petitions for the delivery of the ships of the English merchants detained by the Spaniards. Horace recounts the various secret services which his brother has performed for the latter power :—

> "'Consider how oft himself he exposed,
> And 'twixt you and Great Britain's just rage interposed !
> When her fleets were equipp'd, you must certainly know,
> By him they were hinder'd from striking a blow.
>   Thus Hosier the brave
>   Was sent to his grave,
>   On an errand which better had fitted a slave ;
> Being order'd to take (if he could) your galleons,
> By force of persuasion, not that of his guns.' "

The Don replies in a tone of astonishment :—

" Quoth the Don, ' What you say, my good friends, may be true,
But I wonder that you for such varlets will sue.
Merchants! had they were once *sturdy beggars*, I think,*
And, were I in your p'ace, I would let them all sink.
    They opposed your excise ;
    Then if you are wise,
    Reject their petitions, be deaf to their cries ;
And let us like brothers together agree,—
You excise them on land, I'll excise them at sea.' "

The minister's answer is in perfect accordance with the senti
ments of the Don :—

    " ' Noble Don,' quoth the knight, ' I should heartily close
    (For hugely I like it) with what you propose.
    Our merchants are grown very saucy and rich,
    And 'tis time to prepare a good rod for their breech :
        Were I once to speak *true*,
        Give the Devil his due,
        I love them as little, nay, far less than you ;
    And would willingly crush them, but that I'm afraid
    Of this a bad use by my foes might be made.' "

In the sequel, a private arrangement is made; the Spaniard
takes a bribe, and agrees to appear more moderate; and the
King and the nation are equally deceived by a specious story
of the terror inspired by the renown of the British arms.

The outcry against the insolence of the Spaniards continued
unabated in 1739, and the "convention," signed at Madrid on
the 14th of January, was designated as an "infamous" betrayal
of the natural rights of Englishmen, because it did not insist
upon claims which really had never been allowed by Spain.
When Parliament met, the opposition had increased in violence ;
their clamours against the articles and principles of the "con-

* During the debates on the Excise scheme in the beginning of 1733, the
House of Commons was beset by a tumultuous mob, who not only solicited
the members to vote against the ministerial measure, but even employed
threats. Smollett informs us, that one day "Sir Robert Walpole took
notice of the multitude which had beset all the approaches to the House.
He said it would be an easy task for a designing seditious person to raise
a tumult and disorder among them : that gentlemen might give them what
name they should think fit, and affirm they were come as humble suppliants ;
but he knew whom the law called *sturdy beggars*, and those who brought
them to that place could not be certain but that they might behave in the
same manner. This insinuation was resented by Sir John Barnard, [the
member for London,] who observed that merchants of character had a right
to come down to the Court of Requests and lobby of the House of
Commons, in order to solicit their friends and acquaintances against any
scheme or project which they might think prejudicial to their commerce :
that when he came into the House, he saw none but such as deserved the
appellation of *sturdy beggars* as little as the honourable gentleman himself,
or any gentleman whatever."

vention " were loud in both Houses, and Jenkyns' "car" made a
greater figure than ever. In this debate William Pitt, then a
young man, first distinguished himself in the ranks of the opposition. The minister, however, still carried the day by his
majorities; and a portion of the opposition, led by Sir William
Wyndham, had recourse to the dramatic effect of a public secession from the House, a measure very acceptable to the
Government, and which was far from producing the results
expected from it. But the overbearing conduct of Spain soon
seconded the efforts of the English " Patriots" in hurrying the
two countries into a war, which was declared on the 19th of
October, 1739, amid the enthusiastic shouts of the mob. The
French court showed anything but a friendly aspect towards
England on this occasion; and, by its threats and persuasions,
Holland was induced to remain neutral, and withhold the aux-
iliary troops which the States were bound by treaties to furnish
to their ally; so that England was left to fight single-handed,
with a small army and not a well-manned fleet, and a Parliamentary opposition who cried out against every method of increasing the former or raising sailors for the latter, and yet who
began soon to blame the Government for their want of vigour in
carrying on hostilities. The behaviour of the Dutch was the
subject of a caricature, entitled "The States in a Lethargy," in
which they are represented by a lion asleep in a cradle, rocked
by Cardinal Fleury.

DUTCH FRIENDSHIP.

The caricatures began now to be more numerous and more
spirited than at any previous period. Among those which

appeared towards the end of the year, we may mention one,
bearing date the 8th of October, 1739, and entitled "Hocus
Pocus; or, The Political Jugglers," which is divided into four
compartments. In the first an Englishman is seen fighting
with a Spaniard, while "Hogan" (the Dutchman) takes the
opportunity of picking his pocket. The second compartment
represents Commerce, in the form of a bull, baited by all
the powers concerned on this occasion. In the third, Cardinal
Fleury appears as a negotiator, with money on a table; while
the fourth represents Gibraltar besieged by the Spaniards.
This port had now begun to be looked upon as one of vital
importance for English commerce. Another caricature, published about the end of the year, under the title of "Fee Fau
Fum," and like the former divided into four compartments,
pictures the minister in the character of Jack the Giant-killer.
In the first compartment the political hero has betrayed a
mighty giant, the personification of the Sinking Fund, into a
pit, and is destroying him with his pick-axe. On the giant's

THE POLITICAL JACK THE GIANT-KILLER.

girdle is inscribed the word "Convention," and round his
garter "*The Ear*," of course the celebrated *ear* of Captain
Jenkyns, which, with the subsequent convention, had brought
on the war that had obliged the Government to draw heavily
upon the Sinking Fund in order to defray its expenses. In the
second compartment Jack is encountering the giant Fleury.
In the third he is pursuing a two-headed giant, armed with a
club (? Spain and France.) In the fourth, the minister, in
his character of the hero, is knocking boldly at the castle gate,
while a three-headed giant (Spain, France, and Sweden) is

looking upon him from a window above. The English government had narrowly escaped a war with
the latter of these three powers;
France, as we have already seen, acted
a part calculated to excite the apprehensions of the English; and Spain
was engaged in open hostilities, and
inflicting on the merchants much
greater injuries than they had sustained from her guarda-costas.

The war with Spain was carried on
with no great activity; and the only
event which threw any credit upon it
was the taking of Porto Bello, in the
Isthmus of Darien, on the 22nd of
November, 1739, by Admiral Vernon,
with six ships of the line. It appears
that this success was owing more to
the cowardice of the garrison, than
to the conduct of the English

JACK IN HIS GLORY.

admiral, who was a vain man with no great capacity. But
he was a personal enemy of the minister, and he was on
that account cried up by the opposition, and became in consequence the popular hero of the mob, who were made to believe
that the Government was jealous of him because he was a
"patriot." When the news reached home in March, 1740,
his friends in England fed his discontent, by telling him that
the Court opposed the public acknowledgment due to his
merits; and he wrote back to his friends that he was checked in
his victorious career by the neglect of the ministers at home.
It was hinted that the Government would willingly see
Vernon's armament perish in inactivity, as they had suffered
that of Admiral Hosier to die away on the same station
in 1726. This was a means of reviving old clamours and
animosities, for the fate of poor Hosier had excited great
sympathy. A print was published, entitled, "Hosier's Ghost,"
and representing the spectres of the unfortunate brave who had
thus perished in those unhealthy seas, calling upon Vernon's
sailors for revenge; and a pathetic ballad was distributed, which
has retained its popularity even in modern times, from the circumstance of its insertion in the "Reliques" of Bishop Percy. It
was attributed to Pulteney; but the true writer is understood
to have been Glover, the author of "Leonidas."

ADMIRAL HOSIER'S GHOST.

"As near Porto Bello lying
  On the gently swelling flood,
At midnight with streamers flying
  Our triumphant navy rode ;
There while Vernon sate all-glorious
  From the Spaniards' late defeat,
And his crews with shouts victorious,
  Drank success to England's fleet,

" On a sudden, shrilly sounding,
  Hideous yells and shrieks were heard ;
Then, each heart with fear confounding
  A sad troop of ghosts appear'd,
All in dreary hammocks shrouded,
  Which for winding sheets they wore,
And with looks by sorrow clouded
  Frowning on that hostile shore.

" On them gleam'd the moon's wan lustre,
  When the shade of Hosier brave
His pale bands was seen to muster
  Rising from their watery grave.
O'er the glimmering wave he hy'd him,
  Where the Burford* rear'd her sail,
With three thousand ghosts beside him,
  And in groans did Vernon hail.

" ' Heed, oh heed, our fatal story,—
  I am Hosier's injured ghost,—
You who now have purchased glory
  At this place where I was lost !
Though in Porto Bello's ruin
  You now triumph free from fears,
When you think on our undoing,
  You will mix your joy with tears.

" ' See these mournful spectres sweeping
  Ghastly o'er this hated wave,
Whose wan cheeks are stain'd with weeping—
  These were English captains brave !
Mark those numbers pale and horrid,—
  Those were once my sailors bold !
Lo, each hangs his drooping forehead,
  While his dismal tale is told.

" ' I, by twenty sail attended,
  Did this Spanish town affright :
Nothing then its wealth defended
  But my orders not to fight.
Oh ! that in this rolling ocean
  I had cast them with disdain,
And obey'd my heart's warm motion,
  To have quell'd the pride of Spain !

* The name of Admiral Vernon's ship.

" ' For resistance I could fear none,
    Bot with twenty ships had done
  What thou, brave and happy Vernon,
    Hast achiev'd with six alone.
  Then the bastimentos never
    Had our foul dishonour seen,
  Nor the sea the sad receiver
    Of this gallant train had been.

" 'Thus, like thee, proud Spain dismaying,
    And her galleons leading home,
  Though, condemn'd for disobeying,
    I had met a traitor's doom,
  To have fal en, my country crying
    He has play'd an English part,
  Had been better far than dying
    Of a griev'd and broken heart.

" 'Unrepining at thy glory,
    Thy successful arms we hail;
  Dot remember our sad story,
    And let Hosier's wrongs prevail.
  Sent in this foul clime to languish,
    Think what thousands fell in vain,
  Wasted with disease and anguish,
    Not in glorious battle slain.

" 'Hence with all my train attending
    From their oozy tombs below,
  Thro' the hoary foam ascending,
    Here I feed my constant woe:
  Here the bastimentos viewing,
    We recal our shameful doom,
  And our plaintive cries renewing,
    Wander thro' the midnight gloom.

" 'O'er these waves for ever mourning
    Shall we roam deprived of rest,
  If to Britain's shores returning
    You neglect my just request.
  After this proud foe subduing,
    When your patriot friends you see,
  Think on vengeance for my ruin,
    And for England shamed in me !' "

For a while nothing was talked of but Vernon and Porto
Bello, and even the French were said to have become alarmed at
our rising power in America. A caricature, published in July,
1740, under the title of "The Cardinal in the Dumps, with the
Head of the Colossus," represents Fleury looking with amazement on the portrait of Admiral Vernon, and exclaiming,
" G—d, he'll take all our acquisitions in America ! His iron will
get the better of my gold !" In the background the head of
Walpole appears raised on a pole, under which is written, "The

THE CARDINAL IN THE DUMPS.

preferment of the Barber's Block;" and still lower, through an aperture of the wall, is seen the picture of "Poor Hosier's — " [Ghost.]

In several prints issued during this year Walpole was caricatured as the Great Colossus, as the idol to whom all must bow who would obtain Court favour; and the clamour daily became louder against the possession of too much power by a prime minister.

No actions of importance followed the capture of Porto Bello, while the merchants suffered much more seriously from the Spanish cruisers and privateers than from the petty aggressions of their guarda-costas, and they filled the country with their complaints against the mismanagement of the war. This, joined with a great scarcity of provisions in consequence of an unfavourable season, increased so much the general dissatisfaction, that riots of the most serious character took place in different parts of the island, attended in some instances with bloodshed, and the name of Walpole became exceedingly unpopular. The opposition looked forward with confident hopes to the effect of this excitement on the elections, which were to come on in the spring of 1741, and for which they were making active preparations before the end of the year. In November appeared a bitter metrical lampoon on Walpole, entitled, " Are these Things so ? The previous question from an Englishman in his Grotto to a Great Man at Court," pointing out all the political sins ascribed to his administration in very strong language, and taking for its significant motto the words of Horace —

> " Lusisti satis, edisti satis, atque bibisti,
> Tempus abire tibi."

It was immediately followed by another pamphlet in the same strain under the title " Yes, they are;" and these, with one or two answers and rejoinders, seem to have made a considerable sensation. In the beginning of 1741 all the old subjects of clamour against the Government were revived, and almost every opposition paper was filled with new attacks on the

excise project and on the "infamous" convention. Lists of
the members who voted for and
against the latter measure were
industriously spread among the
electors. Amidst a variety of
political squibs, there appeared on
the 9th of January a caricature
entitled "'The Devil' upon Two
Sticks. To the worthy Electors
of Great Britain;" in which
two of the members are represented carrying the minister
over a slough or pond upon their
shoulders, whilst some have got
over in safety, though not without evident marks of the wet
and dirt through which they
had passed. Britannia and her
"Patriots" remain behind. Underneath are written the words

THE DEVIL UPON TWO STICKS.

"Members who voted for the Excise and against the Convention."

The expectations of the opposition had now become so sanguine, that they determined not to wait for another session to
impress upon the minister the truth of the motto which had
been applied to him in the title-page just alluded to. Sandys,
one of the most discontented of the discontented Whigs, and
who, for the readiness with which he always put himself forward on such occasions, had obtained the name of "The Motion
Maker," was again chosen to take the lead. On the 13th of
February, 1741, at the conclusion of a long and violent attack
upon Walpole, reviewing the whole of his foreign policy, stig-
matising him as a tool of France, who had sacrificed the real
English interests on the Continent to the aggrandisement of
the House of Bourbon, and charging him with arrogating to
himself the "unconstitutional" place of sole minister, and with
unnecessarily burthening his country with debts and taxes,
Sandys moved an address to the King, "that he would be gra-
ciously pleased to remove the Right Honourable Sir Robert
Walpole from his Majesty's presence and councils for ever."
This motion was seconded by Lord Limerick and warmly supported by Pulteney, Pitt, and others. As the opposition seemed
to approach nearer to the attainment of power, the discordant

materials of which it was composed began to show their want
of cordiality, and on Sandys' motion the Jacobites and many of
the Tories left the house before the division. The consequence
of this desertion was, that the minister, who made an able
speech in his own defence, triumphed by an unusually large
majority. On the same day, Lord Carteret (who had become
one of Walpole's most violent opponents, and aspired to his place)
produced a similar motion in the House of Lords, and was
seconded by the Duke of Argyle, and supported by the Duke of
Bedford and other opposition peers; but the victory of the
court party was here as complete as in the other house.

The opposition shrunk back confused and mortified; and
Walpole's friends and supporters set no bounds to their exultation. Within a few days appeared a print entitled " The Motion," of which a copy is given in the accompanying plate. It
was one of the most spirited, and became one of the most
celebrated, caricatures of the day. The background represents
Whitehall, the Treasury, and the adjoining buildings, as they
then stood. Lord Carteret, in the coach, is driven towards the
Treasury by the Duke of Argyle as coachman, with the Earl of
Chesterfield as postilion, who, in their haste, are overturning the
vehicle; and Lord Carteret cries " Let me get out ! "   The
Duke brandishes a wavy sword, instead of a whip; and between
his legs the heartless changeling Bubb Dodington sits in the
form of a spaniel. Their characters are thus set forth in the
verses printed beneath the original engraving :—

" Who be dat de box do sit on ?
'Tis John, the hero of North Briton,
Who, out of place, does place-men spit on,
        Doodle, &c.

" Between his legs de spaniel curr see,
'Though now he growls at Bob so fierce,
Yet he fawn'd on him once in doggerel verse.
        Doodle, &c.

" And who be dat postilion there,
Who drive o'er all, and no man spare ?
'Tis Ph—l—p e—le of here and there.
        Doodle, &c.

" But pray who in de coaché sit-a ?
'Tis honest J—nny C—t—ritta,
Who want in place again to get-a.
        Doodle, &c."

Lord Cobham holds firmly by the straps behind, as footman;
while Lord Lyttelton follows on horseback, characterized equally

by his own lean form, and by that of the animal across which he strides.

> "Who's dat behind? 'Tis Dicky Cobby,
> Who first would have bang'd, and them try'd Bobby.
> Oh! was not that a pretty jobb-e?
>   Doodle, &c.

> "Who's dat who ride astride de poney,
> So long, so lank, so lean, and bony!
> Oh! be be the great orator, Little-Tonry!
>   Doodle, &c.

In front, Pulteney, drawing his partisans by the noses, and wheeling a barrow laden with the writings of the opposition, the *Champion*, the *Craftsman*, *Common Sense*, &c., exclaims, "Zounds! they are over!"

> "Close by stands Billy, of all Bob's foes
> The wittiest far in verse and prose;
> How he lead de puppies by de nose!"

To the right, Sandys, dropping in astonishment his favourite Place Bill (which had been so often thrown out of the House), cries out "I thought what would come of putting him on the box!"

> "Who's he dat lift up both his handes?
> Oh! that's his wisdom, Squire S——s!
> Oh! de Place Bill drop! oh! de army slandes!"

The prelate, who bows so obsequiously as they pass, is Small-brook, Bishop of Lichfield.

> "What parson's be dat bow so civil?
> Oh! dat's de bishop who split de devil,
> And made a devil and a half, and half a devil!"

Several editions of "The Motion" were published, and one, in the collection of Mr. Burke, is fitted for a fan. Another, very neatly drawn and etched on a folio plate, and dated February 19th, contains great variations, and wants much of the pointed meaning of the genuine print. They here appear to be driving into a river; Pulteney and Sandys are omitted; two prelates hold on by the straps behind the coach, which seems in no imminent danger of falling; yet Carteret cries out to his driver, "John, if you drive so fast, you'll overset us all, by G—d!"

Horace Walpole, who received a copy of "The Motion" at Florence, writes to his friend Conway, "I have received a print by this post that diverts me extremely—'The Motion.' Tell me, dear, now, who made the design, and who took the likenesses; they are admirable; the lines are as good as one sees on such occasions."

K

On the 2nd of March the "Patriots" retaliated with a caricature entitled "The Reason," in which we have another carriage,
with the portly form of Sir Robert Walpole as coachman :—

> "Who be dat de box do sit on ?
> Dat's de driver of G—— B——,
> Whom all de Patriots do spit on."

The verses, as it will be seen by this specimen, are a parody
on those attached to "The Motion," to which it is inferior in
point and spirit. On one side of the foppish and effeminate

LORD FANNY.

Lord Hervey, so well known by
Pope's satirical title of "Lord
Fanny," who had distinguished
himself on the ministerial side
in the debate in the House of
Lords, is represented as riding
on a wooden horse, drawn by
two individuals, one of whom
says, encouragingly, "Sit fast,
Fanny, we are sure to win."
The verses referring to this
figure, are—

> "Dat painted butterfly so prim-a,
> On wooden Pegasus so trim-a,
> Is something—nothing—'tis a whim-a."

Lord Hervey was in the habit of painting his face to conceal
the ghastly paleness of his countenance. Another copy of this
caricature, with some variations, was published so quickly after
the original, that, in the advertisement of the latter in the
London Daily Post of March 3rd (the day after the date engraved on the plate), the public are desired to beware of a
"piratical print" under the same title.

Another rather elaborate caricature was published about the
same time under the title of "The Motive ; or, Reason for his
Honour's Triumph ;" directed, like the last, against the ministry, and with similar verses at the foot. Walpole, in the same
character of coachman, drives the carriage inscribed as the
"Commonwealth," with the King within it, and, with the Duke
of Marlborough as his second, goads on Merchandize, the Sink-
ing-fund, and Husbandry as his horses. A number of different
groups bear allusion to the various methods by which the bribery
and corruption with which Walpole was charged influenced his
supporters.

On March the 6th was advertised a caricature entitled " A Consequence of the Motion." The *Daily Post* announces the publication, on Saturday the 7th of March, of another caricature against the opposition, under the title of "The Political Libertines; or, Motion upon Motion." In this print the coach is again broken down in front of the Exchequer, and most of the characters are reproduced who had figured in the former print of "The Motion," in very similar positions. Lord Lyttelton is as before riding on "poor Rosinante;" Chesterfield is again postilion; Pulteney disapproves of the driver; and Sandys, with the Pension Bill hanging from his pocket, shrugs his shoulders and exclaims, "Z—ns! it's all over!"

> "Grave Sam [*Samuel Sandys*] was set to put the motion,
> For his honour's high promotion,
> But the House disliked the notion."

Bishop Smallbrook also makes his appearance again, accompanied by a hog, which grunts fiends from its mouth; while the churchman says, "I can pray, but not fast!"

> "Next the prelate comes in fashion,
> Who of swine has robb'd the nation,
> Though against all approbation."

There are in the same print many other allusions to the minor subjects of political agitation of the day. An advertisement in the same number of the *Daily Post* (the 7th of March) states that "on Monday next will be published (to supply the defects of 'The Reason' and 'The Motive') 'The Grounds;' a print setting forth the true reasons of the motion, in opposition to a print called 'The Motion.'" In the same paper of the 10th of March, "The Grounds" is advertised for sale. This caricature, which is rather gross, was intended to expose the various ways in which the minister extorted money from the country, and expended it in bolstering up his own power in office. He is represented, under the title of Volpone the Projector, cutting up an infant, intended to represent the Sinking Fund, on a machine which is called the money-press. It is drawn by a pack of his supporters, yoked and harnessed; and, in its way, manufactures, trade, honesty, and liberty are crushed under the wheels. Behind it, the *Gazetteer* and *Freeman's Journal*, with others of the minister's paid organs of the press, are beating for recruits. In the foreground "Bribery and Corruption," personified by a fair and gaily dressed lady, is distributing bishoprics and law appointments to prelates and judges, who likewise have yokes round their necks: one of the former exclaims "Thy yoke is easy, and thy

K 2

burden light;" while a judge says, with equal eagerness, " Your
will to us shall be a law !" Behind the prelates are a crowd of
yoked excisemen, longing for a general excise; and on the other
side the officers of the army standing in a similar predicament.
In the distance are Torbay with the English fleet, and the har-
bours of Brest and Ferrol with the fleet of France: Walpole is
emitting two winds, one of which hinders the English fleet from
leaving its station in Torbay, while the other blows the French
fleet on its way to the West Indies. Contrary winds had
delayed Admiral Ogle's departure from Torbay to reinforce
Vernon at this critical moment, which the opposition unjustly
attributed to Walpole's mismanagement.

"Do Register Bill be take lately in hand,
Dat de forces by sea, as well as by land,
Might be slaves to his will and despotic command.

Fifteen years he withold dem from curbing deir foes,
Who plunder and search dern ; den, to add to deir woes,
In place of redress would de convention impose.

Brave Vernon resolve deir proud enemies' ruin ;
But, instead of sending any forces to him,
Doth de French and Spanish fleets were let loose to undo him."

This famous " motion" was the subject of several other caricatures besides those mentioned above. One, entitled " The
Funeral of Faction," was a satire on the opposition, and had
beneath it the inscription " Funerals performed by Squire
S——s" [Sandys]. Two or three are too gross to bear a description. The exultation of the ministerial party was shown also in
a few ballads, and in pamphlets in prose and verse. The old
comparison of Sisyphus, who toiled everlastingly without approaching any nearer to the object of his labour, was again
applied to the Patriots.

But this comparison was no longer true, for the days of Walpole's reign were already numbered. Age was creeping upon the
veteran statesman ; and that energy, with which for so many
years he had discovered and defeated the intrigues of his enemies,
seemed to be forsaking him. The Court party rated too high
the triumph they had just obtained over the opposition, and lost
themselves by their self-confidence. On the 13th of March the
news of the taking of Porto Bello by Vernon came to raise up the
spirits of his party. The admiral was selected at the same time
for several towns in the general elections in May, which were
carried on with great violence, and in which it was evident that
the so-called "country interest" was gaining ground. The
utmost influence of the Prince of Wales, the heir-apparent, was

exerted on this occasion. A print in compartments, entitled "The Humours of a Country Election," advertised in the newspapers of the 6th of May, 1741, represents the general demeanour of the candidates for popular favour, and is thus described in the "explanation" beneath:—"The candidates welcomed into the town by music and electors on horseback, attended by a mob of men, women, and children. The candidates saluting the women, and amongst them a poor cobbler's wife, very big with child, to whom they very courteously offer to stand godfather. The candidates very complaisant to a country clown, and offering presents to the wife and children. The candidates making an entertainment for the electors and their wives, to whom they show great respect. At the upper end of the table, the parson of the parish sitting, his clerk standing by him. The members elect carried in procession on chairs upon men's shoulders, with music playing before them, and attended by a mob of men, women, and children buzzing them."* It will be seen that a great change had taken place since, under George I., complaints were first heard of the indecency of candidates soliciting the votes of the electors. The election at Westminster in 1741, at which Admiral Vernon was an unsuccessful candidate, being defeated by a large majority, presented a scene of tumultuous riot, and was the subject of a parliamentary investigation, carried on with much warmth, at the opening of the ensuing session. It also was the subject of caricature.

While faction was thus active at home, the affairs of the Continent were becoming every day more confused and complicated. The French diplomatists, since the breaking out of the war between England and Spain, had been actively employed, and with some success, in forming an European confederacy against the former power, when new fuel was thrown into the flames by the death of the Emperor Charles VI., on the 20th of October, 1740. By the Pragmatic Sanction, guaranteed by all the great powers of Europe, the emperor was to be succeeded in all his hereditary states by his daughter Maria Theresa, who was usually spoken of in England by the title of Queen of Hungary. At first, the Elector of Bavaria, who laid claim to a large portion of the Austrian inheritance, alone opposed her succession, on the pretence that the female line could not legally inherit. Next, the King of Prussia revived some old claims to Silesia, and

* It appears, by the advertisements in the newspapers, that this caricature was published separately, and also stitched up with a pamphlet upon the elections. I have not been able to meet with the pamphlet, but a copy of the caricature is in the collection of Mr. Burke.

invaded it with a powerful army. The King of France was anxious to obtain a share in the spoils; and, eventually, England was the only power which fulfilled its engagements towards the unfortunate queen, who, however, defended herself against the formidable confederacy with courage and resolution. In England the cause of Maria Theresa was very popular; and when her claims were brought before the Parliament early in April, 1741, a subsidy of 300,000*l* was readily granted for her; King George went over to Hanover, and assembled an army upon the Prussian frontier; and Russia was also induced to support the injured queen. But, in spite of this assistance, the Prussian army met with an almost uninterrupted success, and Maria Theresa was forced to throw herself entirely upon the devotion of her Hungarian subjects. France, anxious now not only to share in the spoils, but to effect the grand dream of the politics of Louis XIV., the entire destruction of the house of Austria, declared herself more openly, and French armies were poured into Germany. The King of England, suddenly overcome with fear for his Hanoverian dominions, concluded a neutrality for one year, and returned to England without having done anything for his ally. The French and Bavarians thereupon threw themselves into Austria, and penetrating into Bohemia, captured Prague before it could be relieved; and there the Elector of Bavaria caused himself to be crowned King of Bohemia. Immediately after-. wards, a diet assembled hurriedly at Frankfort elected him emperor as Charles VII. He was crowned in the February of 1742, when the cause of the Queen of Hungary seemed almost hopeless.

When the neutrality which George had accepted for Hanover became known in England, it raised the greatest excitement, and promised to give as strong a hold to the opposition as the convention, or even as the excise scheme. Numbers of pamphlets and ballads placed before the public the wrongs and misfortunes of the persecuted queen; and the English king was no more spared on this occasion than his ministers. In one ballad he was attacked under the title of the "Balancing Captain,"* who yearly, under one pretence or another, took to Hanover (which had become a sort of bug-bear in Englishmen's ears) all the money he could raise among his English subjects.

> "I'll tell you a story as strange as 'tis new,
> Which all who're concern'd will allow to be true,

* King George II., on account of his attachment to the army, was commonly designated by the Jacobites as "the Captain."

Of a Balancing Captain, well known hereabouts,
Returned home (God save him!) a mere king of clouts!

This captain he takes in a *gold-ballasted* ship,
Each summer to *terra damnosa* a trip,
For which he begs, borrows, scrapes all he can get,
And runs his poor owners most vilely in debt.

The last time he set out for this blessed place,
He met them, and told them a most piteous case,
Of a sister of his, who, though bred up at court,
Was ready to perish for want of support.

This *Hun-gry sister*, he then did pretend,
Would be to his owners a notable friend,
If they would at that critical juncture supply her.
They did—but, alas! all the fat's in the fire!"

In the sequel of the ballad, which is a remarkable example of
the seditious violence that characterized many of these productions, we are told that the Captain, having fingered the money,
immediately made a peace with his sister's enemies, and left her
to her fate :—

" He then turns his sister adrift, and declares
Her most mortal foes were her father's right heirs.
'G—d s—de!' cries the world, 'such a step was ne'er taken!'
'Oh, ho!' says Noll Bluff, 'I have saved my own bacon

" ' Let France damn the Germans, and undam the Dutch,
And Spain on Old England pish ever so much ;
Let Russia bang Sweden, or Sweden bang that,—
I care not, by *Robert!* one kick of my hat!
         *   *   *   *   *

" ' Or should my chous'd owners begin to look sour,
I'll trust to mate *Bob* to exert his old power,
Regit animos dictis, or *nummis,* with ease,
So, spite of your growling, I'll act as I please!'"

The conduct of the Captain is represented as calculated to
bring ruin on his owners, unless they look more closely into his
proceedings :—

"This secret, however, must out on the day
When he meets his poor owners to ask for his pay ;
And I fear, when they come to adjust the account,
A sero for balance will prove their amount."

The caricatures on the affairs of the Queen of Hungary were
very numerous, both on the Continent and in England ; but the
majority of the foreign ones appear to have been against her,
while the English caricatures were all in her favour. In one,
the background of which shews Prague bombarded, the Queen
is represented as a ragged gipsy (a pun upon the French word

A ROYAL GIPSY.

Bohémienne) kneeling before the King of France, to whom she offers her jewels, with the prayer, "*Sire, ayez pitié d'une pauvre Bohémienne !*" The King, who thinks them worthy of the acceptance of his favourite mistress, replies disdainfully, "*Portez les à Pompadour.*" In another print, entitled "The Slough," of which there appeared several copies with slight variations, the Queen of Hungary is driven in a coach, with the King of France as coachman, Count Bruhl riding as postilion, and the new King of Poland holding on behind as lackey. They are running head foremost into a slough. The King of Prussia, who stands near in the character of a sentinel, asks, "Where are you going, Madame?" The Queen, in evident consternation, replies, "Ask my driver." In a third caricature, entitled "The Negotiators," the various powers who had interfered are represented as conspiring to ruin the Queen for their own aggrandizement. In another, entitled "The Consultation of Physicians; or, the Case of the Queen of Hungary," published

THE CUNNING PHYSICIAN.

in February, 1742, the French minister, Cardinal Fleury, in the character of a cunning physician, after having administered a strong dose of emetic, which is evidently producing its effects, is proceeding to bleed her with his pen. A print, entitled "French Pacification; or, the Queen of Hungary stript," published also in the beginning of February, 1742, seems to have had an especial popularity; and a number of imitations appeared, some under the simple title of "The Queen of Hungary stripped." The Queen is here represented in a state of complete nudity, while the different continental powers are carrying off portions of her garments, bearing the names of the different provinces of her empire. Cardinal Fleury, more pitiless than any, is in the act of depriving her even of the slight covering afforded by her own hand. The treacherous conduct of France is severely pointed at in these caricatures, some of which are not quite delicate. In one print, of a rather later date, while England is courteously attempting to assist the Queen over a stile or gate, France takes the moment of defenceless exposure to proceed to unwarrantable liberties. In another, entitled, "The Parcæ; or, the European Fates," the intriguing cardinal

CARDINAL "LACHESIS."

is represented under the character of Lachesis, spinning the web of European politics, on a wheel which bears the title of "Universal Monarchy;" while King George, as Atropos, is cutting the thread.

It was in the midst of this hurly-burly abroad, that Walpole's power was at length broken. The minister had lost much strength in the elections of 1741, chiefly in Scotland and Cornwall; and in one way or other the opposition had succeeded in making him unpopular. Long before the session of Parliament was opened, the opposition papers spoke with more than ordi-

KING "ATROPOS."

nary confidence of success, and they became proportionally violent in their personal attacks. The mob was encouraged, as they had been at the commencement of the reign of George I., to shew themselves on every favourable occasion. On the 12th of November Horace Walpole writes, " It is Admiral Vernon's birthday, and the city shops are full of favours, the streets of marrow-bones and cleavers, and the night will be full of mobbing, bonfires, and lights;" and he adds in a subsequent letter, " I believe I told you that Vernon's birthday passed quietly, but it was not designed to be pacific; for at twelve at night, eight gentlemen, dressed like sailors, and masked, went round Covent Garden with a drum, beating up for a volunteer mob; but it did not take, and they retired to a great supper that was prepared for them at the Bedford Head, and ordered by Whitehead, the author of 'Manners.'" Walpole seems to have been himself full of apprehension, for his son, who returned from his travels just in time to witness his father's defeat, writes of him on the 19th of October, that he who in former times " was asleep as soon as his head touched the pillow, (for I have frequently known him snore ere they had drawn his curtains), now never sleeps above an hour without waking; and he, who at dinner always forgot he was minister, and was more gay and thoughtless than all the company, now sits without speaking and with his eyes fixed for an hour together. Judge if this is the Sir Robert you knew."

The Parliament was opened on the 4th of December. On the 16th, on the election of a chairman of committees, by the desertion of some of his supporters and the absence of others, Walpole was in a minority of four. A day or two after he had only a majority of seven on an election petition; and on another election petition he was again in a minority. The minister seemed to cling to power more than ever, now that he was on the point of losing it; and, instead of taking the advice of his intimate friends, who urged him to resign, he made an unsuccessful attempt to gain over the Prince of Wales, and then resolved to make another effort to carry on in the House. On the 21st of

January, after the Christmas holidays, Pulteney brought forward a motion with the same object as that of Sandys, which had been so triumphantly defeated not quite a year before. Walpole defended himself with as much vigour and eloquence as ever ; but the motion was rejected only by a majority of *three*. On the 28th of January, again, on an election petition, he was defeated by a majority of one. Walpole now made up his mind to resign, and the next day announced his intention to the King. On a division upon the same petition on the 2nd of February, the opposition majority had increased to sixteen. On the 3rd the Houses were adjourned, at the King's request, for a fortnight ; on the 9th Sir Robert Walpole was created Earl of Orford ; and on the 11th he formally resigned all his places.

The intelligence of Walpole's resignation was received in some towns in the country with ringing of bells and other demonstrations of joy ; and there were mobs and bonfires in London ; but, according to Horace Walpole, this feeling was much less general than might have been anticipated. The more violent of the opposition newspapers, however, teemed with ungenerous insults on the fallen minister : they held out threats of inquiry into his conduct, and talked of hunting him to the scaffold ; and they advised him to follow the example of Bolingbroke, in flying from his country. Walpole was almost the only commoner who had ever been admitted to the order of the Garter, and his blue ribbon was an especial object of envious attack. The *Champion* of February 16, 1742 (a more scurrilous paper even than the *Craftsman*), contains the following epigram, which may be taken as a sample of effusions to which the ex-minister was exposed daily :—

> "Sir —— [*Robert*], his merit or interest to shew,
> Laid down the red ribbon * to take up the blue :
> By two strings already the knight hath been ty'd,
> But when twisted at —— [*Tyburn*], the third will decide."

The more violent of the opposition went so far as to get petitions sent to the House, urging an impeachment ; and, in a moment of triumph and excitement, it is difficult to foresee what might have been the result of such a measure, had not the King stood firm to his old friend, and made it to a certain degree a condition of the accession of his enemies to power, that they should screen him from persecution. The *Craftsman* and the *Champion* continued to assail their old enemy with scurrilous

* Sir Robert was created knight of the newly-revived order of the Bath, before he received that of the Garter.

insults: the latter paper, on the 23rd of February, in double allusion to his former influence among the monied and mercantile interests, and his later unpopularity in the city of London, published the following paragraph :—"In regard to the good understanding which has so long subsisted between his *late honor* and the *city*, it is hoped that that great man, in *compliment* to his *old friends*, will pass through the principal streets thereof at noon, in an *open landau*, on his way to his PALACE of H——n." And the same violent journal, on the 17th of August, drags the veteran statesman from his retirement at Houghton :—"From the neighbourhood of H——n *palace*. We are informed that the *annual* NORFOLK CONGRESS is held there as usual (though the *Gazetteer* has not been authorized to set forth a list of the Powers of which it is composed) ; and that, if the *puffs* still continued in *pay* are to be depended upon, ways and means are *already* concerted to terminate the next winter's campaign as *successfully* as the last."

When Walpole was created Earl of Orford, his daughter by his second wife, but born before their marriage, was given precedency as an Earl's daughter by a separate patent, a measure which raised a great storm among the aristocracy of the opposition, and which excited odium even among the mob. An insulting poem, stated to be written by a lady of "real quality," was printed in folio, and distributed abroad, under the title of "Modern Quality ; an Epistle to Miss M—— W——" [Maria Walpole]. This clamour, joined with the disappointment of the Tories and the young "Patriots," who were not allowed to share in the spoils, obliged the Court to agree, at the beginning of April, to the appointment of a secret committee to examine into the conduct of Walpole during the last ten years of his administration ; but the inquiry led to no results of any importance. The populace, however, seem to have been indulged with the hope of a new state tragedy. On the 8th of April, Horace Walpole writes: "All this week the mob has been carrying about his effigies in procession and to the Tower. The chiefs of the opposition have been so mean as to give these mobs money for bonfires, particularly the Earls of Lichfield, Westmoreland, Denbigh, and Stanhope. The servants of these last got one of these figures, chalked out a place for the heart, and shot at it. You will laugh at me, who, the other day, meeting one of these mobs, drove up to it to see what was the matter. The first thing I beheld was a mawking in a chair, with three footmen, and a label on the breast, inscribed ' Lady Mary.' "

The disappointment of Walpole's persecutors, when they saw

that there was no real intention of bringing him to what they called justice, showed itself in newspaper paragraphs and ill-natured caricatures. The old device of the screen was brought up again, and was the subject of more than one print. In one of these, entitled "The Night-Visit; or, the Relapse; with the pranks of Bob Fox the Juggler, while steward to Lady Brit, displayed on a screen," the ex-minister is represented in council with the King at night. George, seated at a table, demands of his old servant, "What is to be done?" Walpole replies, "Mix and divide them." Several other courtiers are introduced, con-

sulting on the change of af-fairs, one of whom, who overhears the conversation just alluded to, remarks, "'Tis good advice!" Through the window are seen a party of men, who are not courtiers, gazing on the heathens with a telescope. One observes, "It must be a comet!" The other replies, "No, by Jove! 'tis Robin Goodfellow from R—chm—d!" [Richmond]. A third exclaims, "I wish the telescope was a gun!" The screen, forming the back-ground of the picture, repre-

GOOD ADVICE.

sents all the evil deeds with which Walpole was charged, and which are described at length in the "Explanation" printed at the foot. The last compartment represents a distant view of the gallows, with an axe, and a head elevated on a pole, the doom of traitors. The devil, for (to judge by the caricatures) all parties seem to have been convinced that Satan was busy among them, peeps from behind the screen, and cries out exult-ingly, "Hah! I shall have business here again!" This caricature is dated the 12th of April, 1742.

On the 16th of November following, when the cry against Walpole was still kept up, a caricature was published, entitled "Bob, the Political Balance-Master." The fallen minister is here decked in his coronet and seated at one end of a balance held up by Britannia, who sits mourning over sleeping trade. At the other end of the balance sits Justice, who is unable to weigh down effectually the bulky peer, assisted as he is by his bags of treasure; but, in spite of this help, his position

THE BALANCE-MASTER IS DANGER.

is critical, and in his terror he cries out to the Evil One, who appears above, "Oh! help thy faithful servant Dob! Satan gives him a look anything but encouraging, and, holding out an axe, replies to his invocation, "This is thy doe!"

It was thus that party-spirit forgot, as it had so often done, the feelings of generosity and justice, and sought vengeance which could have no other object than that of gratifying personal hatred. Within no great length of time from these transactions, we shall find individuals, less powerfully defended, made sacrifices to the same unworthy spirit.

CHAPTER V.

GEORGE II.

IN one of his speeches during the struggles in the House of Commons which preceded his fall, Walpole, analysing the strength of the opposition, had divided it into three classes, the Jacobites and Tories, the discontented Whigs, and the "Boys." The chiefs of the Tories in the House of Commons were Sir William Wyndham (now dead), "honest" Will. Shippen, and Sir John Hynde Cotton. The discontented Whigs were led in the Commons by Pulteney and Sandys, and in the Lords by Carteret and Argyle. Among the Boy Patriots—the young men who were marching fast towards power—were William Pitt, George Grenville, Sir George Lyttelton, and Henry Fox. In the moment of victory these discordant materials fell to pieces, and those who had individually done most towards driving Walpole's ministry out, the leaders of the old "Patriots," seemed now to think of nothing but providing for themselves. Pulteney, Carteret, and Sandys first secured places for themselves, before they looked any farther; and then, intimidated by the threatening looks of their old colleagues, they found minor offices for a few of the others. The Duke of Newcastle, (Walpole's jealous and treacherous colleague), his brother Mr. Pelham and Sir William Yonge were allowed to retain their places. Lord Wilmington was the nominal head of the new ministry; Lord Carteret was appointed secretary of state, and, by flattering the King's propensities, soon engrossed the royal favour. Pulteney took no place himself, but before the end of the session he followed Walpole into the other House, by the title of Earl of Bath; Sandys was made chancellor of the exchequer, and the Earl of Winchelsea was made first lord of the admiralty. The King, who had made a cold reconciliation with the Prince of Wales, acceded to these arrangements with an unwilling consent, and acted by the advice of Walpole, whom he consulted in secret. The position of the Monarch amid these changes is well described in a ballad, which made a great noise, published in the following October, and understood to have been written by Lord Hervey, one of the old ministers who had lost his place :—

> "O England, attend, while thy fate I deplore,
> Rehearsing the schemes and the conduct of power ;
> And since only of those who have power I sing,
> I am sure none can think that I hint at the King.

> "From the time his son made him old Robin depose,
> All the power of a King he was well known to lose ;
> But, of all but the name and the badges bereft,
> Like old women, his paraphernalia are left.

> "To tell how he shook in St. James's for fear,
> When first these new ministers bullied him there,
> Makes my blood boil with rage, to think what a thing
> They have made of a man we obey as a King."

In the midst of the royal embarrassments Carteret comes to the Monarch's relief :—

> "At last Carteret arriving, spoke thus to his grief :
> 'If you'll make me your doctor, I'll bring you relief.
> You see to your closet familiar I come,
> And seem like my wife in the circle—at home.'

> "Quoth the King, 'My good lord, perhaps you're been told
> That I used to abuse you a little of old ;
> But now bring whom you will, and eke turn away,
> Let but me and my money and Walmoden stay.'*

> " 'For you and Walmoden I freely consent,
> But as to your money, I must have it spent ;
> I have promised your son (nay, no frowns) should have some,
> Nor think 'tis for nothing we Patriots come.' "

Carteret then goes on to declare the changes he must have in the ministry,—who are to be turned out, and who to be kept in. Among the latter, the only one of any consequence was the Duke of Newcastle :—

> " 'Though Newcastle's as false as he's silly, I know,
> By betraying old Robin to me long ago,
> As well as all those who employ'd him before,
> Yet I leave him in place, but I leave him no power.

> "For granting his heart is as black as his hat,
> With no more truth in this than there's sense beneath that ;

---

* The King's mistress, who had been created an English peeress under the title of Countess of Yarmouth. George II. is in serious history, as well as in popular satire, represented as of a very avaricious disposition.

Yet, as he's a coward, he'll shake when I frown—
You call'd him a rascal, I'll use him like one.

" 'And since his estate at elections he'll spend,
And beggar himself without making a friend ;
So whilst the extravagant fool has a sous,
As his brains I can't fear, so his fortune I'll use.' "

Among the new men to be brought in, the most important is
Pulteney—

" All that weathercock Pulteney shall ask we must grant,
For to make him a great noble nothing I want ;
And to cheat such a man demands all my arts,
For though he's a fool, he's a fool with great parts.

"And, as popular Clodius, the Pulteney of Rome,
From a noble, for power, did plebeian become,
So this Clodius to be a patrician shall choose,
Till what one got by changing, the other shall lose."

The King is appeased by the flattery of his soldier-loving
propensities :—

" ' For, your foreign affairs, howe'er they turn out,
At least I'll take care you shall make a great rout :
Then cock your great hat, strut, bounce, and look bluff,
For, though kick'd and cuff'd here, you shall there kick and cuff.

" ' That Walpole did nothing they all need to say,
So I'll do enough, but I'll make the dogs pay ;
Great fleets I'll provide, and great armies engage,
Whate'er debts we make, or whate'er wars we wage.'

" With cordials like these, the Monarch's new guest
Reviv'd his sunk spirits and gladden'd his breast ;
Till in rapture he cried, ' My dear Lord, you shall do
Whatever you will,—give me troops to review.' "

The new ministers were bitterly satirised in a caricature, entitled " The Promotion," and in a clever ballad by Sir Charles
Hanbury Williams, the great political balladist of the day, entitled, " A New Ode to a great Number of great Men, newly
made." The satire was most pointedly levelled at the new Lord
Bath, who, in a few months, was exposed to more ridicule than
his whole party had been able to heap upon Walpole during
twenty years. He was everywhere looked upon as having betrayed his party for the bribe of a coronet. Some said that he
had been lured into the snare by Walpole ; others believed that
he had been pushed into it by Carteret, who was jealous of his
popularity ; while many supposed that he had been urged into
it merely by the vanity and avarice of his wife, to whom they
gave the satirical title of " The Wife of Bath," and a ballad made

L

upon her under that title is said to have given the Earl great annoyance.

It was the universal belief that Pulteney and his Patriot friends had purchased their elevation by an agreement to shield their predecessors, and to follow in their steps. A singular accident happened in July, which was quickly seized upon as a subject for a joke against the new ministers. "Last Sunday," Horace Walpole tells us in a letter of this period, "the Duke of Newcastle gave the new ministers a dinner at Claremont, where their servants got so drunk, that when they came to the inn over against the gate of New Park [now Richmond Park, of which Lord Walpole was ranger], the coachman, who was the only remaining fragment of their suite, tumbled off the box, and there they were planted. There were Lord Bath, Lord Carteret, Lord Limerick, and Harry Furnese in the coach. They asked the innkeeper if he could contrive no way to convey them to town; 'No,' he said, 'not he; unless it was to get Lord Orford's coachman to drive them.' They demurred; but Lord Carteret said, 'Oh, I dare say Lord Orford will willingly let us have him.' So they sent, and he drove them home." Horace says in the sequel of the letter, "Lord Orford has been at court again to-day: Lord Carteret came up to thank him for his coachman, the Duke of Newcastle standing by. My father said, 'My Lord, whenever the Duke is near overturning you, you have nothing to do but to send to me, and I will save you.'" The following ballad, attributed to Sir C. Hanbury Williams, was published on the occasion. Lord Bath, as the ex-writer in the *Craftsman,* retains his name of Caleb: the old coach and its driver, in the caricature of "The Motion," is not forgotten :—

"THE OLD COACHMAN."

"When Caleb and Carteret, two birds of a feather,
Went down to a feast at Newcastle's together :
No matter what wines or what choice of good cheer,
'Tis enough that the coachman had his dose of beer.
        Derry down, down, hey derry down.

"Coming home, as the liquor work'd up in his pate,
The coachman drove on at a damnable rate.
Poor Carteret in terror, and scared all the while,
Cried, 'Stop ! let me out ! is the dog an Argyle ?'
        Derry down, &c.

"But he soon was convinced of his error; for, lo !
John stopt short in the dirt, and no further would go,
When Carteret saw this, he observed with a laugh,
'This coachman, I find, is your own, my Lord Bath.'
        Derry down, &c.

"Now the poets quit their coach in a pitiful plight,
Deep in mire, and in rain, and without any light;
Not a path to pursue, nor to guide them a friend—
What course shall they take then, and how will this end!
    Derry down, &c.

"Lo! Chance, the great mistress of human affairs,
Who governs in councils, and conquers in wars;
Straight with grief at their case (for the goddess well knew
That these were her creatures and votaries too),—
    Derry down, &c.

"This Chance brought a passenger quick to their aid,
'Honest friend, can you drive?'—'What should ail me!' he said.
'For many a bad season, through many a bad way,
Old Orford I've driven without stop or stay.
    Derry down, &c.

"'He was once overturn'd, I confess, but not hurt.'
Quoth the peers, 'It was we help'd him out of the dirt:
This boon to thy master, then, prithee requite,—
Take us up, or here we must wander all night.'
    Derry down, &c.

"He took them both up, and through thick and through thin,
Drove away for St. James's, and brought them safe in.—
Learn hence, honest Britons, in spite of your pains,
That Orford, old coachman, still governs the reins.
    Derry down, &c."

The Duke of Argyle had at first insisted upon forming a ministry upon what he termed a "broad bottom," in which all classes of the old opposition were to have a place; but this plan was overthrown by the King's determined hatred of the Tories, who therefore continued in the opposition. The young Patriots, after several vain attempts to obtain places in the new ministry, joined them, and were even more violent against Lord Bath, who had fast sunk into what Lord Hervey termed a "noble nothing," than the Tories themselves. This party of the opposition, from their leaders being chiefly nephews and cousins of Lord Cobham, was sometimes designated as the "Nepotism." In the session of 1743 they renewed their attacks upon the old ministers, chiefly in the hope of embarrassing the new ones; but the latter not only had with them the main body of their party, but they were supported by the adherents of Walpole, and they carried their measures by large majorities, and often without divisions. During 1743 and 1744 there was less political agitation than the country had seen for many years; the old worn-out question of the Hanoverian troops and an act for the repeal of the Gin Act alone made any noise. Lord Bath bore the attacks of the press with far less equanimity than had been shown

by Walpole, and complained bitterly of "scurrilous libels." To
him was commonly attributed a pamphlet, published early in
1743, under the title of "Faction detected," in which the opposition and its organs were severely attacked, and which made
much noise for a short time, being roughly handled in some of
the opposition papers.

At the close of the session the King went to Hanover, with
his son the Duke of Cumberland and his now favourite minister
Lord Carteret, and joined the army of English and Hanoverians
under the Earl of Stair, which he had already ordered to cross
the Rhine to assist the Queen of Hungary. The affairs of this
Queen had, during the previous year, suddenly recovered from
their desperate posture, and the French and Bavarians were now
in their turn labouring under the reverses of war. England was
nominally at peace with France, and her soldiers were only
fighting under the banners of Austria. The Hanoverian army,
which King George, the Duke of Cumberland, and Lord Carteret
had just joined, was on its way to Hanau, when it was attacked
at Dettingen by the French under the Duke de Noailles, who
were signally defeated. A battle on land gained by English
troops was a new thing in England, for there had been no war
of any importance since the days of Marlborough, and the whole
country resounded with exultation. Dettingen was in a moment the theme of every ambitious or popular scribbler, and
pamphlets in prose and verse, ballads and songs, and epigrams,
were showered upon the public. But amid this apparently universal joy were sown the seeds of political disagreement. The
English troops were without provisions, and in an ill condition
to fight; and, though they did fight bravely, their loss had
been severe. They complained that they had not been properly
supported; for the horse, which was chiefly Hanoverian, had not
behaved so well in the battle as the foot. The commander-in-
chief, Lord Stair, had strongly urged that the enemy should be
pursued; but his opinion was overruled by that of the foreign
generals. A second remonstrance, after the troops had been refreshed, was equally unsuccessful; and the Earl, with several
other officers, threw up their commissions in disgust, and returned to England, where a great outcry was immediately raised.
On the 22nd of October was published a caricature, under the
title of "The Hanoverian Confectioner-General," in which the
French are represented as flying from the field hotly pursued by
the British. The former cry out "S'ils nous poursuivent, nous
sommes perdu!" The Earl of Stair, urging on the pursuit,
shouts, "Pursue 'em, lads! and mow 'em awe!" The King, as

the Hanoverian horse, riding on the starved British lion (a hard hit, as the discontented party had always said that England was starved to fatten Hanover,) cries out to the Hanoverian cavalry, " La victoire est gagnée, où vous êtes vous fourrés ?" Their commander replies, " N'importe, j'ai conservé nos gens ;" while his soldiers exclaim, " We will not be commanded by the English. An Austrian commander, who is equally urging the pursuit, calls them "cowardly mercenaries." A label from the lion's mouth bears the words " Starv'd on Boupournicole."

THE BRITISH LION OUT OF ORDER.

The opposition, and many who were not actually in opposition, rejoiced in these divisions ; they talked ironically of making Carteret commander-in-chief (he is said to have remained in his carriage in the neighbourhood of the battle all the day, without *showing any fear*, and he wrote a vaunting despatch) ; and jokes passed about on the trio of successive *Johns*—John Duke of Argyle, who had refused the place because he was not allowed to bring any Tories into the ministry, John Earl of Stair, and John Lord Carteret. The following lines "on the Johns" appeared in some of the papers :—

"John Duke of Argyle
We admired for a while,
Whose titles fall short of his merit.
His loss to repair,
We took John Earl of Stair,
Who like him had both virtue and merit.

"Now he too is gone ;
Ah ! what's to be done ?
Such losses how can we supply ?
But let's not repine ;
On the banks of the Rhine
There's a third John his fortune will try.

"By the Patriots' vagary
He was m de S—— ; [*secretary*]
By himself he's P—— M—— [*prime minister*] made ;

And now, to crown all,
He's made G——l, [*general*]
Though he ne'er was brought up to the trade.

At the same time the death of Lord Wilmington, who had
presided at the Treasury board, gave rise to new changes in the
ministry, in which Lord Orford's secret influence soon overthrew
the schemes of Carteret and Lord Bath. Pelham, who had held
the office of Paymaster of the forces, became first Lord of the
Treasury, and was allowed to bring into inferior places his
friends Henry Fox and Lord Middlesex. Lord Gower resigned
the Privy Seal, which was given to Lord Cholmondeley. Pelham
also obtained the office of Chancellor of the Exchequer, which
was taken from Sandys, who was appeased with a place in the
household and a peerage. The following verses on " the Triumvirate" in the *London Magazine* for January, 1744, (the magazine which had been set up in opposition to the *Gentleman's
Magazine*, and which had been from the first the monthly advocate of the country party,) show the public estimation in which
Carteret, Sandys, and Pulteney (Lord Bath) stood at that
time:—

"John, Sam, and Will combined of late
To form a new triumvirate ;
To share authority and money,
Like Cæsar, Lepidus, and Toney.
But mark what followed from this union :—
John left his countrymen's communion,
And, though in office he appear'd,
Was neither honour'd, lov'd, or fear'd.
Sam in the sunshine buzz'd a little ;
Then sunk in power, and rose in title.
Will with a title out would act,
But place or power ne'er could get.
So Will and Sam obscure remain'd,
And John with general odium reign'd."

Towards autumn it became publicly known that serious dissensions existed in the Cabinet between Carteret, who had now
by his mother's death become Earl Granville, and the Pelhams ;
and, in the sequel, the Duke of Newcastle and his brother compelled the King to dismiss Granville, who had lost his political
influence, on the 23rd of November. Lord Winchelsea, General
Cavendish, and the other Lords of the Admiralty, with some
other inferior placemen, also resigned. The Pelhams now
effected their long-projected plan of a " broad-bottomed" cabinet.
Lord Harrington succeeded to the place of Lord Granville ; the
Jacobite Sir John Hynde Cotton was made Treasurer of the
Chamber in the royal household ; the Tory Lord Gower was

made Privy Seal; Lyttelton obtained a seat at the Treasury
board; Bub Dodington was appointed Treasurer of the Navy;
Pitt joined in supporting the Government, on the promise of
being made Secretary at War as soon as the King's personal antipathy could be overcome; and Lord Chesterfield, who was also
personally disliked by the King, was made Lord Lieutenant of
Ireland; the Duke of Bedford was made first Lord of the Admiralty, with the Earl of Sandwich as second Commissioner; and
Mr. Grenville was made one of the junior Lords of the same
board. The arrangement of the Admiralty seems to have
given most difficulty from the number of applicants; and it
formed the subject of a caricature, entitled " Next Sculls at the
Admiralty," published on the 27th of December, 1744, which
contains a number of figures, all evidently intended for portraits.

In the back is a view of the
Admiralty, with Winchelsea,
Cavendish, and their col-
leagues " going out." Winchelsea, with his characteristic spectacles, advances
forwards, gravely observing,
" We shall see," (apparently
intended as a pun upon his
name;) while Cavendish,
with his hand raised to his
mouth in the attitude of
bidding adieu, and exclaiming " I must eat," turns off
to one side. One of the
groups in front, of those who
are " coming in," or wanting
to come in, represents to the
left the Duke of Bedford in

GOING OUT.

a stooping posture, exclaiming " Bed for 't." In the middle the
tall upright figure of Anson, who had in the course of the year
arrived from his circumnavigation of the world, says, " Round
the world and not in."[*] Before him, an older man resting on a
staff, but not so easily identified, cries out " Next scull!" In
this " broad-bottomed " coalition every party, except the small
number of adherents of Carteret and Lord Bath, had a representative; and the consequence was, that, during the ensuing ses-

---

[*] Anson had a rough unpolished manner, and it was said jokingly of him,
that he had been all round the world, but not in it. He had amassed great
wealth by his voyage.

sion, there was scarcely a division. Lord Orford, who had been called to town by the King to give him his advice in his minis-

COMING IN.

terial embarrassments, returned to Houghton, and died there on the 18th of March, 1745.

This "broad-bottomed" ministry had, however, very little substantial unanimity in itself; the chief tie by which its members were linked together seems to have been the mere love of place, to which they had sacrificed the principles that many of them had been supporting boisterously for so many years; and, f there was not much opposition in the House, there was abundance of dissatisfaction without. During the formation of this ministry, Horace Walpole represents the aspirants to place as standing like servants at a country fair to be hired; and he adds, "One has heard of the corruption of courtiers; but, believe me, the impudent prostitution of patriots, going to market with their honesty, beats it to nothing. Do but think of two hundred men, *of the most consummate virtue*, setting themselves to sale for three weeks!" Within a few days after the publication of the caricature mentioned above, on the 15th of January, appeared a "New Ballad," entitled the "Place-book; or, the Year 1745," which was soon followed by a bitter lampoon on the people in power, under the title of "The Triumvirate; or, broad-bottomry." Several other caricatures, among which we may particularize one, entitled "The Claims of the Broad-bottoms," exhibit the venality complained of by Horace Walpole. The ministry soon became distracted by internal jealousies and dissensions; and these, with the disappointments of the old Tories, again raised the spirit of Jacobitism, which had been so long kept under by the policy of Sir Robert Walpole. The partizans of the exiled family abroad were further encouraged by the battle of Fontenoy, which, though not inglorious to the British arms, was a defeat, and was exaggerated beyond measure in France, Spain, and Italy.

In the summer of 1745 the minstrel of the north began again to chant aloud his hatred to King George and the Whigs, and his wishes for the return of the Stuarts. The arrival of Prince Charles Edward, the young Pretender, on the coast of the highlands of Scotland, in the latter days of July, was the signal for the rising of the clans, and he soon found himself at the head of an army, the more formidable, because the authorities in Scotland were taken by surprise, and not only that country but England itself were in no posture of defence. Having passed the small English army under Sir John Cope, the Pretender entered Perth in triumph on the 4th of September; and in the middle of the same month, still leaving Cope behind him, he obtained possession of Edinburgh. On the 21st Cope was defeated in the brief but celebrated battle, known as that of Preston Pans, from whence, with a small portion of his army, he fled to Berwick, and Scotland was left almost in the power of the rebels. After remaining some time in Edinburgh, the castle of which was still in the hands of the English garrison, the Pretender began his March on the 1st of November, with an army considerably reinforced by new supplies of Highlanders, towards the English borders, and, crossing the Tweed at Kelso, moved directly into Cumberland; and the Scots made themselves masters of Carlisle on the 15th, and, proceeding into Lancashire, they reached Preston on the 27th and Wigan on the 28th, and the same day an advanced party entered Manchester. By this time, however, the royal troops were in motion, numerous volunteers were armed in most of the southern and eastern counties, and Dutch and English troops, under the Duke of Cumberland, had been hastily brought over from the Continent; so that by the time the rebels had reached Derby, they became aware of the perils with which they were surrounded, and began a rapid retreat, closely pursued, towards Scotland. Prince Charles re-crossed the border on the 20th of December, and his army was collected together at Glasgow by the end of the year. On the 17th of January the English troops in Scotland met with as signal a defeat on Falkirk Moor as they had previously experienced at Preston Pans; but better troops and more experienced commanders were rapidly approaching the scene of action, and the hopes of the Jacobites in Scotland were destined to have a speedy and fatal conclusion.

In England the contradictory and vague information daily spread abroad caused the greatest consternation, ill concealed even to us by the contemptuous manner in which the press generally treated the rebellion. The citizens of London showed their fears rather than their courage by their anxious precautions; and their alarm was so great on the day when intelligence was brought of the advance of the rebels to Derby, and of their consequent position between the Duke of Cumberland's army and the metropolis, as to cause it to be long remembered as the "Black Friday." A rush was made upon the Bank, the fatal effects of which it is said to have escaped only by the expedient of refusing to pay in any other coin than sixpences, which enabled the directors to gain time until the panic was over. The songs of exultation and scorn which resounded in Scotland were, however, replied to by satirical caricatures and loyal songs, of which there was no want in the south. In one of the former the British lion is represented as the true support of King George and the Protestant succession against the designs of the French King. The Pretender addresses the King of France, the Pope, and the devil, who were looked upon popularly as the grand encouragers of this enterprize, "We shall never be a match for George, while that lion stands by him."

The popularity of the Pretender was not assisted in England by the belief that he was bringing with him the religious principles of Rome and the political principles of France. The feeling on this subject is strongly exhibited in a caricature, entitled "The Invasion; or, Perkin's triumph," in which the Pretender is represented triumphantly driving in the royal stage-coach, drawn by six horses, which are named Superstition, Passive Obedience, Rebellion, Hereditary

THE PROTESTANT CHAMPION. Right, Arbitrary Power, and Non-Resistance, and riding over Liberty and all the public funds. The Pope acts as postilion, and the King of France as coachman; two monkeys and the devil perform the office of footmen, and various disastrous consequences of the success of the rebellion are represented in different parts of the picture. A group of Scottish soldiers follow a standard, on which are figured a pair of wooden shoes and the motto "Slavery." St. James's palace occupies the background, with Westminster Abbey on one side, and on the other Smithfield and a martyr at the stake. This print was from the pencil and graver of C. Mosley.

Another print is entitled "Britons' Association against the Pope's Bulls," and was published on the 21st of October, 1745.

The river Tweed divides the picture in two. On one side the Pretender is trying to force over the river an importation of bulls, from the mouths and nostrils of which issue lightning mixed with decretals, "massacres," "rods and whips," "everlasting curses," the "fire of purgatory," &c. The Pretender, with the exclamation "Now or never!" holds by the horns, and drags towards the river, a bull laden with indulgences, penances, confessions, absolutions, holy water, and a whole cargo of such Popish furniture. In the distance, Edinburgh Castle appears, well manned with loyal troops, and beneath it a

AN IMPORTATION.

group of Highlanders following their standard with some reluctance, their different opinions showing the want of unanimity in the directors of the rebellion. One says "I'll go home!" while his companion cries "To Newcastle!" and the recommendation of a third to "Cross the Tweed" is backed by the words "Good plunder!" uttered by another. The devil, booted and spurred, and mounted on a broomstick, approaches this group, and accuses them of treason, adding, "I'll tell France, Spain, and the Pope." The other side of the picture represents a troop of volunteers, issuing from a city gate, (perhaps intended to represent London,) and preparing to hinder the Pretender from invading their land. They are led by a man armed with a spear and equipped as a commander, who proclaims, somewhat ostentatiously, "I am your independent officer!" One, who does not seem very eager in advancing, cries, "King and country! Shop and family!" A drummer says, "I wont go out of the parish!" His next companion, with more valour, exclaims, "O God, I'd go five miles to fight!" while another moves on rather doggedly, with an exclamation of regret, "I wish they'd go to dinner!" This portion of the

AN INDEPENDENT OFFICER.

print appears intended to convey no very flattering picture of the courage and zeal which are supposed to have characterized the volunteer defenders of their country in this pressing emergency. In the distance we have a view of the ocean covered with British shipping, and Britannia seated on an islet and encouraged by Neptune. This print, which is tolerably well executed, and is a fair example of the style of caricatures of this period, is accompanied by the following verses, more remarkable for reason than rhyme :—

"I Perkin, young and bold,
    My father me has sent here ;
He is himself too old,
    And tim'rous, too, to venture.

"His spirit and '15
    To break did much contribute,
When many friends were seen
    To grace the fatal gibbet.

"He open'd then his coffers,
    And shew'd 'em what rewards
To those he freely offers,
    Who seize the king and guards.

"Pack up your awls, and post,
    And homewards wisely run ;
Or in a month at most,
    By George, you'll be undone!"

BRITANNIA DANCING TO A NEW TUNE.

Another caricature published at this period was entitled "The
Plagues of England; or, the Jacobites' Folly," and was aimed
especially at the conduct of our French allies on this occasion.
The Pope, the devil, and the Pretender are here raised up as
idols, and worshipped by Jacobite devotees. The King of France
acts as fiddler, while Britannia is seen
dancing to a French tune, led by Folly,
who is carrying Poverty on his back.
Behind them, Industry lies "neglected"
and almost famished. A satirical medal, in the collection of Mr. W. D.
Haggard, represents on the reverse the
same personages as those which the
caricatures figure as the prime movers
of the rebellion (the Pope, the devil,
and their associates), here overcome by
the force of truth. The obverse exhibits a bust of the King
in armour, with the inscription "GEORGIUS II. D. G. REX."

REBELLION DEFEATED.

A caricature, which had been published in the March of this
year, when the Jacobite rising was already foreseen, but it was
at least wished to be believed that the grand conciliation of
"broad-bottomry" would be a sufficient defence against it, represented the King on his throne, attended by his two sons, the
Prince of Wales, and the Duke of Cumberland. On each side,
the Lords and Commons are offering their swords and fortunes
for the defence of the crown. In the foreground, a party of
Jacobite conspirators are unmasking themselves and taking to
flight. One cries, "All's lost!" another, "Detected!" a third,
"D—n their unanimity!" and so on. On the walls of the
apartment are two pictures, one representing English bull-dogs
fighting among themselves; while, in the other, they are united
in attacking a bull, distinguished as "the Pope's bull;" the inscription which runs under the two paintings is, "English bull-
dogs, united against the enemy." This print, entitled "Court
and Country united against the Popish Invasion," is dated the
6th of March, 1744 (i.e. 1744-5).

This unanimity, however specious in appearance, was but an
imaginary one, and we shall soon find the pretended patriotism
of ministers and placemen giving way to their personal interests
and jealousies in the very midst of the dangers which threatened
their country. The question of national rights and liberties,
which wise men saw involved, was looked upon as a secondary
matter by those whose only banner was political or religious
party, or the still more unworthy one of place and emolument,

In a print which appeared in the autumn of 1745, under the title of "A Hint to the Wise; or, the surest way with the Pretender," the church militant is represented on one side offering but a weak resistance to the Pretender, while the standard of broad-bottom, set up by the courtiers against the Jacobites, promises no great strength of resistance, but the mass of the people crowd together to fight successfully under the banner of liberty. The Church was represented by Herring, Archbishop of York, who, after the defeat of Sir John Cope at Preston Pans, had exhibited extraordinary activity in raising and reviewing in person the volunteers of his diocese, though his troops did no great service in the sequel. The warlike prelate is represented in a caricature, entitled "The Mitred Soldier; or, the Church militant." The raising of volunteers was carried on with the more activity, as it was made a profitable job even by many of the nobility, who obtained the pay of officers in the army. In one county the fox-hunters were formed in a corps and armed. One of the Scottish Jacobite (or at least semi-Jacobite) songs of the day gives the following amusing description of the forces collected together from all quarters to suppress the rebellion:—

> "Horse, foot, and dragoons, from lost Flanders they call,
> With Hessians and Danes, and the devil and all;
> And hunters and rangers led by Oglethorpe;
> And the Church, at the bum of the Bishop of York.
> And, pray, who so fit to lead forth this parade,
> As the babe of Tangier, my old grandmother Wade !
> Whose cunning's so quick, but whose motion's so slow,
> That the rebels march'd on, while he stuck in the snow !"

Cope himself, the object of so much satire in the Scottish Jacobite songs, was not spared in the English caricatures, one of which, entitled "A race from Preston Pans to Berwick," is accompanied by a parody on the well-known old ballad against Sir John Suckling. Among the many whose behaviour at this time exposed them to satire, the Duke of Newcastle, whose conduct as minister had made him a general object of derision, was not spared; he was well known to be attached to the pleasures of the table, and was one of the few who then kept French cooks, and on his own cook, named Cloe, who was both a Frenchman and a Catholic, he set especial store: it was pretended that this hero of the kitchen would be included in the proclamation ordering Papists and others to be removed from the metropolis, and the chagrin of the Duke was portrayed in a caricature, entitled "The Duke of Newcastle and his (French) Cook," in

which the Duke is made to exclaim "O Clou! if you leave me,
I shall be starved !"

This rebellion, while it caused in England more fear than
hurt, had been a very advantageous diversion for our enemies
abroad, and our foreign relations were suffering considerably.
Even the Dutch had entered into a neutrality, and gave no
further assistance than they were absolutely obliged to do by
the strict words of existing treaties. A caricature, published on

THE BENEFIT OF NEUTRALITY.

the 26th of December, 1745, under the title of "The Benefit of
Neutrality," was especially directed against our allies of Holland.
France, Spain, and England were represented as struggling to
obtain more shadowy advantages, while Holland in the meantime
was enriching herself with the substance :—

"Ambitious France and haughty Spain
    Unite, the horns of power to gain ;
Against them England drags the tail,
    While the sly Dutchman fills his pail."

In the beginning of the year 1746 the war in Scotland continued to be carried on in the same careless and unskilful manner, which, in the previous year, had chiefly contributed to the
temporary success of the insurrection, until, towards the end of
January, the Duke of Cumberland was sent to the north to take
the command of the English forces. The Prince had scarcely
arrived in Scotland, when he received intelligence that the discontent of persons and party in the South had broken out in a
ministerial revolution. Lord Granville still enjoyed in private
the King's favour and confidence, and was suspected of secretly
thwarting many of the ministerial measures. It was said to

have been by his advice that the King neglected the Scottish
rebellion so long, and thus allowed it to gain head. The ministers, on the other hand, eager to get rid of Granville's influence,
made an attempt to turn out those of that party who still remained in office, and bring in more of their own supporters.
The King refused to accede to their wishes on this point, and,
perceiving from other symptoms that Lord Granville's party
was intriguing against them, on the 10th of February the
Pelham administration resigned. Lord Granville madly undertook to form a new administration, and Lord Bath accepted the
Treasury and Exchequer, Lord Carlisle the Privy Seal, and Lord
Winchelsea returned to the Admiralty. But this strange administration went no further, for its chief, finding himself without influence in the Houses, and seeing that it was impossible to
carry on, made a sudden retreat, after having remained in power
only three days. The old administration were restored immediately to their places, and the King, feeling his own weakness,
gave up his friend Granville to their resentment, and allowed
them to bring in those whom, a few days before, he had posi-
tively refused to admit to his councils. Among these was
William Pitt, who was making rapid strides towards that eminence and popularity which has given him so much celebrity as
Earl of Chatham. One of the best caricatures relating to these
transactions was published in March, un-

der the title of "The noble Game of Bob-
cherry, as it was lately played by some
unlucky boys at the Crown, in St. James's
parish." It appears to have been a very
popular print, for there are two or three
different copies of it, probably pirated
editions, with some variations in the
figures and grouping. The would-be
ministers are represented as jumping at
offices represented by cherries, whilst the
chief members of the late administration
and some of their friends are looking on.
Lord Winchelsea, known by the capacious wig for which he was celebrated,
and his spectacles, is making a jump at a
cherry labelled as Secretary of State.
Lord Bath has just made an unsuccessful
attempt at another, which is labelled
"High Treasurer;" and Chief Justice
Willes is preparing to jump at one marked

BOB-CHERRY.

"High Chancellor." The Earl of Granville, who had swallowed a cherry marked "Secretary of State," is seized with a fit of sickness, which obliges him to disgorge it. Behind him stands the old Tory and half Jacobite, Sir John Hynde Cotton, holding a cherry in his hand, and looking with a smile at the efforts of the eager candidates for the others. Cotton had already obtained a place in the ministry, and he seems to have cared little for the changes which were taking place. William Pitt and Mr. Walpole are standing by, laughing at the vain efforts of the candidates for cherries; and on the other side of the picture the two brothers and ex-ministers, the Duke of Newcastle and Mr. Pelham, are looking quietly on. Among the numerous political pamphlets and prints brought forth by this sufficiently ridiculous transaction, we may specify, "A History of the Long Administration," published in a very diminutive size, "price one penny."

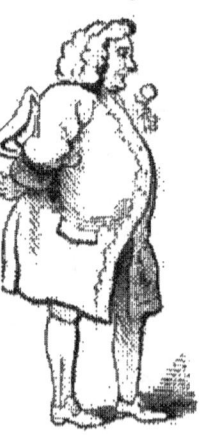

A CHERRY IN HAND.

The Duke of Cumberland, who was warmly attached to the old Whig principles, to which he looked for the support of his House on the throne, and who had been alarmed by the intelligence of the ministerial crisis, was relieved from all his fears, when, a few days afterwards, he heard of the restoration of the Pelhams, and he proceeded vigorously with the work with which he was now entrusted in the north. The fear and anxiety which had so long prevailed throughout England were entirely expelled by the news of the sanguinary and decisive battle of Culloden, fought on the 16th of April; and for several weeks the English papers and prints were filled with nothing but congratulatory poems and songs on the Duke of Cumberland, and satires on the unfortunate Scots; and these subjects, with the trials and executions of the rebels, occupied public attention through this and a great part of the following year. It need hardly be stated that the weak, and we may probably add worthless, Pretender, after passing through many dangers and hardships, disappointed his enemies by making good his escape to France. One of the English ballads sums up his enterprise, by telling us punningly that

" His descent was from Sky,* as thereby he'd declare,
His design was strange castles to build in the air."

London had, during these events, presented a strange physiognomy. With perhaps more general excitement, there was less
of street-mobbing than in 1715; but the consciousness of danger seems to have been stronger. The pamphlet shops were
filled with tracts against Popery and tyranny, and similar publications were hawked about the streets; and the newspapers
spread abroad daily a new cargo of exciteable matter. The
Penny London Post, for example, had the words " No Pretender! No Popery! No slavery! No arbitrary power! No
wooden shoes!" printed round its margins in conspicuous letters. Prints, exhibited in the shop windows, represented the
Popish cruelties and massacres, the ceremony of cursing by bell,
book, and candle, and a variety of similar performances, which,
it was said, were to be re-enacted on the Pretender's arrival in
the metropolis. In the beginning of 1746, although the Pretender had returned to Scotland, yet people were so far from
believing that the danger was entirely averted, that the newspapers and magazines gave directions and illustrative figures for
exercising volunteers in the use of their arms. The gates of
London were regularly closed at an early hour in the evening,
and the city trained bands were kept in constant movement.
Troops, both regulars and volunteers, were brought together in
the neighbourhood of the metropolis, and a strong camp was
formed on Finchley Common to protect this part of the kingdom from danger. Yet, in spite of all these precautions and
preparations, Jacobite agents were actively employed in spreading sedition even in London: numbers of people were arrested,
as in 1715, for drinking the health of the Pretender; ballad-
women and low persons were seen vending seditious papers, not
only in the streets of London, but in the very heart of the
camp; and, in the latter, agents of the Pretender were actually
detected in attempting to seduce the soldiers from their duty.
It is not surprising, that, in such a state of things, the victory
of Culloden should have given universal and deep-felt joy, and
that the victor should have become widely popular throughout
England. Within a few months the Duke of Cumberland's head
was a tavern sign in every country town; and his name contributed to give popularity to one of the prettiest of our common
garden-flowers. Some verses, current at this time, told us that

* The Young Pretender first put foot on Scottish ground in the Isle of
Skye.

> " The pride of France is *lily* white ;
> The *rose* in June is Jacobite :
> The prickly *thistle* of the Scot
> Is northern knighthood's badge and lot ;
> But, since the Duke's victorious blows,
> The *lily, thistle,* and the *rose*
> All droop and fade, all die away,
> *Sweet-William* only rules the day—
> No plant with brighter lustre grows,
> Except the laurel on his brows."

" The agreeable Contrast between the British Hero and the Italian Fugitive," a caricature published shortly after this event, represents the Pretender on one side, his hopes defeated and broken, and on the other the portly Duke, who exclaims, " Britain gave me life ; for her safety I will readily risk it !" Underneath is inscribed the distich—

> " Here happy Britain tells her joyful tales,
> And may again since William's arm prevails."

It was this period of agitation which suggested to Hogarth the admirable picture of the march of the guards to Finchley, on their way to the north against the Scots. The disorder and want of discipline, which characterized the movements of the troops on this occasion, are shewn in the most striking manner. Here you have a group in which the actors appear unconscious of the riot and confusion with which they are surrounded : it represents, we are told, a French spy, who is communicating to a disguised Jacobite a letter of intelligence, announcing that the King of France had sent ten thousand men to the assistance of his party. There, theft and dishonesty and licentiousness, though on a small scale, tell us but too plainly of the low moral character of the British

PRIVATE INTELLIGENCE.

army little more than a century ago. Here, again, a sturdy grenadier is exposed to a disagreeable cross-fire from a brace of females, who are selling ballads. An old explanation of this engraving states that these are the soldier's wife, whom he has deserted, and a woman whom he has deceived, and that they are upbraiding him for his treachery and inconstancy ; but they are evidently two ballad-singers of different political parties, for one carries a paper inscribed "God save our noble King,"

CROSS-FIRE.

and a print of the Duke of Cumberland, while the other holds up a number of the *Remembrancer*, a journal in opposition to the Government. Hogarth's print was given to the world in 1750, several years after the events it commemorates: the painting was exhibited to George II., as it is said, at that monarch's own request; but his only feeling appears to have been that of anger, that his favourite soldiers should be exposed to ridicule, and he returned it without an observation. Hogarth, indignant at the little patronage he received from the Court, satirically dedicated his engraving to the King of Prussia.

There were, however, soldiers exposed to much greater ridicule than those who on this occasion marched through Finchley, or even than those who had fled at Preston and Falkirk, and those were the warriors of the city companies, the trained bands of London. The municipal troops of the capital, which had presented so formidable an array in the middle ages, and which had acted no unimportant part in the civil commotions of the seventeenth century, had degenerated from their ancient character; but they still continued to be mustered and exercised for the defence of the metropolis, and during the earlier part of the century they had been from time to time drawn out in the outskirts of the town to perform battles and sieges, in harmless imitation of the movements of the more dangerous armies on the Continent. They were especially active during the first years after the accession of the House of Hanover to the English throne, and the newspapers of that period contain frequent paragraphs detailing satirically their pretended exploits. As late as the year 1731, *Read's Weekly Journal*, of September 11, announces, that, "On Tuesday, the Cripplegate, Whitechapel,

St. Clement's, and Southwark grenadiers rendezvous'd in Bridgewater Gardens; from whence they marched through the city, and afterwards attacked Cripplegate, both posterns, and Great Moorgate, with *their usual bravery*, and thence proceeded to attack a dunghill near Bunhill Fields, which gloriously completed their exercise of arms." We have already seen these domestic troops, in a caricature on the invasion of the Pretender, exhibited as loving better the enjoyments of home than the rude service of war. They figure in the last plate of Hogarth's series of the " Idle and Industrious Apprentices," and in several caricatures of the time. In one of these, in the collection of Mr. Burke, (without date or title,) these city troops appear, some of them, armed with pipes as well as guns; others on duty in undress, and some deficient of legs and eyes. A large and rather well-drawn caricature, also in the possession of Mr. Burke, and of which the accompanying engraving is a reduced copy, represents these troops under the characters of different animals, led by the self-important and ponderous elephant, with the hog for a standard-bearer, their device being the good roast beef and plum pudding of Old England. They are assembled at the sign of the Hog-in-Armour,* and one of the troop carries a bill with the proclamation—

TRAINED BANDS.

" Come, taylers and weavers,
And sly penny shavers,
All haste and repair
To the Hog in Rag Fair,
To 'list in the pay
Of great Captain Day,
And you shall have cheer,
Beef, pudding, and beer."

Underneath this print, which is dated in 1749, are the lines :—

* There was an inn with the sign of the Hog-in-Armour on Saffron Hill. It may be observed, that, as the figures are all left-handed, and the city arms reversed, the artist probably drew the sketch on copper without reversing it; so that, as far as it may be supposed to represent a locality, it is reversed in the print. This was an ordinary practice with Hogarth, many of whose prints are thus reversed.

> "Hark, now the drum assaults our ears,
> Thus beating up for volunteers;
> Who fight, besiege, and storm amain,
> And yet are never hurt or slain.
> Sad work! should this same army meet
> The late pacific Spithead fleet."*

As the danger of the Rebellion passed over, the Pelham administration, shaken internally by personal jealousies and intrigues, began to be assailed from without by the outcries of a violent, if not a powerful opposition. It was supported by its great parliamentary influence, which the accession of William Pitt to office had rendered complete; and it was carried on with quite as much corruption as had ever characterized the government of Sir Robert Walpole. The breaking out of the Rebellion had furnished an excuse for the repeal of the Habeas Corpus Act; and the power thus obtained being exercised more frequently against those who attacked the ministry than against the enemies of the Crown, had increased the unpopularity of the former. William Pitt, who had not long touched a legacy of 10,000*l.*, left him by the old Duchess of Marlborough for his "patriotic" opposition to the favourite measures of the Hanoverian dynasty, followed the example of so many patriots who had preceded him, and was assailed on every side for the "unembarrassed countenance" with which he suddenly, on his admission to office, advocated the very measures he had been condemning so long and with so much perseverance. In the caricatures of the day, the ghost of the deceased Duchess is represented as reproaching him for his apostacy. The "unembarrassed countenance" was the subject of a caricature and of a ballad. The latter sneers at the eloquence of "a fellow who could talk and could prate," and tells us how, before his accession to the ministry,

> "He bellow'd and roar'd at the troops of Hanover,
> And swore they were rascals who ever went over;
> That no man was honest who gave them a vote,
> And all that were for them should hang by the throat.
>   Derry down, &c."

By his apparent zeal in this cause he soon extended his popularity through the land.

> "By flaming so loudly he got him a name,
> Though many believed it would all end in shame;

* Alluding to a recent naval expedition, which had returned without performing any exploit of consequence.

But nature had given him, ne'er to be harrass'd,
An unfeeling heart, and a front unembarrass'd.
Derry down, &c.

"When from an old woman, by standing his ground,
He had got the possession of ten thousand pound,
He said that he cared not what others might call him,
He would shew himself now the true son of Sir Balaam.*
Derry down, &c."

Reproaches or rebukes had little effect upon him, we are told,
whether they came from friend or foe; and, having once cast
the die, he outdid every one in his barefaced dereliction of his
former principles.

"Young Balaam ne'er boggled at turning his coat,
Determin'd to share in whate'er could be got;
Said, 'I scorn all those who cry, impudent fellow!
As my front is of brass, I'll be painted in yellow.'†
Derry down, &c.

"Since yellow's the colour that best suits his face,
Old Balaam aspires at an eminent place;
May he soon in Cheapside stand fix'd by the legs,
His front well adorn'd and daub'd over with eggs.
Derry down, &c."

Pitt's apostacy was celebrated in other ballads equally bitter,
and he was violently attacked in the opposition papers, especially
in an evening paper entitled *The National Journal, or Country
Gazette,* which was commenced on the 22nd of March, 1746, and
the object of which seems to have been chiefly to expose the
false and exaggerated information relating to the affairs of Scotland published by the Government news-writers. The misuse of
the Duchess of Marlborough's legacy, the "unembarrassed
countenance" of the orator, (the term had been first applied to
him in the House of Commons,) and a variety of other circumstances, are dwelt upon with increasing banter by the writer of
this journal, who makes a lengthened comparison of Orator
Pitt with Orator Henley. But all was in vain: Pitt's eloquent
"oratory" swayed the senate, ministerial bribes defeated opposition without, and on the 12th of June the printer of *The National Journal* was thrown into Newgate, whence he crept
only upon the expiration of the suspension of the Habeas Corpus
Act, in February, 1747.

In the midst of the intrigues of the cabinet, the Prince of

* An allusion to the character of Sir Balaam in Pope's *Moral Essays,*
Epist. iii. l. 339—360.
† A list of the names of those who voted for the Hanover troops two
years before, which Pitt had then vehemently opposed, and which he now
as vehemently advocated, had been printed in yellow characters.

Wales, dissatisfied with the ministry, in the formation of which he had had so large a share, and jealous of the popularity of his brother, again threw himself into the opposition. From this moment there was not only a sensible increase in the attacks against the Government, but every expedient was tried to blacken the character of the Duke of Cumberland. The cruelties exercised against the Scottish rebels were pressed on people's attention in every manner, and with every kind of exaggeration; and the victor of Culloden became generally known by the epithet of "The Butcher." Even his fatness, and the lowness of some of his amours, were turned to derision. The caricature of "The agreeable Contrast," mentioned above as published after the battle of Culloden, was responded to by a parody entitled "The agreeable Contrast—shews that a greyhound is more agreeable than an elephant, and a genteel person more agreeably pleasing than a clumsy one, a country lass better than a town trollop, and that Flora was better pleased than Fanny." The allusion is to the adventures of Flora Macdonald in aiding the escape of Prince Charles Edward, and to a woman of low origin, who had been taken into keeping by the Duke. An extraordi-

THE BEAU.

nary notion of the elegant figure and graceful manners of the Pretender was zealously spread abroad by the Jacobite emissaries, and in this caricature he is represented as the accomplished beau, emblematically figured by his attendant, the courtly greyhound. He, too, is made to proclaim, "Mercy and love, peace," &c.; while Flora exclaims, "Oh! the agreeable creature! What a long tail he has!" On the other side of the picture

stand the bloated " Butcher"
and his attendant emblem,
the elephant. The Duke is
made to exclaim, "B——d
and w——ds!" and a lady
near him expresses strongly
her dissatisfaction at his
figure.

THE BUTCHER.

All the political passions
found a full vent in the
general elections in 1747,
which were unusually violent
throughout the country; and
the ministers are understood
to have attained their majority only by the most lavish
expenditure of the public money. At Westminster the two
parties were brought into violent collision, and the Duke and
the Prince of Wales are said to have taken an active part on the
two sides. The Government candidates were Lord Trentham,
the eldest son of Earl Gower, and Warren, who were elected by
a considerable majority, against the opposition candidates,
Phillips and Clarges. This party struggle was the subject of
several spirited caricatures, in which the " Butcher" is made to
cut a prominent figure. One
of the best of these, published in June, 1747, bears
the title of "The Two-shilling Butcher," and alludes
to the open bribery carried
forward on this occasion. It
is described in an advertisement in the journals as "a
curious parliamentary print."
The Duke gravely observes,
"My Lord, there being a
fatality in the cattle, that
there is 3000 above my cut,
though I offered handsome."
The individual thus ad-
dressed, an elegantly dressed
figure, intended apparently
to represent Lord Trentham,
exclaims in reply, dissatisfied

THE TWO-SHILLING BUTCHER.

at the low price which the Duke had offered for votes, "Curse me! you'd buy me the brutes at two shillings per head, *bona fide.*" On one side of the print a person is seen picking Britannia's pocket, to give the money to Phillips and Clarges, while Britannia exclaims, "O God! what pickpockets!" Among other caricatures on this election, one published in July bore the title, "The Humours of the Westminster Election; or, the scald miserable independent electors in the suds." The agitation of a Westminster election was, however, soon to be renewed with still greater violence. In 1749, Lord Trentham having been appointed one of the Lords of the Admiralty, had to vacate his seat, and every exertion was made by the opposition to hinder his re-election. "Those who styled themselves the independent electors of Westminster," says Smollett, "being now incensed to an uncommon degree of turbulence by the interposition of ministerial influence, determined to use their utmost endeavours to baffle the designs of the Court, and at the same time take vengeance on the family of Earl Gower, who had entirely abandoned the opposition, of which he was formerly one of the most respected leaders. With this view they held consultations, agreed to resolutions, and set up a private gentleman named Sir George Vandeput as the competitor of Lord Trentham, declaring that they would support his pretensions at their own expense; being the more encouraged to this enterprise by the countenance and assistance of the Prince of Wales and his adherents. They accordingly opened houses of entertainment for their partisans, solicited votes, circulated remonstrances, and propagated abuse: in a word, they canvassed with surprising spirit and perseverance against the whole interest of St. James's. Mobs were hired, and processions made on both sides, and the city of Westminster was filled with tumult and uproar."

This election occurred in the midst of a violent popular anti-Gallican feeling, which had been shewn particularly against a company of French players who were performing at the Haymarket, and who were spoken of by the mob as the "French vagrants." An attempt had been made to hinder them from acting, and they had been protected only by a mob hired by Lord Trentham, who appears to have affected Gallic manners, and to have been vain of his proficiency in the French language. The night after his ministerial appointment there was a great riot at the French theatre, in which Lord Trentham was accused of being personally active, although he denied it to the electors. This was made the most of by his opponents, who stigmatised him in ballads and squibs as "the champion of the French *strollers ;"* and common people said that learning to talk French was only a step towards the introduction of French tyranny. In one of the ballads they said,—

> " Our natives are starving, whom nature has made
> The brightest of wits, and to comedy bred ;
> Whilst apes are caress'd, whom God made by chance,
> The worst of all mortals, the strollers 'rom France."

Admiral Vernon, who took an earnest part in the opposition, said in a letter, which was printed and extensively circulated, " For the patrons of French strollers, a nation who are now undermining us in our commerce, and endeavouring to deprive us of it, I heartily detest them, as I think that every honest Briton should that wishes for the prosperity of his country." Lord Trentham's party retaliated by accusing Sir George Vandeput of being a Dutchman, and a partisan of the Dutch, who were at the moment not much more popular than the French ; and all the sins of that people, from the time of the massacre at Amboyna, were raked up and published. This West-minster election is said to have been one of the most expensive contests that the Government had as yet experienced. The following epigram described a supposed conversation between Lord Trentham and his father :—

> " Quoth L—d G—r [*Lord Gower*] to his son, ' Boy, thy frolic and place
> Full deep will be paid for by us and his *g—e* [*grace*] :
> Ten thousand twice over advanced ?—' *Veritable,*
> *Mon père,*' cry'd the youth ; ' but the D—e [*duke*] you know's able :
> Nor blame my *French frolics ;* since all men are certain,
> You're doing behind, what I did 'fore the curtain.' "

An immense number of papers of different kinds, some of them in the highest degree scurrilous, were printed and circulated by both parties. The Ministers were accused of having set at liberty prisoners confined for small debts, that they might secure their votes ; numbers were brought to the place of polling on horseback, and every kind of dishonest trickery was practised on both sides. The same person was, in many cases, smuggled in to vote more than once, and such notices as the following were placarded on the walls :—

" This is to inform the publick, that there is now to be seen in Covent Garden the celebrated Mr. More, so well known to the curious for his astonishing variety of voices, who we hear intends to give them all in favour of Sir G. V——L."

" This day is publish'd,

" An Essay on Multiplication, wherein it will be incontestably proved, that man, like those surprising creatures called Polypuses, may be cut into

6, or 10, or more pieces, and each piece become a perfect animal; as is exemplify'd in the case of several voters for the present W—— election, now living in the parishes of St. Clement's and St. Martin's le Grand."

At the conclusion of the polling there appeared a majority for Lord Trentham, but his opponents demanded a scrutiny; and this scrutiny proved so laborious and difficult, or the parties interested in opposing the Court threw so many obstacles in the way, that it led to a quarrel with the House of Commons, which lasted some months, and gave a double celebrity to the Westminster election of 1749.

In spite, however, of the popular dissatisfaction without, which was thus from time to time exhibited in scenes of uproar and turbulence, the opposition in Parliament was weaker than it had ever been before, and its voice was still further silenced about this time by the admission of the Duke of Bedford into the administration. But, while thus enlarging itself by the admission of not very accordant materials, a consequent division was gradually manifesting itself within the cabinet, which was soon formed into two distinct and rival parties, one represented by Mr. Pelham, the Duke of Bedford, and Fox, and the other by the Duke of Newcastle, who was jealous of his brother's talents and influence, and Pitt, who already looked forward to stepping over their quarrels to the summit of power. These discussions were gradually mixed up with the foreign transactions of the country, until they became in a manner identified with the two questions of peace and war.

The war into which England had been hurried after the downfall of Sir Robert Walpole was carried on unskilfully, and had produced no advantages to this country, although the latter had been involved in an enormous expenditure. The rebellion in Scotland had been a most advantageous diversion for the enemy; and at its close the French were capturing fortress after fortress in the Low Countries, until the fears and the turbulent dissatisfaction shewn by people throughout Holland obliged the Dutch to elect the Prince of Orange to the office of Stadtholder. The King of Prussia held aloof, attentive only to his private views of aggrandisement; the movements of the Russians and Austrians were too slow to be effective; and a number of petty allies were only enriching themselves with English subsidies. On the 2nd of July, 1747, the allied army under the Duke of Cumberland was entirely defeated at the battle of Lauffeld, which spread a general feeling of discouragement. About the same time an English caricature, under the title of " Europe in Masquerade; or, the Royal farce," threw deserved ridicule on

this war without principle, in which the peace and welfare of
Europe were sacrificed to the intrigues of its cabinets. The following lines, under the same title, were reprinted in the *Foundling Hospital of Wit*, and describe with tolerable accuracy the
state of politics in the latter part of 1747 :—

> "The States, at last, with one accord,
> Have made themselves a sov'reign lord.
> For public good ?—Be not mistaken,
> It was to save their own dear Bacon.
> The King most Christian does his work,
> By leaguing with the heathen Turk ;
> The haughty Turk and Kouli Khan
> Are friends or foes, as suits their plan ;
> The Russian lady plays her game,
> As fits her interest or fame.
> You've seen two curs for bone at bay,
> A third has run with it away ;
> Just so the Pr—n [*Prussian*] slily watches,—
> While others fight, the prey he snatches.
> At home behold a mighty pother,
> Friends worrying friends and brother brother,
> Pushing and elbowing one another.
> To Westminster but turn your eye,
> And the whole mystery you'll descry :
> The independents there you'll see
> Bawling aloud for liberty ;
> But if you follow in the dance,
> They'll lead you blind to Rome or France."

The reverses of the allies on the Continent were, however,
balanced by several decisive victories gained by the English at
sea, which destroyed the commerce of France, and crippled her
resources so much that the French monarch shewed a strong inclination to treat for peace. The English prime minister was also
desirous of a pacification ; but his brother, the Duke of Newcastle, joined with the King and the Duke of Cumberland in
wishing for a continuation of the war ; and it was not until
many petty difficulties and obstacles had been overcome, that
the congress at Aix-la-Chapelle was agreed upon. The negotiations were continued through the greater part of the year 1748,
and the treaty of Aix-la-Chapelle was not signed until the 7th
of October.

The English ministers were too much occupied with their
own cabals and private interests to take care of the interests of
their country, and her allies alone gained any advantages by the
peace. The moment the preliminaries were announced, they became an object of attack, and the newspaper and pamphlet warfare was carried on long after the war itself had ceased. That

part of the treaty which caused the greatest discontent in this country was the stipulated restoration to France of Cape Breton, which had been taken by the English shortly before the breaking out of the Scottish rebellion; and this discontent was very considerably heightened by the English government having submitted to the indignity of sending two noblemen, the Earl of Sussex and Lord Cathcart, to France as hostages until the restitution of this conquest should be completed. In the beginning of 1748 a loud cry was also set up against ministers, for allowing English bread to be exported to our enemies of France, who were suffering from famine, which was partly a consequence of the protracted hostilities. The popular arguments on this occasion may be summed up in an epigram printed in the *General Advertiser* of Feb. 1:—

> "To fast and pray, that heav'n our arms may bless,
> Is wise and pious—we can do no less ;
> We might howe'er, methinks, something more do :
> ' What's that, pray !' Why, sir, make the French fast too."

In the same journal, two days later, is advertised a caricature on the same subject, entitled "The Political Bitters; a satirical print." Another subject of complaint, and a more reasonable one, was the practice of insuring French ships in England, so that this country was actually making good the losses which the French merchants sustained in the capture of their ships by the English cruizers. In May, 1748, appeared a caricature, entitled "The Preliminary Congress," directed especially against the surrender of Cape Breton, and against the unsatisfactory conclusion of the sacrifices made by England, who is helping the empress queen over a stile, while France is seizing the opportunity of her exposed position to take liberties with her person. A print published at the same time was entitled "The Congress of Beasts; or, the milch cow." In another caricature, under nearly the same title, "The Congress of the Brutes at Aix-la-Chapelle," the different powers are represented under the forms of animals assembled in council, the Gallic cock presiding, to whom the British lion is, with all due humility, offering his recent conquest: "Pray accept Cape Breton!" In November, after the treaty was signed, appeared "The Grinner from Aix-l-a Chapelle;" and in December appeared a number of spirited caricatures on the subject of the hostages, under such titles as "The two most famous Ostriches;" "The Hostages; a political Print," &c. In one of these, entitled "The Wheelbarrow Cry of Europe," the Earl of Sussex and Lord Cathcart are represented in a barrow wheeled by King George, who cries, "Hostages, ho!

two a penny before they go!" And
in another, dated December 8,
Cromwell appears on the scene with
furious threats, which he is only
hindered from executing by the
devil; but he exclaims in his wrath,
" Was it for this I sought the Lord
and fought?" In January, 1749,
appeared " The Hostages; an hero-
ico-satirical poem;" and at the end
of the same month was advertised
a pamphlet, (accompanied with a
large caricature,) entitled " The
Congress of the Beasts, under the
mediation of the Goat, for negotiating a peace between the Fox,
the Ass wearing a Lion's skin, the
Tygress, the Horse, and other

THE HOSTAGES.

quadrupeds at war." At the same time appeared a number
of pamphlets and ballads against the surrender of Gibraltar,
which it was pretended that the English government contemplated yielding up to Spain. In the *British Magazine* for
January, 1749, is announced " A humorous print, called the
Peace-offering."

Yet, in spite of these marks of dissatisfaction at the terms of
the treaty of Aix-la-Chapelle, peace under any form appears to
have been acceptable, and it was followed by general demonstrations of joy. The fireworks in the Green Park were unusually
magnificent, and these and the jubilee masquerade at Ranelagh
were represented in multitudes of prints, which were eagerly
bought by the multitude. In one of these prints the fireworks
are satirically called " the grand whim for posterity to laugh
at." The Dutch, who had been reduced to a far worse position
than the other allies, and who were now almost destitute of
money and resources, rejoiced louder than anybody else, and
their fireworks far exceeded those of the Green Park in magnificence. The British public thought that Holland had been too
much favoured in the treaty, and that power was suspected of
having had the intention of treating in private for its own interests. These extravagant demonstrations of joy by the Dutch
were accordingly caricatured somewhat ungenerously in an English print, entitled " The Contrast," in which the prosperity of
England (for England had really been increasing rapidly
in commercial importance and wealth) is represented under

the form of a portly individual, with his pockets full of money, laughing at the miserable figure of a Dutchman with

PEACE AND PLENTY.

his empty pockets turned out. The inscription under the Englishman is, "Money with Commerce;" that under the Dutchman, "No money with fireworks!"*

In the midst of these popular subjects of discontent, the divisions in the ministry were becoming every day more apparent, and the open accession of the Prince of Wales raised again the spirits of the parliamentary opposition. The old intriguer Bolingbroke was again brought into play, and new plots were constantly hatching, either at his house at Battersea or at the Prince's at Leicester House. It was not long before the ministry was weakened by several defections; Bubb Dodington first relinquished his place of treasurer of the navy, and returned to a post he had formerly held in the Prince of Wales's household, and he took the lead in the Prince's party. A regular opposition was now again organised in the House of Commons, and the printed attacks on measures and persons became more energetic, as well as more numerous. One of the most violent of these, published under the title of "Constitutional Queries," was levelled at the Duke of Cumberland, who was compared in it to the "crook-backed" Richard III., and it was generally supposed to have come from Leicester House, and to have been written by Lord Egmont. These "Queries" raised a violent heat in the two Houses; the open attempt to sow dissension between the two royal brothers was strongly animadverted upon, and the paper in question was ordered to be burnt by the common hangman,

* In the *British Magazine* for May, 1749, a caricature is announced under the title, "The Contrast; or, such is the folly of no money with fireworks, or money with commerce." I am uncertain if this be the same print as the one described above, or (as was not unusual) a different edition of it.

and measures were taken, but in vain, to discover and punish the author. But the Prince's party in the House opposed these proceedings, and Sir Francis Dashwood and others spoke in palliation of the libel. These party intrigues occupied the whole of the year 1750, and were proceeding with increased activity in the beginning of 1751, when the opposition received a sudden blow from an event totally unexpected. On the 5th of February, 1751, appeared the royal proclamation of a reward of a thousand pounds for the discovery of the author of the "Constitutional Queries." The Prince of Wales died suddenly on the 20th of March, after a short illness, and relieved his father's ministry from one of its most dangerous opponents.

For several years after the treaty of Aix-la-Chapelle, the publication of political caricatures seemed almost suspended, and we shall find them of comparatively rare occurrence till the breaking out of the war in 1755. In the October of 1749 appeared "The true Contrast between a Royal British Hero and a frighted Italian Bravo," occasioned by the movements of the Pretender on the Continent, (who was shut out from France and Spain by the treaty of peace,) and shewing that his name still excited some interest in England; and "The Laugh; or, Bub's compliments to Ralpho," alluding, probably, to some circumstance in the opposition movements, of which Dodington was so active a promoter.

The opposition sustained a further loss in Lord Bolingbroke, who died on the 15th of December. The old actors, who had played their parts under George I., were rapidly disappearing from the stage, and we are entering upon the politics of an entirely new generation.

CHAPTER VI.

GEORGE II.

Changes in the Administration, and Incipient Opposition—Old Interest and New Interest—Elizabeth Canning—The Bill for the Naturalization of the Jews—Elections; Hogarth's Prints—Death of Mr. Pelham, and Consequent Changes in the Ministry—War with France—Trial of Admiral Byng—New Convulsion in the Ministry, and Accession of William Pitt to Power—The Seven Years' War—Popular Discontent; Beer *versus* Gin—Conquest of Canada—Death of George the Second.

THE incipient opposition at Leicester House, as we have just seen, was overthrown by the death of the Prince of Wales; and its ostensible leader, Bubb Dodington, and others, tried to sell themselves at the highest price they could to the people in power. All the great political questions which had so long agitated the country seemed, indeed, now to have become extinguished, and to have given place to a far less honourable partisanship of private jealousies and private interests, in which it was the object of the minister to strengthen himself, by giving place to as many individuals as he had any reason to fear in the opposition, and the simple and only object of opposition was to establish a claim for admission to place. This was so universally felt, that, instead of the old distinctions of Whig and Tory, Hanoverian and Jacobite, or Court Party and Country Party, the supporters of ministers and the opposition had almost involuntarily taken the distinctive titles of the New Interest and the Old Interest; the New Interest being that of men in place, the Old Interest that of men who wanted to be in place. The parliamentary opposition, however, raised its head a little in the June of 1751, upon the dismissal of Lord Sandwich, and the consequent resignation of the Duke of Bedford and Lord Trentham. Lord Granville was again admitted into the ministry as one of the secretaries of state, and Anson was placed at the Board of Admiralty. The year 1751 passed off with great quietness; and the only remarkable parliamentary act in the portion of the session which closed it was the alteration of style, by correcting the calendar according to the Gregorian computation, then adopted by most other nations in Europe, it being decreed that the new year should begin in future on the

1st day of January, and that eleven intermediate nominal days, between the 2nd and 14th days of September, 1752, should for that time be omitted; so that the day succeeding the 2nd should then be denominated the 14th of that month. An alteration so useful in every point of view did not pass without some show of discontent; it was declaimed against as a Popish innovation, and long afterwards many people adhered tenaciously to the old practice.

In 1752, the opposition, though weak, shewed more signs of life. At the end of January, the Duke of Bedford attacked the subsidiary treaty with Saxony, by which the elector was bribed to give his vote for the Archduke Joseph as King of the Romans, the question which was now agitating Germany, and which paved the way for the celebrated Seven years' war. The Pelhams, alarmed, now tried to buy over Bubb Dodington; but the negotiation again failed, and the opposition became a little more spirited, and it shewed itself much stronger on two bills for the naturalization of Jews, and the regulation of marriages. Fox gave violent offence to the Lord Chancellor Hardwicke by his conduct in opposing this latter bill, which, to use the words of Horace Walpole, was "invented by my Lord Bath, and cooked up by the chancellor." It may be observed, *en passant*, that, on the 4th of February, 1752, died Sir John Hynde Cotton, the last of the English Jacobites who had displayed any activity.

In the midst of this political calm, the newspapers and political essayists, which had increased in number, were obliged to seek matter for agitation in the passing incidents of the day; and these shew us how easy it was, in the last century, to set the passions of the multitude in a flame. A young woman of respectable connexions, named Mary Blandy, was executed at Oxford, in the beginning of 1753, for poisoning her father, and her crime had been attended with remarkable and somewhat romantic circumstances. She persisted at the scaffold in asserting her innocence; a number of pamphlets were published by persons who took part for or against her, and it became the subject of a warm public dispute. This was soon followed by a still more singular affair. A girl named Elizabeth Canning, who lived with her mother at Aldermanbury, in London, declared that on the night of the 1st of January, 1753, two ruffians seized on her as she was passing under Bedlam wall, stripped her of her outer apparel, secured her mouth with a gag, and conveyed her on foot about ten miles, to a place called Enfield Wash, where they brought her to the house of one Mrs. Wells, where she was robbed of her stays, and, because she

N 2

refused to become a prostitute, confined in a cold and unfurnished apartment, where she remained a whole month, without any other food than a few stale crusts of bread and a gallon of water, till at last she forced her way through a window, and ran home, almost naked, to her mother's house, in the night of the 29th of January. The story was an improbable one; but, perhaps, on this very account it gained more popularity, and money was subscribed to prosecute the persons concerned in the outrage. Of three persons charged, Wells (the mistress of the house) was punished as a bawd; her servant, Virtue Hall, turned evidence for Canning to save herself, but afterwards recanted; and an old gipsy woman, named Squires, was convicted of the robbery of the stays, though she produced undeniable evidence that, at the time the offence was said to have taken place, she was at Abbotsbury, in Dorsetshire. At the trial, the court was surrounded by an enraged mob, which threatened with the utmost violence all who were brought as evidence for the accused, or who did not sympathize with Canning. The Lord Mayor, Sir Crispe Gascoigne, made a clear and impartial statement of the case; and at his representation the gipsy woman, Squires, received the royal pardon. This only added fuel to the popular fury. Some of the leading journals had taken up Canning's cause with considerable warmth, and they now turned their resentment against the Lord Mayor. An incredible number of pamphlets, both serious and satirical, on both sides of the question, with many prints and caricatures, issued from the press; and the faction raised throughout the kingdom on this trifling subject was so great, that, to use the words of a contemporary writer, "it became the general topic of conversation in all assemblies, and people of all ranks espoused one or other party, with as much warmth and animosity as had ever inflamed the Whigs and Tories, even at the most rancorous period of their opposition." Prosecutions for perjury were commenced on both sides; and, in the end, after Virtue Hall's recantation, Canning herself confessed that the whole story was a fabrication, and she was condemned to transportation. But her supporters, even now, did not give up her cause; those who were least zealous asserted that she had not acted voluntarily, but that she had been the tool of others; and they subscribed money for her, provided her with every comfort on her voyage, and ensured her a good reception in America.

People's minds were drawn off from this affair by a new subject of political agitation. The act of parliament of 1752, to permit the naturalization of foreign Jews, which was the work of the Pelhams, had not passed without a violent opposition in the House of Commons; and, although the bishops had offered no opposition to it in the House of Lords, the clergy out of doors raised such a general outcry, as reminded people of the High-Church agitation of the days of Sacheverell. The alarm of the Church party had been further excited by the deistical tendency of the posthumous works of Lord Bolingbroke, whom while alive they had almost sanctified as their political champion. The merchants of London began also to be alarmed at imaginary commercial advantages which the Jews were to derive from the measure. As the period for the general elections was now fast approaching, the excitement increased tenfold. Multitudes of controversial tracts were published on this subject, as well as others, the more immediate design of which was to inflame the passions of the mob. Among these were histories of the Jews, written in a partial spirit, and magnifying their pretended sins: fearful prognostications of their increasing power, and of their encroachment on the liberties and on the commercial power of the country; and strange imaginary pictures of the state of the country under Jewish supremacy, when it was supposed that the Jews would gradually have made themselves masters of the estates and property of the English nobility and gentry. Caricatures against the Jews were exhibited in the windows of the print-shops, and ballads equally bitter were sung about the streets. Thus, in August, 1753, a caricature is advertised under the title of "The Circumcis'd Gentiles; or, a Journey to Jerusalem," stated to be "engraved by Issachar Barebone, Jun'; " and in December another caricature was announced, entitled "The Racers Unhors'd; or, the Jews jockey'd." One of the ballads, entitled "The Jew's Triumph," and set to a popular tune, gives a melancholy account of the disasters of the year:—

"In seventeen hundred and fifty-three,
The style it was changed to P—p—ry [Popery],
But that it is lik'd, we don't all agree;
    Which nobody can deny.

"When the country folk first heard of this act,
That old father Style was condemned to be rack'd,
And robb'd of his time, which appears to be fact,
    Which nobody can deny;

"It puzzl'd their brains, their senses perplex'd,
And all the old ladies were very much vex'd,
Not dreaming that Levites would alter our text;
    Which nobody can deny."

The faults of the Jews, and the dangers to be apprehended

from them, are portrayed in equally doggerel verses, and vengeance is finally called down upon those who had now advocated
their cause.

> " But 'tis hoped that a mark will be set upon those
> Who were friends to the Jews, and Christians' foes,
> That the nation may see how Deism grows;
>   Which nobody can deny.

> " Then cheer up your spirits, let Jacobites swing,*
> And Jews in their bell-ropes hang when they ring
> To our sovereign lord great George our king;
>   Which nobody can deny."

"The Jews naturalized; or, the English alienated: a ballad;"
breathes the same spirit, and ascribes the passing of the Naturalization Act to that extensive system of bribery with which
everybody was then familiar. Even the clergy preached against
the Jew bill from the pulpit; and the ministry became so
alarmed for the elections, that they weakly yielded to the foolish
clamour, and repealed their own act at the commencement of
the session at the end of 1753.

The elections, which took place in the April following (1754),
were less clamorous than it was expected, and, with the exception of a violent contest in Oxfordshire, the opposition the court
had to contend with was not great. The chief party-cries related to the Jews, to the alteration in the style, and to the
Marriage Act.† The new Parliament, to use the words of
Horace Walpole, was selected "in the very spirit of the Pelhams." The revival of the opposition in Parliament, and the
agitation naturally attendant on elections under such circumstances, produced a few caricatures, which possessed little merit.
In February was announced "The P. [*Parliament ?*] Race; or
the C. [*court*] jockeys." We are better acquainted with a caricature published on the 11th of June, under the title of
" Foreign Trade and Domestic compared;" in which one of two
compartments represents the King of France raising up French
commerce upon the ruins of that of Great Britain; while, in
the other compartment, the Duke of Newcastle, as minister, is

---

* Alluding to the execution of Dr. Cameron this year, which had excited
compassion rather than exultation, even among a mob which appears to
have been especially greedy of such sights.

† The act for the regulation of marriages had met with great opposition,
and it was far from popular with the multitude. On the banner seen
through the window, in one edition of Hogarth's print of "The Election
Dinner," we see the words, "Marry and multiply in spite of the . . . . ."
In April, on the eve of the elections, a caricature appeared under the title
of "The Eccl—at—l Millers; or, the funeral of Private Matrimony;" and
in the October following was published "The Marriage Act, a Novel!"

oppressing our own trade, and sacrificing our merchant navy, by loading commerce with an accumulation of oppressive taxes. The journals of the month of September announce, among other new prints, a caricature, entitled "The Differences of Time between *those times* and *these times*," no doubt designed in the same spirit.

But the elections of 1754 will ever be memorable in the history of art, as having given rise to Hogarth's four capital prints of the humours of an election, the first of which was published in 1755, and the other three in the following years, and which contain several allusions to circumstances connected with the great contest in Oxfordshire. The first of these prints, as every reader will be aware, represents an election dinner, which was now one of the first and most necessary steps of the candidate towards popular favour. The inscription on the banner, and the effigy of the Duke of Newcastle, with the words "No Jews" (seen through the window), allude to the popular subjects of agitation, and show that one candidate belongs to the "Old Interest." The second plate, which contains more of political satire than the others, represents the canvass for votes. Two Inns, the Royal Oak and the Crown, are the head-quarters of the rival candidates; and a third, the Porto Bello, appears to be neuter. The Royal Oak is evidently in the Old Interest, and a large caricature painted on cloth hangs from the sign-post; in the upper part of which the height of the Treasury is contrasted with the squat solidity of the then new Horse-Guards, the arch of which is so low that the state-coachman risks his head in attempting to drive under it, while the turret at the top is drawn like a beer-barrel. This was designed for a satire on Ware, the architect. Money is thrown from the Treasury window, to be put in a waggon for carriage to the country. In the compartment below, "Punch, candidate for Guzzledown," has a wheelbarrow full of gold, which he is distributing to the electors with a ladle.

> "See from the Treasury flows the gold,
> To shew that those who're *bought* are *sold!*
> Come, Perjury, meet it on the road—
> 'Tis all your own—a waggon-load.
> Ye party fools, ye courtier tribe,
> Who gain no vote without a bribe,
> Lavishly kind, yet insincere,
> Behold in Punch yourselves appear
> And you, ye fools, who poll for pay,
> Ye little great men of a day,
> For whom your favourite will not care,
> Observe how much bewitch'd you are."

The candidate is purchasing trinkets of a Jew to conciliate
the favour of the ladies, whilst a messenger brings him a letter,
addressed, "Tim Parti-toole, Esq." The Crown, which is
stated also to be the excise-office, is attacked by a mob, who are
pulling down the sign, which threatens to crush them in its
fall; while the landlord is shooting at them from the window.
In front an elector is receiving bribes from both parties, whose
agents are presenting him with invitations to dinner at the rival
inns. The only sign of political activity at the third inn consists in two men seated at a table, drinking, and arguing on the
capture of Porto Bello, one of them explaining to the other,
with pieces of tobacco pipe, how the place was taken with six
ships only. At the door of the inn of the opposition member
is a wooden lion, devouring a *fleur de lis*, intimating that the
Old Interest were already urging to those hostilities with
France, which soon followed the period of the elections.

> " Oh, Britain, favourite isle of heaven,
> When to thy sons shall peace be given !
> The treachery of the Gallic shore
> Makes even thy wooden lions roar."

The third plate of Hogarth's series represents the various
tricks and frauds used in " polling for the votes ;" and, in the

fourth, the successful candidate is chaired, and enjoying his turbulent, and
apparently somewhat pe-
rilous triumph, amidst a
scene of wild uproar. It
is generally understood
that Hogarth's *successful
candidate*, who is of the
New Interest, is intended
to represent the celebrated
Bubb Dodington, the in-
triguing manager of the
Leicester House opposi-
tion. In the plate the
artist has represented a
goose flying over his head,

THE SUCCESSFUL CANDIDATE.

which is said to be designed for a parody on Le Brun's engraving of the battle of the Granicus, in which an eagle is represented hovering over the head of Alexander the Great.

On the eve of the elections, an event occurred which opened
a door for new intrigues among the younger statesmen, who

were struggling for power. The prime minister, Henry Pelham, died on the 6th of March, 1754. His brother and colleague, the Duke of Newcastle, who had long divided the cabinet by his personal rivalry, succeeded in obtaining the premiership, and at the same time provoked the hostility (concealed for a while) of two other rivals in ambition, Pitt and Fox, who were left in their subordinate places, although one of Pitt's friends, Mr. Legge, was appointed Chancellor of the Exchequer, while Sir Thomas Robinson succeeded Newcastle as Secretary of State. The Duke had indirectly fomented the King's dislike to Pitt and Fox. In the course of the autumn these two statesmen formed a private coalition against the ministry, under which they held place, and it was a secret article of their league, that, in case of success, the latter should be placed at the head of the Treasury, while the former was to be Secretary of State. Pitt and Fox, together, were all-powerful in the House of Commons; and when the Duke of Newcastle was made aware of the coalition, he hazarded a desperate attempt to separate them, and succeeded in detaching Fox, by introducing him into the cabinet as one of the secretaries of state.

Amid these intrigues at home, Europe began again to be threatened with a general war, in which England was made more especially interested by the encroachment of the French upon our colonies in North America, and by their intrigues against us in India. In America, without any declaration of war, the hostilities of the French had been carried so far, that when the Parliament assembled in November (1754), the King was obliged to ask for extraordinary supplies for the defence of our possessions. All the measures of the ministry now began to take a more warlike tone, and the Duke of Newcastle, although he was far from showing any eagerness for hostilities, became more popular with the multitude. England and France, were, however, soon at war in different parts of the globe, while each pretended to be at peace, and endeavoured to throw the blame of hostilities on the other. The French Government dissimulated its real designs, while hastening forwards its armament with the greatest vigour; the English ministers were wanting in vigilance and foresight, and had been neglecting the navy and the colonies; they even now spoke slightingly of the latter, and of the folly of being plunged into a war for them. In March, 1755, they no longer concealed their belief that hostilities were inevitable, and they sent a fleet, under Boscawen, to North America, although they were so completely deceived by the demonstrations of the French, that they anticipated the attack at home, in England, or at least in Ireland. Boscawen missed the French fleet, which had preceded him, but two French men-of-war were captured, and the news, on its arrival in England, was received with the greatest exultation. This event, which appears to have been equally unexpected to the courts of England and France, made a further complication in their relations, and forced the former into more decided hostilities. Although the English cruisers captured French ships wherever they met them, both governments still persisted in stating that they hoped to preserve peace between the two countries. The backwardness of the Duke of Newcastle in supporting British rights against French encroachments had already been made the subject of a caricature, published on the 4th of April, entitled "The Grand Monarque in a Fright; or

THE BRITISH LION ROUSED.

the British Lion roused from his lethargy." Newcastle is restraining the angry animal, who is hardly pacified by the assurance, "Peace, peace, my brave fellow! Be quiet; rely on the equity and veracity of the most Christian King, and all things shall be adjudged by the commissaries of both nations." The equity and veracity of the French court were certainly not at this moment generally believed in. The capture of the two French ships, and the intelligence brought by every new arrival of preparations in our colonies, raised still further the national spirit, and people began already to dream of the expulsion of the French from America. On the 11th of August, another caricature, entitled "British Rights maintained; or, French ambition dismantled," represented the Gallic cock plucked of his feathers by the British lion, and compelled to utter a sorrowful "Peccavi!" The feathers under the lion's paw are severally inscribed with the names of the French forts in North America, "Beau Sójour," "Fort St. John's," "Crown Point," "Ohio," "Quebec," &c. Britannia, bearing the cap of liberty on her spear, is encouraging her lion, while behind, Mars and Neptune are carving out for her portions in the map of North America with her sword and trident. A negro boy laughs at the unfortunate cock, and exclaims, "Pretty bird, how will you get home again?" On the other side of the picture stands ano-

THE GALLIC COCK PLUCKED.

ther group. The genius of France, weeping, exclaims, "Ave Maria! que ferrons nous? After our massacres and persecutions, must heretics possess this promised land, which we so piously have called our own?" On a hill in the distance is seen a martyr burning at the stake. A Frenchman, with chagrin marked in his countenance and attitude, who is designated as "Mons. le Politicien," bites his hat in his spite, and exclaims, "Garni bleu! If our fleet had not been lost in a fog, we should have trompé les f——— Anglois out of tout l'Amerique Septentrional." A British "jack-tar," taking him by the shoulder, and calling his attention to the operations of Neptune and Mars on the map, says, "Hark ye, Mounseer! was that your map of North America? What a vast tract of land you had! Pity the right owner should take it from you!" In the distance,

FRANCE IN THE DUMPS.

the comet of "universal monarchy," represented as the grand object of French ambition, is falling into the sea.[*]

———
[*] In the previous month of July, another caricature had appeared rela-

Shortly after the appearance of this caricature, the public exultation was considerably damped by the arrival of the news from
America of the disastrous result of General Braddock's expedition against the French on the Ohio; and other news, equally
dispiriting, that followed in quick succession, raised a cry of disappointment in the mother-country, which fell heavy upon
ministers In November, as the session of Parliament approached, another caricature appeared, attacking the half-mea-
sures of the English court, and described in the advertisement as
" Two *utopian* scenes, called Half Peace, Half War."

The opposition was evidently gaining force; and when Parliament met, on the 13th of November, Pitt, who had long been
coquetting with popularity, and who, although he retained his
office of Paymaster of the Forces, had been brooding over his disappointments, suddenly dragged his colleague Legge, the Chancellor of the Exchequer, into open opposition to the measures of
the court. In one of his grandest outbreaks of eloquence, Pitt
assailed the whole system of foreign negotiations pursued by the
ministers, and attacked the subsidy treaties with the continental
powers with the same anti-Hanoverian spirit he had displayed in
his younger days. A week after, on the 26th of November, Pitt
and Legge were dismissed from their offices. Pitt had already
formed a close alliance with the Leicester House faction, and he
now became the acknowledged leader of the opposition, weak as
it still was, in the House of Commons. The ministry, however,
still held on with its large, and, as it was said, paid majorities,
and Fox was left to display his talents in contending in the arena
of oratory with his powerful antagonist. Horace Walpole, in a
letter dated the 12th of February, 1756, describes the House of
Commons as then "divided into a very dialogue between Pitt
and Fox."

In the preceding year, in a letter dated August 4, Walpole,
speaking of the recriminations between the courts of France and
England upon the capture of the French ships in America, had
said, with a sneer, " Mirepoix [the French Ambassador] complained grievously, that the Duke of Newcastle had overreached
him; but he is to be forgiven in so good a cause! It is the first
person he ever deceived!" The Duke's incapacity and unfitness
to guide the councils of his country, under the difficult circumstances in which she was now placed, became more apparent
every day. By pretended preparations to invade England, the

ting to the hostilities in America, entitled "The American Moose Deer; or,
away to the river Ohio." Copies of it are in the collections of Mr. Hawkins
and Mr. Burke.

French court had completely drawn off the attention of the English ministry from its real preparations, on the most extensive scale, for the invasion of Minorca and reduction of Port Mahon, a possession which the English people had been taught latterly to consider as second only to Gibraltar. When our ministers were repeatedly warned of the danger, and when they were fully assured of the intentions of France, they still persisted in keeping our ships at home, and in leaving the weak garrison at St. Philip's Fort, which protected Port Mahon, without reinforcements. At length, with the beginning of January, 1756, the alarm became general; odes and poems on the honour and bravery of Britons were bandied about during the following month; and the newspapers inform us, that, on Wednesday, the 3rd of March, " the hottest press began for seamen that ever was known." It was determined to send forthwith a fleet to the Mediterranean. On the 18th of March, Horace Walpole writes, " We proceed fiercely in armament." The ministers now committed a new fault, in appointing to the command of the Mediterranean fleet an officer of very mean capacity, and with little experience—Admiral Byng, the son of old Admiral Byng of Queen Anne's days, who had been raised to the peerage by the title of Earl of Torrington. Byng sailed on the 5th of April, with ten ships of the line (Newcastle had been persuaded by Anson to send no more), and a small body of troops to reinforce Blakeney's small garrison. The fleet lost some time on its way to Gibraltar, and there it did not receive the additional troops it expected. Owing to these delays, Byng did not reach Minorca till the 18th of May, when the French fleet had preceded him, and landed 16,000 men, who immediately formed the siege of the fortress held by Blakeney. Byng had hardly arrived, when the French fleet, consisting of thirteen ships of the line and four smaller vessels, made its appearance, and the two hostile armaments were formed in line of battle, and watched and manœuvred till night. Next morning the French fleet had disappeared. It returned towards the middle of the day, when the two fleets again formed in order of battle; and about two o'clock Byng gave the signal to engage, but in so contradictory a manner, that it only caused confusion among his ships. Rear-Admiral West, the second in command, acting upon the intention of the order, and not upon the letter, bore away with his division, attacked the enemy with the greatest bravery, and had already driven several of their ships out of the line, when, unsupported by the rest of the English fleet, he was obliged to return. Had the whole fleet followed the example of West, it is probable that the

French would have been defeated, and Minorca saved: but Byng seems to have acted in the utmost confusion; his own ship, the Intrepid, had become for a moment unmanageable, and driven out the next ship in position; and, in spite of the expostulations of his captain, Byng refused to advance for fear of breaking his line. The French Admiral, De la Galissonière, who appeared to be no more desirous of fighting than the English, took advantage of this slowness to effect his retreat. Byng then gave orders for the chase, but the French ships were in better condition, and were soon out of sight. Next day Byng called a council of war, represented to them the bad condition of his fleet, and the superiority of the enemy in men and guns, and it was determined to leave Blakeney to his fate, and return to Gibraltar. The brave little garrison of Fort St. Philip held out five weeks longer against its horde of besiegers, and then made an honourable capitulation.

In England the greatest anxiety was shewn for the fate of Port Mahon, and the public were encouraged in forming extravagant expectations of the success of the expedition under Admiral Byng. When, therefore, his despatch arrived in the month of June, the ministry were overwhelmed with consternation, and the country was thrown into an absolute fury. The public exasperation was increased on the arrival of the French accounts, which exulted over the *defeat* of the English fleet, their own fleet having returned on Byng's disappearance; for, though neither party could establish any fair claim to a victory, it was evident that both had run away.

> " We have lately been told
> Of two admirals bold,
>   Who engaged in a terrible fight ;
> They met after noon,
> Which I think was too soon,
>   As they both ran away before night."

So said one of the popular epigrams of the day ; and it was at first the general belief that Byng had betrayed his country by his pusillanimity, and that, if he had fought, Port Mahon would have been saved.

The English ministers, to whose improvidence and ill-management the loss of Port Mahon was chiefly to be ascribed, in their terror, attempted to save themselves by throwing the odium on the unfortunate admiral. Anson, who presided at the Admiralty, was especially active in fanning up the popular flame. Artful emissaries, we are informed by the writers of the time, mingled with all public assemblies, from the drawing room at St. James's to the mob at Charing-Cross, expatiating on Byng's insolence, folly, and cowardice, and exaggerating the losses which were believed to be occasioned by it. His despatch, which was certainly a very lame explanation of his conduct, but which it was pretended the ministry had curtailed of sundry passages reflecting on their own share in the disaster, was everywhere turned into ridicule, and was even versified in a variety of shapes, of which the following may serve as a sample.

"THE LETTER OF A CERTAIN ADMIRAL.

"Mr. C—— [*Cleveland*], I pray, to their L——s [*lordships*] you'll say,
We are glad and rejoice above measure :
When you've read what is writ you, you'll laugh till it split you,
And so give me joy of *my pleasure.*

"We'd a wind, you must know, as fair as could blow,
And therefore in days just eleven,
We had sail'd from the shore full ten leagues or more,
And saw nought but the ocean and heaven.

"Then seventeen ships came licking their lips,
And crying out '*Fee, faw,* and *fum ;*'
Bigger each than St. Paul ; guns, the devil and all ;
And, egad, looking wondrous glum.

"But no matter for that, who says pit a pat !
We tack'd, and we stood to the weather ;
We tack'd quite about, right and left, brave and stout,
And so we were sideways together.

"Souls five score and two, maugre all they could do,
We took in a tartan alive ;
Six hundred did sail in the vessel so frail,
But our *hundred* had eat up the *five.*

"But of this by the bye ; for now we drew nigh
To each other—quite close—nay, 'tis true :
Six times two of the line, large, grand, bright, and fine ;
Five frigates !—but look'd rather *blue.*

"Fair Honour, quoth I, in thy arms let me die,
And my glory burn clear in the socket ;
Not an ounce more of powder, or a gun a note louder,
So the d—— [*directions ?*] I put in my pocket.

"Brave W—— [*West*] led the van, I followed amain ;
Such *closing* and *rating*, and work,
With *foresails* and *braces* all flutt'ring in pieces,
'Twould have melted the heart of a Turk.

"But the devil, in spite, to blast our delight,
Got aboard the I——d [*Intrepid*], his daughter,
Made her jump, fly, and stumble, reel, elbow, and tumble,
And drove us quite *out of the water.*

* The despatch was directed to Mr. Cleveland, the Secretary of the Admiralty.

" And now, being tea-time, we thought it was the time
    To talk over what we had done ;
So we put on the kettle, our tempers to settle,—
    And presently set the fair sun.

"Our c——l [*council*] next day, in seemly array,
    Met, sat, and debated the story :
We found that our fleet at last might l e beat,
    And then, you know, *where is the glory ?*

"Moreover, 'twas plain, three ships in the van
    Had their glasses and china all broke ;
And this gave the balance, in spite of great talents,
    Against us,—a damnable stroke !

" Without fear of reproaches, as sound as your roaches,
    Of glory we've saved our whole stock ;
'Twere pity, indeed, to lose it, or bleed,
    For a *toothless old man and a rock.*"

The ministers had sent out two new admirals, Hawke and
Saunders, to take command of the fleet of the Mediterranean.
When Byng learnt that he was recalled, he wrote a recri-
minatory letter to the Admiralty, which increased the fears and
anger of the Government. Orders were immediately des-
patched to Admiral Hawke to place Byng under arrest, and
send him home a prisoner. On his arrival at Portsmouth, the
fury of the mob was so great, that it required a strong guard to
hinder him from being torn to pieces. His effigy had been
already burnt in almost every town in England ; and the
number of pamphlets both serious and burlesque, of satirical
poems and incendiary ballads, of prints and caricatures, that
were launched into the world on this question, during the
autumn and winter, is almost incredible. It was long since the
nation had been in anything like such a state of excitement and
fermentation.

The ministers soon found that they were themselves in
danger of being overwhelmed by the storm which they had
thus conjured up ; for the tide of unpopularity was running
fast against them, especially against Fox and Anson, while Pitt
had become the idol of the multitude. The loss of Oswego,
and some other successes of the French in America, came soon
after to increase the dissatisfaction against the men who were
now openly blamed for their want of foresight, for their
disregard of the American settlements, and for the ignorance
they had exhibited in the direction of the naval force of the
country. One of the popular tracts for street sale, (or, as they
are more technically called, chap-books,) published at this time,
bears the title of " A Rueful Story ; or, Britain in tears : being

the conduct of Admiral B—g. . . . London: Printed by Boatswain Hawl-up, a broken-hearted sailor." A large folding broadside, which serves as a frontispiece, is adorned with a coarse wood-cut, representing Byng in chains, with the ghosts of his slaughtered sailors appearing to him in his prison, and surrounded by doggerel verses; and the body of the tract consists of an inflammatory report of Byng's conduct, in which he is represented as the willing tool of ministerial mismanagement; with the addition of a number of doggerel ballads in the same spirit. One of the more remarkable of the caricatures, published under the title of " The Devil's Dance—set to French music," of which there is a copy in the collection of Mr. Hawkins, represents the trio, Fox, Byng, and Newcastle, with cloven hoofs. Fox, with the head and tail of the animal designated by his name, carries a goose,

FOX AND GOOSE.

the representative of Anson, (by a miserable pun upon his name—*anser* being the Latin for a goose,) and is treading under foot a bundle of papre inscribed, " Honour," " Law," " Justice," " Honesty," " Liberty," " Property." The Duke of Newcastle is trampling on " Magna Charta," and " The Constitution;" while Byng, who is dressed as a French beau, in the highest cut of the fashion, with a *fleur de lis* in his heart, is dancing gaily upon " Port Mahon," and the various treaties and great exploits of former commanders. In another caricature, entitled " A Court Conversation," Fox and Anson, with the heads of a fox and a goose, the latter leaning on a broken anchor, and pointing to the *London Gazette*, are conversing upon the ill success of their attempt to ward off the storm from themselves by garbling the admiral's despatches: the goose-head has an admirably reproachful look.

THE CLOVEN-FOOTED ADMIRAL.

o

"Quoth Anser to Reynard, 'Methinks you had better
Have not made so free with this cursed letter.'
Sly Reynard replied, ' Yet your Lordship must own,
Not Byng had been burnt, if the truth had been known.'"

Behind this group is the council-table, where three of the
members are disturbed by the fall of a picture of the siege
of Port Mahon, which is the cause of the overthrow of the
table. A map of North America hangs covered with cobwebs ;
and a pile of useless subsidiary treaties lie near a " place
and pension ledger."   Byng appears to have been known
at home as a fop and man of fashion, (a class which, as
imitators of French manners, were themselves unpopular with
the mob) and as a great boaster; and it appears that he was a
collector of china-ware, which explains one allusion in the

metrical version of his letter given above.
In another caricature Byng is represented
"at home" and "abroad." In the
first compartment he appears in the
full garb of a "beau," with the
muff, and every other accessory to
that character, exclaiming gaily, "Pray,
my lords, let me go, and I'll perform
wonders."   At the side is a parcel of
china, with the inscription " China-ware-
house."   In the other compartment, Byng
"abroad" is represented in chains, with a
halter round his neck, and beneath him the
inscription a "Lost Sheep." In another
print, entitled "The Contrast," in which
Byng is placed in disadvantageous contrast

THE BEAU ADMIRAL.   with Blakeney, the fatal halter is again an
accessory, and the distich which accom-
panies it appears to bear allusion to the "lost sheep" of the
former.

"'Tis Britannia's doom, here's a halter for B—— ,
As he fought like a *sheep*, like a *dog* let him swing."

In several other caricatures Byng is represented either as
designed for the gallows, or, at least, as worthy of it ; and
in one, entitled "Byng Triumphant," which appears to
have been especially popular, the unfortunate Admiral is conducted in a sort of mock triumph through Temple Bar, on
which the emblems of the traitor's fate are fearfully conspicuous, to the place of execution, hooted and pelted by

the attendant mob of English, Irish, and Scots, while a Frenchman exclaims in astonishment, "Le diable! la monseur le grand monarque no serva Monsieur Gallisouière so as dese, for sava his fleet."

It was the universal opinion, until his character in this respect was cleared by the court-martial, that Byng had behaved with cowardice; but it was almost as generally believed that he had been treacherous to his country,—that French gold had secured the capture of Minorca; and in this charge the ministry bore their full share. A medal* was circulated, representing on the obverse a figure of Admiral Byng receiving a bag of money from a hand belonging to a person concealed, with the inscription,

"Was Minorca sold
By B—— for French gold?"

On the reverse Blakeney is represented holding a flag before a fort, from which three guns are fired, and a ship is seen in the distance. The inscription is,

"Brave Blakeney reward,
But to B—— give a cord."

It was represented that the people who governed the country were so much addicted to French luxuries and French vices, that they would willingly have allowed our enemies to get possession of Minorca, and blink at their encroachment in America, rather than have a war, which would cut off the supplies that peace with France administered to their vanities. A clever caricature appeared on the 25th of November, entitled "Bird-

THE SCRAMBLER OVERTHROWN.

* This medal is in the collection of Mr. Haggard.

ime for Bunglers; or, the French way of catching fools;" in which the French intriguer is emptying out of a large bag, money, mixed with articles labelled "wine," "cooks," "valets," "dancers," "fiddlers," &c. The English ministers are scrambling for the prize. Byng is prostrate, crushed by the weight of the fallen ministers; he grasps in his right hand two articles inscribed "wine" and "2 tartans," the latter an allusion to Byng's captures; while the unlucky Admiral, who has lost his wig in the fall, exclaims, "Oh, the devil take your lime! I am limed and twigg'd too, with a p— to you! Murder! murder! was it for this that I had the pleasure of saving the K——'s ships?" Upon Byng lies Fox, with a bag containing three millions in his left hand, yet still in his prostrate position stretching out his right hand for more. Under his knee is a label inscribed, "Large Fees for the bottomless Pitt;" and he exclaims, "In for a penny, in for a pound; for I find I cannot draw back my paw in time." The Chancellor, Hardwicke, greedily snatches at the money with both hands, exclaiming, in allusion to his marriage bill, "Have not I saved thousands from the lime-twigs of matrimony, and shall not I have my fees?" Underneath the picture is written, "Oh! how the mighty are fallen!" The caricature was, in fact, published when the ministry was in dissolution. The French distributor of these good things observes, "By Gar, dis lime vil stick longer to deir ribs den deir fingers; and, now I ave found de grand secret, I vil not only trap de Anglois, but tout le monde." Behind him stands a figure, evidently intended to represent Newcastle, grasping in his hand a bag containing eight millions, and remarking gravely, "An excellent way, 'faith! I find a Fox may be caught as easily as an old woman." The unpopularity of Fox had in some mea-

THE CANDIDATE ENCUMBERED.

sure relieved Newcastle. On the other side of the picture appears Lord Anson, rushing eagerly to share in the spoils; but, encumbered by an E. O. table, an allusion to his passion for gambling, he cries out, "E. O., my heart of gold, tip us a handfull, for I have had a d——d bad run." Above him is a tablet, "To the memory of A. B. [*Admiral Byng*] May 21st, 1756;" and near it, on the wall of the apartment, the picture of Justice is obscured by an immense cobweb, in which a large spider exclaims,

> " Sure no vast difference betwixt us lies,
> Since you catch men as I catch flies."

Among the numerous caricatures and satirical tracts published during this period of excitement, it will be sufficient to mention the titles of the following :—In September, a caricature, "The Fox in the Pit;" in October, a tract entitled "The Resignation; or, the Fox out of the Pitt, and the Geese in, with B——y at the bottom ;" and two caricatures, "The Auction of the Effects of John Bull" (his foreign possessions offered by his rulers for sale to the highest bidder), and "The Downfall, as it will shortly be performed, to the tune of 'M——y's [*Murray's*] Delight;'" and, in November, a pamphlet, "The History of Reynard the Fox, and Bruin the Bear," &c.

To explain these titles, it will be necessary to state, that, on the 27th of October, Fox, terrified at the approach of the new session of Parliament under such a load of unpopularity, and feeling that he was in danger of becoming a scape-goat to some of his colleagues, resigned his place of Secretary of State. The Duke of Newcastle, in his distress, made overtures to Pitt, who now, in the pride of his own strength and popularity, refused to join in any ministry of which Newcastle formed a part. After several vain attempts to form an administration, the Duke was obliged to resign, and he was immediately followed by the Lord Chancellor, Lord Hardwicke. The King was now placed under the necessity of calling in Pitt, against whom he had always indulged strong hostile feelings. Pitt, who had profited by the experience of the consequence of his former eagerness to accept place, and now determined not to lose his popularity, showed no anxiety to listen to the call, but suddenly took upon himself a fit of the gout. Pitt's demands were at first considered so unreasonable, that a new attempt, equally unsuccessful with the former, was made to raise a ministry without him. At length the King was compelled, much against his inclination, to accept an administration in which Pitt succeeded Fox as principal Secretary of State ; his friend Legge was again made Chancellor of the Exchequer ; his brother-in-law, Lord Temple, succeeded Lord Anson at the Admiralty ; and all the other places were filled up by his friends and partisans. The King opened the

---

* Murray was the Attorney-General, one of the best speakers in the House of Commons, who was now going to the upper House as Lord Chief Justice, under the title of Lord Mansfield, and leaving the ministers to fight their own battles in the Commons.

Parliament at the beginning of December, with a speech far more English in his sentiments than he had ever been made to utter before; and Pitt and Temple thwarted the royal inclination in several of his favourite foreign measures, which were distasteful to the English people. But the ministers joined (probably with foresight) in aiding the King of Prussia, who was now fairly entered into that celebrated war which tore Europe to its entrails during seven years. The new ministry met with considerable opposition, besides being disagreeable to the King; for they were beaten in some of the elections rendered necessary by their accession to office, and even their royal speech was ridiculed in a production of so libellous a character, that it was ordered to be burnt in the Palace Yard by the common hangman, and the printer was thrown into prison. The King, who did not conceal his dislike to his ministers, is said to have expressed his opinion in private society, that the libellous speech was better than the original.

In January, 1757, Admiral Byng was brought to his trial before a court-martial, and was found guilty of not having done the utmost he might have done to perform the duty imposed upon him; and therefore his judges were obliged, by a recently enacted and very oppressive law, to condemn him to be shot to death; but they fully absolved him of having shown any want of courage, and he was strongly recommended to the royal mercy. The utmost exertions were made by the Admiral's friends, and even by many who were not his friends, to obtain his pardon; but the gates of mercy had been already shut to him. The Duke of Newcastle had led the King, when petitioned by the city of London, at the moment of greatest excitement, into a solemn promise that he would allow justice to take its course; and now, on the one side, the ministers who were out were anxious to sacrifice him, in order to turn the blame of misconduct from themselves, while those who were in had not the courage to risk their own popularity by saving him. An agitation was got up in the city, and the King was publicly called upon to fulfil his promise; and on the 3rd of March papers were fixed on the Exchange, with the words "Shoot Byng, or take care of your King." This was commonly ascribed to the emissaries of Lord Anson. At length, after much hesitation, the sentence was carried into execution on board his prison-ship, the Monarque, off Spithead, on Monday, the 14th of March. The feeling of the nation at large, as is always the case when a length of time elapses before the passions of the populace are indulged, had been gradually subsiding, or, at least, people had begun to lose sight of Byng in their anger against the late ministers; and the heroic fortitude with which he met his fate moved universal compassion, and rendered his enemies still more unpopular. People now spoke openly of Byng as the scape-goat of ministerial misconduct, and they pitied and lamented his fate in a number of epigrams and short poems which appeared in the daily prints during several months after his death. We meet also with a caricature, published about this time, entitled "Byng's Ghost to the triumvirate." The triumvirate here represented was composed of Newcastle, Anson, and Hardwicke. But, in speaking of this triumvirate, the name of Fox, at this moment the most unpopular of all the late ministers, commonly took the place of that of Lord Anson. In a print published at this time, the three heads of the Duke of Newcastle, Lord Hardwicke, and Fox are represented joined together in a piece of stone, as a remarkable specimen of a *lusus naturæ*, or "A curious Petri-faction." The allusion is to the Duke of Newcastle's secretary, Andrew *Stone*, who had been appointed sub-governor of the Prince of Wales, and who, accused of Jacobitism, had recently been the cause of high disputes at court: he was looked upon as the Duke's creature; and in a collection of caricatures to which we shall shortly allude, one represents Newcastle as the old woman of the fable riding on his ass, Stone. In the "lusus

A LUSUS NATURÆ.

naturæ," we are told that the two outside faces (Newcastle and Fox) represent "two heads imperfect and of a black hue, suppos'd to have been wood." The one in the middle (Lord Hardwicke) is "a stone head, not esteem'd and very dull." The stone on which they are placed is "a sort of petrified fungus, to which they adhere."

Pitt's popularity had increased in the same extravagant degree that Fox had become unpopular; but during the winter which followed his accession to power he was paralysed by continued attacks of the gout, a disease to which he was constitutionally subject. It was commonly said that Pitt's gout was of a convenient kind, and that its attacks were often assumed as excuses for not attending upon the King, with whose aversion for him he was well acquainted. The public, however, believed otherwise, and they looked with the greatest anxiety for his recovery from what they fancied was the sole impediment to his taking ample vengeance on our foreign enemies for the disasters of the previous year.

> " The land to rescue from impending fate,
> Pitt rose, the smooth-tongued Nestor of the state.
> The world in prospect saw our fame advance,
> Our thunder rolling through the realm of France.
> But heav'n (in mercy to the trembling foe)
> Made the gout seize his senatorial toe.
> Thus, when Tydides swept the ranks of fight,
> And drove opposing hosts to realms of night,
> Swift from young Paris flew a whizzing spear,
> Stopt the stern hero in his foll career,
> Quick gliding, through the foot an entrance found,
> And nailed the bleeding warrior to the ground."

So wrote a poet in the *Gentleman's Magazine* on the 12th of February. At this very time, the King, who hated his ministry the more from the humiliation he felt at having had it forced upon him by the Leicester House faction (for it was the Princess of Wales and her new favourite, the Earl of Bute, who had been chiefly instrumental in forming it), was making a vain attempt in private to form another more to his own taste ; and his determination to get rid of Pitt was fixed by the refusal of the Duke of Cumberland to take the command of the allied army in Hanover while that minister remained in power. The King first tried the Duke of Newcastle, who declined hazarding himself until the public discontent had been allowed time to subside ; he then commanded Fox to form an administration in concert with the Duke of Cumberland. But the plan Fox at first drew up was neither practicable in itself nor altogether satisfactory to the King, on account of the unreasonable demands made by the maker for his own friends and family. When the King had been brought to consent to it, Fox found that only one of the persons he had pitched upon for ministers, Bubb Dodington, would venture to enlist under his banners. The King then, driven to desperation, prevailed upon Lord Winchelsea to take the Admiralty, and dismissed Pitt's brother-in-law, Lord Temple. About a week after this, still urged on by the Duke of Cumberland, the King dismissed Pitt himself, who was followed by his friend Legge and several others, who resigned their offices. The cabinet was now virtually broken up, without even the prospect of a ministry to succeed it. Pitt became at once the idol of the people: a few days after his dismissal, the city of London determined to present the freedom in gold boxes to him and Legge; and the example of London was followed by a number of other cities. People compared Pitt's disinterested patriotism with the time-serving greediness of Fox and his friends; and, among a variety of political epigrams and squibs on the occasion, it was suggested in one that a division of the popular offerings might be made, to the satisfaction of both parties.

> "The two great rivals London might content,
> If what he values most to each she sent;
> If was the franchise coupled with the box;
> Give Pitt the Freedom, and the gold to Fox."

The embarrassment into which the court was now thrown, without a ministry, and unable to form one, and the consequent intrigues within and excitement out of doors, gave rise to a swarm of political squibs and caricatures. Among the most remarkable of the latter was a caricature, said to be by the Hon. George Townshend, published about the middle of April, and entitled "The Recruiting Sergeant." It was intended to ridicule Fox's abortive attempt to form a cabinet, and represents that statement leading his few ill-assorted recruits towards an altar, on which is placed the fat Duke of Cumberland, crowned with laurel. One of the foremost is Winchelsea, who had so readily accepted the Admiralty. Then comes the lean figure of Lord Sandwich, carrying his cricket-bat* on his shoulder, and exclaiming, "I love deep play; this or nothing!" He is followed by Bubb Dodington, who was one of those readiest to take office under Fox, and whose extraordinary corpulence was as remarkable as the leanness of the Earl of Sandwich.

A LEAN RECRUIT.

Bubb, overcome with the fatigue of the march, cries with an imploring look, "I can't follow this lean fellow much longer,

* Lord Sandwich was a noted cricket-player. It may be observed that several copies or imitations of this caricature appeared, and the different characters were also published on separate cards.

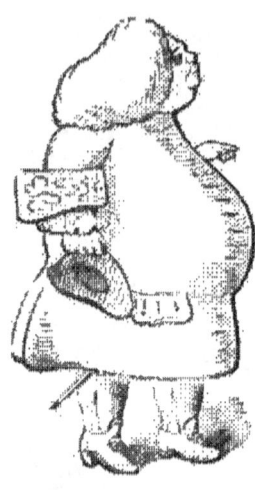

A FAT FOLLOWER.

that's flat."* Early in May was published a pamphlet under the title of "The Chronicle of the short Reign of Honesty," as his admirers called Pitt's administration. In the same month, as we learn from Horace Walpole, came out a bitter caricature against the Pitt party, entitled "The Turnstile." In June, among other satirical prints on the embarrassments in the formation of a ministry, were two, entitled "The Distressed Statesman," and "The Treaty; or Shabear's administration."

The country remained more than eleven weeks without a ministry. At first the King tried some men of inferior rank as statesmen, but met with nothing but refusals; and then he made a new application to the Duke of Newcastle, who attempted a coalition with Pitt and with the Leicester House party. Pitt refused to join in a ministry in which the chief power was not placed in his own hands; upon which Newcastle formed the plan of an administration from which Pitt and his friends were to be entirely excluded; but this also failed. Then followed a new negotiation between Newcastle and Lord Bute for the Leicester House party; and a plan was drawn up, in which Pitt and Lord

* On the 10th of April, Horace Walpole speaks of this caricature in the following terms in a letter to Sir Horace Mann:—

"Pamphlets, cards, and prints swarm again; George Townshend has published one of the latter, which is so admirable in its kind, that I cannot help sending it to you. His genius for likenesses in caricature is astonishing; indeed, Lord Winchelsea's figure is not heightened; your friends Dodington and Lord Sandwich are like; the former made me laugh till I cried. The Hanoverian drummer Ellis, is the least like, though it has much of his air. I need say nothing of the lump of fat, crowned with laurel on the altar. As Townshend's parts lie entirely in his pencil, his pen has no share in them; the labels are very dull except the inscription on the altar, which, I believe, is his brother Charles's. This print, which has so diverted the town, has produced to-day a most bitter pamphlet gainst George Townshend, entitled 'The Art of Political Lying.' Indeed, it is strong."

It is remarkable that two of these figures, those of Bubb Dodington and Lord Winchelsea, were found among the pencil drawings of Hogarth, and engraved in Ireland's "Supplement." Hogarth had written, under Bubb Dodington, "spoil'd," and under Lord Winchelsea "spoil'd also." It may be su pected that Townshend copied the rough sketches of Hogarth.

Temple were to take office with Newcastle, and Fox be excluded;
but the King refused to listen to it. George, now deserted by
every person on whose assistance he had calculated, called Lord
Waldegrave, (who enjoyed his confidence in an especial degree,)
and ordered him to form the best ministry he could. At first
the Dukes of Devonshire and Bedford, the Earl of Winchelsea,
old Lord Granville, and Mr. Fox, were ready to join him; but
after a few days spent in meetings and hesitations, they also
broke down, and left the King entirely at the mercy of Pitt, with
whom and the Duke of Newcastle new negotiations were opened,
which were brought to a conclusion in somewhat more than a
fortnight. On the 29th of June the *Gazette* announced the re-
appointment of Pitt as principal Secretary of State, and he took
office with greater power than ever. The Duke of Newcastle,
with the mere shadow of power, was made First Commissioner
of the Treasury; Anson was placed again at the Admiralty, with
a board composed entirely of Pitt's friends; Lord Granville was
made President of the Council; and Fox, to appease the King,
was made Paymaster of the Forces.

The intrigues and embarrassments of the few months which
intervened between the overthrow of the Duke of Newcastle's
administration in 1756, and the final establishment of Pitt's
power in the summer of 1757, presented, as we have already
hinted, a favourable field for the ingenuity and wit of the caricaturist; and a great number of political prints and, as they
were then termed, cards, were distributed about. These were
often the productions, not of common draughtsmen, but of some
of the distinguished political actors of the day, and especially of
George Townshend. Many of these caricatures appear to have
perished; but two years afterwards upwards of seventy of them
were collected and published on a diminished scale, under the
title of *A Political and Satirical History of the years 1756 and
1757.* These are all directed against the party of Newcastle and
Fox, or rather of Fox and Newcastle, for Fox was now generally
looked upon as the leading man in the old ministry; and the
bitterness of political rancour is shown in the constant allusions
to the axe and the rope. In one, by the side of the heads of
Fox and Newcastle stand two gallowses, entitled the "Pillars of
the State," supporting a reversed ship with a cock crowing over
it—the navy of England made a sacrifice to the vanity of France.
The four most obnoxious ministers, Newcastle, Fox, Hardwicke,
and Anson, were published under the characters of the four
knaves of cards. In a caricature entitled "Punch's Opera, with
the Humours of Little Ben the Sailor," are hung up the wooden

figures of Anson with his box and dice, in the character of Little Isn; Sir George Littleton, as Gudgeon; Fox, as Mr. Punch; Newcastle, as Punch's wife Joan; and Hardwicke as Quibble. They are all *semée* (to use the heraldic expression) with *fleurs-de-lis*, to shew the popular belief in their devotion to French interests. Sir George Littleton (created Lord Littleton in the spring of 1757, by which title he obtained a distinguished place in English literature) had provoked the enmity of the popular party by deserting to the ministerial side a few months before, and his eccentric figure, as well as his weaknesses and vanities, offered a ready butt for satire. In one print the portrait of this orator of the party (for after Fox he was looked upon as one of their better speakers in the House of Commons) is caricatured under the name of *Cassius*. In another he is drawn at full length, proffering the support of his tongue, and declaring that

CASSIUS.

"What oratory can do shall be done ;
But then, good sir, you know I am but one."

The influence of French councils (and even of French gold) on this side of the Channel, is a frequent subject of satire in this collection of prints, and the figures of the Duke of Newcastle and his ministers seldom appear without the characteristic mark of the *fleur-de-lis*. In one caricature, Newcastle, Fox, and Byng are represented as entrapped into their own destruction by golden baits laid before them by the evil one. In another, the ministers have addressed Britannia in gawdy French garments of the newest fashion, which fit so tight, that she complains of being unable to move her arms. Newcastle, as her *femme-de-chambre*, tells her that she has no need to move her arms, since there is nothing for her to do. Fox offers her a *fleur de-lis*, as a becoming ornament to place over her breast. Two pictures are suspended in the room, one that of an axe, the other representing a halter, the rewards of traitorous ministers. Poor Britannia is indeed cruelly baited with the various vanities and vices of her governors. In one caricature she is seated in a chariot, drawn by geese and turkeys, and driven by the devil. Britannia is getting

angry, as she reflects upon her ridiculous position; while a
Frenchman by the way-side is clapping his hands and laughing
at her. Among the patrician extravagances of the year 1756,
Lord Rockingham and Lord Orford had made a match of 500l.,
about the middle of October, between five turkeys and five geese,
to run from Norwich to London. The geese and the turkeys
were easily seized upon by the caricaturists, and were applied to
the statesmen of that day with persevering ingenuity. In
others of these prints the ministers are bitterly attacked for
sending out money instead of men to fight our battles abroad,
for bringing foreign troops into this country, and for their
neglect of the navy, the natural defence of Great Britain. Their
ill-arranged and ill-directed armaments are burlesqued in a caricature entitled "The Triumph of Neptune." The ship "The
Old England," in a dreadful state of dilapidation, with the word
"neglect" under it, is seen out at sea, with three French sail in
the distance. Winchelsea, as the head of the Admiralty in one
of the attempted ministerial combinations, is putting out to sea
in a tub, in tow of "The Old England." A personage swimming
behind him, apparently intended to represent the Duke of New-

A GRAND EXPEDITION.

castle, cries " Hard a port, Sir! Blood! you run all to leeward!"
Winchelsea replies, "Don't you see I am in tow, and the wind
sits exactly as it did when Matthews and Lestock did the
thing?"* Another personage, who swims in front of the tub,
with a speaking-trumpet, hails Fox, who is perched on the poop
of the ship, " Huzza! all we; we shall soon head the French if
we hold on! Keep your loof, Reynard, we have the weather
gage." The Fox replies, "Thus and no nearer." The fat

* An allusion to the ill-conducted naval expedition to the Mediterranean,
when Lord Winchelsea was at the head of the Admiralty in 1743, which
ended in a quarrel between the two admirals.

figure of Bubb Dodington is seen sinking in the sea, and crying
out for help: "Oh! oh! I'll give it up. Help! help! or I
sink!" Beneath the group is inscribed the distich,—

> "Will France pretend to face us now?
> No, no, not they, by Jove! Bow, wow!"

Anson is treated with great severity in these caricatures, and
his gambling propensities are made the most of; while the attacks upon his unfortunate victim, Admiral Byng, are equally
severe. In one, the Admiral is represented letting the cat out
of the bag against his employers, (which he had made bold
threats of doing:) the ministers are in a panic, none of them
quite sure on whom the enraged animal will fix itself; but Fox
shews the greatest terror, and rushes to the door, exclaiming,
"S' blood! open the door! Let me out, or I'll break out!"—an
allusion to his resignation, the first signal of the dissolution of
the ministry of which he had formed so prominent a part. His
rival Pitt appears everywhere triumphing over him, and raised
up on the favour of his countrymen,—the patriotic statesman.
In a caricature entitled "The Fox in the Pit," Justice riding
upon Integrity is pursuing Fox, who falls into a deep *pit*,
weighed down by a heavy sack inscribed "£8,000,000," in allusion to Fox's known eagerness for the spoils of office. In
another, the motto of which is "*Magna est veritas, et præva-
lebit*," Pitt alone in one scale is made to weigh down a whole
scale-full, including Newcastle, Fox, Hardwicke, Anson, and
Littleton. The volume concludes with a portrait of the popular
orator, with Justice and Truth for his supporters.

These hot political contentions gave birth to two or three
periodical papers, among which the most remarkable was the
Test, commenced on the 6th of November, 1756, under the
editorship of, and chiefly written by, Arthur Murphy. This
paper, an organ of the ex-ministers, was a barefaced and violent
attack upon Pitt; and was followed by another paper, on the
other side, entitled the *Con-Test*, which attacked Fox in a
manner no less outrageous. Horace Walpole observes, with
justice, that the virulence of these papers made him "recollect
Fogs and *Craftsmen* as harmless libels." The *Test*, in its
weekly attacks upon the "unembarrassed orator," raked up all
his old political offences, and even made his constitutional gout
an object of sarcastic burlesque. In one paper, about the beginning of 1757, it satirised his pretensions to political skill under
the character of a quack doctor, by the name of Gulielmo Bom-

basto de Podagra, in allusion to his oratory and to his gout, and he is made to put forth the following

"*Advertisement.*

"Lately arived in this town the celebrated *Gulielmo Bombasto de Podagra*, the most renowned physician now in Europe. He hath made the system of the animal œconomy his study for many years past: he restores health and vigour to a decayed constitution, makes an old body young, and gives firmness and strength to *weak members*; and promises instant relief in all cases whatever—the more difficult the better.

"N.B.—As the doctor *does not love money*, he gives his advice *gratis*. Beware of *counterfeits*, for such are abroad."

It is further added, in allusion to his almost constant confinement by the gout during the session, "P.S.—The doctor receives visits in bed." Among the "cases" which are given as proofs of the physician's skill, the following may be cited as an example:—

"John Bull had eat too much *Newcastle salmon*, was troubled with a *Stone*,[*] contracted a scorbutic habit by a voyage round the world,[†] and was held by his lawyer:[‡] to be non compos mentis. His friends advised him to have recourse to exercise, and follow a *Fox*, without suffering himself, as heretofore, to be thrown out, but to see the *Fox* frequently. Doctor Bombasto being sent for, ordered him to abstain entirely from *Newcastle salmon*, unless *he had* a mind to have the *jowl*, and absolutely forbad him ever to see a *Fox*. He then prescribed quiet to the old gentleman, and promised to go to bed for him; which *he* accordingly did: and we hear from *White's* that the knowing ones have *pitted* the old gentleman against the most healthy person now in Europe."

The virulence of the *Test* is especially exhibited in its attacks upon Byng, who was made an object of cruel ridicule, even while he lay under sentence of death. On the 20th of March, when the ministerial interregnum was commencing, it attacked Pitt's pride and haughtiness in the following paragraph:—

"*Minutes of one of a Great Man's Valetudinarian Soliloquies.*

"*Yes, I dare, I dare, I dare! I am exceedingly glorious, even beyond the scale of intellectual beings.*—I will not henceforward use any word that is not compounded.—What! *do the wretches kick at the draught?* They shall swallow it; and yet I must keep some measures with them—at the next audience they shall kiss my slipper—but who first? Sir John—or the alderman?—Let the reptiles adjust their own ceremonies.—I am tired of trampling on such bare necks.—The neck of the most august is the best remedy for an inflamed toe.—. . . . . [*Hiatus valde deflendus.*]

---

* An allusion to Andrew Stone, Newcastle's private secretary, mentioned above, and who now and subsequently was active in the undercurrent of the political intrigues of the day.

† An allusion to Lord Anson.

‡ Lord Chancellor Hardwicke.

The thirty-fifth number of the *Test* was published on the 9th of July, 1757, after which time it was discontinued, for the men it advocated were nearly all taken into Pitt's ministry.

The difficulty of forming a ministry being settled, people began again to turn their thoughts to foreign affairs; for the spirit of the nation had been growing more warlike amid its partial reverses and disappointments. Hogarth gratified this rising spirit in 1756 by his two prints of "France" and "England;" in the former of which the Frenchmen are represented roasting frogs and preparing for their threatened invasion of England, that threat which had so entirely misled the Duke of Newcastle and his colleagues. The French standard bears the inscription, "*Vengence et le bon bier et bon beuf de Angletere;*" and the still existing horror of Popery represented the invaders as bringing over with them all the instruments of persecution. In the other print, the alacrity with which recruits joined the standard of their country, to resist the invader, appears in a youth apparently under age and under height, who is doing his best to prove his qualifications. The courage which was believed to animate the nation at this conjuncture is shewn by the manner in which they turned to

A WILLING RECRUIT.

THE PATRIOTIC PAINTER.

ridicule their expected invaders: a merry group are looking on whilst a soldier is drawing a caricatured figure of King Louis holding a gallows in his hand; and on a label issuing from his mouth are written the words, " You take my fine ships, you be de pirates, you be de tiefes! Me send my grand armies and hang you all ! Morblu !" It is hardly necessary to say that this is a satire upon the memorial of the French king to the English ministers on the captures made by our ships.

There was, nevertheless, during this period much discontent throughout the country, which was increased by a prevailing scarcity of corn and provisions, and which made people lay hold of the slightest cause for complaint. The importation of a body of Hanoverian troops as a defence against the expected invasion was loudly reprobated; and the somewhat severe law passed at this time for the protection of game was represented as an expedient for disarming the people, under pretence of forbidding the keeping of guns for poaching, and thus rendering them incapable of resisting Hanoverian tyranny. Yet, singularly enough, when the Militia Act was passed, and the country was placed under the protection of a truly constitutional force, that was looked upon popularly as an act of insupportable tyranny, and in many counties the attempt to put it in force was the signal for alarming riots. The gin question had also risen again into notoriety, and during the latter years of the reign of George II. there had been going on a vigorous contest between two parties, on the relative effects of gin-drinking and beer-drinking. Gin has been long the bane of society among the lower classes in London. In 1751 appeared a revived print of the " Funeral Procession of Madame Geneva." The same year Hogarth attacked the prevalent vice in his two prints of " Beer Street" and " Gin Lane," the latter of which is a fine but revolting picture of the horrible consequences of the facility given to the sale of spirituous liquors, for the heavy prohibitive duties established in the time of Sir Robert Walpole had now been taken off. A new law was passed restricting the granting of licences, which seems to have had little effect in correcting the evil. A caricature was published in 1752, entitled " A Modern Contrast," which appears to have been designed as a satire on the

ENGLISH BEER.

F

Government for its interference, and represents a licensed seller of good English beer, the wholesome effects of which are shewn in the plumpness of the landlord and his wife, exulting over a dealer in spirituous liquors, who is seized for selling without licence, and his family turned out and his liquor staved. The beer-drinkers carouse without fear, but the gin-drinkers are in distress; and poor Justice lies prostrate in the street, in a state of total drunkenness. Under the peculiar political bias of the day, every subject of discontent was in some way or other identified with the popular hatred of the French. Thus, it was said that beer was the natural beverage of Englishmen, and that wine and spirituous liquors were more French inventions, calculated to corrupt and destroy British bravery and patriotism. A song was very popular in the May of the year 1757, under the title of

"THE BEER-DRINKING BRITON.

" Ye true honest Britons, who love your own land,
  Whose sires were so brave, so victorious, and free ;
Who always beat France when they took her in hand—
  Come join, honest Britons, in chorus with me.
      Let us sing our own treasures, Old England's good cheer,
      The profits and pleasures of stout British beer ;
      Your wine-tippling, dram-sipping fellows retreat,
      But your beer-drinking Britons can never be beat !

" The French with their vineyards are meagre and pale,
  They drink of the squeezings of half-ripen'd fruit ;
But we who have hop-grounds to mellow our ale,
  Are rosy and plump, and have freedom to boot,
      Let us sing our own treasures, &c.

" Should the French dare invade us, thus arm'd with our poles,
  We'll bang their bare ribs, make their lanthorn-jaws ring.
For your beef-eating, beer-drinking Britons are souls
  Who will shed their last blood for their country and king.
      Let us sing our own treasures, &c."

There was, however, a commercial interest involved in this question, which it was necessary to consider. In 1758, at the moment when the scarcity of corn was felt most severely, a bill was passed hastily through the House for the temporary prohibition of its exportation and of the distillation of spirits, which it was believed tended much to increase the scarcity. In 1760 the question of continuing or repealing this law as far as regarded distillation was discussed with considerable animosity. Petitions were got up in the country, stating that since the prohibition the lower orders had become more sober, healthy, and industrious ; and it was observed by grand juries in the metropolis, that not only had individual cases of violence, murder, and suicide followed the use of spirituous liquors in numerous instances, but that the gin-shops were known to be the constant harbour of highwaymen and rogues of every description, and that some of the most extensive robberies of the time had been planned in them. The malt-distillers made their counter-petitions, and, besides shewing the inexpediency of the prohibition in a commercial point of view, and as it affected the revenue, they represented that the excessive use of malt liquors might bo as injurious to the moral character of the population as gin-drinking, yet no person ever thought of prohibiting the practice of brewing in order to prevent the use of ale. The dispute was carried on with some warmth; a number of pamphlets were published on both sides; the old prints against gin became popular again, and new ones were added to them, among which was one, which appeared in January, entitled "Beelzebub's Oration to the Distillers." Public opinion, indeed, appeared to be against the distillers, and the prohibition was continued.

The ill-concerted measures of the Newcastle administration, for the defence of the country and the defeat of its enemies, had become an object of derision to all people of sense, and had made all feel the necessity, under the present circumstances, of a more vigorous government. It is true that England had fleets; but her sailors were ill-fed and neglected, and were commanded by officers who had obtained their promotion by money and court favour, and most of whom were distinguished rather by their foppery, or ignorance of naval affairs, than by any of the requisite qualifications of a naval commander. He who would understand the character of the English navy in the middle of the last century, must study it in the novels of Smollett. The uncertain kind of hostilities which had been carried on during the latter part of 1755, and the beginning of 1756, had given satisfaction to none, for it had exposed the country to all the inconveniences of war, without any of its advantages. Even the prizes were not allowed to be confiscated for the benefit of the captors, but were placed under embargo until the two governments of England and France should choose to determine whether they were really at war or at peace. A caricature, already alluded to, published November 13th, 1755, and entitled "Half-War," ridicules this state of things under the figure of an Englishman, who is committing an assault upon a Frenchman, from whom he is snatching rolls of paper inscribed "Merchantmen" and "Nova Scotia." The Englishman exclaims, "By way of reprisals only!" and the Frenchman, instead of defending himself, is satisfied with the reflection, "Westphalia

shall pay for this!" for the French seemed more intent on
making acquisitions in Germany, than on resenting the insults

HALF-WAR.

to which their flag had been subjected at sea. In the background are seen the different European powers, looking on in
expectation of English subsidies. The inscription at the bottom
of the print, " By our own native foreiguers betray'd," exhibits
the popular belief that the backwardness of the rulers of the
destiny of Britain at that time in making war, had for its only
motive the fear that it would cut off the supply of the
foreign luxuries which they valued more than the honour of
their country. Under these circumstances, it is not surprising
that Pitt's popularity as a minister was established by the
energy which distinguished his foreign policy. He soon gave
full scope to the warlike spirit of the country; and, as he had
silenced opposition by admitting into his ministry the chiefs of
the different parties, he found no further obstructions to his will.
He pacified and conciliated the King, by giving a greater support than ever to his German politics; while he carried into our
other foreign relations that vigour and activity which had been
so signally wanting under his predecessors. William Pitt, indeed, was the minister of war, as Walpole had been the minister
of peace. Yet the first hostile operations under Pitt's administration were singularly unsuccessful. The Duke of Cumberland
had, at the commencement of his father's ministerial embarrassments, gone over to Hanover to take the command of the con-
federate army assembled for the defence of the electorate. The
Duke took the field towards the end of April. After a number

of unskilful movements and useless skirmishes, he retired before the French, and passed the Weser; and on the 26th of July he was totally defeated in the battle of Hastenbeck. The French now became virtually masters of Hanover; and the Duke of Cumberland, allowing himself, by his want of foresight, to be driven into a corner from which he could not escape, was compelled on the 7th of September to sign the disgraceful convention of Closter-Seven, by which the electorate was to be left in the hands of the French till the conclusion of a peace, and the Hanoverian army was to lay down its arms, and be dispersed into different cantonments, under the obligation of remaining inactive during the rest of the war. King George, although he is said to have privately authorized this transaction, expressed openly the greatest anger; and the Duke of Cumberland came home, resigned all his appointments, and retired from an active part in the political intrigues. The name of Hanover was far from popular in England, and the Duke's disastrous campaign soon became a subject of scorn and ridicule.

A GENERAL IN DISTRESS.

In one of the bitter caricatures published on this occasion, a Frenchman is seen on one side of a river, carrying off a horse, the emblem of Hanover; while on the opposite bank the portly figure of the Duke exclaims in dismay, "My horse! my horse! a kingdom for a horse!" The Frenchman retorts by promising to give the horse something "better than turnips." It had been for some years a standing joke to call Hanover the King's *turnip-field;* and in another caricature Hanover is represented as the city of *Turnipolis,* on the bank of a river, on one side of which the French general with his troops, in pursuit, invites the Duke to halt,—"Sar, sar, mon ami! Vat! you no stay for me? Stay one little vile, den I come." The Duke, carrying a standard with the Hanoverian emblem of the horse, is running at his utmost speed on the other side of the river (the Weser, of course), and exclaims, "Oh! for my recruiting-sergeant, with more men and money!" The *recruiting-sergeant* was Fox, in whom, as minister, the Duke of Cumberland had placed his confidence. In a third caricature on the Duke's disaster, the city, placed in the same position as in the foregoing, has over it the inscription, "Save our turnips, oh!"

Another failure came almost at the same moment to increase the popular excitement, and was also made the subject of ridicule and caricature. Pitt had hoped to distract the attention of the French from Germany, by making a descent on their coast nearer home, and in the summer a secret expedition was sent out, with much mystery, against the town of Rochefort; but, owing to disagreement among the commanders, the fleet returned home at the beginning of October, without having achieved any of the objects for which it was sent. The consequence was another court-martial, which ended in the acquittal of those who were brought to trial. Pitt had gained strength by the mishaps of the Duke of Cumberland in Hanover, and his popularity was now so firmly established, that the blame of the failure of the naval expedition was easily thrown from his own shoulders upon the agents who conducted it. The successes of the King of Prussia emboldened the King of England to break the convention of Closter-Seven, on pretext of the outrages committed by the French, and the electorate was soon recovered out of their hands. The nation was cheered by the intelligence of great and substantial advantages gained by our armies in India; and Pitt was taking active steps to secure our possessions in America. The two following years presented a constant succession of victories by sea and land, which shed an unusual glory on the administration of William Pitt, while they ruined the finances of France at home, destroyed her navy and her commerce, and stripped her of her distant colonies. In 1758 the French settlements in Senegal were captured by a small English force; Cape Breton was recovered from the French; and other advantages were gained on the continent of America. In 1759 the French Islands in the West Indies were taken possession of; the capture of Quebec, by the brave but ill-fated Wolfe, made England master of North America; the victories of Boscawen and Hawke completed the destruction of the French navy; and the British empire in India had been firmly established by the wonderful successes of Clive, and the brave officers who were acting with him. The expulsion of the French from North America was in a measure Pitt's own work; and, as Wolfe was one of his own military *protégés*, the public exultation on the taking of Quebec raised still higher the minister who had planned it. The battle of Minden added to the glory of the British arms on the continent of Europe. In the beginning of 1760 rumours had already spread abroad of approaching negotiations of peace; and the English people, in their exultation at the extensive conquests of the last two years, began to express their fears lest any of these advantages should be relinquished, in the same manner in which it was believed that so much had been unnecessarily surrendered in former treaties.

It was in the midst of this glory of conquest that George the Second quitted the stage. He died suddenly and quite unexpectedly, on the morning of the 25th of October, 1760, leaving his family at length firmly established on the throne of England.

CHAPTER VII.

GEORGE II. AND III.

Progress of Literature : Magazines and Reviews ; Dr. Hill—The Reign of Pertness—Prevalence of Quackery and Credulity : the Bottle Conjuror ; the Earthquake ; the Cock Lane Ghost—The Stage and the Opera : Garrick and Quin ; Handel ; Foote—Influence of French Fashions ; National Extravagance, and Social Condition—Exaggerated Fashions in Costume : Hoop-Petticoats and Great Head-Dresses : the Macaronis—Neglect of Literature, and Quarrels of Authors : Hogarth and Churchill ; Smollett ; Johnson ; Chatterton.

LITERATURE continued to experience the neglect of the court through the whole of the reign of George II., and it had been entirely excluded from the palace after the death of Queen Caroline. Some countenance was, it is true, shewn to literary men in the opposition court of Leicester House, but it was rather a parade of patronage, than an efficient or judicious encouragement, and produced little more than a few panegyrical odes. At the same time the literary taste of the day was gradually improving, and it was spreading and strengthening itself in new classes of publications. The newspapers had long been in the habit of devoting a portion of their space to literature, in a form somewhat resembling the French *fruilletons* of the present day, but this was most frequently filled with burlesque, ill-natured criticism, or half-concealed scandal ; or, when such productions were harmless, they were of so dull and flimsy a character, as to give us a very low estimate of the taste of the readers who could receive any satisfaction from their perusal. The *Gentleman's Magazine*, the first attempt at a monthly repository of this kind, was begun by Cave, in 1731 ; its main object at first being to give a summary of the better literary essays which had appeared in the more perishable form of the daily and weekly press, although this part of the plan was soon made subservient to the publication of original papers. This magazine was looked upon as belonging politically to the Whig party, then in the plenitude of power under Sir Robert Walpole, and the *London Magazine* was immediately set up in opposition to it. The success of these two publications led in the course of a few years to a number of imitations, and in 1750 we count no less than eight periodicals of this description, issued monthly, under the titles of the *Gentleman's Magazine*, the *London Magazine*, the *British Magazine*, the *Universal Magazine*, the *Travellers' Magazine*, the *Ladies' Magazine*, the *Theological Magazine*, and the *Magazine of Magazines*. The latter was an attempt, by giving the pith of its monthly contemporaries, to do the same by them as the *Gentleman's Magazine* had first done by the newspapers.

With these periodicals there gradually grew up a new class of writers, known as the Critics. The magazines had from the first given monthly lists of new books, and these lists were subsequently accompanied by short notices of the contents and merits of the principal new publications, while longer notices and abstracts of remarkable works were given as separate articles. This was the origin of the reviews, in the modern sense of the title, which were becoming fashionable in the middle of the last century. In the year 1752 there were three professed reviews, the *Literary Review*, the *Monthly Review*, and the *Critical Review*, the latter by the celebrated Smollett. The critics formed a self-constituted tribunal, which the authors long regarded with feelings of undisguised hostility ; and an unpalatable review was often the source of bitter quarrels and desperate paper-wars. Their design was looked upon as an unfair attempt to control the public taste. There can be little doubt, however, that the establishment of reviews had an influence in improving the literature of the country.

About the same time that the reviews began to be in vogue, the periodical essayists came again into fashion, and a multitude of that class of publications represented in its better features by the *Adventurers, Connoisseurs, Ramblers*, &c., that have outlived the popularity of the day, were launched into the world, most of them combining political partisanship with a somewhat pungent censorship of the foibles and vices of the age. This class of periodicals became most numerous soon after the accession of George III. Besides the personal abuse with which many of them abounded, they published a large mass of private scandal, which was perfectly well understood, in spite of the fictitious names under which it was issued, and which formed probably the most marketable portion of the literature of the day. Even in the highest class of the romances of that age, those of Smollett and Fielding, as well as in a multitude of memoirs and novels of a lower description, the greatest charm for the reader consisted in the facility with which he recognised the pictures of well-known individuals, whose private weaknesses were there cruelly brought to light in false or exaggerated colours. It was this peculiar taste in literature which gave the character to the mode of life of that class of writers who then lived by their pen: their days and nights were spent in the coffee-house, the theatre, or the rout, in raking up scandalous anecdotes and intrigues, which they lost no time in drawing up for the papers, which were in daily readiness to receive them. Among the earlier of the essayists of the class alluded to was the *Inspector*, which first brought into notoriety the celebrated Sir John Hill, the "orator Henley" of the literature of his day, who may be taken as the type of the literary quackery of the age of which we are now speaking. The *original* orator Henley was just quitting the scene in which he had gained so much celebrity—he died in 1757.

John Hill was born in 1716. His father, who was a clergyman, placed him as apprentice with a surgeon at Westminster, and, having married early, he set up for himself in that profession, but soon dissatisfied with it, he applied himself to the study of botany, and obtained the patronage of the Duke of Richmond and Lord Petre. This pursuit he also relinquished, and he next applied himself to the stage, and made several unsuccessful attempts as an actor at Drury Lane, and the little theatre in the Haymarket; in the latter of which he performed the part of the quack-doctor in "Romeo and Juliet." He afterwards indulged the spleen occasioned by this failure by decrying the best actors of the day, and he wrote a book on the art, under the title of "The Actor," chiefly with this object. Hill now returned to surgery and botany, and was taken up by Martin Folkes, the president, and some other leading members, of the Royal Society, and under their auspices published, in 1746, a tolerably well-executed translation of Theophrastus on Gems. He became thus introduced to the booksellers, and was employed to write a Natural History in three folio volumes, to compile a supplement to Chambers's Dictionary, and then to edit the *British Magazine*. With the latter Hill set up in the full character of a popular writer, and at the same time broke with his patrons in science. On the publication of his Supplement to Chambers, he made an attempt to obtain admission into the Royal Society; but, his unprincipled character being now well known, he was rejected, and, in revenge, abused Folkes and his former friends, and attacked the Society in a scurrilous review of its publications, and published a hoax upon it in a clever though ridiculous pamphlet (under the pseudonym of Abraham Johnson) entitled "Lucina sine Concubitu," in which he pretended to shew that generation might take place without the intercourse of the sexes.

This book made some noise at the time, and gave birth to several other pamphlets. Hill now obtained a foreign diploma of doctor in medicine, drove about in his chariot, and took upon himself all the airs of a fashionable author. His overweening vanity made him an object of ridicule: he strutted about with an affected air, was a regular attendant at the theatres and places of amusement, exhibited himself at the fashionable lounges, aped the manners of a fop, and *pretended* to enjoy the favours of ladies of quality. Yet he was a ready and prolific writer, and he now attempted to shine in almost every walk of literature, as well as in science. The so oft parodied lines were again applied to him, in connexion with orator Henley and a noted quack of the time named Rock :—

> " Three great wise men in the same era born,
> Britannia's happy Island did adorn :
> Henley in cure of souls displayed his skill,
> Rock shone in physic, and in both John Hill ;
> The force of nature could no farther go,
> To make a third she join'd the other two."

Of his lighter productions, the " Memoirs of Lady Frail" (a false history of the frailties of Lady Hurriet Vane) made considerable noise. In fact, no writer was so unscrupulous as Hill in publishing private scandal, and in adding to it from his own invention. After a while he was seized with a passion of writing for the stage ; but it was not till 1758, that he prevailed on Garrick to bring out his farce of " The Rout," which was damned on the second night. Garrick's epigram on the occasion will not soon be forgotten :—

> " For physic and farces, his equal there scarce is :
> His farces are physic, his physic a farce is. "

Perhaps no man was ever so bold an adept in literary quackery as Dr. Hill. As if with the intention of throwing all his contemporary essayists in the shade, he commenced, in the spring of 1752, a *daily* essay, under the title of the *Inspector*, which was first published in the *Daily Advertiser*, and was afterwards collected into two octavo volumes. During this year the pen of Dr. Hill was so active, that he is said to have cleared by his writings no less a sum than fifteen hundred pounds ! Some of the *Inspectors* consisted of essays on subjects connected with natural history (especially of microscopic observations), described in an absurdly conceited and pompous style.* On the

* In some of his scientific (!) essays in the *Inspector*, Dr. Hill attained the very perfection of the *bathos.* Some of his antagonists delighted in

Saturday of each week he gave a sort of moral discourse, intended to be suitable for the following day. But many of the essays were composed of the scandal which he had gathered up in his daily or nightly perambulation of the town; others contained unprovoked and unjust attacks on his contemporaries; in some he hinted at his own successes among ladies of quality; and by no means unfrequently he wrote letters to himself, setting forth in no measured terms the praise of his own talents and virtues. It is not to be wondered at if he thus provoked hostility in every quarter. One of the first persons who shewed his resentment was Woodward, the actor, who went to George's coffee-house with the intention of giving Hill a public castigation; but missing his man, he first published a violent pamphlet against him, in which he made public all his early disappointments in seeking stage notoriety, and then he brought him on the stage in a farce under the character of the " Mock Doctor."* Another quarrel took a still more serious character. The *Inspector* of the 30th of April embodied a scurrilous attack upon an Irish gentleman of the name of Brown, giving, as usual, a distorted account of some private transactions, and holding up that gentleman in the character of a rake, a coxcomb, and a coward. Although Brown's name was not mentioned, the allusions could not be mistaken, and he called upon Dr. Hill for an explanation. The latter made a shuffling answer, treated Brown with insolence, and in another *Inspector* gave a vain-glorious account of his own conduct, and treated the character of his offended antagonist with greater contempt than ever, accusing him, among other things, of being so illiterate that he could not write his mother-tongue correctly. On the evening of the 6th of May Brown went to Ranelagh, and meeting Dr. Hill in the passage, he demanded proper satisfaction for the attack, and, on this being refused, insulted him publicly by pulling him by the ear. Dr. Hill made a great uproar, procured a warrant against his

pointing out descriptions like the following. Speaking of a little stream or ditch : " The translucent waves coursed one another down the light declivity, with an inexpressibly pleasing variety of form, and a confused but very soft noise of bubbling, lashing, and murmuring, among, against, and along the inequalities and meanders of its rough sides and various hollows." Of a pond : " The surface of the basin was a polished plane, unfurrowed by the least motion, unruffled by the gentlest breeze ; the setting sun threw a glow of pale splendour over one half of it, the rest was silent shade." Of weeds, &c. gathered to one corner of a ditch : " The fresh breeze had blown together into this part of the watery expanse whatever floated on or near its surface," &c.

* The " Mock Doctor" was given repeatedly at Drury Lane in 1751 or 1752.

assailant, pretended that an attempt had been made to murder
him, that he had been overpowered by numbers and beaten till
he was seriously injured, and took to his bed. Brown surrendered himself to the magistrate, and, it being stated that Dr.
Hill was in no danger, he was allowed to give bail for his appearance on a future day, to answer any charge brought against him;
and, when that day arrived, no one appearing against him, he
was discharged. But Dr. Hill and his friends published and
spread abroad sedulously all kinds of false statements, magnifying his own courage and the brutality of his pretended assailants, and making up a story that was aptly compared with Fal-
staff's relation of his encounter with the redoubtable men in
buckram.. The affair made an extraordinary noise, and a multitude of pens and pencils were raised against the unpopular
Doctor. On the 29th of May two large caricatures were published; the first of which represents a view of the entrance to
Ranelagh, in which Brown is seen pulling the car of the Doctor,
whom he addresses with the words, "Draw your sword, swag-
gerer! if you have the spirit of a mouse!" Hill replies,
"What? 'gainst an illiterate fellow, that can't spell! I prefer
a drubbing;" and imploringly calls for constables. Two of
these are seen hastening to the spot, between whom the following brief conversation takes place : " 'Zounds, Dick, the I———r
[*Inspector*] has no money to pay us withal!"—"No matter,
Tom; we'll swear through thick and thin to put him in cash."
In the other print the Inspector is shewn in bed, the subject of
a consultation of doctors, and supposed to be near his end.
They are probably portraits of some of the eminent medical
practitioners of the day. They seem to be embarrassed with his
case, but above all unwilling to let him off without paying his fees,
while a friend proposes that he should raise money by selling
his sword, which is " only an encumbrance." It was said that
Hill produced a quantity of blood, which he pretended that he
had lost by the injuries inflicted upon his person at Ranelagh.
In the picture before us the face of a man is peeping from behind
the bed, and interrogating another who is entering by the door:
" Dick, did you get the three basons of blood we sent you for ?"
The latter informs him, with some concern, " Lord, sir, we're
out of luck ! Fay, whom you and I swore against, went to Ireland three weeks before the affair happened." About the bed
and the floor are a number of labels, with inscriptions relating
to Hill's pusillanimous conduct and assumed danger. The print
is entitled " Le Malade Imaginaire ; or, the consultation." A
satirical tract against Hill (under the fictitious appellation of

Dr. Atall) appeared about the same time, parodying the title of one of his own books by that of "Libitina sine Conflictu; or, a true narrative of the untimely death of Dr. Atall, who departed this life on Wednesday the 13th of May, 1752 : with some account of his behaviour during his illness." This tract gives a burlesque account of the whole affair, and intimates that it was probably a deeply-laid plot of the French government to get out of the way a political writer of such overwhelming importance as the English Inspector.

Although this affair had turned greatly to Dr. Hill's disgrace, it put no check upon his personal criticisms. Among others who were outraged by his pen were Fielding and Garrick, the latter of whom he attempted to depreciate in comparison with his rival Quin. Fielding, under the assumed name of Sir Alexander Drawcansir, in retaliation, commenced the *Covent Garden Journal,* in which he treated the character of Dr. Hill with the greatest contempt, and proclaimed a general war against the old forces of Grubb Street, and the new squadron of the critics headed by Smollett. It was a spirited attack on the depraved popular taste. These literary quarrels always merged into the great rivalries of the day, and such was the case in the present instance; for Fielding not only entered on a crusade against Hill and literary quackery, but he took up the cudgels for Garrick and Drury Lane against Quin and Rich, who occupied the rival stage at Covent Garden. Dr. Hill also found partisans

THE INSPECTOR GLORIFIED.

to support him. As the Inspector had been brought on the stage in one theatre, so now there was performed on the boards at Covent Garden, "A new dramatic satire, called 'Covent Garden Theatre; or, Pasquin turned Drawcansir, censor of Great Britain.'" A scurrilous opposition paper was also started, under the title of *Have at you all; or, the Drury Lane Journal.* The *Covent Garden Journal* was carried on for several months, until Fielding's declining health obliged him to relinquish it: he died in 1754. The Inspector was attacked from a variety of other quarters, and the two prints above described were not the only caricatures in which he figured. A print undated appears to represent this pseudo-philosopher occupied in his morning studies, with papers before him on some of his trifling subjects of natural history, and surrounded by the books from which he compiled his lucubrations. The figure of folly, with the ears of an ass, is decking his vain head with peacock's plumage.

Dr. Hill's personal criticisms became every day more and more petulant and general, until at length he actually made an attack upon himself. On the 13th of August, 1752, he published the first number of a new periodical, under the very appropriate title of the *Impertinent*, in which he wrote a critique on himself, Fielding, and Christopher Smart, a contemporary poet of some repute, but now nearly forgotten, the object of which was more especially to abuse the writings of the latter. The critique commenced with stating, in his flippant style, that "There are men who write because they have wit; there are those who write because they are hungry; there are some of the modern authors who have a constant fund of both these causes;" and proceeds to illustrate the sage remark by observing, "Of the first, one sees an instance in Fielding; Smart, with equal right, stands foremost among the second; of the third, the mingled wreath belongs to Hill." The *Impertinent* never reached a second number. As soon as its failure was publicly known, the *Inspector*, with matchless effrontery, took notice of it in the following terms:—

"Of all the periodical pieces set up in vain during the last eighteen months, I shall mention only the most pert, the most pretending and short-lived of all. I have in vain sent for the second number of the *Impertinent*. There must have been indignation superior even to curiosity, in the sentence passed on this assuming piece ; and, the public deserves applause of the highest kind, for having crushed in the bud so threatening a mischief. It will be in vain to accuse the town of patronizing dulness or ill-nature, while this instance can be produced, in which a load of personal satire could not procure purchasers enough to promote a second number. It will not be easy to say too much in favour of that candour, which has rejected and despised a piece that cruelly and unjustly attacked Mr. Smart," &c.

Within a few days it was generally known that the author of the first number of the *Impertinent* was the same Dr. Hill who thus exulted over its fall in the *Inspector;* and the magazines, at the end of the month, joined together in making still more public this instance of literary cowardice in the man who, when his new attempt had been thus contemptuously rejected, joined in the popular censure, " as a detected felon, when he is pursued, cries out ' Stop thief!' and hopes to escape in the crowd that follows him." The person more especially attacked, Christopher Smart, turned round upon his assailant, and published a bitter satire under the title of " The Hilliad," in which his principles and pursuits are set forth under the character of Hillario. This rather remarkable poem opens with an indignant address to the prototype of its hero:—

> " O thou, whatever name delight thine ear,
> Pimp ! Poet ! Puffer ! 'Pothecary ! Player!
> Whose baseless fame by vanity is buoy'd,
> Like the huge earth self-center'd in the void.

Hillario is brought into communication with a fortune-telling gipsy, whose prophecy of future celebrity induces him to fly from the apothecary's shop. On his entrance to publicity he is received and welcomed by a group of assistants, " the miscellaneous throng," consisting of Petulance, Dulness, Malice, Scandal, Nonsense, Falsehood, Vanity, and their associates. The subjects on which he was accustomed to hold forth, and which were to support his fame, are next described :—

> " Moths, mites, and maggots, fleas (a numerous crew !)
> And gnats and grub-worms, crowded on his view ;
> Insects, without the microscopic aid,
> Gigantic by the eye of dulness made."

The noise Hillario makes in the midst of these occupations disturbs the gods in their conclave above, and Jupiter inquires angrily what the turbulent creature is. Mercury (the patron of thieves), and Venus, whose favour the vain Doctor pretended that he enjoyed, speak in his favour. The goddess dwells especially on the foppery of his character :—

> " If there be any praise the nails to pare,
> And in soft ringlets wreathe th' elastic hair,
> In talk and tea* to trifle time away,
> The minds so easy and the dress so gay—

* Tea was still an article used only in fashionable society ; and Dr. Hill, in his writings, seeks every occasion of letting his readers know that he indulges in this beverage in the morning, that they may appreciate the kind of society he wishes it to be understood he moves in, and the fashionable elegance of his private life.

> Can my Hillario's worth remain unknown ?
> With whom coy Sylvia trusts herself alone ;
> With whom, so pure, so innocent his life,
> The jealous husband leaves his bosom wife.
> What though he ne'er assume the port of Mars,
> By me disbanded from all amorous wars,
> His fancy (if not person) he employs,
> And oft ideal countesses enjoys.
> Though hard his heart, yet beauty shall controul
> And sweeten all the rancour of his soul ;
> While his black self, Florinda ever near,
> Shows like a diamond in an Ethiop's ear."

Other deities interfere, and speak with contempt of the hero ;
and it is proposed that he shall be allowed to proceed in his
course, as a thing too insignificant to occupy the attention of
the celestials. Momus, the god of ridicule, at last gives him
his true character, and Fame blows it abroad.

Nevertheless, in the latter years of the reign of George II.,
Hill obtained the favour of Lord Bute ; and, his literary reputation failing him, he returned to surgery and botany, obtained
a temporary establishment in the gardens at Kew, was knighted,
and was enabled, by Lord Bute, to give to the world some magnificent, if not very meritorious, botanical works. He married,
in second wedlock, a sister of Lord Ranelagh, who, after his
death (which occurred in 1775), published a pamphlet which
seemed to say that he had not derived any permanent advantage
from the patronage of Lord Bute. In 1779, an extravagantly
panegyrical memoir of Sir John Hill was printed at Edinburgh,
price sixpence.

Dr. Hill has deserved our notice, as a somewhat exaggerated
type of the fashionable literary men of the latter half of the
reign of George II. Dulness, the goddess who presided over
Grub Street in the days of Pope, was resigning her sceptre to
another goddess not less fatal to good taste, Pertness, who was
removing the seat of power farther west. It was a sovereignty
which had risen up with the critics and feuilletonists. A popular satire that appeared about the end of 1752, under the title
of "The Pasquinade," when the notoriety of Hill was at its
height, has celebrated this new empire. This poem opens with
an invocation to the doctor, with allusions to his Chloes,
Daphnes, and Amandas :—

> "O chief in verse ! O ev'ry Muse's care !
> Pride of each mortal and immortal fair !
> Whether compar'd with Urania's charms,
> Or sunk in Culoe or Amanda's arms ;

Q

> Whether eternal bays thy temples grace,
> Or thy lac'd night-cap well supplies their place ;
> Whether with goddess, or with earthly qual,
> You saunter down Parnassus, or the Mall ;
> Or, in philosophy profoundly wise,
> You pore intent with microscopic eyes,
> New worlds discover in a Catherine pear,[*]
> Or monsters animate in sour small beer."

Hill boasted perpetually of his familiarity with the Muses,
who are therefore invoked for their pretended favourite :—

> " Hear, then, ye daughters of immortal Jove!
> By the soft vows of your Inspector's love,
> If not, too jealous of each other's flame,
> You slight the lover for a rival's claim ;
> Or, if his gallantry superior charms,
> And all the nine, in concert, fill his arms,
> Like his familiar Daphnes here below,
> Blooming at once the poet and the beau ;
> Hear and support me in your favourite's cause,
> Inspire my song, and crown me with applause."

Dulness, whose empire had been placed by Pope among " the
tatter'd ensigns of Rag-Fair," now raised her head higher and
took possession of the Mansion House and the city, when the
new sovereign appeared and established her head-quarters in
the vicinity of May-fair. The latter had for her subjects the
critics and the journalists, and she was sometimes obliged to seek
support even among the boxers of Broughton's.

> " Where now behold, in glitt'ring pomp ascend
> A sister queen, a goddess, and a friend :
> Immortal Pertness, sprung from chaos old,
> Inconstant, active, giddy, light, and bold,
> Restless and fickle as her rumbling sire,
> Blind as her mother, Night, could well desire.
> Wrought by some power divine, in equal pride,
> Her throne ascended by her sister's side.
>   Where hunted ducks traverse the muddy stream,
> And dogs initiate their whelps to swim,
> Monsters and fools assemble once a year,
> And juggling Hymen[†] celebrates May-Fair,

[*] In one of the *Inspectors* the Doctor had detailed some extraordinary
observations made on a rotten pear, in an affected style of extravagant and
bombastic description, of which the following may be taken as a specimen :
—" It was but a very small portion of the covered surface of the pear that
could be brought within the area of the microscope ; but this appeared,
under its influence, *a wide extent of territory, varied with hills and lawns,
with winding hollows, open plains, and shadowy thickets.*"

[†] An allusion to Keith's chapel, where the Marriage Act was evaded on
a very extensive scale. These lines describe the district of May-Fair as it
appeared in the middle of the last century. The " palace" was May-Fair

This goddess dwell. Just raised above the ground,
Her palace varnish'd, silver deck'd around.
Here stood her Mercury, here she nursed her apes ;*
Here magpies chatter'd in a hundred shapes ;
Jackdaws and parrots join'd the surrounding noise
Of templars, coxcombs, prigs, and 'prentice boys.
Far hence the goddess spreads her kingdom wide,
To Dulness, as in birth, in power allied.
She, from her native Grub Street to Rag-Fair,
South to the Mint and west to Temple-bar,
Included every garrison'd retreat—
Bedlam, Crane-court, the Counters, and the Fleet :
Her sister boasted as extensive sway ;
Fierce Broughton's bruising sons her power obey ;
St. Giles's, George's, and the famous train
Of Bedford, Bow Street, and of Drury Lane.
Even to the licens'd Park her chiefs resort,
And seize the priv'lege of great George's court."

The two goddesses determine upon a strict alliance, celebrate a grand festival, and review their several forces, consisting of a multitude of obscure names, then active in their different departments in the field of literature, but now so entirely forgotten, that it would be of little utility to rehearse their titles. At length Pertness discovers her favourite Hill :—

"All these the sister queens with joy confess'd,
For lo ! their essence glow'd in every breast !
But Pertness saw her form distinctly shine
In none, immortal Hill ! so full as thine.
Drinking thy morning chocolate in bed,
She saw thy Daphne's neck support thy head ;
Saw thee slip on thy night-gown, and retire
To muse profoundly by thy parlour fire :
By turns thy slippers dangling on thy toes—
Slippers that never were disgraced from shoes !
Saw where thy learning in huge volumes stood,
Part letter'd sheep, part gilt and painted wood."

The goddess points him out with pride to her sister Dulness :—

"When thus the goddess of May-Fair bespoke
Her royal sister : 'Gentle sister, look ;
See where my son, who gratefully repays
Whate'er I lavish'd on his younger days ;

Wells, where there was a private theatre, much resorted to by "clerks and 'prentices," where young aspirants to dramatic fame made their appearance. Hill, before he attained so much celebrity, is said to have acted here, but unsuccessfully.

* Pope had said of Dulness, "Here stood her opium, here she nurs'd her owls." The difference between the attributes of Dulness and Pertness, of the old school and the new one, is marked.

Whom still my arm protects to brave the town,
Secure from Fielding, Machiavel, or Brown ;
Whom rage nor sword e'er mortally shall hurt—
Chief of a hundred chiefs o'er all the *Peri!*
Rescued an orphan babe from Common-sense,
I gave his mother's milk to Confidence,—
She, with her own ambrosia, bronz'd his face,
And changed his skin to monumental brass :
This Shame, or Wit, successless shall oppose,
Unless, so will the Fates, they seize his nose.
This luckless part the young Achilles lick'd ;
And though he cannot blush, he may be kick'd.
Yet still his pen provokes the Fates' decree,
In scandal dipt and elemental tea.' "

Dulness and Pertness agree to adopt this hero as their
common favourite, and to put an end to the war between their
respective hosts ; and the former promises to stifle the ire which
had been nursed in the breast of *her* Smart, whose rivalry with
the new constellation had agitated so violently their different
realms.

Dr. Hill stands forth as a type not only of literary but also
of medical quackery, the wide prevalence of which was among
the distinguishing characteristics of the period of which we are
now speaking. We have, in the pages of " Roderick Random," a
good picture of the usual character of the medical practitioners
of the middle of the eighteenth century. Amid the general
venality, degrees and honours were not always a proof of merit
in the individual upon whom they were bestowed ; and from this
cause, or from the wide-spread spirit of credulity, people sought
with more eagerness the nostrum of the quack than the experience of the proficient. Under these circumstances, a host of
pretenders preyed upon the health and constitutions of their
fellow-countrymen, and the newspapers are filled during many
successive years with the never-failing virtues of the panaceas of
Dr. Rock, of the Anodyne-Necklace man (Burchell), and their
fellows. For several years, about the middle of the century, a
sort of diminutive crusade was carried on against quackery, but
with little success, and it seems in a great measure to have
turned upon, or dwindled into, personal quarrels. A number of
serious pamphlets on the pernicious effects of the system of pills,
powders, and draughts, which were trumped forth into the world
by newspaper advertisements, were published under respectable
names, or anonymously ; while satires and burlesques tended to
turn them to ridicule, and the more remarkable quacks of the
day were set forth in their true colours and attributes in prints

FAMILY PILLS.

and caricatures.* In a mock letter from Dr. Rock "to a physician at Bath," the popular empiric is made to improve upon the
extraordinary properties of the numerous quack medicines then
in vogue. "Imprimis," he says, "there is my famous *sympathe-
tical family pill.* Let the master of any family, or the mistress
if she be master, take one of these at night going to bed, and
another in the morning fasting, and they shall not only be well
purged themselves, but the whole family, men, women, and
children, shall equally participate of the same benefit." Among
the various other advantages of these pills, we are told, "For
instance, when a fine lady has been to go to a rout or to a
ridotto, what does the ill-natured husband do, but take my
pills very privately, and then, poor soul, she dares not venture
out of doors, and, if she did, can have neither coachman nor
footman to attend her." After these are, "Secondly, my *intentional purging pills. . . . The person who takes them need
only say to himself, ' It is my intention these pills should purge
my wife as much as they do me; my boy Jack half as much as
they do me; my daughter Molly once less than Jack; that
liquorish hussey Nan, that steals half the sweetmeats, and eats
half the fruit in the garden, ten times as much as they do me;
and that rascal Tom, that is perpetually at the ale-house, twenty
times as much as they do me, for five days successively.' Upon
this the wished-for event infallibly follows." There was perhaps
in this a sly sarcasm at the doctrine of sympathies, which
merged into animal magnetism.

Among the multitude of nostrums of doubtful efficacy or of an
injurious character which were manufactured at this period, sprung
up some of the best recommended remedies, and the greatest
improvements in modern medicine, which were as much satirised
and objected to at first as the claims of the lowest pretenders.
At the time when there was an absolute rage for Bishop Berke-
ley's tar-water, the introduction of inoculation for the small-pox
was cried down with the most persevering obstinacy. The
fever-powder of Dr. James, a man of high respectability in his
profession, was long violently opposed by the faculty; in spite
of which (perhaps we might say, by favour of which) it quickly
rose in popularity, and enriched its inventor. Horace Walpole
was an enthusiastic votary of James's powder, which he seems

* A general satire on the Medical profession, under the title of "The
Quackade, by Whirligig Dolus, Esq.," was published in 1752; but its
allusions are too obscurely personal and uninteresting, to call for any
further notice here.

to have regarded as a sovereign preventive for almost all diseases.
He writes to Sir Horace Mann, in October, 1764, "James's
powder is my panacea, that is, it always shall be, for, thank
God, I am not apt to have occasion for medicines; but I have
such faith in these powders, that I believe I should take it if
the house were on fire." When Dr. James's opponents found
that they could not hinder the sale of his powders, they turned
round and said that he was not the inventor, but that he had

stolen the recipe from a man named
Baker, who had it of a German Baron
Schwanberg. In a caricature published against him in 1724, entitled
"A Reply for the present to the unknown Author of Villany Detected,"
the Doctor is represented stepping
from his carriage to act the part of a
highwayman towards the right claim-
ant to the secret, who is administer-
ing charity to a poor man, and receiving his blessing in return. Dr. James
takes the opportunity of stealing the
powders from his pocket (some of the
packets falling to the ground), and
at the same time holds a dagger to
strike him, while he says, *aside*, "By
which I keep my chariot, in luxury

THE MEDICAL HIGHWAYMAN.

live, and think of no hereafter." The ghost of a man (perhaps
the German baron) rises from the ground beside him, and exclaims, "Thou perjured villain! thou hast robbed my friend of
the fever-powders!"

The easy credulity and superstition of the English people at
this period, cherished and increased by the preaching and
writings of a number of fanatical sectarians, was exhibited in
many other circumstances besides their belief in quack medicines,
and made them the dupes of several practical jokes, and intentional or involuntary impositions. The ridiculous imposture of
the rabbit-woman of Godalming, which had been favoured by
some members of the medical profession, had afforded a striking
instance of national credulity in the earlier part of the century.
The "gullibility" of the public was illustrated in a still more
remarkable manner in 1749, when some facetious individual (who
he was has never been discovered) put in effect a practical
joke of no ordinary description. On the 16th of January, the

daily papers contained the following advertisement, slightly varied :— *

"At the New Theatre in the Haymarket, this present day, to be seen a person who performs the several most surprising things following ; viz. First he takes a common walking cane from any of the spectators, and thereon he plays the music of every instrument now in use, and likewise sings to surprising perfection. Secondly, he presents you with a common wine-bottle, which any of the spectators may first examine ; this bottle is placed on a table in the middle of the stage, and he (without any equivocation) goes into it, in the sight of all the spectators, and sings in it : during his stay in the bottle, any person may handle it, and see plainly that it does not exceed a common tavern bottle.

"Those on the stage or in the boxes may come in masked habits (if agreeable to them), and the performer (if desired) will inform them who they are.

"Stage, 7s. 6d.　Boxes, 5s.　Pit, 3s.　Gallery, 2s.
"To begin at half an hour after six o'clock."

It was added in a postscript, that the performance had been witnessed by most of the crowned heads of Asia, Africa, and Europe; and the operator promised, for a further gratuity, some other extraordinary exhibitions. In spite of the absurdity of this announcement, and of another advertisement in some of the papers, of the arrival of the wonderful Signor Jumpedo, who, among other things, undertook to jump down his own throat, no suspicion appears to have been entertained of the real character of the hoax, and at the hour advertised a very crowded audience had assembled in the theatre, a large portion of which consisted of persons of quality, and among them was the Duke of Cumberland. There was no music, and the only apparatus on the stage was a table covered with green baize, with a common quart bottle on it. The company sat quietly till towards seven o'clock, when they became extremely impatient, and the house resounded with cat-calls and other equally intelligible expressions of dissatisfaction. A man then came forward to announce that the performer had not yet made his appearance, and some one (it was said to have been Samuel Foote, who performed at this theatre, and was then in the boxes), apparently with the idea of pacifying the audience, said "that the money would be returned if he did not come." A man in the pit shouted out at the same time waggishly, that if they would come again the next night, and double the price, the conjuror would go into a pint bottle. Upon this a candle was thrown from one of the boxes on the stage, which was the signal for a general uproar. The ladies and the more peaceful visitors rushed out of the theatre, and escaped

* It is here given from the *General Advertiser* of Jan. 16, 1749.

only with a general loss of hats, coats, &c. The Duke of Cumberland lost his diamond-hilted sword; and on this being known, some in the crowd shouted, " Billy the Butcher has lost his knife!" Those who remained in the theatre proceeded from one outrage to another, until they had broken up the boxes, benches, and every particle of woodwork that could be removed, and torn down the curtains and scenes, which were soon piled up in the street before the house in one immense bonfire. In the meantime the alarm had been given, and a party of footguards hurried to the spot; but the rioters had fled, and the soldiers arrived only in time to warm themselves at the fire.

The next day John Potter, the proprietor of the theatre, inserted a letter in the newspapers, making an apology to the public for having let the house unwittingly to the impostor, and complained of the injustice done to him personally by the destruction of his property ; and Foote, who was suspected by some of having been accessory to the imposition, wrote a similar letter excusing himself. These letters were continued as advertisements during several days. But others took up the matter much less seriously; and for a week or two after the newspapers contained not unfrequently burlesque announcements of extraordinary performances, like the following, which is found in the *General Advertiser* of the 21st of January :—

" *Lately arrived from Ethiopia,*

The most wonderful and surprising Doctor Benimbo Zanimampoango, oculist and body surgeon to the Emperor of Monœmungl, who will perform on Sunday next, at the little P—— in the Haymarket, the following surprising operations ; viz.—

" 1st. He desires any one of the spectators only to pull out his own eyes, which as soon as he had done, the doctor will show them to any lady or gentleman then present, to convince them that there is no cheat, and then replace them in the socket as perfect and entire as ever.

" 2nd. He desires any officer or other to rip up his own belly, which when he has done, he (without any equivocation) takes out his guts, washes them, and returns them to their place without the person suffering the least hurt.

3rd. He opens the head of a J—— of P——[*justice of peace*], takes out his brains, and exchanges them for those of a calf; the brains of a beau, for those of an ass ; and the heart of a bully, for that of a sheep ; which operations render the person more sociable and rational creatures than they ever were in their lives.

" And to convince the town that no imposition is intended, he desires no money until the performance is over.

" Boxes, 5 gu. Pit, 3. Gal., 2.

N.B.—The famous oculist will be there, and honest S—— F——.*

* This probably means Samuel Foote. The next initial perhaps refers to Dr. Hill. The oculist was a noted quack of the time, and the orator was of

H—— will come if he can. Ladies may come masked, so may fribbles. The faculty and clergy gratis. The Orator would be there, but is engaged."

"The Man in the Bottle" became immediately the hero of several satirical pamphlets on the folly and credulity of the age, besides making his appearance in ballads and caricatures. Two of the caricatures, published in the course of January, were entitled "The Bottle-Conjuror from Head to Foot, without equivocation," and "English Credulity; or, ye're all bottled." In the latter Folly is leading by a string to the bottle-conjuror's table, a group of characters distinguished in arms, law, physic, &c. A sword, alluding to the Duke of Cumberland's loss, is flying away, and a fiend is in pursuit for the proffered reward of thirty guineas. Britannia turns away her face in shame—"Oh! my sons!" In another print, as a companion to the Bottle, harlequin is represented in a very ingenious manner, jumping down his own throat. On the 26th of January, and for some time after, the play-bills added to the announcement of the pantomime of Apollo and Daphne, "In which will be introduced a new scene of the escape of harlequin into a quart-bottle;" and in the summer, a new comedy, called "The Magician; or, the bottle-conjuror," was acted at the smaller theatres. For many years afterwards the bottle-conjuror was a standing joke upon English folly. Yet, within a year, the credulity of our countrymen was again exhibited in a still more extraordinary occurrence. Several smart shocks of earthquakes were felt throughout England about the middle of the last century. The beginning of the year 1750 had been unusually stormy and tempestuous. On the 8th of February, the inhabitants of London were alarmed by a rumbling noise, and a shock, which shook all the houses with such violence that the house-bells rang, and the furniture and utensils were moved from their places. On the same day of the next month a second shock was felt, between the hours of five and six in the morning, which was considerably more intense than the former, and caused the greater consternation, because it awoke people from their sleep. Smollett, who was present in London at the time, tells us that it was preceded by a succession of thick, low flashes of lightning, and a rumbling noise like that of a heavy carriage rolling over a hollow pavement. "The shock itself," he says, "consisted of repeated vibrations, which lasted some

course Henley. It is a satire on the different sorts of quackery then prevalent. During this year the quacks were brought on the stage in several farces, such as "The Mock Doctor," at Covent Garden, "The Anatomist, or the Sham Doctor."

seconds, and violently shook every house from top to bottom. Many persons started from their beds, and ran to their doors and windows in dismay." The alarm occasioned by these two earthquakes was seized upon by the religious enthusiasts of the day as an opportunity for admonishing their fellow-countrymen against the immorality and profaneness which then so widely pervaded English society, and they hesitated not to declare that the earthquakes had been sent as special marks of the displeasure of heaven against the prevailing sins of the people. The Church, in some degree, caught up the same cry, and a pastoral letter of the Bishop of London became the subject of severe strictures. Books on earthquakes and their effects were bought up with great eagerness, and issued from the press with equal rapidity; and people began to look forward with apprehension to the probability of a third shock, which might be still more severe. These apprehensions were gaining ground towards the end of March, when a soldier of the life-guards, who had been driven mad by attending the preaching of religious enthusiasts, ran about the town, crying out that on the same day four weeks after the last shock (which would be Thursday, the 5th of April) another earthquake, of a much more formidable character, would swallow up the whole metropolis and destroy its inhabitants, as a punishment for their sins; and that Westminster Abbey would be buried in the ruins, and disappear for ever. The prophet was arrested, and placed in a mad-house, but this did not calm the fears of the multitude, which increased us the fatal day approached; and even many of those who had at first combated these ridiculous fears, began insensibly to imbibe the contagion. The popular credulity was so great, that on the 1st of April some hundreds of people went through a heavy rain to Edmonton, upon the report that a hen had laid an egg there the day before, on which was inscribed in large capital letters the words "*Beware of the third shock !*" During the following days, many people, who possessed the means of absenting themselves, left London under different excuses, and repaired to various parts of the kingdom. Read's *Weekly Journal* of the 7th of April informs us, that "Thirty coaches, filled with genteel-looking people, were, at Wednesday noon, at Slough, running away from the prognosticated earthquake;" and adds, "and it is known that 34 l'——s, 94 C——rs, and two l'——ds of ——, fled to different parts of the kingdom this week on the same account, in order to avoid the vengeance denounced against them by a late pastoral letter." All the roads leading from London to the country were thronged; and in the course of

Wednesday afternoon, whole families locked up their houses, and went into the open fields outside the metropolis, which were filled with an incredible number of people, assembled in chairs and carriages as well as on foot, who waited in trembling suspense until the return of day convinced most of them of the groundlessness of their apprehensions. Many, however, still insisted that it was a mistake in the day, and that the earthquake would occur on Sunday the 8th, as they should have counted the day of the month, and not that of the week.

The ridicule thrown upon this affair, after the day was past, was as great as the apprehensions which had preceded it. In the account given in the *Universal Magazine*, we are told, "It is observed by the hackney-coachmen and chairmen, that none of the great folks went out of town to avoid the fulfilling of the madman's prophecy about the earthquakes, but such whose curiosity led them to see the conjuror creep into the glass bottle." Lists of the "nobility, gentry, and others," who had fled from the town, were printed and handed about; and satirical tracts were published under such titles as "A full and true Account of the dreadful and melancholy Earthquake," which were so arranged as to furnish a meal of political and private scandal to those who loved to fatten on such food. Other pamphlets dwelt more seriously on the impiety of setting up to be interpreters of the inscrutable designs of Providence. In the course of the month of April this event produced two caricatures, the first entitled "The Military Prophet; or, a flight from Providence;" the other, "The Panick; or, the force of frighted imagination."

For twelve years, English credulity was allowed to spend itself in trifling ebullitions, and it offers little to arrest our attention. But at the end of that period, an affair more ridiculous, if possible, than any of the preceding, agitated the public; it had had its conjuror and its earthquake— the new subject of attraction was *a ghost*. The fame of the Cock Lane ghost has in some sort outlived the memory of bottle-conjuror or military prophet. A Mr. Kent, who lived with the sister of his deceased wife, had occupied lodgings in Cock Lane, Smithfield, at the house of a Mr. Parsons, but, having quarrelled with his landlord, he removed to a house in Clerkenwell, where his companion, who is known in the story by the name of Miss Fanny, died of the small-pox. Parsons, to revenge himself upon Mr. Kent, declared that the ghost of Miss Fanny haunted the room of his daughter, (with whom she had slept during Kent's absence from town,) and had charged Kent with having poisoned her. On examination, mysterious knockings and scratchings were heard at night about the girl's bed; and the report being spread abroad by papers and pamphlets, a concourse of people, many of them of the highest rank and character, visited the house during successive nights: the surrounding streets were filled with mobs, and an extraordinary sensation was created throughout London. Suspicions of trickery, however, soon arose among the more sensible part of the visitors; the child was removed to another house, and separated from her friends, when the result was unsatisfactory, and the ghost failed in its promise to signify its presence in the vault where Miss Fanny was buried, which had been visited by a select party. After this, the child was detected, and made a confession, and all the persons concerned in the imposture were prosecuted and severely punished. The details of this affair, which occurred in the beginning of the year 1762, are too ridiculous to deserve repeating; it gave rise to a number of pamphlets; made ghost stories popular throughout the country for several months, and brought them on the stage; and produced the long rambling satirical poem of "The Ghost" from the pen of Churchill.

The stage was exciting public attention in an unusual degree for some years, at the middle of the last century, from a variety of circumstances; and the moral tendency of the stage itself, the policy of its advocates, the characters of the performers, their personal disputes, and the rivalry of different companies, afforded matter for a continual issue of pamphlets in prose and verse, and a few prints and caricatures. The general character of the performances differed little since the reign of George I.; for pantomimes and burlesques had established themselves permanently in popular favour, and they now went on hand in hand with the regular drama. Amid the rivalries alluded to, and supported by some of the best actors who have ever trod the English stage, the plays of the great English bard were gaining daily in popularity.

It has already been noticed, that, besides the licensed theatres, there was a theatre far east in Goodman's Fields, where a company of players had long been allowed by forbearance to act, because it was thought probably that they did not much affect the audiences of the houses at the West End. It was here that amateurs sometimes gratified their vanity without risk, and it served also as a sort of school for many who afterwards figured on the boards of Drury Lane and Covent Garden. It was at this theatre, that, on the 19th of October, 1741, David Garrick first made his appearance on a London stage; and, in the character of Richard the Third, he gained such universal admiration, that within a few days the larger theatres were almost deserted, and Goodman's Fields presented the unusual spectacle of crowds of carriages from St. James's and Grosvenor Square. Quin, who had been engaged at Drury Lane, had hitherto been considered as the first tragic actor on the English stage, and, alarmed at Garrick's success, he did all in his power to cry him down, but in vain. The patentees of the two great theatres were still more alarmed at the deficiency of their receipts, and they prepared at last to take those measures against the unlicensed theatre of the east end, that forced the latter into a composition, which ended, some months after, in Garrick's final removal to Drury Lane. About the same time, Quin went over to Covent Garden, to oppose Garrick, his jealousy of whom continued unabated. The patent of Drury Lane was at this time in the hands of Charles Fleetwood, who had bought it at a moment when the mismanagement of the former proprietors had reduced it to a very low state, and driven away the best performers. The latter had opened the little theatre in the Haymarket, with some success, but they returned to Drury Lane under Fleetwood, and left their theatre in the Haymarket to a company of French actors. Fleetwood was a man utterly devoid of dramatic taste, and, to the disgust of Garrick, he had brought the tumblers and rope-dancers of Sadler's Wells on the boards of Drury. Other ill-conduct on the part of Fleetwood drove the Drury Lane company to a new revolt; they seceded from the theatre under Garrick and Macklin, and tried to obtain a new patent from the Lord Chamberlain, but in vain. The consequence was, that they were obliged to come to terms with Fleetwood, in which Macklin was made a sacrifice, and quarrelled with Garrick for deserting him. The town took part with Macklin; and when Drury Lane re-opened towards the end of 1743, the theatre presented, for two or three nights, a scene of violent uproar between the partisans of the two actors, which threatened, at one moment, to put a stop to Garrick's acting. Garrick spent the year 1745, and part of 1746, in Dublin, from whence he returned in the May of the latter year, and engaged himself at Covent Garden, under Rich. Fleetwood had, meanwhile, sold his interest in Drury Lane, and it was now under the management of Lacy, who had a good share in the proprietorship.

In 1747 began the great rivalry between the two large theatres, under Rich and Lacy, which agitated the theatrical world for some ensuing years. Rich, much against his will, had

made a momentary sacrifice of his passion for pantomime, in
favour of the regular drama, and engaged Garrick, Quin, Woodward, Mrs. Cibber, Mrs. Pritchard, and several other good
actors. The Drury Lane company numbered among its chief
performers, Barry and Macklin, Yates, Mrs. Clive, and Peg
Woffington. It was the first time that Garrick and Quin had
played together, and the superiority of the former was soon acknowledged, to the great mortification and discontent of his
rival. Yet, in spite of the superiority which the great actor had
given Covent Garden over the rival theatre, Rich was weak
enough to treat him with neglect; and Mr. Lacy having obtained a new patent for Drury Lane, ceded one half of it to
Garrick, who thus, in the summer of 1747, became joint proprietor and stage-manager of Drury Lane theatre. Mrs.
Pritchard, Mrs. Cibber, and others, followed Garrick to Drury
Lane, which was opened with great *éclat* on the 20th of September, 1747; and the following season witnessed a complete
revival of Shakspeare and the older dramatists on the stage.
Jealousies and frequent quarrels, however, soon broke out in
Garrick's company, which furnished materials for the caricaturist during the season of 1748, and the consequence of which
was the desertion of Barry and Mrs. Cibber to Covent Garden
in 1749, where they joined with Quin and Mrs. Woffington, and
thus formed under Rich a dangerous rivalry to the other theatre.
In October, 1749, the Covent Garden company opened the
theatrical campaign with "Romeo and Juliet," a play in which
Barry, and especially Mrs. Cibber, had shone with peculiar
excellence. Garrick had armed himself for the contest; he had
prepared a rival actress in Miss Bellamy, and he produced, to
the surprise of his opponents, the same play of "Romeo and
Juliet" at Drury Lane, on the very night it came out at Covent
Garden. It was a repetition of the war of rival harlequins in
the preceding reign. The town was divided for a long time between the two "Romeos and Juliets," which produced a mass of
contradictory criticism, and finished by almost emptying both
houses, for everybody began to be tired of the monotonous repetition of the same play. A popular epigram of the day spoke
distinctly the public feeling—

> "*On the Run of 'Romeo and Juliet.'*
> " 'Well, what's to night?' says angry Ned,
> As up from bed he rouses;
> 'Romeo again!' and shakes his head,
> 'Ah! plague on both your houses!'"

Personal jealousies, not only among the actors themselves,

but between them and their manager Rich, soon broke up the
harmony of the Covent Garden company. Garrick retaliated on
their efforts to outshine him by attacking Rich in his own peculiar walk; and at the beginning of 1750 brought out a new pantomime, entitled "Queen Mab," in which Woodward acted the
part of harlequin. The great success of this piece, which brought
crowded houses for forty nights without intermission, gave rise
to a very popular caricature, entitled "The Theatrical Steelyard,"
in which Mrs. Cibber, Mrs. Woffington, Quin, and Barry, are
outweighed by Woodward's harlequin and Garrick's Queen Mab.
Rich, dressed in the garb of harlequin, lies on the ground ex-

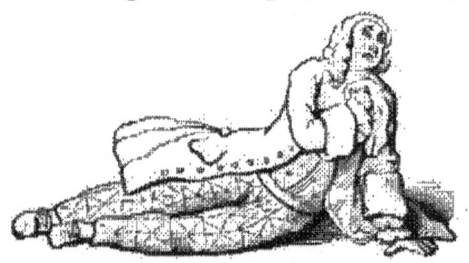

AN EXPIRING HARLEQUIN.

piring. The rivalry of the two theatres continued in this state
in the year 1752, in the literary warfare of which period we
have seen them so deeply involved. Garrick's backwardness in
bringing out new plays had embroiled him with several of the
critics of the day.

But, in the middle of his success, an untoward accident came
to disturb the triumphs of the English Roscius. The popular
feeling against the employment of French actors, which had
been shewn so remarkably in the Westminster election of 1749,
was now at its height, having been kept up by several squibs
and caricatures. One of the latter, published in 1750, under
the title of "Britannia disturb'd; or, an invasion by French
vagrants," represents the foreigners forced on Britannia by a
band of aristocratic rioters, while she holds in her lap her favourite English players and pantomimists. In 1754, with the
hope of raising still higher the theatrical pre-eminence of Drury
Lane, Garrick first planned his grand spectacle, brought out in
the beginning of November, 1755, under the title of "The
Chinese Festival." It had been found necessary to employ a
great number of French dancers in this spectacle, the report of

which having gone abroad, while the hatred of the French was increased by the breaking out of hostilities and by their conduct in America, a mob assembled in the theatre on the first night with the determination of putting a stop to the performance. Garrick, who had expended a large sum of money on this entertainment, did his utmost, but in vain, to appease the ill-humour; but the fashionable people in the boxes took his part, and the war between the two parties continued with doubtful success during five nights. The sixth night of representation was an opera night, and the strength of the boxes was weakened by the absence of many people of quality. When the riot began several gentlemen of rank jumped from the boxes into the pit, and attempted to seize the ringleaders, and the ladies, who remained in the boxes, pointed out to them the obnoxious persons; but after a long and rude contest, in which some blood was drawn, the united pit and galleries triumphed, and they now wreaked their vengeance on the materials of the theatre, demolished the scenes, tore up the benches, broke the lustres, and soon effected a damage which it required several thousand pounds to repair.

The young writers who had formerly found a great part of their employment in writing new pieces for the stage, became more and more irritated at the dramatic taste which deprived them of a part of their bread, by raising up Shakspeare and the older drama, and, being mostly connected with the different papers, magazines, and reviews of the day, they took their revenge by severe and often unfair criticisms on the different performers, which made them objects of dread among the players. The natural consequence of this was, that the stage attracted more and more the attention of the literary world, until, in the March of 1761, the first, and one of the most remarkable poems of one of the most remarkable poets of that day, the " Rosciad " of Charles Churchill, stole anonymously into the world. In this poem, distinguished by remarkable vigour of design and execution, the poet introduces the actors of the day contending for the throne of Roscius, and he satirises with great critical severity the individual defects of the players, as well as those of the writers for the stage. Garrick, whose claim is allowed as the successor of Roscius, was the only one who escaped his lash. This poem, to which the author affixed his name in a second edition, met at once with the most extraordinary success, and passed quickly through a great number of editions, although it was bitterly attacked by the critics, not only in the reviews, but in an incredible number of pamphlets, under every form that the provoked anger of the disputants could imagine. These are too obscure and too dull to merit even that their titles should be enumerated. But Churchill was stung to the quick, and in another poem, under the title of the "Apology," he attacked with extreme bitterness the reviewers and the stage in general, to which he attributed the shoal of abusive pamphlets that had been showered upon him for his theatrical criticisms He stigmatises the critics as an upstart brood of literary assassins, who from their dark concealment stabbed at unprotected genius, when it had with difficulty escaped from the coldness of the great and the persecutions of bigotry :—

> " Unhappy Genius ! placed by partial Fate
> With a free spirit in a slavish state,
> Where the reluctant Muse, oppressed by kings,
> Or droops in silence, or in fetters sings.
> In vain thy dauntless fortitude hath borne
> The bigot's furious zeal and tyrant's scorn.
> Why didst thou safe from home-bred dangers steer,
> Reserved to perish more ignobly here !
> Thus when, the Julian tyrant's pride to swell,
> Rome with her Pompey at Pharsalia fell,
> The vanquished chief escaped from Cæsar's hand,
> To die by ruffians in a foreign land."

The extraordinary power which the critics, though self-elected, had now usurped, is next glanced at :—

> " How could these self-elected monarchs raise
> So large an empire on so small a base !
> In what retreat, inglorious and unknown,
> Did Genius sleep when Dulness seized the throne ?
> Whence, absolute now grown, and free from awe,
> She to the subject world dispenses law.
> Without her licence not a letter stirs,
> And all the captive criss-cross-row is hers."

He next attacks the reviewers for dragging people's names from intentional concealment, whilst they remain themselves carefully screened from view : they had, in fact, attacked several persons by name, as the authors of the "Rosciad," before Churchill had affixed his own to it. This seems at first to have been the great complaint of the authors against the reviewers ; for, while they did not flinch from the old wars of pamphlets, they objected to being regularly brought for judgment by a hidden and irresponsible conclave, who were not accessible to retaliation.

> " Founded on arts which shun the face of day,
> By the same arts they still maintain their sway.
> Wrapped in mysterious secrecy they rise,
> And, as they are unknown, are safe and wise.

R

At whomsoever aim'd, howe'er severe,
The envenom'd slander flies, no names appear :
Prudence forbid that step : then all might know
And on more equal terms engage the foe.
But now, what Quixote of the age would care
To wage a war with dirt, and fight with air ?'

The poet then turns with increased rage upon the actors,
whom he accuses of having a troop of mercenary writers in their
pay to cry up their deserts, and of wishing thus to impose upon
the taste and judgment of the public :—

" Doth it more move our anger or our mirth,
To see these things, the lowest sons of earth,
Presume, with self-sufficient knowledge graced,
To rule in letters and preside in taste ?
The town's decisions they no more admit,
Themselves alone the arbiters of wit,
And scorn the jurisdiction of that court
To which they owe their being and support.
Actors, like monks of old, now sacred grown,
Must be attack'd by no fools but their own."

The lighter amusements of the town had not lost their popularity amid what certainly must be looked upon as the regeneration of the legitimate drama ; and, in spite of the severe attacks
of the moralists, with which they had been assailed at their first
introduction into this country, masquerades or ridottos long continued to sustain their ground. In the summer of 1730, a day
masquerade in the open air was introduced as a novelty at Vaux-
hall, under the name of a *ridotto al fresco*, and, although it provoked new outcries against the immoral tendency of this sort of
entertainment, it was for a time extremely popular, and made
considerable noise. On the first day (Wednesday, the 7th of
June) there were about four hundred persons in masquerade
dresses, and it was announced in the newspapers that one of
them had his pocket picked of fifty guineas. The taste for
ridottos al fresco seems soon to have subsided ; and indeed night
was best calculated for the multitude of intrigues that were constantly carried on at these assemblies. It is impossible to enter
into the history of fashionable society at this period, without
perceiving the injurious effects of the passion for masquerades on
the public morals. To keep outward decorum, it was necessary
to announce in the advertisements and bills that guards were
stationed in the rooms to prevent any offensive conduct. A few
years later, the indignation of the moralist was again excited by
the report that ladies were in the habit of frequenting the masquerades in men's clothing ; and even greater improprieties than

this appear to have been at times perpetrated. The satirical *Drury Lane Journal*, of April 9, 1752, contains the following burlesque announcement :—

"ADVERTISEMENT.

" Whereas there will be a very splendid appearance at Ranelagh Jubilee, C. Richman takes leave to inform the nobility, and no others, that he can furnish them with—

" New-invented masks for those who are ashamed of their own faces, or have no face at all.

" Naked dresses, in imitation of their own skin,
" And all other natural disguises."

Only three years previously to this announcement, in 1749, one of the Princess of Wales's maids of honour, Elizabeth Chudleigh, afterwards the notorious Duchess of Kingston, had carried the second of these ideas into actual practice, by appearing at a masquerade given by the Venetian ambassador at Somerset House, in the character of Iphigenia, in a close dress of flesh-coloured silk, so as to expose, unembarrassed by the covering of her looser garments, much more than strict delicacy allowed. The Princess gave her a gentle rebuke by throwing her own veil over her ; but the story soon became public, and was tortured into a variety of shapes, and a number of prints appeared pretending to be portraits of the maid of honour in her " naked dress," some of which would make us believe that she had exhibited herself almost in a state of nature.[*] This exaggeration of immodesty seems to have thrown the masquerades into some disrepute, and a vigorous stand was made against them in the spring of 1750, on occasion of the panic caused by the earthquakes in London ; the attempt to suppress them, defeated now but repeated again after the fearful earthquake which effected the destruction of Lisbon, at the end of 1755, was in the latter case so far effectual, that we hear little of masquerades for several years. Horace Walpole says, in a letter dated March 22, 1762, " We have never recovered masquerades since the earthquake at Lisbon." Yet, in the first year after the accession of George III., the example of reviving them began to be set by the court. On the 7th of June, 1763, Walpole, with the earthquake still in his recollection, describes the magnificence of the masquerade and fireworks given at Richmond House :—" A

---

[*] It is said that on this occasion, the King, provoked by the wayward damsel's costume, having requested permission to place his hand on her breast, she replied that she would put it to a still softer place, and immediately raised it to his royal forehead.

masquerade," he says, " was a new sight to the young people,
who had dressed themselves charmingly, without having the
fear of an earthquake before their eyes, though Prince William
and Prince Henry were not suffered to be there." When the
King of Denmark was in England in 1768, he gave a masquerade at Ranelagh "to all the world;" and Walpole observes
sarcastically, " The bishops will call this *giving an earthquake;*
but, if they would come when bishops call, the Bishop of Rome
would have fetched forty by this time. Our right reverend
fathers have made but a bad choice of their weapon in such a
cold, damp climate." An unsuccessful attempt was made to
revive public masquerades in 1771.

As Rich had found a successful rival in Garrick, so Heidegger
was eventually eclipsed by a great composer, who, towards the
middle of the century, introduced a new style of musical performance. George William Handel settled in London about the
year 1710. He soon obtained the patronage of the Earl of Burlington; and subsequently, in connexion with Senesino and some
others, set up what he called an academy of music in the Haymarket. This, however, was broken up, in consequence of his
quarrels with his colleagues, and, finding little patronage in
England, where the fashionable world were still mad after the
Italian singers, he retired to the Continent. He returned to
England in the beginning of 1742; and in the subsequent years
he produced those noble oratorios, which soon gave him celebrity
and riches. Handel, who was celebrated for his love of luxurious living, and his power of deglutition, was as remarkable for
his corpulence as Heidegger had been for his ugliness; and in
"The Scandalizade," a satirical poem published in 1750, when
Handel was at the height of his celebrity, the former is introduced ridiculing the unwieldy figure of his rival.

> " 'Ho, there! to whom none can, forsooth, hold a candle,'
> Call'd the *lovely-faced* Heidegger out to George Handel,
> 'In arranging the poet's sweet lines to a tune,
> Such as God save the King! or the fam'd Tenth of June!
> How amply your corpulence fills up the chair—
> Like mine bust at an inn, or a London lord-mayor;
> Three yards at the least round about in the waist;
> In dimensions your face like the sun in the west.
> But a chine of good pork, and a brace of good fowls,
> A dozen-pound turbot, and two pair of soles,
> With bread in proportion, devour'd at a meal,
> How incredibly strange, and how monstrous to tell!
> Needs must that your gains and your income be large,
> To support such a vast *unsupportable* charge!
> Retrench, or ere long you may set your own dirge.' "

The composer retorts on his antagonist, and expresses indignation at the charge of over-eating, which appears not to have
been exaggerated, in the foregoing lines :—

> " ' Would'st upbraid with ill-nature, as monstrous and vast,
> My moderate eating and delicate taste,
> When I paid but two hundred a year for my board !
> True, my landlord soon after the bargain deplor'd ;
> Withdrew, became bankrupt, a prey to the law,
> His effects swallow'd up in disputing a flaw
> ' Mong counsel, attorneys, commissioners, and such,
> And all the long train so accustom'd to touch.
> But what is this matter of bankrupt to me ?
> All folks must abide by the terms they agree :
> If guilty my stomach, my conscience is free."

In two prints, nearly alike, and evidently copied from the
other, published in 1754, Handel is represented under the title
of "The Charming Brute," as an overgrown hog, performing on
his instrument, in the midst of a vast assemblage of his favourite
provisions, hung round the apartment and against the organ.

THE CHARMING BRUTE.

The opera, during the theatrical wars, had lost none of its
popularity among fashionable society, and was regularly re-
cruited by a succession of Italian singers and dancers, who furnished subjects of ridicule to the multitude in their personal
quarrels, or in their impertinent vanity. Among the "cargoes
of Italian dancers" announced by Horace Walpole on the 10th
of November, 1754, as having newly arrived in the London
market, was the celebrated Mingotti, whose rivalry with Vanneschi subsequently disturbed the peace of the theatre in the
Haymarket as much as those of Cuzzoni and Faustina had done
in former days. Walpole, who noted all these important trifles
in his correspondence, says, in the October of 1755, "I believe I

scarce ever mentioned to you last winter the follies of the opera:
the impertinences of a great singer were too old and too common
a topic. I must mention them now, when they rise to any improvement in the character of national folly. The Mingotti, a
noble figure, a great mistress of music, and a most incomparable
actress, surpassed anything I ever saw for the extravagance of
her humours. She never sang above one night in three, from a
fever upon her temper ; and never would act at all when Ricciu-
relli, the first man, was to be in dialogue with her. Her fevers
grew so high, that the audience caught them, and hissed her
more than once : she herself once turned and hissed again. . . .
Well, among the treaties which a Secretary of State has negotiated this summer, he has contracted for a *succedaneum* for the
Mingotti. In short, there is a woman hired to sing when the
other shall be out of humour !" The contest between Mingotti
and the manager, Vanneschi, which ended in the ruin of the
latter, made the proud dame sovereign of the opera, and her airs
were proportionally increased. A caricature published on the
8th of October, 1756, represents this creature of fashionable
adoration under the title of "The Idol," raised on a stool inscribed with "£2000 per annum," and receiving the homage of
her worshippers of all classes. A fashionable lady, with a pug-
dog, exclaims, " 'Tis only pug, and you I love !" A divine, on
his knees before the stool, ejaculates, " Unto thee be praise, now
and for evermore !" A nobleman, bringing his subscription of
£2000, says to his lady, " We shall have but twelve songs for
all this money." His lady replies, " Well, and enough, too, for
the paltry trifle !" Other persons are expressing their admiration in various ways. The idol, from her throne, sings with
contempt—

> " Ra, ra, ra, rot ye,
> My name is M—— [*Mingotti*] ;
> If you worship me until
> You shall all go to pott."

The moral of the whole is told in a distich below :—

> " Behold with most indignant scorn the soft enervate tribe,
> Their country selling for a song : how eager they subscribe !"

While the old drama was thus progressing side by side with
the more recently established opera, another class of pieces
became extremely popular in the hands of Samuel Foote, who
then a young actor, had joined Macklin, when, after his quarrel
with Garrick in 1743, he betook himself to the little theatre in
the Haymarket, where Foote made his first appearance on the

6th of February, 1744. We have had frequent occasions for observing how the passing events of the day were carried on the stage in comedies and pantomimes, as objects of satire. This species of farce was brought to perfection by Foote, whose great talent was that of mimicry, and who delighted his audience by the exact manner in which he imitated the peculiarities and weaknesses of individual contemporaries. He was in all respects the great theatrical caricaturist of the age. The personality of the satire was the grand characteristic of Foote's performances, and one which rendered them dangerous to society, and certainly not to be approved. An affront to the actor was at any time enough to cause the offender to be dragged before the world; and matter in itself of the most libellous description was published without danger, under the fictitious name of a character, the resemblance of which to the original was sufficiently evident to the town. From such tribunals, neither elevation in society, nor respectability of character, are a protection. After working a few years together, Foote and Macklin disagreed, and the latter left him to set up an oratory, under the title of "The British Inquisition," for Henley's success had made the name of oratory popular, and a sort of passion was at this time springing up for lecturing and speechifying. Several oratories arose about the same time, besides a variety of debating clubs, like the celebrated Robin Hood Society. Horace Walpole says, on the 24th of December, 1754, "The new madness is oratories." Foote immediately brought out "Macklin and the British Inquisition" on the stage at the Haymarket. From the Haymarket, Foote went to Drury Lane, and enlisted for a while under Garrick, with whom, however, he was never on terms of cordial friendship. His "Englishman in Paris," at the commencement of his Drury Lane connexion, was extremely popular; but another piece, "The Author," although equally well received by the mob, was eventually stopped by the Lord Chamberlain, at the complaint of an individual who was unjustly attacked in it. The Haymarket was an unlicensed theatre, and Foote evaded the law by serving his audience with tea, and calling the performance in his bills, "Mr. Foote's giving tea to his friends."* Churchill, who attacked Foote with some bitterness in his

---

* Foote's advertisement ran, "Mr. Foote presents his compliments to his friends and the public, and desires them to drink tea at the little Theatre in the Haymarket every morning, at playhouse prices." The house was always crowded, and Foote came forward and said, that, as he had some young actors in training, he would go on with his instructions while tea was preparing.

"Rosciad," and who judged rightly that his performances
tended to lower the character of the stage, alludes to this
circumstance, and to the similar character of Tate Wilkinson,
whom he looked upon as Foote's shadow :—

> "Foote, at Old House, for even Foote will be
> In self-conceit an actor, bribes with tea ;
> Which Wilkinson at second-hand receives,
> And, at the New, pours water on the leaves."

At the beginning of the reign of George III. Foote occupied
the house alluded to more regularly as a summer theatre, and
brought out his farce of the "Minor," which, independent of its
personalities, was a violent satire upon the Methodists, and
through them upon the more religious part of the community,
and contained a considerable quantity of coarse language, and
some rather exceptionable morality. The appearance of this
piece was the signal for a violent paper war. Foote and his
farces were attacked in every way, and the moral tendency of the
stage was thus again brought into question under disadvantage
for itself. The clergy interfered, and the "Minor" was no
longer allowed to be acted. In 1766, Foote obtained a patent
for the theatre in the Haymarket, upon which he purchased and
pulled down the old house, and built the new one, which was
ever after known as the Haymarket Theatre.

The course of the theatrical caricaturist was, however, anything but smooth. In 1762 Foote brought out "The Orators,"
the design of which was to ridicule the prevailing taste for
speechifying, the affair of the Cock Lane Ghost, and especially
the debating society held at the Robin Hood. Among other
persons who were to be exposed to satire and ridicule on this
occasion, was Dr. Johnson, who had taken an active part in the
investigation of the Cock Lane Ghost, and contributed to the
exposure of the imposture : Johnson was informed of Foote's
design before the farce came out, and intimated to him immediately, that he should be in the theatre with a stout cudgel,
ready to fall upon the first person on the stage who attempted
to mimic or throw ridicule upon him. The character of the
Doctor was omitted, when "The Orators" appeared on the stage.
In 1772, Foote's farce of "The Nabob," a satire on the East
India politics, nearly involved him in a serious quarrel with
some of the directors of the India Company. In 1775, having
gathered abroad some scandalous anecdotes of the Duchess of
Kingston, he wrote a farce, entitled "The Trip to Calais," in
which that notorious woman was grossly caricatured under the
name of "Lady Kitty Crocodile." The attack was cruel,

because the Duchess was in the midst of her embarrassments relating to the trial for bigamy; and she had sufficient influence with the Lord Chamberlain, to obtain a refusal to allow it to be acted. Foote expostulated in vain with the Lord Chamberlain, and then threatened the Duchess he would print the farce, unless she gave him two thousand pounds to suppress it. The haughty dame entered into a war of letters with him, and showed that she was no match in caustic satire; but there is a certain brutality in his way of trampling on an unfortunate woman, which makes us feel how pernicious to society a character like Foote must ever be. A Rev. Mr. Jackson, a writer in some of the newspapers of the day, was the Duchess's agent in her transaction with Foote. The latter, finding he was likely to get nothing out of the Duchess of Kingston, altered the name of his farce to "The Capuchin," omitted all that related to the Duchess, but brought in her agent, the parson, on whom he expended his full measure of scorn and ridicule, and it was thus brought on the stage the following summer. Jackson (it was said, at the instigation of the Duchess of Kingston,) revenged himself by charging Foote with a revolting offence; and, although he was honourably acquitted, the disgrace bore so heavy upon his mind, that he never recovered it. Foote died on the 21st of October, 1777.

A good print, by Boitard, entitled "The Imports of Great Britain from France; humbly addressed to the laudable associations of Anti-Gallicans, and the generous promoters of the British arts and manufactories," and published March 7, 1757, exhibits some of what the mob considered the most objectionable articles which France sent over to corrupt the manners and principles of Englishmen. The various groups are described at the foot of the engraving. The rage for French fashions is represented by "Four tackle porters staggering under a weighty chest of *Birth-Night Clothes*," addressed to a right honourable viscount in St. James's, and doubtless comprising a magnificent costume for the ball on the King's birthday. The love of French cookery appears in "several emaciated high liv'd epicures familiarly receiving a *French cook*, acquainting him, that, without his assistance, they must have perished with hunger." The affected conceit of a French education is pictured in "a lady of distinction, offering the tuition of her son and daughter to a cringing *French abbé*, disregarding the corruption of their religion; so they do but obtain the true French accent; her frenchified well-bred spouse readily complying, the English chaplain regretting his lost labours." The passion for French *artistes* appears in "another woman of quality, in raptures, caressing a *French female dancer*, assuring her that her arrival is to the

honour and *delight of England;*" the negro page is laughing at the strange taste of his mistress. The other prominent features of the picture are described as follows:— "On the front ground, a cask overset, the contents, French cheeses from Normandy, being *raffiné*, a blackguard boy stopping his nostrils, greatly offended at the *haut-goût;* a chest well examined with tippets, muffs, ribbons, flowers for the hair, and other such *materiel bagatelles;*

FOREIGN MERCHANDIZE.

underneath, concealed cambricks and gloves; another chest, containing choice beauty-washes, pomatums, l'eau d'Hongrie, l'eau de luce, l'eau de carme, &c. &c. &c.; near, French wines and brandies. At a distance, landing, swarms of milliners, tailors, mantua-makers, frisers, tutoresses for boarding-schools, disguised Jesuits, quacks, valet-de-chambres, &c. &c. &c." Such was the merchandize, which, it was popularly believed, hindered English ministers from defending our national honour from the insults of our neighbours.

The outcry against the influence of French fashions and principles was indeed at its height at the time of publication of this print, and not altogether without reason. Corruption had been progressing so long, that society seemed to be rotten to the very heart, and to require some violent remedy before it could be restored to its normal state. The evil was deeply rooted in the manners of the age, and was imbibed with the first rudiments of fashionable education, of which it was considered a necessary part that young men of family should make the continental tour with a tutor before they were introduced into society at home. They were thus snatched from the indulgences of a university life, to be thrown, unrestrained, amid the vices of France and Italy, which they returned to practise in their own country. The evils of this system were generally felt, and many a moral sermon or bitter satire was written against it, but in vain. The travelling tutors, who were frequently as immoral as their pupils, and encouraged, rather than restrained, them in their worst propensities, went popularly by the title of *bear-leaders.* In England, the common life of a man of fashion, presented a strange mixture of frivolousness and brutality—the day spent over the toilette, or at the boudoir of women of fashion, whose principles were no more delicate than their own, lisping scandal and gallantry, and trifling with a pantin,* or some other equally childish plaything, ended commonly in tavern debauchery and street riot, the object of emulation being—

> " To run a horse, to make a match,
> To revel deep, to roar a catch ;
> To knock a tottering watchman down,
> To sweat a woman of the town."

In these riots blood was frequently shed, and they sometimes ended fatally, for the sword was always ready in the fray. The exaggeration of this spirit of riot and debauchery produced private associations like the " Hell-fire Club," of the earlier part of the reign of George II., and the fraternity whose voluptuous devotions at Medmenham were so notorious at the beginning of that of George III.

The peculiar frame of society tended to diffuse the evil; for what was looked upon as the *beau-monde* then lived much more in public than now, and men and women of fashion displayed their weaknesses to the world in public places of amusement and resort with little shame or delicacy. The women often rivalled the men in libertinism, and even emulated them sometimes in their riotous manners. It was this publicity of manners that made the fashionable world collectively and individually, as it were, the property of the town, and not only caused the latter to take a personal interest in it, but produced numerous imitators on an humbler scale among the middle and lower classes, and thus spread the poison through every vein. This filled the literature of the day with so much personal scandal; and hence arose the great success which attended Foote's attempt to drag

---

* A puppet of pasteboard, strung together so that by every touch of the finger it was thrown into a variety of grotesque attitudes. From 1748 to 1750, it was in high vogue among the *beau-monde* as a diverting plaything for gentlemen and ladies. The pantin was the subject of several caricatures and ballads in 1748, the year in which it came into fashion in England : one of the former, published in September 1748, was entitled, " Pantin à la Mode : or, Polite Conversation." Another, published in August 1749, is advertised as " A new emblematic print in high taste, representing Folly playing with his pantin." I have not seen these prints, which appear to be very rare. This of course was also one of the fashionable importations from France.

it on the stage. Every man (or woman) who made himself remarkable in fashionable society was a public character, and the satire cast upon him by the writer or by the actor needed no explanation to make it understood. The scandal and disgrace which were thus heaped so plentifully on those who provoked public observation by their extravagance, although long set at defiance, must, in the end, have contributed towards changing the tone of society, by forcing vice to retire into privacy.

The general extravagance showed itself in nothing more remarkable than in the fashions of dress, which furnished a subject of never-failing satire from the earlier part of the reign of George II. to the middle of that of his grandson. The hoop-petticoats had been a subject of scandal in the time of George I., but the circular hoops of that period were moderation itself in comparison with the extent of robe given to the ladies of the following generation. At the middle of the century, the hoop began to be made of an oval form, instead of circular, and an immense projection on each side of the body made some of the satirists of the day compare a fashionable woman to a donkey with a pair of panniers. The unsightliness of this costume was increased by the use of a loose flowing robe, called a sack.* In 1747 the great objects of scandal in the dress of the ladies were hoop-petticoats and French pockets, both of which are represented as being very indecorous. The hoop-petticoat and its inconveniences, were made the subject of innumerable caricatures, many of them in the highest degree indelicate. A print, entitled "The Review," without date, but evidently of the latter part of the reign of George II., exhibits the inconvenience of the hoop-petticoat in a variety of ways, and suggests different methods of remedying it. One of the most ingenious is, that of coaches with moveable roofs, and a frame and pulleys to drop the ladies in from the top, so as to avoid the decomposing of their hoops, which necessarily attended their entrance by the door. The great outcry at this time was occasioned by the practice

MODERN CONTRIVANCES.

* An example of this dress will be seen above in the cut on p. 250. For

of leaving bare too much of the neck and shoulders, and wearing the hoop-petticoats short. A poetical description of the ladies' dress, in 1773, directs,

> "Your neck and your shoulders both naked should be,
> Was it not for vandyke, blown with chevaux de-frise,
>
> * * * *
>
> Make your petticoats short, that a hoop eight yards wide
> May decently shew how your garters are tied."

But the attention of the satirist was shortly to be called from the garb of the body to that of the head. Hoop-petticoats disappeared early in the reign of George III., and were followed by enormous head-dresses. The poem just quoted describes the dress of the head as being at that time by no means a very prominent part of the costume.

> "Hang a small bugle cap on, as big as a crown,
> So put it off with a flower, vulgo dict. a pompoon."

The first grand advance in decorating this part of the person, was made at the same time with the introduction of cabriolets, in 1755. Horace Walpole writes on the 15th of June of that year, "All we hear from France is, that a new madness reigns there, as strong as that of Pantins was. This is *la fureur des cabriolets*, *Anglicè*, one-horse chairs, a mode introduced by Mr. Child:[*] they not only universally go in them, but wear them; that is, every thing is to be *en cabriolet*; the men paint them on their waistcoats, and have them embroidered for clocks to their stockings; and the women, who have gone all the winter without anything on their heads, are now muffled up in great caps, with round sides, in the form of, and scarce less than, the wheels of chaises." The fashion was quickly communicated to England, where the cabriolet head-dress was soon improved into *post-chaises, chairs and chairmen*, and even *broad-wheeled waggons !* The following description is taken from a short poem, entitled "A Modern Morning," written in 1757; the lady, after taking her chocolate, has arisen from bed.

> "Then Cœlia to her toilet goes,
> Attended by some fav'rite beaux,
> Who fribble it around the room,
> And curl her hair and clean the comb,
> And do a thousand monkey tricks
> That you would think disgraced the sex.

a more full account of the dress of this period, the reader is referred to Mr. Fairholt's excellent work, "Costume in England," 8vo. 1846. It will only be necessary to notice on the present occasion some of its more extravagant features.

* Josiah Child, brother of the Earl of Tilney.

'Nelly ! why, where's the creature fled !
Put my *post-chaise* upon my head.'—
'Your *chair-and-chairmen*, ma'am, is brought.'—
'Stupid ! the creature has no thought !'—
'And, ma'am, the milliner is come,
She's brought the *broad-wheel'd-waggon* home,
And 'tis the prettiest little thing.
Upon my honour !'—'Bring ! bring ! bring !
How can you stand and talk about it !
You know I die, I die without it !'
  In *broad-wheel'd-waggon* thus array'd
By beaux, and milliner, and maid,
Dear Cœlia treads the toilet round,
Iu her fair faithful glass 'tis found,
And so employs her every sense
'Twould take a team to draw her thence."

A satirist of the day foretells the speedy adoption of similar head-dresses by the gentlemen, and suggests that, as emblematic of the political consistency of the day, the men of one party should wear *windmills*, and the others *weathercocks*.

With the commencement of the reign of George III. hair-dressing became an intricate and difficult science, and was made the subject of several elaborate publications. To raise up the lofty pile of hair, and fill it out with materials to give it due elasticity, to arrange the vast curls that flanked it, and to give grace to the feathers and flowers with which it was crowned, was not within the capacity of every vulgar *coiffeur*. The interior of the mass which rose above the head was filled with wool, tow, hemp, &c., and the quantity of pomatum, and other materials used with it, must have produced an effect calculated to disgust all who were not absolutely mad upon fashion. An ode to the ladies in 1768, printed in the "New Foundling Hospital for Wit," describes the lover's astonishment at his mistress's head-dress :—

"When he views your tresses thin
  Tortur'd by some French friseur ;
Horse-hair, hemp, and wool within,
  Garnish'd with a diamond skewer.

"When he scents the mingled steam
  Which your plaster'd heads are rich in,
Lard and meal, and clouted cream,
  Can he love a walking kitchen !"

When we consider that the great labour of arranging this strange structure hindered its being refreshed often, and that it was sometimes kept two or three weeks before it was broken up, being merely retouched externally, and covered with fresh odours, to conceal any disagreeable smell which might issue from the interior, we shall readily believe the accounts given by those who wrote and preached against the ridiculous enormities of fashion, and who assure us that the interior of the ladies' head-dresses was commonly filled with vermin. In the *London Magazine* for August, 1768, a correspondent on this subject says, "I went the other morning to make a visit to an elderly aunt of mine, when I found her pulling off her cap, and tendering her head to the ingenious Mr. Gilchrist, who has lately obliged the public with a most excellent essay upon hair. He asked her how long it was since *her head had been opened or repaired.* She answered, *not above nine weeks.* To which he replied, that *that was as long as a head could well go in summer,* and that there-fore it was proper to deliver it now; for he confessed that it began to be a little *hazardé.*"

The description of the open-ing of the head which fol-lows is almost too disgusting to repeat.

The caricaturists, as might be expected, were busy with these monstrous decorations of the head, and they did their best to improve upon the originals. A print pub-lished on the 8th of May, 1777, represents what is de-scribed as " a new-fashioned head-dress for young misses of three-score and ten," which is a picture not much ex-aggerated of the fashion prevalent in that year. Two men are required to place the enormous fabric *in situ.* The large nosegay, and the long waving plumes are strictly in character.

A HEAD-DRESS IN 1777.

"But above all the rest
A bold Amazon's crest
Waves, nodding from shoulder to shoulder;
At once to surprise,
And to ravish all eyes,
To frighten and charm the beholder."

The satirists of the day lament over the devastation committed throughout the feathered creation in order to supply this borrowed plumage; and represent the unfortunate bipeds of the

A NEW OPERA-GLASS.

wing wandering about in unnatural and unprovoked bareness, while their two-legged rivals in the ranks of humanity were rendering themselves no less ridiculous in thus appropriating their spoils.

The immense curls on each side of the head were peculiar also to the year just mentioned. In a spirited caricature entitled "A new opera-glass for the year 1777," it is suggested that these spacious curls should be turned to a useful purpose.

" Behold how Jemmy treats the fair,
And makes a telescope of hair!
How will this suit high-headed lasses,
If curls are turned to optic glasses ?"

The extravagant costume of this and the following years is best caricatured in a plate representing four ladies playing at cards,—a reflection, at the same time, upon the violent passion

A BIRD OF PARADISE.

for gaming which characterized this age, and which was attended with so many tragical consequences. Two of the ladies are here quarrelling; one having accused the other of bad play, her antagonist is preparing to decide the dispute with the candlestick. This print, entitled "Settling the odd trick," was "published by M. Darley, Feb. 26, 1778."

Caps now came into fashion to cover the immense heap of hair; and these were equally remarkable for their extravagance, rising high above the head, and spreading out at the sides into a pile of ribands and ornament. In there, caricature could hardly improve upon the strange unwieldy form

of the originals, and it will be enough to give two or three specimens of the fashionable head-dresses, as they were actually worn. The first, of the date 1780, is taken from a print entitled "The bird of Paradise," but is understood to represent the celebrated Mary Anne Robinson (the Perdita of the amorous history of the Prince of Wales, afterwards George IV). A card beside her, inscribed, "Admit Mrs. M—— to the masked ball," shows that she is in full dress; yet there is nothing extravagant in her costume except the enormous *coiffure* and

cap, which look as though they had been stolen from some gigantic dame of the land of Brobdignag. Another cap, equally preposterous, and of nearly the same date, is represented in our next cut, which is said to be a portrait of Mrs. Cosway, the artist. It would be in vain to go on giving examples of the different forms of head-dresses which now came into vogue; for the characteristic of fashion seems to have become suddenly variety instead of uniformity, and it was almost impossible to meet two ladies of high *ton* the outlines of whose costume at all resembled each other.

"Now drest in a cap, now naked in none,
Now loose in a mob, now close in a Joan;
Without handkerchief now, and now buried in ruff;
Now plain as a Quaker, now all of a puff,
Now a shape in neat stays, now a slattern in jumps;
Now high in French heels, now low in your pumps;
Now monstrous in hoop, now trapish, and walking
With your petticoats clung to your heels, like a maulkin;
Like the clock on the tower, that shews you the weather,
You are hardly the same for two days together."

One description of cap or bonnet continued, however, for a long time in favour. It was called a calash, and is said to have been invented in 1765, by the Duchess of Bedford. The calash was formed like the hood of a carriage, and was strengthened with whalebone hoops, so that by means of a string in front, connected with the hoops, it could either be

MISS CALASH IN CONTEMPLATION.

drawn forwards over the face, or it might be thrown backwards over the hair. In the above cut, taken from a print engraved in 1780, the calash is thrown back, and the string hangs loosely over the face. In the next cut the calash is shown as drawn forwards; and the second lady wears another of the numerous extravagant head-dresses of the day. This group is taken from a print published in 1783, and entitled "A Trip to Scarborough." Several other ladies, with equally grotesque head-dresses, though dissimi-

LADIES OF FASHION.

lar, are of the party. Within a few years, however, after this date, these extravagances had disappeared, and the heads of our fair countrywomen were reduced somewhat nearer to their natural size.

Extravagance in male fashions, among the more restricted number of individuals who indulged in it, followed close upon the heels of extravagance in the other sex. The grand phenomena of the years 1772 and 1773 were the *Macaronis.* Men of fashion in the earlier part of the reign of George II. had been commonly designated by the appellation of *beaux;* about the year 1749 they began to be termed *fribbles,* a name which continued in use during the first years of the reign of George III. Then a number of young men who had made the tour, and had returned from Italy with all the vices and follies they had picked up there, formed themselves into a club, which, from the dish which peculiarly distinguished their table, was called the *Macaroni Club.* The members of this club soon became distinguished by the title of *Macaronis;* it was their pride to carry to the utmost excess every description of dissipation, effeminacy of manners, and modish novelty of dress. The *Macaronis* first inundated the town in the year 1772, as just stated. "One will naturally inquire," says a satirical writer in the *Universal Magazine* for the April of that year, "whence originated the prolific family of the Macaronis? who is their sire? To which I answer, that they may be derived from the *Homunculus* of Sterne; or it may be said the Macaronis are indeed the offspring of a *body*, but not of an *individual.* This same body was a many-headed monster in Pall Mall, produced by the demoniac committee of depraved taste and exaggerated fancy, conceived in the courts of France and Italy, and brought forth in England." Horace Walpole, writing in the same month of April, 1772, gave a somewhat different pedigree; he ascribed the growth of this monster to the enormous wealth imported from our conquests in India, and its extravagance was already converting back wealth into poverty —" Lord Chatham begot the East India Company; the East India Company begot Lord Clive; Lord Clive begot the Macaronis; and they begot poverty; and all the race are still living." The Macaronis, in 1772, were distinguished especially by an immense knot of artificial hair behind, by a very small cocked-hat, by an enormous walking-stick, with long tassels, and by jacket, waistcoat, and breeches, of very close cut. The accompanying caricature is taken from the number of the *Universal Magazine* above alluded to.

A MACARONI IN 1772.

The Macaronis soon made an extraordinary noise; everything that was fashionable was à la Macaroni. Even the clergy had their wigs combed, their clothes cut, " their delivery refined," à la Macaroni. The shop-windows were filled with caricatures and other prints of this new tribe; there were portraits of " turf Macaronis," and " Parade Macaronis," and " Macaroni divines," and " Macaroni scholars," and a variety of other species of this extensive genus. Ladies, who carried their head-dress to the extreme of the mode, set up for female Macaronis. Macaronis were the most attractive objects in the ball, or at the theatre. Macaroni articles abounded everywhere. There was Macaroni music, and there were Macaroni songs set to it. The most popular of these latter was the following :—

THE MACARONI.

"Ye belles and beaux of London town,
　Come listen to my ditty;
The Muse in prancing up and down
　Has found out something pretty,
With little hat, and hair dress'd high,
　And whip to ride a pony;
If you but take a right survey,
　Denotes a Macaroni.

"Along the street to see them walk,
　With tail of monstrous size, sir,
You 'll often hear the grave ones talk,
　And wish their sons were wiser.
With consequence they strut and grin,
　And fool away their money;
Advice they care for not a pin,—
　Ay,—that's a Macaroni!

"With boots, and spurs, and Jockey-cap,
　And breeches like a sack, O;
Like curs sometimes they'll bite and snap,
　And give their whip a smack, O.
When this you see, then think of me,
　My name is Merry Crony;
I'll swear the figure that you see
　Is called a Macaroni.

"Five pounds of hair they wear behind,
　The ladies to delight, O;
Their senses give unto the wind,
　To make themselves a fright, O.
This fashion who does e'er pursue,
　I think a simple-tony;
For he's a fool, say what you will,
　Who is a Macaroni."

A MACARONI IN 1773.

The fashion of the Macaronis was too extravagant to last long. Their dress received some alterations between 1772 and 1773, the most remarkable of which were the elevation of the hair, and the adoption of immense nosegays in the bosom. Walpole writes, on the 17th of February, 1773, "A winter without politics . . . . . even our Macaronis entertain the town with nothing but new dresses, and the size of their nosegays. They have lost all their money and exhausted their credit, and can no longer game for twenty thousand pounds a-night." The accompanying cut of a Macaroni of this period, with his lofty head-dress and large nosegay, is taken from a print published on the 3rd of July, 1773, and is stated to be "a real character at the late masquerade." Soon after this period, men of fashion gave up the name of Macaroni, and returned to their original title of beaux.

A large print, bearing the date 1767, and entitled "The present Age," "addressed to the professors of driving, dressing, ogling, writing, playing, gambling, racing, dancing, duelling, boxing, swearing, humming, building, &c." represents the chief subjects of complaint in the manners of the first years of the third George. In the background are three large buildings; the first of which has the sign, "The academy of the noble art of boxing. N.B. Mufflers provided for delicate constitutions." Through the window, a nobleman, with ribbon and star, is seen giving his personal encouragement to the "noble art." The next building is a theatre, with people of all ranks and professions crowding to the door: on a stage in front Folly is pointing with his bauble to the bill of performance, which is inscribed—"Britannia humm'd; or, the Tragedy of the Secret Expedition, a mock tragedy; to which is added a farce, called the Pregnant Rabbit-Woman; together with the adventures of the Bottle Conjuror and the Polish Jew; as likewise the taking the standard at the battle of Dettingen." Behind the figure of Folly are seated on a bench, Elizabeth Canning and the witch, the rabbit-woman, the bottle-conjuror with the quart-bottle on his head, the Polish Jew, and an English dragoon with the captured standard, as so many witnesses of English credulity and gullibility. The third building is a great man's mansion, a sample of taste in modern architecture, "the Corinthian, Venetian, Gothic, and Chinese, huddled in one front;" while, from a garret-window, an old woman is warning a group of individuals from the door—this is described as "modern hospitality in the character of old age, left to take care of furniture, and answer duns, that the family is in the country." The foreground is filled with a number of groups, all described in the margin. In front is a carriage full of ladies in the height of the fashion, described as "British nobility disguised." They are accosted by a foppish personage, with cringing politeness, stated to be one "returned from the *polite tour.*" Near them a French valet is beating an old soldier, who, crippled by the loss of an arm and a leg, is abandoned to beggary; it is "foreign insolence, expressed by the French *valet-de-chambre*, daring to insult English bravery in distress, reduced to ask alms in his native country, after having courageously lost his limbs in defence of it on board a privateer, and unjustly kept out of his prize-money." Another fop, looking unmoved on this scene through an eye-glass, is designated as "the optical ogle, or polite curiosity." Behind the coach is seen a hearse, stated to contain "the corpse of a blood, who boldly lost his life in a duel defending the reputation of a prostitute." In the background two individuals are weighed in a scale—"the balance of merit in this happy climate for useless exotics, a French dancing-master obtains £300 per annum, and

A PLAYER.

a clear benefit, worth nearly £300 more, while the ingenious English shipwright, though assistant to the honour, profit, and

defence of his country, barely obtains £40 per annum." In the far distance, the sea appears covered with ships, one of which is marked as "one British buss, of more service to the community than ten Italian singers." On the other side of the picture is the door of a gentleman's house, "the industrious tradesman thrust off with contempt, expecting a just debt to be paid, to make room for a high-life gambler, politely ushered in to receive his *debt of honour.*" In front appears "a player," carried in a chair, and preceded by his footman; while still more prominently "an author" walks on foot, the picture of want and misery.

Literature was not, indeed, the most lucrative profession during the period of which we are speaking; the House of Hanover was never

AN AUTHOR.

its patron, and the booksellers were not in general liberal
paymasters. Even Dr. Johnson was reduced at one period to
depend upon what he derived from contributions to the magazines and newspapers, and the memorandum found in the pocket-
book of the unfortunate Chatterton, of receipts apparently scattered over several weeks, shows us how such contributions were
remunerated :—

		£	s.	d.
"Received to May 77, of Mr. Hamilton for Mid- d'esex [Journal] . . .		1	11	6
„ of B.		1	2	3
„ of Fell, for the Consuliad . .		0	10	6
„ of Mr. Hamilton, for Candidus and Foreign Journal . . .		0	2	6
„ of Mr. Fell . . .		0	10	6
„ Middlesex Journal . .		0	8	6
„ Mr. Hamilton, for 16 songs (!) .		0	10	6."

Politics was the only subject that found much encouragement ;
and even this brought but the hope of future reward from the
party who were aiming at power, or from those who had obtained
it. There was truth in the statement contained in one of Chatterton's letters:—" Essays fetch no more than what the copy is
sold for," which we have just seen was not much ; " as the
patriots themselves are searching for a place, they have no gra-
tuities to spare. On the other hand, unpopular essays will not
be accepted, and you must pay to have them printed ; but, then,
you seldom lose by it. Courtiers are so sensible of their deficiency in merit, that they generally reward all who know how
to daub them with an appearance of it." The unproportionate
rewards bestowed upon literature and the stage, satirised in the
print described above, had become a subject of invidious remarks,
and produced a pamphlet by Ralph, under the title of " The case
of authors by profession," which attracted some notice. The
generally debased condition of the press, weighed down by political faction, is dwelt on in " The Author," a poem by one of
those who made most by the profession, Charles Churchill, who
describes his fellow-writers as—

> " The slaves of booksellers, or (doom'd by Fate
> To baser chains) vile pensioners of state."

Lord Bute had, indeed, after his accession to power under the
young king, caused pensions and places to be bestowed, with the
professed object of encouraging literature and art, but his choice
had been made without judgment, and those on whom it fell
only became involved in the popular odium gathered round the
name of their patron. A print, dated in 1762, and accompanied

with doggerel verses, represents the unpopular favourite distributing his rewards to a motley crew, described as "the hungry mob of scribblers and etchers." Bute seems to have formed the project of establishing a body of political writers in defence of the court, and of breaking down that formidable power of the press of which almost every ministry of the preceding reign had felt the effects, though all affected to treat it with neglect; but he contrived to bring to notice principally Jacobites and Scotchmen, two classes of personages especially unpopular at that time, and the patronage bestowed on them led to many desperate literary quarrels. Among Lord Bute's pensioners of the better class were, Hogarth, Johnson, Smollett, Shebbeare (who had suffered in the pillory during the preceding year for his virulent attacks upon the House of Hanover,)* Arthur Murphy (the quondam editor of the *Test*), and others.

No single person, entirely unconnected with state affairs, was perhaps ever so much caricatured as the grand caricaturist, Hogarth. He had done in picture what Foote practised on the stage; and his constant practice of introducing contemporaries into his moral satires had procured him a host of enemies on the town, while his vain egotism, and the scornful tone in which he spoke of the other artists of the age, offended and irritated them. The publication of Hogarth's portrait by himself, with his well-known dog in the corner, exposed the painter to an attack in the *Scandalizade* (written in 1750), which shews that even then he was not popular in the literary world. To a doubt expressed as to the meaning of the picture,—

> " Quoth a sage in the crowd . . . ' I'd have you to know, sir,
> 'Tis Hogarth himself, and his friend honest Towzer,—
> Insep'rate companions! and, therefore, you see
> Cheek by jowl they are drawn in familiar degree;
> Both striking the eye with an equal eclat,
> The biped *this* here, and the quadruped *that.*'—
> ' You mean—the great dog and the man, I suppose;
> Or the man and the dog—be't just as you chuse.'"

A dispute on this point is settled abruptly,—

---

* It is amusing to hear Smollett (in his History) speak of the sufferings of "this good man," "for having given vent to the unguarded effusions of mistaken zeal, couched in the language of passion and scurrility." The "Letters to the People," for one of which Dr. Shebbeare was placed in the pillory by the ministers of George II., abound in language like the following, here applied to King George's foot grenadiers, who bore on the front of their caps the Hanoverian symbol of the white horse.—"Such confusion and dread dwelt on the dastard faces of all who, sold to the H——n interest, stand branded in the forehead with the *white horse,* the ignominious mark of slavery."

"Split the diff'rence, my friend, they're both great in their way.
  * * * they're alike, as it were,
A respectable pair! all spectators allow,
And that they deserve an inscription below
In capital letters, *Behold we are two!*"

The publication of his "Analysis of Beauty," at the end of 1753, became the signal for a general attack; and what was termed his line of beauty, an S-shaped curve, in which he seems to have fancied that that quality chiefly consisted, and which he had illustrated by two very droll plates, became an object of unceasing ridicule. A great number of caricatures were, in consequence, launched forth against him in the course of the year 1754. In one, entitled "A new Dunciad—done with a view of [fixing] the fluctuating ideas of taste," the painter is represented with a stupid, vacant face, playing with a pantin, with a fool's cap on the ground, adorned with the line of beauty in front: a black harlequin standing behind him. In another he is represented as the mountebank painter, demonstrating to his admirers and subscribers that crookedness is the test of beauty: the hump-backed and deformed are crowding forward to attract his notice. In a third, entitled (in allusion to his having turned scribbler,) "The Author run mad," he is pictured as a maniac, chained by a foot to the floor, while, with his line of beauty in one hand, he is painting wild subjects on the wall. Another, in allusion to the title of his book, represents the unfortunate "analyst" in great consternation and distress, resting his book upon his celebrated line of beauty, while in the distance copies of it are being thrown into the caves of Dulness and Oblivion. In a larger and more finished print, Hogarth is represented in the act of undermining the sacred monument of all the best painters, sculptors, &c., in imitation of the Grecian Herostratus, who is seen in the distance setting fire to the Temple of Diana, to gratify his morbid desire of fame. A portly individual is lighting Hogarth at his envious work, perhaps intended to represent Dr. Morell, who assisted him in passing his work through the press.

AN UNFORTUNATE ANALYST.

Other caricatures represented him in his studio, painting after coarse and ugly models, burlesqued his attempts at historical painting (such as

the picture of Paul before Felix), or parodied some of his famous
works. Thus, in a print entitled "The Painter's March from
Finchley," Hogarth is seen pursued from the village by every
kind of persecutor, biped and quadruped, and assailed by a

A PAINTER IN DISTRESS.

mingled din produced from the various vocal organs of woman
and child, goose and donkey, cow and pig. Underneath we read
the lines :—

"Patrons of worth, encouragers of arts,
Lo! from his seat the son of folly starts
At Nature's call.—How cheap is —— come!
For see a wit holds burlesque for his ——.
O Hogarth, born our wonder to engage,
Thou low refracting mirror of the age!"

In 1758 Hogarth was exposed to a new onslaught of caricatures. In the previous year the question of founding an
academy for the fine arts had been agitated (a plan which was
carried into effect some years later by George III.), and some
steps were taken towards a general encouragement of art in this
country. The interest caused by this project is shown by
several prints relating to the progress of the arts, published at
that time. Hogarth set his face violently against it, and again
provoked the imputation of enviously keeping back artists in
general, in the fear that they might in the end intrench upon
his own fame. One or two new caricatures against him appeared
in consequence, in which he is represented as the patron of
coarseness and ugliness, surrounded with models in which those
qualities are set out in the most forbidding forms. In one of

these, entitled "Pugg's Graces, etched from his *original daubing*," the painter is represented executing a picture of Moses before Pharaoh's daughter, his pug's legs resting on three volumes, the lowest of which is his own "Analysis of Beauty." His fat encourager (Dr. Morell?) is directing his attention to his model Graces, three naked females, whose forms exhibit everything that is coarse and revolting. Near him lies an open book, on one page of which is the title, "Reasons against a Public Academy, 1758," and on the other the words "No Salary." Above, among the models of various kinds, flies a head in the fashionable *coiffure* of the day, with the

PAINTER PUG.

line of beauty in its mouth, described as "a modern cherubim." Another of the painter's patrons leans in admiration against his chair, holding in his hand the book in which the line of beauty is set forth. Among the different grotesque articles scattered about the room are several described as "A Diana's crescent; B. A multiplying glass; 76. A gammon of bacon; 14. Rays of light; 4. Beauty stays (a pair of stays, to give elegance to the female shape); 68. A jack-boot." This print is accompanied with the lines,—

> "Behold a wretch whom Nature form'd in spite;
> Scorn'd by the wise, he gave the fools delight.
> Yet not contented in his sphere to move,
> Beyond mere instinct and his senses drove,
> From false examples hoped to pilfer fame,
> And scribbled nonsense in his daubing name.
> Deformity herself his figures place,
> She spreads an ugliness on every face,
> He then admires their elegance and grace.
> Dunce connoisseurs extol the author Pug,
> The senseless, tasteless, impudent hum-bug."

From the introduction of the jack-boot into the print just described, we may presume that Hogarth already enjoyed, or

was believed to enjoy, the patronage of Lord Bute, before the
death of George II. The slight shown to his talents by that
monarch was enough to procure him favour in the household of
his grandson. Soon after the accession of the latter to the
throne, when the chief power had been lodged in Bute's hands,
Hogarth was appointed to the office of serjeant painter to all his
Majesty's works, which his enemies jeeringly interpreted as chief
" pannel-painter ;" and this mode of distinguishing talent and his
historical painting of Sigismunda, executed about the same
period, were subsequently made the ground of no little ridicule.
The picture was parodied in a vulgar print entitled, " A harlot
blubbering over a bullock's heart; by William Hogarth."
    In an unlucky hour, Hogarth's zeal in the cause of his patron,
or, as others said, the desire of obtaining an increase in his pension, led him into the arena of politics, from which he had
hitherto kept tolerably clear, and he entered the field against his
old friends, Wilkes and Churchill. In the September of 1762
appeared the political print of " The Times," which was labelled
" No. I.," as though intended only to be the first of a series. It
was an attack upon the ex-minister, Pitt. Europe was represented in a conflagration, and the flames were already communicating to Great Britain. Pitt was blowing the fire, which Lord
Bute, with a party of soldiers and sailors, assisted by Highlanders, was endeavouring to extinguish ; but he was impeded in
his design by the Duke of Newcastle, who brought a barrow-full
of *Monitors* and *North Britons* to feed the flames. Wilkes had
received information of the intended caricature before its
publication, had expostulated in vain with Hogarth, and had
threatened retaliation; the Saturday after the appearance of
" The Times," Wilkes fulfilled his threat in the seventeenth
number of the *North Briton*, an attack upon Hogarth, written
with so much bitterness, and striking not only at his professional
but at his domestic character, that he appears never to have
recovered it. A coarse woodcut portrait of Hogarth headed
this paper, the motto of which was,—

        " Its proper power to hurt each creature feels,
        Dulls aim their horns, and asses lift their heels."

    In his anger, Hogarth repaired to Westminster Hall, when
Wilkes was the second time brought thither from the Tower,
and, in Wilkes' own words, " skulked behind the counter in
the Court of Common Pleas ;" he thence sketched a caricatured
portrait of the pretended " patriot," in which his ill-favoured
features are made ten times more demoniacal than the ori-

ginal. The publication of this portrait drew another combatant into the field, Wilkes' friend, the poet Churchill; who, soon after its appearance, in the summer of 1763, published that bitterest of poetic invectives, the "Epistle to William Hogarth." This piece added canker to the wound which already rankled in Hogarth's breast; he again took up the pencil, and produced a picture of Churchill under the figure of a canonical bear, with a pot of porter in one hand, and a knotty club in the other, each knot being labelled as "lie 1," "lie 2," &c. In one corner below, Hogarth's own dog is treating the "Epistle" in the most contemptuous manner. Other emblems are scattered about; and in a second edition he added on a label a group representing himself as a bear-master forcing the bear, Churchill, and the monkey, Wilkes, to dance, under the infliction of a severe castigation. The monkey holds a *North Briton* in his hand. The picture was en-

A PATRIOT.

A BEAR-MASTER.

titled, "The Bruiser, C. Churchill, (once the Rev.,) in the character of a Russian Hercules, regaling himself after having killed the monster Caricatura, that so severely galled his virtuous friend, the heaven-born Wilkes."

This quarrel drew upon Hogarth another flood of caricatures, which held him up now as the pensioned dauber of the unpopular Lord Bute, and the calumniator of the friends of liberty. In one, entitled "The Butyfier, a touch upon the Times," Hogarth is represented on a large platform, daubing an immense boot, (the constant emblem of the obnoxious minister,) while in his awkwardness he bespatters Pitt and Temple, who happen to be below. It is a parody on Hogarth's own satire on Pope. Beneath the scaffold is a tub full of *Auditors, Monitors,* &c. labelled "The Charm: Butifying Wush." A print entitled "The Bruiser Triumphant," represents Hogarth as an ass, painting the Bruiser, while Wilkes comes behind, and places horns on his head—an allusion to some scandalous intimations in the *North Briton.* Churchill, in the garb of a parson, is writing Hogarth's life. A number of other attributes and allusions fill the picture. A caricature entitled "Tit for Tat," represents Hogarth painting Wilkes, with the unfortunate picture of Sigismunda in the distance. Another "Tit for Tat," "Inv¹ et del. by G. O'Garth, according to act or order is not material," represents the painter, partly clad in Scotch garb, with the line of beauty on his palette, glorifying a boot surmounted by a thistle. The painter is saying to himself, "Anything for money : I'll gild this Scotch sign, and make it look glorious, and I'll daub the other sign, and efface its beauty, and make it as black as a Jack Boot." On another

THE BEAUTIFIER.

easel is a portrait of Wilkes, "Defaced by order of my L— by O'Garth," and, in the foreground, "a smutchpot to sully the best and most exalted characters." In another print, "Pug the snarling cur" is being severely chastised by Wilkes and Churchill. In another, he is baited by the bear and a dog ; and in the background is a large panel, with the inscription, "Panel painting." In one print Hogarth is represented going for his pension of £300 a-year, and carrying as his vouchers the prints of "The Times," and Wilkes. "I can paint an angel black and the devil white, just as it suits me." "An Answer to the print of John Wilkes, Esq." represents Hogarth with his colour-pot, inscribed "Colour to blacken fair characters ;" he is treading on the cap of liberty with his cloven foot, and an inscription says, "£300 per annum for distorting features." Several other prints, equally bitter against him, besides a number of caricatures against the Government, under the fictitious names of O'Gurth, Hoggart, Hog-ass, &c., must have assisted in irritating the persecuted painter.

Hogarth died on the 26th of October, 1764, as it was generally believed of a broken heart, caused by the persecution to which he had exposed himself. He left an engraving of

"The Times, Plate II.," in which Wilkes was represented on the pillory by the side of "Miss Fanny," but it was not given to the world till many years after his death. He was soon followed by his adversary, Churchill, who died at Calais on the 4th of November, 1764, in consequence of a sudden attack of fever.[*]

Among the writers whom Lord Bute, on his appointment to the head of the ministry, employed in his Quixotic crusade against the opposition press, was Doctor Smollett, who was not only a Scotchman, but whose principles leaned strongly towards Jacobitism. Smollett had no regular pension; but he was paid to write the *Briton*, a violent weekly paper, the object of which was to abuse Pitt, and all the popular party. It was this injudicious government paper which provoked the publication, by Wilkes and Churchill, of the *North Briton*, which has attained to so much celebrity in the history of the earlier years of this reign. Churchill detested Smollett both as the Critical Reviewer and as the author of the *Briton*, and speaks of him with bitterness in several passages in his poems. After the appearance of the *North Briton*, Bute set up another rather scurrilous paper in support of his *Briton*, which was named the *Auditor*, and which was written or edited by Arthur Murphy, an author of small merit and chiefly known as a translator and adapter of plays from the French to the English stage. The first number of the *Briton* appeared on the 29th of May, 1762; the *North Briton* came out on the 5th of June; and the first number of the *Auditor* followed it on the 10th of June. A shoal of popular papers, bitterly attacking Bute and his "hirelings," was roused by this new Government organ, and literature was suddenly drawn into the troubled arena of politics far more fiercely than had ever been the case before. The "pensioners," as they were termed, were held up to public scorn in every possible shape. Smollett especially, the paid Scottish advocate of Scotchmen, was an object of general attack; and in a caricature published at the end of May, immediately after the appearance of the *Briton* and the *North Briton*, under the title of "The Mountebank," in which Lord Bute, in the character of the quack-doctor, is boasting of the efficacy of his gold pills, Smollett acts the part of the mounte-

---

[*] Dr. Johnson persisted in looking upon Churchill's poetry with unmerited contempt. It is too temporary in its allusions to be generally interesting to the present age; but Mr. Tooke, in his recent edition (3 vols. Pickering, 1844), has done much to make it popular among modern readers.

bank to call attention to them.   They are on a stage, addressing
a multitude of people.   The following speech is put into the
mouth of Smollett, who holds under his arm a roll which
is inscribed as the *Briton*, while the *North Briton* lies under his

THE MOUNTEBANK.

feet :—" By my saul, laddies, I tell ye truly I went round about,
and I thank my gued stars I found a passage through Wales,
which conducted me to aw the muckle places in the land, where
I soon got relief, and straightway commenced doctor for the
benefit of mysel and countrymen.   See here, my bra' lads, in
these bags are contained the gowden lozenges, a never-failing
remedy, that gives present ease famous throughout the known
world for their excellent quality.   Now, as ye are a' my countrymen, and stand in most need of a cure, I will gie every mon
o' ye twa or three thousand of these lozenges once a year,
to make ye hauld up your heads, and turn out muckle men."
The quack-doctor, Bute, adds, " Awa wi' ye to the deel, ye
southern loons ; but aw ye bonny lads fra the north o' Tweed,
mak haste and come to me, I am now in a capacity to gie ye aw
relief, I ken fu' weel your distemper,—I donna mean that so
peculiar to our country, occasion'd by the immoderate use
of oatmeal.   But it is the gowden itch wi' which ye are
troubled (and, in truth, most folk are,) that I learnt the art to
cure.   I mysel was ne'er fra' this muckle itch while I liv'd in
the North, but having a gud staff to depend upon, I resolved
to travel into the South to seek a cure."   A female figure looks

from behind the curtain, intended to represent the Princess-Dowager of Wales (who was popularly called *the witch*).

Neither the *Briton* nor the *Auditor* endured many months, for it was soon found that they answered ill the purpose for which they had been started. But their authors, and the other pensioners of Lord Bute, continued to serve against the popular cause with political pamphlets, and by other means. Dr. Johnson continued long silent, and his pension seemed only to have rendered him mute. Churchill, who hated Johnson, and ranked him among the " vile pensioners of state," makes the distinction between those who were paid to write, and those who only abstained for their pay :—

> " Some, dead to shame, and of those shackles proud
> Which Honour scorns, for slavery roar aloud ;
> Others half-palsied only, mutes become,
> And what makes Smollett write, makes Johnson dumb."

Johnson had, in fact, given an unfortunate definition of the word *pensioner* in his dictionary, compiled when he received nothing from government, which laid him open to the sneers of the popular party ; but it was not till 1770 that the doctor ventured openly to enter the field of politics by an attack on Wilkes in a pamphlet entitled " The False Alarm." It is probably to that period that we must ascribe a caricature repre-

A PATRIOT WORRIED.

senting the "patriot" Wilkes, worried by two dogs, one of which (that to the left) bears the features of the lexicographer, and the other, those of some other writer of the court-party, of

T

the identity of whom we are less certain. Dr. Johnson, the general decrier of talent in others, was by no means a favourite among the writers on the popular side in the great political warfare of the last century, and he was made the subject of a variety of caricatures, most of them published at a later period than that of which we are now speaking.

AN OWL.

One of these, published on the 10th of March, 1782, on the occasion of the prejudiced character of some of his lives of the English poets, represents the doctor, in the shape of an owl, standing upon the " Lives of the Poets " and the Dictionary, and leering at Milton, Pope, &c., who are surrounded with starry rays. It is entitled, " Old Wisdom blinking at the stars."

Johnson himself partook violently in those strong political prejudices which were the bane of literature at the commencement of the reign of George III., and which then were felt still more injuriously, because they even influenced the judgment of the critics in those new tribunals, the reviews, who too often punished the political creed of the writer by speaking bitterly or contemptuously of his talents as an author. It is to be wished that the effects of this political barbarism had died with the age which produced it. But it is too certain that literature, in this country, neglected by the first two monarchs of the house of Hanover, and persecuted at the commencement of the reign of the third, has never since been allowed to obtain its fair share of court or ministerial favour.

One of the most remarkable victims to the neglect of literature at this period of political strife was the unfortunate, though talented Chatterton. Genius was, in this instance, as in so many others, drowned in the rage of party. The young poet threw himself upon the world, reckoning for success on his own talents. He gave way to the prevailing taste for virulent satire, and, amidst a profusion of hopes and promises, he found himself, like so many of his contemporaries in the profession he had chosen, reduced to hopeless poverty, and he escaped from it by a crime which was then fearfully common among all classes of society, and which had closed the career of several other votaries of the Muse—suicide.

CHAPTER VIII.

GEORGE III.

Accession of George III.—Breaking up of the Pitt Ministry—Rise of Lord Bute, and Inundation of Scotchmen —The Peace —Bute's Resignation— "Wilkes and Liberty ;" the Mob—The North Briton, and the " Essay on Woman"—Attempt to Tax the Americans—The Rockingham Ministry—Pitt's Re-appearance, and Temporary Restoration to Power as Earl of Chatham—Outlawry of Wilkes ; the Pillory—Bute's Secret Influence ; his Puppets—Wilkes at Brentford, and in the King's Bench —Wilkes Lord Mayor of London, and his subsequent History.

THE political heroes of the first ten years of the reign of George III. were William Pitt, Lord Bute, and John Wilkes. It was a period at which faction raged with extraordinary violence; and which carried off from the scene nearly all the great political intriguers that remained of those who figured in the events contained in the former part of the present volume.

When George III. ascended the throne, he had entered his twenty-third year ; his education had been notoriously neglected, and, from the character of his instructors, it was generally believed that they had instilled into him very exalted notions of the prerogatives of the crown, if they had not taught him to aspire to arbitrary power. Everybody know the pains which had been taken to keep him under the influence of his mother ; and the close connexion between her and Lord Bute, which had been made a subject of scandal alternately by all parties, led most people to look forward with apprehensions to a reign of favouritism, apprehensions which were not calmed by the good promises under which it opened.

John Stuart, Earl of Bute, was originally a poor Scotch nobleman, by disposition proud and ambitious, but not remarkable for his talents. He first attracted the notice of Frederick Prince of Wales at a private dramatic entertainment, given by the Duchess of Queensbury, where he performed the part of Lothario in " The Fair Penitent." Frederick invited him to Leicester House, and took him into favour; and after the Prince's death, he became the still more special favourite of the Princess-Dowager, who made him her groom of the stole, and he was the chief actor in all the Leicester House intrigues. We have no

T 2

reason to doubt that, from the moment George III. ascended the throne, Lord Bute's ambition led him to grasp at the chief power, but he began cautiously, and his plans were assisted by the old and treacherous rivalry of the Duke of Newcastle and some other members of Pitt's administration. At first the only changes were made in the Bed-Chamber. Horace Walpole has handed down to us a bon-mot of a lady observer, who said at the beginning of December 1760, that the great question was whether the King would burn in his chamber *Scotch*-coal, *Newcastle*-coal, or *Pitt*-coal; and he adds that "a bon-mot very often paints truly the history or manners of the times." At the beginning of January people were already complaining of the undue partiality shown to Scotchmen. The scandal attached to Bute's intimacy with the Princess-Dowager was not allowed to die. Walpole, who has preserved so much of the political small-talk of the day, writes on the 3rd of March, 1761,— "There has been a droll print: her mistress [the princess] reproving Miss Chudleigh [one of the maids of honour, afterwards Duchess of Kingston] for her train of life; she replies, 'Madame, chacun a *son Bute!*'" Within a few days after this date, Legge was suddenly dismissed from the Chancellorship of the Exchequer, and Lord Holderness was ordered to give up the Seals, which the King immediately delivered to Lord Bute. All this was done without consulting Pitt, who, however, shewed no resentment. The parliament was dissolved towards the end of March, and faction seemed to have been so entirely subdued under Pitt's administration, that the elections were attended with none of the usual excitement. But when the new parliament had been ensured, the favourite proceeded towards his object more boldly and openly.

Many circumstances connected with the resignation of Pitt at the beginning of this reign, bore a close resemblance to those of the fall of the Whigs under Queen Anne. In each case, the ministry had become popular by a long and glorious war, which their successors closed by a hasty and not very advantageous peace; and in both, the revolution was brought about by the insidious influence of favouritism. In the latter case, as well as in the former, we shall see that an attempt was made to influence the mob; but the circumstances of the times had changed, and rendered the latter part of the project less practicable. In both cases, too, the court influence in the House of Lords was strengthened by a numerous creation of new peers. France, reduced almost to despair by the successive losses of her colonies, which were but slightly balanced by what she had gained in Germany, and impoverished by her exertions in the war, began to talk of peace with England immediately after the accession of the new King, and the French ministers soon opened negotiations, and evidently thought that they might obtain it on easy terms from Bute. But Pitt haughtily and obstinately demanded greater concessions to the glory of England than they seemed willing to make. His opponents immediately set up the cry, that he advocated war merely because his own position as minister depended upon it. It was soon, however, found that France was insincere in its proceedings, and that, under cover of negotiations for peace, that government was secretly forming an alliance with Spain to make that power a party in the war against England in the colonies. The "Family Compact" between the two countries was signed on the 15th of August, 1761, and ratified on the 8th of September, and Pitt, aware of this circumstance, and informed of the great preparations carried on in Spain, proposed a bold and decisive line of conduct for this country. It was his advice to recal our ambassador from Madrid, unless a satisfactory explanation were given by the Spanish government, and to issue an immediate declaration of war against Spain. But Pitt's advice was overruled in council, which preferred temporizing, and when he declared that he could not remain in office and be responsible for measures which were not his own, he found that his power in the ministry was gone, and on the 6th of October he delivered up his seal of office. The King offered him, through Lord Bute, any rewards in the power of the crown to bestow, and he accepted a pension of £3000. a year, with a peerage for his wife, who was created Baroness of Chatham. Pitt was followed in his resignation by his friend and brother-in-law, Lord Temple.

Although the resignation of Mr. Pitt spread alarm among a large portion of that class which we are in the habit of calling thinking people, the popular excitement occasioned by it was much less than might have been expected. The City of London, indeed, voted public thanks to the ex-minister, instructed their members in parliament to look to him as their leader, and took every opportunity of shewing their strong sympathy; and two or three other cities followed the example. Even the popular newspapers were far from violent, although they were not wanting in warm expressions of regret and apprehension. At the coronation, which had taken place on the 22nd of September, one of the largest jewels had fallen from the crown, which was looked upon by superstitious people as a sinister omen; and now there were many who saw its fulfilment.

> " When first, portentous, it was known,
>   Great George had jostled from his crown
>   The brightest diamond there ;
>   The omen-mongers, one and all,
>   Foretold some mischief must befall,
>   Some loss beyond compare.
>
> " Some fear this gem is Hanover,
>   Whilst others wish to God it were ;
>   Each strives the nail to hit.
>   One guesses that, another this,
>   All mighty wise, yet all amiss ;
>   For, ah ! who thought of Pitt !"

Another similar effusion, which was afterwards reprinted in the "New Foundling Hospital for Wit," made the following recapitulation of the various ministers who had held rule under the House of Hanover ; Walpole, the Pelhams, Newcastle or, as it was more generally considered, Fox and Pitt :—

"CORINNA VINDICATED.

> " Corinna, Virtue's child, and chaste
>   As vestal maid of yore,
>   Nor sought the nuptial rites in haste,
>   Nor yet those rites forswore.
>
> " Her, many a worthless knight to wed
>   Pursued in various shapes ;
>   But she, though choosing not to lead,
>   Would not be led by—*apes.*
>
> " Roysters they were, and each a more
>   Penelope's gallant ;
>   They ate and drank up all her cheer,
>   And loved her into want.
>
> " See her by Walpole first address'd,
>   (But Walpole caught a Tartar) ;
>   Him while an ill-earn'd riband graced,
>   She wore a nobler garter.
>
> " A pair of brothers next advance,
>   Alike for business fit ;
>   The filly 'gan to kick and prance,
>   And spurn the Pelham bit.
>
> " But who comes next ? Ah ! well I ken
>   Him playing fast and loose.
>   Cease, Fox, the prey will ne'er be thine,
>   Corinna's not a goose.
>
> " See last the man by heaven design'd
>   To make Corinna bless'd ;
>   To every virtuous act inclined,
>   All *patriot* in his breast.
>
> " He woo'd the fair with manly sense,
>   And, flattery apart,

By dint of sterling eloquence
Subdued Corinna's heart.

" She gave her hand—but, lest her hand
So given should prove a curse,
The price omitted, by command,
For better and for worse."

It was the court-party which now blew the spark of faction into a new blaze. No sooner had Pitt quitted his office, than he was attacked by a host of carica-tures, newspapers, and pamphlets, in the interest or pay of Bute. They represented him as the "distressed statesman," disappointed and over-thrown in his ambitious projects, and now obliged to retire from public ob-servation to conceal his chagrin. They spoke of him as the general incen-diary, the demon of war, who cared not how he burdened or embroiled his country, while he gratified his love of slaughter and confusion. They blazoned forth his venality, and ex-patiated continually on his pension and his wife's peerage. They talked of his factiousness, and of his intended measures of opposition. In one of the caricatures, entitled "Gulliver's Flight, or the

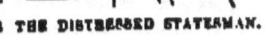

THE DISTRESSED STATESMAN.

GULLIVER'S FLIGHT.

Man-mountain," the " Great Commoner," as he was popularly

termed, is represented flying away from St. Stephen's upon his own bubbles, amid the acclamations of the multitude below. The large bubble on which he is seated, is inscribed with the words, " Pride, Conceit, Patriotism, Popularity." The smaller ones beneath it, are "Vanity," " Adulation," "Self-importance." Those just falling from him, are inscribed, "North America," "Spanish War," " Honesty," as being the bubbles that preceded his resignation. And the one just issuing from the pipe is " Moderation." a sneer at the moderation which he professed after his resignation. This print is accompanied by a violent attack on Pitt's political conduct, in the form of an allegory or dream.

These attacks upon the great statesman were ill-timed, and only produced a violent reaction in his favour. The opposition papers began to take a bolder tone; portraits of Pitt, and pictures that glorified him, had a ready sale; and the caricatures upon Bute and his Scotchmen became more numerous and more violent. In one of the prints alluded to, Pitt, carrying the cap of Liberty, and treading on Faction, is presented to Britannia by Pratt Lord Camden, and is supported by Justice and Victory. The ministry of Pitt, during the last years of George II., seemed, indeed, to have trodden faction under foot; and party, which had for some years been a mere distinction of ins and outs, appeared to be almost extinguished. It was now that the name of Tories, which had always been considered as identical with Jacobites, and which had scarcely been heard of for some time, again made its appearance. In the late reign, the crown had been a moderator of parties; it now entered the field of political warfare as a party in the strife, and the early prejudices of youth identified George III., during the rest of his reign, violently and obstinately with those who, modified considerably from the old Jacobites, were henceforward denominated Tories.

The wisdom and foresight of William Pitt was as quickly demonstrated by the course of events. The English government temporized and showed its weakness during three months; it gave Spain time to make all its preparations for war, and receive all its treasures from America, which came at this period of the year; and then, at the end of December, it was obliged, under disadvantages, to make the declaration of war which Pitt would have made under every advantage at the beginning of October. The manifesto of the King of Spain, was a personal attack upon Pitt, and did not fail to raise him in the estimation of his countrymen; the English government was obliged to tread in the very steps which he had been obliged to resign for indicating; yet the ex-minister was still abused for his warlike propensities. The state of foreign relations in 1761 is represented in a rather popular caricature of the day, entitled "The present state of Europe, a political farce of four acts, as it is now in rehearsal by all the potentates, A.D. 1761." The distant part of the print represents the island of Corsica, and the bombardment of Bastia. On the left a weeping Genoese sighs and exclaims, "I see and bewail the error too late of my country's severity to these brave islanders." Considerable sympathy was felt at this time in England for the Corsicans, who were struggling under their brave general Paoli against the French. In the same part of the picture, the Russian bear growls against a Danish dog gnawing a bone. A Swedish dog stands and snarls over Pomerania, at a Prussian attempting to throw a collar over his neck, charging him to "fly from our Prussian Pomerania, or else, you meddling cur, I'll chain you." The King of Prussia plays the Black Joke on a flute; and the Queen of Hungary, dancing to it, falls, exclaiming, "Deuce take his joke, I have crack'd my crown by it!" The Empress of Russia says, calmly, "Oh, sister, keep it up for the joke's sake." The British Lion treats the Gallic Cock with contempt, and behind stands a quadruple alliance of the pope, the kings of France and Spain, and the devil. The pope urges the Spaniard, "My son, assist your most Christian brother against the heretics; it will be more meritorious than a crusade." The Spaniard replies, "I own I love them not, but dread their power." France entreats, "Dear brother, assist me now, or I am lost for ever!" Satan consoles them all, by promising them a retreat in his dominions.

In "The present state of Europe; a political farce in four acts, part four; published at the commencement of 1762, the designs of the King of Spain appear to be still doubted. The monarchs of Europe are playing at dice. King George and the King of Prussia sit in close alliance at one end of the table; the former throwing the dice, with his drawn sword in his hand, is made to say,—"Play on, brave Prussia, proud Poland's down. Faithful Britons will never submit to sharpers." The King of Poland and Elector of Saxony, has made a bad throw, and his crown is falling from his head. He cries,—"I am undone, d——n Bruhl—I've lost my own by playing a game for that ambitious Hungary Queen." At the other end of the table sit the Kings of France and Spain; the former urges his brother monarch to risk a bold stroke for Gibraltar, in order to ensure

to himself Hanover at the end of the contest, but the wily King
of Spain is made to reply, "Most Christian Brother, I will recover Gibraltar establish my right to the fishery, but as to your
conquest of Hanover, I would not
venture an ounce of logwood to it."
The King of Spain is, however,
himself a victim, and a personage
described as "The sure gamester
Minheer Trickall, a Dutch politician, with his pockets full of ducats
and louis-d'or " (to show his cunning and the profit he was making
out the war), is represented picking the King of Spain's pocket of
a bag of "dollars," with the reflection, "Let them play on, mine
is the sure game—Minheer shall
win from all without hazard."
Behind him appears the Genoese,
reduced to distress by his exertions
for the assistance of France; and
at the extreme left, the devil is
peeping in, and exulting over the scene thus laid open to his
view.

DUTCH POLICY.

The King's first speech to parliament had, indeed, expressed
the old sentiment of attachment to the King of Prussia, and
sympathy in his cause, which was still that of England. But
as soon as Pitt was got rid of, these sentiments were rapidly
modified, and Bute openly declared the intention of deserting
our German allies in the same manner that they had been
deserted by the Tory ministry of Queen Anne. Some of the old
ministry were, however, opposed to this dishonourable conduct;
and at length, on the 26th of May, 1762, the Duke of Newcastle, the nominal head of the administration, indignant at the
intended treatment of the King of Prussia, and not till it seems
that he had received broad hints that he was no longer acceptable, resigned his office, upon which, the same day, Lord Bute
was made first Lord of the Treasury. This was a change which
had evidently been contemplated for some time. Lord Egremont had been appointed to the place of Secretary of State,
vacated by Pitt; George Grenville was now made the other
Secretary of State; and Lord Bute's creature, the dissipated
and incapable Sir Francis Dashwood, Chancellor of the
Exchequer.

The popular attacks upon the favourite, through the instrumentality of the press, had been gradually increasing in number and violence, before he made himself Prime-minister. The complaints against the patronage of Scotchmen were especially loud. As early as the 12th of January, 1761, the newspapers advertise " A new copper-plate ballad called Boot-all;" with an additional announcement of " A new collection of Scotch collops, screens, curtains, &c., with those curious prints of the *Quere*, and *We are all a coming.*" After Lord Bute had become Prime-minister, the number of caricatures increased amazingly, and the mere titles of the political prints issued during the next two or three years would almost fill a volume. A large proportion of them, however, are ill-designed, and still worse engraved, and some of them revolt us by their gross indecency.[*] Yet they answered their purpose in inflaming the passions of the mob. Walpole writes on the 20th of June 1762, " The new administration begins tempestuously. My father was not more abused after twenty years than Lord Bute is after twenty days. Weekly papers swarm, and, like other swarms of insects, sting." Bute's attempt to combat the opposition of the press with its own weapons only added fuel to the fire. The *Monitor*, the warm advocate of Pitt and his measures, contained on the 22nd of May (two days before Newcastle's resignation) a bitter article on royal favourites. Bute established the *Briton*, the first number of which contained a reply to the *Monitor*, and this, as well as another government paper, the *Auditor*, continued weekly to pour forth a torrent of not very delicate abuse on all the popular party. The *Briton*, as it has been already stated, produced the *North Briton*, edited by Wilkes and Churchill, which attacked the court party with quite as much scurrility as distinguished the government organs, and which eventually contributed not a little towards overthrowing the Bute administration.

Bute seemed intoxicated with his power, and, paying little attention to the popular complaints, he set no bounds to his injudicious patronage of his countrymen, heaping preferment on his brother, James Mackensie, to whom he gave, in 1763, the highest offices in Scotland. Bute's patronage of his brother and countrymen is satirized in a caricature entitled "The flying

---

[*] A newspaper paragraph of October 15, 1762, reprinted in the *Gentleman's Magazine* for that month, very justly says, " Many of the representations that have lately appeared in the shops, are not only reproachful to government, but offensive to common sense ; they discover a tendancy to inflame, without a spark of fire to light their own combustibles."

machine from Edinburgh in one day, performed by Moggy Mackensie at the Thistle and Crown." A northern witch is

A JOURNEY FROM THE NORTH.

conducting the Scottish adventurers to the land of promotion, on a monstrous broomstick :—

> " On broomstick, by old Moggy's aid,
>   Full royally they rode,
> And on the wings of northern winds,
>   Came flying all abroad."

Other caricatures represent the high roads from the north, crowded with ragged Scots who were deserting their bleak and barren mountains for the milder climes of the south; while in others ship-loads sought the land of promise by sea. Even the post from the north-country was suspected of bringing its share of the noxious importation; and one of the caricatures of

A SCOTCH MISSIVE.

a somewhat later period represents a Scotchman dispatched to London under cover of a franked envelope.

The favourite himself, who was commonly spoken of as the "Thane," was attacked under every shape that inveterate hatred could suggest. He was the "jack-boot" (a poor pun on his name) from which all our mischiefs flowed, the thistle, the "political bag-piper." The "boot" was the favourite object in caricatures. One of these, entitled "The Whipping Post," represents poor Britannia stripped naked and bound to the whipping-post, while a Scotchman is scourging her mercilessly with thistles. The caricatures and satires on Bute's private relations with the young King and his mother, the Princess of Wales, were libellous in the highest degree, and not unfrequently obscene. He was compared with Mortimer, the favourite of Queen Isabel, and a celebrated mock dedication to him by Wilkes, of a new edition of the tragedy of Mortimer, expresses the wish that he might share that wicked favourite's fate. Others parodied a scene in Hamlet, and represented our "thane" instilling poison into the royal ear, in order that he might rule in his stead. In one caricature, entitled "The royal dupe," the Princess of Wales is seated on a sofa, lulling the young king to sleep in her lap, while Lord Bute is stealing his sceptre, and Fox is represented picking the king's pocket. Two pictures on the wall of the apartment represent the garden-scene in Hamlet and the Fall of Mortimer.

Pitt's old rival, Henry Fox, was the minister who enjoyed chiefly the confidence of the favourite, and who promoted his measures with the greatest zeal, and, as might be expected, shared largely in his unpopularity. His name became as closely identified with the Bute administration as it had formerly been with that of the Duke of Newcastle. This statesman seems to have been equally remarkable for the looseness of his private morals, and the dishonesty of his public conduct; and, during the long period he held the lucrative office of paymaster of the forces, he became extravagantly rich out of the plunder of the public money. In 1769, the petition of the city of London for the redress of public grievances adverted especially to his defalcations, and stigmatized him as "the public defaulter of unaccounted millions," an expression which was long attached to his memory. In one of the caricatures which appeared before Newcastle's resignation, entitled "The State Nursery," where the Bute ministry are occupied in children's games, Fox, as the whipper-in of the ministerial majority in the Commons, is mounted on the back of Bute—

"First you see old sly Volpone-y
Riding on the shoulders brawny
Of the muckle favourite Sawney."

The Duke of Newcastle is employed in rocking the cradle.
From this time Fox and Bute are constantly joined together,
and even after they had been driven from
ostensible power, they were popularly
believed to share in secret influence. In
another caricature, entitled "The ever-
memorable Peace-Makers settling their
accounts," Fox and Bute are joined in a
trio with the king. The book in which
Fox is writing bears the inscription,
"Unaccounted Millions;" and the rolls
before the King are entitled "West Indies," "North America," "Manillas,"
&c. In the original print, the devil, with
an axe in one hand (the reward of treason), holds the inkstand, from which Fox
replenishes his pen.

THE FOX ELEVATED.

The great aim of the court intrigues
appears, indeed, to have been to gain
popularity for the favourite by making
him the author of peace;* and as soon
as he had been raised to the nominal
head of the ministry, he began to make
indirect advances for the renewal of the
negotiations. The condition in which
Pitt had left the national forces, and the energy which he had
impressed on all their operations, continued to produce their

THE PEACE-MAKERS.

* On the renewal of negotiations for peace, Bute's first step was to write
a letter to the lord mayor of London, to inform him of his intentions, with
the evident intention of conciliating the City.

effect, and the war with Spain was, on our part, a series of brilliant successes, which made us master of the Havanna and Manillas, and most of the Spanish and French West Indian islands; so that the two powers were glad to listen to offers of peace on almost any terms. Bute had begun his administration, at least not very honourably, by deserting the King of Prussia and our German allies, and they were now left out of the treaty, to make terms for themselves. No doubt England might have exacted much more advantageous terms; for she gave up a large portion of her conquests; but she retained all Canada, with Cape Breton, (which had been so often a bone of contention,) and other possessions, which rendered the British empire in Northern America compact and safe.

Whatever might have been the general wish for a peace, the popular feeling in England was not in favour of a peace to be made by Lord Bute, and it was easy to raise an outcry against the extent of the concessions made to our enemies. As soon as the negotiations were formally opened, in the month of September, 1762, caricatures, and ballads, and pamphlets, flew about in rapid succession. In one of the former, entitled " The Congress; or, a device to lower the Land Tax, to the tune of Doodle, doodle, do," advertised on the 13th of September, 1762, the favourite is represented treating with the Frenchman, and giving up Guadaloupe, Martinico, &c., while he retains merely " barren Canada," and " part of Newfoundland." A Scotchman carries the standard of the boot and petticoat. Bute is made to say, " Tak aw again, Monseir, and gie us back what ye please;" to which the Frenchman replies, " Der is Canada and N. F. Land; now tank de grande monarch for his royale bountee." The British lion is held down by a chain, with the *Auditor* and *Briton* weighing heavy upon his neck; and on the other side of the picture is a tombstone, with the inscription, " English glory. Obiit 1762." The following song is attached to this caricature:—

> " Here you may see the happy congress,
> All now is done with such a *bon-grace*,
> No English wight can surely grumble,
> Or cry, our treaty-makers fumble.
>> Doodle, doodle, do, &c.

> " Who would not for a peace like this,
> Replete with every kind of bliss,
> Give all our conquests, all our gain-s,
> And glory in the Highland Thane-s!
>> Doodle, &c.

> "Our manners now we all will change-s,
> Talk Erse and get the Scottish mange-s,

An oatmeal haggiso we will feed-a,
And Smithfield boasts no more shall bleed-a.
            Doodle, &c.

"A tartan plaid each chield shall wear-a ;
With bonnets blue wo'll deck our hair-a ;
And make so act that no one may put
A felt or beaver on his *caput*.
            Doodle, &c.

"Then strut with Caledonian pride ;
Shakspeare and Milton fling aside ;
On bagpipes play, and learn to sing all
Th' achievements of the mighty Fingal.*
            Doodle, &c.

"In gratitude all this we owe-a,
For saving us from beaten foe-a ;
And 'tis the least we surely can do,
For to regain lost Newfoundland-o.
            Doodle," &c.

Another caricature, published in the course of September, was
entitled " The Caledonian Pacification ; or, All's well that ends
well." Bute is here seated by a muzzled lion, on an elevation ;
he holds the sceptre, and proclaims, " Be this our r—l [*royal*]
will and pleasure known." The Kings of France and Spain are
making their own terms. Pitt and his friends are going to the
assistance of Britannia, who sits weeping in a corner. It was
at this time that Hogarth published his caricature, or rather
emblematical print, of " The Times," defending Bute's peace,
and stigmatizing Pitt, Temple, and Newcastle as public
incendiaries. This print, as we have already seen, only served
to increase and embitter the attacks on the government.
Immediately after its publication, appeared a large print, entitled
" The Rare Show, a political contrast to the print of The Times
by William Hogarth," in which the Scots are seen on one side
dancing and rejoicing at the fire which is consuming John Bull's
house. The centre of the picture is occupied by a great acting-
barn, from the upper window of which Fox shews his cunning
head, and points to the sign representing Dido and Æneas going
into the cave, and announcing that the play of these two
worthies is acted within. This is, of course, an allusion to the
presumed intimacy between Bute and the princess-dowager, who
are exhibited as the hero and heroine on a scaffolding in front,
Smollett on one side, blowing a trumpet, entitled " The *Briton*,"
and Murphy on the other, beating a drum, entitled " The

* Macpherson's " Ossian " had been published in this year, 1762, and was
now exciting general attention.

Auditor." There are many other groups allusive equally to the political events of the day. In one corner sits the mercenary Dutchman, receiving the wages of his interested neutrality from " mounsieur."

It appears that even the members of the cabinet were not unanimous in approval of the peace ; at least some of them were unwilling to compromise themselves by signing it. This led to some

NEUTRALITY.

changes in the ministry, the most important of which was the resignation of the Duke of Devonshire at the beginning of November; upon which the king in council ordered the duke's name to be struck out of the council book, an act of ignominious treatment totally unmerited, and said to have been intended to intimidate others from following his example. This resignation was followed by those of the Marquis of Rockingham and the duke's relatives, Lord George Cavendish, and Lord Besborough. The Duke of Cumberland, who had received some slights, also joined the opposition, which tended to increase its popularity. At the end of November, when the parliament met, Lord Bute could not pass the streets without being hissed and pelted by the mob, and a strong guard was necessary to secure his person from still greater violence.

Parliament met on the 25th of November, and the preliminaries of the treaty were laid before both houses. Pitt, who was suffering from his gout, came to the House of Commons, wrapped up in flannels, to attack the peace, and the debate there was very animated, but the ministers found themselves secure of a large majority. In the Lords, Bute gloried in his own work, and declared that he wished for no other epitaph to be inscribed on his tomb than that he was the adviser of this peace. The phrase was snatched at by the opposition, and gave rise to an epigram, which was soon in everybody's mouth :—

> "Say, when will England be from faction freed ?
> When will domestic quarrels cease ?
> Ne'er till that wished-for epitaph we read,
> 'Here lies the man that made the peace.' "

U

The moment Bute felt assured of his majorities in parliament, he shewed his resentment against his opponents by tyrannically ejecting from their offices, even to the lowest, every person who had received an appointment from the Duke of Newcastle and other leaders of the opposition when in office.

Between one hesitation and another, the peace was not concluded until the month of February, 1763; and perhaps no peace was ever received by the body of the people with greater dissatisfaction. The popular hatred of the French increased with the cessation of hostilities; and there was a new cry against the importation of French fashions, which, it was pretended, were the only return we should receive for so many sacrifices. Churchill expressed the popular feeling—

> " France, in return for peace and power restored,
> For all those countries, which the hero's sword
> Unprofitably purchased, idly thrown
> Into her lap, and made once more her own ;
> France hath afforded large and rich supplies
> Of vanities full-trimmed ; of polish'd lies,
> Of soothing flatteries, which through the ears
> Steal to and melt the heart ; of slavish fears
> Which break the spirit, and of abject fraud—
> For which, alas ! we need not send abroad."

The minister tried to console himself for the unpopularity of his peace by getting up addresses[*] of congratulation, but they found few who would address, and they met everywhere with discomfiture. An address was very reluctantly wrung from the city of London, and was carried to St. James's on the 11th of May, by Sir Charles Asgill (as *locum tenens* in the absence of the lord mayor), accompanied by six other aldermen, the recorder, sheriffs, chamberlain, and town-clerk. The procession was accompanied by a great mob, which hissed and hooted during the whole route; as it passed along Fleet Street the great bell of St. Bride's began to toll, and a dumb peal struck up; and it received a similar salutation from Bow-bells on its return. When the mob approached the palace, they became still more uproarious, and the whole transaction tended only to throw disgrace on its promoters, and make them an object of the popular ridicule and contempt. Churchill, in the fourth book of " The Ghost," published shortly after this event, speaks of processions which move on slowly—

> " —— to the melancholy knell
> Of the dull, deep, and doleful bell,

[*] There were several caricatures on these patched-up addresses, the best of which is entitled, " A sequel to the knights of Baythe, or the One-headed Corporation."

Such as of late the good Saint Bride
Muffled, to mortify the pride
Of those who, England quite forgot,
Paid their vile homage to the Scot,
Where Argill hold the foremost place,
Whilst my lord figured at a race."

Caricature prints of the procession for the proclamation of the peace were circulated under the title of "The Proclamation of Proclamations," in which the proclaimer was represented with a large *boot* on one leg, and riding upon a donkey (the latter being the mob emblem of the young king.) Beneath were the doggerel lines :—

" See here, fellow-subjects (so fine and so pretty)
A show that not long since was seen in the City,
With marshals, and heralds, and horse grenadiers,
And music before 'em to tickle our ears ;
To tell us proud Sawney has patched up a peace,
That our foes may take breath and our taxes increase.
Oh ! who could have thought we should e'er see the day
When a Scotchman should over the English bear away,
Thus bully and swagger and threaten and dare,
Till the credulous lion falls into the snare.
But though coward-like from his post he has fled,
Let's hope yet his lordship wont die in his bed."

Lord Bute had, indeed, after a short but stormy reign, deserted his post. The arrears and various liabilities incurred by the war, had produced the necessity of new taxation, the odium of which fell entirely upon the Scotch minister. Early in 1767, a tax was laid upon beer, which raising the price of that article, had exasperated the mob, on whom such a tax fell with disproportionate heaviness. The tax was made immediately the subject of ballads and caricatures against the king and his favourite ; and the popular discontent was shown in several instances in a way which could not fail to reach the royal ears. The *Royal Magazine*, under the date of February 15, informs us that " some evenings ago, while their majesties were at Drury Lane Theatre, to see the Winter's Tale, as Garrick was repeating the two following lines of the occasional prologue to that celebrated piece :—

" For you, my hearts of oak, for your regale,
Here's good old English stingo, mild and stale,"

an honest fellow cried out of the shilling gallery, ' At threepence a pot, Master Garrick, or confusion to the brewers!' which," it is added, "was so well received by the whole house, as to produce a plaudit of universal approbation." Several other taxes were proposed or talked of; but in the spring of 1763, Bute suddenly proposed an excise on cider, and a law was passed, rather hastily and ill-digested, in spite of the most violent opposition and the most threatening demonstrations in some parts of the country. People compared the rash disregard of popular opinion with which this measure was pushed through, with the conduct of Sir Robert Walpole, who had bowed to the public demonstrations against his far wiser system of excise; and when the resignation of Lord Bute was suddenly announced on the 8th of April, 1763, many ascribed his retreat to the terror raised by the popular indignation on this occasion. Others (and this seems to have been the general opinion) said that he had been driven out by the Duke of Cumberland, who, with the Duke of

THE FRIEND OF LIBERTY.

Newcastle, led the opposition in the House of Lords. A caricature, entitled "The Roasted Exciseman; or, the Jack Boot's exit," represents the enraged mob burning the effigy of a Scotchman suspended on a gallows; a great worn boot lies in the bonfire, into which a man is throwing an "excised cider barrel" as fuel. A Scotchman, in great distress, cries out, "It 's aw over with us now, and aw our aspiring hopes are gone." In one corner is Liberty drooping over her insignia and a number of the *North Briton*, and comforted by a portly personage, apparently intended for the Duke of Cumberland: she says, "your R. H—gh—ness was always my firm friend, and I well know feels for my distress." Another caricature published on this occasion is entitled "The Boot and the Blockhead. Oh! Garth fec'. 1762." A wooden head raised upon a boot, and adorned with Hogarth's line of beauty, is erected as the idol to be worshipped. Hogarth with his print of "The Times" as a shield, is defending it against the attacks of Churchill, armed with the *North Briton*. It is attended by a crowd of worshippers, who are chiefly Scotchmen. Through an entrance doorway to the right a bright sun is seen rising, and the Duke of Cumberland enters with a whip in his hand, followed by a sailor. The duke turns back to his companion, and says, "Lend 's a hand, Ned, to scourge the worshippers of a blockhead! I'll warn 'em presently, as I did in '45." The sailor cries, "I'll lend you a hand, my prince of bold actions!" Others said that the minister had been killed politically by the *North Briton*. The truth, however, probably is, that Lord Bute was suddenly terrified at the degree of popular hatred to which he had exposed himself, and thought that he should escape it by giving up his place. We can hardly help feeling convinced that in the first years of the reign of George III. a desperate attempt was made to raise the royal prerogative to a very undue position in regard to the constitution, and that no means were left untried to secure success; the experiment was a dangerous one, and it failed; Bute is said to have confessed that he was terror-struck at the perils with which he was surrounded, and that he was afraid of involving the king in his own fate.

THE IDOL.

The fallen minister, however, soon recovered his courage, and the only difference was that he ruled from behind the curtain, instead of reigning in public. Fox, who seems to have shared in the panic, retired at the same time, and was raised to the peerage, under the title of Lord Holland. Sir Francis Dashwood, Bute's incompetent chancellor of the exchequer, also resigned, and was created Lord Despenser. The other changes were trifling; George Grenville was made first lord of the treasury and chancellor of the exchequer; and the machine of state was still guided secretly by the hand of Bute.

The court seems to have been provoked in the highest degree by the opposition which its measures had received from the press; and it now began a

THE IDOL'S FOOTAGE.

violent persecution, the only effect of which was to give an
unusual importance to the mob, of which for many years after
no efforts could deprive it. On the 19th of April, three
days after the change in the ministry, the King closed the
session of Parliament with a speech in which he dwelt upon
the advantages of the peace. On the 23rd of April appeared
the celebrated "No. XLV." of the *North Briton*, which consisted of a very severe criticism of the King's speech, taken,
as it is always considered, as the speech of the minister,
and of a violent attack (but less so than many previous ones)
on the public conduct of the Earl of Bute. There is nothing
treasonable or unusually libellous in this paper, or which had
not been said over and over again in the House of Commons;
its only fault is a want of moderation in language. But the
North Briton had contributed very largely in raising the popular
hatred which had forced Lord Bute to resign; and the court,
blinded by resentment, rushed headlong and inconsiderately on
the prospect of vengeance. A *general warrant*, to seize all persons concerned in the publication of the *North Briton*, without
specifying their names, was immediately issued by the secretary
of state, and a number of printers and publishers were placed in
custody, some of whom were not concerned in it. Late on the
night of the 29th of April, the messengers entered the house of
John Wilkes (the author of the article in question), and produced their warrant, with which he refused to comply. The
next morning, however, he was carried before the secretary of
state, and committed a close prisoner to the Tower, his papers
being previously seized and sealed, and all access to his person
strictly prohibited. The warrant was considered as an illegal
one, and had only been resorted to in one or two instances, and
under very extraordinary circumstances, of which there were
none in the present case. Wilkes's friends immediately obtained
a writ of *habeas corpus*, which the ministers defeated by a mean
subterfuge; and it was found necessary to obtain a second before
they could bring the prisoner before the court of King's Bench,
by which he was set at liberty, on the ground of his privilege as
a member of parliament. He then opened on an angry correspondence with the secretaries of state on the seizure of his papers,
which led to no result. But in the meantime, the attorney-
general had been directed to institute a prosecution against him
in the King's Bench for libel; and the King had ordered him
to be deprived of his commission as colonel in the Buckinghamshire militia. The King further exhibited his resentment by
depriving Lord Temple of the lord-lieutenancy of the same

county, and striking his name out of the council book, for an expression of personal sympathy which had fallen from him.

George Grenville's administration had hardly lasted three months, when it was weakened by the death of one of the secretaries of state, Lord Egremont; upon which, without any communication with the ministers, and to the surprise of everybody, Lord Bute, by the King's command, repaired to Mr. Pitt to negotiate his return to office, and the formation under him of a new cabinet. Pitt consulted his friends, and waited twice upon the King, but the latter insisting on certain arrangements to which the statesman would not agree, the negotiation failed; and Grenville remained minister. The Duke of Bedford, whose name was very unpopular in connection with the peace, was now brought into the ministry, and the Earl of Sandwich was made secretary of state.

When the parliament met on the 15th of November 1763, its attention was at once called to the affair of Wilkes, whose cause was taken up warmly by the opposition. The court, however, was still master of large majorities in the house, and it was resolved that the article in the *North Briton* was a " false, scandalous, and seditious libel," and that it should be burnt by the hands of the common hangman. It was further proposed to expel Wilkes from the house, and they talked of condemning him to the pillory. Wilkes replied by a complaint of the manner in which the privileges of the house had been violated in his person, and raised a question, the consideration of which was postponed for a week. The court party, however, was not satisfied with the fair open course of proceeding which lay before them, but they had a new attack in store, intended to throw a moral odium on their victim, and got up in a manner which threw disgrace on every one concerned in it. Although he has probably been condemned more severely than he deserved, Wilkes's moral character, like that of many of his eminent contemporaries, was very low. But he appears to have learnt his immorality in the society of Lord Sandwich, Sir Francis Dashwood (Lord le Despencer), Thomas Potter, M.P. for Aylesbury, and son of Potter, Archbishop of Canterbury, and some other men of fashion and dissipation, who formed with him a club, which, in its private meetings, held at Medmenham, in Buckinghamshire (the seat of Lord le Despencer), set all religion and decency at defiance. Potter and Wilkes together composed an obscene parody on Pope's Essay on Man, which they entitled "An Essay on Woman;" and which, in imitation of Pope's poem, was accompanied with notes under the name of Bishop

Warburton. Wilkes had read this production to Lord Sandwich and Lord lo Despencer, who *highly approved* of it, but he
had communicated it to no other person. He had printed
twelve copies of it at a private press in his own house, which
were to be distributed among the members of the club, and he
had taken the greatest precaution to hinder its being carried
abroad by his workmen. One of them, however, had purloined
some fragments of it, and shown them to a needy parson named
Kidgell, who gained his living by writing for the press, and who
was employed by the government to obtain a copy of the work
alluded to by bribing one of Wilkes's compositors, in which, with
some difficulty, he succeeded. On the very day when Wilkes's
alleged libel was brought before the House of Commons, the
stolen copy of the " Essay on Woman " was laid before the
lords, and, of all other persons, the notoriously profligate Earl
of Sandwich, who had privately approved of this very production, was selected to bring it forward, and comment upon its
profane indecency. This was as bad a burlesque as the book
itself; and it only led to the publication of a load of scandalous
stories of the impiety and immorality of the hypocritical
accuser; for Lord Sandwich is said to have been expelled from
the Beefsteak Club for blasphemy; and Horace Walpole tells
us, on this occasion, that " very lately, at a club with Mr.
Wilkes, held at the top of the play-house in Drury Lane, Lord
Sandwich talked so profanely that he drove two harlequins out
of the company." To make matters worse, Kidgell, the ministerial tool in this unworthy affair, published a quarto pamphlet,
giving an indecent account of Wilkes's poem, which was spread
abroad rather copiously, and brought Kidgell and his employers
into equal contempt.

In parliament the ministerial majorities were supreme, and
both houses joined in the severest censures on the *North Briton*
and on the poem. But it was different out of doors, where the
court persecution of Wilkes had made him a perfect idol with
the mob. When, on the 3rd of December, the Sheriff of London, Alderman Harley, with the City officers and hangman,
proceeded to carry into effect the sentence of the House of
Commons against the *North Briton*, by burning it in a fire in
Cheapside, the mob attacked them with the greatest violence,
forced the sheriffs to make a hasty retreat to the Mansion
House, drove away the officers from the fire, and, snatching from
the hangman the half-burnt " libel," carried it in triumph to
Temple Bar, where they made a bonfire and burnt a large jack-
boot, for all these unpopular acts were laid to the account of

the favourite. Among the numerous epigrams passed about on this occasion, one of them shows strongly the popular sentiment in this respect :—

> "Because the *North Briton* inflamed the whole nation,
> To flames they commit it, to shew detestation :
> But throughout old England how joy would have spread,
> Had the real North Briton been burnt in its stead !"

In consequence of this riot, the government nearly quarrelled with the City ; and to increase the mortification of the former, Wilkes and the printers arrested by the general warrant, who had all commenced prosecutions for illegal imprisonment, obtained rather heavy damages from the under secretary of state, who had put the warrant in execution ; and a violent opposition to the system of general warrants was raised in parliament, which ultimately effected their abolition. The opposition to the proceedings against Wilkes was headed in the House of Lords by the Duke of Cumberland.

Wilkes himself did not again face his opponents in the House of Commons. In a duel, which arose out of the debate on the first day, he had received a severe wound, which afforded an excuse for not attending ; and, when the parliament met after the Christmas holidays on the 19th of January, 1764, he had made his retreat to Paris, from whence he sent medical certificates that he could not come back. The House of Commons thereupon passed a vote of censure on the *North Briton*, and then proceeded to expel Wilkes from the house. Kidgell about the same time became involved in some discreditable money transactions, and was obliged also to leave the country, and this double elopement gave rise to the following epigram :—

> "When faction was loud, and when party ran high,
> Religion and Liberty join'd in the cry ;
> But, *O grief of griefs !* in the midst of the fray,
> Religion and Liberty both ran away."

It is difficult to conceive the excitement produced by this affair, which continued during the spring. The debates in parliament were angry and obstinate ; Pitt came frequently to his place in the house, wrapped in flannels, to head his party in defending the constitutional liberty of the subject which had been infringed by the proceedings of the government ; and three remarkable men (besides others), who acted a prominent part in subsequent events, were pettishly turned out of their places, and two of them deprived of their commissions in the army, for joining in the opposition, Lord Shelburne, Colonel Barré, and

General Conway. The court carried this sort of intimidation to such an excess, that a writer in the *Royal Magazine* in February 1766, informed us that "a curious gentleman" had made a calculation that down to that time since Legge had been discharged in May 1761, there had been no less than five hundred and twenty-three changes of places by ministerial influence.

Few of the popular party effusions produced by the prosecutions against Wilkes appear to be preserved; and the caricatures connected with it are not of great interest. In one, published 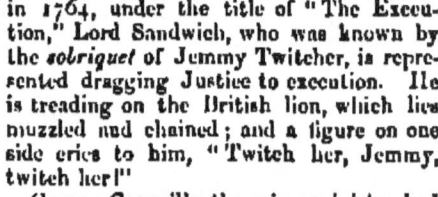 in 1764, under the title of "The Execution," Lord Sandwich, who was known by the *sobriquet* of Jemmy Twitcher, is represented dragging Justice to execution. He is treading on the British lion, which lies  muzzled and chained; and a figure on one side cries to him, "Twitch her, Jemmy, twitch her!"

George Grenville, the prime minister, had also (like most of his colleagues) his *sobriquet*. In the debate on the cider bill, the last measure of Bute's administration, Grenville contended that the government did not know where else to lay a tax, and turning to Pitt, who was warm in the opposition, exclaimed, "Let him tell me where— THE EXECUTIONER. only tell me where!" Pitt replied only by humming in his place the words of a popular tune, "Gentle Shepherd, tell me where!" The house was thrown into a roar of laughter, and ever after the minister carried with him the title of the Gentle Shepherd. It was this gentle shepherd who now, when the affair of Wilkes was for the present ended, by a new scheme of taxation, laid the foundation of the American war and the loss of those important colonies which now form the United States. The magnitude of the question seems not at first to have been fully appreciated in this country, and the opposition, though brisk, was not very strong, to a measure which was, nevertheless, felt to be neither constitutional nor politic, the taxing of a people who were not represented in parliament, except as far as, as was suggested by one member, North America was considered, by a sort of constitutional fiction, as forming parcel of the manor of Greenwich, in Kent. Even Pitt was not present at these debates. The custom duties on goods imported into America now levied, and the

threat of a stamp-tax, excited a violent ferment in America, and
met with a resolute opposition there; yet in the next session
(January 1765), the King's speech urged the parliament to persist in taxing the Americans, and in enforcing obedience.

In the meantime the English government became involved in
new changes. In the summer of 1764 Pitt, who appears to
have been more and more ambitious of being thought above the
partizanship of faction, emancipated himself from the league he
had formed with the Duke of Newcastle, and declared his intention of acting entirely upon his own judgment in opposing or
supporting the measures of ministers. The apparent disorganiza-
tion of the opposition alone saved Grenville's ministry during the
remainder of the year. In February 1765, the American stamp
act was carried through parliament, in spite of the representations
of Benjamin Franklin and a deputation sent from America to
expostulate; but still Pitt, suffering under the gout, kept away.
Immediately after it had passed, in the latter part of March, the
young king experienced the first attack of that derangement
under which he laboured in the latter years of his life, and, on
his recovery, ministers brought in a hasty and ill-digested plan
of a regency bill, by which they grievously affronted the
Princess of Wales, and gave little satisfaction to the king.
From this moment their doom was certain, and it was said that
Bute fixed the king's determination. In the middle of May, the
king sent for his uncle, the Duke of Cumberland, and dispatched
him to Mr. Pitt, at his seat at Hayes, in Kent, to beg him to
form a new ministry, but he refused. The duke then, by the
king's desire, tried to form a ministry among the opposition, but
nobody would engage without Pitt. The monarch was then
driven to the alternative of asking his old ministers to remain;
which they now refused to do, unless the king would promise
never again to consult Lord Bute, to dismiss Bute's brother,
Mackenzie, from his office in Scotland, and Fox (Lord Holland)
from his place of paymaster of the forces, (which he still retained,) and appoint Lord Granby captain-general. The king
gave a flat refusal to the first and last of these demands, and his
ministers were satisfied by the sacrifice of Lord Holland and Mr.
Mackenzie, and the promise that Bute should not be permitted
to interfere. The king, however, was still determined to get rid
of his ministers, and towards the end of June he made a new
communication to Pitt, who now took some steps to form an
administration, which were rendered abortive by the objections of
Lord Temple. Upon this the Duke of Cumberland again
addressed himself to the more moderate part of the opposition,

and succeeded in forming an administration under the Marquis of Rockingham, who brought into parliament his private secretary, the celebrated Edmund Burke, and raised to the peerage, as Lord Camden, the popular chief-justice Pratt.

During the ministerial changes the country was in a troubled state, which was increased by several causes of popular excitement. The disputes with the American colonies was a hindrance to commerce, and was felt heavily by the merchants, and thus their cause found advocates in England. The English mob was increasing in power and insolence, and the Grenville ministry persisted in provoking it by unpopular exhibitions. Wilkes had escaped the pillory by retiring to France, and the other persons concerned in the original publication of the *North Briton* had beaten their persecutors, with the exception of Kearsley, the bookseller, who had been ruined, but who was re-established in trade in the beginning of 1765, by the exertion of some of Wilkes's partizans. Another bookseller, named Williams, re-published about this time the set of the *North Britons* in two small volumes. He was immediately prosecuted by the court, and sentenced to stand in the pillory in Palace Yard for one hour, which was put into execution on the 1st of March, 1765. Williams was conducted to the place of punishment amid the shouts and acclamations of a vast concourse of people, in a hackney-coach, numbered 45.[*] When he mounted the pillory, as well as when quitting it, he bowed to the spectators, and during the whole time he held a sprig of laurel in his hand. While he stood there, the mob erected a gallows of ladders opposite to him, on which they hung a jack-boot, an axe, and a Scotch bonnet; which articles, after a while, were taken down, the top of the boot cut off with the axe, and then both boot and bonnet thrown into a large bonfire. In the meantime a gentleman drew out a purple purse, adorned with orange-ribbons, and made a collection of two hundred guineas for the sufferer, who was con-

[*] The number of the *North Briton* was the more popular from its fortuitous coincidence with that of the year of the great Scottish rebellion. Long after the events themselves had ceased to be a matter of general interest, patriotic tradesmen continued to give popularity to their merchandize by distinguishing it with the favoured number 45. It is said that even within a few years the favourite article in a snuff-shop in Fleet-street, was extracted from a canister marked 45, and the mixture known by no other name. Mr. Tooke, from whose notes to Churchill this fact is taken, adds, that, on the other hand, so obnoxious were these numerals to royalty itself, as well as its retainers, that the young Prince of Wales, in 1772, thought he could not exhibit his resentment for some privation or chastisement he had undergone more provokingly towards his royal father than by roaring out repeatedly the popular cry, "Wilkes and No. XLV. for ever!"

ducted from the scene of his punishment in the same triumphal
manner in which he had been brought there. One of the spectators took out a pencil and wrote on the scaffold the extempo-
rary lines :—

> " Martyrs of old for truth thus bravely stood,
> Laid down their lives, and shed their dearest blood ;
> No scandal then to suffer in her cause,
> And nobly stem the rigour of the laws :
> Pulpit and desk may equally go down,
> A pillory's now more sacred than a ——." [crown.]

The popular excitement caused by this new act of ministerial
(and, as it was interpreted, Scotch) persecution, raised a great
clamour. Ballads were sung about the streets on Williams and
on the pillory ; and several prints appeared, representing the
various circumstances of the exhibition in New Palace Yard, with
a fair sprinkling of caricature. On one of them the pillory is
entitled the "Scotch Yoke ;" and the print is accompanied with
a ballad, which, as this was one of the affairs that threw the
pillory into disuse as a punishment for political offences, is
perhaps worth repeating :—it is entitled—

"THE PILLORY TRIUMPHANT ; OR, No. 45 FOR EVER.

> "Ye sons of Wilkes and Liberty,
>   Who hate despotic sway,
> The glorious forty-five now crowns
>   This memorable day.
>   And to New Palace Yard let us go, let us go.

> "An injur'd martyr to her cause
>   Undaunted meets his doom :
> Ah ! who like me don't wish to see
>   Some great ones in his room !
>   Then to New Palace Yard let us go, let us go.

> "Behold the laurel, fresh and green,
>   Attract all loyal eyes ;
> The haughty thistle droops its head,
>   Is blasted, stinks, and dies.
>   Then to New Palace Yard let us go, let us go.

> "High mounted on the gibbet view
>   The *Boot* and *Bonnet's* fate ;
> But where's the *Petticoat*, my lads !
>   The *Boot* should have its mate.
>   Then to new Palace Yard, let us go, let us go.

> "What acclamations burst around !
>   Victoria is the cry :
> Hear, hear, oh Jeffreys ! and turn pale,
>   Thy malice we defy.
>   Then to New Palace Yard let us go, let us go.

"Look up and blush with guilt and shame,
  Ye vile *informing* crew,
While Williams thus with *honour* stands,
  The gallows groans for you.
    Then to New Palace Yard let us go, let us go.

" When wicked ministers of state
  To fleece the land combined,
As guardian of our liberties,
  The *Press* was first designed.
    Then to New Palace Yard let us go, let us go.

" But now the *scum* is uppermost,
  The truth must not be spoke ;
The laws are topsy-turvy turn'd,
  And justice is a yoke.
    Then to New Palace Yard let us go, let us go.

" In vain the galling *Scottish* yoke
  Shall strive to make us bend ;
Our monarch is a Briton born,
  And will our rights defend.
    Then to New Palace Yard let us go, let us go.

" For ages still might England stand,
  In spite of Stuart arts,
Would heaven send us men to rule
  With better heads and hearts.
    Then to New Palace Yard let us go, let us go.

At the same time there was much rioting in different parts of the country, against the exportation of flour, and for other supposed grievances. A little later, in May, when the ministerial embarrassments commenced, the London weavers arose in great numbers, and attacked the house of the Duke of Bedford, whom they accused of having negotiated the obnoxious peace which had brought French silks and poverty into the land, and they were not dispersed without bloodshed.

THE COURIER.

The rest of the year passed over quietly ; and a few caricatures without much point, shew that there was the latent will

to stir up mischief, without the resolution to act. The party who had been thrown out of power began to exert themselves to destroy the reviving popularity of Pitt, and some attacks were made upon him in print, accompanied by several caricatures. One of these, under the title of "The Courier," makes a joke of the Duke of Cumberland's unsuccessful visit to the gouty foot at Hayes: the sign is that of a blown bladder, inscribed "Popularity," with the further inscription "By W. P." underneath.

When the Parliament reopened in January, 1766, the gout was gone, and Pitt again made his appearance in the house, and delivered one of his grand philippics. He condemned all the measures of the late ministry, and stigmatized in the strongest terms the attempt to tax the Americans, in which the king in his opening speech had just recommended the house to persevere. He expressed his personal regard for the members of the new administration, but declared his want of confidence in it as a ministry; and then burst into an eloquent attack upon the

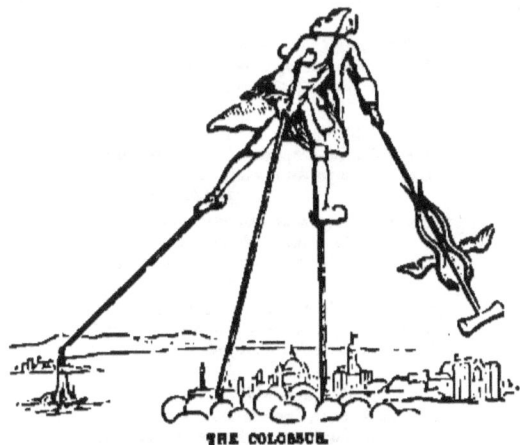

THE COLOSSUS.

secret influence, which he intimated had paralyzed his own efforts in the service of the country, and had been the cause of all the mischief that had happened since. Ministers denied the secret influence; but the nation believed implicitly in it, and Pitt became again the idol of the mob on this side of the Atlantic, and of the dissatisfied and angry colonists on the other. The attacks on the popular orator by the court-party now increased in violence. In the month of February appeared a poem, entitled "The Demagogue," stated to be written "by Theophilus Thorn," in which Pitt is attacked as a mere pretender to patriotism, and he is accused of stirring up mischief in America with the mere object of gaining the shouts of the mob. A caricature, published about the same period, under the title of "the Colossus," represents the statesman raised on lofty stilts, his gouty leg resting on the Royal Exchange, in the midst of London and Westminster, which are surrounded by a cloud of bubbles, inscribed "War," "Peace," &c.; this stilt is called "Popularity." The other stilt, called "Sedition," he stretches over the sea towards New York (the town seen in the distance), fishing for popularity in the Atlantic. The long staff on which he rests, is entitled "Pension." Above the orator's head hangs the broad hat of the commonwealth, and raised in the air on one side, Lord Temple is occupied in blowing the bubbles which support the "great commoner's" fame. Below are the lines :—

> "Tell to me, if you are witty,
> Whose wooden leg is in de city,
> Eh bien drole, 'tis de great pity.
> 　　　　Doodle do.
>
> "De broad-brim hat he thrust his nob in,
> De while St. Stephen's throng are throbbing,
> One crutch in America is lubbing.
> 　　　　Doodle do.
>
> "But who be yonder odd man there, sir !
> Building de castle in de air, sir ?
> Oh ! 'tis de Temple, one may swear, sir !
> 　　　　Doodle do.
>
> "Stamp act, le diable ! dat's de job, sir,
> Dat stampt it in de stiltman's nob, sir,
> To be America's nabob, sir.
> 　　　　Doodle do.
>
> "De English dream vid leetle vit, sir ;
> For de French dey make de Pit, sir,
> 'Tis a pit for them who now are bit, sir.
> 　　　　Doodle, noodle, do."

The acts of the Rockingham administration were in general popular; but it was feeble in itself, and was soon further weakened by defections. Early in July, 1766, Pitt again received a message from the king, desiring him to form a new administration, and on this occasion the king left him to make his own terms. The orator now found his greatest difficulty in getting together his own party. He quarrelled with Lord

Temple, who seems to have thwarted him rather largely in his plans; and at length he was obliged to compose a motley ministry, formed of men taken from several parties, and the chief tie of which consisted in his own name, the popularity of which was suddenly diminished by his reception into the House of Lords, under the title of Lord Chatham. Lord Chatham's ministry, however, brought together a number of young statesmen who figured more prominently in subsequent times. He himself took the office of lord privy seal; Lord Camden was made chancellor; Lord Shelburne one of the secretaries of state, and General Conway the other; the Duke of Grafton was made first lord of the treasury; Lord North was associated with Mr. George Cooke in the office of paymaster-general; Mr. Willes was made solicitor-general; and the Duke of Portland was lord-chamberlain. It was in every respect a liberal government, and it is difficult to account for the extraordinary odium which was attached to Pitt's elevation to the peerage. Few attempted to defend the "great commoner's" ambition to sit in the House of Lords. An almost solitary epigram, amidst a heap of abuse, made a half apology.

> "The Tories,* 'od rat 'em,
> Abuse my Lord Chatham,
> For what—for commencing a peer
> But is it not hard
> He should lose his reward,
> Who has purchas'd a title so dear?"

> "In every station
> Mr. Pitt serv'd the nation,
> With a noble disdain of her pelf;
> Then where's the great crime,
> When he sees a fit time,
> If a man should for once serve himself?"

But the populace looked upon the peerage as a bribe, for which Pitt had sold himself to the Scottish favourite, and they refused to look upon him as anything more than a tool of the court. In spite of everything that could be said to the contrary, it was still confidently believed that Bute ruled there, and that none could be ministers, except by placing themselves at his disposal; and the mob would probably never have been persuaded to the

---

* The name of Tories (it has already been observed), which had been always an unpopular one, and had generally been combined more or less with Jacobitism, was almost lost in the latter years of George II. Bute brought it up again by introducing into place professed Tories, and within a few years the title, with a modified meaning, became the general appellation of the supporters of court influence.

contrary, except by the public hanging or beheading of the object of their hatred. A caricature given with the *Political Register* for October 1767 (the publication of Wilkes's friend Almon) represents, under the title of " The wire-master and his puppets," the members of the present ministry as so many puppets moved by wires directed by the Scotch favourite from

THE WIRE-MASTER AND HIS PUPPETS.

the palace of St. James's. The gouty Lord Chatham stands prominent in front, with one of his crutches broken. On one side Lord Holland (who was believed to have had a hand in Lord Bute's secret influence) peeps in, and gives his signal—" A little more to the left, my lord." On the other side Britannia sits weeping, and exclaims, " It is sport to you, but death to me." Below, those who are out of place, among whom the Duke of Newcastle is conspicuous, are looking on at the performance, while the devil is pulling away the prop of the stage on which the puppets are moving, to make greater diversion for the spectators. Four lines from Swift explain the scene:—

> " The puppets, blindly led away,
> Are made to act for ends unknown ;
> By the mere spring of wires they play,
> And speak in language not their own."

It is a matter of considerable doubt at what time the Earl of Bute's influence at court really ended; but it is certain that it was popularly believed in long after it had ceased to exist. It can hardly be supposed that Lord Chatham would have submitted, as represented by his enemies, to be the mere tool of what was described at that very time as—

> —- "that haughty, timid, treacherous thing,
> Who fears a shadow, yet who rules a king."

When the Duke of Cumberland died rather suddenly, in September, 1765, he was sincerely regretted by the popular party, who believed that he was the most powerful opponent to the influence of the Scottish "thane," and prints and caricatures immediately subsequent to that event, represented the latter as dancing over the prince's tomb, rejoicing in the recovery of power. In one of these an inscription on the tombstone describes the deceased duke as the defeater of Scottish treason and supporter of the Protestant throne, and adds, in allusion to the formation of the then existing Rockingham ministry, that he had "elected a ministry out of those virtuous few, who gloriously withstood general warrants, America-stamps, stamps of excise, &c." In 1767, there began to be great talk among the medical profession of the virtues of the *carduus benedictus*, or blessed thistle, as a universal remedy; and the plant worshipped by the quacks was soon adopted as an emblem of that thistle to which it was pretended that all Englishmen were to be forced to bow the head. Bute was said to have been aiming at the recovery of power on the resignation of Lord Chatham in 1768. A caricature subsequent to this

THE CARDUUS BENEDICTUS.

period, at a time when Lord North and Mansfield were in place, represents the thistle glorified, and the two nobles just mentioned looking on and admiring; behind them, Satan attends as musician, playing on the bagpipe. A print, dated in 1770, and suggested as a design for a new crown-piece, gives the converse and reverse of the coin. On the latter, Britannia is repreented in bonds, while Bute

THE REIGNING TRIO.

mounting a jack-boot, with the

THE BOOT.

tramples on her shield, and the sun is shining brightly upon a thistle: the inscription around it is, "Le soleil d'Ecosse aux Angloises feroce." The other side represents the head of Bute between those of the king and the Princess of Wales, with the inscription, "Tria juncta in uno." Still later, when Wilkes was elected Lord Mayor of London in 1774, a medal was struck in his honour,[*] bearing on the obverse a bust of the popular idol in his mayoralty robes, and on the other side the figure of Bute's head surmounting a jack-boot, with the axe by its side, and the inscription, "Britons strike home;" a device and motto which had been frequently used in the earlier period of the excitement raised by the proceedings against Wilkes.

Lord Chatham's ministry went on slowly and inefficiently till 1768, without enjoying the confidence of the country, although composed of men, most of whom were regarded as patriotic in their principles. Lord Chatham, confined with the gout, took no share in public business; and the Duke of Grafton, who was at the head of the treasury, and whose administration it was commonly called after 1767, gave most of his attention to Newmarket and to his mistresses. Other offices were filled with as little efficiency. Nevertheless, after Lord Chatham's resignation, the Duke of Grafton remained at his post as prime minister, until the change in 1770 placed Lord North at the head of affairs.

It was during the least active period of Chatham's adminis-

---

[*] This medal is in the collection of Mr. Haggard.

tration, that John Wilkes again made his appearance. Having
suffered the indictment against him in the Court of King's
Bench to run to an outlawry, he had been residing at Paris ever
since, and had made several vain attempts to get the sentence
reversed. He arrived in London early in February, but did not
shew himself publicly until the dissolution of parliament in
March, when he suddenly presented himself as a candidate for
the City of London. He was received by the mob with boiste-
rous enthusiasm, and people paraded the streets with poles on
which were suspended a boot and a yellow petticoat, but he was
unsuccessful in the poll; upon which he immediately offered
himself for Middlesex, the election for which took place at
Brentford, on Monday the 28th of March, 1768. Before day-
break on that day, Piccadilly and all the roads leading to
Brentford were occupied by mobs, who would suffer no one
to pass without blue cockades and papers inscribed "No. 45,
Wilkes and Liberty," and who tore to pieces the coaches of the
two other candidates. They are said to have been provoked to
this violence by the appearance of the latter at Hyde Park
Corner, accompanied with a procession carrying flags, on which
were inscribed "No blasphemy!" and "No sedition!" A newspaper of the day says, that "There has not been so great a
defection of inhabitants from London and Westminster, to ten
miles distant in one day, since the lifeguardsman's prophecy of
the earthquake, which was to destroy both these cities in 1750."
At Brentford, Wilkes had sufficient influence over the mob to
keep it quiet, but, it being announced at the close of the poll
that he was far a-head of his opponents, they behaved with some
violence on the way back, stopping people's carriages and
chalking them all over with "No. 45," and forcing everybody
to shout for Wilkes. At night they compelled people to illu-
minate, and broke the windows of those who refused; and
violent attacks were made on the Mansion House (the lord
mayor having displayed hostility towards the popular candidate), and the house of Lord Bute in Audley Street, the rioters
being only at length dispersed by the arrival of the guards.
Next day Wilkes was returned member for Middlesex; and at
night the mob rose again, the illumination was still more general,
and further outrages were committed. The turbulence of the
mob was not confined to London; in many parts of the country
the elections were unusually riotous, and a number of persons
were killed. It was said that some of the leaders of the opposition in parliament encouraged the popular demonstration; there
were many wise enough to see that there was little to fear in it.

The Duke of Newcastle is said to have declared that he loved a mob, that he had once been the leader of a mob himself, and that he thought a mob inseparable from the true interests of the Hanoverian succession. Yet the court was suddenly seized with great apprehensions; and imprudent threats were held out against Wilkes and the populace. It was this unwise persecution alone that made Wilkes a hero.

After he had secured his election, Wilkes declared his intention of surrendering himself to the court which had outlawed him; for this purpose, he presented himself in the court of King's Bench on the 20th of April; but, in consequence of some legal informalities, he was then allowed to depart, and a writ having been issued, he was brought before the court on the 27th, and then committed to the custody of the marshal of the King's Bench prison. He left the court in a hackney coach, but the mob, which was again numerous and riotous, took off the horses at Westminster Bridge, and after forcing the marshal in whose custody he was, out of the coach as they passed Temple Bar, drew their favourite through the city to a public-house in Spitalfields. But as soon as the mob had partially dispersed, Wilkes escaped at midnight by a back door, and repaired to the King's Bench prison, where he surrendered himself into the marshal's custody. When it was known next day that he was in prison, a mob collected outside the walls, and shouted all day for Wilkes and Liberty. A body of horse-guards, sent to the spot, and stationed near the prison, only served to irritate the populace; the latter, who assembled daily at the same place, committed, as we are told, no further riot than shouting " Wilkes and Liberty," yet the guards were always brought out in an ostentatious manner to watch them, and each party abused and threatened the other, until the 10th of May, when the new parliament was to meet, and when the mob believed that Wilkes was to be taken out of prison to attend in his place in the house. They accordingly attended in greater numbers than usual. A large force of soldiers had been stationed in front of the prison, and, by an unfortunate coincidence, they were a Scottish regiment, and they appear to have shewn somewhat too openly their hatred of the English mob. The latter became exceedingly riotous, and dirt and stones were thrown. Two of the Surrey magistrates read the riot act, but it is said not to have been heard; the soldiers fired, as it appears, with great haste and rashness, and many of the mob were killed and wounded. Three of the soldiers quitted their ranks, to follow one of the rioters whom they had singled out, and at some distance from the scene of riot entered a cow-house, where they deliberately shot a young man named Allen, who had taken no part whatever in the proceedings of the day. The mob now became infuriated, and they added to the general excitement by parading the body of Allen through the streets. Prosecutions for murder were lodged against the soldiers and an officer implicated in the death of Allen, and against the Surrey magistrates, who had ordered soldiers to fire at the mob, and verdicts were given against the former; but they were screened by the court, which, in a very unadvised manner, publicly approved and praised the conduct of the soldiers, whereas the three who had killed Allen were at least guilty of a breach of military discipline in quitting their ranks. This only added to the popular irritation: the riot was long remembered as the " massacre of St. George's Fields ;" and the mob increased in strength, and became more violent.

Several other mobs arose in London at the same time, who, as Horace Walpole observes, " only took advantage of so favourable a season. The coal-heavers began, and it is well," Walpole observes, " it is not a hard frost, for they have stopped all coals coming to town. The sawyers rose too, and at last the sailors, who had committed great outrages in merchant ships, and prevented them from sailing. The last mob, however, took an extraordinary turn ; for many thousand sailors came to petition the parliament yesterday (May 11), but in the most respectful and peaceable manner; desired only to have their grievances examined; if reasonable, redressed ; if not reasonable, they would be satisfied. Being told that their flags and colours with which they paraded were illegal, they cast them away. Nor was this all ; they declared for the king and parliament, and beat and drove away Wilkes's mob." These riotous proceedings dwindled into a sort of civil war between the sailors and coal-heavers, which, strange to say, was allowed to continue for several weeks, although many lives were lost. On the 22nd of June, Walpole writes, " The coal-heavers, who, by the way, are all Irish whiteboys, after their battles with the sailors, turned themselves to general war, robbed in companies, and murdered wherever they came. This struck such a panic, that in Wapping nobody dared to venture abroad, and the city began to find no joke in such liberty." It required again the active intervention of the guards to quell this disturbance.

In the meanwhile the court of King's Bench had reversed Wilkes's outlawry on account of some informalities in the proceeding: and judgment was given on the original sentence, by which he was condemned to pay a fine of 500*l.*, and be imprisoned ten calendar months for writing the *North Briton*, No. 45, and to pay another fine of 500*l.*, and be imprisoned twelve calendar months in addition to the former term of imprisonment for publishing the " Essay on Woman," which in reality had been published by the ministers. Whatever excuse may be made for the first part of the sentence, none can be found for the extreme injustice of punishing a man for the publication of what he had carefully concealed from public view, and a copy of which had only been procured by the basest treachery. The natural consequence was, that Wilkes, in his imprisonment, became a more formidable opponent than when at liberty, and that he only sank into insignificance when he ceased to be an object of persecution. Soon after the Middlesex election, Cook, the other member, died, and on the issuing of a new writ, Wilkes, from his prison, recommended his friend and supporter, Serjeant Glynn, who beat the court candidate, Sir William Proctor, by a large majority. The latter had recourse to Wilkes's own weapons, and hired a mob, which acted with so little moderation, that one of the popular party, named Clarke, was killed. Two of Proctor's chairmen were immediately brought before a jury at the Old Bailey, charged with murder, and one of them, turning out to be a Scotchman, was condemned, but received a pardon, to the great disappointment of the London mob. On the meeting of parliament in November, the affair of Wilkes was again debated fiercely during several weeks, and on the 3rd of February, 1769, he was again expelled the House of Commons. It was on this occasion that Edmund Burke, who spoke with great force against the expulsion, described the proceedings of the government, as " the fifth act of the tragi-comedy acted by his majesty's servants, for the benefit of Mr. Wilkes, at the expense of the constitution."

A new writ was issued for Middlesex, and Wilkes again offered himself as a candidate. The election took place at Brentford, on the 10th of March, when a Mr. Dingley undertook to be the ministerial champion, but he could not approach the hustings or find any one who would venture to propose him, and Wilkes was re-elected without opposition. The ministerial majority in the House of Commons flew into a rage, and, after another violent debate, declared the prisoner incapable of re-election, and issued a new writ next day, and Colonel Luttrell, then member for Bossiney, was engaged to stand for Middlesex. Wilkes, however, was again elected by a large majority, and London was as usual illuminated. But on this occasion the house voted that the sheriff had made a wrong return, and that Luttrell's name should be inserted instead of that of Wilkes as the member for Middlesex. Thus ended the war between "the two kings of Brentford," * as people jokingly termed King George and John Wilkes.

The mortifications of the court were not, however, confined to the "war" at Brentford; the ministers had again tried the unwise experiment of getting up a popular demonstration in their own favour. The first attempt was made in the county of Essex, "which," Horace Walpole observes, "being the great county for calves, produced nothing but ridicule." Dingley, the unsupported candidate for Middlesex, was the hero of this attempted demonstration, which miscarried through his own imprudence. Another attempt was made, and some signatures were obtained to a loyal address, which was to be presented to the king on the 22nd of March, by a procession of six hundred merchants and others. They set out amid hisses and outcries of every description, but they made their way in tolerable order as far as Temple Bar. There the mob had assembled in great force, and, having closed the gates against them, received them with a shower of mud and stones, which obliged them to disperse and save themselves in any streets and lanes that were not blocked up. This was popularly termed "The battle of Temple Bar." About a third of the loyal addressers re-assembled at some distance in advance of the scene of their discomfiture, and formed again in procession; but they were soon overtaken by the mob, which had obtained a hearse drawn by four horses, on one side of which hung a large escutcheon, with a coarse representation of the "massacre of St. George's Fields," while a similar escutcheon on the other side, represented the slaughter of Clarke at Brentford. This was marched slowly at the head of the procession, and thus, in the midst of a dreadful uproar, they reached St. James's, where the mob became more riotous than ever. The king and his ministers were obliged to wait a considerable length of time before the address could be presented; the mob had tried to seize the important document, and they had so pelted the chairman of the committee of merchants with mud that he was unfit to appear with it. Lord Talbot came down and seized one of the rioters, but the mob pressed round him and broke the steward's staff in his hand. Other unpopular noblemen received ill-treatment. At length, after fifteen persons had been captured by the guards, the mob dispersed, and the

* An allusion, of course, to the two kings of Brentford, introduced in the Duke of Buckingham's celebrated satire, "The Rehearsal."

address was presented. In the popular prints representing these disturbances, which were sold in great numbers, the tumult before St. James's is entitled "the sequel to the battle of Temple Bar."

It was about this period of agitation that some of the most violent of the political caricatures were ushered into the world, with a host of publications of different kinds, calculated to inflame people's minds. Political magazines were now established, such as the *Oxford Magazine* and the *Political Register*, bringing their monthly cargoes of caricatures and inflammable matter, and the engravings which had appeared singly during the earlier years of the reign were re-published, and in several instances collected into volumes. But new political heroes were coming on the scene, as objects of popular worship or hatred. Wilkes's career may be said to have closed with his release from imprisonment in 1770. A committee of men who called themselves "The supporters of the Bill of Rights," raised a subscription which relieved him from the pecuniary embarrassment into which he had been thrown by his own improvidence as much as by the persecutions to which he had been exposed; and a week after he left the prison he was admitted an alderman of London. In 1774, he and his friend Serjeant Glynn were elected members for Middlesex without opposition, and he was now allowed to take his seat in the house unmolested. The same year he was elected lord mayor, and he subsequently obtained the more lucrative and permanent office of chamberlain. In 1780, he was re-elected for Middlesex, and in 1788 he obtained a vote of the

house to expunge from its journals the declarations and orders formerly passed against him. He had now, however, become a very insignificant member of the House of Commons; and, having made the most of his patriotism, he exhibited himself as a remarkable instance of tergiversation, disclaiming his own acts, and making no scruple of expressing his contempt for the opinions of his former friends. In 1784, several caricatures celebrated the reconciliation of the "two kings of Brentford." The best of these, published on the 1st of May, of that year, is entitled "The New Coalition," and represents the king and Wilkes embracing, the latter holding the cap of liberty reversed. The patriot says to

THE RECONCILIATION.

the monarch, "I now find that you are the best of princes." King George replies, "Sure! the worthiest of subjects, and most virtuous of men!" Another caricature, published on the 3rd of May, represents the King, Lord Thurloe, and Wilkes, leagued in amity together; while a third, the work of some unscrupulous democrat, represents Wilkes and the king hanged on one tree, with the inscription, "Give justice her claims." The "two kings of Brentford" were now indeed equally unpopular with the mob; and at the general election in 1790, Wilkes received the most humiliating defeat on the very hustings where he had so often triumphed in his days of "patriotism." He died on the 26th of December, 1797, and was interred in a vault in Grosvenor Chapel, South Audley Street, where a plain marble tablet, described him simply as "a friend of liberty."

CHAPTER IX.

GEORGE III.

Violent Political Agitation—The North Administration—The Foxes—Remonstrances and Petitions—The Button Maker—Liberty of the Press—
Caricatures of the American War—Admiral Keppel—War with France
and Spain—No Popery ; the London Riots—Attacks on the Earl of
Sandwich and on Lord North ; the Political Washerwoman—Overthrow
of Lord North's Ministry—Rodney's Triumphs—Rockingham and Shelburne Administrations—America.

A T the moment that John Wilkes was losing his personal
importance, Lord Chatham re-appeared on the stage with
redoubled energy, and he continued for several years to support,
by his voice and example, the opposition in Parliament. The
result was a continuance of stormy sessions, such as had seldom
been seen in either house before ; and attacks were made within
the walls of St. Stephen's not only on the ministers, but on the
Crown also, which far exceeded anything that had appeared in
the *North Britons* without. The latter also were succeeded by
papers of a still more violent character ; and the language with
which the press had attacked Bute was feeble in comparison with
the powerful and fearless hostility of the celebrated Junius, or
the abuse of the *Whisperer*, a political paper established at the
beginning of 1770, which seldom deigned to apply to the king's
ministers more gentle epithets than that of " diabolical villains."
This journal contained articles openly exciting the people to rebellion ; and indeed everything seemed to threaten a great
national convulsion.

The opposition made its muster in attacking the address at
the opening of parliament in the beginning of January, 1770,
and shewed strong in talent, if not powerful in numbers ; and
this first question was productive of important, and, as appears,
rather unexpected results. The opposition was, moreover, acting
with greater unity than had distinguished it for some time ; for
Lord Chatham had formed a close alliance with the Rockingham
party, and the Marquis of Rockingham, who carried weight by
his integrity of character and his parliamentary abilities, was

personally a valuable ally in the House of Lords.* The two principal subjects of contention were, the ministerial policy with regard to America, where affairs were progressing fast towards civil war, and, at home, the infringement of the constitution in the case of Wilkes and the Middlesex election. On the first debate on this question in the House of Lords (Jan. 9), the chancellor, Lord Camden, to the surprise of everybody, seconded Lord Chatham, expressed his opinion strongly against the proceedings of the ministers in the case of Wilkes, and declared that, as a minister of the Crown, he had long disapproved the arbitrary

THE MARQUIS OF ROCKINGHAM.

measures pursued by his colleagues. Lord Camden was, as might be expected, immediately deprived of the seals, and one of the only men who brought any popularity to the court party was thus thrown into the opposition. The place of Lord Chancellor of England, refused by everybody, literally went a-begging, and, after the suicide of the Hon. Charles York, who had been with difficulty prevailed upon to accept it, was at length put in commission.

Among the foremost leaders of the opposition in the House of Lords were now, after Lord Chatham, the Marquis of Rockingham, the Dukes of Richmond, Portland, and Devonshire, and Lords Shelburne and Temple. In the lower house, the principal leaders and ablest speakers were Edmund Burke, Colonel Barré, George Grenville, Dowdeswell, and others. Colonel Barré was particularly distinguished by the boldness

COLONEL BARRÉ.

* The subjoined portrait of the Marquis of Rockingham, as well as that of Colonel Barré which follows, is taken from the series of slightly caricatured portraits etched by Sayer, and published in 1782. They are valuable keys to the caricatures of the day.

and vehemence with which he attacked the measures of government. He had been first thrown into the opposition by personal slights received from the Court ; and his resentment was
afterwards embittered by ill-treatment which he experienced in
his profession, the army. The debate on the address produced
effects in the House of Commons similar to those we have just
seen in the House of Lords ; the Marquis of Granby, the popular commander-in-chief of the army, joined the opposition, and
subsequently threw up his appointment. The opposition was
here further strengthened by the acquisition of Mr. Wedderburn,
the solicitor-general, who followed his friend, Lord Camden, and
by several other defections from the ministry. The latter, however, seemed but little weakened, when suddenly, at the end of
January, the Duke of Grafton gave in his resignation as prime-
minister. Upon this the ministry underwent some slight modifications, and Lord North was raised to the dignity of premier.
The celebrated North administration thus began on the 28th of
February, 1770.

At this moment some of the men began to take their place
on the political stage, whom we shall find acting a prominent
part in the stirring events of the latter part of the century.
Among these was the celebrated Charles James Fox, the second
son of Lord Holland, who, now little more than a youth, was
exerting his extraordinary talents in support of the measures of
the Duke of Grafton and Lord North, and he thus began the
world under the weight of unpopularity which had attached
itself to the names of those ministers. Charles Fox, as well as
his elder brother, had been early initiated into the dissipations
of the time by their father ; and his passion for gambling had
already reduced him to neediness. He was under age at the
time he entered the House of Commons, where the hope of place
made him a staunch supporter of the Court ; and he was the
most energetic opponent of Burke (his subsequent friend) in
the debate on the address. In the changes which followed the
Duke of Grafton's resignation, Fox was made a junior lord of
the Admiralty, and within three years after he was made a lord
of the Treasury. Horace Walpole writes, on the 2nd of February, 1770, the day after Fox's first appointment to office,
" Charles Fox shines equally there [at the hazard-table] and in
the House of Commons ; he was twenty-one yesterday se'nnight,
and is already one of our best speakers. Yesterday he was
made a lord of the Admiralty." A few months later (April
1772), Walpole went to the house to hear the young orator, and
he tells us that " Fox's abilities are amazing at so very early a

period, especially under the circumstances of such a dissolute life. He was just arrived from Newmarket, had sat up drinking all night, and had not been in bed. How such talents make one laugh at Tully's rules for an orator, and his indefatigable application! His laboured orations are puerile in comparison of this boy's manly reason." On the 27th of November, 1773, Walpole writes again, "Lord Holland is dying, is paying Charles Fox's debts, or most of them, for they amount to one hundred and thirty thousand pounds! Ay, ay; and has got a grandson and heir. I thought this child a prophet, who came to foretell the ruin and dispersion of the *Jews;* but while there is a broker or a gamester upon the face of the earth, Charles will not be out of debt."*

While Fox continued in his speeches sneering openly at "the voice of the people," it is no wonder that, with his father's unpopularity hanging over him, he became a mark for the popular satirists and caricaturists, who gave him the title of "the Young Cub," and made the most of his private vices. A print in the *Oxford Magazine* for February, 1770, immediately after Charles Fox's appointment to a seat at the Admiralty board, is entitled "The Death of the Foxes." It represents an old fox and a young fox hanged side by side on a gallows, while the farmer, John Bull, and his wife, are rejoicing at the liberation of their poultry-yard from such vermin. The youthful statesman was already remarkable for his corpulence. The same number of the *Oxford Magazine*, which is illustrated by the print just mentioned, contains a series of political cross-readings from news-

* At this period the passion for gambling was carried to absolute madness among the young aristocracy. The magazines and papers of the day contain numerous examples of their extravagances. Thus, in the *Oxford Magazine* for October, 1770, we are told, "A few days since some sprigs of our hopeful nobility, who were dining together at a tavern at the west end of the town, took the following sensible conceit into their heads after dinner. One of them observing a maggot come from a filbert, which seemed to be uncommonly large, attempted to get it from his companion, who not choosing to let it go, was immediately offered five guineas for it, which were accepted. He then proposed to run it against any other two maggots that could be produced at table. Matches were accordingly made and the poor insects were the means of five hundred pounds being won and lost in a few minutes." On another similar occasion, some hundreds of pounds were hazarded on the relative velocity of two drops of rain running down a pane of glass, which, however, disappointed the gamesters by joining in one before they reached the appointed goal. Statesmen and prime-ministers were affected with the same infatuation. We are told in the *Town and Country Magazine* for March, 1770, that "the late premier (the Duke of Grafton) was at one period of his life so addicted to gaming, that he lost his seat of E—n-hall (Euston-hall) one night to the late Duke

papers, one of which is, "Speakers on the side of Admin——n,*
the Hon. C. Fox, Esq.—He is reckoned the fattest man in
England next to Mr. Bright." In December, 1773, the *Oxford
Magazine* published another caricature against the family of the
Foxes. The old fox is seated at the table, apparently giving
the young ones his serious advice, to which the son and heir,
seated to his left, appears to listen with attention. The "young

A NEST OF FOXES.

cub," Charles, who, from his dark visage had already obtained
the nickname of Niger, sits on the other side, picking his
father's pocket. In the original, over his head, is the inscription "*Hic niger est;*" beneath him, on the ground, lie *Hoyle's
Games* and a brace of dice, and the devil concealed under the
table, holds him chained by the feet. The inscription under
the plate is, "Robbed between sun and sun." The old Fox,
Lord Holland, died at the beginning of July, 1774; but his son
Charles, who seems to have been no longer held in check by the
paternal politics of the house, had already quarrelled with the
minister, and was throwing himself into the ranks of the
patriots. On the 24th of February, 1774, Walpole announces to

of C——d (Cumberland), who generously returned it to him, on condition
of his never losing above a hundred pounds at one sitting." Horace
Walpole, July 10, 1774, tells of a still more extravagant amusement. One
of these gamblers, he informs us, "has committed a murder, and intends to
repeat it. He betted £1500 that a man could live twelve hours under
water; hired a desperate fellow, sunk him in a ship, by way of experiment,
and both ship and man have not appeared since. Another man and ship
are to be tried for their lives, instead of Mr. Blake, the assassin."

* Administration. Parliament, and especially the court party, was at this
time so jealous of any publication of what passed within doors, that it was
necessary thus to make indirect or concealed allusions even to the names of
the speakers.

his correspondent in Italy, "The famous Charles Fox was this morning turned out of his place as lord of the Treasury, for great flippancies in the house towards Lord North. His parts will now have a full opportunity of showing whether they can balance his character, or whether patriotism can whitewash it." It is due to Fox's character to say, that from this moment he continued during his life steady and consistent in the political principles he now embraced.

While things were going on anything but peaceably within the walls of the legislature, the agitation through the country without was increasing, and the North administration soon found itself engaged in a violent war with the city, and involved in the most vexatious and unprofitable hostilities with the old enemy of the court—the press. The year 1769 had seen the commencement of the letters of Junius; and at the end of May in the same year a petition from the city of London was presented to the King in full levee, violently attacking the court measures, and asking for the dismissal of ministers and the dissolution of the Parliament, which by its venality had lost the confidence of the country. Many of the counties, cities, and towns throughout the kingdom followed the example of the capital; but the King, who seemed resolved to push the war between royal prerogative and popular freedom to a crisis, refused to listen to their complaints, and, in opening the session at the beginning of 1770, the King's speech spoke of a disease that prevailed among horned cattle, instead of alluding to the violent agitation under which the kingdom then laboured. This was greedily seized upon by the satirists of the day; it was commonly said, that the King cared more for his own farmyard than for the interests of his subjects; and from this time he was often sneered at under the title of "Farmer George." It was further understood, that the royal leisure at Kew was often occupied in turning on the lathe and other similar amusements, and that royal ingenuity had gone so far as to construct "a button;" and the crime of button-making was in popular ridicule long coupled with the dignities of the British crown. The caricaturists made the horned cattle story tell upon other branches of the royal family; for the Duke of Cumberland, one of the King's brothers, had just been surprised at St. Alban's in an intrigue with Lady Grosvenor, for which he paid dear; and before many days had passed over the royal speech, a caricature on the court appeared under the title, "The Trial of Mr. Cumberland for spreading the distemper among the horned cattle at St. Alban's and other parts."

Y

The King himself seemed bent upon desperate measures. The *Whisperer* (of Feb. 24, 1770) asserts, that, "when the Marquis of Granby resigned his employments, the King said to him, 'Granby, do you think the army would fight for me?' To which the marquis nobly replied, 'I believe, sir, some of your officers would, but I will not answer for the men.'" Whether this be true or not, it is certain that Lord Marchmont, one of the most zealous of those whom the King now began to term "his friends," was so indiscreet as to talk in the House of Lords of the possible necessity of calling in foreign assistance. Expressions like these were repeated and commented upon abroad; and the citizens of London, who had voted the petition to which no answer had been returned, were further irritated by a report that some high persons about the throne had designated them as "*the scum of the earth* and *dregs of the people*." They determined to lay their complaints again before the King; and a very strongly-worded document was got up, under the title of an "Address, Remonstrance, and Petition," which complained of the dangers to which the country was exposed from secret and evil counsellors and a corrupt majority of the House of Commons, and called to the King's memory the fate of Charles the First and James the Second. The King is said to have consented only with extreme reluctance to receive this remonstrance: it was carried to St. James's on the 14th of March by the lord mayor, attended by a numerous body of the common-councilmen and city officers, and accompanied by an immense mob; and the King received it on the throne, but he is said to have shown a lowering countenance, and he returned a rebuking answer, concealing his anger with difficulty. Some of the courtiers also are said to have used impatient gestures, and to have held out indecent threats of depriving the city of its liberties. The court, indeed, at once resolved to proceed with rigour against the persons chiefly concerned in getting up this petition; and some very angry proceedings took place in the House of Commons; but these were subsequently relinquished by the urgent advice of Lord North and the more moderate of the ministers. The King is said to have complained in private that his ministers had not supported him in bridling the insolence of his subjects.

A number of caricatures, in rapid succession, exhibited the bitter sentiments of the popular party on the treatment experienced by their petitions and remonstrances. The *Oxford Magazine* for April, 1770, contains a caricature, entitled "The Button-Maker," which represents the mayor and sheriffs pre-

senting their " Remonstrance," to which the King refuses to
listen, exclaiming, as he shews his buttons to two noblemen in
attendance, " I cannot attend to your remonstrance! Do not
you see that I have been employed in business of much more
consequence?" One of the noble attendants observes, " What
taste! what elegance! Not a prince in Europe can make such
buttons!" while the other courtier, in the same strain, adds,
" What a genius! why, he was born a button-maker!"

However rude the language of petitions and remonstrances in
speaking of the House of Commons may have appeared, the
great corruption of that branch of the legislature, at the period
of which we are now speaking, was notorious; and it was the
money of the court only that overbalanced the eloquence of the
opposition. The latter only became more violent by the consciousness of its numerical weakness. In the March of 1770
the popular leaders in both houses were again declaiming against
the secret influence behind the throne, and the cry was quickly
caught by the mob, and chalked up against every wall in execrations against the Dowager Princess of Wales. Men who had
been ministers declared openly that their counsel had become
unpalatable to the royal ear the moment it savoured of constitutional liberty. On the 23rd of May, the lord mayor (Beckford), with some aldermen, and a numerous train of city worthies,
presented a new remonstrance to the King, less violent in its
language, but complaining of their treatment on former occasions. The reply was, a new rebuke; upon which the bold lord
mayor obtained leave, in the confusion of the moment, to make
an extempore speech, which roused the King's anger so much,
that he immediately issued orders that no lord mayor should be
allowed thus to address the throne again. The indignation of
the city was so great, that, if some moderate men of their own
party had not persuaded them otherwise, they were on the point
of refusing to congratulate the King on the birth of a Princess;
but very shortly afterwards, on the 21st of June, city patriotism
experienced a serious loss in the death of Beckford. About a
fortnight before this event, the Princess Dowager of Wales, the
object of so much popular odium, had left England on a visit to
Germany—an event which, as we learn from Horace Walpole,
was immediately sung about the streets in a ballad, the burden
of which was " The cow has left her calf!"

Although these events were succeeded by an appearance of
tranquillity, the fate of the city remonstrances continued long to
be a subject of discontent; and the occupation of button-making
was sung about the streets in ballads and lampoons with obsti-

nate perseverance. Most of these, to judge by an example now in my possession, entitled "A New Dialogue between the Devil and Mr. King, the Button-maker," were too scurrilous and doggerel to be quoted. A rather extensive class among the popular literature of this period consisted of jest-books, which were sometimes fertile in political satire. Thus, in the April of 1770 was published a collection entitled, in allusion to the *sobriquet* of Lord Sandwich, "Jemmy Twitcher's Jests." In the following November appeared "The Button-maker's Jests," with a coarse caricature on the King for a frontispiece. We may perhaps rest satisfied with the opinion expressed in a contemporary review, that it was a piece of "low scurrility." But the subject was revived again and again in a variety of forms; and in February, 1771, when the peace between England and Spain was nearly broken by the quarrel concerning the Falkland Islands, the two monarchs, said to have been both distinguished for the same sort of mechanical ingenuity, are introduced in a caricature in the *Oxford Magazine*, settling their differences over a paper of buttons. The bag of money on the Spanish King's lap is described as "A bribe for the P—— D—— of W——s;" and

BUTTON-MAKERS.

the Don says, "His M—m—'s directions are very good: we'll let him breathe a little, while she and I undermine the constitution." The mind of King George is entirely absorbed with one subject: he exclaims to his rival, "I say you never made so good a button in all your life." The preceding number of the same magazine contains one of the latest caricatures on the petitions, entitled "The Fate of City Remonstrances," in which the King is represented as giving the petitions of his subjects to the boyish Prince of Wales as materials for kites. In another print, published a few weeks later, Farmer George is seen in slovenly garb, attending to his nursery and the state of the weather, and utterly unconscious of the grievances of his country.

It was just at this moment that a new source of contention arose to embroil the ministers with the city of London. The former were constantly occupied with prosecutions against the Letters of Junius and other violent political papers, from which they derived no advantage, and which passed over without attracting more than a very temporary notice; but there were strong things said within the walls of Parliament, which it was the interest of ministers, satisfied with carrying all their measures by a large bought majority, to keep from the public ears. At no period was the English Parliament so absurdly jealous of the publication of its proceedings as at this time, when the licence of the press out of doors was almost unbounded; and the most extraordinary precautions were taken to conceal what was said within from the knowledge of those without. At the beginning of 1771, some newspapers ventured on giving reports of the parliamentary debates, notes of which they of course obtained through members of the house, when Col. George Onslow, one of the lords of the Treasury, who had been spoken of by his popular nickname of "Cocking George," brought forward the question of privilege in rather an angry manner. At the end of February and the beginning of March, there were several warm debates on the subject, and warrants were issued to arrest the printers, who dwelt in the city. The latter also stood upon its privileges: no one would give information where the offenders were to be found; and when some of them were seized, they were set at liberty by the city magistrates. Another person arrested was not only set at liberty, but he charged the messenger of the House of Commons with an assault; upon which the lord mayor (Crosby) with two aldermen (Oliver and Wilkes) signed a commitment against him, and he was obliged to find bail. On the 18th of March, the House of Commons, in a heat, summoned the lord mayor to attend in his place, which he did the next day, attended thither by a prodigious mob. Some members who had been insulted by the mob, such as Charles Fox, spoke in great anger. Every day, while the house was occupied with this question, it was surrounded by the infuriated populace, who hissed and hooted the members distinguished by their support of the court. Within the house the debates became at last almost as stormy as the riot without. A party of the opposition publicly seceded, and Colonel Barré told the house that their conduct was infamous, that no honest man could sit amongst them, and then walked away. On the 28th of March it was resolved to commit the lord mayor and Alderman Oliver to the Tower. The house avoided attacking Alderman Wilkes, who was probably the chief offender. The mob on this day had been unusually violent, having dragged Charles Fox and his brother from their chariot, and assaulted them violently; and Lord North's chariot was destroyed, and he himself narrowly escaped being torn to pieces. The next day the King went to the house, when the mob, which is said to have assembled to the number of at least eighty thousand, hissed and insulted his Majesty, and again attempted to vent their fury on Charles Fox, a large stone thrown at him having passed through both windows of his carriage. Fox was looked upon as one of the chief promoters of these violent measures; and one of the daily newspapers tells us, that "the resentment of the populace would probably not have been carried so far as it was, but for the indecent and most shocking behaviour of Mr. Charles Fox, who is supposed to have great influence with his Majesty, and already assumes the style and post of minister. This youth, for about half an hour, was leaning out of a coffee-house window in Palace Yard, shaking his fist at the people, and provoking them by all the reproachful words and menacing gestures that he could invent. George Selwyn stood behind, encouraging him, and clapping him on the back, as if he was a dirty ruffian going to fight in the streets." The prisoners remained in the Tower till after the prorogation of the Parliament, and were quite as formidable there as in the Mansion House. The fashionable toast in London was, in allusion to Alderman Oliver, "Success to Oliver the Second!" Mobs continued to encumber the streets. At mid-day, on the 5th of April, two carts, preceded by a hearse, were dragged in slow procession through the city to Tower Hill, amidst a vast concourse of people. The two carts had each a gallows stretched across, with large pasteboard figures hung upon them; those in the first cart being labelled on the back "L—d B—n" (Lord Barrington), "L—d H—x" (Lord Halifax), and "Alderman H—," the latter being an unpopular member of the court of aldermen, from his known attachment to ministers. The figures in the second cart were labelled "L— the Usurper," "De G—y" (De Grey), "J—y T—r" (Jemmy Twitcher, *i.e.* Lord Sandwich), and "C—g G—e" (Cocking George, *i.e.* Col. Onslow). At the Tower Hill, the gallowses and figures were committed to the fire; and the dying speeches of "some supposed malefactors" were subsequently cried about the streets. A rudely engraved print of this mock procession, with the speeches put into the mouths of the malefactors, is in the collection of Mr. Hawkins.

The court party now made an attempt to strengthen themselves a little in public opinion, by working upon the fears and
prejudices of the populace, and by other similar means, and with
a certain degree of success. They raised suspicions of foreign
designs on this country, and excited jealousy of foreign aggrandizement, as well as of domestic treason. Among reports used for
this purpose, was a pretended plot to embarrass our naval preparations by burning Portsmouth dockyard, and two or three
very humble individuals were arrested on this charge. This
affair seems to have caused no great excitement; and we hardly
trace it in the journals of the time, except by a caricature published in the *Oxford Magazine* for September, 1771, designed as
a satire upon the venality and partiality of the police-courts
under the celebrated Justice Fielding. Fielding had occupied
his prominent seat on the magisterial bench for a great number
of years; and he was now old, and remarkable for his fatness
and his blindness. In a satirical list of imaginary masquerade
characters in the *Westminster Magazine,* for December, 1771,
the watchful, but now blind magistrate, is thus introduced—
"Argus, whose eyes were sealed by Mercury, Sir J. Fielding."
The caricature alluded to is entitled, "The blind justice, and the
secretaries One-eye and No-head examining the old woman and
little girl about the firing Portsmouth dockyard." Justice
herself is represented as fat and
bloated, and as venal as her
official representative. The
latter, blind as he is, addresses
himself to the prisoners: "I see
plainly you are guilty, you have
a hanging look." One of the
secretaries of state, who has
his eye covered, adds, " Somebody must be hanged for this,
right or wrong, to quiet the
mob and save our credit." The
other secretary, being represented not only as intellectually
but bodily without a head, says
nothing. The woman accused
replies, "No more than your
worships have: I'm a poor
honest woman: my betters
know more of the fire than I."

JUSTICE.

The ministers were now actively working in the city of London, by indirectly influencing elections, &c. to obtain a majority

or at least a greater influence, in the city councils: and in this they had at times considerable success. The death of Beckford, in the summer of 1770, had shaken the strength of the city patriots; and their weaknesses had been increased by division among themselves. In May, 1772, we find a caricature on the ministerial influence in the city under the title of "The difference of weight between court and city aldermen;" in which their regard for the principles they profess, is estimated at a very low rate. On one side the cap of liberty is treated with the utmost disgrace; and in a framed picture on the wall above, poor

Britannia, whom we have so often seen abused and ill-treated by one party or the other, is represented as having arrived at the last degree of ignominy, by being hanged on a gallows. In the October of the same year we have another caricature, entitled "The City junta, or, the ministerial aldermen in consultation." These political divisions in the city were productive of serious domestic riots; and at the lord mayor's feast in 1772, the civic party were disturbed at their festivities in Guildhall by the violence of the mob without.

AN EXECUTION.

Several of the caricatures we have been describing were published with different monthly magazines, which from 1769 to 1772, had been largely illustrated with such subjects. The lull of political agitation is at this time made evident by the altered tone of these publications, which become suddenly tamer in style, and contain less of politics, and the caricatures give place to views of towns and of gentlemen's seats, or to pictures of birds and flowers. Caricatures, indeed, begin now to be scarce, and in general spiritless, till the violence of political agitation began to be felt again about 1780, towards the end of the North administration. The convention with Spain in 1771, and the management of our increasing Indian empire about the same time, were the subjects of considerable discontent, and gave rise to a few prints; and, when the agitation excited by the remonstrances and the imprisonment of the lord mayor began to subside, the ministers were attacked more generally for their support of arbitrary power at home, and for the want of dignity in their foreign policy, and especially for their neglect of the navy, the natural defence of this country, which was under the direction of the unpopular Lord Sandwich. The first number of the *Westminster Magazine* for December, 1772, contains a political satire, entitled, "A conversation which passed between the lion and the unicorn at St. James's, after the meeting of Parliament in 1772." It is a bitter complaint against the corruptions of the Government, and sneers at the King's taste for making snuff-boxes and buttons, instead of occupying himself with the wants of his subjects. The neglect of the navy is accounted for by the supposition that the King cared only for the defence of his own person against his subjects, for which soldiers were far more necessary than sailors, and it exhibits a little of the old jealousy against a standing army. Sandwich, says the lion, cared little how the sailors were provided for :—

> "LION.
> "Ah, the sailors are what Master George should observe;
> But Sandwich declares all the heroes shall starve :
> For by keeping them hungry, you keep 'em all keen,
> That like half-famish'd crows, which on carrion you've seen,
> They will fly at the French with the stomachs of hogs,
> And, like storks, in a trice clear the sea of the frogs.
>
> "UNICORN.
> "'Tis a comical maxim, and much out of nature,
> For me, Master Sandwich, faith, never shall cater;
> But if they don't quiet these terrible storms,*
> All our men and our ships will be eat by the worms.
>
> "LION.
> "The ships! what are they to our sensible master?
> 'Tis the horse and the foot which devour all the pasture.
> Will shipping defend him at London and Kew?
> No,—then what, pray, with shipping has Georgy to do?
>
> "'Tis the soldiers, my boy, upon Wimbledon Common,
> That tickle his eye, and the gigg of each woman;
> Their buttons he makes, and he cocks all their hats,
> With them he rides out too, and merrily chats."

The same magazine, for February, 1773, contains a caricature entitled "The state cotillion," founded on the rage for dancing then prevalent, and conveying a general satire on the administration. Lord Mansfield, the chancellor, is represented dancing on Magna Charta; and North is dancing on the national debt and on bills of grievances. Other bills are trampled upon by different ministers. The King peeps through a door on one side, and seems to enjoy the sport. On the other side, Lord

---

* The weather that season was extraordinarily tempestuous, and a great number of ships of all sorts had perished.

Bute is represented playing on the bagpipes the tune of " Over the water to Charley." The *Oxford Magazine* of the following May was adorned with a caricature representing the King with North and Sandwich in council, getting up a sham war, as an excuse for raising money for the court, while they receive secret subsidies from France to keep the nation quiet.

It was at this time, however, that our foreign relations were becoming every day more complicated and threatening. The dispute with the American colonies had now continued for several years ; and it became almost the sole question in debate between our political parties at home. But, even among those who complained most of the want of foresight shewn by our ministers in their measures with regard to the Americans, the cause of the latter was not everywhere viewed in the same light; for many condemned equally the violent conduct of the insurgents, and the evident design, already encouraged by a number of ambitious men amongst them, to throw off their allegiance to the English Crown. This was the real hindrance to a reconciliation. There were others, however, in the mother-country who took up the cause of the colonists with less reservation. Among the numerous pamphlets on this subject announced in the month of May, 1770, soon after the first collision between the mob and the soldiers in Boston, in which the blame most

A STRONG DOSE OF TEA.

certainly belonged to the former, two bear the titles of " A short narrative of the horrid massacre in Boston," and " Innocent blood crying from the streets of Boston." Prints of these, and of other alleged acts of violence, were distributed abroad ; yet the subsequent conduct of the Bostonians, and of the inhabitants of

Rhode Island, exasperated the English people, and gave unpopularity to the cause of the Americans. This, however, did
save the English ministers from the charge of obstinate folly
and imprudence ; while conciliation might have availed, they
were insolent and tyrannical, and while they provoked the
Americans more and more to resistance, they overlooked the
magnitude of the question, and took measures of defence totally
inadequate to avert the danger which was thus allowed to gain
head, until conciliation was no longer available. The tea bill was
represented in popular squibs and caricatures as a bitter dose,
which Lord North was forcing upon an unwilling patient *usque
ad nauseam*. One caricature represents America held down by
Lord Mansfield, the lord-chancellor, and compiler of the late
obnoxious acts against the colonies, while Lord North pours
the tea down her throat ; Britannia is seen behind, weeping at
her distress. In another caricature, published with the *Westminster Magazine* for
April, 1774, under the
title of " The White-
hall Pump," poor Bri-
tannia is thrown down
upon her child, Ame-
rica, while Lord North,
who was remarkable
for his shortness of
vision, viewing her
through his glass, is
pumping upon her,
and appears to be en-
joying her distress.
Underneath fallen Bri-
tannia, a multitude of
acts and bills are scat-
tered over the ground,
bearing the titles of
" Magna Charta,"
" The Bill of Rights,"
" Coronation Oaths,"

BRITANNIA IN DISTRESS.

" Remonstrances," " Petitions," &c. The chancellor, Lord Mansfield, holding an act of Parliament in his hand, stands by the
prime-minister, to encourage and support him. The other members of the cabinet, who are also in attendance, have joy marked
strongly on their countenances. The pump is surmounted by
the not very intellectual features of King George. Other peo-

ple—for there were many shades of opinion with regard to America—deceived by the outward declarations of the colonists, seized upon every new breath of apparent conciliation to preach up the advantages of amity and concord. A caricature, undated, entitled "A Political Concert," represents Britannia and her disobedient daughter reconciled, and united in supporting the cap of liberty. It was, indeed, the common outcry of the extreme opposition in this country, that the attack upon the civil rights of the American colonists was only a step towards the destruction of popular liberty at home.

CONCORD.

Among the caricatures on ministerial improvidence, one published in October, 1774, represents Lord North in the character of blustering "Boreas" (the sobriquet which was commonly applied to him), eyeing the distant colonies through his glass, and shewing his ignorance of the difficulties with which he had to contend by the flippant and vaunting threat "I promise to reduce the Americans in three months."

BOREAS.

It was the American question which finally, 'in 1774, placed Charles James Fox in opposition to the ministers, and which stirred up the ancient fire of Lord Chatham's eloquence during the latter years of his life. The English Parliament, with bill after bill, irritated the colonists, until they threw themselves into open war with the mother-country; while the insulting language of the Americans only gave an excuse for the English acts of Parliament against them, and so much disgusted the people of England, that the strength of the English ministry was daily increased. The general election of 1774 added so much to their majority in the House of Commons, that they were relieved of all fears from the opposition there. The war with America, which may now be said to have commenced, was a series of blunders and follies, which involved this country

in perpetual disasters. The memorable battle of Bunker's Hill
was fought on the 16th of June, 1765; and the same year the
"United States of America" made their declaration of independence. The war was now carried on with great animosity
during this and the following year, the Americans no longer
concealing the real object of the struggle, which was not relief
from a trifling grievance, but the resolution to break their allegiance to the mother-country, and establish themselves as a
separate empire. Now the popular complaint against the
ministers was, that their preparations to reduce the colonists to
obedience were inadequate and ill-directed, and that England
was betrayed into danger by her own rulers. In a caricature
published in April, 1776, under the title of "The Parricide,"
Young America is represented in the act of making a ferocious
attack on her mother, Britannia, who, held down by the
ministers, is unable to defend herself. The British lion is
roused into a state of furious agitation, ready to throw himself
upon the assailant, but he is bridled and restrained by Lord
Mansfield. There were many who already foresaw what must
be the ultimate result of the contest; and they looked forward
with apprehension to a period when liberty and civilization
would fly from the shores of Britain, to establish themselves in
greater glory in the New World. The following spirited poem,
published in the June of the year 1775, and placed in the
mouth of Lord Chatham, embodies these ideas:—

LORD CHATHAM'S PROPHECY.

"When boasting Gage was hurried o'er
To dye his sword in British gore,
  And plead the senate's right,
E'en Chatham, with indignant smile,
Harangued in this prophetic style,
  Illumed by freedom's light!

"Your plumed corps though Percy cheers,
And far-famed British grenadiers,
  Renowned for martial skill;
Yet Albion's heroes bite the plain,
Her chiefs round gallant Howe are slain,
  And fallow Bunker's Hill.

"Some tuneful bard, who pants for fame,
Shall consecrate one deathless name,
  And future ages tell,—
For Spartan valour here renown'd,
Where laurels shade the sacred ground,
  Heroic Warren fell!

"Erewhile a Howe indignant rose,
Against his country's, freedom's foes;
  Those glorious days are past.

A coward's orders to perform,
Lo, yon sea-Alva,* rides the storm,
    And drives the furious blast.

"Though darkness all the horizon shroud,
And from the east yon thunder-cloud
    Menace destruction round;
Yet Franklin, versed in Nature's laws,
From her dire womb the lightning draws,
    And brings it to the ground.

"Around him Sydneys, Hampdens throng;
His ardent philosophic tongue
    Can Roman zeal inspire;
The Amphyctyon council, hand in hand,
Like the immortal Theban band,
    Catch its electric fire.

"Can fleets or troops such spirits tame,
Although they view their cities flame,
    And desolate their coast !
'Midst distant wilds they'll find a home,
Far as the untamed Indians roam,
    And *freedom's luxury* boast.†

"Midst the snow-storm ‡ yon hero § shines,
Pierces your barrier, breaks your lines,
    With splendour marks his days;
He falls, the soldier, patriot, sage !
His name illumes th' historic page,
    Crown'd with immortal praise.

"Brighten the chain, the wampum tie,
Those painted chiefs raise war's fell cry,
    And hail the festive hour ;
The Congress binds the savage race,
As Heaven's own æther rules through space,
    Arm'd with attraction's power.

"Canadians scorn your vile behest,‖
Indignant passions fire each breast,
    And freedom's banner waves ;

* Lord Howe.

† An allusion to the words of the "Address of the twelve United Provinces to the Inhabitants of Great Britain:"—"We can retire beyond the reach of your navy, and without any sensible diminution of the necessaries of life, enjoy a luxury, which from that period you will want—*the luxury of being free.*"

‡ The account of the attack on Quebec, published by the Congress, said, "When everthing was prepared, the general waited the opportunity of a snow-storm to carry his design into execution,—being obliged to take a circuit, the signal for an attack was given, and the garrison alarmed before he reached the place; however, pressing on, he forced the first barrier, and was just opening to attempt the second, when he was unfortunately killed."

§ General Montgomery, who was slain in the attack on Quebec.

‖ The Canada, or lawyer's bill, as it was called, the work of Lord Mansfield.

Whole years they felt her flame divine ;
Its cheering light can they resign,
   And sink again to slaves !

"No more will kings court Britain's smiles,
No longer dread this Queen of Isles,
   No more her virtues charm ;
See her pursue th' ignoble strife
By the dire Indian's scalping-knife,
   And by the bravo's arm.

"Vain France, and Spain's vindictive power,
Exulting, wait the auspicious hour,
   To spread war's dire alarms,—
No more our fleets triumphant ride ;
This isle of bliss with all her pride,
   May feel the Bourbon arms.

"America, with just disdain,
Will break degenerate Britain's chain,
   And gloriously aspire ;
I see New Lockes and Camdens rise,
Whilst other Newtons read the skies,
   And Miltons wake the lyre.

"Behold her blazing flag unfurl'd,
To awe and rule the western world,
   And teach presumptuous kings,
Though lull'd by servile flattery's dream,
The people are alone supreme,
   From whom dominion springs !

"Heaven's choicest gifts enrich her plain,
The red'ning orange, swelling grain,
   Her genial suns refine ;
For her the silken insects toil,
The olive teems with floods of oil,
   And glows the purple vine !

"Her prowess Albion's empire shakes ;
Her cataracts, her ocean'd lakes,
   Display great Nature's hand ;
And Europe sees with dread surprise,
Æthereal tow'ring spirits rise
   To rule the wondrous land !

"Bold Emulation stands confest ;
Through the firm chief's and yeoman's breast
   The heroic passion runs ;
Imperial spirits claim their place!
No venal honours lift the base,
   When Nature ranks her sons !

"Lo, Britain's ancient genius flies
Where commerce, arts, and science rise,
   And war's dire horrors cease ;
Exulting millions crowd her plains,
Escaped from Europe's galling chains
   To liberty and peace !"

In the beginning of November, 1775, the Duke of Grafton, disagreeing with his colleagues, was dismissed from the ministry, and joined the opposition. This was followed by other changes in the cabinet, the most important of which was the appointment of the unpopular Lord George Germaine (the Lord George Sackville of Minden notoriety) to be secretary of state for America. The war there dragged on with various vicissitudes, sometimes flattering the British government with the hope of recovering its supremacy, while at other times it promised the immediate independence of the colonies; but the final result each year seemed more and more discouraging to the British cause. At length, on the 3rd of December, 1777, the Court was thunderstruck with the disastrous intelligence of the surrender of General Burgoyne and his army at Saratoga, on the 17th of October. The opposition could hardly conceal their exultations; the disgrace and loss which had fallen on the British arms were exaggerated, and chanted about the streets in doggerel ballads. An "Ode on the Success of his Majesty's Arms," written in December and printed in the *Foundling Hospital for Wit*, celebrates, ironically, the glorious results of the campaign, and the skill and prudence of the ministers at home, and ends with a congratulation on the old tale of King George's mechanical amusements :—

> "Then shall my lofty numbers tell,
> Who taught the royal babes to spell,
> And sovereign arts pursue ;
> To mend a watch, or set a clock,
> New pattern shape for Hervey's frock,
> Or buttons make at Kew."

In Parliament, the opposition burst into a violent storm; they reproached ministers with the imbecility of their measures, and laid all the faults and disasters on Lord George Germaine, with whom they were said to have originated. The thunder of Chatham's eloquence was again heard in the House of Lords, undiminished in force ; and Burke, Fox, and Barré overwhelmed the ministerial organs in the House of Commons. A new ground of complaint against the manner of conducting the war had now presented itself in the employment of the American Indians in the British army, whose cruel ravages on former occasions were still remembered with feelings of horror. It does not appear that the Indians now employed in the British army had committed any serious disorder; but the opposition not only saw them burning and massacring the King's own subjects—men whose veins flowed with English blood, but they conjured up fearful pictures of cannibalism; and in a caricature (in the collection of Mr. Burke) entitled, "The Allies—*par nobile fratrum,*" King George, whose private will, it was universally believed, governed in the cabinet, was represented in close league with his savage

TE3 ALLIES.

ally, gnawing the remains of the revolting feast.

Lord Chatham directed all the movements of the opposition on this important question. Indignation at the way in which the American war was misconducted seemed alone to keep the veteran statesman alive. Whenever there was to be an attack upon the ministers on that subject, he was carried into the house, wrapped up in flannels, and supported on crutches, and he rose up like a ghost from the grave to thunder forth his condemnation of the past, and his warning for the future. On these occasions he seemed suddenly animated with the full vigour of his youth. General Burgoyne, liberated on his parole, had now returned to take his place in the ranks of the opposition in the House of Commons, of which he was a member; and he was said to be a better debater than a general; it was, indeed, commonly reported, that his appointment to the command of the army in America was a mere stratagem of the ministry to get him away from his place in the house. When he made his reappearance there, in the month of March, 1778, he declared his willingness to undergo any kind of trial, and threw the blame of the failure of the expedition on the

GENERAL BURGOYNE.

z

secretary for America, Lord George Germaine. A grand debate was expected in the House of Lords on the 5th of April; and then Chatham was again in his place, but he looked more like a man that was come there to die, than one who would take any part in the political passions which agitated his country. There had been a division in the ranks of the opposition, and some now believing that the reduction of the colonies to obedience was hopeless, advocated the immediate acknowledgment of their independence. Chatham arose, and, held up by two of his friends, spoke with eloquence and indignation against the threatened separation of the colonies from the mother country. When he had resumed his seat, the Duke of Richmond, who represented that portion of the opposition which now looked upon that separation as inevitable, spoke against him, and when he had ended, Lord Chatham rose to reply. But, overpowered by his feelings, his strength failed him, and the orator fell back into the arms of his friends, and was carried out of the house in a state of insensibility. He was taken next day to his seat at Hayes in Kent, where, after lingering a little

ADMIRAL KEPPEL.

more than a month, he died on the 11th of May, at the age of seventy years.

At this very moment secret negotiations were going on between the American colonies and France to obtain the assistance of the latter country against England. The former had already received indirect encouragement, and it appears to have been only the reluctance of Spain, which had such extensive colonies of its own in the other hemisphere, to join with France, that hindered an open acknowledgment of American independence. By the month of June, the English government was fully informed that a treaty had been concluded between the rebellious colonies and the French King, and a fleet was immediately sent out to watch the French coasts, under Admiral Keppel,* another active member of the opposition,

* The portraits of Admiral Keppel and that of General Burgoyne,

whom the Court was glad to remove from his place in the House of Commons. Keppel at once commenced hostilities, and after making two or three small captures, he discovered that a large French fleet was at Brest, ready to put to sea. He immediately returned to Portsmouth for reinforcements. On the 9th of July both fleets put to sea, Keppel's forces being considerably inferior to those of the French under the Count d'Orvilliers. The two fleets came in sight of each other on the 23rd, but the French being unwilling to fight, and having the advantage of the wind, Keppel could not engage them till the 27th, when a dark squall brought them close together off Ushant; then the order was given for engaging, and a furious cannonade was kept up for full two hours as the fleets ran past each other, in which the French lost many men, and the English ships sustained considerable damage in their rigging, especially the division under Sir Hugh Palliser. When Keppel attempted to renew the engagement, Palliser was unable or unwilling to obey the signal, and the delay thus occasioned enabled the French fleet to escape.

This action led to events that again raised up the mob of the metropolis, which, not many months afterwards, was urged into acts of violence of a more serious character than any of which a London mob had been previously guilty. In his official dispatches, Keppel had generously screened Sir Hugh Palliser from blame in not having seconded him properly in pursuing the enemy. It has already been hinted that Keppel, as one of the opposition, was an object of aversion at Court; while Palliser, "that black man," as Horace Walpole styles him, was not only in favour at Court, but one of the lords of the Admiralty. Rumours had gone abroad, and letters had appeared in the newspapers, which were less sparing of Palliser's character than his superior officer had been; whereupon Sir Hugh wrote a letter in vindication, and demanded of Admiral Keppel an authentication of all his statements, which the latter declined to give. The subject was brought before the House of Commons at the beginning of December, and led to a rather angry debate, in which Palliser charged his superior officer with misconduct. The Court seized on this question in the hope that they would be able to crush Admiral Keppel, and the Admiralty ordered him to be brought to trial before a court-martial; a proceeding which gave great dissatisfaction to the officers of the navy in general, and which was indignantly condemned by the popular party.

given above, with others in this chapter, are taken from the series published by the caricaturist Sayer in 1781.

The trial began at Portsmouth on the 7th of January, 1779, and lasted thirty-two days; the result, which was an honourable acquittal of Keppel, was made known on the 11th of February. The mob of London, which had been all along in a state of agitation, waited impatiently for this intelligence, and, when it arrived, between nine and ten o'clock in the evening, the popular exultation knew no bounds, and, between joy at the event, and fear of the populace, every house in London is said to have been illuminated before eleven. The houses of Lord North and Lord George Germaine were attacked, and the windows broken. The windows of the Admiralty were also broken, and the large gate forced off its hinges; besides other violence. The effigy of Sir Hugh Palliser was hanged and burnt in various parts of the town. His house in Pall Mall was protected by a strong body of soldiers till after midnight; but, they having been then wholly or partially withdrawn, the mob burst in, and carried all the furniture into St. James's Square, where they burnt it. Young men of rank gave encouragement to, and even joined with, the populace. Mr. Pitt, who began his political life in the ranks of the popular party, is said to have assisted in breaking windows, and the young Duke of Ancaster was taken among the rioters, and passed the night in the watch-house. The next day was one of triumph to Keppel: the city of London voted him its freedom, to be presented in a box made of heart-of-oak, richly ornamented, and votes of thanks to the admiral were passed in both houses of Parliament. Another general illumination took place the following night, but with less rioting. Palliser resigned his seat at the Admiralty board, and vacated his seat in the House of Commons; and he also was brought to trial before a court-martial; but the influence of the Court is said to have been exerted to save him from a severe sentence. From this moment the King looked upon Admiral Keppel as a personal enemy, and it is said that at the subsequent elections the influence of the Castle was used in the most undisguised manner to hinder his re-election to represent the borough of Windsor.

The attempt at individual persecution had by no means increased the strength of the ministry; Keppel's triumph led to a violent attack on the board of Admiralty, and especially on the first lord, Lord Sandwich; and the cabinet was not a little embarrassed by the united attacks of naval and military commanders, including among the latter the two commanders in the American war, Generals Burgoyne and Howe, who now stood forth with the opposition, and laid all the misfortunes in

America to the charge of ministerial imbecility. The King of France was now at open war with us, and the summer of 1779 brought the King of Spain into the hostile confederacy. A popular song of the Americans long afterwards continued to speak of Louis XVI., as a mark of their gratitude for the assistance thus bestowed, by the title of the "patriot" King:—

> " Let us in rapture sing,
> Of Louis the patriot King,
> Virtue's support :
> Who with unshaken zeal
> Aided our common weal,
> And fixed friendship's seal
> To the New World."

The two monarchs derived in the sequel little advantage from this war, into which they had entered unprovoked ; and it may be doubted if it was of any great benefit to the Americans. Although the final independence of the American colonies was a thing which everybody now foresaw, the campaigns of 1779 and 1780 were not favourable to their cause.

Amid the incessant attacks to which its foreign policy exposed

BRITAIN'S STATE PILOT.

it, the North administration was gradually losing its strength. Some of its own supporters began to feel that the weight of increasing taxation was hardly compensated by any advantages gained by the extravagant expenditure which called for it; others began to desert it merely because the opposition was gaining force, and promised ere long to be the surest way to place; and thus its numerical majority in the House of Commons became daily less. Towards the end of June, 1779, when an open rupture had taken place with France and Spain, and the friendship of Holland was already doubtful, appeared a rather boldly executed caricature, representing "Britain's State Pilot foundering on Taxation Rock, to the great amusement of Lewis Baboon, Don Strut, and Nic Frog." These three personages (the frog emblematical of the Dutchman) are looking on in mockery, while North, in the character of the sloth, (he was remarkable for his laziness,) is piloting Britannia's boat, which, its sail torn from its hold by the wind, is striking on the fatal rock. At the masthead is the unpopular thistle, the influence under which it was pretended the state boat sailed; for Bute still presented an object of apprehension. In allusion to this, the engraving bears the inscription "Stuart pinxit—Yanky fecit." A few months later, (December, 1779,) in a caricature, entitled "The Botching Tailor cutting his cloth to cover a button," King George is again accompanied by his Scottish assistant, cutting up his cloth (the United Kingdom), while Lord North and his cabinet are looking on. Under the stall,

are the Bill of Rights, Magna Charta, Remonstrances, &c., cut into shreds and thrown away. The walls of the tailor's shop are ornamented (as was usual) with broadside ballads, on one of which we read the title, "Taxation no Tyranny, a new song, as sung at the Theatre Royal; the words by Jocky Stewart." Another is entitled "The Button-maker's downfall; or, Ruin to Old England; to the tune of Britons Strike Home;" a third proclaims the virtues of "Dr. Cromwell's effectual and only remedy for the king's evil;" and at the foot of the fourth, which contains a parody on "The Highland Laddie," is seen the popular emblem of the boot. A

THE BOTCHING TAILOR.

picture suspended behind, is a parody on the flight into Egypt, and represents the King and his family making a hasty exit on their way "to Hanover." Between the dates of these two caricatures, there had been one or two resignations in the cabinet, which shewed that even among the ministers there was not entire unanimity. Lord Gower, who had resigned the presidency of the council, declared, in his first speech in the ranks of the opposition at the end of November, that "he had seen such things pass of late at the council-table, that no man of honour or conscience could any longer sit there." The unusually large expenditure of the last few years, and the consequent increase of the national debt, and of the taxation of the country, began now to excite loud complaints, and associations were formed throughout England, with the object of opposing the extravagance of the government, and obtaining a reform in the parliamentary representation, the corruptions of which, people began to look upon as one of the principal causes of the evils under which they suffered. But these complaints were rather suddenly interrupted by a new subject of excitement, which led to fearful scenes of violence in the metropolis. For some time the dread of popery had been gaining ground, excited in some degree by the outcries of those who were opposed to the question of Catholic emancipation, which was now beginning to be agitated. Some bigoted people were even weak enough to believe that King George himself had a leaning towards the Church of Rome. This was especially the case in Scotland, where there had been serious no-popery riots in the beginning of 1779. It was a Scottish madman, the notorious Lord George Gordon, whom Walpole designates as "the Jack of Leyden of the age," who led the cry in England, and who had placed himself at the head of what was called the Protestant Association. After having troubled the House of Commons with inflammatory speeches during the whole of this session, Lord George gave notice on the 26th of May, 1780, of his intention on the 2nd of June to present a petition against toleration of Roman Catholics, signed by above a hundred thousand men, who were all to accompany him in procession to the House. We are told that the only precaution taken against the threatened mob was an order of the privy council on the previous day, empowering the first Lord of the Treasury to give proper orders to the civil magistrates to keep the peace, which the first lord of the Treasury forgot to put into effect.

On Friday, the 2nd of June, an immense multitude assembled in St. George's Fields, where Lord George addressed them in an inflammatory style, and then they marched in procession, six abreast, over London Bridge and through the city to Old Palace Yard, where they behaved in a most riotous manner. Many members of both houses were ill-treated, and one or two narrowly escaped with their lives. The confusion within doors, especially in the House of Lords, was very great; the Lords broke up without coming to any resolution, and made their escape. The House of Commons behaved with more firmness. But it was not till late in the evening that the mob was prevailed upon to disperse. In their way home, they attacked and burnt two Catholic chapels, that of the Bavarian ambassador in Warwick Street, Golden Square, and that of the Sardinian ambassador in Duke Street, Lincoln's Inn Fields. The mob assembled again on the night of Saturday, in the neighbourhood of Moorfields, and continued during the night to molest the Catholics who inhabited that part of London. Some military were ordered to the spot on Sunday morning, but no efficient measures were taken to suppress the rioters, and on Monday morning, when there was a drawing-room for the King's birthday, the disturbances had become much more serious. Under the cry of "No Popery," all the worst part of the population of the metropolis had now collected together, and London was entirely in their power during the rest of the day and the whole of the following night. Early on Monday morning they robbed and burnt the house of Sir George Saville, in Leicester Fields, because he had been the prime mover of a proposed act for shewing religious tolerance towards the Catholics. Several chapels and some private houses were plundered and destroyed, and fires were seen in various parts of the town. Both houses met, but some of the members were attacked on their way, and Lord Sandwich fell into the hands of the populace, and was with difficulty torn from them after he had been severely hurt. The House of Lords adjourned immediately, but in the Commons there were hot debates, and several strong resolutions were passed. As evening approached, the mob, which had increased, and consisted now of all the lowest rabble of London, rushed to Newgate, set fire to the prison, which was entirely destroyed, and liberated all the criminals. These joined the rioters, who now became more ferocious, and went about ravaging and plundering in the most fearful manner. A print of the time has given us a characteristic portrait of these would-be religious reformers.* The new prison at Clerkenwell was also

* He is in the act of shouting, "Down with the Bank!" The print is entitled "No Popery, or Newgate Reformers."

broken into, and the prisoners set at liberty. They next attacked and plundered the house of Sir John Fielding, the police magistrate, and they burnt down the house of Lord Mansfield, in Bloomsbury Square, destroying in it, among other things, a valuable library of ancient manuscripts. All day on Tuesday, and through Tuesday night, the populace went about robbing and burning, and drinking,—and this latter occupation only added to their fury. On Wednesday, the King's Bench, the Fleet, and the other prisons were burnt, and two at-

A MOB REFORMER.

tacks were made on the Bank of England, but the assailants were driven back with great loss by the soldiers who guarded that important building. Various other public buildings were marked for destruction. People, now, however, began to recover from their panic, and voluntarily armed in defence of their property, and troops, as well of the regulars as of the militia, were pouring into London; yet during the Wednesday night the town was on fire in no less than thirty-six places, and the destruction of property was immense. On Thursday the 8th of June, after many had been killed by the soldiery, and a still greater number had perished through intoxication in the burning houses, tranquillity was restored, and the capital was saved from the hands of a mob which seemed at one moment to threaten its entire destruction. On Saturday, Lord George Gordon was committed to the Tower; and he was subsequently brought to trial for high-treason, but was allowed to escape conviction, and he eventually shewed sufficient proofs of mental derangement.

These dreadful riots had been allowed at first to gain head entirely by the culpable negligence and pusillanimity of the civil authorities, who seem to have lost all presence of mind; and by a want of foresight on the part of the government. The conduct of the city rulers, with the exception of Wilkes, had been especially disgraceful, and the lord-mayor was punished for his cowardice. A few coarse and not well executed caricatures, and some ballads and songs, held them up to public ridicule and indignation. Lord Amherst, who, after Wolfe's death, obtained the credit of conquering Canada from the French, and who was now a courtier, an active man in the politics of the day, directed the military operations against the rioters, and became unpopular for his severity.* He was made

LORD AMHERST.

the butt of a considerable number of caricatures, in one of which he is represented as killing geese, and, in allusion to some threat which he had uttered, he is made to declare, "If I had power, I'd kill twenty in an hour." The King, as we have already seen, was openly stigmatized as being a Catholic at heart. A caricature, published at this time, and entitled "A great man at his private devotions," represents him kneeling before an altar, and wearing the dress of a monk, embroidered with the words "The holy Roman Catholic faith;" a crucifix stands on the altar, and portraits of Boreas and Jemmy Twitcher decorate the walls of his private chapel. A picture of the pope hangs above an open door, and petitions from Surrey and Middlesex lie within it as waste paper. A print of Martin Luther drops in neglected fragments from the wall. Burke, as the great advocate of Catholic emancipation, was especially odious to the fanatical party; and he obtained on this occasion the character which was so often afterwards applied to him of being a concealed Jesuit.

The "No-Popery!" cry was coupled with new apprehensions (though not very generally felt) of the Pretender, at whose return the imaginary Scottish influence was supposed now to aim. I have already mentioned a caricature in which this is slightly alluded to. In another caricature published this year, under the title of "Argus," King George is lulled into a profound slumber, while some cunning plunderers are stealing his sceptre, and others, apparently Scotchmen, are cautiously lifting the crown. One of them, in a plaid and bonnet (Bute), asks of another, in a large wig and ermined robe, "What shall be done with it?" the reply is "Wear it yoursel', my laird." But another of the party exclaims, "No, troth, I'se carry it to Charley, and he'll not part with it again." A miserable figure in rags on the opposite side, supposed to be a personification of the English community, clasps his hands, and cries, "I have let them quietly strip me of everything." An Irishman, de-

* This caricature portrait of Lord Amherst is taken from the series by Sayer.

parting, protests "that he will take care of himself and family." An American, leering upon the dozing sovereign, says, "We in America have no *crown* to fight for or lose." Behind the hedge which forms the background, a Dutchman feeds upon honey, during the absence of the bees from their hives. In one corner Britannia sits weeping, and her lion reposes in chains close to a map of Great-Britain, from which America is torn.

BRITANNIA IN SORROW.

The strength of the administration was evidently in a rapid decline, and its popularity had not been assisted by the turbulent scenes we have just described, or by any favourable change in the prospects of the war. Before the London riots, the government had been embarrassed by a signal defeat on a question of a very significant character. The petitions crowding in from all parts of the country had already alarmed the Court; when, on the 6th of April, Mr. Dunning moved in the House of Commons his famous resolution against the overgrown influence of the Crown, which was carried against the Court, and was followed by the adoption of other motions equally unpalatable. On the 10th of April the opposition was still in the majority, and other strong resolutions against prerogative were passed. Everybody was in astonishment, and expected an immediate dissolution of the cabinet and a change of measures. A caricature on this occasion, published on the 20th of April, and entitled "Prerogative's defeat; or, Liberty's triumph," is in the collection of Mr. Hawkins; it represents the downfall of Scottish influence, while Ireland and America are both rejoicing, the latter exclaiming, "Now we will treat with them." But the ministers had had time to recover from their surprise, and an adjournment of the house to the 24th of April was employed in negotiating with those who had on this occasion deserted their ranks. On that day the ministers recovered their majorities, although they were not now very large ones. In another caricature, entitled "The Bull over-drove; or, the drivers in danger," the British bull is represented in a rage, kicking at the ministers, one of whom

(Lord George Germaine) exclaims, "This is worse than the battle of Minden!" The Kings of France and Spain stalk away, the former exclaiming, "By gar! my friend America, I must leave you; dis hull will play le diable!" the other, "I wish I was safe out of his way; he beats the bulls of Spain." America replies, "I fear, monsieur, I shall get little by your friendship."

The ill-treatment which Keppel and other liberal officers received from the Court brought unpopularity on those who were put forward by the ministry, and this often embarrassed them in their operations. Rodney had begun the year prosperously by a decisive victory over the Spanish fleet off St. Vincent on the 16th of January, which was followed by the relief of Gibraltar, now besieged by the Spaniards; but the unwillingness of his captains to obey a Tory commander deprived him, in the middle of April, of gaining a much more signal victory over the French fleet in the West Indies. The French escaped, and took shelter

in a friendly harbour, and both sides boasted of the superiority. A caricature, entitled "National Discourse," published after the intelligence of these events arrived in England, represents the mutual feelings of the sailors of the two nations on this occasion; the lean and vain-glorious Frenchman's taunt, "Ha, ha, we beats you!" receives from the sturdy Englishman the somewhat unpolite reply, "You lie!" Rodney's miscarriage led soon

NATIONAL DISCOURSE.

after to the junction of the French and Spanish fleets, and nothing but the sickness which fell upon them and weakened them, and the mutual mistrust between these two allies, saved our West Indian islands from conquest. The close of this year saw Holland openly added to the number of our enemies. In America the events of the war continued to be in general discouraging to the colonists, until the latter part of the year 1781, when it suddenly took a decided turn to their advantage, and the capture of Lord Cornwallis and his army may be looked upon as having left no longer any doubt in people's minds as to what must be the final result.

At the beginning of the year (on the 17th of January, 1781,) when the prospects of the British arms in America seemed to be in the highest degree promising, a caricature was published, representing Britannia and her enemies weighed in the balance. America is seated in one scale in an attitude of sorrow, sighing forth the unwilling avowal, "My ingratitude is justly punished." The Spaniard and the Frenchman stand in the scale with her, and the Dutchman is hanging on with his whole weight in the effort to pull it down. The first of these exclaims, "Rodney has ruined our fleet!" The Frenchman addresses himself to their new ally the Dutchman, "Myn-

A LIGHT COMPANY.

heer, assist, or we are ruined;" and receives for reply, "I'll do anything for money." But the Dutchman is a loser, apparently unknown to himself, for his money is falling from his pocket, with papers inscribed, "Demerara," "Essequibo," "St. Eustatia," "St. Martin," and other colonies which had fallen into the hands of the British. In spite of their exertions, Britannia, standing alone in the other scale, is outweighing them all; she holds a drawn sword, inscribed "Justice," in her hand, and exclaims, "No one injures me with impunity." Other caricatures, marking the popular exultation, appeared about the same time.

In the general elections in the autumn of 1780, the ministerial majority was not as usual (and, perhaps, as was expected) increased. The opposition, feeling its strength, commenced a resolute attack on the ministry, criticising its measures abroad and at home, and exaggerating its errors, and the consequences that resulted from them. They fell first upon Lord Sandwich, and brought forward the old grievance relating to Admiral Keppel and Sir Hugh Palliser, the latter of whom had been rewarded with the governorship of Greenwich Hospital. They next entered upon the alleged ill-management of the navy, and complained that it had been deprived of some of its ablest officers in a time of great danger, by the political partialities of the Court. After Christmas, they returned to the charge, and accused the ministers with having unnecessarily driven this country into a war with Holland. The charge of mismanagement of the navy was then renewed. Burke next brought forward a motion for

LORD SANDWICH.

economical reform, with a view also to a reform in the representation of the country, founded on the petitions of the different political associations now formed throughout England; he was supported by the whole force of the eloquence of the opposition, and the debate, on the second reading of his bill, on the 26th of February, 1781, brought on his legs, for the first time in the house, young William Pitt, the second son of the great Earl of Chatham, who entered the political arena as a disciple of Charles Fox. Sheridan and Wilberforce also made their first speeches on this occasion, as zealous members of the opposition. The next subject of attack was Lord North's financial arrangements. Through all these attacks, and many more which followed, the ministers were supported by the encouraging accounts of the success of our arms in America and other parts; but in the autumn even this prop began to give way, and when, on the 25th of November, the news of the surrender of Lord Cornwallis's army arrived, they were filled with dismay. Parliament opened two days afterwards, and the debates occasioned by this disaster were violent in the extreme. Until the Christmas recess, the house was almost entirely occupied with the American war, and the state of the navy. In the midst of this warfare of words, young William Pitt was rising daily into distinction.

After Christmas, the war between the opposition and the ministry was renewed with increased vigour. Lord Sandwich was again the first object of attack. Charles Fox moved for an inquiry into the causes of the constant ill success of our naval forces, and a bitter declamation was made on the improvidence of the Admiralty, and on the narrow policy which had deprived our ships of some of their best commanders, such as Keppel, Howe, and others, because their political opinions were not agreeable at Court. Ministers agreed to the inquiry, and there was no division; but in a motion for a vote of censure on the Admiralty board, a few days afterwards, the ministerial majority was only twenty-two. After the arrival of the news of Lord Cornwallis's surrender, most people began to look forward to a total change in the cabinet as not far distant; and the venal supporters of the Court in the House of Commons were already beginning to desert, to join those who were likely to succeed to power. On the 20th of February, Fox renewed the attack on Lord Sandwich, and the ministerial majority was reduced to nineteen.

It was evident that the affairs of America would not long be allowed to remain untouched, and, at the beginning of February, Lord George Germaine had been allowed to resign the colonial secretaryship, and as a reward for his staunch support of the King's policy, he was raised to the peerage by the title of Viscount Sackville. On the 22nd of February General Conway moved for an address to the King, praying him to put an end to the American war : and on this occasion, after a long and warm debate, the ministerial majority was only one. Still, however, North did not resign, but on the 25th of February he calmly brought forward his budget. The opposition was furious, and attacked his ways of raising money in the most violent terms. Some new taxes proposed on this occasion were very unpopular out of doors, especially one on soap, which was made the subject of a host of ballads and caricatures, that continued to be hawked about long after North's ministry had fallen. In these the premier was ridiculed under the title of "Soap-suds," the political "Washerwoman," and a variety of other similar appellations. It was pretended that people would now have to learn to wash without soap; and in one of the caricatures, entitled "The M-n-s-r reduced ; or, Sir Oliver Blubber in his proper station," the new washerwoman is occupied, as it appears, in this experiment, for, on the wall behind is the notice, "Linen wash'd 50 per cent. cheaper than at any other place in London.

by Mary North, author of the treatise upon washing without soap, and many other ingenious performances." At a window before the portly figure of the metamorphosed minister, two washerwomen of the old practice are looking in at his work and laughing.

Two days after the announcement of the budget, on the 27th of February, General Conway made a new motion for an address for pacification with America, when, after another warm debate, ministers were in a minority of nineteen. When this was known next day,

THE WASHERWOMAN.

the town was filled with manifestations of joy; many houses were illuminated in the evening, and papers were cried about the streets announcing "Good news for England! Lord North in the dumps, and peace with America!" The King returned rather an evasive answer to the address, on which the ministers, instead of retiring, as it was expected they would do, proposed to bring forward some half measures, with the hope of appeasing the opposition. The latter now raised a loud cry against the obstinacy with which Lord North clung to his place, and Charles Fox in particular, whose unfortunate love of dissipation and gambling had reduced him to necessitous circumstances,* could hardly conceal his eagerness to get the ministers

* Fox, as we learn from various sources, was at this time in great pecuniary difficulties. Towards the end of May, 1781, Walpole writes, "As I came up St. James's Street, I saw a cart and porters at Charles's door; coppers and old chests of drawers loading. In short, his success at Faro had awakened his host of creditors; but unless his bank had been swelled to the size of the Bank of England, it could not have yielded a sop for each. Epsom, too, had been unpropitious, and one creditor had actually seized and carried off his goods, which did not seem worth removing. As I returned full of this scene, whom should I find sauntering by my own door but Charles. He came up and talked to me at the coach-window, on the Marriage Bill, with as much *sangfroid* as if he knew nothing of what

out, that he might share in the spoils. On the 8th of March, Lord John Cavendish again brought forward the question of American mismanagement, and moved a direct vote of censure on the English ministry; the latter on this occasion had a majority of ten. On the 15th, Sir John Rouse made a new and still more direct attack, in a motion declaring that the house no longer placed confidence in the present ministers, whose majority was now only nine. Lord Surrey immediately gave notice that he should bring forward another motion to the same effect on the 20th; but when that day came, the debate was prevented by Lord North's announcement to the house of the resignation of ministers.

The tenacity with which Lord North apparently clung to office through so many defeats was generally attributed, and in all probability with justice, to the King's unwillingness to accept his resignation. It was widely believed that the King's will had for some time been the rule according to which his ministers shaped their measures, and that he showed the greatest reluctance to admitting to any share in the government of the country those who were not "his friends." Most of the leaders of the liberal party were to him objects of personal animosity.

The opposition itself, since Lord Chatham's death, had become more clearly divided into two sections, one of which acknowledged Lord Rockingham for its leader, whilst the other was ranged under the banners of Lord Shelburne; the former numbered in its ranks Charles Fox, Edmund Burke, and Admiral Keppel, while with Lord Shelburne were Colonel Barré and the young and aspiring William Pitt. The rivalry of these two parties was at present rather personal than founded on any especial principle; but the King had less repugnance to the Shelburne party, because they still shared in Chatham's objections to acknowledging the independence of the Americans; while the Rockingham party insisted that the time was now come when peace must be made with the Americans at any rate, and they called for the sacrifice of all claims to supremacy on the part of the mother-country. The King is said to have tried to negotiate privately with Lord Shelburne; but, the only leader under whom the whole opposition could be brought to serve

had happened. I have no admiration for insensibility to one's own faults, especially when committed out of vanity. Perhaps the whole philosophy consists in the commission. The more marvellous Fox's parts are, the more one is provoked at his follies, which comfort so many rascals and blockheads, and make all that is admirable and amiable in him only matter of regret to those who like him, as I do."

A A

being Lord Rockingham, he was sent for, and he undertook the task of forming a new cabinet. The only one of the old ministers whom the King was allowed to retain was the lord-chancellor Thurlow, and he remained but as a thorn in the sides of his colleagues, for he was never prevailed upon to act cordially with them. It appears that, even at last, the negotiations between the King and Lord Rockingham were carried on in great part by the mediation of Lord Shelburne, which increased the jealous feelings of the more liberal party towards the latter. The new ministers were, Lord Rockingham as first lord of the Treasury; the Earl of Shelburne and Mr. Fox, secretaries of state; Lord Camden, president of the council; Lord Thurlow, chancellor: the Duke of Grafton, privy seal; Lord John Cavendish, chancellor of the Exchequer; Admiral Keppel, created a viscount, first lord of the Admiralty; General Conway, commander-in-chief; the Duke of Richmond, master-general of the Ordnance; and Dunning, now created Baron Ashburton, chancellor of the duchy of Lancaster. Burke, without a seat in the cabinet, was made paymaster; Colonel Barré, treasurer of the Navy; William Pitt, who refused to take a subordinate place, was allowed to stand aloof, and was evidently looking forward to greater things. Three conditions had been insisted upon in forming the new administration, and had been conceded by the King; they were, 1. peace with the Americans, and the acknowledgment of their independence; 2. a substantial reform in the civil-list expenditure; and 3. the diminution of the influence of the Crown.

The ministers proceeded immediately to carry out their projected reforms, and evidently with good-will, but that they were not especially palatable to the King was sufficiently clear from the constant opposition they received from the Chancellor Thurlow, with whom Fox had expressed great reluctance to take office. Keppel brought at least new vigour into the Admiralty department; and many of the old veteran officers, who had resigned after Keppel's trial, were restored to the service. Rodney, a staunch Tory, who had not yet performed what was expected from him with the fleet in the West Indies, was recalled, and Admiral Pigot was sent out to supersede him. Rodney was at this time so little popular in England, that his constituents in Westminster, which he represented in Parliament, had declared their intention of nominating Mr. Pitt in his place for the next election. The position of England at this moment was discouraging on every side; and our enemies, both in America and in Europe, refused to treat except on humiliating conditions. In the midst of these embarrassments, on the 18th of May, the whole country was struck with astonishment, and thrown into what has been described as "a delirium of joy," by the arrival of the news of the glorious victory of the 12th of April gained by Rodney over the French admiral De Grasse, which in one day restored England to the sovereignty of the ocean. The English ministers, who had blamed so much all the naval schemes and operations of their predecessors, were much embarrassed by this success, the honour of which really belonged to Lord North, and by their own proceedings with regard to Rodney. An express was sent to prevent Admiral Pigot sailing, but it was too late. A cold vote of thanks was given by both houses to the victorious Rodney, and he was raised to the peerage, but only as a baron, and was voted a pension of but 2,000*l.* a-year. Such were the effects of the violence of political faction in this country under George III. The other officers received honours and rewards in different degrees.

The popular rejoicings on Rodney's victory turned less against the ministry than might have been expected, but they were attacked with vigour by their predecessors, who were now in the opposition, and they were glad to make the best excuses they could. Those sure concomitants of a struggle of parties in this country, the caricatures, had already been launched against them, and Rodney's successes furnished abundant materials. One of these, entitled, "Rodney introducing De Grasse," published on the 7th of June, represents the conqueror presenting his illustrious captive at

RODNEY AND DE GRASSE.

the foot of the throne. On one side of the sovereign stands Admiral Keppel; on the other, Fox. The latter is represented as

A A 2

soliloquizing, "This fellow must be recalled; he fights too well for us; and I have obligations to Pigot, for he has lost 17,000*l.* at my faro bank." The insinua-

REWARD.

tion thus conveyed against the secretary of state was to all appearance perfectly unjust. Keppel is represented as jealous of Rodney's glory; he is reading a list of the captures, among which we can distinguish the name of the *Ville de Paris* (De Grasse's ship), and he observes, "This is the very ship I ought to have taken on the 27th of July." Another caricature, published on the 13th of June, is entitled "St. George and the Dragon." St. George (Sir George Rodney) is overcoming a mighty dragon, and forcing it to disgorge a quantity of frogs (perhaps an allusion to the Dutch). King George is running towards him with the reward of a baron's coronet, and exclaims (in allusion to Rodney's recall and elevation to the peerage), "Hold, my dear Rodney, you have done enough! I will now make a lord of you, and you shall have the happiness of never being heard of again." These two prints are reckoned to be the first attempts of the celebrated Gillray, whom we shall soon find for many years almost monopolizing, by his remarkable talent, this branch of art.

LORD SHELBURNE.

The somewhat sudden death of the Marquis of Rockingham, on the 1st of July, brought on quite unexpectedly a new ministerial crisis. It was soon known that the King, who always preferred communicating with Lord Shelburne, intended to place him at the head of the ministry. The Rockingham party, and more especially Fox and Burke, (the former was accused by his opponents of aiming at the place himself), held a meeting, and most of them determined to resign. Fox had already complained that he was in a situation where he was thwarted in his principles by a superior power, and, although in a position of great pecuniary difficulty, he refused under any condition to act in a ministry of which Lord Shelburne was head. He was followed by Burke, Lord John Cavendish, John Townshend, and others. Colonel Barré took Burke's place, and was himself succeeded by Dundas : Thomas Townshend succeeded Fox as foreign secretary ; and William Pitt was raised to the post of chancellor of the Exchequer, in the place of Lord John Cavendish. Thus began the Shelburne administration, with no great hopes of success, for it was notoriously weak in parliamentary influence.

These changes led to acrimonious recriminations in the House of Commons, in which Pitt shewed the commencement of his future hostility towards Fox. The King is said to have received the resignation of the latter with unconcealed satisfaction ; all kinds of abuse were thrown upon Fox and Burke out of doors, and the most selfish and factious motives were attributed to them. One of the earliest caricatures by Sayer, a large print published on the 17th of July, and entitled "Paradise Lost," represents the unfortunate pair cast out of the gate of the ministerial paradise, which is adorned with the faces of Shelburne, Barré, and Dunning.

> " To the eastern side
> Of Paradise, so late their happy seat,
> Waved over by that flaming brand, the Gate
> With dreadful faces thronged and fiery arms !
> Some natural tears they dropt, but wiped them soon.
> The world was all before them, where to choose
> Their place of rest, and providence their guide.
> They, arm in arm, with wand'ring steps, and slow,
> Thro' Eden took their solitary way."

Dunning and Barré had both received pensions through Lord Shelburne, the latter upwards of 3,000l. a-year, and they were naturally among his most staunch supporters. The large pension given to Colonel Barré, for no apparent services to the state, was made the subject of loud and bitter complaints by the Tories, who compared it with the smaller reward which had been doled out to Rodney for one of the most glorious victories of the age. Another large print by Sayer, published on the 24th of August, under the title of "*Date obolum Belisario,*" represents the colonel receiving his pension from Lord Shelburne at the Treasury door.

> " Rome's veteran fought her rebel foes,
> And thrice her empire saved ;
> Yet through her streets, bow'd down with woes,
> An humble pittance craved.

"Our soldier fought a better fight,
    Political contention;
And grateful ministers requite
    His service with a pension."

ENVY.

One of the few efforts of Gillray
at this early period of his career,
related to the hostilities of faction,
and was aimed against Fox, who
is represented in a parody on
Milton's Satan, envious of the
happy pair, Shelburne and Pitt,
who are counting their money on
the Treasury table.

          "Aside he turned
For envy, yet with jealous leer malign
Eyed them askance."

These are but a small portion of
the caricatures of which Fox and
his friend were now made the
butt.   In one, the discomfited
ex-secretary of state is seen under
the character of "Ahitophel in
the dumps," riding away dolefully on his mule towards a gallows and block.   In another, Fox

AHITOPHEL IN THE DUMPS.

and his staunch supporter Burke, are placed in the stocks as personifications of Hudibras and his squire.

The Parliament, however, was prorogued on the 11th of July, and the summer and autumn were occupied in fruitless negotiations to secure a majority for the Shelburne cabinet in the ensuing session. Their apprehensions were so great, that, as the time for the opening of Parliament approached, Pitt was employed in a private interview with Fox to gain him over to the ministry, but he persisted in his resolution of not taking office under Lord Shelburne.

HUDIBRAS AND HIS SQUIRE.

His party, indeed, now began to fear that, elated by Rodney's victory over the French fleet, Lord Shelburne, who had always been opposed to the recognition of American independence, might be induced to yield to the King in countenancing the sovereign's favourite measure of the war against America. The signal overthrow of the French navy had struck the Americans with dismay, and some of them began to despair; but they were encouraged by the conduct of Washington, and they still looked with coldness on all conciliatory advances. On this side the Atlantic, the King of Spain had risen almost to an imbecility of self-confidence in the magnitude of his preparations for the reduction of Gibraltar; and he and the King of France put forward pretensions to which the English ministry could on no conditions listen. Other successes, however, attended our fleets at sea; and the hopes of our confederated enemies were at length entirely broken down by the wonderful defeat of the Spanish armament against Gibraltar in the grand attack on the 13th of September 1782, and by the subsequent arrival of the fleet under Lord Howe for the relief of the garrison, actions which have made the names of General Elliot and Admiral Howe immortal. All parties began now to talk with more sincerity of their desires for peace; and the signing of preliminaries, which was executed by the Americans and their European allies independent of each other, was hastened by their mutual jealousies. The independence of the United States of America was thus acknowledged; but King George acceded to the wish of his subjects on this point with a very bad grace, and his ill-humour was even shewn in the speech with which he opened his Parliament at the beginning of December. The King long detested the very name of anything American; and his personal hatred of Franklin, who had certainly been one of the least conciliating and least candid of the factious "patriots" on the other side of the water, was afterwards exhibited even in the peculiar colour given to his patronage of science and literature. It is said that Sir John Pringle was driven to resign his place as president of the Royal Society by the King's urgent request that the Royal Society should publish, with the authority of its name, a contradiction to a scientific opinion of the rebellious Franklin; the president replied, that it was not in his power to reverse the order of nature, and resigned, and Sir Joseph Banks, who, like a true courtier, advocated the opinion which was patronized by the King, succeeded him in the society's chair.

Feelings like these, long persisted in, tended to perpetuate that estrangement of interests between the mother-country and her now separated colonies, which was naturally enough generated by a long and obstinate war, which, considered from the beginning as a civil war, was accompanied with all that bitterness of animosity that usually accompanies civil contentions. The royalists and the Tories of this country, long after the contest was over, could think and speak of the Americans only as rebels; and the latter, who seemed to have adopted as their national character too much of the bullying manners and passions of the worst of the demagogues who urged them into the war, never forgave the insult which they felt to be conveyed to them by this reproachful term. They expressed their sentiments of unabating hostility in many a lampoon upon their ancient brethren in Britain. The following ballad, founded upon an incident that occurred while Philadelphia was in the hands of the royalist troops, was especially popular; and, as will be seen, particularly in the latter stanzas, expresses in a marked manner the irritation occasioned by the indiscriminate use of the term "rebel" among the officers of the British army.

THE BATTLE OF THE KEGS.

(Tune *Maggy Lauder*.)

"Gallants, attend and hear a friend
Trill forth harmonious ditty;
Strange things I'll tell, which late befell
In Philadelphia city.

" 'Twas early day, as poets say,
  Just when the sun was rising,
A soldier stood on log of wood,
  And saw a sight surprising.

" As in amaze, he stood to gaze,—
  The truth can't be denied, sir,—
He spied a score—of kegs, or more,
  Come floating down the tide, sir.

" A sailor, too, in jerkin blue,
  The strange appearance viewing,
First d—d his eyes, in great surprise,
  Then said—'Some mischief's brewing.

" 'These kegs now hold the rebels bold,
  Packed up like pickled herring;
And they're come down t' attack the town,
  In this new way of ferrying.'

"'The soldier flew, the sailor too,
  And, scared almost to death, sir,
Wore out their shoes, to spread the news,
  And ran till out of breath, sir.

" Now up and down, throughout the town,
  Most frantic scenes were acted ;
And some ran here, and some ran there,
  Like men almost distracted.

" Some 'fire' cried, which some denied,
  But said the earth had quaked ;
And girls and boys with hideous noise,
  Ran through the town half naked.

" Sir William,* he, snug as a flea,
  Lay all this time a-snoring ;
Nor dreamt of harm, as he lay warm
  In bed with Mrs. L——g.

" Now, in a fright, he starts upright,
  Awak'd by such a clatter ;
He rubs both eyes, and boldly cries,
  'For God's sake, what's the matter ?'

" At his bed-side he then espied
  Sir Erskine† at command, sir ;
Upon one foot he had one boot,
  And t' other in his hand, sir.

" ' Arise ! arise !' Sir Erskine cries,
  'The rebels—more's the pity—
Without a boat, are all on float,
  And rang'd before the city.

"' 'The motly crew in vessels new,
  With Satan for their guide, sir,
Pack'd up in bags, or wooden kegs,
  Come driving down the tide, sir.

* Sir William Howe, who commanded in America from 1776 to 1778.
    † Sir W. Erskine.

" 'Therefore prepare for bloody war :—
   These kegs must all be routed,
Or surely we despis'd shall be,
   And British courage doubted.'

" The royal band now ready stand,
   All ranged in dread array, sir,
With stomach stout, to see it out,
   And make a bloody day, sir.

" The cannons roar from shore to shore :
   The small arms make a rattle :
Since wars began, I'm sure no man
   E'er saw so strange a battle.

" The 'rebel' vales, the 'rebel' dales,
   With 'rebel' trees surrounded,
The distant woods, the hills, and floods,
   With 'rebel' echoes sounded.

" The fish below swam to and fro,
   Attack'd from ev'ry quarter :
'Why sure,' thought they, 'the devil 's to pay
   'Mongst folks above the water.'

" The kegs, 'tis said, though strongly made
   Of 'rebel' staves and hoops, sir,
Could not oppose their powerful foes,
   The conquering British troops, sir.

" From morn to night, these men of might,
   Display'd amazing courage ;
And when the sun was fairly down,
   Retir'd to sup their porridge.

" A hundred men, with each a pen,
   Or more, upon my word, sir,
It is most true, would be too few
   Their valour to record, sir.

" Such feats did they perform that day
   Upon these wicked kegs, sir,
That years to come, if they get home,
   They'll make their boasts and brags, sir."

CHAPTER X.

GEORGE III.

Overthrow of Lord Shelburne—The Coalition—Attacks on the Coalition—Fox's India Bill—Carlo Khan—Back-stairs Influence—The Interference of the King, and Dismissal of the Ministry—Quarrel between the Crown and the House of Commons—William Pitt Prime Minister—The Opposition in Majority in the House ; Dissolution of Parliament—The Westminster Election—The Duchess of Devonshire—Caricatures and Squibs against the Defeated Coalitionists.

THE peace put an end to the weak administration of Lord Shelburne. From the moment the leaders of the old Rockingham party separated from Shelburne, the latter was looked upon by most people as little more than a provisional minister ; and young William Pitt, who had been aiming at popularity by his repeated advocacy of reform in the parliamentary representation (which was now beginning to be the watchword of a party), seems already to have been fixed in the King's mind as the minister of his choice. But William Pitt was hardly yet in the position to command a party, even though backed by the King.

Shelburne's party were evidently embarrassed by the secession of so many of the old Whigs, and they did not attempt to conceal their anger ; Pitt, especially, exhibited an irritability which he was not in the habit of shewing. We have seen with what bitterness the conduct of Fox and his friends was criticised in the caricatures, which represented Fox hurled from his hopes of treasury profits to the poverty and wretchedness of the gambler, and Burke retiring to his supposed Jesuitical reflections in the privacy of his chamber. One of the best of those on the latter subject, published on the 23rd of August, 1782, is entitled "Cincinnatus in retirement ; falsely supposed to represent *Jesuit Pad* driven back to his native potatoes." The metamorphosed orator is taking his frugal meal out of an utensil, inscribed "Relic No. 1, used by St. Peter," surrounded with various emblems of fanaticism and whisky-drinking. Fox and Burke, in return, accused Lord Shelburne of treachery and selfishness ; and these charges were re-echoed in satires which came more direct from the Tories, and attacked indiscriminately both divisions of the Whigs. Thus, in a print entitled "Guy Vaux and Judas

RECRIMINATION.

Iscariot," Shelburne, in the latter character, is walking off with a bag inscribed "Treasury," while the Guy is detecting the traitor by the light of his lanthorn. The Fox exclaims, "Ah! what, I've found you out, have I? Who armed the high priests and the people? who betrayed his man...?" Judas retorts, "Ha, ha! poor Gunpowder's vexed—he, he, he! Shan't have the bag, I tell you, old Goose-tooth." With similar sentiments, others looked upon these rapidly

A SLUMBERING MONARCH.

changing ministries as so many parties of mischief-makers; and in one caricature, published during the present year, King George is seen slumbering on his throne, while his ministers are dispatched rather unceremoniously to a very warm habitation.

As the time for the meeting of Parliament approached, people began to look with more anxiety to the position which each of the three parties that now divided it was likely to take. It was roughly estimated that the ministerial votes in the House of Commons were about a hundred and forty, that about a hundred and twenty members followed the standard of Lord North, and ninety that of Fox, the remainder being uncertain; and it was evident, under these circumstances, that Fox could give the majority in the house to either of the two parties with which he chose to join. Lord North professed moderation, and a wish to stand on neutral ground; and he did not threaten the Court with any serious attack. When Parliament met on the 5th of December, the preliminaries of the peace were made known, and the King's speech was warmly attacked by Fox and Burke, to

whom a spirited reply was made by Pitt; but the opposition
shewed itself but slightly till after the Christmas recess. When
the house met again towards the end of January, the interval
had produced a union of parties which seems to have struck
most people with surprise. The preliminaries of peace had been
signed at Paris on the 20th of January (1783), and their consideration in the House of Commons was fixed for the 17th of
February, when the ministers moved an address of approval.
The amendment, which accepted the treaty, but demanded
further time to consider the terms before expressing a judgment
upon them, and was evidently intended as a mere trial of
strength, was moved by Lord John Cavendish. The debate
which followed was long and animated, and merged into strong
personalities. The famous coalition between Fox and North,
which had for some days been talked of, was now openly avowed,
and both parties attacked the peace with the greatest bitterness.
It was observed that, during the earlier part of the debate, Fox
and North spoke of each other in terms of indulgence to which
they had long been strangers; and the ministerial speakers, in
their reply, fell with the greatest acrimony upon what they
termed the monstrous alliance between two men who had previously made such strong declarations of political hostility.
Burke first spoke, in defence of the coalition; he was followed
by Fox, who openly avowed it, and both he and Lord North declared that, even when they were most opposed to each other,
they had regarded one another personally with mutual respect;
that their ground of enmity—the American war—being now at
an end, it was time for their hostility to cease also, and that they
had joined together for the good of the country. The debate
was prolonged through the whole night, and it was nearly eight
o'clock in the morning when, on a division, the amendment was
carried by a majority of sixteen. Four days after this, on the
21st of February, the united opposition brought forward a motion of direct censure on the terms of the treaty and on the conduct of ministers, which lasted till after four in the morning,
and was carried by a majority of seventeen. The coalition was
again the main subject debated; it was now defended warmly by
Lord North, and bitterly attacked by Pitt, who called it "a
baneful alliance" and an "ill-omened marriage," dangerous to
the public safety.

This second defeat was the death-blow of the administration,
and Lord Shelburne immediately resigned. The King, who
literally hated Fox, and who was enraged at the coalition, made
a fruitless attempt to form a ministry under Pitt. In the
beginning of March, the King had several interviews with Lord

North, whom he attempted to detach from his new alliance, and then he tried to form a half coalition ministry, from which Fox was to be excluded. On the 24th of March, when the country had remained more than a month without a Cabinet, an address was voted in the House of Commons almost unanimously, praying the King to form immediately such an administration as would command the confidence of the country. The King, however, remained obstinate in his personal animosities; and, on the 31st of March, another and much stronger address was moved by the Earl of Surrey; upon which Pitt, who had all this time retained his office of chancellor of the Exchequer, and whom it was evidently the King's wish to make prime minister, announced that he had that day resigned. On the 2nd of April, the King again sent for Lord North, and, through him, gave full authority to the Duke of Portland, who was considered as the head of the Rockingham party, or old Whigs, to form an administration. The Duke of Portland himself was made first lord of the Treasury, with Lord North as Secretary of State for the Home Department, and Fox as Secretary for Foreign Affairs. Lord John Cavendish was made chancellor of the Exchequer; Keppel, first lord of the Admiralty; Lord Stormont (the only person admitted into the Cabinet to please the King), president of the council; and the Earl of Carlisle lord privy seal. Lord Thurlow was rejected, and the great seal was put in commission, the commissioners being Lord Loughborough, Sir W. H. Ashurst, and Sir Beaumont Hotham. The other members of the ministry were, the Earl of Hertford, lord chamberlain; Viscount Townshend, master-general of the Ordnance; the Honourable Richard Fitzpatrick, secretary at war; Edmund Burke, paymaster of the forces; Charles Townshend, treasurer of the Navy; James Wallace, attorney-general; Richard Brinsley Sheridan and Richard Burke, secretaries to the Treasury; the Earl of Northington, lord-lieutenant of Ireland; William Windham, secretary for Ireland; and William Eden, who is said to have been the chief negotiator in the formation of the coalition, vice-treasurer.

There seemed to be much greater cordiality in this alliance of two parties than had been visible in any former coalition of the same kind; and, to all appearance, the new ministry might have been an efficient one, and beneficial to the country, had it not been regarded from the first with bitter dislike by the King, who took little pains to conceal his intention of getting rid of it as soon as possible. Still there was something anomalous in its character, which was far from giving general satisfaction, and at first the liberal leaders lost much of their popularity. Caricatures were hurled against them in greater numbers, and in a better style of execution, than had been witnessed for several years. In the windows of the print-shops the heads of the two leaders were contrasted in their new fraternity in a variety of shapes, so as to exhibit the opposite character of their passions and qualities. The sleek face and fashionably-dressed and powdered hair of Lord North seemed to reject all comparison with the dark countenance and the black and disordered locks of Charles Fox. In one of these, by Sayer, the profiles of the two chiefs of the coalition are joined together on the face of a medallion; in another, by the same artist, entitled "The Mask," and inscribed "*fronti nulla fides*," the coalition is pictured by a full face formed of one half of the face of each joined in a vertical line; that of Fox, on the left, is made to convey a rather vulgar intimation of successful cunning, while the more candid features of Lord

COALITION.

North represent a strange compound of vexation and satisfaction.

WAR.

Among the earliest of the caricatures against the coalition is one by Gillray, published on the 9th of March, representing in two compartments the position which the coalescing parties held towards each other before and after their union. The first is entitled "War," and exhibits Fox and Burke thundering against North, as minister, their eloquent denunciations, and stigmatizing as "infamous" the very idea of their ever consenting to act under the same banner with him. North's condemnation of his two adversaries is equally energetic. Beneath the figures, which give us a characteristic sketch of the oratorical attitudes of the three speakers, are inscribed extracts from their speeches when thus opposed to each other. In the second compartment, or plate, entitled "Neither Peace nor War," the three orators, now united in one cause, are placed in the same attitudes, attacking the articles of the preliminaries, from beneath which a dog makes its appearance and barks with an angry look at the trio.* Under them we read the words, "The astonishing Coalition." A caricature by Sayer, published on the 17th of March, represented North painting white the dark features of his new friend, alluding to his declaration in the house, "I have found him a warm friend, a fair though formidable adversary." The motto of the print is, "*Qui color ater erat, nunc est contrarius atro.*" One of the rarer prints of Gillray, published in the month of April, 1783, satirises the new administration under the representation of a "coalition dance," in which the principal characters in it figure under the various garbs given to them by the prejudices of party faction.

A JESUIT.

Edmund Burke appears here as the concealed Jesuit, a character which, as we have already seen, the extreme Protestant party had conferred upon him ever since his exertions for Catholic emancipation. A large caricature by Sayer, published on the 5th of May, is founded on a speech made by one of the opposition lords in the upper house immediately after the formation of the new ministry, who, speaking of Lord North, had expressed himself in these terms:—"Such was the love of office of the noble lord, that, finding he would not

* The dog is said to be intended as an allusion to an occurrence in the

be permitted to mount the box, he had been content to get up behind." The new Whig coach, with the Fox's crest on the panels, is drawn by two meagre hacks of horses through a rough road, jogging every minute against some of the great stones thrown in its way by the opposition, by which one of its wheels has received a serious fracture. Lord North is riding behind, with an air of alarm; whilst Fox and the Duke of Portland, seated together on the box, are joining in their efforts to draw in the reins. A guide-post indicates the way they are going, "To Bulstrode, through Bushy Park." On the 21st of April, Sayer had satirized the whole ministry in a caricature, entitled, "Razor's Levee; or, the heads of a new Whig Ad——n on a broad bottom." The scene is the shop of a barber, who is busily engaged in arranging a number of block-heads, representing the members of the coalition ministry. He is especially occupied on the heads of North and Fox, joined on one stand. On the wall, immediately behind, are suspended in juxtaposition the portraits of Cromwell and Charles I., to intimate that the principles now

THE DRIVERS OF THE STATE.

brought together were in reality as hostile to each other as those two historical personages. Distributed through the room are the heads of Lords Portland, John Cavendish, Stormont, Carlisle, and Keppel, and Edmund Burke, each on its separate stand. A broadside ballad is stuck against the wall immediately behind Keppel, of which enough is legible to inform us that it is "Rule Britannia, set to a new tune," on the "27th July;" an allusion to Keppel's partial engagement with the French, which the Tories still threw in Keppel's teeth as an act of incapacity, if not of cowardice. Over the fire-place is "A new

House of Commons during the last defensive declamation of Lord North, on the eve of his resignation. A dog, which had concealed itself under the benches, came out and set up a hideous howling in the midst of his harangue. The house was thrown into a roar of laughter, which continued until the intruder was turned out; and then Lord North coolly observed, "As the new member has ended his argument, I beg to be allowed to continue mine." The dog is made to accompany Lord North in some of the subsequent caricatures.

map of Great Britain and Ireland," from which Ireland is
nearly torn away.   The celebrated publican and politician, Sam

House, whom we shall soon meet again
as a prominent actor in politics, sits in
front with a pot of beer in his hand,
and looks on admiringly.   Under the
barber's table are thrown away three
blocks, Shelburne, Dundas, and the
Duke of Grafton.   The latter, who
had formed a part of so many successive ministries, and who was accused
by his enemies of deserting or betraying them all, seemed now to have fallen
entirely in political importance.

Among the miscellaneous caricatures
against the coalition we may mention
one which represents the three chiefs,
Portland, Fox, and North, as a strange

THE DUKE OF GRAFTON.   *lusus naturæ*, examined by the King, who
refers it for further examination and dissertation to "his friend
Jenkinson."   Mr. Jenkinson, afterwards Earl of Liverpool, was
popularly looked upon as the hero of the back-stairs influence by
which this administration was eventually overthrown.   In

another, represent-
ing Fox and North
partaking of their
bowl of pottage,
the fox is made to
take the place of
the satyr of the
fable, who found a
host who blew hot
and cold with the
same breath.   Ano-
ther large print, or
rather series of
prints, in nine divi-
sions, is entitled

BOON COMPANIONS.

"The loves of the Fox and the Badger; or, the Coalition
Wedding," and represents a burlesque pictorial history of the
friendship between Fox and Lord North, the latter of whom
was commonly designated by the *sobriquet* of "the badger."
Another caricature in compartments is entitled, "Slides to the
State Magic Lantern," and ridicules the history of the coali-

tion. In one of the divisions, the two political friends are joined under one coat, and placed on a pedestal as the new idol of the state, which everybody was required to worship. The crown and sceptre are thrown on the ground; and, indeed, it was clear to all that the idol was only allowed to stand because the King could not help himself, and that to him it was not an object of voluntary worship. The caricaturist would have us believe that it was equally unacceptable to the country; and another of the slides represents the two candidates for power rejected by Britannia, who points to a distant view of the gallows and the block as their proper destination.

THE NEW STATE IDOL.

The first acts of the coalition ministry showed, however, that it was strong in parliamentary influence. A rather heavy loan,

THE COALITION CANDIDATES REJECTED.

rendered necessary by the condition in which Lord Shelburne had left the finances of the country, and a stamp-duty on receipts, were carried by large majorities, in spite of the violent efforts of the opposition; and the favourite measure of William Pitt, whenever he was out of office, a motion for parliamentary reform, which he now brought forward to embarrass the cabinet, was thrown out in a manner equally decisive. In the middle of July, parliament separated, and the new ministers were left to prepare in quiet the great measures which they intended to bring forward for the consideration of the legislature.

The chief of these were two bills for the better regulation of our extensive possessions in the East. The public had been long dazzled by the brilliance of our conquests in Asia, and astonished at the riches which were daily brought home; but, in the transition from a company of traders to a body which held sovereign power over mighty empires, the India directors now stood in a position which called for the interference of the British legislature. India had hitherto been looked upon chiefly as an extensive field of plunder and aggrandizement, and it was known to the mother-country principally by the so-called English "nabobs," who returned home with immense fortunes, which they had amassed by every description of injustice and rapacity. The vices of this system had attracted attention for some time, and the measures now brought forward by Fox were intended to bring a remedy. He proposed to vest the affairs of the East India Company in the hands of certain commissioners, for the benefit of the proprietors and the public, who were to be nominated first by the Parliament, and subsequently by the Crown, and whose power was to last during limited periods; and to add to them other officers for the more immediate government of India, with powers, and under responsibilities, which were calculated to put an end to tyranny and oppression, and to improve the condition of the people throughout our Indian possessions. The plan was, of course, obnoxious to the company, and they employed freely their immense riches in raising up opposition to it: it was even hinted at by many that the King himself had indirectly taken money from the company to overthrow it.

Parliament met on the 11th of November, and then the first measure brought forward was the bill for the regulation of India. Pitt, Dundas, Jenkinson, and other members of the opposition, spoke with warmth against it, yet it passed through the House of Commons with large majorities, the third reading taking place on the 8th of December. But anxiety was already felt for its fate in the Lords. Walpole writes on the 2nd of December, "The politicians of London, who at present are not the most numerous corporation, are warm on a bill for the new regulation of the East Indies, brought in by Mr. Fox. Some even of his associates apprehended his being defeated, or meant to defeat him; but his marvellous abilities have hitherto triumphed conspicuously, and on two divisions in the House of

Commons he had majorities of 109 and 114. On *that* field he will certainly be victorious; the forces will be more nearly balanced when the Lords fight the battle; but though the opposition will have more generals and more able, he is confident that his troops will overmatch theirs; and in parliamentary engagements a superiority of numbers is not vanquished by the talents of the commanders, as often happens in more martial encounters. His competitor, Mr. Pitt, appears by no means an adequate rival. Just like their fathers, Mr. Pitt has brilliant language, Mr. Fox solid sense, and such luminous powers of displaying it clearly, that mere eloquence is but a Bristol stone when set by the diamond reason."

The main grounds of opposition to this India bill were, that it was an infringement of vested rights as regarded the company, and that its tendency, and, probably, its object, was, by the immense influence it gave to ministers, who had the appointment of the India governors, to increase their power to such an extent as to make them independent of the Crown. Some people hesitated not to say that Fox aimed at establishing in his own person a sort of supreme India Dictatorship, and they gave him the title of Carlo Khan. Caricatures, squibs, pamphlets, were showered upon him from every side. In a caricature by Sayer, published on the 25th of November, and entitled, "A Transfer of East India Stock," Fox is represented as a giant carrying the India House on his shoulders to St. James's. Sayer was courting the favour of William Pitt, who was now evidently on the point of grasping at power, and a few days after the appearance of the caricature last mentioned, on the 5th of December, he published his more celebrated print of "Carlo Khan's Triumphal Entry into Leadenhall Street," his most famous production, though certainly much inferior to many of his subsequent works. Fox, in his new character of Carlo Khan, is conducted to the door of the India House on the back of an elephant, which exhibits the full face of Lord North, and he is led by Burke as his imperial trumpeter; for he had been the loudest supporter of the bill in the House of Commons. A bird of ill-omen from above croaks forth the would-be monarch's doom. Fox is said to have acknowledged that his India Bill received its severest blow in public estimation from this caricature, which had a prodigious sale, and its effect was increased by the multitude of pirated copies and imitations. When Pitt came into power he rewarded the author with a profitable place.[*]

* James Sayer was the son of a captain merchant at Yarmouth, and

The sentiment which is said to have weighed most with King George, after his personal dislike to his ministers, was the dread of diminishing the influence of the Crown, which was often and carefully instilled into him by Lord Thurlow; for the King held private communication with the chiefs of the opposition, with whom he was concerting measures for bringing them back to power. The King's behaviour to his present ministers was, indeed, most uncandid. He never informed them that he disapproved of the India Bill; yet when the 15th of December, the day appointed for the second reading in the House of Lords, approached, he gave Lord Temple, with whom he had had several private interviews, a note in his own handwriting to the effect "that his majesty would deem those who voted for the bill not only not his friends, but his enemies; and that if Lord Temple could put this in still stronger words, he had full authority to do so." This note was shewn pretty freely to all those peers who were supposed to be influenced by the royal inclinations; and the King further commanded the lords of the Bedchamber to vote against his ministers. The consequence was that the latter were beaten by a majority of eight. On the 17th of December the bill was finally thrown out by a majority of nineteen. In the night of the 18th the King dismissed his ministers, and gave the seals into the hands of Lord Temple.

The opposition—which, in this instance, was the Court party—burst into loud exultation, which was as loudly re-echoed by the newspapers, and trumpeted forth by their agents in a variety of different shapes. On the 24th of December, appeared a sequel to Sayer's caricature, with the title of "The Fall of Carlo Khan," in poor imitation of Sayer's style; the elephant, goaded by the opposition, has thrown its rider, Carlo, who is falling to the ground with the words, "secret influence" in his mouth. Burke, having thrown down his trumpet, and a large sack, inscribed "plans of economy," is running away at full speed. Sayer himself now produced a series of prints, in the first of which, entitled "The Fall of Phaeton," and published on the 6th of January, 1784, Fox is represented as falling headlong from the car of state, the reins of which are held by the hand of royalty. In another, published on the 12th of January, under the title of "Pandemonium," the caricaturist has again

was by profession an attorney, but having a moderate independency, he did not much pursue business. Pitt gave him the offices of marshal of the Court of Exchequer, receiver of the sixpenny duties, and carrstorship. He was the author of many political songs and squibs. He died in the earlier part of the present century, no long time after his patron, Pitt.

attempted a parody on a passage of Milton, by exhibiting Fox as the political Satan, surrounded by his satellites, Lords Portland, Carlisle, Cavendish, Keppel, North, and Burke, &c. with rueful countenances, whom he is encouraging after their fall.

> " All these and more came flocking, but with looks
> Downcast and damp, yet such wherein appeared
> Obscure some glimpse of joy, to have found their chief
> Not in despair, to have found themselves not lost
> In loss itself, which on his countenance cast
> Like doubtful hue; but he, his wonted pride
> Soon recollecting, with high words that bore
> *Semblance of worth,* not *substance,* gently raised
> Their fainting courage and dispell'd their fears."

At this time, indeed, the representatives of the nation were rallying round the ex-ministry, and throwing the court into the greatest embarrassment. The King was in the somewhat difficult position of having appointed a ministry in opposition to the majority in the House of Commons, at the same time that he had thrown their predecessors out by a manifest unconstitutional interference with parliamentary privileges. Some strong remarks on back-stairs influence, and on the note understood to have been given by the King to Lord Temple, were made in the House of Lords; but the House of Commons proceeded much more energetically. On the 17th of December, the very evening when this underhand influence was brought into play in the other House, a violent debate arose upon the subject in the Commons, and they passed, by a majority of nearly two to one (the numbers being one hundred and fifty-three to eighty), a resolution, " That it is now necessary to declare, that, to report any opinion, or pretended opinion, of his Majesty upon any bill, or other proceeding, depending in either House of Parliament, with a view to influence the votes of the members, is a high crime and misdemeanour, derogatory to the honour of the Crown, a breach of the fundamental privileges of Parliament, and subversive of the constitution of this country ;" and further, " that this House will, upon Monday morning next, resolve itself into a committee of the whole House, to consider the state of the nation." This was followed by a resolution equally strong, and carried by a majority in the same proportion, declaring the necessity of a legislative act for the government of India. On the 19th of December, after the ministers had been dismissed, the Court party, on a question of adjournment, found themselves in so small a minority, that they did not dare to divide. On Monday, the 22nd, it was notified that Earl Temple, who had been appointed one of the new secretaries of state, had resigned his office in consequence of what had transpired in the House on the 19th. A very strong address to the King was then voted without a division, and was presented on the 24th, to which the King returned an evasive answer, but made a distinct declaration that he would not prorogue or dissolve the Parliament. On the 12th of January, the first day of meeting after Christmas, when there was a full attendance of members, the Court having made every exertion to increase its number of votes, there was a majority of thirty-nine against the ministers, on the question of going into committee to consider the state of the nation. Fox then stated, that it was necessary to come to some specific resolution to prevent the present ministry from making an improper use of their power " the short time they had to exist ;" and moved, " That it was the opinion of the committee, that any person in his Majesty's treasury, exchequer, pay-office, bank of England, or any person whatever entrusted with the public money, paying away, or causing to be paid, any sum or sums of money voted for the service of the present year, in case of a dissolution or prorogation of Parliament, before a bill, or bills, were brought in for the appropriation of such sums, would be guilty of a high crime and misdemeanour, highly derogatory to the honour of the House, and contrary to the faith of Parliament." This resolution was carried without a division, as well as another, " That it is the opinion of the committee, that there should be laid before them an account of all sums of money expended for the use of the public service between the 19th of December, 1783, and the 12th of January, 1784, specifying each sum, and for what expended." In moving this resolution, Fox said that it might appear an extraordinary method ; but, as extraordinary measures had been taken by the present ministry to come into power, it required extraordinary motions to prevent them doing mischief now they were in power. Other resolutions were passed, especially two moved by the Earl of Surrey, " That it is the opinion of the committee, that in the present situation of his Majesty's dominions, it is highly necessary that such an administration should be formed as possesses both the confidence of this House and of the public ;" and " that it is the opinion of the committee, that the late changes were preceded by extraordinary rumours, dangerous to the constitution, inasmuch as the sacred name of Majesty had been unconstitutionally used for the purpose of affecting the deliberations of Parliament ; and the appointments that followed were accompanied by circumstances new and extraordinary, and such as were evidently calculated not to conciliate the affections of that House."

This last motion was violently opposed by Pitt, Dundas, and Scott (afterwards Lord Eldon), but it was carried by a majority of fifty-four. On the 15th of January, Pitt obtained leave to bring in his India bill. On the 16th the House again resolved itself into a committee; and, after a very warm debate, the following resolution was passed by a majority of twenty-one:— "That it is the opinion of this committee, it having been declared by this House, that, in the present situation of his Majesty's dominions, an administration should be formed, which possessed the confidence of this House and the public; and the present administration being formed under circumstances new and extraordinary, such as were not calculated to conciliate the affections or engage the confidence of this House; that his Majesty's present ministers still holding high and responsible offices, after such a declaration, is contrary to true constitutional principles, and injurious to his Majesty and his people." The debates on these resolutions were sometimes exceedingly violent, and led to much personal recrimination, especially between Pitt and Fox; but the former bore everything with the passive coldness for which he was remarkable, and the King remained obstinate in pursuing his own course. On the 23rd of January Pitt's India bill was thrown out by a majority of eight, and Fox obtained leave to bring in a new bill on the same subject. The House was still labouring under the fear of a dissolution; and, on the 26th of January, a resolution was passed to avert it, on which Pitt declared that he should not advise his Majesty to dissolve the Parliament. An attempt was now made by some persons of influence, who were alarmed at the threatening aspect of affairs, to form a new coalition; to which the King and Pitt professed themselves favourable; but it was soon seen that this was merely done for the purpose of gaining time, and in the hope of being able to soften down the opposition. On the 2nd of February, Mr. Grosvenor, who had been the chief actor in this attempt, declared to the House his failure, and moved a resolution, which was carried without a division, setting forth the necessity of an "united administration." This was followed by a much more important resolution, moved by Mr. Coke of Norfolk, and carried, after a warm debate, by a majority of nineteen, "That it is the opinion of this House, that the continuance of the present ministry in power is an obstacle to the formation of such an administration as is likely to have the confidence of this House and the people." Next day it was resolved, by a majority of twenty-four, that a copy of the resolutions of the preceding day should be laid before the King. On the day after (Feb. 4), the House of Lords passed a resolution, by a majority of forty-seven, that it was contrary to the letter and spirit of the constitution that one branch of the legislature should pass any resolutions impeding the progress of the whole, and tending to deprive the Crown of its prerogative in nominating and keeping in office its own servants ; and, on the 5th, a loyal address of the House of Lords was presented to the King. The Commons resented this with warmth, and passed a string of resolutions in defence of their own conduct. On the 18th of February, Mr. Pitt coldly informed the House "That his Majesty, after considering the present situation of public affairs, had not dismissed his ministers, nor had those ministers resigned." On the 20th, another resolution against the ministers was passed by a majority of twenty, and an address to the King in the same spirit was passed ; and similar motions and addresses were repeated, until, on the 24th of March, the Parliament was prorogued, with a discontented speech from the throne, and it was dissolved on the day following, March 25th. Thus ended for the moment this threatening contest between the Crown and the most important branch of the Legislature ; and the result of the elections hindered it from being revived in the subsequent session.

During these rough proceedings within doors, the nation without was violently agitated, and the press entered hotly into the dispute, and dealt largely in personal abuse. The ministerial caricaturists were not inactive. On the 9th of February, Sayer engraved a plate representing the heads of Fox and North, decapitated and laid on the table of the House, with a parody on Fox's motion for the adjournment of the consideration of the mutiny act :—

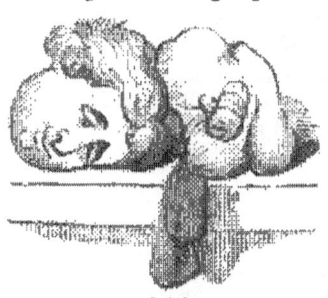

HEADS.

" *Cui bono ?—publico bono.*

" *Die Lunæ,* 9° *Februarii,* 1784.

" In a committee on the sense of the nation,—Moved—that for preventing future disorders and dissensions, the *heads* of the Mutiny Act be brought in, and suffered to lie on the table to-morrow.

" Ordered.

" That all further proceedings upon the act for dividing the Commons, &c. be adjourned *sine die.* " Ordered.

" VOX POPULI, *Cler. Par.*"

One or two other clever prints by Sayer were produced on this occasion. An engraving by Gillray, published in the month of February, represented Pitt under the character of the infant Hercules, strangling the two serpents of the coalition,

YOUNG HERCULES AND THE SERPENTS.

Fox and North. The coalition was attacked in songs and ballads, as well as in caricatures; and the political tergiversations, either real or pretended, of the chiefs of the opposition, were chanted incessantly, not only in public, but even in private parties.

"Lord North, for twelve years, with his war and contracts,
The people he nearly had laid on their backs;
Yet stoutly he swore he sure was a villain,
If e'er he had bettered his fortune a shilling.
Derry down, down, down, derry down.

"Against him Charles Fox was a sure bitter foe,
And cried, that the empire he'd soon overthrow;
Before him all honour and conscience had fled,
And vow'd that the axe it should cut off his head.
Derry down, &c.

"Edmund Burke, too, was in a mighty great rage,
And declared Lord North the disgrace of the age;
His plans and his conduct he treated with scorn,
And thought it a curse that he'd ever been born.
Derry down, &c.

"So hated he was, Fox and Burke they both swore,
They infamous were if they enter'd his door;
But, prithee, good neighbour, now think on the end,
Both Burke and Fox call him their very good friend!
Derry down, &c.

"Now Fox, North, and Burke, each one is a brother,
So honest, they swear, there is not such another;
No longer they tell us we're going to ruin,
The people they serve in whatever they're doing.
Derry down," &c.

Against the evils under which the country was in danger of being brought by this confederacy, there was, it is pretended, only one hope of salvation.

> " But Chatham, thank heaven ! has left us a son ;
> When he takes the helm, we are sure not undone ;
> The glory his father revived of the land,
> And Britannia has taken Pitt by the hand."

The Court party, indeed, did all they could to have it believed that the opposition was a mere faction, unpopular throughout the country ; and they expressed with great confidence that an appeal to the nation would end in their own

favour. A boldly-drawn caricature, entitled " Britannia Aroused ; or, the coalition monsters destroyed," represents Britannia hurling the two chiefs of the coalition from her, as enemies to that liberty of which she carries the symbol by her side.

The coalition had, indeed, for a time become unpopular, not only from a sort of repugnance to the sudden union of parties who had been so bitterly opposed to each other, but from the pertinacity of the attacks which had been directed against it. There were others who held back in a certain degree of neutrality, equally opposed to the extension of the prerogative on one side, and fearful on the other that the violence of the other was paving the way for the encroachments of demo-

BRITANNIA AROUSED.

A LONG PULL AND A STRONG PULL.

cracy. The voice of this party is heard at times, but not very loud. A caricature, entitled "The Unfortunate Ass," published on the 11th of March, 1784, burlesques the long struggle between King George and Charles Fox, which had preceded the dissolution of Parliament. The ass represents the people laden with taxes; the King, armed with the sword of "prerogative," is pulling in one direction, which is designated by a finger-post as the "road to absolute monarchy." Fox is pulling with equal obstinacy in the other direction, which is similarly pointed out as the "road to republicanism." Fox exclaims, "I humbly insist upon the management, or else will not grant any supplies."

The popular party had also its numerous caricaturists, who held up to scorn not only the measures and designs of the new ministers, but the means by which they had been brought into power. In one of these, published on the 12th of January, the King is represented with two faces, giving his hand openly on one side to Fox, who has the India bill in his hand, and to North, while with the other face he thrusts his hand through a screen to a lord who has mounted by the back-stairs. Behind North and Fox a picture is suspended on the wall, representing Bute in the character of a Scottish cat, booted, with an inscription in French, intimating that it is "the celebrated Scottish cat which obtained a place in the royal cabinet twenty-four years ago: it is represented booted, and fierce, especially to the King's ministers." Over the back-stairs entrance is an empty frame, with the inscription, also in French, "The frame for the companion to the Scottish cat, which is not yet found."

Among a number of patriotic caricatures which appeared during the parliamentary struggle described above, and on the eve of the elections, we may mention three, which bear considerable resemblance to the style of Rowlandson, and are probably to be reckoned among his early works. In the first, published on the 11th of March, Fox is represented as "The Champion of the People," armed with the sword of justice and the shield of truth, and combating the many-headed hydra, whose various mouths breathe forth "Tyranny," "Assumed prerogative," "Despotism," "Oppression," "Secret influence," "Scotch politics," "Duplicity," and "Corruption." The two latter, with some others, are already cut off. Behind the dragon, the Dutchman, Frenchman, and other foreign enemies, are seen dancing round the standard of sedition. The champion has on his side strong bodies of English and Irish, bearing aloft the "standard of universal liberty;" the former shout, "While he protects us, we will support him;" the latter, "He gave us a

free trade, and all we asked; he shall have our *firm* support."
Still nearer him, the East Indians are on their knees praying for
his success. The second of these caricatures, published on the
26th of March, is entitled, " The State Auction." Pitt, as the
young auctioneer, is knocking down with the hammer of " prerogative" most of the valuables of the constitution. Dundas,
as his assistant, is holding up for sale a heavy lot, entitled "Lot
1. The Rights of the People." Pitt cries, " Shew the lot this
way, Harry—a'going, a'going—speak quick, or it's gone—hold
up the lot, ye Dund-ass !" To which the assistant replies, " I
can hould it na higher, sir." On the left, the " chosen repre-
senters," as they are termed, are leaving the auction-room, mut-
tering complaints, or encouragements, such as, " Adieu to
liberty !" " Despair not," " Now or never !" Fox alone stands
his ground, and makes a last effort,—" I am determined to bid
with spirit for lot 1 ; he shall pay dear for it that outbids me !"
Beneath the auctioneer stand what are termed the " hereditary
virtuosis;" the foremost of whom (apparently intended to represent the lord-chancellor) leads them on with the exhortation,
" Mind not the nonsensical biddings of those common fellows."
The auctioneer's secretary observes, " We shall get the supplies
by this sale." The third of the caricatures alluded to, published
on the 31st of March, when the elections were beginning, alludes
more especially to the dissolution which had just taken place.
It is entitled " The Hanoverian Horse and British Lion ;—a
scene in a new play. lately acted in Westminster with distinguished applause, act 2nd, scene last." Behind is the vacant
throne, with the intimation, " We shall resume our situation
here at pleasure, Leo Rex." In
front, the Hanoverian horse, without bridle or saddle, neighing
"pre-ro-ro-ro-ro-rogative," is
trampling on the safeguards of
the constitution, and kicking
out with violence its " faithful
commons." The young minister,
mounted on the back of the
prancing animal, cries " Bravo !
—go it again !—I love to ride
a mettled steed ; send the vaga-
bonds packing." On the opposite side of the picture, Fox is
borne in, with more gravity, on
the back of the British lion, and

THE BRITISH LION AND ITS RIDER.

holding a whip and bridle in his hand. The indignant beast exclaims, " If this horse is not tamed, he will soon be absolute king of our forest!" The lion's rider warns his rival horseman of his danger,—" Prithee, Billy, dismount before yo get a fall, and let some abler jockey take your seat."

William Pitt, though only in his twenty-fifth year, was thus, by the royal will, firmly established prime minister of England. His colleagues were either those who were already well known as " The King's friends," or those young aspirants to power who were willing to tread in their steps. Pitt joined in himself the offices of first lord of the Treasury and chancellor of the Exchequer. Lord Camden was president of the Council; Viscount Sydney and the Marquis of Carmarthen, secretaries of State for Home and Foreign Affairs; Earl Gower, privy seal; Earl Howe, first lord of the Admiralty; Lord Thurlow, chancellor; the Duke of Richmond, master-general of the Ordnance; Mr. W. Grenville and Lord Mulgrave, joint paymasters of the Forces; Mr. Dundas, treasurer of the Navy; Mr. (afterwards Lord) Kenyon, attorney-general; and Mr. Pepper Arden, solicitor-general. The opposition were fully aware of the disadvantages under which they would labour in a general election at the present moment, and they had been anxious to avert a dissolution; their fears were confirmed by the event. The elections were in many cases obstinate; but Court influence, and even the King's name, were used openly, and from being the majority, the party which had been led by Fox and North numbered but a comparatively small minority in the House of Commons. A few passages from Horace Walpole's Correspondence will give us the best picture of the feelings of the day. On the 30th of March, ho writes, " My letters, since the great change in the administration, have been rare, and much less informing than they used to be. In a word, I was not at all glad of the revolution, nor have the smallest connexion with the new occupants. There has been a good deal of boldness on both sides. Mr. Fox, convinced of the necessity of hardy measures to correct and save India, and coupling with that rough medicine a desire of confirming the power of himself and his allies, had formed a great system, and a very sagacious one; so sagacious, that it struck France with terror. But as this new power was to be founded on the demolition of that nest of monsters, the East India Company, and their spawn of nabobs, &c., they took the alarm; and the secret junto at Court rejoiced that they did. The Court struck the blow at the ministers; but it was the gold of the company that really conjured up the storm, and has

diffused it all over England. On the other hand, Mr. Pitt has
braved the majority of the House of Commons, has dissolved
the existent one, and, I doubt, given a wound to that branch of
the legislature, which, if the tide does not turn, may be very
fatal to the constitution. The nation is intoxicated; and has
poured in addresses of thanks to the Crown for exerting the
prerogative *against* the palladium of the people. The first consequence will probably be, that the Court will have a considerable majority upon the new elections. The country has acted
with such precipitation, and with so little knowledge of the
question, that I do not doubt but thousands of eyes will be
opened and wonder at themselves." And, on the 11th of April,
" The scene is wofully changed for the opposition, though not
half the new parliament is yet chosen. Though they still contest a very few counties and some boroughs, they own themselves totally defeated. They reckoned themselves sure of 240
members ; they probably will not have 150. In short, between
the industry of the Court and the India Company, and that
momentary phrenzy that sometimes seizes a whole nation, as if
it were a vast animal, such aversion to the coalition, and such a
detestation of Mr. Fox, have seized the country, that, even where
omnipotent gold retains its influence, the elected pass through
an ordeal of the most virulent abuse. The great Whig families,
the Cavendishes, Rockinghams, Bedfords, have lost all credit
in their own counties; nay, have been tricked out of seats where
the whole property was their own: and, in some of those cases,
a *royal* finger has too evidently tampered, as well as singularly
and revengefully towards Lord North and Lord Hertford . . . .
Such a proscription, however, must have sown so deep resentment
as it was not wise to provoke ; considering that permanent fortune
is a jewel that in no crown is the most to be depended upon."

The most remarkable event in the history of these elections
was the obstinate contest for Westminster, which agitated the
metropolis in the most extraordinary manner during several
weeks. Westminster had been represented in the Parliament
just dissolved by Fox and Sir Cecil Wray, who had been nominated by Fox, but he had deserted the standard of his political
leader. The Court was resolved, if possible, to turn Fox out of
the House, and Wray and Lord Hood (the admiral) were on the
present occasion proposed for Westminster, the former being more
especially held forth as the antagonist of the "man of the
people." The poll was opened on the 1st of April, and
continued without intermission until the 17th of May. For
the first few days, in consequence of the extraordinary exertions of their party, the two ministerial candidates were

decidedly in the majority: but afterwards Fox gradually gained ground, until, at the close of the election, he had a majority of 236 votes over his rival, Sir Cecil. For a great portion of the six weeks during which this contest lasted, the western part of the town and, more especially, the streets in the neighbourhood of Covent Garden, (where the election for Westminster always took place), presented a scene of indescribable riot and confusion. At the beginning of the election, Lord Hood had brought up a considerable body of sailors, or, as others represented them, they were chiefly hired ruffians dressed in sailors' clothes, who occupied the neighbourhood of the hustings, and hindered many of Fox's friends from approaching to register their votes. When not thus employed, they paraded the streets, insulting and even striking Fox's partizans. On the third day they came in greater numbers, armed with bludgeons, and surrounded the Shakespeare, where Fox's committee met, and committed various outrages during the day. At night they besieged the Shakespeare still more closely, until the gentlemen within, provoked by their insulting behaviour, sallied out and beat them away. This defeat only added to the excitement, for on the morning of the fourth day of the election the sailor mob made its appearance with a great accession of force, and took up its position about the hustings as usual. But there was a mob on the other side also, for the hackney-chairmen, a numerous body, who were chiefly Irishmen, were almost unanimous in their support of Fox; and, aggravated by the conduct of the sailors, when the latter began at the close of this day's poll to return to their usual outrages, the chairmen, whom the newspapers in the interest of the opposition termed the "honest mob," fell upon them and handled them so roughly that we are told that several had their skulls fractured, and that others were afterwards picked up with arms, legs, and ribs broken. The sailors then left the neighbourhood of Covent Garden, and proceeded to St. James's Street, where chiefly the chairmen plied for custom, with the avowed intention of breaking their chairs; but the chairmen beat them again, and the riot was at length put an end to by the arrival of a body of the guards. The next day, which was Tuesday. the sailors re-assembled in a threatening attitude in Covent Garden, but when, towards the end of the poll, the rival mob, composed now of a multitude of butchers, brewers, and other people, in addition to the chairmen, made its appearance, the sailors left Covent Garden, and hastened towards Charing Cross, to intercept Fox, who was understood to be on his way to Westminster to canvass. Fox escaped by taking refuge in a private

house; and the mob, having visited Westminster without
meeting with the object of their search, returned to the Strand,
where another combat took place between the adverse factions,
and the sailors were again defeated. They met with no better
success in two other battles that occurred in the course of the
same evening. Wednesday presented the same scenes of riot,
and, in the evening, a still more obstinate battle was fought in
Covent Garden between the two mobs, in which the sailors were
utterly defeated, and no less than twenty or thirty of them are
said to have been carried to the hospitals with severe injuries.
Next day few sailors made their appearance, and no more serious
rioting occurred until measures were taken by the civil
authorities to prevent any violent outbreak of popular feeling
which might occur at the close of the poll. The special constables were assembled at the places where Hood and Wray's
committee met, and behaved in a manner so evidently hostile to
the friends of Fox, that their presence tended rather to provoke
riot than otherwise. On the 10th of May, a party of constables
from Wapping were brought by order of Justice Wilmot,* in
opposition, it was said, to the opinions of the other magistrates,
and they went about shouting "No Fox!" and impeding and
insulting the liberal voters. Just as the poll closed, a slight
disturbance gave the excuse for an attack by the constables.
The sound of marrow-bones and cleavers, the old signal for an
insurrection of the populace, was immediately heard, and a
rather serious scuffle ended in the death of one of the constables.
The party of Fox's opponents endeavoured to fix the death of
the constable on some individuals of the Foxite mob, who were
indicted for the murder, but acquitted; and it appeared pretty
evident on the trial that the victim had been knocked down by
mistake by one of his fellow-constables in the heat and confusion
of the moment. But the violence of party faction was so great,
that one or two men of notoriously bad character were brought
forward, apparently hired, to swear that they had seen the
constable killed by the persons indicted; and a further attempt
was made to create a new affray, by carrying the body for
burial to Covent Garden church, attended by a tumultuous

* "Justice Wilmot" appears to have had no great reputation for the extent
of his judicial capacity. One of the Foxite newspapers pretends that, a
short time before the catastrophe mentioned in the text, he had addressed
to one of the chief booksellers in London a note worded as follows:

"MR. EVANS,
  "Sir, I expects soon to be calld out on a Mergensey, so send me all
the ax of parlyment re Latin to a Gustis of Piece. I am,
                        "Yours to command, &c.
                                "GUSTIS WILMOT."

cavalcade, with flags, and incendiary handbills, on the 14th of May, in the midst of the day's polling. This was prevented by the firmness of the parish officers, and by the proposal to close the poll at two o'clock on that day.

Perhaps no single occasion ever drew forth, in the same space of time, so many political squibs, ballads, and caricatures, and so much personal abuse on both sides, as this election for Westminster. The newspapers were filled daily with this subject, which seemed exclusively to occupy all the wits and fashionable politicians of the metropolis. The popular charges against Sir Cecil Wray were, his ingratitude towards Fox, for which his opponents treated him with the title of Judas Iscariot; a proposal which he was said to have made to suppress Chelsea Hospital; and a project of a tax upon maid-servants. To these were added the more general cries against his party, of undue elevation of the prerogative and back-stairs influence. The particular crimes laid against Fox, were the Coalition and the India-bill; but he was taxed with private immorality and with revolutionary principles. His opponents represented that his attack on the East India Company's charter was but the commencement of a general invasion of chartered rights of corporate bodies :—

> "This great Carlo Khan,
> Some say, had a plan
> To take all our charters away;
> But his scheme was found out,
> And you need not to doubt,
> Was opposed by the staunch Cecil Wray."

It was but a new link in his chain of political delinquencies; his whole life, they said, had been characterized by the same want of sober principles :—

> "When first young Reynard came from France,
> He tried to bow, to dress, to dance,
> But to succeed had little chance,
> The courtly dames among;
> 'Tis true, indeed, his wit has charms;
> But his grim phiz the point disarms,
> And all were fill'd with dire alarms
> At such a *beau garçon.*

> "He left the fair, and took to dice;
> At Brooks's they were not so nice,
> But clear'd his pockets in a trice,
> Nor left a wreck behind.
> Nay, some pretend he even lost
> That little grace he had to boast,
> And then resolved to seize some post,
> Where he might *raise the wind.*

> "In politics he cou'd not fail ;
> So set about it tooth and nail ;
> But here again his stars prevail,
>   Nor long the meteor shone.
> His friends,—if such deserve the name,—
> Still keep him at a losing game ;
> Bankrupt in fortune and in fame,
>   His day is almost done."

The grand enemy of the Crown, the Court agents said, was
no doubt at his last gasp, and they began already to sing their
triumph over his grave :—

> "Dear Car, is it true,
>   What I've long heard of you ?
> 'The man of the people,' they call you, they call you !
>   How comes it to pass,
>   They're now grown so rash,
> At the critical moment to leave you, to leave you ?
>
> "Oh ! that curs'd India bill !
>   Arrah, why not be still,
> Enjoy a tight place and be civil, be civil ;
>   Had you carried it through,
>   Oagh ! that would just do,
> Then their charters we'd pitch to the Devil, the Devil."

The other party, by dwelling continually on Sir Cecil's
project of saving money to the state by abolishing Chelsea
Hospital, arrayed against him the numerous class who, one way
or other, derived benefit from that establishment ; and they
loudly represented that his proposed tax on maid-servants
would throw a great number of servants out of places, and that
it would thus not only produce great distress, but that it would
indirectly increase the prevalence of prostitution.   There was
also a satirical story of his keeping nothing in his cellar but
small-beer, and some other little incidents, which were stretched
one way or another into objects of ridicule, if not of odium.
The sort of papers that were daily placarded and distributed
about, may be conceived from the following specimen, belonging
to a class of parodies which were then not uncommon :—

The first Chapter of the Times.

  "1. And it came to pass, that there were great dissensions in the West,
amongst the rulers of the nation.
  "2. And the counsellors of the back-stairs said, let us take advantage
and yoke the people even as oxen, and rule them with a rod of iron.
  "3. And let us break up the Assembly of Privileges, and get a new one
of Prerogatives ; and let us hire false prophets to deceive the people. And
they did so.
  "4. Then Judas Iscariot went among the citizens, saying, 'Choose me
one of your elders, and I will tax your innocent damsels, and I will take
the bread from the helpless, lame, and blind.

"5. 'And with the scrip which will arise, we will eat, drink, and be merry.' Then he brought forth the roll of sheep-skin, and came unto the gin-shops, cellars, and bye-places, and said,—'Sign your names,'—and many made their marks.*

"6. Now it came to pass, that the time being come when the people choose their elders, that they assembled together at the hustings, nigh unto the Place of Cabbages.

"7. And Judas lifted up his prerogative poll, and said, 'Choose me, choose me!' But the people said, 'Satan, avaunt! thou wicked Judas! hast thou not *deceived* thy best friend? would'st thou *deceive* us also? Get thee behind us, thou unclean spirit!

"8. 'We will have the man who ever has and will support our cause, and maintain our rights, who stands forth to us, and who will never be guided by *Secret Influence!*'

"9. And the people shouted, and cried with an exceeding loud voice, saying, 'Fox is the man!'

"10. Then they caused the trumpets to be sounded, as at the feast of the full moon, and sang, 'Long live Fox! may our champion live for ever! Amen.'"

Every new proclamation or placard issued by Fox's party harped on the story of Chelsea Hospital and the maid-servants; nor was the old symbol of France and slavery—wooden shoes—forgotten. The following, put out early in the canvass, may serve as an example; the allusion being more especially to the extensive polling of soldiers for Hood and Wray at the beginning of the election:—

"All *Horse-guards, Grenadier-guards, Foot-guards,* and *Black-guards,* that have not polled for the destruction of *Chelsea Hospital* and the *tax on maid-servants,* are desired to meet at the Gutter Hole, opposite the Horse-guards, where they will have a full bumper of 'knock-me-down,' and plenty of soap-suds, before they go to poll for Sir Cecil Wray, or eat.

" N.B.—Those that have no shoes or stockings may come without, there being a quantity of *wooden shoes provided for them.*"

The obnoxious tax upon the maids was a sufficient set-off to the new taxes, especially that on receipts, which had been proposed by Fox while in office, and were loudly cried down by his Tory opponents:—

"For though he opposes the stamping of notes,
'Tis in order to tax all your petticoats,
Then how can a woman solicit our votes
For Sir Cecil Wray?"

The ladies are, therefore, especially warned against countenancing such a pretender, whose only claim was the love of

* This alludes to a loyal address sent from Westminster a little while before the election, and said to have been smuggled by Sir Cecil Wray without the knowledge of the greater part of the electors, and signed only by a few ignorant people.

back-stairs intrigue, and whose crooked politics were not embellished even by generous feelings :—

> " For had he to women been ever a friend,
> Nor by taxing them tried our old taxes to mend,
> Yet so *stingy* he is, that none can contend
> For Sir Cecil Wray.
>
> "The gallant Lord Hood to his country is dear,
> His voters, like Charlie's, make excellent cheer;
> But who has been able to taste *the small beer*
> Of Sir Cecil Wray!
>
> "Then come ev'ry free, ev'ry generous soul,
> That loves a fine girl and a full flowing bowl,
> Come here in a body, and all of you poll
> 'Gainst Sir Cecil Wray!
>
> " In vain all the arts of the Court are let loose,
> The electors of Westminster never will choose
> To run down a Fox, and set up a *Goose*
> Like Sir Cecil Wray."

The exertions of the Court against Fox were of the most
extraordinary kind. The King is said to have received almost
hourly intelligence of what was going on, and to have been
affected in the most evident manner by every change in the
state of the poll. The royal name was used very freely
in obtaining votes for Hood and Wray, even in threats. On
one occasion, two hundred and eighty of the guards were sent
in a body to give their votes as householders, which Horace
Walpole observes, " *is* legal, but which my father (Sir Robert),
in the most quiet seasons, would not have dared to do." All
dependents on the Court were commanded to vote on the same
side as the soldiers. When the popular party cried out against
this sort of interference, their opponents charged Fox and his
friends with bribery, and with using various other kinds of improper influence; they insulted his voters by describing them
publicly as the lowest and most degraded part of the population ; and their language became more violent as Fox gradually
rose on the poll. " It is an absolute fact," one of their papers said,
" that if a person, on going up to the Shakespeare, can shew a
piece of a shirt *only*, the committee declares him *duly qualified*."
Another paper announces, " This day the *elegant* inhabitants of
Borough-clink, Rag-fair, Chick-lane, &c., go up with an address
to Mr. Fox, at his *ready-furnished lodgings*, thanking him for
his interest in the late extraordinary *circulation of handkerchiefs.*" Forgetting their own sailors, they exclaimed against
the employment of persons of no better character than Irish

chairmen; and after the unfortunate affair on 10th of May,
they headed their bills with such titles as, "No murder! no
club-law! no butchers' law! no petticoat government!" It was
now, however, the turn of the Foxites to triumph in their
increasing numbers of votes, and a shower of exulting squibs
and songs fell upon their opponents. Placards like the following
were scattered abroad before the end of April :—

> "*Oh! help Judas, lest he fall into the Pitt of Ingratitude!!!*
>
> "The *prayers* of all bad Christians, Heathens, Infidels, and Devil's-agents,
> are most earnestly requested for their dear friend,
>
> JUDAS ISCARIOT, *knight of the back-stairs*,
>
> lying at the period of political dissolution; having received a dreadful
> wound from the exertions of the lovers of liberty and the constitution, in the
> poll of the last ten days at the Hustings, nigh unto the Place of Cabbages."

They published caricatures, in which the unsuccessful candidate
was driven away by a maid-servant's broom and a pensioner's
crutch; or pursued by a hooting crowd, bearing on their
banners "No tax on maid-servants," &c.; or riding dolefully on
a slow and obstinate ass, while the successful candidates are
galloping onwards to the end of the race, on high-mettled
horses, and leaving him far in the distance. Even the Irish
chairmen were given their fling at the discomfited candidate in
a "new" ballad, entitled "Paddy's farewell to Sir Cecil :"—

> "Sir Cecil, be aisy, I wont be unshivil,
>   Now the Man of the Paple is chose in your stead;
> From swate Covent-Garden you're flung to the Divil,
> By Jasus, Sir Cecil, you've boulder'd your head.
>   Fa-ra-lal, &c.
>
> "To be sure, much avail to you all your fine spaiches,
>   'Tis nought but palaver, my honey, my dear,
> While all Charly's voters stick to him like laiches,
> A frind to our liberties and our *small beer*.
>   Fa-ra-lal, &c."

The ladies are then represented as rejoicing in his defeat, with
the exception of his canvassing friend, Mrs. Hobart; and
the songster concludes :—

> "Ah now! I pray let no jontleman prisunt take this ill,
>   By my troth, Pat shall nivir use unshivil wards;
> But my varse sure must plaise, which the name of Sir Cecil
> Hands down to oblivion's latest recards.
>   Fa-ra-lal, &c.

"If myself with the tongue of a prophet is gifted,
Oh! I sees in a twinkling the knight's latter ind!
Tow'rds the varge of his life div'lish high he'll be lifted,
And after his death, never fear, he'll discind.
Fa-ra-lal, &c."

The young Prince of Wales, who was now the intimate
friend of Fox, and the warm supporter of the coalition, exerted
himself as actively against the Court in this Westminster
election, as his father's ministers did in favour of it, and his conduct is said to have given extreme provocation to the King and
Queen. Members of his own household were employed in canvassing for voters; and some of the ministerial papers, which, in
their paragraphs shewed little respect for his character, declared
that he had canvassed in person; one of them states, with an
appended observation, the wit of which is not very remarkable,
that "The Prince appeared at Ranelagh last week with a *Fox
cockade* in his hat, and a sprig of *laurel; if he should ever be
sent a *bird's-nesting* by Oliver, it is to be expected he will
prefer the *laurel* to the *oak*." At this time is said to have
arisen the hostile feeling which the Prince ever afterwards
entertained towards Pitt, and which was increased by the
minister's stiff and haughty bearing towards him. The Prince
gave a magnificent party in
honour of Fox's triumph at
Westminster.

A PATRIOTIC PUBLICAN.

Another active and re-
markable partizan of Fox
was "honest" Sam House*
the publican, an old resident
in this character in Westminster, remarkable for his
oddities† and for his political
zeal. During this election he
kept open house at his own
expense, and was honoured
with the company of many
of the Whig aristocracy.
An early caricature by Gillray, entitled "Returning
from Brooks's," represents
the Prince of Wales in a
state of considerable ine-
briety, wearing the election

* The picture of Sam House occurs in many caricatures of the time.
The cut given above is copied from a plate by Gillray.
† Sam House was remarkable for his clean and perfectly bald head, over

cockade, and supported by Fox and the patriotic publican. The wit of the ministerial papers was often expended on honest Sam. At the beginning of the election, when Fox seemed to be in a hopeless minority, one of them inserted a paragraph stating that the publican had committed suicide in his despair. He is said to have been a very successful canvasser in the course of the election.

> " See the brave Sammy House, he's as still as a mouse,
> And does canvass with prudence so clever :
> See what shoals with him flocks, to poll for brave Fox,
> Give thanks to Sun House, boys, for ever, for ever, for ever !
> Give thanks to Sam House, boys, for ever !
>
> "Brave bald-headed Sam, all must own, is the man,
> Who does canvass for brave Fox so clever ;
> His aversion, I say, is to small beer and Wray !
> May his bald head be honour'd for ever, for ever, for ever !
> May his bald head be honour'd for ever !"

But the most active and successful of Fox's canvassers, and the most ungenerously treated by the opposite party, was the beautiful and accomplished Duchess of Devonshire (Georgiana Spencer). Attended by several others of the beauties of the Whig aristocracy, she was almost daily present at the election, wearing Fox's cockade, and she went about personally soliciting votes, which she obtained in great numbers by the influence of her personal charms and by her affability. The Tories were greatly annoyed at her ladyship's proceedings ; they accused her of wholesale bribery ; and it was currently reported that she had in one instance bought the vote of a butcher with a kiss, an incident which was immediately exhibited to people's eyes in multitudes of pictures, with more or less of exaggeration. But nothing could be more disgraceful than the profusion of

BRIBERY.

which he never wore hat or wig. His unvaried dress consisted of nankeen jacket and breeches, brightly polished shoes and buckles, and he had his waistcoat constantly open in all seasons, and wore remarkably white linen. His legs were generally bare ; but, when clad, were always in stockings of the finest quality of silk.

scandalous and indecent abuse which was heaped upon this noble lady by the ministerial press, especially by its two great organs, the *Morning Post* and the *Advertiser*. The insult in some cases was merely coarse, such as the following from the *Morning Post* :—"The Duchess of Devonshire yesterday canvassed the different alehouses of Westminster in favour of Mr. Fox ; about one o'clock she took her share of a pot of porter at Sam House's in Wardour Street." The same paper makes her write to the candidate :—"Yesterday I sent you three votes, but went through great fatigue to secure them ; it cost me *ten kisses* for every *plumper*. I'm much afraid *we are done up*,—will see you at the *porter-shop*, and consult about ways and means." Others of these newspaper paragraphs were more pointedly insulting to the feelings of a virtuous female, such as "We hear that the D——ss of D—— grants *favours* to those who promise their votes and interest to Mr. Fox."—"A certain beautiful lady of quality, who has for some days past canvassed on foot for her favourite candidate, met lately with such a reception as she might reasonably expect ; one man offered a hundred votes *for one of her favours*."—"A certain lady of great beauty and high rank, requests that in future when she condescends to favour any shoemaker, or other mechanic, with a salute, that he will *kiss fair*, and not take improper liberties." Multitudes of these paragraphs contained innuendos and aspersions far too infamous to allow of their being transferred to our pages; we merely quote as one of the least objectionable,—"*Ladies of Pleasure* have ever been of prodigious service to *conspirators ;* not only Catiline, but also the famous Jacques Pierre, and several other contrivers of mischief, have carried on their operations through the medium of a *courtezan*."

But the newspaper paragraphs were nothing in comparison with the disgraceful manner in which the duchess was treated in the caricatures, in many of which she was figured and exhibited to public view in the shop windows, in indecent postures, accompanied with allusions of the most infamous kind. The Queen, who had all the caricatures on this occasion brought to her, and was extremely amused with the manner in which the opponents of the Court were turned to ridicule, is said to have been much shocked by some of these coarse caricatures against the Duchess of Devonshire, which had been accidentally brought to her among the other political prints. The "canvassing duchess" figured also in many caricatures of a much less objectionable character. Thus, in one entitled "Wit's Last Stake, or, the cobbling voters and abject canvassers," the

duchess is represented seated on Fox's knee, and holding her
shoe to be mended by a cobbler, for which she is paying his wife

A GROUP OF CANVASSERS

with gold; Fox is shaking hands with another voter, who is
treated by Sam House with a pot of porter. In others she is
represented marching about with
troops of canvassing ladies, bearing
banners with appropriate mottoes ;
or practising various arts to convince unwilling voters. In a caricature published immediately after
the election, entitled " Every man
has his hobby-horse," the successful
candidate is carried in triumph by
his fair and zealous supporter.
Charles Fox may truly be said to
have been carried into the House
of Commons in 1784 by the Duchess
of Devonshire.*

THE SUCCESSFUL CANDIDATE.

We ought not to pass over another zealous actor in this exciting
scene of turbulence, who helped at
least to enliven it—the celebrated
convivial songster, Captain Morris,
whose effusions were unfortunately not always of an unexception-

* An immense mass of newspaper paragraphs, placards, squibs, songs,
&c., relating to this election, with a certain number of caricatures, were
published collectively under the title of a " History of the Westminster
Election ;" and, although but a selection, they form a large quarto volume
in small print. On the whole, these records of party feeling are much more
distinguished by scurrility than by wit. The following anecdotes of Fox's
personal canvass are related. He and his friends were often subjected to

able character. We shall soon meet with him again as one of the boon companions of the heir apparent. The captain had begun his career as a political songster in the ranks of the Tories, and had composed a bitter song against the Fox and North administration, under the title of "The Coalition Song." His conversion to the other party was probably effected by the example of the Prince of Wales. During the Westminster election of 1784, he was a constant attendant at Fox's convivial parties, for which several of his best political songs were composed, especially one against the King and his young minister Pitt, entitled "The Baby and Nurse," which was enthusiastically called for over and over again at the election dinners, and, oddly enough, while he was himself singing this new song to the Whigs, the Tories were singing his old song against the coalition. Another song against Pitt, by Captain Morris, was popular during and after the election, under the title of

"BILLY'S TOO YOUNG TO DRIVE US."

"If life's a rough journey, as moralists tell,
Englishmen sure made the best on 't ;
On this spot of earth they bade liberty dwell,
While slavery holds all the rest on 't.
They thought the best solace for labour and care,
Was a state independent and free, sir ;
And this thought, though a curse that no tyrant can bear,
Is the blessing of you and of me, sir.
    Then while through this whirlabout journey we reel,
    We'll keep unabused the best blessing we feel,
    And watch ev'ry torn of the politic wheel—
    Billy's too young to drive us.

"The car of Britannia, we all must allow,
Is ready to crack with its load, sir ;
And wanting the hand of experience, will now
Most surely break down on the road, sir.
Then must we, poor passengers, quietly wait,
To be crash'd by this mischievous spark, sir !
Who drives a d—d job in the carriage of state,
And got up like a thief in the dark, sir.
    Then while through this whirlabout, &c.

personal insult ; but this was one of the charms of electioneering in the olden time.

"Mr. Fox, on his canvass, having accosted a blunt tradesman, whom he solicited for his vote, the man answered, 'I cannot give you my support ; I admire your abilities, but d—n your principles !' Mr. Fox smartly replied, 'My friend, I applaud you for your sincerity, but d—n your manners !' "

"Mr. Fox having applied to a saddler in the Haymarket for his vote and interest, the man produced a halter, with which, he said, he was ready to oblige him. Mr. Fox replied, 'I return you thanks, my friend, for your intended present ; but I should be sorry to deprive you of it, as I presume it must be a family piece.' "

"They say that his judgment is mellow and pure,
And his principles virtue's own type, sir;
I believe from my soul he's a son of a ——,
And his judgment more rotten than ripe, sir,
For all that he boasts of, what is it, in truth,
But that mad with ambition and pride, sir,
He 's the vices of age, for the follies of youth,
And a d—d deal of cunning beside, sir.*
    Then while through this whirlabout, &c

"The squires, whose reason ne'er reaches a span,
Are all with this prodigy struck, sir ;
And cry, ' it's a crime not to vote for a man
Who 's as chaste as a baby at suck,' sir.

"It 's true, he 's a pretty good gift of the gab,
And was taught by his dad on a stool, sir ;
But though at a speech he 's a bit of a dab,
In the state he 's a bit of a tool, sir.
For Billy's pure love for his country was such,
He agreed to become the cat's paw, sir ;
And sits at the helm, while it 's turn'd by the touch
Of a reprobate fiend of the law,† sir.
    Then while through this whirlabout," &c.

The Westminster election of 1784 was the most remarkable struggle of the kind that has ever been witnessed in this country, and is an event of importance in the political history of the last century, because it was the only very serious check that the Court met with at this time in its successful attempt to obtain a strong Tory House of Commons. The superior power of the Crown in the legislature, and the political influence of William Pitt, were from this moment firmly established ‡ The principal measures of the new ministers during the present year (1784) were (with the exception of Pitt's India-bill, a performance so

* To explain some parts of this song, it may be necessary to state, that, although very strongly addicted to the bottle, Pitt, who was of a cold, phlegmatic disposition, had none of the wild habits of the young men of his day, and was held up by the Court as a contrast to the irregularities of Fox and his companions. Two stanzas and a half are omitted.

† An allusion to Lord Thurlow, who was celebrated for his swearing propensities.

‡ The hostility against Fox at Westminster did not end with the election; the Court party had, from the first, declared their intention of demanding a scrutiny if Fox succeeded, because it was known that, under the circumstances, this would be a long, tedious, and expensive affair. The returning officer acted partially; and, on the demand of Sir Cecil Wray for a scrutiny, refused to make a return. Fox had been elected member for Kirkwall in Scotland, so that he was not hindered from taking his seat in the House ; and, after some months' delay, the high-bailiff was not only obliged to return him as member for Westminster, but Fox brought an action against him, and recovered heavy damages.

crude that his own friends were obliged to emendate it from
beginning to end as it passed through the House, and several acts
were subsequently called for to explain it,) of a financial character; and their object was to provide for the debts incurred in
the late war by new taxes, or commutations of old ones. A
feeble opposition was made to the government plan of taxation,
and the public began to cry loudly against the burthens under
which they laboured. "Master Billy's Budget" was the burthen
of more than one satirical song; and the following lines
" On the Taxes," published towards the end of the year, give a
tolerably comprehensive view of the various items of which it
consisted :—

"Should foreigners, staring at English taxation,
Ask why we still reckon ourselves a *free nation,*
We'll tell them, we pay for the light of the sun ;
For a horse with a saddle—to trot or to run ;
For writing our names ;—for the flash of a gun ;
For the flame of a candle to cheer the dark night ;
For the hole in the house, if it let in the light ;
For births, weddings, and deaths ; for our selling and buying ;
Though some think 'tis hard to pay threepence for dying ;
And some poor folks cry out, ' These are Pharaoh-like tricks,
To take such unmerciful tale of our bricks !'
How great in financing our statesmen have been,
From our ribbons, our shoes, and our hats may be seen ;
On this side and that, in the air, on the ground,
By act upon act now so firmly we're bound,
One would think there's not room one new impost to put,
From the crown of the head to the sole of the foot.
Like Job, thus John Bull his condition deplores,
Very patient, indeed, and all cover'd with sores."

The opposition, indeed, seemed at this moment to be sunk so
low in public opinion,
that the patriot's
" occupation" might
truly be said to be
gone. The serious pa-
pers and the burlesque
caricatures joined in
treating the efforts of
the country party
with contemptuous
derision. The support
they derived from the
Prince of Wales was
the only thing which

PRECEPTOR AND PUPIL.

gave uneasiness; and it provoked the King and Queen to the highest degree. They looked upon Fox with abhorrence as the corruptor of the royal youth; and a caricature, published in May, at the conclusion of the Westminster election, entitled "Preceptor and Pupil," represents the opposition leader, in loathly form, whispering his doctrines into the ear of the sleeping heir to the throne. Fox's friend and ally, the sleepy and inactive Lord North, is figured in another caricature as "Ignavia,"—the personification of Sloth. Burke was equally an object of attack to the resentful exultation of his political opponents. His warmth of feeling and his splendid eloquence made him one of the foremost champions in the desultory warfare which was carried on against the ministerial majorities in the House of Commons; and the caricaturists made war upon his pretended Jesuitism, and even upon his worldliness; and they pictured the writer on the Sublime and Beautiful as a raving demon

IGNAVIA.

of sedition, one of the foremost of the followers of the political Satan, who is seen on the other side of the picture smarting under the mortification of his defeat, yet still rallying his dispirited troops, and urging them on to the attack.

The Tories, in their derision, recommended the opposition leaders to turn their talents to more profitable labours; a ballad, addressed to their leader, in October, and a nearly contemporary caricature* embodying the same sentiment, recommend him to turn his talents to preaching, and, since the sinners had left him in the lurch, to aim at the support of the saints. The various pretences of the opposition, says the song, were quite worn out:—

SOME OF SATAN'S TROOPS.

* Entitled, "More ways than one; or, the Patriot turn'd Preacher," published on the 2nd of November, 1784.

"Dear Charles, whose eloquence I prize,
To whom my every vote is due,
What shall we now, alas! devise
To cheer our faint desponding crew?

"Well have we fought the hard campaign,
And battled it with all our force :
But self-esteem alone we gain,
Outrun and jockey'd in the course.

"Within the Senate, and without,
Our credit fails ; th' enlighten'd nation
The boasted Coalition scout,
And hunt us from th' Administration.

"We've carp'd at this, and carp'd at that,
And who hath heeded what we said?
The house is coy, they smell a rat,—
The time is past, and we are sped.

"And shall we then, like fools, despair?
Can we no thriving scheme invent?
Yes :—let cameleons feed on air,
Such diet will not thee content.

"But why invent? the plan is ready,
Form'd by a wag of late in jest :
Let us adopt it, firm and steady,
And, drowning, clasp it to our breast."

"Fox, the Preacher," occupies the pulpit, and has assumed his most engaging and persuasive looks :—

"Quick let thy soul with *grace* be fill'd!
Expect no other *call* but mine ;
With penitence I see thee thrill'd,
With new-born light I see thee shine.

"I see *subscribers* throng around,
(Can Brooks's e'er supply such prizes?)
The pious *herd*—and from the ground,
Behold a *Tabernacle* rises!"

The sleek and good-humoured North is placed in the seat below :—

"How spruce will North beneath thee sit!
With joy officiate as thy clerk!
Attune the hymn, renounce his wit,
And carol like the morning lark!

"Or, if thy potent length of prayer,
By chance induce a kindly doze,
Wake in the nick with accent clear,
To cry, amen! and bless the close!"

Sheridan, who now shone as one of the opposition leaders, is to
act as pew-keeper :—

> "To comic Richard, ever true,
>   Be it assign'd the curs to lash,
> With ready hand to ope the pew,
>   With ready hand to take the cash."

Burke, who has passed through
another metamorphosis, puts on
the garb of feminine devotion, and
leads in the harmonious chorus :—

> 'For thee, O *beauteous and sublime !*
>   What place of honour shall we find !
> To tempt with money were a crime ;
>   Thine are the riches of the mind.

"MISTRESS" BURKE.

> "Clad in a matron's cap and robe,
>   Thou shalt assist each *wither'd crone !*
> And, as the piercing threat shall probe,
>   Do 't thine to lead the choral groan !

> "Thine to uplift the whiten'd eye,
>   And thine to spread th' uplifted hand !
> Thine to upheave th' expressive sigh,
>   And regulate the *hoary band !*"

Such a plan as this, it was represented, could not fail to be
profitable to the ranks of the defeated opposition, and might
raise up in another sphere those whose ambition seemed for ever
disappointed in the arena of politics :—

> "Dear Charles, with speed this plan essay,
>   On dreams of power no longer muse ;
> For, faith ! thou'rt in a piteous way,
>   And not a moment hast to lose !"

CHAPTER XI.

GEORGE III.

Low State of the Opposition—Caricatures against Fox and his Colleagues—
The Probationary Odes—Ireland; Grattan and Flood—The Fortifica-
tion Scheme — India; Warren Hastings; the Impeachment — The
Prince of Wales; Royal Parsimony and Royal Extravagance—The
Trial of Warren Hastings—Ministerial Corruption; Antipathy of
Parties; the Installation Supper—First Indisposition of the King;
The Regency Bill.

THE consequences of the defeat of the liberal party in the
elections of 1784 were very apparent in the Parliamentary
session of 1785, and are best described in a few words of Horace
Walpole, written on the 2nd of February :—" The Parliament,"
he says, " is met, but as quietly as a quarter-session; the opposition seems quelled, or to despair." Rarely indeed has so
entire a change in popular feeling been effected in so short a
space of time; but, like all sudden changes, it was not long
before it began to experience a gradual reaction. Under the
absurd persecution of the Westminster scrutiny, the popularity
of Charles Fox was already beginning to revive; and the proud
and scornful bearing of the young minister were not calculated
to conciliate people's esteem. When, at the beginning of April,
the scrutiny ended in favour of Fox, the defeat of the Court was
celebrated by a general illumination on two successive nights,
attended with some rioting.

The overbearing temper of the minister on one side, and the
mortification of the opposition on the other, caused the debates
in the House of Commons during the present session to degenerate much more than was usual into attacks and recriminations
of a personal character. On the 9th of February, 1785, when
Fox complained in sufficiently gentle terms of the Westminster
scrutiny as an act of persecution against himself, Pitt, turning
up his nose with more than usual scorn, (a characteristic of the
orator which is never forgotten in the caricatures in which he
figures,) fell upon his rival in the following insulting language :—
" I am not surprised if he should pretend to be the butt of
ministerial persecution; and if, by striving to excite the public
compassion, he should seek to reinstate himself in that popularity

which he once enjoyed, but which he so unhappily has forfeited.
For it is the best and most ordinary resource of these political
apostates to court and to offer themselves to persecution for the
sake of the popular predilection and pity which usually fall upon
persecuted men. It becomes worth their while to suffer, for a
time, political martyrdom, for the sake of the canonization that
awaits the suffering martyr; and, I make no doubt, the right
honourable gentleman has so much penetration, and at the same
time so much passive virtue about him, that he would be glad
not only to seem a poor, injured, persecuted man, but he would
gladly seek an opportunity of even really suffering a little persecution, if it be possible to find such an opportunity." Such
scenes were of frequent occurrence. On one occasion, the 9th of
March, when the same subject was in debate, Fox broke into an
ironical commendation of the present Parliament, a large portion
of which consisted of new faces that had never been in the
House before.* He said, that he highly approved of their
general conduct, although they had been "called together by an
unfortunate political delusion." "They were gentlemen with
whom he was entirely unacquainted, men whose faces were un-

known to any person; but,
emerged from obscurity as they
had, he was happy to find that
they possessed great candour
and impartiality." Pitt replied
in rather an angry tone, which
led to another violent alterca-
tion.

A scene of this description was
the foundation of a print by
Sayer, published on the 17th of
March, under the title, "Cicero
in Catilinam." The leader of
the opposition, in the character
of Catiline, is represented as
seated on the opposition benches,
quailing beneath the eloquent
invective of the political Cicero,
Pitt. Lord North is seated by
his colleague, his face concealed

CATILINE REPREHENDED.

---

* No less than a hundred and eighty of Fox's ordinary supporters had
been thrown out in the election of 1784, and replaced by new members,
who had not been in the House before. The rejected candidates received
the popular appellation of *Fox's Martyrs.*

in a bundle of papers in which his attention appears to be absorbed.
In another caricature, by the same artist, the two leaders (Fox
and North) are represented blowing up the fire of opposition
and discontent, fed by a host of petitions, &c., to burn the
Irish emblem of the harp, and the ministers' "Propositions"
relating to the sister isle. A few days before (April 6), Sayer
had represented the eloquent but rather discursive Burke, setting
the House asleep by the length of his perpetual invectives
against ministers. He is supported on the shoulders of two of
the most active members of the opposition in the present Parliament—Powis and Sawbridge—the former holding in his hand a
bundle of papers inscribed "Memoranda of important observations for reform in the representation, &c." The print is
entitled " * * * * (Burke) on the Sublime and Beautiful,"
alluding to the celebrated work published by the orator before
he had become distinguished as a statesman. In another larger
print by Sayer, published on the 7th of June, the opposition are

joining their strength to get
up a concert. Fox and one
of his colleagues are practising on the fiddle; the
former treading the music of
"God save the King" under
his foot. The Duke of Portland is occupied with the
piano; Burke plays the
trumpet; North performs
upon the trombone; the
Earl of Derby figures with
the pipe and tabor; and so
on with the rest, not omitting
the celebrated parliamentary
dog which joins its howl
with the general concert.
Against the wall hangs a pair
of bagpipes, the representa-

PRACTITIONERS.

tive of Lord Loughborough. The portrait of the Prince of
Wales is suspended behind, with a large picture on each side,
representing, in one, Fox exhibiting a dancing bear, and in the
other, North playing the pipe to three dancing dogs, while Fox
is teaching a hare to beat the tabor. On the chimney-piece lie
the "Probationary Odes for the Laureateship," and the "Rolliad" and "Critique on the Rolliad," witty satires against the
ministers, which had just been published, the work of some

young aristocratic poets of talent, but too minute in their personal allusions to have much interest at the present day.* The "Probationary Odes" were especially clever; the vacancy in the laureateship was supposed to have called forth a host of candidates in rivalry of Thomas Warton (who succeeded to it), and each of his Majesty's ministers enters into the competition, and contributes an ode more or less characteristic of himself, or descriptive of his political conduct. First in the list of candidates stands Sir Cecil Wray, who appears by the election squibs of the preceding year, to have been guilty of some attempts at poetry, and who now takes a magnificent flight in the regions of namby-pamby. After a somewhat magniloquent exordium, he goes on to flatter the King,—

> "Yes, Joe and I
> Are em'lons!—Why!
> It is because, great Cæsar, you are clever—
> Therefore we'd sing of you for ever!
> Sing—sing—sing—sing—
> God save the King!
> Smile then, Cæsar, smile on Wray!
> Crown at last his poll with bay!—
> Come, oh! bay, and with thee bring
> Salary, illustrious thing!—
> Laurels vain of Covent Garden,
> I don't value you a farding.
> Let sack my soul cheer,
> For 'tis sick of small beer!
> Cæsar! Cæsar! give it!—do!—
> Great Cæsar, giv't all!—for my muse 'doreth you!"

After being wrapt for a while in the poetical contemplation of his own grandeur, he ends by a sublime threat against the presumption of his rival.

* Horace Walpole writes on the 30th of October, "As to your little knot of poets... we have at present here a most incomparable set, not exactly known by their names, but who, till the dead of summer, kept the town in a roar, and I suppose, will revive by the meeting of Parliament. They have poured forth a torrent of odes, epigrams, and part of an imaginary epic poem, called the 'Rolliad,' with a commentary and notes, that is as good as the 'Dispensary' and 'Dunciad,' with more ease. These poems are all anti-ministerial, and the authors very young men, and little known or heard of before. I would send them, but you would want too many keys: and, indeed, I want some myself; for, as there are continually allusions to parliamentary speeches and events, they are often obscure to me till I get them explained." The principal writers of these satires were, we are told, Mr. Ellis, a lawyer named Lawrence, Colonel R. Fitzpatrick, and John Townshend, second son of George Viscount Townshend.

> "Yet if the laurel prize,
>   Dearer than my eyes,
> Cursed Warton tries
>   For to surprise,
> By the eternal God, I'll *scrutinize!*"

A number of candidates of obscurer name follow. Michael
Angelo Taylor, who had obtained the nickname of "the
Chicken," stands forth as "a Chicken of the Muse," and
rejoices in the figure he makes in the House,—

> "Lo! how I shine, St. Stephen's boast!
> There, first of *chicks*, I rule the *roast!*
>   There I appear,
>   Pitt's *Chanticleer*,
> The *bantam-cock* to oppositions!
>   Or like a *hen*,
>   With watchful ken,
> Sit close and watch—the Irish propositions!"

These minor constellations are all thrown into the shade by
the appearance of the Scot, Dundas,—

> "Hoot! hoot awaw!
> Hoot! hoot awaw!
> Ye Lawland bards! wha' are ye aw?
> What are your sangs? what aw your lair to boot?
> Vain are your thoughts the prize to win,
> Sae dight your gobs, and stint your senseless din;
>   Hoot! hoot awaw! huot! hoot?
>   Put oot aw your attic feires,
> Burn your lutes, and brek your leyres;
> A looder and a louder note I'll streike:—
> Na watter drawghts fra Holicon I breed,
> Na wull I mount your winged steed,—
> I'll mount the Hanoverian horse, and ride him whare I leike!"

Among the candidates of higher note comes the profane-
swearing chancellor, of whose ode the exordium, as being the
least outrageous portion, may serve as a specimen.

> "Damnation seize ye all,
> Who puff, who thrum, who bawl and squall!
>   Fired with ambitious hopes in vain,
> The wreath, that blooms for other brows, to gain.
>   Is Thurlow yet so little known?
> By G—d! I swore, while God shall reign,
> The Seals, in spite of changes, to retain,
> Nor quit the woolsack till he quits the throne.
>   And now, the bays for life to wear,
> Once more, with mightier oaths, by G—d, I swear;
> Bend my black brows, that keep the peers in awe,
> Shake my full-bottom wig, and give the nod of law."

In the conclusion, the chancellor's ode loses itself in a

magnificent phalanx of wild comminations against "the factious crew" collectively and individually. Among the especial objects of his hostility are Lord Loughborough, whose ambitious eye was fixed upon the woolsack—"D—n Loughborough! my plague,—would his *bagpipe* were split." Lord Loughborough was regarded as the leader of the opposition in the House of Lords, and as the inciter and backer of Lord Stormont, who also was now a bitter opponent of the ministry. On the 30th of July, 1785, a discussion arose on the Irish Propositions, in which Stormont (for himself and Lord Loughborough, who was absent) threw some obstacle in the way of the arrangements proposed by Lord Sidney, the Secretary for Home Affairs. Next day (July 1) appeared a caricature by Sayer, in which "yesterday's business" is represented in the light of "boring a secretary of State." Lord Loughborough, whose face is turned away, is represented as using his instrument, Lord Stormont, to bore Lord Sydney, who appears as a

A BORE.

piece of timber with two knots, inscribed " 1st Proposition" and " 2nd Proposition."

Among the difficult questions with which the new ministry had to contend, the state of Ireland was by no means the least. The discontented inhabitants of the sister isle, amongst whom agitation had been more or less actively at work since the beginning of the century, had watched the progress of the American insurrection with interest, and shewn a great inclination to follow the example. The clamour for free-trade and exemption from duties had drawn concessions even from Lord North ; and a caricature published in 1780, represents Hibernia, with the acquisition of her free-trade, exposed to the cajolery and flattery of a host of foreign suitors, who demand an entrance into her ports. In 1782, Grattan received from the Irish Parliament a very handsome grant, in consideration of his exertions in securing its independence. Grattan continued to shine conspicuously among the Irish patriots for many years; but his patriotism was not of the ultra-violent character which was now alone gaining credit among the Irish democrats, who

began to rebel even against their own legislators. The leader of these ultra-patriots was the celebrated Henry Flood, Grattan's rival and opponent. Delegates of this party were chosen throughout Ireland, and held a sort of national convention in Dublin, which began by demanding a radical reform of their own Parliament, and urged their countrymen to arm for the purpose of obtaining it. Flood, who, like Grattan, was a member of the Parliament, laid their complaints and demands before the legislative assembly; but they were rejected by large majorities, indignant at the kind of intimidation which was

GRATTAN.

held out towards them. The debates were often violent and personal in the highest degree. One of these scenes is represented in a print published in London, on the 25th of November, 1783, in which a violently caricatured portrait of Grattan, copied in

the cut above, is represented exposing the principles and designs of the Irish agitator of the day. An equally caricatured figure of Flood, launches as violent an invective against his assailant, as he walks doggedly out of the House. The convention, which afterwards, in still closer imitation of the Americans, took the title of a national congress, continued to hold its ground, and was acknowledged by a large portion of the population of Ireland as the true parliament of the island. There were thus two rival governments existing at the same time. Pitt brought forwards in the session of 1785, as a measure of pacification, his two propositions or provisions, to allow the

FLOOD.

produce of our colonies to be imported into England through Ireland, and to establish a free trade between Ireland and Great Britain; in return for which advantages Ireland was to contribute a certain annual sum out of her revenue towards the general expenses of the empire. These propositions soon excited the jealousy of the British merchants; and they seem, indeed, in their original form, to have been very defective. The merchants were heard by counsel in the English Parliament; numerous petitions against the measure were presented; and it was attacked bitterly in both Houses. The minister was obliged to yield in some degree to the popular feeling, and he modified his measure, and brought it forwards in an entirely new form on the 12th of May. It was these propositions which, in the House of Lords, subjected Lord Sydney to the bore depicted above. Among the foremost to attack them in the House of Lords was Lord George Germaine, who is represented in a caricature by Sayer, backed in the onslaught by Lords Stormont and Derby. Lord George was now in the opposition, and, singularly enough, the court threw into his face the very charges relating to his conduct at the battle of Minden, from which, while he supported King George's measures, he had been so pertinaciously screened. The following verses were at first placed on this caricature; but they were afterwards erased,—

> "'Gainst France opposed on Minden's plain,
>   When Brunswick gave the word—
> 'Bring all your power, my Lord Germaine;'
>   The noble lord demurr'd.
>
> "Pitt's propositions now the foe,
>   He boldly mounts the breach,
> Obeys command, and aims a blow
>   With all his power—of speech!"

In a caricature published by the other party, Pitt is represented in the utmost dismay, riding off to Dublin on a wild Irish bull, to seek shelter from the English mob, to whose execrations he is exposed by his accumulating taxes, and especially that on shops, and that on maid-servants, which had now been carried by Pitt, and was a subject for endless jokes; both had excited great dissatisfaction. This print, which is very coarsely executed, is entitled "Paddy O'Pitt's triumphant exit," and was published on the 20th of June, 1785. People cried out that Pitt was treating the Irish with undue partiality, while he was crushing Englishmen with insupportable burthens.

It was during this session that Pitt made his last show of attachment to the liberal principles he had so warmly advocated while out of power, by bringing forward a bill for a reform in Parliament; but it was so inefficient a measure, that it was only ridiculed by the opposition, and, as he did not use his own parliamentary influence to support it, it was clear he never intended it should pass. He was ever after a resolute opponent of parliamentary reform, in whatever shape it was presented. In other matters, the young premier met with several slight crosses and disagreements. The foreign policy of his ministry was an object of incessant attack to the liberal opposition; and a plan of national fortifications, brought forward by the Duke of Richmond, who had deserted his old colleagues to take office as master-general of the Ordnance, was an object of great ridicule. After several animated debates, in which the Duke of Richmond's apostasy was said more of than his fortifications, and which showed how much party spirit entered into the profession of patriotism, on a division, the numbers on both sides of the question were equal, and the government scheme was thrown out by the casting vote of the speaker. This was the subject of several caricatures and squibs, in which the unceremonious extinction of the fortifications by the speaker is made a subject of no little mirth. In a print by Gillray, published in the year following, the Duke of Richmond is made to swallow his own fortifications by another individual, apparently intended to represent Lord Shelburne.

A BITTER DOSE.

The affairs of India had been made doubly prominent by the succession of bills for the regulation of that distant empire,—bills which, as we have seen, underwent so many vicissitudes; and the attention began to be directed rather against individuals who had misgoverned, than to the general subject of misgovernment. Several persons were successively pointed out to popular execration for the tyranny and rapacity they had exercised in different stations of our Indian empire; but at length the whole indignation of the opponents of eastern oppression was concentrated on the person of the governor-general of Bengal, Warren Hastings. The other members of the opposition are said to have been dragged, somewhat unwillingly, by Edmund Burke into the long and tedious proceedings against this man, who, having only done as others had done before him under the same circumstances, and that in the service not only of the company by whom he was employed, but of the English Crown, was not a little astonished, on his return home, to find himself on the eve of being subjected to a state prosecution. The proceedings of the Company's servants in India were exactly of that kind which, if made public in this country, where they were only imperfectly understood, could not fail of exciting general indignation, especially when dressed up by a man of ardent imagination, like Burke. The delinquencies of the governor-general had been not unfrequent objects of Burke's declamation, although it was not till the beginning of the year 1786 that he made the open declaration of his design to bring this great offender to justice. He had moved for the production of Indian papers and correspondence as early as the month of February in this year, and on the 4th of April he stood up in the House of Commons to charge Warren Hastings with high crimes and misdemeanours, exhibiting against him nine distinct articles of accusation, which, in a few weeks, were increased to the number of twenty-two. The first charge was brought forward on the 1st of June, and, after a long and warm debate, the House of Commons threw it out as untenable, by a very large majority. On the 13th of June, the second charge, relating to the treatment of the Rajah of Benares, was brought forward; and then an equally large majority declared, "That this charge contained matter of impeachment against the late governor-general of Bengal." Hastings, who was supported by the whole strength of the East India Company, and who was understood to enjoy the King's favourable opinion in a special degree, had calculated on the support of his ministers; and everybody's astonishment was great when they now saw Pitt turn round and join with his enemies. Hastings felt this desertion with great acuteness, and it is said that he never forgave it. Some accounted for it by supposing that Pitt, and more especially Dundas, were jealous of Hastings's personal influence, and feared his rising in Court favour; and a variety of other equally discreditable motives were assigned for this extraordinary change.

The return of the ex-governor's wife had preceded his own, and Mrs. Hastings was received at Court with much favour by Queen Charlotte, who was generally believed to be of a very avaricious disposition, and was popularly charged with having sold her favour for Indian presents. The supposed patronage of the Court, and the manner in which it was said to have been obtained, went much further in rendering Hastings an object of popular odium than all the charges alleged against him by Burke, and they were accordingly made the most of by that class of political agitators who are more immediately employed in influencing the mob. At the very moment when the impeachment was pending, a circumstance occurred which seemed to give strength—or, at least, was made to give strength—to the popular suspicions. The Nizam of the Deccan, anxious at this moment to conciliate the friendship of England, had sent King George a valuable diamond of unusual dimensions; and, ignorant of what was going on in the English Parliament, had selected Hastings as the channel through which to transmit it. This peace-offering arrived in England on the 2nd of June, while the first charge against Hastings was pending in the House: and on the 14th of June, the day after the second charge had been decided on by the Commons, the diamond, with a rich bulse or purse, containing the Nizam's letter, were presented by Lord Sydney at a levee, at which Hastings was present. When the story of the diamond got wind, it was tortured into a thousand shapes, and was even spoken of as a serious matter in the House of Commons; and Major Scott, the intimate friend and zealous champion of Hastings in the House, was obliged to make an explanation in his defence. It was believed that the King had received not one diamond, but a large quantity, and that they were to be the purchase-money of Hastings's acquittal. Caricatures on the subject were to be seen in the window of every print-shop. In one of these Hastings was represented wheeling away in a barrow the King with his crown and sceptre, observing, "What a man buys, he may sell ;" and, in another, the King was exhibited on his knees with his mouth wide open, and Warren Hastings pitching diamonds into it. Many other prints, some of them bearing evidence of the style of the best caricaturists of the day, kept up the agitation on this subject. It happened that there was a quack in the town, who pretended to eat stones, and bills of his exhibition were placarded on the walls, headed, in large letters, " The great stone-eater ! " The caricaturists took the hint, and drew the King with a diamond between his teeth, and a heap of others before him, with the inscription, " The greatest stone-eater ! " Songs and epigrams on the diamond were passed about

in all societies, and others, of a less refined character, were
sung about the streets, or sold to the populace by itinerant
ballad-dealers. One of these, now before me, printed on a slip
of coarse paper, with the title, " A full and true account of the
wonderfull diamond, presented to the King's Majesty, by
Warren Hastings, Esq., on Wednesday the 14th of June, 1786,
being an excellent new song, to the tune of Derry down,"
deserves to be reprinted (with a slight necessary alteration) as a
good example of the class of literary productions to which it
belongs :—

> " I'll sing you a song of a diamond so fine,
> That soon in the crown of our monarch will shine ;
> Of its size and its value the whole country rings,
> By Hastings bestow'd on the best of all kings.
> > Derry down, &c.

> " From India this jewel was lately brought o'er,
> Though sunk in the sea, it was found on the shore,
> And just in the nick to St. James's it got,
> Convey'd in a bag by the brave Major Scott.
> > Derry down, &c.

> " Lord Sydney stepp'd forth, when the tidings were known—
> It 's his office to carry such news to the throne ;—
> Though quite out of breath, to the closet he ran,
> And stammer'd with joy ere his tale he began.
> > Derry down, &c.

> " ' Here 's a jewel, my liege, there 's none such in the land ;
> Major Scott, with three bows, put it into my hand :
> And he swore, when he gave it, the wise ones were bit,
> For it never was shown—to Dundas or to Pitt.'
> > Derry down, &c.

> " ' For Dundas,' cried our sovereign, ' unpolish'd and rough,
> Give him a Scotch pebble, it's more than enough.
> And jewels to Pitt, Hastings justly refuses,
> For he has already more gifts than he uses.'
> > Derry down, &c.

> " ' But run, Jenky, run ! ' adds the King in delight,
> ' Bring the queen and the princesses here for a sight ;
> They never would pardon the negligence shown,
> If we kept from their knowledge so glorious a stone.
> > Derry down, &c.

> " ' But guard the door, Jenky, no credit we'll win,
> If the prince in a frolic should chance to step in :
> The boy to such secrets of state we 'll ne'er call,
> Let him wait till he gets our crown, income, and all.'
> > Derry down, &c.

> " In the princesses run, and, surprised, cry, ' O la !
> ' 'Tis as big as the egg of a pigeon, papa ! '
> ' And a pigeon of plumage worth plucking is he,'
> Replies our good monarch, ' who sent it to me.'
> > Derry down, &c.

" Madam Schwellenberg peep'd through the door at a chink,
And tipp'd on the diamond a sly German wink ;
As much as to say, ' Can we ever be cruel
To him who has sent us so glorious a jewel !'
　　　　　　　　Derry down, &c.

" Now, God save the queen ! while the people I teach,
How the king may grow rich while the Commons impeach ;
Then let nabobs go plunder, and rob as they will,
And throw in their diamonds as grist to his mill.
　　　　　　　　Derry down, &c."

The extreme frugality of the King and Queen in private life, and the meanness which often characterized their dealings, had already become subjects of popular satire, and contrasted strongly with the reckless extravagance of the Prince of Wales. This became still more generally a subject of conversation, when, in the session of 1786, an application was made to the House of Commons for a large sum of money to clear off the King's debts, which in spite of the now enormous civil list, he had latterly incurred. As there was no visible outlet by which so much money could have disappeared, people soon made a variety of surmises to account for King George's heavy expenditure ;

some said that the money was spent privately in corrupting Englishmen to pave the way to arbitrary power, and most people believed that their monarch was making large savings out of the public money, and hoarding them up either here or at Hanover. It was said that the royal pair were so greedy in the acquisition of money, that they condescended to make a profit by farming; and the royal farmer and his wife figured about rather extensively in prints and songs.

FARMER GEORGE AND HIS WIFE.

In these the royal pair are represented as haggling with their tradesmen, and cheapening their merchandize. Pictures represented them as visiting the shops at Windsor, to make their bargains in person.

Carlton House, as has just been observed, presented a very different scene, for the Prince of Wales seemed ambitious only of taking the lead in every wild extravagance and fashionable vice that characterized the age in which he lived. With the tradition of the family feuds, which seemed inseparable from the history of the princes of the House of Brunswick, the prince was on very bad terms with the King, his father, and more especially with the Queen. They disliked him because he was profligate; they disliked his politics, and they disliked him still more because he took for his companions the very men towards whom King George nourished the greatest aversion. In 1783, when the coalition ministry was in power, and the prince had just come of age, the ministers proposed that he should have a settlement of a hundred thousand a-year; but the King insisted on allowing him no more than fifty thousand, making him dependent on his bounty for the surplus. From this moment the prince became the inseparable friend and companion of Charles Fox, and among his principal associates were Sheridan and Lord North. The King and Queen were further irritated by the report of the prince's private marriage—which, of course, could not be a legal one—with Mrs. Fitzherbert. This was a sore subject at Court; and even Pitt was encouraged to look at the prince with some sort of disdain. The ministerial writers were by no means sparing in their allusions, and the failings of the heir-apparent were laid open to the public in frequent paragraphs in the newspapers. As might be expected, the prince was rapidly involving himself in debt, and his difficulties had become so great in the summer of 1786, that he found it necessary to apply to the King for assistance; but he met with a peremptory refusal. In his distress, the Duke of Orleans, proverbial for his immense riches and for his dissipation, who had been in England as Duke of Chartres in 1783 and 1784, and had then formed a close intimacy with the Prince of Wales, and who was now again on a visit to this country, offered his assistance, and the prince appears to have been only prevented by the earnest expostulations of some of his private friends from borrowing a large sum of money of the French prince to relieve himself.

When he found that no assistance was to be expected from the King, the Prince of Wales determined to make a show of magnanimity, and adopted the resolution of suppressing his household establishment, and retiring into a life of strict economy. The works at Carlton House were stopped, the state apartments shut up, and his race-horses, hunters, and even his coach-horses, were sold by public auction. He at the same time vested forty thousand a year—the greater part of his income—for the payment of his debts. The prince's friends, and a large portion even of the populace—for, in spite of his irregularities, the prince was at this time far from unpopular,—trumpeted him forth as the model of honesty and noble self-denial. But the King was highly displeased, and the prince's conduct was represented at Court as a mere peevish exhibition of spleen, and as an attempt to make the King and his ministers unpopular. The press—that portion of it which was under government influence—published forth the prince's failings in an indecent manner; his riotous life, his connexion with Mrs. Fitzherbert, and all his promiscuous amours, were commented upon, and represented in not very decorous prints and caricatures, which again were imitated in others of a far more vulgar character. The supposed alliance with Mrs. Fitzherbert was more especially an object of pictorial scandal; the prejudices of the mob were worked upon by representations of the danger which threatened the constitution from the marriage of the heir-apparent with a Catholic, which was represented as being the work of Fox and Sheridan. Burke, under the character of a Jesuit, was seen officiating at the marriage, and blessing the union. The alleged poverty of the prince, it was said, had not put a stop to his riotous living, and his doings at Brighton during the autumn —for Brighton was already his favourite place of residence— were not overlooked. In one print, said to be by Gillray, the party at Brighton are pictured (in allusion to the prince's cir- cumstances) as "The Jovial Crew; or, Merry Beggars" The

LANDING AT BOTANY BAY.

prince's companions are Mrs. Fitzherbert, Fox, Sheridan, Burke, Lord North, Captain Morris, and two others. Several other well-executed engravings, undoubtedly by Gillray, embody severe attacks on the prince and his friends. One, published on the 1st of November, 1786, and entitled " Non-commission officers embarking for Botany Bay," represents the same party, with the exception of the lady, setting out in a boat for the newly-established penal settlement. The prince is here seated on a butt of "imperial tokay ;" and Burke is equipped in a bishop's mitre. A sequel to this, published on the 16th of November, is entitled "Landing at Botany Bay." The prince and his party are now arrived at their destination. A man who takes the lead carries a standard inscribed, "The Majesty of the People." He is followed by Burke, with his mitre and pastoral staff, who reads the service from the Newgate Calendar. Captain Morris comes next, with the legs and lower extremities of a goat. The prince is carried on shore on the shoulders of two convicts, supported on each side by Fox and North, the former equipped in armour. The ship which had borne them over the ocean is entitled the "Coalition Transport—C⁴ Morris, Commander."

Captain Morris was now the constant attendant on the prince's revelry, which he enlivened by his songs and by his wit. Both,

it is hardly necessary to say, were too often of a licentious description; but the captain's minstrelsy deserved the reputation it enjoyed among his contemporaries. He was the best song-writer of his day, and many of his effusions have been thrown into unmerited oblivion. At the time of which we are now speaking, in the first struggles between Whigs and Tories under the ministerial dictatorship of William Pitt, he composed more political songs than at any other period. The above portrait is taken from

CAPTAIN MORRIS.

a sketch by Gillray, in 1790, and represents the minstrel in the moment of joviality. Amongst other caricatures against the prince was one published on the 18th of January, 1787, in which he is represented in the character of the prodigal son, compelled to tend upon and associate with swine. Near him are the "prince's feathers," thrown into the dirt; and the inscription on his garter is reduced to the word "*honi*." Amid the shoal of such caricatures, of which the Prince of Wales was at this time made the butt, those published in his defence, or, rather against his alleged persecutors, were comparatively few, and not very remarkable. But there is a large and rare print, published in 1786, and understood to be a work of Gillray (who not unfrequently worked for both sides of the question), entitled "A New Way to pay the National Debt." The King and Queen, attended by their band of pensioners, are issuing from the Treasury gateway, all so laden with money that it is rolling out of their pockets. Pitt, nevertheless, is adding large bags of the national revenue to the royal stores, to the very evident joy of their majesties. On the wall, on this side of the picture, are

THE PRODIGAL SON.

several torn placards, one entitled "Charity, a romance;" another contains the commencement of "God save the King." One, that is not torn, has the announcement, "From Germany, just arrived, a large and royal assortment . . . .;" and another professes to contain the "Last dying speech of fifty-four male-factors executed for robbing of a hen-roost;" an allusion to the severity with which the most trifling depredators on the King's private farm were prosecuted. Beneath them is seated a crippled soldier, seeking in vain for relief. On the other side of the picture, a little in the background, we see the prince, all tattered and torn, left by his father in poverty, and receiving the offer of a check for two hundred thousand pounds from a foreigner, the courtly Duke of Orleans. Behind them, the walls are also placarded. On one bill we read, "Œconomy, an old song;" on another, "British property, a farce;" on a third, "Just published, for the benefit of posterity, 'The dying groans of liberty;" and two torn bills immediately over the prince's head bear, one, the prince's feathers, with the altered motto, "Ich starve;" the other, two hands joined, with the word "Orleans" underneath. This bitterly satirical picture is stated to be "design'd by Helogabalis," and "executed by Sejanus." The allusions are sufficiently obvious.

POVERTY RELIEVED.

After the prince had carried on his œconomical project some months, finding that it had little effect upon the court, he agreed with his confidential advisers that the subject should be laid before the House of Commons. This was accordingly done on the 20th of April, 1787, by Alderman Newnham, who gave notice of a motion for an address to the King, praying him to take the situation of the prince into consideration, and to grant him such relief as he in his wisdom should think fit. This proceeding appears to have thrown the Court into great embarrassment. On the 24th, Pitt brought up the question again, declaring that the prince would receive no assistance from the government; pressed Newnham to drop his intended motion; and held out a threat that if he did otherwise, he (Pitt) should be driven to the disclosure of circumstances which he should have thought it otherwise his duty to conceal. On the 27th, Alderman Newnham acquainted the House with the purport of his intended motion; on which Mr. Rolle, the member for Devonshire, a pertinacious supporter of all the measures of the Court, and the hero of the very remarkable satire entitled "The Rolliad" (already mentioned), spoke against the introduction of such a motion, declaring that the question involved matter tending immediately to affect the constitution in church and state. This was understood to refer to the rumoured marriage with Mrs. Fitzherbert. Pitt supported Rolle, and again talked of the delicate investigation which he wished to avoid. On this, the Prince's friends, Sheridan and Fox, fired up, and a

E E 2

warm debate ensued, in the course of which Fox and Sheridan denied that the prince was married to Mrs. Fitzherbert; a declaration which was never believed by the mass of the people. They declared, moreover, that the prince was ready to submit to any investigation, and that the motion should be persevered in. This statement had its desired effect; the ministry determined not to expose themselves to the inconveniences that might arise from the discussion of the motion itself, and, by the King's desire, Pitt had an interview with the Prince of Wales, who consented that the motion should be withdrawn on the express promise that everything should be settled to his royal highness's satisfaction. On the 24th of May, the House of Commons agreed to an address to the King to allow the prince a hundred and sixty-one thousand pounds out of the civil list, to defray his debts, and twenty thousand pounds to complete the works at Carlton House, it being understood that he had promised to refrain from contracting debts in future. Thus ended, not very much to the credit of any party, an affair which for some months had drawn public attention from other matters.* The prince and his friends had sacrificed the character of Mrs. Fitzherbert, much, as it was said, to her indignation; and several pamphlets were published, one by Horne Tooke, vindicating her honour from the blot it had sustained from the light in which her connexion with the Prince of Wales was placed by the declarations of his friends in the House of Commons.

With the parliamentary session of 1787, Burke re-commenced his attack upon Warren Hastings. Pitt had already acknowledged that the second charge involved sufficient grounds for an accusation; and when, on the 7th of February, this second charge, relating to the spoliation of the Begum, or Princess, of Oude, had been brought forwards in the wonderful speech of Sheridan, admired equally for its length, its perspicuity, and its poetry,—by which, no doubt, the sins of the governor-general were clothed in intensely exaggerated horror,—in the adjourned debate on the following night, the premier declared his full con-

---

* On the 2nd of August, 1786, when the prince's affairs were first in agitation, and soon after the reduction of his domestic establishment, occurred the very feeble attempt to assassinate the King, made by a mad woman, Margaret Nicholson. It was made the utmost use of by the ministers to strengthen themselves and the Crown, and addresses of congratulation were got up from every corner of the kingdom, to a degree that had never been witnessed before. The King was so much offended at the prince, that he did not allow any communication to be made to him on the subject; and when the latter repaired to Windsor, to give his personal congratulations on the escape, it is said that the King refused to admit him to his presence.

THE POLITICAL BANDITTI ASSAILING THE SAVIOUR OF "YDIA

viction of the criminality of the accused; and charge after charge was now carried against him, until at the end of the session it was resolved that ulterior proceedings should be immediately commenced. On the 10th of May, Burke accordingly repaired to the bar of the House of Lords, and, in the name of the House of Commons, and of all the Commons of Great Britain, impeached Warren Hastings of high crimes and misdemeanours, at the same time announcing that the Commons would with all convenient speed exhibit articles against him.

The trial of Warren Hastings took place in Westminster Hall, which was fitted up for the occasion with great magnificence, and commenced on the 13th of February, 1788. Burke's preliminary speech occupied four days, and produced an extraordinary effect on all his hearers. The Benares charge, and that relating to the Begums of Oude, were proceeded with in February and April. The proceedings, as a matter of course, closed with the session of Parliament. Domestic events at home, and, after them, still more extraordinary events abroad, came to retard the progress of the impeachment. The dissolution of Parliament in 1790, while the trial was still pending, created a further embarrassment; the parties originally united in the prosecution broke up their mutual friendship; the public indignation, which at first they had so effectively stirred up, gradually cooled, or was turned off into other channels,—and, after dragging on feebly through several subsequent years, it ended in the April of 1795 in an acquittal on all the charges.

The party in Parliament, who were believed to represent the King's private feelings, and especially the Lord Chancellor Thurlow, had defended Hastings throughout his trial,—thus leaving no doubt of the royal sentiments. It is difficult to assign any very plausible motives for the part acted by Pitt, and especially for his sudden change at the commencement of the trial; but it is a very remarkable circumstance that, of the two great political caricaturists, while Gillray (who first took part with Hastings) changed with the minister, and subsequently published caricatures against him, Sayer, although notoriously patronized by Pitt, continued to the end to ridicule the accusers. Some of the earlier works of the latter artist on this subject are too minute in their allusions to interest us much at the present day.

On the 11th of May, 1786, Gillray published one of the best of his earlier prints, under the title of "The political banditti assaulting the saviour of India," in which Warren Hastings is represented as defending himself with the shield of honour

against Burke, who fires a blunderbuss at him in front, while
Fox is attacking him with a dagger from behind. Lord North,
in the mean time, is robbing him of some of his money-bags.
The supporters of the impeachment represented Hastings as
another Verres, called upon by the modern Cicero to answer for

A MODERN CICERO AGAINST VERRES.

his oppressive government of the provinces entrusted to his
care. A bold sketch of the orator was published on the 7th of
February, 1787,—the day on which proceedings against Hastings
were resumed in the House of Commons,—under the title of
"Cicero against Verres." Fox and North are seen behind the
eloquent accuser. In 1788, the year of the impeachment, the

BLOOD ON THUNDER.

caricatures on this subject
became more numerous.
One by Gillray, published
on the 1st of March, under
the title of "Blood on
Thunder fording the Red
Sea," represents Hastings
carried in safety on the
shoulders of the Lord Chancellor Thurlow through a
sea of blood, strewed with
the bodies of mangled In-
dians. In another print by
Gillray, entitled "A Dish
of Mutton-chops," the head
of King George is served on
a dish at a table, round
which sit Pitt, Hastings,

and Thurlow; the premier is eating the tongue, while Hastings is employed in picking out the eyes, and the chancellor devours the brains. Among those published by Sayer at this period were, 1. a print, published on the 11th of April, entitled, "The Managers in distress, in which Burke, Fox, and his fellow-accusers are thrown from the bridge they designed to pass over, owing to the giving way of the piers. Fox exclaims, "D——n the piers, they wont support us!" 2. "The first Charge," published on the 14th of April, and relating to a rather frivolous article of accusation, that an Indian prince had been deprived of his hookah, or pipe, and so hindered from smoking. The accuser (Burke), with one of his most energetic gestures, eloquently appeals to the feelings of his audience—"Guilty of not suffering him to smoke for—two days!" 3. One published on the 26th of April, under the title of "A Reverie," an allusion

A Benares Flea.   A Begum Wart.   Begum's Tears.   An Ouzle.

OBJECTS MAGNIFIED.

to some curious information produced by Burke relating to the private history of the Begum or princess. 4. "The Princess's Bow, alias the Bow Begum," published on the 1st of May, and representing the Eastern princess seated, and receiving the homage of Burke, Fox, and Sheridan; beneath her seat we perceive the face of Sir Philip Francis, the bitter personal enemy of Hastings, and the prompter in many of the proceedings against him: he says, "I am at the bottom of all this!" On the wall above hangs a picture, illustrative of the old saying, "*Parturiunt montes, nascetur ridiculus mus.*" 5. "The Galante Show," published on the 6th of May. This is the best of the set; it represents Burke as the showman, exhibiting, by means of a magic lantern, the magnified figures of different objects on the wall. The objects are, "A Benares Flea," which takes the form of an elephant; a Begum wart, as large as Olympus, Pelion, and Ossa piled one on the other; "Begum's Tears," of proportionate dimensions; and "an ouzle," which appears in the semblance of a whale. The spectators are delighted with the exhibition; one remarks that the objects are "finely magnified;" another exclaims, with poignant feelings, on observing the dimensions of the tears, "Poor ladies—they have cried their eyes out!" a third, evidently intended to represent Lord Derby, remarks, that the last object is "very like an ouzle."

In 1795, at the end of the trial, Sayer published a large print, entitled "The last scene of the manager's farce," in which the bust of Warren Hastings is represented rising pure from the black clouds of calumny with which it had been obscured, and now surrounded with a halo of glory. Above are two figures in the characters of good and bad angels, Thurlow and Loughborough, the former declaring, "Not black, upon my honour!" the latter, "Black, upon my honour!" The clouds of darkness are rising from a cauldron, filled with the various charges as so many poisonous ingredients, more of which are in the hand of the conjurer (Burke), who is described as "one of the managers and a principal performer; who, having out-Heroded Herod, retires from the stage in a passion at seeing the farce likely to be damned." The conjurer and his cauldron are sinking through trap-doors in the stage; the latter is inscribed with the words, "*Exit in fumo.*" Fox appears in the manager's box as "another manager, a great actor, very anxious about the fate of the farce." Behind him are several "other managers, very well dressed, but not very capital performers, some of them tired of

A SNAIL'S PROGRESS.

acting." The face of Sir Philip Francis is seen peeping from behind a scene— "the prompter, no character in the farce, but very useful behind the scenes." The manager's box is old and torn; a rat has made its way through the crevices, and holds in its mouth one of the tickets of admission to the trial in Westminster Hall; and a snail, gradually crawling its slow course through year after year, 1787, 1788, 1789, and so on to 1795, represents the dull progress of this tiresome impeachment. Beneath the stage we have a glance of the evil one in a warm place, designated as "a court below, to which the managers retire upon quitting the stage." Satan mutters the rhyme,—

> " By the pricking of my thumbs,
> Something wicked this way comes!'

The trial of Warren Hastings was indeed, in its result, a farce, and an expensive one ; but, perhaps, like many other such farces, which have little utility in themselves, it was the cause of the reformation of much evil, and led the way to a more enlightened and just policy with respect to our eastern empire.

The proceedings against Warren Hastings were the only subject which produced much excitement during the spring and summer of the year 1786. The ministers continued to carry all their measures by large majorities, or without division ; and the opposition in the house was reduced almost to an opposition of words. Out of Parliament, however, the feeling of discontent at this state of things was gaining ground upon the strong reaction which had taken place at the beginning of Pitt's reign, and the subject of parliamentary reform, which had been driven out of the House of Commons, was in public canvassed more and more every day. The more general publication of the debates in Parliament fostered the liberal spirit, and gave the speeches of the opposition a weight out of doors which they seemed no longer to possess within. The accusations against the court and ministers, of purchasing power by corrupt means, were repeated more extensively, and it was commonly believed that no small portion of the burdensome civil list was expended for this purpose. A clever caricature by Gillray was published on the 2nd of May, 1786, under the title of "Market-Day—every man has his price;" in which the ministerial supporters are represented as horned cattle exposed for sale. The scene is laid in Smithfield ; and the dark, scowling figure of Chancellor Thurlow, as the state farmer, stands forth as the principal purchaser. At the window of a public-house adjoining appear Pitt and Dundas, a jovial pair, drinking and smoking, as if almost regardless of the scene. Hastings is riding off with the King, in the guise of a calf which he has purchased ; the influence of Indian money and diamonds on the palace was an article of universal belief. Fox,

A BUYER OF CATTLE.

Burke, and Sheridan are thrown from a sort of van, on which they were driving, by the overwhelming rush of the cattle.

The appointment of Lord Hood in the beginning of July to a place at the board of Admiralty, rendered necessary a new election for the city of Westminster, when that city was contested on the opposition interest by Lord John Townshend. The latter was well supported by his friends and party; and, after an obsti-

nate canvass, the Court candidate was thrown out by a very large majority. This was a severe defeat to the ministers, who are said to have used every kind of influence to secure the return of Lord Hood. On the 14th of August, ten days after the close of the poll, the corrupt practices of the ministerial agents on this occasion drew forth from Gillray a caricature with the title, "Election troops bringing in their accounts to the pay-table." A motley assemblage, consisting of newspaper-writers, soldiers, ballad-singers, mob-exciters, false voters, Jews, and a variety of other characters, besiege the door of the Treasury. Among the rest, a worthy disciple of St. Crispin, with the cockade of Lord Hood in

AN INDEPENDENT VOTER.   his hat, presents a claim "for voting three times;" a practice which appears to have prevailed among this constituency on a large scale.

It was just at the moment when the proceedings against Warren Hastings absorbed public attention, that Gillray brought out a remarkable caricature, the only object of which appears to have been to bring together, in a sort of unnatural familiarity, the figures of the persons at that moment most strongly contrasted by political antipathies, personal intrigues, or other causes. This print, which is now become one of the rarest of Gillray's works (because probably its form renders it more difficult to preserve from injury,) is entitled "The Installation Supper, as given at the Pantheon by the knights of the Bath, on the 26th of May, 1788." To explain the title, it may be observed that there had been a grand installation of knights of the Bath in Westminster Abbey on the 19th of May; and that the satirist supposes them to have given a supper in consequence. The Pantheon, the well-known scene of Mrs. Cornelys's masquerades, had witnessed many assemblies which presented an appearance equally anomalous with that here offered to our view. At a long table, not over-well provided with the good things of this world, the company is distributed in groups of

gentlemen and ladies in familiar conversation, generally so
selected as to form the greatest outrage upon probability. Near
one extremity, the leaders of the two grand political parties, Fox

FRIENDSHIP BEHIND THE BACK.

and Pitt, whose mutual personalities at this time so frequently
disturbed the equanimity of the House of Commons, are quietly
hob-nobbing behind the back of the gruff chancellor, Thurlow,
while the latter is eagerly employed on the contents of his plate,

WANT AND ABUNDANCE.

totally unaware of this singular conciliation. Almost at the
other end of the table sits the ex-governor of India, Warren

Hastings, and his lady all bedizened with diamonds. Hastings has appropriated to himself a whole ham; and his antagonist, Burke, who sits solitary and unserved on the opposite side of the table, is petitioning in vain for a share in the spoil. Others of the remarkable men, and of the remarkable women, are easily recognised. The Duke of Richmond is seen in close conference with his political antagonist, Lord Rawdon. Lord Shelburne shakes hands with Lord Sydney; and Lord Derby is closely engaged in conversation with Lady Mount Edgecumbe, an antiquated member of the *bon-ton*, who still dreamt of conquest. The princes are each seated between a couple of ladies; the Prince of Wales, besieged by Lady Archer (of gambling memory) on his right, and Lady Cecilia Johnson on his left, listlessly picks his teeth with his fork. Next to them Mrs. Fitzherbert is conversing in the most amiable familiarity with the ex-patriot, Alderman Wilkes.

A PRINCE CLOSE BESET.

Since the arrangement of his debts, and while the unsupported eloquence of the opposition fell harmless upon the all-powerful ministers, the Prince of Wales had become to a certain degree reconciled with his father, and he was received at court; but a few months brought about a new and very serious cause of rupture. On the 11th of July the King had prorogued the Parliament to the 25th of September, and it was thence re-prorogued to the 20th of November. The two Houses met at that time under circumstances of extraordinary embarrassment. As early as the month of July a change was observed in the King's health which gave considerable uneasiness to his physicians, who recommended a progress to Cheltenham, in the hope that he might derive benefit as well from the change of scene as from drinking the mineral waters. The King had at an early period in his reign given some slight indications of a tendency to mental derangement; and that tendency seems to have been confirmed, rather than relieved, by the excitement caused by the enthusiastic greetings with which he was received in the country through which he had to pass. Early in October, after his return, the symptoms became much more alarming, and by the

end of the month the truth began to be whispered abroad, and
hints of the insanity of the highest personage in the realm found
their way into the newspapers. At length, on the 5th of November, while seated at the dinner-table with his family, the
King became suddenly delirious, and from this moment he
remained in a state in which he could be communicated with by
none but his physicians. The condition of the sovereign was
publicly known before the period for the assembly of Parliament,
and the greatest anxiety was felt throughout the kingdom.
When the two houses met on the 20th of November, they
adjourned to the 4th of December, without entering upon business of any kind; on that day a report of the privy council
relating to the King's malady was laid on the table, and they
adjourned again till the 8th. From this time parliament was
occupied in anxious deliberation, without even taking its usual
holidays at Christmas.

The two great political parties were suddenly thrown in face
of each other under very extraordinary circumstances. It was
generally feared that there was no hope of the King's recovery;
and the Prince of Wales, as heir-apparent to the throne, being
of age, was naturally the person who would be selected, as regent,
to exercise the royal authority. Pitt, who was neither personally
nor politically the prince's friend, knew well that his nomination
to the regency was tantamount to the dismissal of his ministry,
and the return of the Whigs under Fox to power. He was
anxious, therefore, either to shut the door against him, or, if
that could not be done, to restrict as much as possible his power
of action. He hardly condescended to conceal his motives from
the world. The opposition, on the other hand, were already
exulting in the prospect of place; and Fox, who was on a tour
in Italy for the benefit of his health, was hurried home in a
condition ill able to bear the fatigue and excitement which
awaited him. In their haste to drive out their opponents, the
leaders of the liberal party blindly took up a doctrine which
was quite inconsistent with their usual principles, and which
probably under other circumstances they would have combated
with the greatest pertinacity; they asserted that the prince, as
next heir to the throne, had an inherent right to the regency,
and that his right did not depend upon the will of the Parliament; and, in defence of this doctrine, Fox put forth his
eloquence, and Burke his invective. Pitt and the Tories, with
equal inconsistency, threw themselves on the most popular principles of the constitution, and asserted that the prince had no
more right of himself to assume the government than any other

individual in the country; but that the right of providing for the government of the country, in cases where it was thus suddenly interrupted, belonged to the peers and to the nation at large, through its representatives, and was to be regulated entirely by their discretion. It was simply two factions striving for power, neither of which cared to abide by abstract principles as long as these stood in the way of their ambition. The debates were consequently warm, and often personal. Fox, at the commencement, had hastily and rashly used words to the effect that the Prince of Wales possessed the inherent right to assume the government, or, at least, expressions that admitted of that interpretation. Scarcely had the words escaped his lips, when the features of the proud and stiff premier gave place to an unusual smile, and slapping his thigh with exultation, he exclaimed to a member who was seated next to him, " I'll un-Whig the gentleman for the rest of his life." During the rest of the debates, he confuted Fox's arguments by asserting the extreme doctrines of the liberal party. Fox's remarks were commented upon in the same spirit by Lord Camden in the House of Lords. On the 12th of December Fox rose in his place in the House of Commons, and recurred to this matter to protest against the construction which had been placed upon his words; he stated, that he did not say that the prince might *assume* the administration in consequence of his Majesty's temporary incapacity, but that the *right of administration* subsisted in him, and the assertion of his having such right to govern was different from saying that he might assume the reins of government,—he had the right, but not the possession, which latter he could not legally take without the sanction of Parliament,—he might appeal to the two Houses to recognise his claim, in the same manner as persons who are entitled to particular species of property apply, before they take possession, to the proper court for a formal investiture,—the adjudication of his right belonged to the Parliament.

This explanation was far from answering the full purpose for which it was designed; people still looked upon Fox's original declaration as a temporary assertion of ultra-Tory principles to serve an object; and they now accused him of trying to escape the consequences by eating his own words. Among the multitude of caricatures which appeared on this occasion, one represents him under the title of "The Word-eater," exhibiting his skill before the assembled legislature, and holding in his hands his "speech" and his "explanation." It is accompanied with an

"ADVERTISEMENT EXTRAORDINARY.

"This is to inform the public, that this extraordinary phenomenon is just arrived from the Continent, and exhibits every day during the sittings of the House of Commons before a select company. To give a complete detail of his wonderful talents would far exceed the bounds of an advertisement, as indeed they surpass the powers of description. He eats single words and evacuates them so as to have a contrary meaning—for example, of the word *treason* he can make *reason*, and of *reason* he can make *treason*.* He can also eat whole sentences, and will again produce them either with a double, different, or contradictory meaning ; and is equally capable of performing the same operation on the largest volumes and libraries. He purposes, in the course of a few months, to exhibit in public for the benefit and amusement of the electors of Westminster, when he will convince his friends of his great abilities in this new art, and will provide himself with weighty arguments for his enemies."

Towards the end of the year, numbers of caricatures were launched against the adherents of the Prince of Wales, satirizing their eagerness for power, their presumed designs, and the prospects of the country under such a government as the Whigs desired. One of these, entitled "A Touch on the Times," and published on the 29th of December, 1788, appears to have been very popular, as there was, at least, one imitation of it. Britannia is represented as handing the prince to the throne, which her lion seems to bear with anything but equanimity. The foundation step of the throne, on which the prince is placing his foot, is, "The voice of the people ;" the second step, " Public safety," is cracked and broken ; the emblem of virtue, inscribed on the back of the throne, is a full purse. The prince is backed by a motly group of pretenders to patriotism, who seek to benefit by his accession : one, who carries the ensign of liberty, is purloining the prince's handkerchief from his royal pocket. The genius of commerce sits in the corner, a victim to gin-drinking.

COMMERCE UNDER THE REGENCY.

When the minister had demonstrated by the force of his majorities that the ap-

* Fox, in one of the debates on this occasion, had accused Pitt of uttering doctrines that were a treason against the constitution.

pointment of a regency was a matter which lay entirely at the
discretion of Parliament, he next brought forwards a string of
resolutions, which, though obstinately opposed, were passed on
the 19th of January, and which had the effect of placing the
executive in the hands of the Prince of Wales, under restrictions
which deprived him of any substantial power, the latter being
either placed in abeyance, or given to the Queen, who was Pitt's
friend.   These resolutions were,—"That as the personal exercise of the Crown is retarded by the illness of his Majesty, the
Prince of Wales be requested to take upon himself, during the
continuance of his Majesty's illness, and in his name (as a
regent), the execution of all the royalties, functions, and constitutional authorities of the King, under such restrictions as shall
be hereafter mentioned.   That the Regent shall be prevented
from conferring any honours or additional marks of royal
favour, by grants of peerage, to any person, except to those of
his Majesty's issue who shall obtain the age of twenty-one.
That he shall be prevented from granting any patent place for
life, or any reversionary grant of any patent place, other than
such as required by law to be for life, and not during pleasure.
That the care of his Majesty being to be reposed in her Majesty,
the officers of his Majesty's household are to be under the
direction of her Majesty, and not subject to the control of the
Regent.   That the care of his Majesty be reposed in the Queen,
to be assisted with a council."

Pitt made no secret that his restrictions were mainly intended
to abridge the power that would fall into the hands of what he
almost openly designated as a cabal, and the speeches of the
ministerial party generally set out on the assumption that the
prince would be surrounded by bad advisers.   The prince himself was in a very ill-humour with the minister, and held
frequent consultations with the opposition.   When Pitt communicated to him his intentions, on the 30th of December, his
Royal Highness consented to take the regency, but expressed
strongly his dissatisfaction at the restrictions, in a letter which
is understood to have been written by Sheridan.   The general
feeling out of doors, except among the staunch adherents of the
opposition in Parliament, seems to have been against the prince;
but there were a few bitter caricatures on what was looked upon
by some as an unnecessary spoliation of the crown which he was
virtually to wear.   In some of these the prince was represented
as a child in leading-strings, placed under the guidance of
William Pitt.   In a bold print by Gillray, published on the 3rd
January, 1789, the premier is represented as on over-gorged

vulture, which has fixed its claw on the crown and sceptre, and is tearing the prince's feathers from his coronet.

THE VULTURE OF THE CONSTITUTION.

The more numerous class of caricatures, however, were directed against the party who demanded the unrestricted regency, and the person of the prince was by no means spared, even in publications which were known to come from people who were generally looked upon as acting under the immediate patronage or pay of the government. The private vices and weaknesses of the prince and his companions were again raked up and exhibited to the public. The former they represented as a mere tool in the hands of a parcel of political adventurers, who aimed at gratifying their own ambition at the expense of the constitution of their country. The circumstance, soon known, that the prince's letter to Pitt had been written by Sheridan, and shewn for approval to the other Whig leaders, was seized upon as another proof that he was not acting by his own independent judgment. Sayer, who we have already seen was an ultra-Pittite, and a paid one, represented the heir-apparent under the form of a horse (the old emblem of the family of Hanover), taught by Sheridan to write a letter "to Mr. Pitt," while Lord Derby, as a monkey, is perusing the rough draught. Beneath the table is a rat-trap, in which are captured several political rats. Under it is the announcement, "To be seen at Mr. S——n's (Sheridan's) menagery, the wonderful learned Han—r colt, who writes a letter blindfolded. N.B. He is in training for several other useful purposes. Also, a very curious monkey, who can read and write a little, and imitates the human voice. Also, several very extraordinary rats, from Holland, Buckinghamshire, Milton, and other places." This print was published on the 27th of January, 1789; Sayer had already introduced the Hanoverian colt in a

F F

caricature published on the 17th of January, under the title of " A mis-fire at the Constitution."

A CONVENIENT SCREEN.

Sheridan is here holding the colt by the head ; and Fox, as a bandit, is using it for a screen, while he aims over its back at the British lion, which is holding the rights of the people and supporting the insignia of royalty. Fox's discharge turns out but a flash in the pan. The royal colt is treading underfoot petitions and a vote of thanks to Mr. Pitt from the city of London. Sheridan treads on the "oath of allegiance ;" while a number of papers fall from his pocket, entitled " Paragraphs against the ministers," " Puffs direct for the P——e," "Oblique puffs for the P—— of W——," " Abuse of the ministers." It would appear from this that Sheridan was looked upon as the writer or prompter of a large portion of the newspaper paragraphs in the interest of the prince.

The rats in the caricature first mentioned allude to a number of little intrigues that were going on behind the curtain, among men who were anxious to secure their interests in the event of the prince ascending the throne. The greatest of political rats was the chancellor, Lord Thurlow. In the conviction that the King was past recovery, he at first held himself aloof under different excuses from the consultations of the Cabinet, and entered into secret communication with the prince, with the view of securing the chancellorship under the regency, to the exclusion of his rival, the Whig Lord Loughborough, who, it was universally understood, was to take the office of lord chancellor, whenever his party came into power. The prince's advisers snatched at the prospect of detaching Thurlow from the ministerial party, and gave encouragement to his advances. When Fox arrived from Italy, he found things in this state ; and, strongly prejudiced against Thurlow, he was persuaded only with difficulty to use his personal influence in prevailing with Lord Loughborough to waive his claims for the present. The Whigs, however, soon saw reason to be distrustful of Thurlow, and

Loughborough was restored to his hopes of the chancellorship. Thurlow, now perceiving that he was losing ground with his own party, and not really gaining ground with the other, and having obtained some rather strong glimpses of a near prospect of the restoration of the King to his mental faculties, suddenly appeared on the woolsack with all his old zeal for the ministers, and gave his utmost support to Pitt's regency bill.

This bill was brought into the House of Commons on the 5th of February, and it increased the number of restrictions and enumerated them in greater detail. One clause restrained the regent from marrying a Papist, and in committee the zealous Mr. Rolle, still harping upon the old story of Mrs. Fitzherbert, moved to introduce a paragraph, providing that the regent should be incapacitated if he "is or shall be married in law or fact to a Papist." This amendment, though rejected at once, was a fruitful subject of new scandal out of doors. After several very hot debates, the bill passed the Commons on the 12th of February. It had scarcely reached the other House, when the reports of the King's recovery became stronger, and the Lords adjourned from day to day, until the 10th of March, when the complete restoration of the King was officially announced, and the Parliament regularly opened by commission, with a speech from the throne. The regency bill was immediately thrown aside, and the country was relieved from a great embarrassment, which must, under the circumstances, have led to much confusion. One important result of the agitation of the question, was the establishment of a great principle in the constitution, which was thus stamped with the sanction of that party in the state who might have been expected to be most decidedly opposed to it.

The embarrassment of the situation was increased by the somewhat factious conduct of the Parliament of Ireland, where both Houses, it has been supposed at the secret instigation of Burke, and by the active intervention of Grattan, had passed resolutions in the precise spirit of the opposition in England, for addresses to the Prince of Wales, to request him to assume of his own right the regency of Ireland, without any restrictions. The lord-lieutenant refused to be the medium of transmission; and the two Houses elected a deputation to wait on the prince in London, where he received them with marked favour, but informed them of the circumstances which now rendered their measures unnecessary. This was contrasted with the cold manner in which he had received the English deputation under Mr. Pitt. The prince's conduct throughout had been most obnoxious to the Queen, and gave great offence to the King, who, after his recovery, expressed very openly his displeasure. The caricatures and satirical paragraphs against the prince and his party, were repeated with new spirit and violence. In one of these, published by Gillray on the 29th of April, under the title of "The Funeral Procession of Miss Regency," the bier is preceded by Burke, who, as a Jesuit priest, under the title of "Ignatius Loyola," reads the service of the dead. The chief mourner is entitled "The Princess of W—s,"—it is Mrs. Fitzherbert; the second mourners are Fox and Sheridan, who are designated as "The rival Jacobites." There is an allusion throughout to the rumours relating to Mrs. Fitzherbert, and the dangers with which the Protestant church was supposed to be threatened by the prince's connections.

The conduct of the Lord Chancellor Thurlow was not forgotten in the royal displeasure; and the confidence between him and his colleagues was never restored.

The rejoicing throughout England on the king's recovery was loud and universal, and the joy was certainly sincere. The metropolis was illuminated with unusual brilliancy on the 12th of March; and the spontaneous burst of devotion to the royal person which accompanied the grand procession to St. Paul's on the 25th of April, the day fixed for public thanksgiving, shewed how much the King had gained in popularity. The odes and poems, usual on such occasions, filled the journals of the day.*

The popularity of the ministers did not increase in the same proportion, for it was too evident to every one that they had

---

* Among these loyal effusions, the following is given as the *bonâ fide* production of an honest parish clerk in North Wales; it may, perhaps, be taken as a measure of the popular *feeling* among the mass, and the magazine in which it was printed thinks it "is not unworthy of being recorded."

"*Few lines upon the recovery of his Majesty upon the old poem way.*

"Happy recovery for the king,
   This matter is mighty surprising,
   God be thankd, 'tis the next thing
   As deliver the dead a living.

"Not by the facle turn of the faculty,
   It provd the providence of the Almighty,
   He has the mode of remedy,
   Or turn us to eternity.

"We ought not to thought such thing,
   As Pitt is to appoint us a sovring,
   Nor keen Fox has the fixing,
   God has the care to send us a king."

been actuated more by the spirit of political faction, which was equally prevalent with both parties, than by true patriotism. We must not overlook a rather celebrated caricature by Gillray, entitled "Minions of the Moon," published a little later (it is dated the 23rd of December, 1791), but generally understood to refer to this affair. It is a parody on Fuseli's picture of "The Weird Sisters," who are represented with the features of Dundas, Pitt, and Thurlow; they are contemplating the disc of the moon, which represents on the bright side the face of the Queen,

THE WEIRD SISTERS.

and on the shrouded side that of the King, now overcast with mental darkness. The three "minions" are evidently addressing their devotions to the brighter side.

CHAPTER XII.

GEORGE III.

The French Revolutionary Period—Effect of the Revolution in England—Desertions from the Liberal Party in Parliament; Burke's Philippics—Revolutionary Sympathy in England; Dr. Price, Dr. Priestley, and Thomas Paine—Anti-Gallican Agitation—Satires on the King and Queen—Agitation throughout the Country, and Government Measures affecting the Liberty of the Subject—Foreign Policy; War with France.

KING GEORGE awoke from the darkness of his mental malady to be a witness of the most fearful social storm that had struck Europe since the days when the broken empire of Rome was overrun by the barbarian hordes of the North. To the eyes of profound observers, France had been long labouring under a complication of evils, which must eventually lead to some great national calamity. Reckless corruption, and a selfish contempt of the interests of the people, had, during many years, been aggravating the irritation of the populace, while a school of so-called philosophers were as industriously disseminating principles which tended to undermine and dissolve the existing frame of society. The increasing difficulties of the domestic policy of France, was watched with interest in England, where one party looked upon it as a grand struggle between liberty and despotism; another, less zealous in the cause of the former, still rejoiced in the embarrassments at home, which hindered France from being formidable to her neighbours, while they felt a sort of exultation in seeing the government thus punished for the part it had acted in the war of American independence. Amid so many elements of discord, it was the misfortune of France to be governed by a weak monarch, in every respect unfitted to grapple with the difficulties of his position,—a people ill-disposed, an enormous national debt, and an administration filled with abuses, were the legacies bequeathed to him by his predecessors. A winter unusually severe, accompanied with famine and its other concomitant disasters, ushered in the year 1789, and drove the mass of the people to little short of despair. The French King endeavoured to avert the danger by repeated concessions, which always came too late, and only exposed to his discontented subjects the weakness of his position. The attention of Englishmen had been called from the affairs of France by the serious calamity which threatened them at home, and by the rejoicings after they had been relieved from their fears by the King's recovery; for several months the news from France had occupied but a secondary place among our foreign intelligence, when the extraordinary revolution of the months of June and July, came suddenly to astonish all classes of society in this country.

The French revolution at first excited considerable sympathy in England, although, as it proceeded, and its true character became developed, that sympathy soon diminished. During the latter part of the year 1789, the tone of the moderate English papers was decidedly favourable to the movement, which, it was believed, would end in the establishment of free institutions. Thus, the *European Magazine*, a periodical extremely moderate in its politics, makes the following reflections in the month of September:—"The political phenomenon exhibited by France, at this moment, is perfectly unparalleled throughout the annals of universal history. If the constitution now forming, under circumstances so peculiarly favourable, be finally established, if the deliberations and wisdom of the philosopher be not circumscribed by the intrigues of the politician, or destroyed by the sword of faction, the result will be a *chef-d'œuvre* of government."

The interest which the English populace felt in the troubles now going on in Paris, is shown by the frequency of allusions to them on the stage. In some instances the scenes of the incipient revolution were introduced in theatrical pageantry. The popularity of such representations, and the class they were intended to captivate, are testified by the words of an epilogue pronounced on the 21st of August, in the private theatre of Lord Barrymore, at Wargrave, in presence of the Prince of Wales, which places these subjects in the same category with wonderful animals, boxers, and wrestlers, in that age the favourite spectacles of the mob.

> "But though, all anxious, every nerve we strain,
> How can we hope your plaudits to obtain !
> Here the spectator no dark Bastille sees,
> *Pasteboard* Versailles, and canvas Tuileries;
> No keen remarks concerning French affairs;
> No dancing turkies and no drumming hares;
> Nor (as must fit in a gymnastic age)
> Does Ben with Johnson fist to fist engage ;
> Nor Humphreys here, Antæos-like, renew
> His stubborn contest with the rival Jew."

As we advance towards the end of the year, we find these attempts to bring French politics on the stage more frequent, and the feeling was evidently extending itself to the higher theatres; but at the same time the sentiments of the court begin to be apparent in the proscription of them. On the 13th of November, an opera, entitled "The Tale of St. Margaret," was brought out at Drury Lane in a mutilated form. It is stated in the periodicals of the day that this performance was originally designed for a representation of the assault and destruction of the Bastille, with which was blended the story of the Iron Mask; but, when it came before the licencer, every part of the piece that bore immediate resemblance to the late popular events in Paris, was, from political considerations, forbidden, and therefore it was "unavoidably brought forward in a maimed and mutilated state." The prologue, spoken by Bannister, concluded with the following lines, which tended to propitiate the power that had curtailed the piece, as well as the feelings of the populace. Britain, it says, stands as a blessed beacon amid the storm which was raging abroad.

> " Nations of freemen, yet unborn, shall own
> Thee parent of their rights.—Thou who alone,
> By storms surrounded, fixt on Albion's rock,
> With pity from on high behold'st the shock
> Of jarring elements—thyself at rest !
> Conscious that thou, above all nations blest,
> Free from revolt alike and slavish awe,
> Art doubly safe where liberty is law !"

An "occasional address" spoken at the Royal Circus in November, on occasion of one of these political representations, being intended more especially for the populace, was much stronger in its expression of sentiments.

> " How I have strove your kind applause to gain,
> The interest of the scene will best explain.
> To-night we lead you to a neighbouring shore,
> Where swelling Tyranny shall reign no more ;
> Where Liberty has made a glorious stand,
> And spread her lustre e'en o'er Gallic land.
> Yes ! Albion's spirit has at length inspired,
> Warm'd every heart, and every bosom fired.
> Oppression shrinks ; his hosts in terror fly,
> And France is blest with England's liberty !
> The goddess, rising in her native charms,
> In one bright moment called her sons to arms.
> True to her call, her glorious sons obey,
> Beneath her banners work their rapid way.
> And, oh, for ever be the band adored
> Who first the Bastille's horrid cells explored,

> Freed each pale inmate from a wretched doom,
> And fixed their fame for ages yet to come. —
> Such glowing scenes to paint be ours to try.
> Oh, should they move the heart, impearl the eye,
> With gratitude increased we'll nightly strive
> To keep the blest emotions still alive !
> What scene more suited to a British stage,
> Than that where Freedom glows with honest rage ;
> Warms a whole kingdom to confess its cause,
> And fix indelible its sacred laws,
> Firm as the rocks which girt our Albion's shore,
> To stand revered till time shall be no more !
> Oh ! may such laws to other shores extend,
> And prove to all a universal friend !
> May proud Oppression from his throne be hurl'd,
> And Freedom reign—the mistress of the world !"

The same call for stage representation of French politics, and
the same jealousy on the part of the government, extended into
the provinces. At Bath, on the 2nd of November, the following
lines of an epilogue to the tragedy of " Earl Goodwin," were
expunged by command of the Lord Chamberlain, and were not
allowed to be spoken in the theatre.

> " Lo ! the poor Frenchman, long our nation's jest,
> Feels a new passion throbbing in his breast ;
> From slavish, tyrant, priestly fetters free,
> For *Vive le roi !* cries *Vive la liberté !*
> And daring now to act as well as feel,
> Crushes the convent and the dread Bastille."

In theatres of a less public character, other sentiments were
occasionally pronounced. At Mr. Fector's " private " theatre
at Dover, at a representation on the 4th of November, an
epilogue closed with the lines,—

> " But can we sit supine at others' woe ?
> For royal sufferings loyal tears will flow ;
> A generous nation mourns a fallen foe.
> With grief our sympathising bosoms wring
> At the sad fate of Gallia's captive king.
> The monarch's palace is no prison here,
> Free as his people—what has George to fear ?
> His happy home no fishwomen beset,
> Virtue and worth dissever faction's net ;
> Beloved he executes the sacred trust,
> And foes proclaim him both benign and just.
> Oh, may our loyalty its charm diffuse,
> And every daring demagogue confuse ;
> In every clime defeat sedition's plan,
> Preserve the peace, and guard the rights of man."

The leaders of both the great political parties seem at first to have accepted the French revolution as a good omen for the future prospects of Europe, although their eyes were soon opened to the real character of the movement, and the dangers that were engendered by it. For some time, however, they spoke with caution, and seemed anxious to avoid every occasion of bringing the subject into discussion, however strongly several of them may have expressed themselves in private. When the parliament opened on the 21st of January, 1790, the speech from the throne omitted even the name of France, though it spoke of the "continued assurances of the good disposition of all foreign powers," but a passing allusion was made to "the internal situation of different parts of Europe." The addresses of both houses were agreed to with slight discussions; the movers spoke of the excellence of the English constitution, and compared the constitutional liberty enjoyed in this country with the anarchy and licentiousness which reigned in France. Most of the speakers took it for granted that it had been the intention of the revolutionists to form a government in imitation of our constitution. The House of Commons next proceeded to the consideration of the slave trade, for the abolition of which Wilberforce was now contending; and no further allusion to France was made until the 5th of February, when a discussion arose upon the army estimates.

Although the ministerial speakers had expressed no disapprobation of the attempt of the French people to relieve themselves from a ruinous and despotic government, it was well known that their private sentiments were hostile to the present state of things. The atrocious character which the popular movement in France had now taken had already disgusted a large portion of those who at first viewed it with favour, and it was destined to break up, in a more disastrous manner than any previous question, the ranks of the opposition. The grand explosion of hostility against the French revolution came from a quarter in which it might have been least expected. In the debate just alluded to, Fox praised the conduct of the French soldiers in refusing to act against the people, and said that it took away many of his objections to a standing army. This dangerous sentiment drew forth some severe remarks, especially from the military part of the House. Fox, it was well known, had accepted the revolution, in spite of all its sinister accompaniments, as the dawn of European regeneration; and to the last he defended its principles, and persisted in his hopes of its favourable termination, while he disapproved of the conduct of those who had driven it into so many excesses and calamities.

One section of the Whig party fully partook in his sentiments on this subject; but there were many of his old friends who disagreed with him. When the debate on the army estimates was resumed on the 9th of February, Fox repeated his remark on the conduct of the French soldiers, and openly avowed his opinion of the revolution, declaring that he exulted in the successful attempt of our neighbours to deliver themselves from oppression, intimating at the same time his confident belief that the present convulsions would, sooner or later, give way to constitutional order. This declaration roused Edmund Burke, who deprecated the countenance given to the French revolution by his old political friend and leader, made an eloquent declamation on the errors and dangers of that extraordinary catastrophe, and expressed his fears that the movement might eventually reach our own country, where, he said, there were people watching only for the opportunity to imitate the French. When Burke rose, he was evidently labouring under great agitation of feeling; and, in the warmth of his declamation, he declared that he was prepared to separate himself from his oldest friends, in order to defend the constitution of his country against the encroachments of the baneful democratical spirit which had produced so much havoc in France. Fox replied with moderation, reasserted his own sentiments on the subject, and lamented in feeling terms the difference of opinion which had arisen between them; but Sheridan, less temperate, burst into something like an invective against Burke, and described his speech as one disgraceful to an Englishman, a direct encomium of despotism, and a libel on men who were virtuously engaged in labouring to obtain the rights of men. Burke rose again, expressed great indignation against Sheridan, and declared that he considered their political friendship at an end for ever.

Pitt had sat quietly on the Treasury bench, inwardly rejoicing at the division which had taken place among his opponents; but he also rose after Burke's second speech, and, without making any direct attack upon the French, he spoke of the necessity of rallying round our own constitution, complimented Burke on the sentiments he had that day expressed, and declared that he had earned the gratitude of his country to the latest posterity. Several others of the ministerial party followed Pitt in applauding Burke's conduct. Fox felt personally for the disagreement, and the whole Whig party took the alarm. Great exertions were made to effect a reconciliation, but without any satisfactory results, for Burke continued cold and distant; and Sheridan, who seems to have displeased his own party by his violence on this occasion, took little part in the parliamentary proceedings during the remainder of the session.

Burke was correct in stating that there was a number of discontented people in this country who admired the conduct of the Gallic democrats, and who were most anxious to establish their principles and follow their practice in this country. The political agitation of the earlier part of the reign of George III., and the warm partizanship to which it had led, had given a tendency to the formation of clubs and private societies for the discussion of political questions, which were scattered over the country, and not only assisted the opposition in elections, but were extremely useful allies in getting up petitions to the House on questions likely to embarrass the ministers. Beyond this their influence was not great, and there was nothing in their character to cause any apprehensions. Some of them were at times attended, and even presided over, by distinguished members of the opposition in both Houses of Parliament. One of the most remarkable and the oldest of these clubs was that known by the name of the "Revolution Society," which consisted of a number of the old Whig party, who met every year on the 4th of November to celebrate the memory of the revolution of 1688. In 1788 this society celebrated the centenary anniversary of that great event with more than usual solemnity, and with a very large attendance; among those present was a secretary of State, and several persons high in office and confidence at Court. The sentiments expressed on this occasion were of the most loyal description; but a year seems to have altered very much the complexion of the society. Most of the members shared in Fox's opinion of the French revolution; and, by a strange misunderstanding of its true character, and of that of the French populace, they imagined that it would bear a strict comparison with that which had hurled James II. from the English throne. The society met as usual on the 4th of November, 1789, under the presidency of Lord Stanhope, a nobleman whose love of republican principles was carried almost to insanity. Among the more enthusiastic members of this society was an old man, a preacher of the gospel, who (singularly enough) had been, on more occasions than one, the financial adviser of young William Pitt, who had not taken alarm at his zeal for the cause of American independence as he now did at those outbursts of the same zeal which merited for him the title of

"That revolution-sinner—Dr. Price."

On the morning of the anniversary dinner of the Revolution

Society in 1789, in the midst of the excitement produced in this country by the earlier acts of the French revolution, Dr. Price preached at a dissenting chapel in the Old Jewry, before the members of the society, a sermon " On the love of our country," which was subsequently printed, and was the cause of considerable agitation. In this discourse, Price accepted the French revolution as a glorious event in the history of mankind, as one fraught with unmixed good to the whole human race. At the conclusion, he burst into a rhapsody of admiration. " What an eventful period is this! I am thankful that I have lived to it : and I could almost say, ' Lord, now lettest thou thy servant depart in peace, for mine eyes have seen thy salvation.' I have lived to see a diffusion of knowledge which has undermined superstition and error; I have lived to see the rights of men better understood than ever, and nations panting for liberty which seemed to have lost the idea of it; I have lived to see thirty millions of people indignantly and resolutely spurning at slavery, and demanding liberty with an irresistible voice; their king led in triumph, and an arbitrary monarch surrendering himself to his subjects. After sharing in the benefits of one revolution, I have been spared to be a witness to two other revolutions, both glorious; and now methinks I see the ardour for liberty catching and spreading, and a general amendment beginning in human affairs—the dominion of kings changed for the dominion of laws, and the dominion of priests giving way to the dominion of reason and conscience. Be encouraged, all ye friends of freedom, and writers in its defence! The times are auspicious. Your labours have not been in vain. Behold kingdoms admonished by you, starting from sleep, breaking their fetters, and claiming justice from their oppressors! Behold the light you have struck out, after setting America free, reflected to France, and there kindled into a blaze, that lays despotism in ashes, and warms and illuminates Europe!"

Such were the sentiments which at this moment were gaining ground in England; and the enthusiasm of the preacher seems to have communicated itself to his audience. At the meeting of the society, which was very fully attended, a motion proposed by Dr. Price was agreed to by acclamation for a formal address of " their congratulations to the National Assembly on the event of the late glorious revolution in France." This address was transmitted by the chairman, Lord Stanhope, and was received with strongly marked satisfaction by the body to which it was sent; but it had the double effect of misleading the revolutionary government as to the real feelings of the population of this

country in their subsequent transactions with England, and of
encouraging those attempts at political propagandism which
soon followed. A close correspondence was soon established
between the discontented party in this country, and the democrats in Paris, from which Fox himself was not altogether free;
and many new political societies were formed in different parts
of the island, some of them much more violent in their language
and professed objects than the London Revolution Society.
Counter societies were likewise established, to combat the revolution societies with their own weapons of agitation. We shall
soon witness the effects of this popular antagonism.

Two other individuals stood prominent among the violent
revolutionists of this country. The first was a man of low
origin, only half educated, but talented in that style of writing
which has its effect among those classes of society which were
now most agitated, and reckless in his attacks on all existing
institutions, political or religious. This was Thomas Paine,
originally a stay-maker at Thetford, who had subsequently been
an exciseman, then a sailor, after which he emigrated to America,
where his ardent revolutionary propensities had been blown up
into a blaze. He had now returned to England, was active
among the political clubs, and had attracted the notice of the
chiefs of the opposition, having even been admitted to a certain
degree of intimacy by Edmund Burke. Joseph Priestley merited
a more honourable celebrity by his researches and discoveries in
science, than by his political and religious opinions, in both of
which he was violently opposed to the established order of things.
Dr. Priestley was a Unitarian preacher, resident at Birmingham,
and belonged to a sect which had become numerous in various
parts of England, and which generally entertained political
opinions of a very liberal character. In the hands of people like
these, the clubs multiplied, and became more violent in their
language; among the more celebrated of these were the Constitutional Society, the "Club of the 14th of July," (the day of
the capture of the Bastille,) and the Corresponding Society, the
latter being the most violent of them all.

At the same time that these clubs were doing all they could
to spread democratical opinions through England, King George's
disinclination to making concessions to the liberal party, seemed
to increase with age and infirmities; and he now adopted the
conviction that the concessions on the part of the crown had
been the chief cause of the French revolution. The clergy,
terrified by the fate of their Romish brethren on the other side
of the channel, seconded the King's resolution with the cry that

the church was in danger; they had been for some years looking
with alarm at the increase in the dissenting body, and they now
began to agitate against them, and to call for measures of persecution. In face of this feeling from above, other large and
intelligent portions of the community called loudly for legislative
reform, and for religious toleration. The revolution in France
was set up as a sufficient argument against reform in England;
the real or pretended designs of some of the dissenters were
made to justify the continuance of the test and corporation acts;
and even Wilberforce's favourite measure for the abolition of
slavery was stifled by an appeal to the horrors perpetrated in
French republican St. Domingo.

Fox brought forward in the House of Commons a motion for
the repeal of the test and corporation acts, on the 2nd of March,
1790, in a very able speech, to the principles of which no objec-
tion was made. Some members avowed their approval of the
measure, but said they considered themselves bound to obey the
will of their constituents, who, in various instances, had held
public meetings, and directed their representatives to oppose all
concession to the dissenters. Pitt declared that his feelings
were in favour of toleration, but he was afraid that in granting
their wishes he might be overthrowing one of the barriers of the
constitution. It was Burke who, on this occasion, took upon
himself the task of religious persecutor. He also made an
apology for the part he was taking, and then he flew off to his
favourite subject, the horrors and crimes of the French revolution; he avowed general opinions totally at variance with those
with whom he had acted so many years, declared that there was
no such thing as natural rights of men, and condemned the
whole body of the dissenters in the strongest terms, as discontented people, whose principles tended to the subversion of good
government. He even supported his opinions by calling to
memory the proceedings of the mad Lord George Gordon; and to
prove the danger with which the constitution was now threatened,
he spoke of the celebrated sermon of Dr. Price on the love of
our country, and of some political writings of Dr. Priestley.
The motion was rejected by a majority of nearly three to one.

The question of religious toleration was that on which the
Tory party first began to agitate the people, and they succeeded
in exciting the prejudices of the mob, and even of the middle
classes, to an extraordinary degree. It was little short of a
new Sacheverell crusade; for there were "no dissenter" meetings
in all parts of the country, and in some places "no dissenter"
mobs. Besides pamphlets of a more serious character, they were

ridiculed and burlesqued in satirical songs and poems, many of which incited the populace to insult and abuse them. A lawyer of Birmingham, well known by the name of councillor Morfit, (as we find written by a contemporary hand, on a copy in the possession of Mr. Burke,) composed a parody on the national anthem, which soon became extensively popular, and was printed sometimes with a large caricatured representation of the chief dissenters brooding over sedition. It was entitled

"OLD MOTHER CHURCH.

"God save great George our king,
Long live our noble king,
  God save the king!
Send him victorious,
Happy and glorious,
Long to reign over us,
  God save the king !

" Old mother Church disdains
The vile dissenting strains,
  That round her ring ;
She keeps her dignity,
And, scorning faction's cry,
Sings with sincerity,
  God save the king !

" Sedition is their creed ;
Feign'd sheep, but *wolves* indeed,
  How can we trust !
Gunpowder Priestley would
Deluge the throne with blood,
And lay the great and good
  Low in the dust.

" History, thy page unfold,
Did not their *sires* of old
  Murder their king !
And they would overthrow
King, lords, and bishops too,
And, while they gave the blow,
  Loyally sing,

" O Lord our God arise !
Scatter our enemies,
  And make them fall ;
Confound their politics,
Frustrate their knavish tricks ;
On thee our hopes we fix,
  God save us all."

The language of the more violent among the dissenters, it must be confessed, was not calculated to dispel the prejudices of their enemies. Burke, in his speech against the motion for the repeal of the test and corporation acts, had asserted, with truth, that tolerant feelings were a thing unknown amongst the party which was crying loudest for toleration, and all their proceedings at this moment of agitation were strongly tainted with the bitter animosity of the religious parties in the age of the Puritans. Burke said that, according to the doctrines set forth by the dissenters, the church of Rome was a common strumpet, the kirk of Scotland was a kept mistress, and the church of England an equivocal lady of easy virtue, between the one and the other. A rather popular ballad, distributed about during the agitation against the dissenters at the beginning of 1790, before the motion in Parliament for the repeal of the test and corporation acts, under the title of " Now or never ; or, a Réveillée to the Church," pictures the terror of the church at the movement among its opponents,—

> " Oh, who shall blow the brazen trump,
> By famed Sacheverell sounded,
> That spread confusion through the Rump,
> And silenced every Roundhead ?
>
> " Now, now, if ever, loudly bawl
> ' The Church, the Church in danger !'
> Each prebend trembles for his stall,
> And eke his rack and manger.
>
> " Peers, knights, and squires, in league combined,
> Protect your good old mother ;
> For should the beldame slip her wind,
> You'll ne'er see such another."

The church, says this ballad in equally strong language, was unwilling to give up any portion of the loaves and fishes on which it had been so long fattening,—

> " Two hundred years and more the dame
> Has tightly held together ;
> Her glorious motto, ' Still the same,'
> In spite of wind and weather.
>
> " Her babes of grace, with tender care,
> She fed on dainty dishes ;
> And none but they have had a share
> Among the loaves and fishes.
>
> " Shall Presbyterian shrieves and mayors
> Eat custard with the wise men—
> Or meetings hear the pious prayers
> Of searchers and excisemen ?
>
> " The sects they prate of rights and stuff,
> And brawl in fierce committees,
> And soon will put on blue and buff,
> While Price sings *Nunc dimittis.*

G G

"Rouse, then, for shame! ye church-fed race,
 With Tories true and trusty,
 Turn on your foe your fighting face,
 And fit your armour rusty."

The universities next come in for their share of the attack, and
the ballad concludes with an allusion to the part taken by some
of the towns and corporations in appealing to Parliament
against the dissenters.

Among the caricatures produced by this excitement, and designed to keep it up, is a large print by Sayer, published on the
16th of February (about a fortnight before Fox's motion in
the House of Commons), and entitled "The Repeal of the Test
Act, a vision." The three leading dissenters occupy a lofty
pulpit, and beat the "drum ecclesiastic" in the chapel of sedition. Priestley, to the left, with outstretched arms, is breathing
forth flames of "Arianism," "Socinianism," "Deism," and

A TRIO OF INCENDIARIES.

"Atheism." Price, in the middle, is closing his discourse with
a solemn prayer,—"And now let us fervently pray for the
abolition of all unlimited and limited monarchy, for the anni-
hilation of all ecclesiastical revenues and endowments, for the
extinction of all orders of nobility and all rank and subordina-
tion in civil society, and that anarchy and disorder may, by our
pious endeavours, prevail throughout the universe. See my
sermon on the anniversary of the revolution." The doctor holds
in his hand a paper inscribed, "The prayers of the congregation
are desired for the success of the patriotic members of the
National Assembly now sitting in France." Dr. Lindsey, who
occupies the other side of the pulpit, is tearing to pieces a tablet
inscribed with the thirty-nine articles. Among the congregation
we see Fox (shouting "Hear, hear, hear!") Margaret Nichol-

son (the would-be regicide), Dr. Rees, Dr. Kippis, Lord Stanhope (who is tearing to pieces the "Acts of Parliament for the
uniformity of the Common Prayer and Administration of the
Sacraments"), and several others, some of whom are busy
clearing away rubbish, including mitres, communion cups,
Bibles, and other similar articles. Through the window we
perceive that people are at work pulling down church steeples,
and an angel is flying away with the cross. The door of the
"Sanctum Sanctorum" on the other side reveals to our view a
picture of Cromwell suspended within. The following lines,
inscribed at the foot of the print, express the spirit of the
whole,—

> " From such implacable tormentors,
> Fanatics, hypocrites, dissenters,
> Cruel in power, and restless out,
> And, when most factions, most devout,
> May God preserve the church and throne,
> And George the good that sits thereon.
> Nor may their plots exclude his heirs
> From reigning, when the right is theirs !
> For should the foot the head command,
> And faction gain the upper hand,
> We may expect a ruin'd land."

The agitation against the dissenters, and the alarm caused by
the disorderly and sanguinary turn which the revolution in
France had taken, were seized as offering a favourable opportunity for the elections, and Parliament was dissolved on the
10th of June. The new Parliament seems to have differed
little in its character from the old one; and the only incident of
much importance, as depicting the political movement of the
day, was the appearance of John Horne Tooke (so well known
in the earlier part of the reign as Parson Horne of Brentford),
who offered himself as a candidate to contest Westminster with
Fox and Lord Hood. Neither Fox, nor his seconder, Sheridan,
were a match in mob-eloquence with Tooke, and the latter held
his place manfully on the hustings ; but, at the end of the poll,
he was in a considerable minority. This man, who is best
known to the public by his " Diversions of Purley,"—a work
which has long enjoyed a much better reputation than it merits,
—had been in the political contentions of the beginning of the
reign a violent Wilkite : he had subsequently quarrelled with
Wilkes, and done everything in his power to vilify his private
and public character ; since that he seemed almost to have disappeared from the political stage, until the French Revolution
and the English political societies again brought him to life.

On his rejection at Westminster he presented a petition against the return, in a tone that gave great offence to the House of Commons. We shall soon see him still more active in the political factions of the day. The Westminster election of 1790 was, like its predecessors, the scene of much mobbing and violence, and produced abundance of electioneering squibs. A few poor caricatures were directed chiefly against Fox, who, it was pretended by his opponents, gained his election by coalescing with Lord Hood. When the Tories wished to be very severe on their great parliamentary enemy, they tried to get up some charge of a "coalition."

The new Parliament met on the 26th of November, when any direct allusion to the affairs of France was again omitted in the King's speech, and the subject seemed to be avoided for a while in the debates in either house. But, while it appeared thus to have been discarded by the Court, it had absorbed the whole mighty intellect of Burke, who, a short time before the opening of the session, had published his eloquent Reflections on the French Revolution. In this remarkable production he had painted in exaggerated colours its errors and enormities, and he had no less undoubtedly exaggerated the danger of the extension of republican principles to this country. The English political societies, the dissenters, and their acknowledged or covert designs, and especially Dr. Price's sermon, all became objects in turn of his indignant declamations. Perhaps no single book ever produced so powerful an effect as these "Reflections;" their publication marked an epoch in the history of the country, and we find that immediately after the appearance of this pamphlet, not only did the general feeling throughout England become more decidedly hostile to democratic France, but the English government began to take bolder steps for the suppression of sedition at home. An admirable caricature by Gillray, published on the 3rd of December, 1790, represents the long, spectacled nose of the author of these Reflections, armed with the crown and the cross, penetrating into the secret study of Dr. Price, and surprising him, surrounded by all the evidences of sedition against Church and State.[*] The King and his ministers, and all the Tory party, expressed unbounded admiration of this splendid defence of their policy; but it gave great dissatisfaction to the ultra-Whigs, who complained that Burke had misrepresented the conduct of the French in order to

---

[*] It is entitled, "Smelling out a Rat; or, The Atheistical Revolutionist disturbed in his midnight Calculations." An exact copy of this caricature is given in the accompanying plate.

render them odious, and that he had advanced principles which
led to despotism and arbitrary power. Burke's book was
answered in an elegant essay by Mackintosh, who then figured a
young man as one of the boldest Whigs, and more violently and
coarsely in a celebrated work entitled "The Rights of Man,"
by Thomas Paine, who, after having studied republicanism and
democracy in the congress of America, and in the worst clubs in
Paris, had now returned to England in the hopes of finding
here a soil fitted for their reception. At first Paine's "Rights
of Man" was approved by Fox, and thousands of copies were
printed, distributed through the country, and read with eagerness. Dr. Priestley also entered the field against Burke's
"Reflections," and a number of more insignificant writers took
up the pen. Pamphlets for and against the French Revolution, now issued from the press in extraordinary numbers.

The satisfaction which Burke's pamphlet gave to ministers,
was soon increased by his entire defection from the standard of
opposition. The Whigs seemed to have designedly urged him
on to his grand outbreak on this subject. For weeks their
journals teemed with attacks on his book, and with hints at his
apostasy from the cause of freedom. When he rose in the
house to speak on French politics, they put him down by their
murmurs, although Fox and Sheridan were ready to seize upon
any occasion of declaring their admiration of the revolution.
Burke kept silence during a large part of the session, or
said little; the more moderate of the Whig party counselled
him to act thus, in order to avoid making a schism in their
ranks. But it was a task in which Edmund Burke was not the
man to persist, and, after entering into a warm debate on the subject on the 15th of April, in connexion with the pending measure for the government of Canada, and having given one or two
intimations that his heart was full of a burthen which he was
resolved to discharge, on the 16th of May he delivered his
second grand philippic in the House of Commons against the
French Revolution and its authors. He dwelt especially on the
horrible massacres which had devastated the French Isle of St.
Domingo, and returned from them to depict the state of France,
which at that time was every day sinking deeper in anarchy and
blood. He was interrupted for a while by the impatience
of some members of the opposition, and Fox seized the opportunity of declaring how entirely he differed with him on this
grand topic, and of speaking somewhat disrespectfully of his
book. It was then that Burke rose again, with more warmth
than ever, and, after complaining of the interruptions and

attacks to which he had been exposed, proceeded to dilate
in eloquent and forcible language on the new principles propagated in France, and the way in which they were propagated, on
the treasonable conduct of certain unitarian and other dissenting preachers in this country, who corresponded with the
French democrats, and held them up for imitation—he alluded,
of course, to Priestley and other instigators of sedition; Dr.
Price had died on the 19th of April,—and on the danger
that the French might be tempted to use a portion of their
large military force in assisting to revolutionize England; he
said that love of his country was a feeling above private
affections, and proclaimed that his friendship with Fox and
his party was at an end. Fox, than whom no man possessed a
kinder or more affectionate heart, rose to reply with tears
rolling down his cheeks; he appealed to their long friendship
and familiar intercourse; to his own unaltered attachment; he
cited Burke's former opinions and exertions in the cause of
liberty; and he deprecated the idea that their personal friendship should be destroyed by a difference of opinion on one
particular subject. He, however, intermixed his reply with
some personal recriminations and observations which only
increased the irritation; Burke remained cold and inexorable,
and all intercourse between the two statesmen was discontinued.

The loss of Burke was a severe blow to the party, and was a
subject of no small exultation to the ministry and to the
court. He became an object of unbounded admiration in
the Tory papers, while those of the opposition were equally
pertinacious in their attacks and in their abuse. Several clever
caricatures have remained to us as testimonies of the former
feeling. One of those in which the sentiment is more coarsely
expressed, entitled "The wrangling friends; or, Opposition
in disorder," published on the 10th of May, and an evident
attempt at imitating the style of Gillray, depicts the affecting
scene in the House of Commons in broad caricature, and shews
favour to neither of the two principal actors. Pitt, seated
quietly on one side exclaims, "If they'd cut each other's
throat, I should be relieved from these troublesome fellows."
The Tories represented Burke as one who had turned King's
evidence against his accomplices, who they expected would
now be convicted and condemned. A caricature by Gillray,
published on the 14th of May, represented Fox as the Guy
Faux of his party, on the point of blowing up the King,
Lords, and Constitution, when he is detected and brought

to light by the vigilant watchman, Burke, who here appears in the service of the crown. Sheridan and others of his colleagues are seeking safety in flight. That he had entered the service of the crown, and was to be paid accordingly, many believed, or pretended to believe ; and both parties seemed not unwilling that this impression should go abroad. In one print, published at this time, Burke is represented as receiving from Pitt a coronet as the reward of his desertion. Another caricature by Gillray, published in May, about the same time as the former, represents the great impeacher pointing out his two colleagues Fox and Sheridan, to justice, with the declaration,

THE VIGILANT WATCHMAN.

"Behold the abettors of revolution!" It is entitled, "The impeachment ; or, The father of the gang turned King's

AN IMPEACHMENT.

evidence." Both parties, in the scene described above, described the other chiefs of the opposition as the political offspring of Burke. From this time the face of Burke appears much more rarely in the caricatures. A severe, and an unjust caricature by Gillray, published on the 16th of November, 1791, after Burke had accepted a pension from the crown, represents him under the title of "A uniform Whig."

He is seen leaning with his right arm on a pedestal supporting the bust of King George, and holding in his hand his "Reflections on the French Revolution." On this side of his body, his garb is new and fashionable, and his pockets are overflowing with money. On the other side he is dressed in rags, his empty pockets turned inside out, and he holds a cap of liberty in his hand. The supposed changeableness of his principles is intimated by a figure of Fame, making with its toe a tangent on the extremity of the sail of a windmill. Underneath is inscribed a sentence from his own "Reflections,"—"I preserve consistency by varying my means to secure the unity of my end." Burke was the last person in the world to condescend to use means, or to listen to motives, that were mean or dishonourable.

Encouraged by the desertions which were weakening the opposition in parliament, and by the extraordinary effect produced throughout the country by Burke's "Reflections," the government now began to take a higher tone towards France, and their agents neglected no means of exciting the popular feelings throughout the nation, against dissenters and revolutionists. The caricaturists, especially, began now to be unusually active. In the caricatures, the leaders of the opposition in parliament were ranked in the same category as the incendiaries of the clubs— they were all equally democrats and king-haters. The four leaders—associates in council and in arms—were Fox, Sheridan, Priestley, and Paine. The latter had gained an extraordinary importance by his "Rights of Man," — the answer to Burke's "Reflections." Gillray burlesqued this low agitator in a caricature, published on the 23rd May, 1791, entitled, "The Rights of Man; or, Tommy Paine, the American tailor, taking the measure of the crown for a new pair of revolution breeches." Paine is here represented with the

A BAD MEASURER.

conventional type of face which in the caricatures of this and the subsequent period was always given to a French democrat;—his tricoloured cockade bears the inscription, "*Vive la liberté!*" And the following almost incoherent soliloquy is placed in his mouth:—

"Fathom and a half! fathom and a half! Poor Tom! ah! mercy upon me! that's more by half than my poor measure will ever be able to reach! —Lord! Lord! I wish I had a bit of the stay-tape or buckram which I used to cabbage when I was a prentice, to lengthen it out.—Well, well, who would ever have thought it, that I, who have served seven years as an apprentice, and afterwards worked four years as a journeyman to a master tailor, then followed the business of an exciseman as much longer, should not be able to take the dimensions of this bauble!—for what is a crown but a bauble! which we may see in the Tower for sixpence a piece? —Well, although it may be too large for a tailor to take measure of, there's one comfort, he may make months at it, and call it as many names as he pleases!—and yet, Lord! Lord! I should like to make it a Yankee-doodle night-cap and breeches, if it was not so d—d large, or I had stuff enough. Ah! If I could once do that, I would soon stitch up the mouth of that barnacled Edmund from making any more Reflections upon the Flints—and so Flints and Liberty for ever! and d—n the Dunga! Huzza!"

It was represented that those who were opposed to Pitt's government aimed directly at the overthrow of the throne and the constitution—that reform was a mask for republicanism—that dissent from the church was equivalent to atheism. Fox and his party, in the prints which were now spread about the country, appeared as regicides *in embryo*, and the fate of Charles I. and the sins of the puritans were made to ring constantly in people's ears. These anticipations were set forth graphically, in a large engraving by Gillray, entitled "The hopes of the party," published in July, 1791. Amid the horrors of the successful revolution here pre-supposed, the Queen and the prime minister are seen on one side, each suspended to a lamp. This was an example borrowed from recent proceedings of the French democrats. It was commonly believed that Pitt and Queen Charlotte were closely leagued together to pillage and oppress the

A PAIR OF PENDENTS.

nation, and she was far less popular than the King, whose infirmity produced a general sympathy, and who had many good qualities that endeared him to those with whom he came in contact. In another part of Gillray's picture, the King is brought to the block, held down by Sheridan, while Fox, masked, acts as executioner. Priestley, with pious exhortations, is encouraging the fallen monarch to submit to his hard fate.

The prejudice which such productions were intended to excite soon communicated itself to the populace, which more especially caught up the cry against the dissenters. There was some rioting in several parts of the country, but the weight of the popular ill-humour fell upon Dr. Priestley, who

MARTYRDOM.

then resided at Birmingham. This town was, even then, the place of all others where it was easiest to get together a mob that would hesitate at nothing, with the prospect of mischief and plunder before it. A number of Priestley's friends in Birmingham agreed to celebrate the second anniversary of the capture of the Bastille on the 14th of July, 1791, by a dinner, which it was understood would be accompanied with revolutionary toasts and songs. There were many people in the town who disliked the persons who were to assemble on this occasion as much as they hated the cause in which they were engaged, and the announcement of this dinner caused considerable agitation. It can hardly be doubted that a plot was formed by persons in a better position in society to get up a popular demonstration for the purpose of insulting (at the least) the friends of democratic principles. Two or three days before the appointed day, a violently seditious paper, of which Priestley's friends declared themselves entirely innocent, and which there seemed reason to believe had come from London, was distributed about the town. On the 14th, which was a Thursday, about eighty persons sat down to dinner, but Dr. Priestley himself was not present. A mob had already assembled round the tavern at which the dinner was to be held, who shouted "Church and King," and insulted the guests as they came to the door. The magistrates, instead of taking measures to preserve the peace, were dining at a neighbouring tavern with a party of red-hot loyalists. The mob kept from violence until both parties had broken up; but then, encouraged by the loyalists who were heated with wine and enthusiasm, they broke into the tavern in search of Dr. Priestley, who was not there: and then, disappointed in their design of seizing the arch-revolutionist (as they considered him), they rushed to his chapel, the new meeting-house, and burnt it to the ground. It was now evening, and the mob was greatly increased, having been joined by large bodies of labourers, who had ended their day's work. They then burnt the old meeting-house, and proceeded to the house of Dr. Priestley, about a mile and a half from the town, which they also destroyed, with his library, papers, and philosophical instruments. Priestley and his family had fled; he reached London in safety, and took the charge of Dr. Price's congregation at Hackney. The mob was now master of the place, and for several successive days paraded Birmingham and its neighbourhood, burning and destroying without interruption, until the following Monday (the 18th), when a strong body of military arrived, and the rioters dispersed. An inclination to follow the example of Birmingham was exhibited in some other places, and the outcry against dissenters and revolutionists became loud from one end of the kingdom to the other. The ultra-radicals were strongest in London and in Scotland.

In the autumn, a domestic event came to throw a gleam of joy amid the bitterness of political and religious faction which now reigned throughout the land. On the 29th of September, the Duke of York was married at Berlin to the eldest daughter of the King of Prussia, and he arrived with his bride in London on the 19th of October, where they were received amid the congratulations of all classes of society. For some time nothing was talked of or sung of but the new duchess, and her portrait was to be seen in every print-shop. The marriage became soon the subject of a variety of prints and caricatures.

EXPECTATION.

The latter were very numerous; and one of them, by Gillray, represents the joy of the King and Queen at the arrival of their daughter-in-law as arising chiefly from the riches she was said to have brought with her. It is entitled "The Introduction," and was published on the 2nd of November. The duke is introducing his bride, who carries her apron full of money; the King and Queen are shewing their satisfaction at her golden burthen in unmistakeable gestures, the Queen, especially, holds out her apron in expectation of a share.

It was during this period of danger for thrones and princes, that poets and artists joined in heaping ridicule and satire on the persons of King George and his family. Among the former, by far the most remarkable was Dr. Wolcot, better known by his celebrated pseudonym of Peter Pindar, whose clever but daring infractions of royal inviolability have not yet ceased to amuse his countrymen. These satirists invaded the most private recesses of the palace, and dragged before the world a host of ridiculous incidents with which royal eccentricity furnished them, and which were calculated rather to bring royalty into contempt than to add to its splendour. It appears that both the King and the Queen were in the habit of attending to various minutiæ of domestic economy which are more consistent with a low station in life than with the public dignity of the Crown, and scenes of this description were brought before the eye of the public with the most provoking impertinence. A caricature, published on the 21st of November, 1791, represented the King and Queen in the character of careful farmers, "going to market." The royal pair were described as cheapening bargains, and exulting in the saving of shillings and sixpences. When at their favourite watering-place, Weymouth, they were said to have had their provisions brought from Windsor by the mail, free of carriage, because Weymouth was a dear place. So, at least, says Peter Pindar,—

> " The mail arrives !—hark ! hark ! the cheerful horn,
> To majesty announcing oil and corn ;
> Turnips and cabbages, and soap, and candles,
> And, lo ! each article great Cæsar handles !
> Bread, cheese, salt, catchup, vinegar, and mustard,
> Small beer and bacon, apple-pie and custard :
> All, all, from Windsor greets his frugal grace,
> For Weymouth is a d—d expensive place."

According to the satirist, no occasion of driving a hard bargain was suffered to escape, even if the royal visitor met with it in his ordinary walks. Thus he meets with a drove of cattle, carrying to the market for sale :—

" A batch of bullocks !—see great Cæsar run :
He stops the drover—hargain is begun.
He feels their ribs and rumps— he shakes his head—
' Poor, drover, poor—poor, very poor indeed !'
Cæsar and drover haggle—diff'rence split—
How much !—a shilling ! what a royal bit
A load of hay in sight ! great Cæsar flies—
Smells—shakes his head—' Bad hay—sour hay'—ho buys.
' Smell, Courtown—smell—good bargain—lucky load—
Smell, Courtown—sweeter hay was never mow'd.'
   A herd of swine goes by !—' Whose hogs are these ?
Hay, farme:, hay ?'—' Yours, measter, if you please.'
' Poor, farmer, poor—lean, lousy, very poor—
Sell, sell, hay, sell !'—' Iss, measter, to be zure :
My pigs were made for sale, but what o' that !
You caall mun *lean* ; now, zur, I caall mun *rat*—
Measter, I baant a starling—can't be cort ;
You think, agrah, to ha the pigs vor *nort*.'
   Lo ! Cæsar buys the pigs—he slily winks—
' Hay, Gwinn, the fellow is not *caught*, he thinks—
Fool, not to know the hargain I have got !
Hay, Gwinn—nice bargain—lucky, lucky, lot !' "

On the 28th of November, 1791, appeared a brace of prints, reflecting on the household economy of the palace. In the first the King is represented in very uncourtly dishabille, preparing for breakfast by toasting his own muffins; in the companion print, the Queen, in homely garb, although her pocket is overflowing with money, is frying sprats for supper. A very clever caricature was published by Gillray, entitled " Anti-saccharites," in which the King and Queen are teaching their daughters to take their tea

TOASTING MUFFINS.

without sugar, as " a noble example of economy." The princesses have a look of great discontent, but their royal mother exhorts them to persevere ; " Above all, remember how much expense it will save your poor papa." The King, delighted with the experiment, exclaims, " O delicious ! delicious !" This print appeared on the 27th of March, 1792 ; on the 28th of the following July, the same artist produced a beautiful plate under the title of "Temperance enjoying a frugal meal," in which the King and Queen are seated at their table, eating eggs, and breakfasting with the greatest frugality out of the most sumptuous utensils. All the accessories of the picture offer innumerable examples of the saving habits of the illustrious pair.* Their avaricious disposition, especially that of the Queen (who was never very popular), had now become proverbial. Thus, in a print published on the 24th of May, 1792, entitled "Vices overlooked in the new poclamation," avarice is represented by King George and

FRYING SPRATS.

AVARICE.

Queen Charlotte hugging their hoarded millions in mutual satisfaction, with a book of interest-tables beside them. This print is divided into four compartments, representing avarice—drunkenness, exemplified in the person of the Prince of Wales,—gambling, the favourite amusement of the Duke of

* Gillray at the same time published a companion plate, representing the voluptuousness of the Prince of Wales, and entitled, "A voluptuary under the horrors of digestion." Both these caricatures are rare, and are sought for as two of his best works.

York,—and debauchery, the Duke of Clarence and Mrs. Jordan, —as the four vices of the royal family of Great Britain.

King George was remarkable for slovenliness of manners, for his ungraceful and undignified carriage, for a love of entering into conversation with people of all ranks, and for the volubility with which he poured upon them his *naïve* and often pointless questions. The latter qualification is well known to all readers of the verses of Peter Pindar. It was reported that Dr. Johnson, after his first interview with the King, privately expressed his opinion of the King's intellectual qualities in the following terms:—"His Majesty seems to be possessed of some good nature and *much curiosity* ; as for his *nous*, it is not contemptible. His Majesty, indeed, was *multifarious* in his *questions* ; but, thank God! he *answered them all himself.*" This royal curiosity furnished everlasting subjects for the poet and the caricaturist, and the one might be made to illustrate the other through page after page. A caricature, published by Gillray on the 10th of February, 1795, represents an example of royal "affability." The King and Queen, in their rural walks, arrive at a dirty hut, the occupant of which, no very high sample of humanity, is feeding his pigs with wash. The vacant stare on his countenance shows him overwhelmed with the rapid succession of royal interrogatives,—"Well, friend, where a' you going, hay ?—what's your name, hay ?—where d' ye live, hay ?—hay ?"

ROYAL AFFABILITY.

These satirical attacks on royal manners were continued through the whole of the revolutionary period, and anywhere but in England they could not have failed to bring the person of the sovereign into contempt. The King's familiarity of manners, approaching to vulgarity, was exhibited in another caricature by Gillray, published in the month of June, 1797, representing a scene on the esplanade at Weymouth. The King, distinguished by his awkward and shuffling gait (which is not much exaggerated in the picture), has a word to say to every one of the crowd through which he is walking. The con-

stant practice of taking the air in unceremonious excursions, and his great attachment to hunting, gave frequent occasions for bringing forth these qualities of the King, and led to scenes of a ridiculous kind. One of these furnished the subject of a caricature, published on the 2nd of November, 1797, representing his Majesty " learning to make apple dumplings." The King, in his pursuit of the chase, is represented as having arrived at the cottage of an old woman, occupied in a manner which is said to have drawn forth exclamations of astonishment from the curious and admiring monarch; " Hay! hay! apple dumplings!— how get the apples in!—how? are they made without seams?" This subject had already been treated by Peter Pindar:—

A KING.

THE KING AND THE APPLE DUMPLINGS.

" Once on a time, a monarch, tir'd with hooping,
        Whipping, and spurring,
        Happy in worrying
A poor, defenceless, harmless buck,
(The horse and rider wet as muck),
From his high consequence and wisdom stooping,
    Enter'd through curiosity a cot,
    Where sat a poor old woman and her pot.
The wrinkled, blear-ey'd, good old granny,
In this same cot, illum'd by many a cranny.

Had finish'd apple dumplings for her pot :
 In tempting row the naked dumplings lay,
 When, lo! the monarch in his usual way,
Like lightning spoke, ' What this ! what this ! what ! what !'
Then taking up a dumpling in his hand,
His eyes with admiration did expand ;
 And oft did majesty the dumpling grapple :
' 'Tis monstrous, monstrous hard, indeed !' he cried ;
' What makes it, pray, so hard ?'—The dame replied,
 Low curtseying, ' Please your majesty, the apple.'
' Very astonishing indeed !—strange thing !'
Turning the dumpling round, rejoined the king,—
 ' 'Tis most extraordinary then, all this is—
It beats Pinetti's conjuring all to pieces—
Strange I should never of a dumpling dream !
But, Goody, tell me where, where, where's the seam ?'
' Sir, there's no seam,' quoth she ; ' I never knew
That folks did apple dumplings sew.'
' No !' cried the staring monarch with a grin,
' How, how the devil got the apple in ?'
On which the dame the curious scheme reveal'd
By which the apple lay so sly conceal'd,
 Which made the Solomon of Britain start ;
Who to the palace with full speed repair'd,
And queen, and princesses so beauteous, scar'd,
 All with the wonders of the dumpling art.
There did he labour one whole week, to show
 The wisdom of an apple dumpling maker ;
And, lo ! so deep was majesty in dough,
 The palace seem'd the lodging of a baker !"

In the caricatures on more general subjects of a later period
than that of which we are now speaking, we shall often find

JOYFUL NEWS.

these personal weaknesses of the royal family — the love of
H H

money, the homely savings, the familiar air, the taste for gossip
—introduced. A caricature by Gillray, published in 1792, after
the arrival of the news of the defeats of Tippoo Saib in India,
represents Dundas, in whose province the Indian affairs lay,
bringing the joyful intelligence to the royal huntsman and his
consort. It is entitled, "Scotch Harry's News; or Nincom-
poop in high glee." The exulting secretary of state, who is
thus designated, announces that "Seringapatam is taken —
Tippoo is wounded—and millions of pagodas secured." The
vulgar-looking King, with a strange mixture of ideas of Indian
news and hunting, breaks out into a loud—"Tally ho! ho! ho!
ho!" while his queen, whose head is running entirely on the
gain likely to result from these new conquests, exclaims, "O the
dear, sweet pagodas!"

The caricaturist who thus burlesqued royalty, had a pique
against George III., very similar to that of Hogarth against
George II. Gillray had accompanied Loutherbourg into France,
to assist him in making sketches for his grand picture of the
siege of Valenciennes. On their return, the King, who made
great pretensions to be a patron of the arts, desired to look
over their sketches, and expressed great admiration of the
drawings of Loutherbourg, which were plain landscape sketches,
finished sufficiently to be perfectly intelligible. But when he
came to Gillray's rough but spirited sketches of French officers
and soldiers, he threw them aside with contempt, merely observing, "I don't understand these caricatures." The mortified
artist took his revenge by publishing a large print of the King
examining a portrait of Oliver Cromwell, executed by Cooper,
to which he gave the title of "A connoisseur examining a
Cooper." The royal countenance exhibits a curious mixture of
astonishment and alarm as he contemplates the features of the
great overthrower of kings, whose name was at this moment
put forth as the watchword of revolutionists. The King is
burning a candle-end on a save-all! This print was published
on the 18th of June, 1792; Gillray, who had not the same
dependence on court as Sayer, who was much inferior to him in
talent, seldom loses an opportunity of turning the King to
ridicule.

Nor did Pitt always escape his satire. The young minister,
who had so suddenly risen to the summit of power, and now
somewhat haughtily lorded it over his fellow statesmen, seems
to have given offence to the artist, who, on the 20th of December,
1791, caricatured him as an upstart fungus, springing suddenly
out of the hot-bed of royal favour, which is somewhat rudely com-

pared to a dung-hill. The print is entitled " An excrescence—a fungus,—*alias*, a toad-stool upon a dung-hill." The thin meagre figure of the prime minister was no less fruitful a matter for jest, than that of his fat and slovenly opponent Fox. In one of Gillray's prints, dated the 16th of March, 1792, that caricaturist has seized upon an equivocal phrase in one of the statesman's speeches, and, under the title of a " bottomless pitt," has given us a characteristic sketch of his figure and his gesture.

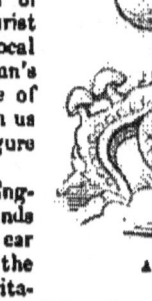

A FUNGUS.

The determination of the English court to resist all demands for reform, and to turn a deaf ear to popular complaints, had the natural effect of provoking agitation. The opposition in parliament, in spite of many defections, became, under its old leaders, Fox and Sheridan, and some of the young and rising debaters, such as Grey, Erskine, Lord Lauderdale, Whitbread, and others, louder and more menacing. Within parliament, every question that would admit of a debate, was contested with the greatest obstinacy. The session of 1792 was first occupied with the foreign policy of the preceding year, which, whether in Europe or in India, was analyzed and bitterly attacked. Wilberforce's question of the abolition of negro slavery embarrassed the ministers, whose

"A BOTTOMLESS PITT."

chief argument against it was that it numbered among its advocates some of the revolutionary reformers, and among the rest Thomas Paine; they disposed of it eventually by a motion for gradual abolition. The detection of a number of flagrant instances of improper interference in elections gave a new force to the question of parliamentary reform, which was brought

forward at the end of April by Grey and Fox, and violently
opposed by Pitt and by Burke. The arguments reproduced by
each successive speaker on the ministerial benches was the
impolicy of the time at which the question was brought forward, and the danger of making concessions to popular violence;
and the court in 1792, seemed resolved to raise the reputation
and importance of Thomas Paine and his " Rights of Man," in
the same way it had, more than twenty years before, raised up
John Wilkes, his *North Briton*, and his " Essay on Woman."
Burke, who opposed this motion with great warmth, and who
declared his belief that the House of Commons was as perfect
as human nature would permit it to be, flew out against French
revolutionists and English political societies, and talked of the
factious men with which England abounded, and who were
urging this country towards blood and confusion. In the heat
of party faction, the ministers exaggerated greatly the real
danger they had to apprehend from people of this description,
while it was equally under-valued by their opponents.

If, however, the question of parliamentary reform was, in
point of numbers, weakly supported in the house, it was making
substantial advances among people out of doors. In the debates
in the House of Commons, Fox took every occasion of remind-
ing those who were now in power of their advocacy of reform

MAJOR CARTWRIGHT.

when in opposition, and
especially recalled to their
memory a meeting on
the subject, held at the
Thatched House Tavern,
in 1782, when Pitt and
the Duke of Richmond
had joined hand in hand
with Major Cartwright
and Horne Tooke. These
men had there been as
decided instigators of sedition as those to whom
they now applied the
epithet. But a few years
of gratified ambition had
made Pitt and Richmond
the most resolute oppo-
nents of liberal measures,
while Cartwright* and

* The figure of Major Cartwright is taken from a print attributed to

Tooke, who had not been exposed to the same seductions, continued to walk in their old path. Parliamentary reform had now become the watchword of several of the political clubs, which were increasing in numbers, as well as in the violence of their language. A few weeks had seen the formation of the "Corresponding Society," which placed itself in immediate communication with some of the most violent clubs in Paris, and which openly demanded universal suffrage and annual parliaments; and now, in the month of April, 1792, arose the "Society of the Friends of the People," which was more moderate in its language and demands, and counted in its ranks several noblemen and leading members of Parliament, and many other persons distinguished in literature and science. It was at the desire of this latter society, that Grey and Erskine, who were both members, brought the question of reform before the House of Commons, in the spring of 1792; and it was resolved that they should bring forward a more formal motion on the subject in the ensuing session.

The ministry dreaded the way in which the opposition was thus strengthening itself with political associations, and determined to take measures to counteract them, and to suppress the quantity of inflammatory materials which were now spread about the country in the shape of seditious writings. The gradual and effective manner in which the ministers paved their way for hostile steps against sedition at home and designs from abroad, by addressing themselves to people's passions, and exciting their apprehensions, is deserving of admiration. They even contrived to make the odium of sedition recoil heavily upon the heads of the leaders of the opposition in parliament, who were represented as nourishing concealed views of ambition, and as close imitators

PATRIOTS AMUSING THEMSELVES.

Gillray, published in 1784, in which he is caricatured as "the Drum-major of Sedition."

of the worst of the ultra-democrats of France. In a caricature by Gillray, published on the 19th of April, 1792, and entitled, "Patriots amusing themselves; or, Swedes* practising at a post," Fox and Sheridan are perfecting themselves in the use of fire-arms. Dr. Priestley stands behind, holding two pamphlets in his hand, entitled "On the glory of revolutions," and "On the folly of religion and order," and says to his colleagues, "Here's plenty of wadding for to ram down the charge with, to give it force, and to make a loud report." Fox, bearing the French cockade, with the inscription "ça ira," is firing a blunderbuss; while Sheridan, loading his pistol, exclaims, "Well! this new game is delightful!—O heavens! if I could but once pop the post!—

> "Then you and me,
> Dear brother P.,
> Would sing with glee,
> Full merrily,
> *Ça ira! ça ira! ça ira!*"

The post at which they are shooting is rudely moulded into the form of King George, surmounted by the royal hunting cap. The success which these attempts on people's fears and prejudices met with, encouraged the ministry to proceed, and they soon ventured to make a direct attack on the liberty—or rather, in this case, on the licence of the press. On the 21st of May appeared a royal proclamation against seditious meetings and writings, but which was more especially aimed at the societies above alluded to. It spoke particularly of the correspondences said to be carried on with designing men in foreign parts, with a view to forward their criminal purposes in this country. This proclamation was violently condemned in parliament, by the opposition, as an injudicious and uncalled-for measure; and it produced debates in both houses, which shewed a number of desertions from the popular party. Among the most important in the House of Lords were the Duke of Portland and the Prince of Wales, who both spoke energetically in favour of the proclamation.

At this moment some divisions shewed themselves also in the midst of the ministerial camp. There had never been any cordiality between the premier and the chancellor, since the treacherous conduct of the latter on the occasion of the regency bill; and Thurlow not only spoke contemptuously of Pitt in private society, but he more than once attacked his measures in

* An allusion to the assassination of the King of Sweden, in the preceding year.

the house. The King had a great disinclination to parting with his chancellor, and things were allowed to go on for some time, until, in the session of 1792, the latter made a gross attack in the House of Lords on some of Pitt's law measures. It is even said that the King, knowing the mutual feelings of his two ministers, and attached by long habit to Thurlow, had hesitated more than once which of them should be the sacrifice; but the Queen was a firm friend to Pitt, and when, at length, at the beginning of the session, the provoked premier forced the King to an alternative, it was notified to Thurlow that he must resign. Thurlow obeyed, much against his inclination; though, on account of business pending in the Court of Chancery, he consented to remain at his post till the end of the session. On the day of prorogation, the 15th of June, he gave up the seals, which were placed in commission, but which were subsequently given to his old rival Lord Loughborough, who was one of the deserters from the Whig phalanx. The caricatures on the dismissal of Thurlow were bitterly sarcastic. One by Gillray, published on the 24th of May, entitled "The fall of the Wolsey of the Woolsack," represents him engaged in a desperate struggle for the insignia of office against the King and his two ministers, Pitt and Dundas. Another caricature by the same artist, published on the 9th of June, and entitled "Sin, Death, and the Devil," is a finely executed parody on the scene between those three characters in Milton, but it involves too coarse an outrage on the Queen, who is represented as the personification of Sin, rushing to separate the two combatants, Death (bearing the semblance of Pitt) and Satan (who exhibits the dark frowning countenance of Thurlow).

It was soon seen that Pitt's agitation against revolutionary principles had a further object than the mere repression of domestic sedition. The countenance shewn by the minister towards France was outwardly mysterious and equivocal, though not absolutely threatening; but in secret the English court was approving if not abetting the continental confederacy which was at the same moment forming with the avowed purpose of restoring monarchy in France by force of arms. A few months left no doubt that England had looked with favour upon the secret treaty of Pilnitz. On the appearance of the royal proclamation in May, the French ambassador, Chauvelin, who had but recently arrived in that capacity, made a formal remonstrance against that part of it which alluded to the correspondence with persons in foreign parts, as calculated to convey an impression that the English government gave credit to reports that France was a party to the seditious practices in England, and that England looked upon her neighbour with hostile feelings. The reply of the English secretary of State for Foreign Affairs, Lord Grenville, breathed the strongest sentiments of peace and amity, and was accompanied with expressions that gave great satisfaction to the French revolutionary government, which had suspected a secret understanding between the English court and those who were leaguing against it on the continent. Encouraged by Lord Grenville's language on this occasion, the French government made a subsequent application, through its ambassador, to engage the English King to use his good offices with his allies to avert the attack with which it was threatened from without. The reply on this occasion was conveyed in a much less satisfactory tone: Lord Grenville said, as an excuse for refusing to accede to the wishes of France, " that the same sentiments which engaged his Britannic majesty not to interfere with the internal affairs of France, equally tended to induce him to respect the rights and independence of other sovereigns, and particularly those of his allies." Down to this moment the French government appears to have placed entire faith in the good intentions of this country ; but the only sense which it could possibly make of this document was that it could no longer reckon on the friendship of England; and this, joined with the arrogant manifestoes now published by the courts of Berlin and Vienna, drove the French to desperation, destroyed entirely the little spirit of moderation that remained, and, no doubt, contributed to the disastrous scenes which followed.

The calamities of that unhappy country now succeeded one another in rapid succession. The proclamations of the allies declared very unadvisedly that for some months the King of France had been acting under constraint, and that he was not sincere in his concessions and declarations. This proceeding only tended to aggravate the French populace, and the fearful events of the 10th of August overthrew the throne, and established the triumph of democracy. The English ambassador was immediately recalled from Paris, on the pretext that his mission was at an end so soon as the functions of royalty were suspended. The French government still attempted to avert the hostility of England, and kept their ambassador in London, although the King and his ministers refused to acknowledge him in a public capacity. The horrible massacres of September quickly followed to add to the general consternation ; and vast numbers of French priests and refugees flocked to this country, to attract the sympathy of Englishmen by their misfortunes, and increase the detestation of French republicanism by their reports of the atrocities which had driven them away. Various acts followed which shewed too clearly the inclination of the French to propagate their opinions in other countries. In the National Convention, which was called together at the end of September, two members were elected from England, Thomas Paine and Dr. Priestley; the latter declined the nomination, but Paine accepted it, and proceeded to Paris to enter upon his legislative duties. Addresses and congratulations, couched in exaggerated and inflammatory language, were sent to the Convention from some of the English political societies, which laid those societies open to new suspicions; and these suspicions, and the fears consequent upon them, were increased by successes of the republican arms, and the arrogant tone now taken by the Convention itself. On the 19th of November the Assembly passed by acclamation, the famous decree,—" The National Convention decree, in the name of the French nation, that they will grant fraternity and assistance to all those people who wish to procure liberty; and they charge the executive power to send orders to the generals to give assistance to such people, and to defend citizens who have suffered and are now suffering in the cause of liberty." This was a plain announcement of a universal crusade against all established and monarchical governments, and, though itself but an empty vaunt, was calculated greatly to increase the alarm which already existed in this country. The seed which had been sown so widely by Burke's "Reflections" was thus ripened into a deep hatred of France and Frenchmen, which was kept up by the activity of the government agents throughout the country. Anti-revolution societies were formed, and exerted themselves to spread the flame; and they published innumerable pamphlets, containing exaggerated narratives of the crimes committed in France, and a variety of other subjects calculated to inflame men's passions in favour of the crown and the church. The political societies were described as secret conspiracies against the constitution, and, as the meeting of parliament approached, the ministers increased the panic by calling out the militia to protect the government against what were probably visionary dangers of conspiracy and revolt.

On the 13th of December, the session of parliament was opened with the evident prospect of a general war; and the King's speech spoke of plots and conspiracies at home fomented by foreign incendiaries, and announced that it had been considered necessary to augment the military and naval forces of the kingdom. The opposition, which had lost

much in numbers, was warm, yet more moderate than usual in
its language; it deplored the occurrence of seditious proceedings, wherever they existed, but blamed the government for
magnifying imaginary dangers and for creating unnecessary
alarm; it deprecated the haste with which ministers were
hurrying the country into an unnecessary and, probably, a
calamitous war, and urged the propriety of re-establishing the
diplomatic communications between this country and France,
with the hope of averting the disasters of war by means of
friendly negotiations. All these efforts, however, were in vain;
our ministers rejected the French offers of negotiation with
contempt; and at the beginning of 1793, M. Chauvelin, whom
the French still considered in the light of an ambassador, was
ordered to leave the kingdom. When all hopes of avoiding
hostilities between the two countries had vanished, the French
Convention anticipated our government by a Declaration of
War on the 1st of February, 1793.

In the caricatures and political prints of this period we have
abundant proofs of the exertions that were made in this country
to raise up a hostile feeling against France and the revolution.
The majority of those prints are coarse pictures of the
sanguinary conduct of the French at home; of the miseries
and atrocities of republicanism; of the altered condition of
England, if French armies or republican propagandism should
obtain the mastery. The guillotine, the dagger, the extempore
gallows, the pike, and the firebrand were exhibited in luxuriant
profusion. In a plate published on the 21st of December, "French

COMPULSATORY FEEDING.

liberty" is compared
with what the repub-
licans of France and the
political societies here
so often designated as
"English slavery:"—
A jolly son of John
Bull, surrounded with
provisions and all kinds
of comforts, is crying out
with the fear of starva-
tion and slavery, on one
side; while on the other
the hungry, ragged
Frenchman is exulting
in his own misery. The
leaders of the opposition

in Parliament, who were not daunted by the storm with which
they had to contend, became marked objects of popular odium.
They were the men who, it was represented, directed the secret
weapon which was to strike at the constitution and prosperity
of the country. A caricature published on the 12th of January,
1793, entitled "Sans-culottes feeding Europe with the bread of
liberty," represents the French propagandists by force of arms
compelling the various states around them to swallow loaves
inscribed with the word "liberty;" in the middle group Sheridan
and Fox, in the characters of sans-culottes, are driving two of
these loaves at the point of daggers into the somewhat capacious
throat of honest John Bull, who seems far from easy under the
infliction. A caricature by Sayer, published on the 15th of
December, under the title of "Loyalty against Levelling," represents the soldier and the sailor as being at this moment
England's only defence against the infectious plague of republicanism.

The caricatures on the other side of the question, at this
time, were few, and seems to have found little encouragement.
On the same day, however, which produced the caricature by
Sayer, just mentioned, the eccentric Gillray published one in an
entirely different spirit. It represents Pitt working upon the
terrors of John Bull, who carries in one arm a gun, while
the other hand is deposited in his capacious pocket, and whose
whole appearance bespeaks an alarm, with the reasons of
which he is totally in the dark. That seditious writings had
not totally seduced him, is evident from the contents of his
waistcoat pockets, in one of which is the so much dreaded
"Rights of Man," while the other contains one of the loyal
pamphlets, entitled "A Pennyworth of Truth;" his estimate of
the danger of cockades is evinced by the simplicity with which
he has placed in juxtaposition on his hat the tricolor and
the true blue, one inscribed, "Vive la liberté," the other, "God
save the King." John Bull and his conductor are placed
within a formidable fortification; the latter is looking through
a glass at a flock of geese which are seen scattered over the
horizon, but which he has metamorphosed into an army of dangerous invaders. The terror of the minister is exhibited in his
incoherent exclamations : a burlesque on his speech at the opening of parliament,—"There, John! there! there they are!—
I see them!—Get your arms ready, John!—they're rising and
coming upon us from all parts;—there!—there's ten thousand
sans-culottes now on their passage!—and there!—look on the
other side, the Scotch have caught the itch too; and the wild

Irish have began to pull off their breeches!—What will become
of us, John!—and see there's five hundred disputing clubs with
bloody mouths! and twenty thousand bill-stickers, with *Ça ira*
pasted in the front of their red caps!—where's the Lord Mayor,

John?—Are the lions
safe?—down with the
book-stalls!—blow up
the gin-shops!—cut off
the printers' ears!—O
Lord, John!—O Lord!
—we're all ruined!—
they'll murder us, and
make us into aristocrat
pies!" John is alarmed
because his master is
frightened, but his own
plain common sense is
only half smothered by
his fears.—" Aristocrat
pies!—Lord defend us!
— Wounds, measter,
you frighten a poor

A BRACE OF ALARMISTS.

honest simple fellow out of his wits! gin-shops and printers' ears!
—and bloody clubs and Lord Mayors!—and wild Irishmen without breeches — and sans-culottes!—Lord have mercy upon our
wives and daughters!—And yet I'll be shot if I can see
anything myself but a few geese gabbling together.—But Lord
help my silly head, how should such a clod-pole as I be able to
see anything right?—I don't know what occasion for I to see at
all, for that matter;—why, measter does all that for I;
my business is only to fire when and where measter orders, and
to pay for the gunpowder.—But, measter o' mine, (if I may
speak a word,) where's the use of firing now?—What can
us two do against all them hundreds of thousands of millions of
monsters?—Lord, measter, had we not better try if they wont
shake hands with us and be friends!—for if we should go
to fighting with them, and they should lather us, what will
become of you and I, then, measter!!!"

It must be confessed, however, that the French democrats on
the other side of the channel, and the demagogues of the clubs
on this side, almost daily gave new provocations to justify the
conduct of the English government, and the fears which were
now spreading universally through English society.   It was
becoming evident that no country could remain long at peace

with the French republic. In the National Convention on the
28th of September, 1792, on the question of making Savoy into
a department of France, Danton declared, amid the loud
applauses of the assembly, "The principle of leaving con-
quered people and countries the right of choosing their own
constitution ought to be so far modified, that we should
expressly forbid them to give themselves Kings. *There must be
no more Kings in Europe. One King would be sufficient to
endanger the general liberty;* and I request that a committee
be established for the purpose of promoting *a general insurrection among all people against Kings.*" It was in this spirit
that the republican government always made a distinction
between the English people and their King and minister; and
showed an inclination to correspond and treat with the people
rather than with their governors. It was William Pitt and
King George, and their aristocrats, they said, who alone were
their enemies; it was they alone who made war, and the
English people were to be appealed to against them. When
General Santerre made his farewell address to the National
Convention on the 18th of May, 1793, on his departure to act
against the royalist insurgents in La Vendée, he concluded with
the words, "After the counter-revolutionists shall have been
subdued, a hundred thousand men may readily make a descent
on England, there to proclaim an appeal to the English people
on the present war." Similar doctrines were propagated by the
revolutionary societies in England, who corresponded with the
democrats of Paris as with brothers, and who, in the latter part
of 1792, were exceedingly active. Before his election to the
National Convention, Paine published the second part of his
"Rights of Man," in which he boldly promulgated principles
which were utterly subversive of government and society in
this country. This pamphlet was spread through the kingdom
with extraordinary industry, and was thrust into the hands of
people of all classes. We are told that, as a means of spreading
the seditious doctrines it contained, some of the most objectionable parts were printed on pieces of paper, which were used
by republican tradesmen to wrap their commodities in, and that
they were thus employed even in wrapping up sweetmeats for
children. Proceedings were immediately taken against its
author, who was in Paris, for a libel against the government and
constitution, and Paine was found guilty. He was defended
with great ability by Erskine, who, when he left the court, was
cheered by a crowd of people who had collected without, some
of whom took his horses from his carriage, and dragged him

home to his house in Serjeants' Inn.   The name and opinions
of Thomas Paine were at this moment gaining influence, in
spite of the exertions made to put them down.

In his speech in court, Erskine acknowledged that the voice
of the country was against him.   The feeling of resistance to republican propagandism in England, had, indeed, become universal,
and the number of loyal societies formed for the purpose of
counteracting sedition, and said to have in many instances
received direct encouragement from the government, was increased.   Of these the most remarkable was the "Society for
preserving liberty and property against republicans and levellers,"
which held its meetings at the Crown and Anchor in the Strand,
and which had distributed abroad penny tracts in large numbers.
These consisted of popular replies to the insidious doctrines
propagated by the disciples of Paine, of encomiums on the
excellence and advantages of the British constitution, of narratives of the horrible atrocities perpetrated by the republicans in
France, and of exhortations to order and obedience.   One of the
most celebrated and successful of these publications was the
tract entitled "Thomas Bull's One penny-worth of Truth,
addressed to his brother John."   These tracts were often
accompanied with loyal and anti-revolutionary songs, such as the
following, which was one of the most popular :—

"A WORD TO THE WISE.

" The Mounseers, they say, have the world in a string,
They don't like our nobles, they don't like our King ;
But they smuggle our wool, and they'd fain have our wheat,
And leave us poor Englishmen nothing to eat.
                                                  Derry down, &c.

" They call us already a province of France,
And come here by hundreds to teach us to dance :
They say we are heavy, they say we are dull,
And that beef and plum-pudding's not good for John Bull.
                                                  Derry down, &c.

" They jaw in their clubs, murder women and priests,
And then for their fishwives they make civic feasts ;
Civic feasts ! what are they ?—why, a new-fashion'd thing,
For which they remove both their God and their King.
                                                  Derry down, &c.

" And yet there's no eating, 'tis all foolish play—
For when pies are cut upen, the birds fly away ;
And Frenchmen admire it, and fancy they see
That Liberty's perch'd at the top of a tree.
                                                  Derry down, &c.

" They say, man and wife should no longer be one,—
' Do you take a daughter, and I'll take a son.'—

And as all things are equal, and all should be free,
'If your *wife* don't suit you, sir, perhaps she'll suit *me*.'
Derry down, &c.

" But our women are virtuous, our women are fair,
Which is more than, they tell us, your Frenchwomen are ;
They know they are happy, they know they are free,
And that Liberty's not at the top of the tree.
Derry down, &c.

" Then let's be united, and know when we're well,
Nor believe all the lies these Republicans tell,
They take from the rich, but don't give to the poor,
And to all sorts of mischief they'd open the door.
Derry down, &c.

" Our soldiers and sailors will answer these sparks,
Though they threaten Dumourier shall spit us like larks ;
True Britons don't fear them, for Britons are free,
And know Liberty's not to be found on a tree.
Derry down, &c.

" Ye Britons, be wise, as you're brave and humane,
You then will be happy without any *Paine*.
We know of no despots, we've nothing to fear,
For this new-fangled nonsense will never do here.
Derry down, &c.

" Then stand by the Church, and the King, and the Laws ;
The old Lion still has his teeth and his claws ;
Let Britain still rule in the midst of her waves,
And chastise all those foes who dare call her sons slaves.
Derry down, &c."

The success of these tracts was so complete, and the opposition to government so much weakened, that it began to
be believed that the year ninety-two would see the end of
faction, and that there would be nothing but unity and
loyalty in

"NINETY-THREE.*

" All true honest Britons, I pray you draw near ;
Bear a bob in the chorus to hail the new year ;
Join the mode of the times, and with heart and voice sing
A good old English burden—'tis ' God save the King !'
Let the year Ninety-three
Commemorated be
To time's end ; for so long loyal Britons shall sing,
Heart and voice, the good chorus of 'God save the King !'

" See with two different faces old Janus appear,
To frown out the old, and smile in the new year ;
And thus, while he proves a well-wisher to crowns,
On the loyal he smiles, on the factious he frowns.
For in famed Ninety-three,
Britons all shall agree,
With one voice and one heart in a chorus to sing,
Drowning faction and party in ' God save the King !'

* This song was composed by Charles Dibdin.

" Some praise a new freedom imported from France :
Is liberty taught, then, like teaching to dance ?
They teach freedom to Britons !—our own right divine !—
A rushlight might as well teach the sun how to shine !
       In famed Ninety-three,
       We'll convince them we're free !
Free from every licentiousness faction can bring ;
Free with heart and with voice to sing ' God save the King !'

" Thus here, though French fashions may please for a day,
As children prize playthings, then throw them away ;
In a nation like England they never do hurt ;
We improve on the ruffle by adding the shirt !
       Thus in famed Ninety-three
       Britons all shall agree,
While with one heart and voice in loud chorus they sing,
To improve ' Ca ira' into 'God save the King !' "

The same activity in resistance to the invasion of French
principles produced a new host of caricatures. These were more
personal than the songs and tracts. The trial which had caused
very considerable sensation in the country, brought a number of
caricatures upon Paine. It had been preceded, on the 10th of
December, by a fine print by Gillray entitled "Tom Paine's
nightly pest," which was so well received that it was published
in imitations and pirated copies. The republican stay-maker, and
so-called citizen of the world, was represented reposing on his

BRITANNIA IN STAYS.

bed of straw, and dreaming of judges' wigs, and of all sorts of
horrors, fears, and punishments. At his bed-head are two

guardian angels, presenting the well-known faces of Fox and Priestley. On the 2nd of January, another caricature, entitled "Fashion for ease; or, a good constitution sacrificed for a fantastic form," represents Paine fitting Britannia with a new pair of stays. The lady appears to suffer under the operation, and she keeps herself steady by clinging to a ponderous oak. Over the door of a cottage on one side is the sign, " Thomas Paine, stay-maker, from Thetford—Paris modes by express." Paine did not venture to return to England, nor did his popularity in France last long; by advocating leniency towards the unfortunate king, he fell under the hatred of the violent party, and was soon after thrown into a dungeon by Robespierre and his associates. In his confinement he composed the most blasphemous of his books, the "Age of Reason." An accident alone saved him from the guillotine; and he sought his last asylum in America, where he lived many years to publish harmless abuse of the laws and institutions of his native country.

In the caricatures of the year 1793, Fox and Sheridan are the two extreme leaders of sedition—the advocates and companions of Paine—pictured *literally* in the character of sans-culottes. The fallen hopes of the great chief of the opposition had given birth, on the 2nd of January, to a caricature by Gillray, in which Fox, as the despairing Christian, eager for place and not obtaining it, with his eyes fixed on the glorious paradise of patriots, the Treasury, is sinking into the "slough of despond." On the 1st of March, the same artist pictured him as "a democrat"—a veritable sans-culotte in all the perfection of vulgarity of which that character was thought susceptible. This print is said to have given especial offence to Fox. Others represented him in all the different phases of sans-culottism. In one he was a sans-culotte advocate—"The solicitor-general for the French Republic"—studying the directions for its defence.—"1st. Insist we have done everything we ought to have done. 2nd. They have provoked us, neglected, and treated us with scorn. 3rd. How desirous we were of peace, fraternity, and equality: N.B., not to mention our under-hand proceedings. 4th. Soften the massacres. 5th. Abuse our adversaries. 6th. If likely to terminate against us, to demur to the matter of form, or move an arrest in judgment." In another, he is represented with his *bonnet rouge*, and his tricolor cockade, armed cap-à-pie with every instrument of rebellion and destruction, as "The Republican Soldier;" his "head-quarters, the Crown and Anchor—parole, Reform—countersign, Anarchy." The result of his efforts was represented in a clever print by Gillray, on the 30th

I I

of March, entitled, "Dumourier dining in state at St. James's,"
dedicated "to the worthy members of the society at the Crown
and Anchor." It appears that the liberal party had their
meeting also in this tavern. Gillray's print represents the
republican general served at table by Fox, Sheridan, and
Priestley. The first brings him the head of Pitt in a dish;
Sheridan serves him with the crown in a pie; and Priestley
offers him the mitre in a tart: all these dishes are garnished
with frogs. Other caricatures exult over the fall of Fox's political power, and the desertions of many of his friends. One of
these, published on the 7th of March, represents the two sans-
culottes, Fox and Sheridan, discarded scornfully by their old
ally, the Prince of Wales, who, a repentant prodigal, is returning
to his father's home; its title is, "False liberty rejected; or,
fraternizing and equalizing principles discarded—no more coali-
tions—no more French cut-throats." The desertion of Burke,
and his continued philippics against the French, were no less a
subject of exultation; it was represented that his former associates were paralysed with fear lest he should divulge their
secrets, and denounce their designs. In one of Gillray's caricatures, dated on the 19th of March, Burke is pictured as the
"Chancellor of the Inquisition marking the incorrigibles." On
one side is seen the door of the Crown and Anchor, (the haunt
of the Anti-Revolutionary Society,) inscribed as the "British
Inquisition." Burke, in his new character, is writing the
"Black List.—Beware of N—rf—k! P—tl—d loves us not!
The R—ss—ls will not join us! The man of the people has
lived too long for us! The friends of the people must be
blasted by us! Sheridan, Ersk . . . ." Here we trace the hand
of the denouncer no further. Fox's private circumstances were,
in the meantime, becoming more and more embarrassed, and the
great statesman—for great statesman he certainly was—was
reduced to a condition of absolute poverty. He was obliged for
a while to resign even the trifling luxuries of life, and it was
doubtful if he would not be compelled to retire from public
business. His friends, however, interfered, and in the summer
of 1793, a meeting was held at the Crown and Anchor to take
his distressed condition into consideration. The popularity
which he still enjoyed was proved by a large subscription, with
which an annuity was purchased for him. His enemies laughed
at his wants, and mocked the charity by which he was supported, in several caricatures published at the beginning of June.
One of these, published by Gillray on the 12th of June, bore the
title, "Blue and Buff Charity; or, the patriarch of the Greek

clergy applying for relief." The chairman of the committee for raising a pension for "the champion of liberty," Mr. Sergeant Adair, is doling out to Fox a bundle of unpaid bonds, dishonoured bills, and other worthless paper; while the receiver is surrounded by the figures of Earl Stanhope, Dr. Priestley, Horne Tooke, and M. A. Taylor. The secretary of the Blue and Buff Charity committee was Mr. Hall, formerly an apothecary in Long Acre, known politically by the sobriquet of "Liberty Hall:" he had married the daughter of the eccentric Lord Stanhope, who chose to prove his sincere love of the French principle of equality and fraternity by marrying his child with a plebeian Mr. Hall is represented in the caricature as a ragged personage, with a phial in his pocket containing poison for Pitt.

Under all these circumstances,—the people influenced by fear on one side and prejudice on the other,—the old popular questions of agitation in parliament had no longer any chance of success. Economy, liberty, reform, were hooted as so many synonyms for spoliation, murder, and republicanism. At the beginning of the year, (Jan. 8, 1793,) the history of reform—if it were allowed to proceed—was represented in a large print in three compartments. First was " Reform advised:" the portly figure of John Bull, seated in the midst of comforts, enjoys his beef and plum pudding, and is only interrupted by three ragged hunters of liberty, who advise him to seek reform. In the second compartment, " Reform begun," John has entered on the path thus pointed out to him, but the prospect is not encouraging; he is reduced in his personal appearance, and hobbles forward on a wooden leg; his three advisers have become victorious mob-revolutionists: they force him, with daggers and clubs, to eat frogs, a diet to which he has evidently some difficulty in accustoming himself. The movement once begun, John has no longer the power to halt: " Reform Compleat " follows, and his three advisers, with the torches of incendiarism blazing in their hands, have thrown him down and are trampling him under their feet.

Such were to be the effects of reform, according to the tracts spread abroad by the anti-revolution societies; and they inculcated the duty of unbounded gratitude to the minister then at the helm, who had saved them from such disasters, and shielded them against such advisers. In one of Gillray's best caricatures, published on the 8th of April, Pitt is represented steering the bark of Britannia, in a mean and safe course through the dangers with which it was threatened, on one side by republicanism, and on the other by despotism, and making direct for the "haven of public happiness." The print is entitled, " Britannia between Scylla and Charybdis ; or, The vessel of the constitution steered clear of the rock of democracy, and the whirlpool of arbitrary power." The ship is closely followed by three " sharks, dogs of Scylla," presenting the features of Fox, Sheridan, and Priestley.

The Reign of Terror which now prevailed in France, was but too vivid a commentary on these exaggerated representations of the dangers of political innovation.

Nevertheless, the war in which this country had engaged was far from being popular. It was soon seen that our government had hurried into it without being well prepared for hostilities, and that they carried it on without much skill. A body of English troops, under the Duke of York, had been sent into Flanders to co-operate with our German allies, but proceedings on both sides were for a while guided almost more by accident than by design, and a considerable diversion was made at the beginning of April by the defection of the French commander Dumourier, who left the service of the republic to throw himself into the hands of the Austrians. Gillray, who was in Flanders about this time, represented the " Fatigues of the campaign in Flanders," in May, in a jovial picture of drinking and licent'ousness. Many began to compare the small advantages war was likely to bring us, with its expenses and its evils. On the 3rd of June, Gillray embodied this sentiment in a print in four compartments, representing the various scenes of " John Bull's progress" in war. At first he appears happy and contented at home, in the midst of his family ; then, persuaded that his duty calls him off, he marches away boldly to encounter his enemies ; next, while the war is prolonged abroad, we are introduced to his home, where his family are reduced by distress to carry all their goods to the pawnbroker ; and, lastly, when John returns, ragged and crippled, he finds his family is as great misery as himself. Towards the end of the year, when the allies began to experience reverses, the caricatures, on one side against the war, and on the other against the French, became more numerous. Success seemed even to have quitted our old safeguard, the navy. Howe had cruised the seas with an English fleet for some weeks, and was popularly accused of having allowed the French fleet to slip away from him out of Brest Harbour, for which he was severely attacked in several caricatures. The populace believed that French gold alone had saved the republican navy ; and Gillray represented the British Admiral blinded

by a shower of guineas, in a print, published on the 10th of
December, and entitled, "A French hail storm; or, Neptune
losing sight of the Brest fleet." On the 10th of February,
1794, a still bolder caricature, by the same artist, entitled
"Pantagruel's victorious return to the court of Gargantua,"
ridicules the warlike expedition of the Duke of York. The
Duke, returned from his Flemish campaign, brings to his royal
father the keys of Paris. The monarch is seated carelessly on
his throne, in his hunting garb, to intimate that affairs of state
were not his favourite amusement. In a room behind, we perceive the Queen carefully hoarding her treasures, and receiving
further contributions from the spirit of evil. Pitt is contriving
new taxes, "Not to be felt by the swinish multitude." This
last phrase, which had been uttered by Burke in his violent
declamations against democratic agitation, was long remembered
by the popular politicians, and became subsequently a sort of
watchword to the ultra-reformers.

In the beginning of 1794, France, by immense exertions, had
rendered herself a formidable enemy to the rest of Europe, and
England at length was seized with the fear of invasion. Within
a few months, indeed, the French had invaded, with success,
nearly every country that bordered upon the French territory.
Howe's victory of the 1st of June, came fortunately to support
the spirits of Englishmen, who, however, had already become
tired of the war. The opposition in parliament now raised their
heads with exultation, and accused the ministry of rashness and
imbecility. The ministerial party subsidized abroad, and raised
soldiers at home, and they affected to laugh at their parliamentary opponents, as a parcel of quacks, who thought they possessed a nostrum against all the evils with which the country
was ever threatened. This nostrum, they said, was Charles Fox,
to be applied as prime minister. It was an old superstition
among the people of Naples, when their fearful neighbour
Vesuvius burst into eruption, to bring forth the head of their
patron saint, Januarius, and hold it forth as a safe shield against
the danger. Fox was, as it were, the political St. Januarius of
the English liberals. A caricature by Gillray, published on the
25th of July, 1794, and entitled, "The eruption of the mountain, or the Head of the protector St. Januarius carried in procession by the Cardinal Archevêque of the Lazzaroni," represents the political volcano that was overwhelming and threatening with destruction the nations of the earth, while the head of
Fox is brought forth by his followers to stop the course of the
danger. The cardinal who officiates is Sheridan; Lord Lauder-

dale carries the book, bell, and candle; the Duke of Norfolk assists with his earl-marshal's staff; Lord II. Petty and Lord Derby support the cardinal's train; Lord Stanhope brings up the rear; and a then well-known general personates a cur which always smelt fire.

Encouraged by its strength in parliament, and by the conservative spirit that had been spread through the country, the court had proceeded to measures of domestic policy, the wisdom of which might well admit of a doubt. The trial of Thomas Paine was the commencement of a series of state prosecutions, not for political offences, but for political designs. To the name of Paine had been given such unenviable notoriety, and it had caused so much apprehension in the minds of quiet people, that his case excited personally no great sympathy, though many dreaded the extension of the practice of making the publication of a man's abstract opinions criminal, when unaccompanied with any direct or open attempt to put them into effect. In the beginning of 1793, followed prosecutions in Edinburgh, where the ministerial influence was great, against men who had associated to do little more than call for reform in Parliament; and two persons, whose crimes consisted chiefly in having read Paine's "Rights of Man," and in having expressed partial approbation of his doctrines, were transported severally for fourteen and seven years! These men had been active in the political societies, and it was imagined that, by an individual injustice of this kind, these societies would be intimidated. Such, however, was not the case, for, from this moment, the clubs in Edinburgh became more violent than ever, and they certainly took a more dangerous character; so that, before the end of the year, there was actually a "British Convention" sitting in the Scottish capital. This was dissolved by force at the beginning of 1794, and two of its members were added to the convicts already destined for transportation. Their severe sentences provoked warm discussions in the English Parliament, but the ministers were inexorable in their resolution to put them in execution. In the similar prosecutions which they now commenced in England, the Court was less successful. A bookseller of London, who had published a pamphlet of a democratic tendency, entitled "Politics for the People; or, Hog's-wash," and some violent democrats of Manchester, for an alleged conspiracy, were all acquitted by the juries which tried them; and in the latter case one of the government witnesses was subsequently convicted of perjury, and sentenced to the pillory. The public agitation was much increased by these prosecutions,

and many parts of the country became the scene of serious
riots ; for there was always a mob for the prosecuted, and there
was in general also a loyal mob—a mob for the prosecutors.
This latter, in several instances, committed great outrages on
the property of individuals. The illuminations in London, on
the occasion of Lord Howe's victory, were attended with considerable uproar, and attacks were made on the houses of some of
the so-called revolutionists. It was generally believed that these
attacks were made under direct incitement from persons of
higher rank in society than those who engaged in them. The
next day, the un-aristocratic and more than eccentric Lord
Stanhope inserted the following advertisement in the newspapers :—

"OUTRAGE IN MANSFIELD STREET.

"Whereas an hired band of ruffians attacked my house in Mansfield
Street, in the dead of the night, between the 11th and 12th of June instant,
and set it on fire at different times ; and whereas a gentleman's carriage
passed several times to and fro in front of my house, and the aristocrat, or
other person who was in the said carriage, gave money to the people in the
street, to encourage them ; this is to request the Friends of Liberty and
Good Order to send me any authentic information they can procure, respecting the names and place of abode of the said aristocrat, or other
person, who was in the carriage above-mentioned, in order that he may be
made amenable to the law.   "STANHOPE.'

Earl Stanhope, the "sans-culotte
peer," figures in a multitude of caricatures, during this and subsequent
years. In the one from which the
accompanying cut is taken, published
on the 3rd of May, 1794, he is represented as the fool of the opposition, holding for his bauble a standard
with the inscription, " *Vive Égalité!*"
throwing away his breeches as a
garment inconsistent with his sans-
culottism, and trampling on his
coronet. The print gives him the
title of "The noble sans-culotte,"
and is accompanied with "a ballad
occasioned by a certain earl's styling
himself a sans-culotte citizen in the
House of Lords."

A SANS-CULOTTE NOBLE.

> " Rank, character, distinction, fame,
>   And noble birth, forgot,
> Hear Stanhope, modest Earl, proclaim
>   Himself a sans-culotte.

" Of pomp and splendid circumstance
The vanity he teaches ;
And spurns, like citizen of France,
Both coronet and breeches."

Lords Stanhope and Lauderdale were coupled together as the
two advocates of extreme democratic principles in the House of
Lords.

In the month of May, the government made a direct attack
on two of the most violent and powerful of the London societies
—the Corresponding Society and the Society for Constitutional
Information. Some of their principal members, including the
Rev. Jeremiah Joyce, (Lord Stanhope's private secretary,)
Horne Tooke, the afterwards celebrated political lecturer John
Thelwall, Thomas Hardy, Daniel Adams, and three or four
others, were arrested and thrown into the Tower on a charge of
high-treason. The papers of the societies were seized, and laid
by a royal message before parliament, and, on a very vague
report of their contents, the ministers succeeded by their overwhelming majorities in carrying hurriedly that extreme measure
under imminent danger, the suspension of the habeas corpus
act. All this violence tended on the one hand to destroy public
confidence, by disturbing the country with unnecessary terrors,
while on the other it was hastening a reaction of the public
mind against the temper into which it had been urged by conservative agitation.

The state trials took place in the months of October, November, and December, and were the cause of very great excitement.
The courts were crowded to excess, and mobs assembled out of
doors. Hardy, who had been secretary of the Corresponding
Society, was first brought to trial, which, after lasting eight
days, ended on the 5th of November in an acquittal by the jury.
The evidence amounted to nothing more than charging him with
holding certain principles, which he had done in no manner that
was absolutely illegal; and, as it appeared, the papers of the
society, on which so much stress had been laid, contained
nothing that had not before been printed in the newspapers.
Horne Tooke was next acquitted, on the 22nd of November ;
and the same fate attended all the other prosecutions. The Court,
mortified at this check, relinquished some other similar proceedings
which it had already commenced, and certainly gained no popularity by what it had done. Many, who were personally hostile
to the opinions of the men prosecuted, rejoiced with others at
their escape, and exulted in the courage and probity of English
juries. The mob carried the prisoners and their legal defenders

home from the court in triumph. The chief advocate in the defence in these state prosecutions, was Erskine.

In the course of these unwise proceedings, the ministry had received strength from a modification in its ranks, and the admission of some of the more moderate of the old Whig party, who had separated from the Foxites at the same time and on the same grounds with Burke. In July, 1794, the Duke of Portland was made third secretary of state; Earl Fitzwilliam president of the council; Earl Spencer received the office of lord privy seal; and Mr. Windham was made secretary at war. In December following, the ministry underwent some other slight modifications, the chief of which arose from the appointment of Earl Fitzwilliam to the office of Lord Lieutenant of Ireland, and of Earl Spencer to be first lord of the Admiralty, in place of Pitt's elder brother, the Earl of Chatham, who took the privy seal in exchange.

CHAPTER XIII

GEORGE III.

THE violent and unnatural agitation of the country towards extreme Toryism was now giving way to a gradual reaction, and with the year 1795 the opposition began for a moment to raise its head again. This was first shewn in the increased clamour for peace. Even some of those who sat on the ministerial benches, such as Wilberforce, expressed their dissatisfaction at the warlike tone in which the session was opened, and at the want of any expression of a pacificatory tendency in the speech from the Throne. The ministers, in defending themselves, spoke of making peace or alliance with a government like that of France as a thing to which England could hardly condescend; they said that no such peace could be lasting, and they held up again the bugbear of republican propagandism. During the spring, motion after motion was made in the House of Lords, as well as in the House of Commons, to force upon the attention of the Court the necessity of negotiating with our enemies on the other side of the water. The leaders of the opposition lost no opportunity of agitating the question ; and petitions against the war began to flow in from different parts of the country.

The Court had recourse to the old stratagem of exciting popular terror, and throwing discredit on the motives of the "patriots." Most of the old leaders of actual sedition had disappeared from the scene in one manner or other ; even Dr. Priestley had now migrated to America; but Fox and Sheridan still fought their old battle in the House of Commons ; and they found able supporters among the young statesmen who were coming forward in the political world. The ministers represented that these men were betraying the interests of their country to France, out of a blind admiration of its republican institutions, and that it was the wish to see those institutions established at home which led them to advocate peace. A caricature by Gillray, published on the 26th of January, 1795, pictures Fox as a "French telegraph making signals in the dark," and pointing out to our enemies the way into our own stronghold. Another, by the same artist, published on the 2nd of February, was entitled, "The Genius of France triumphant, or Britannia petitioning for peace;" and represented Britannia offering her crown, sceptre, spear, shield, and liberties, at the foot of a *sans-culotte* monster, crowned with the guillotine, and resting its feet on the sun and moon. Behind her come Sheridan, bringing for his offering to this new object of worship the English navy, Fox, with the bank, and Lord Stanhope, bringing for his sacrifice the English Parliament. On the 2nd of March, Gillray depicted the conse-

AN OBJECT OF WORSHIP.

quences which we were to expect from thus truckling to our enemies, in a large plate, entitled "Patriotic Regeneration, or, Parliament reformed *à la Française.*" In this "reformed" Parliament, Pitt is brought up as a culprit before the bar of the House, with Stanhope as public accuser, and Lord Lauderdale as executioner. Fox presides, with Sheridan as secretary, and Erskine as attorney-general. The body of the picture presents a wholesale scene of plunder and confusion. The three Whig lords, Grafton, Norfolk, and Derby, are burning Magna Charta and the Bible; and Lord Shelburne, who had long left the Tory camp, is weighing the cap of liberty against the crown.

Pitt's own caricaturist, Sayer, published on the 14th of April a series of what he entitled "Outlines of the Opposition in 1795, collected from the works of the most capital Jacobin artists." In the first of these prints, Wilberforce is represented in the character of a weathercock, blown round by the breath of republicanism till he stretches out his arms to "peace and fraternity with France,"—the dove bringing the olive-branch in its beak and the dagger in its claw. The next represents Whitbread, under the character of a barrel of his own beer, bursting and

driving out the members of the House by its stink; in the
fumes which issue from it we read the words "Reform,"
"Peace," "Liberty," "Equality," "No slave trade." The
speaker, with averted head, is calling to order. In another,
Lord Stanhope is formed into a vessel, urged on by the monster
of republicanism, but sailing against the "current of public
opinion" and the breeze of "loyalty;" it is entitled "The Stanhope republican gunboat, constructed to sail against wind and tide."
A fourth plate is entitled "The Bedford Level," and is aimed
against the Duke of Bedford, now one of the most energetic
opponents of the ministry, and who, on the 27th of January,
had brought forward a motion in the House of Lords for negotiations for peace. At the entrance to Bedford House, a
builder's level, inscribed "Liberty and Equality," is supported
on the heads of a jockey seated on a saddle, and a sans-culotte
seated on a pile of bags of money and a bundle of "title-deeds
of estates in ——." Each figure wears the tricoloured cockade;
and the latter of the two alludes to the liberality with which
the duke expended his money in the "good cause." The next
caricature of this series, entitled "A recruit for opposition from
the *Temple* of British Worthies," represents Fox and Lord
Derby enlisting the Duke of Buckingham. The diminutive
Earl of Derby, mounted on a table, is measuring the Duke's
height by the "standard of opposition;" Fox's flag is inscribed
"Watchword, Peace;" the Duke shows Fox his terms, "Condition, to be first Lord of the Admiralty," and says,—

> "To Pitt I made my proposition,
> But he rejected the condition,
> So I enlist with Opposition."

The last of these plates is a ludicrous burlesque on the apprehension held out by the opposition that the French might be
brought over to invade us in Dutch bottoms; the leaders, Fox,
Sheridan, Lords Stanhope and Lansdowne, and Watson, Bishop
of Landaff, are admiring the fine phantasmagoric effect produced
by this contrivance.

Two caricatures by Gillray, which appeared at this period, in-
volve bitter attacks on the opposition "patriots." The political
and religious excitement of the time, with the wonderful events
that were passing every day before people's eyes, led some persons into bold and extraordinary hallucinations, and drove others
stark mad. When the pulpit of the more sober preachers of the
gospel often resounded with denunciations in general terms of the
designs of providence, as evinced in the dreadful storm that was

now breaking over Europe, and they explained by them the un-
fulfilled prophecies of Scripture, we need not be surprised if
there were others who believed themselves endowed with the
spirit of prophecy, and who undertook to make known more
fully the events of the coming age. Among these, one of the
most remarkable was an insane lieutenant of the navy, named
Richard Brothers, who declared that he was the "nephew of
God," and that he had a divine mission, and boasted that he
was unassailable by any human power. He announced that
London was on the eve of being swallowed up and totally
destroyed, and that immediately afterwards the Jews were
to be gathered together into the promised land. It is extraordinary that an enthusiast like this should have been able
to work upon the superstitious feelings of the populace so as to
make him an object of apprehension to government; but it is
said he was believed to have become the tool of faction, and that
he was employed to seduce the people and to spread fears and
alarms. On the 4th of March he was arrested by two King's
messengers and their assistants, and placed under restraint,
though they had some difficulty in keeping off the mob, who
attempted to rescue him. The next day Gillray published the
first of the caricatures just alluded to, under the title of "The
Prophet of the Hebrews;" but the Jews here carried to the land
of promise are the leaders of the opposition in Parliament, who
are borne away by the genius of revolution towards a fiery
gallows that blazes in the distance. In the other caricature,
published on the 30th of April, under the title of "Light expel-
ling Darkness," Pitt appears drawn in glory by the lion and the
unicorn, harnessed to a triumphal car, and trampling down or
scattering before them the leaders of the opposition.

Another royal union came this year to relieve the monotony
of the usual subjects of political agitation, and this was a marriage
which affected still more the interests of the country,—that of
the heir-apparent, the Prince of Wales. The prince appears to
have been as much terrified as the people by the alarm-cry of
the ministry, and he had for some time discontinued his support
of the opposition in Parliament. The extravagance of his private
life, however, had undergone no change, and he was again deeply
involved in debt. It was under these circumstances that he was
induced to marry the Princess Caroline of Brunswick, and the
marriage ceremonies were performed by the Archbishop of
Canterbury on the 8th of April. The Tories hoped that this
marriage, which was understood to have been a favourite measure
with the King, would entirely estrange the prince from his

Whig connexions, which they always pretended to be the sole
cause of his private irregularities. A fine print by Gillray,
published a few days before the marriage, and entitled " The
Lover's Dream," embodied these sentiments : on one side of the
Prince's bed, Fox and Sheridan, his evil genii, are vanishing in
darkness before the bright vision of beauty which bursts forth
on the other side. The hopes which everybody placed in this
union were sung about in joyful ballads, and exhibited with no
less gladness in the windows of the print-shops. Yet its only
result at the moment was a new application to Parliament for
the payment of the prince's debts, and it eventually ended in
domestic unhappiness and public scandal.

The two questions on which, after that of peace, the country
was most agitated, were those of the increase of taxation and
parliamentary reform. The necessarily great expenditure of the
war, made greater by the utter want of economy shewn everywhere in the application of public money, and the extraordinary
subsidies given to foreign governments to support them in their
exertions against France, were now driving the minister to every
kind of expedient to raise money. Taxes were levied upon
articles which no one ever thought of taxing before. The most
remarkable tax of this kind, granted by Parliament in the
session of 1795, was the tax upon persons wearing hair-powder,
a fashion which was then universal among all who laid claim to
respectability in society. This tax could hardly be complained
of as a serious burden, or even as a grievance; but it was chiefly
remarkable for the extraordinary mistake which the minister
committed in boasting of the great addition which it was to
bring to the revenue; for the use of hair-powder was almost
immediately discontinued, and the produce of the tax was hardly
worth the trouble of collecting it. It became at first a party
distinction; the Whigs wore their hair cut short behind, and
without powder, which was termed wearing the hair à la guillotine; while the Tories, who continued the use of the hair-
powder, were called *guinea-pigs*, because one guinea was the
amount per head of the tax. The hair-powder tax was the
subject of many songs and *jeux-d'esprit*, as well as of several
caricatures, which, from this time to the end of the century,
became so numerous that they form a regular history of every
event that agitated society, even in a trifling degree. The larger
portion of the caricatures of the period alluded to were from the
talented pencil and graver of Gillray, and are much superior to
those of the preceding or following periods. The hair-powder
tax was brought forward by Pitt on the 23rd of February; on

the 10th of March, Gillray published a caricature under the
title of " Leaving off Powder; or, a frugal family saving a
guinea." An anonymous caricature, published on the 15th of
June, represents Pitt under the character of " a guinea-pig,"
and Fox as " a pig without a guinea." On the 1st of June the
artist just mentioned, in a caricature entitled " John Bull ground
down," had represented Pitt grinding John Bull into money,
which was flowing out in an immense stream beneath the mill.
The Prince of Wales is drawing off a large portion to pay the
debts incurred by his extravagance, while Dundas, Burke, and
Loughborough, as the representatives of ministerial pensioners,
are scrambling for the rest. King George encourages Pitt to
grind without mercy. Another caricature by Gillray, published
on the 4th of June, represents Pitt as Death on the white horse
(the horse of Hanover) riding over a drove of pigs, the representatives of what Burke had rather hastily termed the " swinish
multitude." In a caricature, published on the 12th of June,
under the title of " Blind Man's Buff; or, too many for John
Bull," the minister is represented setting all the foreign
powers on poor John to drain him of his money. A caricature
on the different progressive stages of government, as exemplified
in different countries, published on the 1st of September,
represents it first as " The State Caterpillar," its rings composed
of high offices, pensions, and other sources of extravagant
expenditure, devouring England, Scotland, and Ireland, which
are spread before it in the form of a cabbage-leaf; next it is
represented in Holland, in its transition state, as a chrysalis;
and lastly as a glorious butterfly in republican France. This
allegory represented the sentiments then held by many on the
progressive developments of the civil government, as the people
advanced from despotism to liberty.

The popular discontent was increased by the great scarcity,
and consequent dearness of provisions, which began to be felt at
the beginning of summer, and increased to an alarming degree
during the autumn. From this cause, and from grievances
connected with recruiting and press-gangs, there was much
rioting throughout the country. Considerable uneasiness was
caused at Birmingham and other places in that part of England
in the month of June, by mobs demanding " cheap bread," which
led in some cases to collisions with the military. Similar
disturbances took place in London, and the feeling of dissatisfaction extended all over the country. The government appears to
have taken no effectual measures against the increasing distress;
they merely recommended various expedients to lessen the

consumption of bread, by employing other substances, and a bill
was passed to prevent, for a period, distillation from grain; but
the attention of Parliament was chiefly occupied with
providing for the Prince of Wales. Pitt was said to have made
the singular suggestion that people should eat meat to save
bread; and a caricature, published on the 6th of July, represents
the minister as the " British butcher," serving John Bull with
dear meat to stop his cry for cheap bread. Beneath him is the
epigram,—

> *" Billy the Butcher's advice to John Bull.*
>
> " Since bread is so dear (and you say you must eat),
> For to save the expense you must live upon meat ;
> And as twelvepence the quartern you can't pay for bread,
> Get a crown's worth of meat,—it will serve in its stead."

As winter approached, the agitation became still greater, and

AN ORATOR.

the numerous demagogues
who addressed themselves
to the populace and lower
orders, took advantage of
the general discontent to
spread abroad their se-
ditious opinions. A nu-
merous meeting had been
held in St. George's
Fields in June to petition
for annual parliaments
and universal suffrage.
This sort of agitation
went on increasing, and
the London Correspond-
ing Society called a meeting on the 26th of October
in Copenhagen Fields,
where an immense multi-
tude assembled to vote
and sign addresses and
remonstrances on the state
of the country. Three
wooden scaffolds were
raised in different parts
of the field, from which three of the orators of the populace
addressed the assemblage in inflammatory language, which no
doubt contributed towards urging them to the disgraceful
outrage which followed three days later. The most active

speaker was Thelwall, who had just escaped from prison.* The opening of parliament was looked forward to with great anxiety. It was called together early, on account of the extreme distress under which the country was labouring. As the time approached, popular meetings were held in the metropolis, and preparations were made for an imposing demonstration of mob force. During the morning of the 29th of October, the day on which the King was to open the session in person, crowds of men continued pouring into the town from the various open spaces outside, where simultaneous meetings had been called by placards and advertisements, and before the King left Buckingham House, on his way to St. James's, the number of people collected on the ground over which he had to pass is said in the papers of the day to have been not less than two hundred thousand. At first the state-carriage was allowed to move on through this dense mass in sullen silence, no hats being taken off, or any other mark of respect being shewn. This was followed by a general outburst of hisses and groans, mingled with shouts of "Give us peace and bread!" "No war!" "No King!" "Down with him! down with George!" and the like; and this tumult continued unabated until the King reached the House of Lords, the Guards with difficulty keeping the mob from closing on the carriage. As it passed through Margaret Street the populace seemed determined to attack it, and when opposite the Ordnance Office, a shot of some kind, supposed to be a bullet from an air-gun, passed through the glass of the carriage window. The tumult was, if anything, more outrageous on the King's return, and he had some difficulty in reaching St. James's Palace without injury; for the mob threw stones at the state-carriage and damaged it considerably. After remaining a short time at St. James's, he proceeded in his private coach to Buckingham House, but the carriage was stopped in the park by the populace, who pressed round it, shouting, "Bread! bread! peace! peace!" until the King was rescued from this unpleasant situation by a strong body of the Guards.

The Lords were much agitated at this gross insult offered to the royal person, and were some time before they could calm themselves sufficiently to proceed to business. The Tories made a new cry against the spread of revolutionary principles, and the dangerous designs of seditious men; and they said that

* A caricatured picture of this celebrated meeting, was published on the 16th of November, under the title of "Copenhagen House." The cut given in the preceding page is taken from this print, and is understood to represent Thelwall addressing the mob.

it was the opposition shewn to ministers in parliament that encouraged the mob out of doors. Gillray gave to the public a caricature on the 1st of November, in which the attack upon the King was travestied, and each of the opposition leaders had his place in the scuffle. Pitt is seated on the box, as royal coachman; and Lords Loughborough and Grenville, Dundas, and Sir Pepper Arden hold on behind as footmen. The Duke of Norfolk presents the blunderbuss at royalty; Fox and Sheridan are bludgeon-men; and Lords Stanhope and Lauderdale and another old patriot are holding the wheels of the carriage to stop its progress.

The ministers took advantage of this riot to bring forward new bills for the defence of his Majesty's person, and to prevent assemblies of an inflammatory character, where papers were circulated and speeches made calculated to irritate the minds of his Majesty's subjects against his person and government. This measure met with the most violent opposition, and it was extremely unpopular throughout the country. People said that there were already laws enough for the protection of the crown, without any further infringement of the liberty of the subject; they beheld the government forming itself into a sort of inquisition, from the eyes of which no one would be safe; and they augured that King George and William Pitt were goading and irritating the people, until they would produce that very revolution of which they professed to entertain such profound fears. The political clubs throughout the kingdom began immediately to agitate against Pitt's new bill; and the London Corresponding Society called another public meeting. Pitt is said to have shewn the greatest symptoms of alarm on this occasion. His temerity in provoking John Bull by so many coercive measures was satirised on the 21st of November, in a caricature entitled, "The Royal Bull-fight," in which Pitt, on the white horse (the emblem of the house of Hanover,) is encountering the British Bull; the inscription is a parody on the account of a Spanish bull-fight—"Then entered a bull of the true British breed, who appeared to be extremely peaceable till opposed by a desperado mounted upon a white horse, who, by numberless wounds, provoked the animal to the utmost pitch of fury, when collecting all its strength into one dreadful effort, and darting upon its opponent, it destroyed both horse and rider in a moment." Such, it was foretold, would be the fate of King George (the white horse of Hanover), and his rider Pitt, if they urged John Bull too far. Another caricature which appeared on the 26th of November,

represents Fox and Sheridan, whose opposition to the bill
against popular meetings had been very galling to the minister,
tarring and feathering Pitt, their tar being "the rights of
the people," made to boil over by a fire the fuel of which
was "the sedition bill," "ministerial influence," and "informations." The system of spies and informers was now being
organised on a very extensive plan. A caricature, published on
the 1st of December,—one of the earlier works of this class by
Isaac Cruikshank,—represents Pitt as "the royal extinguisher,"
putting out the flame of sedition. Amid the scarcity of
provisions under which people were suffering, a caricature, published on the 24th of December, took revenge upon the minister
for the former joke of making meat a substitute for bread, and
represents him and his party feeding voraciously on English
gold as a still better substitute.

Caricatures, and other satirical productions, attacked Pitt
severely for his apparent neglect, or want of foresight, in not
making some better provision against the visitation of famine.
The premier was addicted somewhat immoderately to the
bottle, and he, as well as his great opponent, Fox, is said to
have taken his place in the House of Commons more than once
in a state of absolute intoxication. We are frequently reminded of this failing in the caricatures of the period of which
we are now speaking. When the scarcity of 1795 was just beginning, a print, published by Gillray on
the 27th of May, represents one of the
jovial scenes at Pitt's country house,
at Wimbleton, between the minister
and his friend Dundas, who was as
great a drinker as himself. It is
entitled, "God save the King! in
a bumper; or, An Evening Scene
three times a-week, at Wimbleton."
Pitt is attempting to fill his glass
from the wrong end of the bottle,
while his companion, grasping pipe
and bumper, ejaculates the words,
"Dilly, my boy — all my joy!"
Another caricature by Gillray, published on the 9th of November,
represents the supposed "fatal
effects of French defeat," upon the
intelligence of an unexpected success

A MINISTER IN HIGH GLEE.

gained by the allies; these effects are "hanging" and "drowning:"

KK2

—the former is supposed to be literal in the case of Fox, who
was always represented by the Tories as the friend of republican
France; but Pitt and Dundas are drowning in wine, the effects of
which are only fatal so far as to lay them helpless on the floor.
Among the new taxes brought forward in the spring of 1796,
was an additional duty of twenty pounds per butt on wine,
which provoked no little discontent; and the minister's wine-
bibbing propensity furnished the subject of aquudance of
satire. Gillray represented him under the character of
Bacchus, and his friend Dundas under that of Silenus, in a
caricature published on the 20th of April, 1796, with the title

BACCHUS AND SILENUS.

of "The Wine Duty; or,
the Triumph of Bacchus and
Silenus." John Bull, with
empty bottle and empty purse,
and a very long face, addresses
his remonstrance: — "Pray,
Mr. Bacchus, have a bit of
consideration for old John;
— you know as how I've
emptied my purse already for
you; and it's waundedly hard
to raise the price of a drop of
comfort, now that one's got no
money left for to pay for it!"
The ministerial Bacchus, from
his pipe of wine (which is supported on the "treasury
bench,") hiccups forth his reply:—"Twenty pounds a t-tun additional duty, i-i-if you d-d-dont like it at
that, w hy, t-t-t-then dad and I will
keep it all for o-o-our own drinking,
so here g-g-goes, old Bu-bu-bull and
mouth!"

A BRANDY-DRINKER.

The bibacious qualifications of the
patriots were, however, no less celebrated than those of the ministers, and
were in their turn brought forward as
subjects of satire or of joke. Fox and
Sheridan were notorious drinkers; and
the former is said to have been sometimes brought from the tavern late at
night to the House, on an extraordi-
nary emergency, in such a condition that he required a long

application of wet towels to his head before he was able to go to his place and speak. In a caricature by Gillray, published on the 4th of February, 1797, representing one of the private parties of the Whig leaders, here described ironically as "the feast of reason and the flow of soul," Sheridan, not satisfied with drinking wine, like his companions, is filling his bumper with brandy.

The additional wine-tax furnished subjects for other caricatures besides that by Gillray. In one, published on the 25th of April, and entitled "The Triumph of Bacchus; or, a Consultation on the additional wine-duty," Pitt is represented as Justice Midas, sitting on the wine-barrel, drinking and smoking. Dundas sits on one side, on a tub, occupied in the same manner, and exclaims, "Who dare oppose wise Justice Midas?" On the other side stands the Duchess of Gordon, Pitt's great political supporter among the ladies. She is dressed in a remarkable transparent vest, leans against a barrel, and she also drinks, while she exclaims, "Oh, what a God is Justice Midas! oh, the tremendous Justice Midas!"

Another tax, now laid for the first time, which excited both discontent and ridicule, was that upon dogs. The debates on this tax in the House of Commons appear to have been extremely amusing. In opposing the motion to go into committee, Sheridan objected that the bill was most curiously worded, as it was in the first instance entitled "A bill for the protection of his Majesty's subjects against dogs:" "from these words," he said, "one would imagine that dogs had been guilty of burglary, though he believed they were a better protection to their master's property than watchmen." After having entertained the house with some stories about mad dogs, and giving a discourse upon dogs in general, he asked, "since there was an exception in favour of puppies, at what age they were to be taxed, and how the exact age was to be ascertained." The secretary at war, who spoke against the bill, said, "it would be wrong to destroy in the poor that *virtuous feeling* which they had for their dog." In committee Mr. Lechmere called the attention of the house to ladies' lap-dogs: "he knew a lady who had *sixteen lap-dogs*, and who allowed them a roast shoulder of veal every day for dinner, while many poor persons were starving—was it not therefore right to tax lap-dogs very high? He knew another lady who kept one favourite dog, when well, on Savoy biscuits soaked in Burgundy, and when ailing, (by the advice of a doctor,) on minced chicken and sweetbread!" Among the caricatures on this subject, one by Gillray (of which there were imitations) represented Fox and his friends, hanged upon a gallows, as "dogs not worth a tax," while the supporters of government, among whom is Burke with " G. R." on his collar, are ranged as well-fed dogs, " paid for."

The ministers carried their bill to prevent seditious meetings through every stage by large majorities ; but in the course of the debates, the most unconstitutional publication that turned up, was a pamphlet, entitled " Thoughts on the English Government," by a Mr. Reeves, an active member of one of the anti-revolutionary societies, in which it was stated that " The monarchy of England was like a goodly tree, of which the Lords and Commons were merely branches; that they might be lopped off, and that the constitution of England might still go on without their aid." The whole pamphlet was read before the House of Commons, and excited considerable warmth ; but, after several debates, the author was sent from the tribunal of the House to a court of justice, in which he was prosecuted for a libel on the constitution ; but he was acquitted by the jury on the ground that his motives were not such as were laid in the information, though the jury condemned the pamphlet as "a very improper publication." The ministers were, at the same time, mortified at having their prosecutions for sedition or treason defeated by the juries, who, in almost every instance, gave a verdict of " not guilty." The societies were not destroyed, as was expected, by the government bill; on the contrary, they were encouraged by the support of some of the richer and more powerful members of the parliamentary opposition, especially of the Duke of Bedford, who now stood foremost in its ranks, and was liberally expending his money in the cause of freedom, which was certainly threatened by the ministerial measures. Gillray, on the 3rd of February, made the manner in which the patriotic duke expended his money a subject of satire in a caricature, entitled " The Generæ of Patriotism, or the Bloomsbury Farmer planting Bedfordshire Wheat." The duke is represented sowing his gold on land ploughed by Sheridan. Fox, as the sun, smiling roguishly from his orb, warms the seeds into productiveness, and they spring up behind the sower in a numerous crop of French *bonnets-rouges* and Jacobin daggers.

In the middle of February Mr. Grey again introduced a motion for peace, which was supported by the opposition, and replied to with much less warmth than formerly, and the minister acknowledged that the government was not averse to seize an opportunity of negotiating. The face of Europe had indeed changed considerab'y within a few months. On one side, our allies, in spite of ·he extraordinary sums expended in subsidies, were becoming faint and falling off before the immense armies of the republic; and, on the other, the republic itself, since the overthrow of the Jacobin party, seemed to be changing its character from a democracy to a despotic oligarchy. The fear of propagandism appeared, therefore, to have vanished, while it left us to the prospect of contending single-handed against so powerful an adversary. In this position of affairs, the English parliament was dissolved in the latter part of May, and another was elected equally subservient to the will of the minister. On the 21st of May, the day after the Parliament was prorogued, Gillray produced a caricature, entitled "The Dissolution, or the Alchymist producing an æthereal Representation," in which Pitt appears with an immense retort, distilling the old House of Commons into a new one, the members of which fall down worshipping at his feet. He heats the fire of his furnace, by which this transmutation is produced, with bright gold coin, which is described as " treasury coals."

When the new Parliament met on the 6th of October, the speech from the throne announced that steps had been taken which had opened the way for a direct negotiation for a European peace, and that an ambassador would be immediately sent to Paris with full powers to treat. It was intimated, moreover, that the wish for negotiation was hastened by the declared intention of France to attempt an invasion of this island. Lord Malmesbury was accordingly sent to Paris to open negotiations, and arrived there on the 22nd of October. The lower orders in France seem to have rejoiced at the prospect of peace, and they exhibited their feelings somewhat tumultuously in the welcome they gave to the ambassador as he passed through the provincial towns; but the Directory, after amusing him with pretended negotiations, and then treating him in a haughty and insulting manner, gave him a peremptory order to leave Paris on the 19th of December, and thus destroyed all hope of obtaining peace, under any circumstances, from the government which now ruled France, and which had imbibed too deeply the thirst for conquest and plunder, and possessed an immense army which it would have been dangerous to recall. England was thus plunged deeper than ever into the war, and, feeling that its only safety lay in conquering, entered upon it with more resolution and unanimity than ever.

The negotiation, perhaps, arose from a sudden misgiving on the part of the minister, for it seems never to have been fully

approved of by his own party, and its expediency appears to
have been very generally doubted. Burke had been the first to
protest against it, in his two eloquent "Letters on a Regicide
Peace," published in the course of the summer.* Earl Fitzwilliam entered a protest against it in the journals of the House
of Lords, on occasion of the debate on the address. Burke's
letters had produced a great sensation, and they were backed by
some bold and spirited caricatures as the period for negotiating
approached. A large print by Sayer, dated the 14th of October,
but said to have been never finished for publication, is entitled
"Thoughts on a Regicide Peace," and represents Burke dreaming of the dangers with which his country was threatened. In
the frightful vision, republican France is dictating its own terms,
while Britannia is practising a French tune, which her lion
accompanies with a dismal howl. Gillray's caricature, dated
the 20th of October (two days before our ambassador's arrival
in Paris), and entitled, "Promised horrors of the French invasion ; or, forcible reasons for negotiating a Regicide Peace," was
published, and exhibits a terrific picture of what was to be
expected if the French revolutionized England (for the French
government still patronized democracy in the countries they
wished to conquer) and made the Foxite reformers masters of
the crown and constitution. In the foreground, Pitt is bound
to a post, and is scourged by Fox, between whose legs M. A.
Taylor struts in the form of a crowing bantam-cock perched on
the handle of the bloody axe. The Duke of Bedford, as a bull,
urged on by the mob orator Thelwall, is tossing Burke into the
air. Lord Stanhope is weighing the head of Lord Grenville
against the ministerial weight of the broad bottom. Erskine,
to whom Lord Lansdowne is offering the Lord Chancellor's wig,
is employed in burning Magna Charta. Jenkinson and Canning
are hanged on the lamps. The princes are assassinated, and
their bodies thrown from the windows of Brooks's. A complicated scene of murder and plunder fills the whole picture, in the
back-ground of which we perceive the Palace of St. James's
enveloped in flames.
  The failure of our negotiations had this advantage, that it
kindled throughout the island a flame of patriotic enthusiasm,
and a determination to resent to the utmost the threat of invasion. In the midst of such feelings, it is not surprising if the
alarming budget which the minister was obliged to announce in
the beginning of the session was allowed to pass with less abso-

* This publication was one of the last of Edmund Burke's political acts.
He died on the 9th of July, 1797.

lute-discontent than usual; and that even a voluntary loan, which the government was obliged to open, was filled up with extraordinary rapidity. On the 17th of November, Gillray published a caricature entitled the "Opening of the Budget; or, John Bull giving his breeches to save his bacon." Pitt, with a large bag inscribed as the "requisition budget" open before him, is obliged to excite John Bull's apprehensions in order to extract his money from his pocket; he exclaims, "More money, John! —more money! to defend you from the bloody, the cannibal French—they're a coming!—why, they'll strip you to the very skin!—more money, John!—they're a coming—they're a coming!" The money was not all expended against French invaders, for Burke, Portland, and Dundas, as representatives of the host of pensioners, are seen behind the bag scrambling for the gold, and seconding Pitt's exhortations with their several assertions—"Ay, they're a coming!"—"Yes, yes, they're a coming!"—"Ay, ay, they're a coming—they're a coming!" John Bull, in his alarm at the report of invasion and his distrust of the professed patriots, throws money and breeches and all into the bag, with the sullen declaration, "A coming! are they? —Nay, then, take all I've got at once, Measter Billy! vor it's much better for I to ge ye all I have in the world to save my bacon, than to stay and be strip'd stark naked by Charley and the plundering French invasioners, as you say!" Charley (Fox) is seen behind declaiming across the Channel (with the fortifications of Brest in the distance)—"What! more money?—Oh! the aristocratic plunderer!—*vite! citoyens, vite!—dépêchez-vous!* —or we shall be too late to come in for any smacks of the *argent!* —*vite! citoyens, vite! vite!*" Gillray also published, at the beginning of December, a caricature on the voluntary loan, in which Pitt is represented in the character of a highwayman, presenting his blunderbuss at John Bull as he is passing by, and asking him for a voluntary contribution. It is scarcely necessary to say that this is a parody on a scene in Gil Blas.

England was now fairly entered upon that desperate struggle which eventually, after great sacrifices, raised our national glory to a far higher pitch than it had attained at any former period. The dangers to which this country was then exposed were of no trifling character—with a great burthen of taxation already weighing upon it, it was threatened with the whole resentment of a powerful enemy, who expected to find disaffection at our very heart, and who had Ireland ready to rise in rebellion at the first signal that France was advancing to its assistance. Although there must have been more of faction than of real patriotism in those who could embarrass the government at such a moment, we yet, perhaps, owe to the obstinate resistance of Fox and his party to the ministerial measures that English liberty was not, in the enthusiasm of the moment, sacrificed to court supremacy to a degree almost as disastrous even as the effects of foreign invasion.

We may trace the parliamentary battle of this session in the caricatures of the day, especially in the works of Gillray. The failure of the French expedition which was to have landed in Bantry Bay, produced from this artist, on the 20th of January, a caricature entitled the " End of the Irish Invasion ; or, the destruction of the French Armada." The faces which here man the sinking fleet, are those of Fox, Erskine, Thelwall, and others, whom the Tory satirists placed in the same rank ; the foul winds that have raised the storm in which they are perishing, are produced by Pitt, Dundas, Wyndham, and the Marquis of Buckingham, who occupy their mythological station in the clouds. The next day Gillray gave to the public another caricature, in which the minister was represented as " the giant factotum amusing himself." Pitt, seated on the canopy over the speaker's chair, in gigantic majesty, is playing at cup and ball with the world ; one foot nearly crushes Fox, Sheridan, Erskine, and other leaders of the opposition ; the other is supported on the shoulder of Dundas, and the head of Wilberforce, while Canning is devoutly kissing the toe, and the members from the Treasury benches are bowing in worship before it. This print was very popular and gave rise to at least one imitation. It is said that the facetious Caleb Whiteford, when he first saw it, made an extempore parody on the words of a well-known song :—

> " Jove in his chair,
> Of the skies lord-mayor,
> When he nods, men, yea gods, stand in awe;
> O'er St. Stephen's school
> He holds despotic rule,
> And his word, though absurd, must be law."

The ministers, indeed, now confident in their power, began to treat the opposition with scornful superiority. When Fox continued to declaim against the dangers to which they were exposing the country by their ill-conduct and improvidence, Dundas is said to have spoken of the Whig alarmist in his reply in the following terms :— " For a dozen years past he has followed the business of a Daily Advertiser, in daily stunning our ears with a noise about plots and ruin and treasons and im-

peachments;—while the contents of his bloody news turn out
to be only a Daily Advertisement for a place and a pension."
The allusion to the Whig paper told with great effect; and
shortly after, on the 23rd of January, the idea was embodied in
a caricature by Gillray, representing Fox, in the character of a
ragged newsman, with his horn, shouting the news of the
"Daily Advertiser," and knocking, but in vain, at the Treasury
gate. In their mortification at the increasing power of their
ministerial opponents, the political societies gave utterance frequently to imprudent sentiments and expressions, which were
turned to the disadvantage of the liberal party as a body. Thus,
the following sentiment is said to have been expressed in the
Whig club, on the 14th of February:—"The tree of liberty
must be planted immediately! this is the something which
must be done, and that quickly, too, to save the country from
destruction." Gillray's pencil immediately pictured the tree of
liberty, the planting of which, in the opinion of the Whigs,
would be the salvation of England—its foundation, a pile of
ghastly heads, at once recognised as those of Sheridan, Stanhope,
Thelwall, Horne Took, and other active agitators in opposition

to government; its stalk, a bloody spear, sus-
taining, as its fruit, the bleeding head of the
arch-agitator, Fox. At the latter end of
February, the French made a descent on the
coast of Wales, without any apparent object or
utility, which ended in the immediate capture
of the invaders. The opposition quickly raised
a cry against the government. A caricature
by Gillray, published on the 4th of March,
represents the hold which the Whigs thought
they had thus gained on the minister, as "Billy
in the Devil's claws," the unfortunate premier
held in the brawny grasp of Fox; but the intelligence of Jervis's brilliant victory over the
Spaniards came to set the captive loose, and
obliged the evil visitor to let go his hold in
chagrin, which is represented in an accompanying picture of "Billy sending the Devil
packing." The whole is entitled "The Tables
turned."

TREE OF LIBERTY.

A new cause of alarm was now furnished by
the embarrassments of the Bank of England,
arising from the immense sums which had been advanced to
government, and the anxiety of people in general to withdraw

their money, under the apprehension of an invasion ; and, in the
month of February, the bank announced its inability to continue
cash payments. Pitt came forward to its assistance with an act
of parliament making bank notes a legal tender, and from this
time the circulation of gold coin became almost obsolete.
Several caricatures appeared on this occasion. In one, the
minister was represented attempting a rape on the old lady of
Leadenhall-street. Another was a parody on the well-known
story of Midas—the political Midas (Pitt) instead of turning
everything into gold, turned it into paper; in the distance,
across the water, a great explosion at Brest blows into the air
a cloud of Jacobin sans-culottes armed with daggers, and the
wind from it moves the reeds (the English opposition), which
sigh forth, "Midas has ears!" The opposition are constantly
thus depicted as causing embarrassment to the government at
home for the advantage of our enemies abroad. In another
caricature on the paper-currency question, Pitt is represented
offering bank-notes to John Bull, while Fox and Sheridan are
persuading him not to take them. John, however, remains
deaf to their arguments.

John Bull's courage and patriotism, indeed, increased in
intensity, and his dislike of war diminished, as the danger
approached nearer and became more imminent. The insolence of the French Directory and of their agents, and
the atrocious threats which they held out against England,
only tended to unite all classes in the defence of their native
land. The commander of the army of invasion, General Hoche,
had already, in imagination, plundered our capital. "Coura-
geous citizens," he said to his followers, in an address which
was circulated through France, "England is the richest country
in the world—and we give it up to you to be plundered. You
shall march to the capital of that haughty nation. You shall
plunder their national bank of its immense heaps of gold. You
shall seize upon all public and private property—upon their
warehouses—their magazines—their stately mansions—their
gilded palaces; and you shall return to your own country loaded
with the spoils of the enemy. This is the only method left to
bring them to our terms. When they are humbled, then we
shall dictate what terms we think proper, and they must accept
them. Behold what our brave army in Italy are doing—they
are enriched with the plunder of that fine country, and they
will be more so, when Rome bestows what, if she does not, will
be taken by force. Your country, brave citizens, will not demand a particle of the riches you shall bring from Great Britain

Take what you please, it shall be all your own. Arms and ammunition you shall have, and vessels to carry you over. Once landed, you will soon find your way to London." These lines, which were published in most of the English newspapers and magazines in the month of March, added to the martial spirit of the people, whose property was thus threatened, and volunteer troops began to be formed in all parts of the country. The metropolis and its volunteers began again to look like Old London and its trained bands, and caricatures on these soldier-citizens soon became numerous. One by Gillray, published on the 1st of March, may be compared with the satires against the city soldiery in the days of George I.—it represents, "St. George's volunteers charging down Bond-street, after clearing the ring in Hyde Park, and storming the dunghill at Mary-bone;" and the assailants are evidently gaining an easy victory over the fashionable loungers of the former locality. A number of pictures representing the horrible consequences of French success, published during March and April, tended to keep the national spirit in a blaze.

Still John Bull grumbled at being taxed, although he was so earnestly assured that it was for his own advantage. One of the taxes proposed during the spring of 1797, which gave most room for satire and ridi-

cule, was a duty on hats, which people evaded by wearing caps. Gillray, in a caricature, published on the 5th of April, entitled "*Le bonnet rouge :* or, John Bull evading the hat-tax," intimates the danger that such taxes might drive John Bull to adopt the re-publican costume of his neighbours, and he cer-tainly does look " trans-formed." John chuckles in contemplation of the astonishment that his ruler

JOHN BULL IN BONNET ROUGE.

must feel when he beholds the strange effect of his taxes—" Wauuds! when Measter Billy sees I in a red cap how he will stare!—egad, I thinks I shall cook 'en at last!—well, if I could but once get a cockade to my red cap, and a bit of a gun—why, I thinks I should make a good stockey soldier." Other caricatures attacked the increasing system of taxation, and the minister with whom it originated, with much greater severity; they represented him as practising a continued deception—of making professions which he never intended to fulfil, and talking of objects which he took no steps to gain—in order to extract the money from John Bull's pocket. A caricature, published on the 15th of August, under the title of "Billy's Raree-Show; or, John Bull en-lighten'd," represents Pitt as the royal showman, picking John's pocket of his "savings," while the latter is looking at his exhibition. The showman, with all due gravity, is directing John's attention—"Now, pray, lend your attention to the enchanting prospect before you—this is the prospect of peace—only observe what a busy scene presents itself—the ports are filled with shipping, the quays loaded with merchandize—riches are flowing in from every

THE DISHONEST SHOWMAN.

quarter—this prospect alone is worth all the money you have got about you." The simple auditor of this fine speech, totally unconscious of the process to which his pocket is being subjected, observes, "Mayhap it may, Master Showman, but I canna zee ony thing loike what you mentions—I zees nothing but a woide plain, with some mountains and molehills upon't—as sure as a gun, it must be all behoind one of those!" The flag of the raree-show bears the inscription, "Licensed by Authority, Billy Hum's grand exhibition of moving mechanism; or, deception of the senses." Great as might be the increase of taxes in one session, the next was sure to bring with it the addition of new ones. Scarcely had the parliament begun business at the end of the year 1797, when it was announced that a heavy addition would be made to the assessed taxes. A caricaturist, in the month of December, in a print entitled, "More visitors to John Bull; or, the Assessed Taxes," represents these unwelcome guests introducing themselves to John Bull in a bodily form. The latter asks in surprise, as well as alarm,

"What do you want, you little devils?—ain't I plagued with enough of you already? more pick-pocket's work, I suppose?" The imps reply, in the most courteous manner, "Please your honour, we are the assessed Taxes."*

WE ARE THE ASSESSED TAXES.

Amid so many subjects of uneasiness, with preparations for invasion without, and when our fleets were in open mutiny at Spithead and the Nore, the question of parliamentary reform was again agitated from one end of the country to the other. In the month of May, Fox and his party made two important efforts in the House of Commons to force the ministry to more liberal measures. On the 23rd, Fox himself moved for the repeal of the acts passed in the preceding session against sedition and treason. The ministers defended warmly their coercive measures, and one of their party declared "that he considered this motion as a tissue of the web that Mr. Fox had been weaving for the last four years, which had tended to degrade this country in the eyes of foreign powers; had it not been for these acts he believed that the French national flag would have been hoisted on the Tower of London." After a long debate, Fox's motion was rejected by two hundred and sixty votes against fifty-two. On the 16th, Mr. Grey moved for leave to bring in a bill to reform the representation in the country, and explained at considerable length the principal details of his plan. The motion was seconded by Erskine, and the debate lasted till three o'clock in the morning, when it was rejected by a majority of a hundred and forty-nine against ninety-one. The leaders of the opposition now declared their

* The only copy of this caricature that I have seen is in the possession of Mr. Burke.

despair of making any impression on the House of Commons, and announced their intention for the present of taking no further part in its proceedings. The voice of Fox was scarcely heard again within the walls of St. Stephen's till after the close of the century. Sheridan alone remained at his post, and it was commonly believed that he had disagreed with his party, and that he was looking out for encouragement to desert to the ministerial side of the House. Upon this occasion the Tories complained louder than ever of the factious behaviour of the opposition; they said that the opposition had remained in the House as long as there remained any prospect of doing mischief, and then shewed their patriotism by leaving their country to its fate. Gillray published a caricature on the 28th of May, the spirit of which is sufficiently explained by its title of " Parliamentary Reform; or, Opposition rats leaving the House they had undermined." A caricature, published some days later, represents Fox slinking away from the neighbourhood of the House, after his partizans have laid the trains that were to blow up the constitution. Other caricatures traced the opposition leaders into their retreats, and shewed them encouraging and aiding sedition without the House, now that their efforts had proved useless within. On the 5th of June appeared a caricature, entitled " Diversions of Purley; or, Opposition attending their private affairs," represents Fox and his political friends in affectionate homeliness nursing two ill-favoured babes, "Sedition and Revolution." Another caricature, published by Gillray on the 16th of June, is entitled " Homer singing his verses to the Greeks;" it represents Fox and his party round the jovial table, listening to their old minstrel Captain Morris, who, all ragged and wretched, is singing them a new song. Still later on in the year, on the 24th of November, in a caricature entitled "Le coup de maître," Gillray represented Fox in the character of a political brigand, practising with his gun at the crown, lords, and commons.

It is certain that, after the secession of the opposition in the House of Commons, the agitation throughout the country became greater, and the activity of the political societies increased. Political meetings to discuss the necessity of Parliamentary reform became more frequent. One of the most remarkable of these meetings was held on the grounds at Guy's Cliff, near Warwick, under the favour of Bertie Greatbead, Esq., the proprietor of that picturesque locality, and was commemorated by a medal, an article at this time very popular as a means of spreading political opinions. Numerous medals had been struck for and against Paine. The reform medal com-memorating the meeting at Guy's Cliff, was parodied by a loyal medal, which represented on the obverse the devil holding three halters over the heads of the demagogues, while on one side the "wrong heads" are applauding them, and on the other the "right heads" are shewing disgust at their proceedings. The newspapers now became more violent and abusive, and less scrupulous in their state-ments, when they could serve their party by falsehood or misrepresentation.

It was to combat the seditious tendency of the opposition press, the attacks of which assailed the ministers with incessant gall, that the celebrated *Anti-Jacobin* was established in the latter part of November, 1797. It was conducted by some of the most talented men connected with the administration, and is remarkable for the bitterness of its satire, and the boldness of its personalities. In this respect one party was quite as little scrupulous as the other. The second number of this paper, published on the 27th of November, contained that admirable burlesque by Canning (one of the principal contributors) on the pains taken by the political agitators and so-called philanthro-pists to instil discontent into the lower orders of society, even when of themselves they were not at all inclined to be discontented:—

THE FRIEND OF HUMANITY AND THE KNIFE-GRINDER.

"*Friend of Humanity.*

" ' Needy knife-grinder ! whither are you going !
Rough is the road, your wheel is out of order—
Bleak blows the blast—your hat has got a hole in 't,
        So have your breeches !

" ' Weary knife-grinder ! little think the proud ones,
Who in their coaches roll along the turnpike-
road, what hard work 'tis crying all day, ' Knives and
        Scissors to grind, O !'

" ' Tell me, knife-grinder, how you came to grind knives !
Did some rich man tyrannically use you ?
Was it the 'squire ? or parson of the parish ?
        Or the attorney ?

L L

" ' Was it the 'squire for killing of his game ? or
Covetous parson for his tythes distraining ?
Or roguish lawyer made you lose your little
                              All in a lawsuit ?

" ' (Have you not read the 'Rights of Man' by Tom Paine ?)
Drops of compassion tremble on my eye-lids,
Ready to fall, as soon as you have told your
                              Pitiful story.'

                    " *Knife-grinder.*

" ' Story ! God bless you ! I have none to tell, sir,
Only last night, a-drinking at the Chequers,
This poor old hat and breeches, as you see, were
                              Torn in a scuffle.

" ' Constables came up for to take me into
Custody ; they took me before the justice ;
Justice Oldmixon put me in the parish-
                              stocks for a vagrant.

" ' I should be glad to drink your honour's health in
A pot of beer, if you will give me sixpence ;
But, for my part, I never love to meddle
                              With politics, sir.'

                    " *Friend of Humanity.*

" ' *I* give thee sixpence ! I will see thee damn'd first !—
Wretch ! whom no sense of wrongs can rouse to vengeance !—
Sordid, unfeeling, reprobate, degraded,
                              Spiritless outcast ! ' "

(*Kicks the Knife-grinder, overturns his wheel, and exit in a transport of republican enthusiasm and universal philanthropy.*)

This burlesque was reprinted in a broadside, on the 4th of December, with a large engraving by Gillray, in which the "friend of humanity" carries the features of Tierney, and it is dedicated "to the independent electors of the borough of Southwark," of which constituency Tierney was the representative.

In their mortification at the steady and overwhelming ministerial majorities in parliament, the opposition seceders seem to have vented their ill-humour in ultra-liberal toasts and speeches at public dinners and entertainments, and under the genial influence of the god to whom their devotions were always fervent, they sometimes uttered sentiments that were not of the most prudent description, and which were eagerly seized upon by their opponents. On the 24th of January, 1798, a grand dinner was held in the rooms of the Crown and Anchor to celebrate the birthday of Charles James Fox. Not less than two thousand persons are said to have been present. The Duke of Norfolk presided, and was supported by the Duke of Bedford,

Earls Lauderdale and Oxford, Sheridan, Tierney, Erskine, Horne Tooke, and others. Captain Morris produced three new songs for the occasion. After dinner had been withdrawn in the great room, the Duke of Norfolk, as reported in the newspapers, addressed the company nearly as follows : " We are met, in a moment of most serious difficulty, to celebrate the birth of a man dear to the friends of freedom. I shall only recall to your memory, that not twenty years ago, the illustrious George Washington had not more than two thousand men to rally round him when his country was attacked. America is now free. This day full two thousand men are assembled in this place. I leave you to make the application. I propose to you the health of Charles Fox." After this toast had been drunk, and warmly applauded, the duke gave successively, "The Rights of the people ;" "Constitutional redress of the wrongs of the people;" " A speedy and effectual reform in the representation of the people in parliament;" "The genuine principles of the British constitution ;" "The people of Ireland, and may they be speedily restored to the blessings of law and liberty." The health of the chairman was then drunk, to which the duke responded by giving "Our sovereign's health —*the majesty of the people!*" The court gave a much less favourable interpretation to these proceedings than it was probable that the actors in them ever contemplated, and the Tory press was loud in its outcries. The result was, that, within a few days after the meeting, the King dismissed the Duke of Norfolk from his offices of Lord Lieutenant of the West Riding of Yorkshire, and Colonel in the militia, which caused no less outcry in the newspapers of the opposition. A print by Gillray, published on the 3rd of February, represents the noble toastmaster, giving "the loyal toast," surrounded by Fox, Bedford, Stanhope, Sheridan, and others. The duke's seat, in place of a coronet bears the figure of a *bonnet rouge.* Above his head appear two hands, one holding a pair of scales, the other with a pair of scissors cutting off

A NOBLE TOASTMASTER.

from a long list of the honours bestowed by the crown upon the Norfolk family the two just alluded to. Just three months later, at a meeting of the Whig club, at the Free Masons' Tavern, on Tuesday, the 1st of May, Fox gave as a toast, "The sovereignty of the people of Great Britain," and accompanied it with a speech strongly condemnatory of the conduct of ministers, whom he compared with the French Directory. A similar mark of resentment was shewn towards Fox, as had already been exhibited in the case of the Duke of Norfolk ; the King immediately ordered his name to be crased from the list of

the privy council. Another caricature by Gillray, published on the 12th of May, represents the dismay of the two disgraced patriots, in a "Meeting of the unfortunato *citoyens.*" Pitt and Dundas stand as sentinels at the entrance to St. James's. Fox, who appears to have just been refused admittance, exhibits a truly rueful countenance, and meeting the duke, exclaims, "Scratch'd off! —dish'd ! —kick'd out,

PATRIOTS IN DISMAY.

dammo !" His companion in misfortune, from whose pocket hangs a paper containing the announcement of his dismissal from the lieutenancy, replies, "How? what I kick'd out !— —ah ! morbleu !—chacun à son tour ! morbleu ! morbleu !"

During these transactions, the French were constantly boasting of their preparations for the invasion of this country, and it was openly declared that they were to be assisted with a rebellion in Ireland, some discontented and ambitious democrats of that country having been in active communication with the governing powers in Paris. Threatening paragraphs from the French papers found their way continually into the English journals, and helped to keep up the alarm. It was announced that Buonaparte, now one of the most distinguished of the generals of the republic, elated with the victories of his Italian campaign, was to lead his veteran armies against England. A paragraph from a Parisian paper of the 26th of November,

1797, proclaimed that "The army of England is created; it is commanded by the conqueror of Italy. After having restored peace to the continent, France is at length about to employ all her activity against the tyrants of the seas." The London newspapers, at the end of December, published the address of the president of the Directory to Buonaparte on his arrival from the south:—"Citizen-general! crown so glorious a career by a conquest which the great nation owes to its outraged dignity. Go, and by the punishment you inflict on the cabinet of London strike terror into all the governments which shall dare to doubt the power of a nation of freemen. Pompey did not disdain to crush a nest of pirates. Greater than the Roman general, go and chain down the gigantic pirate who lords it over the seas: go and punish in London crimes which have remained unpunished but too long. Numerous votaries of liberty wait your arrival; you will find no enemy but vice and wickedness. They alone support that perfidious government; strike it down, and let its downfall inform the world, that if the French people are the benefactors of Europe, they are also the avengers of the rights of nations."

This constant declaration on the part of France that she expected to secure powerful assistance in England, injured the cause of the opposition in this country, and appeared to confirm the charges brought against them by the Tories, whose indignation was raised to the highest pitch, when, in February, the French papers brought over a printed copy of the letter by which the notorious renegade, Paine, conveyed his sentiments on the subject to the council of Five Hundred—"Citizen representatives, though it is not convenient to me, in the present situation of my affairs, to subscribe to the loan towards the descent upon England, my economy permits me to make a small patriotic donation. I send a hundred livres, and with it all the wishes of my heart for the success of the descent, and a voluntary offer of any service I can render to promote it. There will be no lasting peace for France, nor for the world, until the tyranny and corruption of the English government be abolished, and England, like Italy, become a sister republic."

As spring approached, the French papers brought frequent intelligence of preparations and orders for this threatened descent.

In England the alarm was great, and every measure was again practised that was likely to stir up and sustain a flame of patriotism, as well as to make people suspicious of the motives and designs of those who were in opposition to the ministers.

Loyal songs became suddenly more popular than all others, and new ones were regularly given to the world in the columns of the *Anti-Jacobin* and other publications. The following excellent parody appeared in this journal early in December:—

"LA SAINTE GUILLOTINE

"From the blood-bedew'd valleys and mountains of France
See the genius of Gallic invasion advance !
Old Ocean shall waft her, unruffled by storm,
While our shores are all liv'd with the *friends of Reform*.
Confiscation and Murder attend in her train,
With meek-eyed Sedition, the daughter of Paine ;
While her sportive *Poissardes* with light footsteps are seen
To dance in a ring round the gay *guillotine*.

"To London, 'the rich, the defenceless,' she comes—
Hark ! my boys, to the sound of the Jacobin drums !
See Corruption, Prescription, and Privilege fly,
Pierced through by the glance of her blood-darting eye.
While Patriots, from prison and prejudice freed,
In soft accents shall lisp the Republican creed,
And with tri coloured billets, and cravats of green,
Shall crowd round the altar of *Sainte Guillotine*.

"See the level of Freedom sweeps over the land—
The vile aristocracy's doom is at hand !
Not a seat shall be left in the house *that we know*,
But for *Earl* Buonaparte and *Baron* Moreau.
But the rights of the Commons shall still be respected—
Buonaparte himself shall approve the elected ;
And the Speaker shall march with majestical mien,
And make his three bows to the grave *guillotine*.

"Two heads, says our proverb, are better than one ;
But the Jacobin choice is for Five Heads or none.
By Directories only can liberty thrive,
Then down with the *one*, boys ! and up with the *five !*
How our bishops and judges will stare with amazement,
When their heads are thrust out at the *national casement !**
When the *national razor* has shaved them quite clean,
What a handsome oblation to *Sainte Guillotine !*"

A caricature by Gillray, published on the 1st of February, 1798, under the title of "The storm rising ; or, The Republican Flotilla in danger," represents Fox, Sheridan, and their allies, drawing the enemy's flotilla to our coast by means of a capstan and cable, while Pitt, from above, is blowing up the storm that is to drive it away—in the winds we discern the names of Duncan, Howe, Gardiner, &c., the admirals who were now making the name of England respected on the seas. The flotilla has in front the flag of "liberty," but the flag behind is inscribed as

* *La petite fenêtre* and *le rasoir national* were popular terms applied to the guillotine by the mob in France.

that of "slavery." The turrets and bulwarks represent "murder," "plunder," "beggary," and a number of other similar prospects. On the other side of the water are seen the fortifications of Brest, with the guillotine raised on its principal tower, and the devil dancing over it and playing the tune of "Over de vater to Charley!" Plenty of pictures were now published, to shew the disastrous state of things to be expected in this country, when the Whigs should have helped the French to the mastery. Of these the most remarkable was a series of four plates, engraved by Gillray, and published on the 1st of March, and said, in the corner of each plate, to be "invented" by Sir John Dalrymple. They are entitled, "The consequences of a successful French invasion." The first represents the House of Commons occupied by the triumphant democrats; the mace, records, and other furniture of the house, are involved in one common destruction, and the members are fettered in pairs, in the garb of convicts, ready for transportation to Botany Bay. In the second, the House of Lords is the scene of similar havoc; a guillotine, supported by two Turkish mutes with their bows, occupies the place of the throne; and the commander-in-chief, in his full republican uniform, pointing to the mace, says to one of his creatures, "Here, take away this bauble! but if there be any gold on it, send it to my lodging."

In the third plate, the good people of England, in rags and wooden shoes, are forced to till the ground, while their proud republican task-masters follow them with the whip. The fourth is a lesson for Ireland; having come over with the specious pretext of delivering the Catholic faith from Protestant supremacy, they abuse the Catholic clergy and plunder and profane their churches.

A FRENCH REFORMER IN PARLIAMENT.

Ireland was at this time breaking out into open rebellion, and occupied the attention of both political parties in England as seriously as the threatened invasion from France. The Whigs accused the Tories of having provoked the Irish into resistance by their tyrannical measures, and affected sympathy for their sufferings; the Tories accused the Whigs of having encouraged disaffection by their example, and by the propagation of their

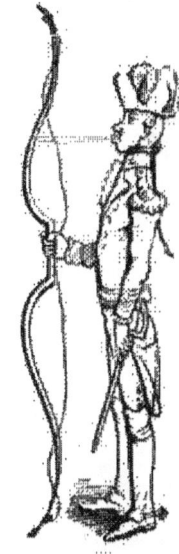

republican doctrines. Among those who preached most about English injustice in the sister island, was Lord Moira, who has been mentioned before as Lord Rawdon, and who was incessant in his declamations against English misrule. A caricature, published by Gillray on the 12th of March, represents him as "Lord Longbow, the alarmist, discovering the miseries of Ireland," and doing his best to blow the diminutive flame across the channel into a blaze with his small breath. On the 20th of March, Gillray published a caricature, entitled "Search Night; or, State Watchmen mistaking honest men for Conspirators," in which Pitt and Dundas, as watchmen, are breaking through the door of the secret apartment in which the "Corresponding Society" are supposed to be deliberating. They find the room full of daggers, caps of liberty, &c., and a party of conspirators brooding over Irish insurrection. The approach of the watchmen

LORD LONGBOW THE
ALARMIST.

has been the signal for a general flight; the Dukes of Bedford and Norfolk make their escape through the chimney; Fox and Sheridan mount through a trap-door; Tierney and two others seek concealment under the table; Moira alone, who boasted that he managed well with both parties, stands his ground: over the mantelpiece are portraits of Robespierre and Buonaparte. In June, people were excited against the Irish by pictures of the atrocities committed by the rebels, which rivalled almost the doings of French republicanism; and, among other caricatures on the same subject, published in October, is a picture of "The allied Republics of France and Ireland," in which the French ally, after enriching himself by plunder, is riding upon poor Ireland transformed into a donkey. This picture is accompanied by a mock song, burlesquing the national burthen of "Erin go bragh :"

"From Brest in the Bay of Biskey
Me come for de very fine whiskey,
To make de Jacobin friskey,
　　While Erin may go bray.

"Me have got de mealy pottato
From de Irish democrato,
To make de Jacobin fat, O,
　　While Erin may go bray.

"I get by de guillotine axes
De wheats and de oats, and de flaxes,
De rents, and de tythes, and de taxes,
　　While Erin may go bray.

"I put into requisition
De girl of every condition,
For Jacobin coalition,
　　And Erin may go bray.

"De linen I get in de scuffle
Will make de fine shirt to my ruffle,
While Pat may go starve in his hovel,
　　And Erin may go bray.

"De beef is good for my belly,
De calf make very fine jelly,
For me to kiss Nora and Nelly,
　　And Erin may go bray.

"Fitzgerald and Arter O'Connor
To Erin have done de great honour
To put me astride upon her,
　　For which she now does bray.

"She may fidget and caper and kick, O,
But by de good help of Old Nick, O,
De Jacobin ever will stick, O,
　　And Erin may go bray."

The Whigs continued to be caricatured as the patrons of French principles, whether in England or in Ireland. Gillray published, on the 18th of April, a series of "French Habits," in which the principal English Whigs were equipped in the gay theatrical costumes of the different officers of the French republican government of that time; Fox led the way as "*le ministre d'état en grand costume.*" On the 23rd of May, a caricature by Gillray parodied Milton in representing "The Tree of Liberty, with the Devil tempting John Bull." Fox, as the serpent, is offering John Bull the apple of "Reform;" but the latter is not to be tempted, for his pockets are filled with better fruit. A caricature by the same artist, published on the 26th of May, represents the "Shrine at St. Anne's Hill;"* Fox worshipping the *bonnet rouge*, which is supported on a republican altar, with the bust of Robespierre on one side, and that of Buonaparte on the other; the heads of the other leaders of the opposition, with red caps on their heads, appear as cherubs attendant on his devotions. In another caricature by Gillray, entitled "Nightly Visitors at St. Anne's Hill," published on the 21st of September, the ghosts of Lord Edward Fitzgerald, and the headless trunks of others who had fallen a sacrifice in their rebellion against the government in Ireland, are made to disturb Fox in his slumber, and accuse him of having been their first seducer.

The threats of France and her ostentatious preparations, had greatly injured the cause of the Whigs in England, where the warlike spirit had been increased by the victories gained by Duncan and other admirals at sea. Our fleet seemed to be rapidly rising in glory since the repression of the memorable mutiny at the Nore. The enthusiasm was kept up by every kind of incentive, even by "loyal" performances at the theatres. On the 9th of February, a tragedy, entitled "England Preserved," an interlude, and the farce of the "Poor Sailor," were acted at Covent Garden Theatre, and the receipts of the house appropriated to the voluntary contribution for the defence of the country. There were present Lord Bridport and Lord Hood, whose healths being drunk in the interlude occasioned such extraordinary bursts of applause, that both those naval heroes were obliged to come forward and shew themselves to the audience. This and other performances were accompanied with appropriate prologues, epilogues, and addresses, all calculated to produce the same effect. Even Captain Morris became loyal, and wrote some truly patriotic songs, of which the following, which was very popular in the month of May, is one of the best:—

A LOYAL SONG.

"Ye brave sons of Britain, whose glory hath long
Supplied to the poet proud themes for his song,
Whose deeds have for ages astonish'd the world,
When your standard you 've hoisted or sails have unfurl'd;
France raging with shame at your conquering fame,
Now threatens your country with slaughter and flame.
But let them come on, boys, on sea, or on shore,
We 'll work them again, as we 've worked them before.

* Charles James Fox's country house in Surrey, to which he retired after the secession of the opposition in the House of Commons.

"Now flush'd with the blood of the slaves they have slain,
These foes we still beat swear they'll try us again;
But the more they provoke us, the more they will see,
'Tis in vain to forge chains for a nation that's free:
All their rafts, and their floats, and their flat-bottom'd boats,
Shall not cram their French poison down Englishmen's throats.
So let them come on, &c.

"They hope by their falsehoods, their tricks, and alarms,
To split us in factions, and weaken our arms;
For they know British hearts, while united and true,
No danger can frighten, no force can subdue;
Let 'em try every tool, every traitor, and fool,
But England, old England no Frenchman shall rule.
So let them come on, &c.

"How these savage invaders to man have behav'd,
We see by the countries they've robb'd and enslav'd;
Where, masking their curse with blest Liberty's name,
They have starv'd them, and bound them in chains and in shame.
Then their traps they may set, we're aware of the net,
And in England, my hearties, no gudgeons they'll get.
So let them come on, &c.

"Ever true to our king, constitution, and laws,
Ever just to ourselves, ever staunch to our cause;
This land of our blessings, long guarded with care,
No force shall invade, boys, no craft shall ensnare.
United we'll stand, firm in heart, firm in hand,
And those we don't sink, we'll do over on land.
So let them come on," &c.

As the summer approached, all fears of invasion vanished away, and the departure of Buonaparte for Egypt shewed that the ambition of France was directed for the present to another quarter. At the beginning of October, the news of the great and decisive victory of the Nile came to cheer all hearts, except those of the seditious few who had built their prospects on the assistance of French bayonets. The Tories exulted over the supposed mortification and chagrin of men who certainly did not lament their country's glory, and a print by Gillray, published on the 3rd of October (the day after the announcement of the battle in the gazette), under the title of "Nelson's victory; or, Good news operating upon loyal feelings," represents the different Whig leaders giving unequivocal evidence of their disappointment. A caricature, published on the 6th, represents Nelson with a club, inscribed, "British Oak" clearing the Nile of its monsters—it is entitled, "Extirpation of the Plagues of Egypt; destruction of revolutionary crocodiles; or, The British hero cleansing the mouth of the Nile." Scarcely a day now passed without bringing intelligence of some new success of the British navy at sea, and John Bull seemed in danger of being surfeited with the multitude of his captures. On the 24th of October, Gillray published his caricature of "John Bull taking a luncheon; or, British cooks cramming old Grumble-Gizzard with *bonne chère*." John sitting at his well-furnished table, is almost overwhelmed by the zealous attentions of his (naval) cooks, foremost among whom, the hero of the Nile is offering him a "fricassee à la Nelson,"—a large dish of battered French ships of the line. The other admirals, in their characters of

cooks, are crowding round, and we distinguish among their contributions to John's table, "fricando à la Howe," "Dessert à la Warren," "Dutch cheese à la Duncan," and a variety of other dishes, "à la Vincent," "à la Bridport," "à la Gardiner," &c. John Bull is deliberately snapping up a frigate at a mouthful, and he is evidently fattening fast upon his new diet; he exclaims, as his cooks gather round him, "What! more frigates!—why, you rogues you, where do you

A GOOD CATLER.

think I shall find room to stow all you bring in?" Beside him stands an immense jug of "true British stout" to wash

them down; and behind him, a picture of "Buonaparte in Egypt," suspended against the wall, is concealed·by Nelson's hat, which is hung over it. Through the window we see Fox and Sheridan running away in dismay at John Bull's voracity. It was now pretty generally the hope of some, and the fear of many, in France as well as in England, that Buonaparte would never be

JOHN BULL TAKING A LUNCHEON.

able to get back to his own country, and all eyes were fixed with anxiety upon the East. Gillray published a caricature on the 20th of November, entitled "Fighting for the dunghill; or, Jack Tar settling Buonaparte," in which Jack is manfully disputing his enemy's right to supremacy over the world; the nose of the latter gives evident proof of "punishment." Jack Tar has his advanced foot on Malta, while Buonaparte is seated, not very firmly, on Turkey. At home the plan of a descent upon England was so far modified, that the invasion was to be made through Ireland, and the command of the army destined for this purpose was given to the republican General Hoche; but, while Jack Tar was thus settling Buonaparte in the

DISPUTED POSSESSION.

East, General Hoche died unexpectedly in France, and so entirely had the success of our fleets restored the feeling of security in England, that his disappearance from the stage would hardly have been perceived, had it not been announced by the grand print of Gillray, entitled "The Apotheosis of Hoche," published on the 11th of December, 1798, and the representing in one vast panorama the horrors of the French revolution crowded around its hero. The same year that witnessed the signal defeat of the navy of France, saw also the overthrow of the French prospects in Ireland, by the suppression of the rebellion.

During the spring and summer of 1798, the prosecutions for political offences had increased in number, and the whole country seems to have been invaded with an army of spies and informers. Men were dragged into court on informations of the most trifling and ridiculous kind, and it was long before this country was relieved from the evils of a disgraceful system, which, in the blindness of momentary enthusiasm, the ministry of William Pitt had been allowed to establish. An amusing caricature on this subject, published on the 2nd of April, and alluding apparently to some incident that had occurred at Winchester, is entitled "The Sedition Hunter disappointed; or, d—g by Winchester Measure." An honest farmer is dragged into court by an informer, who accuses him of having uttered the *treasonable* expression, "D—n Mr. Pitt." The sensation against the informer is unequivocally expressed; and the judge, in this case, comes to the sage opinion in the matter of law, "If a man is disposed to d—n, he may as well d—n Mr. Pitt as anybody else."

The Tories continued to exult over the defeat of "the party." There had taken place at the beginning of the year a sort of coalition between the Foxites and some of the more violent democrats, such as Horne Tooke and Frend, who had formerly repudiated Fox as not sufficiently democratic in his views, but who now expressed themselves satisfied at his declaration in favour of parliamentary reform, and proclaimed the necessity of union. On the 30th of October, after the glorious successes which had added so much to the strength of the ministers in power, Gillray published a caricature entitled, "The Funeral of the Party," in which the bier of party is borne along with a lugubrious procession, Fox, Sheridan, and their friends marching behind it as chief mourners; the Duke of Norfolk leads the procession, bearing the banner inscribed the "Majesty of the People;" and behind him Horne Tooke reads the service from "The Rights of Man." This was followed, on the 6th of November, by "Stealing off; or, Prudent Secession," a caricature alluding to the secession of the Whigs in the previous spring, and representing Fox flying from the House, where the opposition bowed down their heads overwhelmed by the successes of government. On the 17th of November, came "The Fall of Phaeton," Fox struck from his chariot by the lightning of royalty, and the Whig club involved in his destruction. Horne Tooke had now become one of the most prominent members of the reform confederacy; at one period of his career, when acting (as it was said) in the pay of government, he had published a pamphlet under the title of "Two Pair of Portraits," in which he contrasted, much to the advantage of the former, the two Pitts with the two Foxes. A caricature by Gillray on this subject, of which the accompanying plate is an accurate copy, was published on the 1st of December, with the *Anti-*

Jacobin Review; Horne Tooke is redaubing his portrait of Charles Fox, and is surrounded on every side with pictures allusive to the varying principles of his life.

The parliamentary session of 1799, opened at the end of November, 1798, when Fox kept his word of absenting himself from the debates; yet in the caricatures he was always placed foremost in the opposition. The announcement of a property and income tax at the beginning of December, produced a caricature, published on the 13th, under the ironical title of "Meeting of the Moneyed Interest," in which Fox with a begging-box by his side, is exciting against the bill a meeting of which the greater part appears to be anything but "moneyed." It was Fox, according to the same caricatures, who, in his love of faction, was now creating every possible obstacle to Pitt's favourite measure of the Irish union. A caricature by Gillray entitled, "Horrors of the Irish Union," published on the 24th of December, represents Britannia on one side of the channel, reposing amid plenty and happiness, offering to Ireland on the other side a "Union of security, trade, and liberty." The face of Fox is just seen from behind a bush, (which conceals him from Britannia, who appears not to be aware of his presence), whispering across the channel, "Hip! my old friend, Pat!—hip! —a word in your ear!—take care of yourself, Pat! or you'll be ruined past redemption. Don't you see that this d—d Union is only meant to make a slave of you? Do but look how that cursed hag is forging fetters to bind you, and preparing her knapsack to carry off your property, and to ravish your whole country, man, woman, and child!—why, you are blind, sure! Rouse yourself, man! raise all the lawyers and spur up the corporations; fight to the last drop of blood, and part with the last potato to preserve your property and independence!" Pat, who is covered with rags and wretchedness, whose whole property is comprised in a broken pike, his house in flames in the distance, looks, to use his own expression, entirely "bothered." He scratches his head as he makes his reply, "Plunder and knapsacks! and ravishments and ruin of little Ireland!—why, by St. Pathrick, it's very odd, now; for the old girl seems to me to be offering me her heart and her hand, and her trade and the use of her shillolee to defend me, into the bargain! By Jasus, if you was not my old friend, Charley, I should think you meant to bother me with your whisperings, to put the old lady in a passion, that we may not buss one another, or be friends any more."

The year 1799 was that at which the outcry against sedition

was greater than at any previous period, and in which extraordinary measures were taken to restrain the liberty or licence of the press. In July, the ministry put in effect the extreme measure of subjecting printing-presses to a licence. The Tory caricatures still boasted of the absolute defeat of opposition, and they imagined that in its despair it was laying secret trains for the destruction of the constitution, and were continually calling for severer political persecution. The King's Bench, and Newgate, and Coldbath Fields, began to be filled with political offenders; the last had received the popular epithet of the "Bastile." A caricature published with the *Anti-Jacobin Review*, and entitled, "A charm for democracy, reviewed, analysed, and destroyed, January 1st, 1799, to the confusion of its affiliated friends," represents the members of the opposition assembled in the cave of Despair, where Tooke and two of his violent colleagues, as witches, are mixing up the caldron of sedition, under the immediate presidency of the evil one. The incantation is

> "Eye of Straw, and toe of Cade,
> Tyler's brow, Kosciusko's blade,
> Russell's liver, tongue of cur,
> Norfolk's boldness, Fox's fur ;
> Add thereto a tiger's caldron,
> For the ingredients of our caldron."

Above, in the sky, appears the King on his throne, backed by his ministers, throwing a glare of light on the machinations of the disaffected patriots. The King says, "Our enemies are confounded!" Pitt urges, "Suspend their bodies!" But the chancellor, more careful of the forms of law, says, "Take them to the King's Bench and Coldbath Fields."

On the 22nd of January, the proposition for a union with Ireland was laid before Parliament in a message from the Crown. This subject, with the rebellion of the preceding year, caused the affairs of the sister island for some time to occupy a considerable share of public attention in this country. Caricatures on the subject were very numerous, as well as prints exhibiting respectively the violence and cruelty of the rebels, and the consequence of French influence. On the 1st of March was published with the *Anti-Jacobin Review* a print, apparently from the pencil of Rowlandson * (a copy of which is given in the accompanying plate), entitled "An Irish howl." It represents the

---

* Most of Rowlandson's earlier political caricatures were published without his name, and many of them were not engraved by himself, so that

United Irishmen terror-struck at a vision of the consequences of the French republican influence which they had invoked.

The property and income tax was a fruitful source of popular complaint. Gillray published on the 13th of March a caricature entitled "John Bull at his studies, attended by his guardian angel;" in which John Bull is seen puzzling himself over an immense mass of paper, rather ironically entitled, "A plain, short, and easy description of the different clauses in the income tax, so as to render it familiar to the meanest capacity." He remarks very gravely, "I have read many crabbed things in the course of my time; but this for an easy piece of business is the toughest to understand I ever met with. "Above, Pitt appears, as John's guardian angel, playing to him upon the Irish harp,—

A GUARDIAN ANGEL.

> "Cease, rude Boreas, blust'ring railer,
> Trust your fortune's care to me."

A paper on the table bears the descriptive lines,—

> "The sweet little cherub that sits up aloft,
> To keep watch for the *pure* of poor Jack."

Various seizures were made about this time of the persons and papers of some of the active members of the political societies, and the latter were laid before a secret committee of the House of Commons; but, although much noise was made on the subject, very little of importance was found among them. The populace, however, was made to believe the contrary; and a large and elaborate print by Gillray, published on the 15th of April, entitled an "Exhibition of a democratic conspiracy, with its effects upon patriotic feelings," represents the Whig leaders

It is not always easy to recognise them. The plate of which we are here speaking, however, bears very evident traces of his style, especially in some of the faces.

M M

turning away in dismay from the light thrown upon their proceedings by the committee, which illuminates a large transparency, exhibiting in four compartments the expected proceedings of the democrats in power, as they had been described over and over again in the Tory prints during the few years preceding :—first, they plunder the bank,—then they assassinate the Parliament (Fox is stabbing Pitt),—next, they steal the crown and the regalia from the Tower (Fox is carrying off the crown, and a party of sweeps are making a bonfire of the records), —and, lastly, they welcome the entry of the victorious French soldiery into the palace of St. James's. There must have been few persons left who would pay much attention to such exaggerated improbabilities as these. Yet the caricaturists persisted in their tactics of identifying English Whigs with French republicans. On the 7th of May, Gillray published a series of engravings entitled a "New Pantheon of Democratic Mythology," in one of which Fox, in allusion to his secession and retirement to the privacy of St. Anne's Hill is represented under the character of "Hercules reposing;" in another, Tierney, Sir George Shuckborough, and Mr. Jekyl, as "Harpies defiling the feast," are spoiling John Bull's roast-beef, plum-pudding, and pot of porter; and in a third the Duke of Bedford is represented as "the affrighted centaur" flying from the British lion. In another caricature by Gillray, published on the 1st of May, Fox is represented in bed, ridden over by the Hiberno-Gallic republican nightmare. It is a parody on the well-known picture by Fuseli.

During the summer of 1799, domestic agitation seems to have experienced a calm; but, when the Parliament opened at the end of September, the necessity of levying new taxes soon stirred up new subjects of discontent. Among the taxes now announced was one upon beer, which would have the effect of raising the price of porter to fourpence the pot, and which would weigh especially heavy upon the labouring classes. The satirists on the Tory side pretended to sympathize most with the staunch old Whig, Dr. Parr, who was a great porter drinker and smoker, and no less an opponent of the government of William Pitt; and, on the 29th of November, Gillray published a spirited sketch of the supposed "Effusions of a Pot of Porter; or, ministerial conjurations for supporting the war, as lately discovered by Dr. P—r, in the froth and fumes of his favourite beverage." A pot of fourpenny is placed on a stool, with the doctor's pipe and tobacco beside it; from the froth of the porter arises Pitt, mounted on the white horse, brandishing a flaming sword, and breathing forth war and destruction on everything around. The doctor's "reverie" is a satire on the innumerable mis-chiefs which popular clamour laid to the charge of the minister:— " Fourpence a pot for porter!—mercy upon us! Ah ! it's all owing to the war and the cursed ministry ! Have not they ruined the harvest ?—have not they blighted all the hops ?—have not they brought on the destructive rains, that we might be ruined in order to support the war ?—and bribed the sun not to shine, that they may plunder us in the dark ? *(Vide, the Doctor's reveries, every day after dinner.)"*

DEATH IN THE POT.

It took nearly two years to com-plete the union with Ireland; diffi-culties of various kinds arose, and had to be overcome; and some of these led eventually to the resigna-tion of the minister. It was not till the first day of the new century that the two sisters were allowed at last to join in that kindly " buss " which a former caricature insinuated that it was the aim of the Whigs to hinder.* The Union took effect on the 1st of January, 1801, and on the next day appeared the proclamation of the King's new royal titles, from which that of King of France, with the fleur-de-lis, was omitted.

A KISS AT LAST.

With the end of the century the continent of Europe entered upon a new phase of its history. After a long stay in the east, which had no other result than that of ex-hibiting to the world an extra-ordinary picture of the reckless injustice and rapacity of repub-

* This cut is taken from a large caricature by Gillray, published in 1801, entitled "The Union Club." The two figures there occupy the back of the president's chair.

M M 2

lican France, Buonaparte made his escape from Egypt. He
appeared suddenly in France, and succeeded in overthrowing
the Directory, and placing himself at the head of the state,
under the title of first consul, on the 13th of December, 1799.
The republic had now but a nominal existence, and even this
shadow of the so long vaunted French liberty had but a temporary duration. The war had been carried on by England at
sea with unvarying success; and the troops of the republic had
sustained several severe defeats on the continent of Europe
before the allied armies of the new coalition, which had been
formed at the commencement of the year. Buonaparte, immediately after his appointment as first consul, made an attempt to
get himself recognised on the footing of a sovereign prince by
King George, but without success. Yet during the year 1800,
the war seemed to fall spontaneously into a calm, and no actions
of great importance were fought by sea or land. A caricature
by Gillray remains as a memorial of the overthrow of the
French Directory; it was published on the 21st of November,
1799, and is entitled "Exit Liberté à la Française! or, Buonaparte closing the farce of Egalité at St. Cloud, near Paris, Nov.
10th, 1799."

CHAPTER XIV.

GEORGE III.

Society during the latter part of the Eighteenth Century—Costume; Extravagance of Fashions—The Balloon Mania—Gambling and its Consequences; Lord Kenyon and the Gambling Ladies—Revival of Masquerades; Mrs. Cornelys and the Panthron; Licentiousness of the Masquerades—The Opera, and its Abuses—The Stage; Sheridan, Kemble, the O. P. Riots—Private Theatricals; Wargrave and Wynnstay; the Pic-Nics—The Shakspeare Mania; Ireland's Forgeries, and Boydell's Shakspeare Gallery—Art, Literature, and Science—Peter Pindar and the Artists—The Venetian Secret—State of the Periodical Press; Literature in General; Bozzy and Piozzi—Science; the Societies; Sir Joseph Banks.

WHEN we look into the state of society in England, during the latter part of the last century, we must acknowledge the existence of many of the same causes which had led to such a fearful convulsion in the social system in France. Rousseaus and Voltaires were not wanting among our writers, and the fashionable philosophy of the day had made a deep impression. Hand in hand with it went a widely-spreading spirit of immorality and licentiousness. The mania of gambling was rendering people reckless, and throwing numbers on the world who were ready to follow any desperate course, in the hope of retrieving their shattered fortunes. The unjust monopoly of patronage by the aristocratic influence, and the neglect of a large mass of the talent of the country, was gradually teaching disaffection to the latter, and making it eager for any change that promised a chance of reaching the elevation to which it aspired. In all these respects, English society was closely imitating the example set in France; as it was in frivolity of manners, and in the extravagance of modes and dress. This imitation, towards the end of the century, was extending itself more and more into the middle classes of society, and we then, for the first time, hear general complaints that the daughters of tradesmen and farmers were sent for education to fashionable boarding-schools, and were taught to exchange the homely duties of their station for the modish accomplishments of fine ladies.

The strange vagaries in the forms of costume, among the *haut ton*, may be looked upon in some degree as indexes of the manners of the age, and are therefore not unworthy of our attention. For some years preceding the French revolution the dress of the ladies was distinguished by the same superfluity in dimensions and stiffness in form that had shone so conspicuously in the costume of the age of the Macaronis. Tho artificial mass of head-dress had, it is true, been discarded, and the natural hair had been allowed to form the chief ornament of the head, though frizzled into a bush; but this *coiffure* had been followed by enormously broad-brimmed hats, and the dress of the body was gathered into immense projections before and behind. This costume, than which nothing could be less graceful or more absurd, soon became the object of abundance of jokes and ridicule. The prominence before was made to cover the bosom, and to make it seem unnaturally large; it was formed of linen and gauze, and went by the name of a *buffont*. The prominence behind was placed lower, and was equally ugly and ridiculous. Broad caricatures represented the inconvenience of such appendages to the person; whilst others pretended to shew that they might be turned to useful purposes on extraordinary occasions. They originated, it appears, like most other fashions in dress which have prevailed in this country, in Paris, and there it was said that the posterior prominence was turned to a good account for the purpose of smuggling brandy through the gates of the city; a caricature, published in 1786, represents, in a humorous manner, the discovery of the fraud. The purposes to which

such dresses were to be turned in England are described as exhibiting still greater ingenuity. The dress was so artificially built, and so much larger than the body, that it was supposed that the latter might be withdrawn from its covering without seriously deranging it; in a caricature, published on the 6th of May, 1786, entitled, "The bum-bailiff outwitted," a lady is represented as thus escaping from the hands of her pursuer. The bailiff is seizing her from behind, and holding forth his warrant with one hand; while the lady slips away *en chemise* below, leaving the shell without the substance—hat, wig, and dress sustain themselves so well in his grasp, that it is some time before he perceives the trick which

THE BAILIFF OUTWITTED.

has been put upon him. In the January of the year following (1787), when the dimensions of the hats, as well as of the prominences behind and before, had increased considerably, a caricature, entitled "Mademoiselle Parapluie," shews how, in a sudden shower, this dress might be made to serve the purpose of an enormous umbrella, and shelter under its protection a whole family.

As it will be observed in this last caricature, the other sex had begun to adopt a hat resembling in form that worn by the ladies, instead of the cocked hat previously in use. It was with the entire change in the character of the dress of both sexes, which followed the French revolution, that the tall, narrow-brimmed hat for men —the precursor of the hat as worn at the present day—was first introduced.

MADEMOISELLE PARAPLUIE.

At the same time came in large cravats, frilled shirts, and breeches bagging out in the upper part, but contracting to the thighs, and buttoned close down the legs. At the same time came an absolute rage for striped patterns, which procured for the wearers and their apparel the title of "zebras." A fop of this period is here given, from a caricature published on the 29th of March, 1791, entitled "Jemmy Lincum Feadle;" the style is French in the extreme, and the print is accompanied with the lines so often applied in similar cases, but never more appropriately :—

A "ZEBRA."

> "Whoe'er with curious eye has ranged
> Through Ovid's tales, has seen
> How Jove incensed to monkeys changed
> A tribe of worthless men.
>
> "Jove with contempt the men survey'd,
> Nor would a name bestow ;
> But woman liked the motley breed,
> And call'd this thing a beau."

With the opening of the revolutionary period, **the costume of** the ladies underwent a very remarkable change in two of its striking peculiarities; the extraordinary stiffness and redundancy which had characterized the dress of the succeeding period was suddenly changed for extreme lightness and looseness, and the waist, which had formerly been long, was diminished until it disappeared altogether. The buffonts and the rumps " (as they were politely termed), disappeared also; the breasts, instead of being thickly covered, were allowed to protrude naked from the robe, which was very light, and hung loose from the bosom, with thin petticoats only beneath. A turban of muslin was wrapped round the head, surmounted with one, two, or three (seldom more) very high feathers, and often with straw, the manufactures in which had now been carried to great perfection. It appears to have been in 1794 that this fashion first reached so extravagant a point as to become an object of general ridicule; and the caricatures of dress during that and the following years are very numerous. The one here given, from a print ascribed to Gillray, represents an exquisite of each sex in the month of May of the year just mentioned; the gentleman is still distinguished by the great cravat and the zebra vest, which latter is made all of a piece, and so as to give him the appearance of being as lightly covered as his partner. The immense cravats of the men are caricatured in other prints which appeared during this year. In a caricature by Gillray, published in the year following, entitled " A lady putting on her cap," the lady requires the aid of two maids to hold up the immense length of muslin which, seated at her toilet, she is wrapping round her head in the form of a turban. This turban, and its single feather rising high into the air, as well as the naked breasts and the deficiency of waist, are exhibited in the next figure, taken from a caricature entitled " The Graces for 1794," published on the 21st of July in that

EXQUISITES IN 1794.

year. This lady wears another personal ornament in vogue at this period among the ladies—a watch of very large dimensions, with an enormous bunch of seals, &c., suspended from the girdle immediately below the breasts. From this girdle, without any waist, the robe flows loosely, giving the whole person an appearance as if the legs sprang immediately from the bosom.

This peculiarity was carried to still greater extravagance towards the end of the year. On the 1st of December, 1794, a caricature, entitled "The Rage; or, Shepherds, I have lost my waist," represents a lady in this predicament, refusing cakes and jelly offered her by an attendant, because her dressmaker had left her no body wherein to bestow either; it is accompanied with a parody on a popular song:—

ONE OF THE GRACES.

> "Shepherds, I have lost my waist,
>   Have you seen my body?
> Sacrificed to modern taste,
>   I'm quite a hoddy-duddy!"

> "For fashion I that part forsook
>   Where sages place the belly;
> 'Tis gone—and I have not a nook
>   For cheesecake, tart, or jelly.

> "Never shall I see it more,
>   Till common sense returning,
> My body to my legs restore,
>   Then I shall cease from mourning.

> "Folly and fashion do prevail
>   To such extremes among the fair,
> A woman's only top and tail,
>   The body's banish'd God knows where!"

This absolute banishment of the body from the female form is exhibited in the adjoining figure of a lady in full promenade dress, taken from a caricature by Gillray, entitled "Following the fashion," published on the 9th of December, 1794. This caricature, in the original, consists of two compartments: in the first, the figure here given is described as "St. James's giving the *ton*, a soul without a body;" the other presents a coarse fat dame of the city, finely but vulgarly dressed, who'

from her corpulence would find some difficulty in getting rid of
her body—she is an emblem of "Cheapside
aping the mode, a body without a soul."

NO-BODY.

The dress of the man of fashion appears to
have remained much the same from 1791 till
near the end of the century, with the exception of the hat, which, at the period of which
we are now speaking (1794 and 1795), took
several fantastic shapes, having in some cases
an enormously broad brim turned up at
the sides. On the promenade the ladies of
fashion throw their hair back over the shoulders,
and wore a hat resembling in form that
of the other sex, but much smaller, with
immense bushes of straw above. This also
was the period when parasols came into
general use, and they were carried in the
manner represented in the following figures,
taken from a caricature published on the
15th of January, and entitled "Parasols for
1795." The lady's hair, in this instance,
appears to be spread out and plaited at the
ends, and it extends over her back in such a
manner as to answer almost the purposes of a
mantle. The fashionable pair are represented in full promenade
costume, and the hat of the gentleman and the lady's parasol
appear to answer much the same purpose.

During this year, the loose dresses, especially for in-door
parties, continued in fashion with the lofty feathers, which,
to judge by their representation in the engravings of the time,
must have had a picturesque effect in large assemblies. The
short waists also still furnished matter for ridicule. In a caricature published on the 4th of August, 1795, the ladies'
dresses are ridiculed under the title of "Waggoners' frocks,
or no bodys of 1795." The satirists began also at this time to
cry out against short petticoats, and it appears to have become
the fashion to expose the legs. Straw was coming more
and more into vogue, and was more especially used in the head-
dresses, and in the out-of-doors costume, and sometimes so profusely scattered over the head and body that a print published
on the 12th of July, represents a fashionable lady under the
title of "A bundle of straw." It was at this period that
straw-bonnets began to come into use. An epilogue spoken at
Drury Lane, in November, jokes on the prevailing fashion.

> "What a fine *harvest* this gay season yields!
> Some female heads appear like *stubble-fields.*
> Who now of threaten'd famine dare complain,
> When every female forehead teems with *grain!*
> See how the *wheat-sheaves* nod amid the plumes!
> Our *barns* are now transferred to drawing-rooms;
> While husbands who delight in active lives
> To fill their *granaries* may *thrash* their wives.
> Nor wives, alone prolific, notice draw,
> Old maids and young ones, all are *in the straw!*"

The loose style of the frock is ridiculed in a caricature published on the 9th of December, under the title, "A fashionable information for ladies in the country," which is illustrated by an extract from some one of the milliners'

PARASOLS FOR 1795.

announcements for the season—"the present fashion is the most easy and graceful imaginable—it is simply this—the petticoat is tied round the neck, and the arms are put through the pocket-holes."

The fashion of light covering and exposure of the person was increasing at the beginning of 1796. A caricature published on the 20th of January, intended to improve on the actual manners of the day and picture "A lady's dress as it soon will be," represents the loose frock—the only covering—so arranged as to expose to view at every movement the whole of the body below the waist. According to other caricatures, the dresses actually worn were approaching fast towards such a con-

summation; for the body is represented as covered with little more than a mere light frock, the very pocket-holes of which became the subject of many a wicked joke. Gillray, in a caricature published on the 15th of February, 1796, endeavours to shew that these pocket-holes, when placed sufficiently high, might be made useful: a lady of rank and fashion, dressed for the rout, could perform the duties of a mother, while her carriage waited at the door, without any derangement of her garments. The title of this print is, "The fashionable mamma, or the convenience of a modern dress; vide, The Pocket-hole, &c."

If we believe numerous caricatures published at this time, ladies who carried fashion to the extreme were not content with this paucity of covering, but they had it made of materials of such transparent texture, that they rivalled the celebrated costume among the ancients of which Horace has told us—

A FASHIONABLE MAMMA.

> "— Cois tibi pœne videre est,
>   Ut nudam."

In the caricatures of the spring of 1796, we see through the thin frock the tie of the garter and the outlines of the body. We have already had to allude to a print of this date, in which the Tory Duchess of Gordon is represented in one of these transparent vests.* In a caricature by Gillray, entitled "Lady Godina's (for Godiva) Rout; or, Peeping Tom spying out Pope Joan," alluding probably to some forgotten incident of

* See p. 501.

the time, the duchess's daughter, Lady Georgiana Gordon, shortly afterwards married to the Duke of Bedford, is represented in the very height of fashion, with a vest more transparent even than we have here ventured to represent.

The caricatures are of course considerably exaggerated, but they leave no room to doubt that the peculiarities which they ridicule were carried often to an extent that we should now have a difficulty in reconciling with propriety.

Lady Georgiana's head-dress furnishes a good example of the fashionable turban and feathers, which, with most of the other characteristics of the costume of this period, continued more or less during this and the following year. To judge from many of these pictures of contemporary manners, the politeness of our countrymen during the French revolutionary period was not shewn very conspicuously, except between those who were personally acquainted. A caricature, published by Gillray on the 21st of March, 1796, and entitled " High 'Change in Bond Street ; or, la Politesse du Grande

THE HEIGHT OF FASHION IN 1796.

Monde," represents the fashionable loungers in that well-known promenade taking the pavement, while the ladies are obliged to walk in the gutter. One of these, seen from behind, represents a back view of the loose dress, and of the manner in which the hair was turned up over the turban.

The caricatures on dress became less frequent after 1796, until 1799 and 1800, when they were again numerous. The principal change which had then taken place is the altered shape of the ladies' hats, which assume the form of a rounded bonnet, and the reappearance of the waist. The general dress of the ladies now approached nearer the natural form of the body, but there was still an outcry against its transparency, and it is represented as exhibiting distinctly to view the form of the limbs, and even the garters. Examples may be seen in a caricature by Gillray, entitled " Monstrosities of 1799—see Kensington Gardens," published on the 25th of June in that year, and in several others of the same date. It would appear, that this taste for transparencies vanished in the severe winter which closed the year just mentioned, as a caricature, dated on the 5th of January, 1800, represents the ladies forced by the rigour of the weather to cover their bosoms, and adopt drawers and petticoats under their thin robes; it is entitled "Boreas effecting what health and modesty could not do."

The male costume among people of fashion had gone through a greater change during the last years of the eighteenth century, than that of the ladies. Among the "monstrosities" of the June of 1799, in the print already alluded to, is a beau in full dress. He wears large Hessian boots, with a coat of a new construction, buttoned close, and having high bunches on the shoulders; he has a large high cravat, rising above the chin, and a hat approaching nearer in shape to those worn at the present day. This costume, which was extremely ugly, was imported directly from France. The coat, perhaps from its inventor, was known by the name of a "Jean-de-Bry." If in former days of peace with France, which then under its King possessed the most polite court in Europe,

A BACK VIEW.

our countrymen cried out against the importation of French fashions, we need not be surprised if they did the same now that the two countries had been so long engaged in a war distinguished by bitter animosity on both sides, and when Englishmen had been taught to look upon our republican neighbours as models of everything that was barbarous. A caricature by Gillray, published on the 18th of November, 1799, represents a "French tailor fitting John Bull with a Jean-de-Bry." The tailor is equipped in the detested bonnet rouge and its cockade, and appears delighted with his exploit.—"A-ha! dere, my friend, I fit you to de life!—dere is liberté!—no tight aristocratical sleeve to keep from you de vat you like!—a-ha!—begar! dere be only want von leetel national cockade to make look quite à la mode de Paris!" Poor John, who stands in his great Hessian boots on a book of "Nouveaux Costumes," and has evidently no taste for French liberty in any shape, exclaims in disgust, "Liberty!

quoth'a! why, zound, I can't move my arms at all! for all it looks woundy big!—ah! d—n your French à la mode, they give a man the same liberty as if he was in the stocks!—Give me my old coat again, say I, if it is a little out at the elbows!"

But John Bull's disgust availed little in counteracting the infection of French example in this respect; and in the very year when we were about to be terrified with the most extraordinary preparations for French invasion, our enemies sent us a costume which was uglier even than that last spoken of. Its distinguishing features were the coverings of the head, which consisted, in the one sex, of an enormous military cap, and in the other of a bonnet, probably of straw, of a very ungraceful form.

ONE OF THE MONSTROSITIES.

They are represented in the accompanying cut, taken from a caricature entitled, "Two of the Wigginses—tops and bottoms of 1803," published on the 2nd of July in that year.

The frivolity of manners and sentiments which gave rise from time to time to so much exaggeration of bad taste in dress, was no less frequently exhibited in the other paths of life, not only among the votaries of fashion, but through a large portion of society. Routs and balls had become objects of profuse extravagance; masquerades were revived, and became again the fury of the day; gambling and intriguing formed the chief occupation of immense numbers in all classes of society; and novelty, however absurd, was the object of adoration of the multitude as well

JOHN BULL TRANSFORMED.

as of the select who gave the *ton*.

THE MODE IN 1803.

London was never so full of strange sights; and its population were never so ready to be gulled by them. It stands recorded in the newspapers of the time, on the 6th of September, 1785, "Hand-bills were distributed this morning, that a bold adventurer meant to walk upon the Thames from Riley's Tea Gardens." We are further informed that at the hour appointed thousands of people had crowded to the spot, and the river was so thickly covered with boats, that it was no easy thing to find enough water uncovered to walk upon. The man evaded his promise in a dishonest manner, and it was fortunate for him that the indignation of the multitude he had been the instrument of bringing together, did not lead them to open violence. In other fashionable amusements we seemed to be going back to the ages of the Roman gladiators. It was at this period that Astley established his amphitheatre.

One of the most remarkable fashions of this period was a sudden and extraordinary rage for ascending in balloons, which had been brought to a certain degree of perfection by some Frenchmen, for it was from France also that this mania was imported. It was at its height in England during the years 1784 and 1785. As early as the 2nd of December, 1783, when those aerial vehicles were newly come into notice, Horace Walpole writes, "balloons occupy senators, philosophers, ladies, everybody. France gave us the *ton*; and, as yet, we have not come up to our model." They soon became the object of epigrams, satires, speculations, and even prophecies; and people in joke, or in earnest, began to talk of scaling heaven in the face of day. An anonymous writer of a poem entitled, "The Air-balloon ; or, Flying Mortal," published in April 1784, rises from step to step till he concludes in the enthusiastic prospect:—

"How few the worldly evils now I dread,
No more confined this narrow earth to tread!
Should fire or water spread destruction drear,
Or earthquake shake this sublunary sphere,
In air-balloon to distant realms I fly,
And leave the creeping world to sink and die."

The invention was already giving rise to some apprehensions in France, for at the commencement of May a royal *ordonnance* forbad the construction or sending up of "any aerostatic machine," without an express permission from the king, on account of the various dangers attendant upon them, intimating however that these precautions were not intended to let this "sublime discovery" fall into neglect, but only to confine the experiments to the direction of intelligent persons. Blanchard was at this time the most distinguished and enterprising of the French aeronauts; his third "aerial voyage," which took place on the 18th of July, 1784,* made a great noise in England, and was soon imitated. An Italian gentleman, named Lunardi, secretary to the Neapolitan embassy, is said to have been the first person who ascended in a balloon in this country; he left the Artillery Ground in London, in company with an Englishman, at a quarter before two o'clock on Wednesday the 15th of September, 1784, and descended in a field near Ware, in Hertfordshire, at about six o'clock in the evening. In October, Blanchard came to London, and ascended from Chelsea with an Englishman named Shellon, on the 16th of October. On the 12th of November, Mr. Sadler made the first of a numerous series of aerostatic voyages, starting from Oxford. It began now to be generally acknowledged that these locomotive

FOLLY IN A NEW SHAPE.

* His first ascent had taken place on the 2nd of March. The first ascent of a balloon in France occurred on the 21st of November, 1783. The ascents in France during the year 1784 were very numerous, and excited interest even in England.

N N

machines were so liable to accidents, that they were never likely to serve any useful purpose. Yet the fashion for them increased, and for several months they were the subject of continual papers in magazines and newspapers, besides giving rise to a number of pamphlets and prints, and a few caricatures. In one of the latter, the head of Folly occupies the place of the ball, with the inscription "The English Balloon, 1784," on the front of the cap. We may quote as another proof of the extraordinary share of public attention which these machines occupied, a successful farce, entitled "Aerostation; or, the Templar's Stratagem," brought out at Covent Garden on the 29th of October; in it the passion of a lady of fortune for balloons, and her desire to ascend in one, was made to furnish a Templar with the occasion for a stratagem by which he eventually obtains her hand. The prologue to this piece thus declares the future advantages which were to arise from the popular discovery.

> "I make no doubt to entertain you soon
> With a new theatre in a *stage-balloon.*
> No more in garret high shall poets sit,
> With rival spiders spinning cobweb wit ;
> Like ancient barons future bards shall fare,
> In *their own castles* built up *in the air ;*
> Dull poets there *behind a cloud* shall stay,
> Whilst Fancy, darting to the source of day,
> Bold as an eagle, her career shall run,
> And with strong pinions fan the blazing sun."

The chronicle of events given in the magazines of 1785, describes upwards of twenty remarkable balloon excursions made during that year, seven of which occurred in the month of May. Blanchard had crossed the Channel from Dover to France in a balloon, on the 7th of January. On the 7th of May, 1785, Walpole writes from London, "of conversation, the chief topic is air-balloons: a French girl, daughter of a dancer, has made a voyage into the clouds, and nobody has yet broken a neck, so neither good nor harm has hitherto been produced by these aerial enterprises." On the 13th, Walpole adds, "Mr. Windham, the member for Norwich, has made a voyage into the clouds, and was in danger of falling to *earth,* and being *shipwrecked.* . . Three more balloons sail to-day ; in short, we shall have a prodigious navy in the air, and then what signifies having lost the empire of the ocean?" On the 15th of July, M. Rozier and another Frenchman, ascended from Boulogne, and their balloon taking fire at an immense elevation, the aeronauts were both thrown to the earth and killed. This disaster seemed to have checked the passion for travelling in the air a little; yet there were several ascents in this country in July, and an attempt was made to pass the Irish channel, which failed. They became less frequent during the following months, and by the next session they seem entirely to have lost their popularity, to make way for some new object of temporary excitement.

No single vice was contributing so much to demoralize the nation as the passion for gaming, which ran through all ranks in society, but which was carried to an extraordinary pitch in the fashionable circles. It was well known that ladies of rank and fashion in the world associated together to support their private extravagance by seducing young men to the gambling table, and stripping them of their money in the manner professionally termed "pigeoning." Faro-tables for this purpose were kept in the houses of some of the aristocracy. Three ladies in particular enjoyed this reputation, Lady Buckinghamshire, Lady Archer, and Lady Mount Edgcumbe, who from this circumstance became popularly known by the epithet "Faro's daughters." Numerous caricatures, among which are some of Gillray's happiest conceptions, have preserved the features and renown of this celebrated trio. Their infamous conduct had provoked in an especial degree the indignation of Lord Kenyon, who, on the 9th of May, 1796, in summing up a case connected with gambling, and lamenting in forcible terms that that vice so deeply pervaded the whole mass of society, animadverted with great severity on the higher orders who set the pernicious example to their inferiors, adding, with some warmth, "They think they are too great for the law: I wish they could be punished;"—and then, after a slight pause, he added, "If any prosecutions of this nature are fairly brought before me, and the parties are justly convicted, whatever be their rank or station in the country— *though they should be the first ladies in the land*—they shall certainly *exhibit themselves on the pillory.*" If they escaped that pillory to which the angry judge had devoted them, there was another pillory which exposed these gaming ladies to equal scandal, if not to an equal punishment, and instead of being pilloried once, their ladyships stood for the public view, for weeks instead of hours, in the windows of every print-shop in the town. On the 12th of May, Gillray published a caricature entitled the "Exaltation of Faro's daughters," in which Ladies Buckinghamshire and Archer are placed side by side in the threatened pillory, exposed to a shower of mud and rotten eggs which testify the joy of the mob at their disgrace; a placard stuck upon the pillory describes this process as a "Cure for gambling, published by Lord Kenyon in the Court of King's Bench, on May 9th, 1795." An imitation of this print of Gillray appeared on the 16th of May, under the title of "Cocking the Greeks," in which the same ladies are similarly exposed, but the short and

LADIES OF ELEVATED BANK.

plump Lady Buckingham is obliged to stand on the tip of her toes upon her own faro-bank box to raise her neck on a level with that of her taller companion; Lord Kenyon, in the character of public crier, is making his proclamation—"Oh yes! oh yes!—this is to give notice that several silly women, in the parishes of St. Giles, St. James, and St. George, have caused much uneasiness and distress in families, by keeping bad houses, late hours, and by shuffling and cutting have obtained divers valuable articles;—Whoever will bring before me . . . . ."

Lord Kenyon's threat, and the noise it then made abroad, seem to have had equally little effect on the patrician offenders to whom it was designed to serve as a warning. Other caricatures followed with as little success. One, published apparently about the beginning of 1797, represents these gambling dames "dividing the spoil," after a successful night, and compares them with a party of unfortunate women in St. Giles's, who are shewn in another compartment, sharing the various articles they have purloined from the pockets of their casual admirers. On one occasion, at the period just alluded to, Lady Buckingham-shire's faro-bank was stolen, while she and her party were closely occupied at their game. This circumstance produced a carica-ture by Gillray, entitled "The Loss of the Faro-bank," pub-lished on the 2nd of February, 1797, and gave rise to a mock heroic poem entitled "The Rape of the Faro-bank," which made its appearance about the same time. It was not long after this event that the offending ladies did fall into the power of their foe of the Bench. At the beginning of March, 1797, an infor-mation was laid against Lady Buckinghamshire, Lady E. Lut-terell, and some other ladies and gentlemen of rank, for keeping

faro-tables in their houses; and on the 11th of that month they
were convicted of that offence, but Lord Kenyon seems to have
forgotten his former threat, and he only subjected them to
rather severe fines. This disaster furnished matter during
several successive weeks to the newspapers for continual paragraphs, and the caricaturists took care to remind the judge
of the disproportion between his present punishment and
his former threat. In a caricature published on the 25th
of March by Gillray, Lady Buckinghamshire is undergoing the
punishment of being publicly flogged at the cart's tail, while
two of her companions are suffering in the pillory in the
distance; over the cart a board is raised with the inscription,
"Faro's daughters, beware." This print is entitled, "Discipline à la Kenyon." Another, published by the same artist on
the 16th of May, is entitled "Faro's daughters, or the Ken-
yonian blow up to the Greeks." Four ladies here figure in the
pillory, and Fox (who it was said often made one of the
gambling party), himself in the stocks, supports one of the
sufferers on his shoulders. Lord Kenyon is busily occupied in
burning the cards, dice, and faro-bank. The lesson this time
seems to have been more effectual than the former, and we hear
little of Faro's daughters after this scandal had passed away.

The pernicious effects of the passion for gambling on society
are but too evident in the manners and condition of the time.
It was rapidly demoralizing all classes, and was accompanied
everywhere with a general increase of crime, of which we evidently see but a small portion reported in the newspapers.
Various pamphlets on the criminal statistics of the metropolis,
shew us the alarming danger that existed, and the difficulty of
grappling with it. The latter part of the eighteenth century
was proverbially the age of highwaymen. On the 8th of
September, 1782, Horace Walpole writes, "We are in a state of
war at home that is shocking. I mean from the enormous
profusion of housebreakers, highwaymen, and footpads; and,
what is worse, from the savage barbarities of the two latter,
who commit the most wanton cruelties. The grievance is so
crying, that one dares not stir out after dinner but well armed.
If one goes abroad to dinner, you would think one was going to
the relief of Gibraltar."* Walpole repeats this complaint of the
numbers and boldness of highwaymen not unfrequently during
the following years; in January, 1786, the mail was stopped in
Pall Mall, close to the palace, and deliberately pillaged, at so

* It was the time of the celebrated siege of Gibraltar, when that spot was
so gallantly defended by General Elliott.

early an hour as a quarter past eight in the evening. Walpole observes in continuation of the passage just cited, "You may judge how depraved we are, when the war has not consumed half the reprobates, nor press-gangs thinned their numbers! But no wonder—how should the morals of the people be purified, when such frantic dissipation reigns above them? Contagion does not mount but descend." And he adds further, "a new theatre is going to be erected merely for people of fashion, that they may not be confined to vulgar hours—that is to day or night."

Previous to this, the masquerades, which were long discountenanced and forbidden by the Court, had been revived, by an evasion of the order against them. A German singer, named Teresa Cornelys, who had come to England in the latter years of the reign of George II., opened a kind of private opera in Soho square at the commencement of the reign of his successor, which was carried on until she was prosecuted by the manager of the Opera in the Haymarket, and compelled to close her house by the decision of a court of justice. Horace Walpole gives the following account of Mrs. Cornelys on the 22nd of February, 1771:—"Our most serious war is between two operas. Mr. Hobart, Lord Buckingham's brother, is manager of the Haymarket. The Duchess of Northumberland, Lady Harrington, and some other great ladies, without a licence erected an opera at Madame Cornelys's. This is a singular dame; she sang here formerly by the name of Pompeiati. Of late years she has been the Heidegger of the age, and presided over our diversions. Her taste and invention in pleasures and decorations are singular. She took Carlisle House, in Soho Square, enlarged it, and established assemblies and balls by subscription. At first they scandalized, but soon drew in both righteous and ungodly. She went on building, and made her house a fairy palace, for balls, concerts, and masquerades. Her opera, which she called Harmonic Meetings, was splendid and charming. Mr. Hobart began to starve, and the managers of the theatres were alarmed. To avoid the Act, she pretended to take no money, and had the assurance to advertise that the subscription was to provide coals for the poor,—for she has vehemently courted the mob,—and succeeded in gaining their princely favour. She then declared her masquerades were for the benefit of commerce." Mrs. Cornelys's masquerades had made the greatest noise, and been most magnificent, during the year 1770: they were attended regularly by all the principal nobility and gentry in the kingdom, (as we are told, at each representation, by the newspapers of the day,) who went in splendid dresses; and one peculiarity was, that now all the masks acted up to their characters. On one occasion we learn that "Miss Monckton, daughter to Lord Gallway, appeared in the character of an Indian sultana, in a robe of cloth of gold, and a rich veil. The seams of her habit were embroidered with precious stones, and she had a magnificent cluster of diamonds on her head: the jewels she wore were valued at thirty thousand pounds." Some notion may be formed of the sort of performance exhibited at these meetings from the following fragment of a newspaper report:—"Miss G——, in Leonora, looked charming; she sang the favourite air in the 'Padlock' with great sweetness. The situation of her pretty tame bird was envied by many. Mr. Andrews, in the dress of the Calmuc Tartar, was taken great notice of; the character he supported extremely well. The lady run mad for the loss of her lover, was a character well sustained for some time; but she soon recovered her senses; no other madhouse could have administered more effectual remedies. The two jockeys, who pretended to be just arrived from Newmarket, were very little knowing in any respect, and seemed more calculated for a country hop than the turf. The nurse with the child was rather diverting, but the brat very noisy and troublesome." Such remarks as these were continued through the whole assembly. On the 27th of February, 1770, we are informed that "Some of the most remarkable figures were,—a highlander (Mr. R. Conway); a double man, half miller, half chimney-sweeper (Sir R. Phillips); a political bedlamite, run mad for Wilkes and liberty and No. 45; a figure of Adam, in flesh-coloured silk, with an apron of fig-leaves; a druid (Sir W. W. Wynne); a figure of somebody; a figure of nobody; a running footman, very richly dressed, with a cap set with diamonds, and the words 'Tuesday night's club' in the front (the Earl of Carlisle); his Royal Highness the Duke of Gloucester in the old English habit, with a star on the cloak," &c. One of the grandest masquerades at the Soho rooms was that on the 7th of February, 1771, where two royal dukes, and nearly all the fashionable portion of the aristocracy, were present. On this occasion Colonel Luttrell (the same who had opposed Wilkes in the election for Middlesex,) appeared as a dead corpse in a shroud, with his coffin. The taste for political allusions at these assemblies gained ground, and they soon became veritable caricatures, not only upon society itself, but upon the events of the day. At a masquerade in 1784, we are informed in the newspaper report, that "A figure representing Secret Influence, was well-drest, and seasonable in its point. He wore a black cloak, tied round with a girdle, labelled 'Secret Influence,'—a double face, and a wooden temple on the top of his head. A ladder was painted down his back, entitled 'The back stairs.' He had a dark lantern in his hand; but with all these accoutrements he was very dull; he hardly opened his mouth, and when he did, he muttered some jargon in a whisper unintelligible to common ears; but perhaps he was in character to speak in whispers, and his inefficacy was design. He was followed by Public Ruin, which also was well equipped, and very pitiable." One of the characters in a masquerade in 1774 was "a mad politician," who was covered with bills and acts of parliament; "having lost the Boston port bill, he humorously accused Mr. Wedderburn of stealing it."

These masquerades were professedly private meetings, and their pretended object was to raise money for the poor; yet, in spite of the high rank of the people who attended them, great improprieties were allowed, and they led, under cover of the mask, to extraordinary licentiousness. Mrs. Cornelys was prosecuted for giving masquerades without licence, in 1771; and in the same year bills of indictment were preferred against her by the grand jury of Middlesex, in which she is accused of "keeping and maintaining a common and disorderly house," and the fashionable company who frequented it are described as "divers loose, idle, and disorderly persons, as well men as women!" whom she "did permit and suffer to be and remain during the whole night, rioting, and otherwise misbehaving themselves." So far, however, from the masquerades being checked by such scandal, it was at this time that the rival and splendid Pantheon in Oxford Street (then called Oxford Road) was opened, and for several years the two establishments emulated each other in magnificence and gaiety, although Mrs. Cornelys became involved in difficulties, and her establishment experienced a temporary interruption.

The disorders of these assemblies seem, however, to have increased, and the public ear was continually offended with the scenes that took place in them. The want of delicacy in the fashionable company who chiefly supported Mrs. Cornelys had winked at the admission of loose women, and this was gradually carried to such an extent, that in the spring of 1772 it became the subject of so much scandal that it was found necessary to complain. In the following season the bench of bishops thought it their duty to interfere to put down the Pantheon masquerades, but a powerful intercession was made in their favour, and it was represented in this case also that their only object was the charitable one of raising money for the suffering poor. A caricature, representing the Macaronis petitioning the bishops in favour of the masquerades, entitled "'The Pantheon Petition," was published with the *Oxford Magazine* in January, 1773. At a masquerade at the Pantheon on the 18th of February following, the number of people of rank and position in the world who attended was estimated at fourteen hundred. Yet during this and the following year the licentiousness of these mixed assemblies was carried to so alarming a height, that the very actors in them became gradually disgusted,* and they seemed to be rapidly going out of fashion. In 1776 Mrs. Cornelys re-opened Carlisle House in a style of extraordinary splendour, and the masquerades became as much the fashion as ever. In 1778, this lady, who had ruined herself by her exertions, was obliged to quit the management, which was carried on during another year unsuccessfully, and the masquerades at Carlisle House soon gave place to lectures and public assemblies of a totally different character. The *European Magazine* for July, 1789, contains "An Elegy written in Soho Square, on seeing Mrs. Cornelys's House in ruins." Mrs. Cornelys herself was eventually reduced to a state of helpless poverty; she died in the Fleet Prison in 1797.

The masquerades continued to flourish at the Pantheon, and were given also at the Opera House, at Ranelagh, and in other places, but they became gradually more and more degraded in their moral character. One of the newspaper critiques on the masquerade at Carlisle House in February, 1779, laments gravely, "We were sorry to see such spirited exertions so poorly

---

* The report of the masquerade at the Pantheon, in May, 1774, given in the *Westminster Magazine*, (which was far from straight-laced in its morality,) observes,—"The last masquerade has had different accounts given of it, according as individuals felt. But, as one entirely unprejudiced, I do pronounce it uncommonly dull, but more particularly before supper. The champaign made some eyes sparkle, which nothing else could brighten, though a deal of wanton love was exercised to effect purposes most base and dishonourable. The room was crowded with courtezans; there was not a duenna in town who had not brought her Circassians to market; and, towards the conclusion of the debauch, I beheld scenes in the rooms up-stairs too gross for repetition. I saw ladies and gentlemen together in attitudes and positions that would have disgraced the court of Comus; ladies with their hair dishevelled, and their robes almost torn off. In short, I am so thoroughly sick of masquerading, from what I beheld there, that I do seriously decry them, as subversive of virtue, and every noble and domestic point of honour."

rewarded, as scarcely one person of distinction, or one *fille de joye* of note, was present, to give a *ton* to the eveniug's entertainments."   At length we read in the *St. James's Chronicle* of April 23, 1795, the remark, that "No amusement seems to have fallen into greater contempt in this country than the masquerades . . . . . . they have been lately mere assemblages of the idle and profligate of both sexes, who made up in indecency what they wanted in wit."

The extreme licentiousness which appears to have reigned amid these riotous amusements, and the still greater immorality to which they led, was, like the mania of the women for gambling, only one shade of the general profligacy of this age.   The shameless immorality which reigned among the higher classes in general, and which was propagated by example to the middle and lower classes, is but too evident in the popular writings of the day.   The newspapers are full of advertisements offering means of indulgence.   Instead of matrimonial advertisements, we meet with advertisements for mistresses ; and, to quote a particular example, in 1794, the newspapers contain public advertisements of persons whose business it was to furnish means of concealing pregnancy and, when it could no longer be concealed, to deliver privately and dispose of the offspring so as to save the mother from scandal.   The reign of George III. was especially the age of adultery in this country, which had really taken its place among the fashions of the day, and that crime had become almost a mania in the higher classes : there is, unfortunately, no want of evidence to prove that it was common enough in the middle and lower classes.   In many cases, the trials laid open scenes of profligacy in high life of the most revolting character.   Ineffectual efforts were made at different times to check this evil by placing difficulties in the way of divorce.   In the spring of 1779, Shute Barrington, Bishop of Llandaff, introduced into the House of Lords a bill with the object of discouraging this crime, by fixing a brand of infamy on the adulteress that might operate as a terror upon the mind ; and he stated that as many divorces had occurred during the first seventeen years of the present reign as had taken place during the whole recorded history of the country :* the bill passed the Lords, but was thrown out in the House of Commons.   Several similar attempts were made at different times ; and one of these, in 1798, drew the Bishop of Durham into a severe attack upon the dancers of the Opera.

* Morals were infinitely worse in France : it is stated in the *European Magazine* for August, 1785, "Letters from Paris mention that there are no

The Opera had lost somewhat of the novelty which it had possessed under George II., and for a while it seemed to be almost eclipsed by the popularity of Carlisle House and the Pantheon. Foreign singers no longer attracted that extraordinary worship which had been bestowed on them formerly, and towards the end of the century the managers seemed to have aimed at moving the passions of the audience by the small quantity of apparel which was allowed to the *danseuses*, and the freedom with which they exposed their forms to public view. An English dancer, Miss Rose, who joined to a very plain face an extremely elegant figure and graceful movement, enjoyed great reputation in 1796, and seems to have led the new fashion for this kind of exhibition. A caricature picture of her by Gillray, published on the 12th of April, 1796, bears the motto, " No flower that blows is like this Rose." On the fifth of May following, Gillray caricatured this new style of dancing in a caricature entitled, " Modern Grace ; or, the Operatical finale to the ballet of Alonzo e caro." On the 2nd of March, 1798, there was a debate in the House of Lords on a divorce bill, in the course of which the Bishop of Durham took occasion to complain of the frequency of such bills, and laid the fault upon the French government, who, he said, sent agents into this country on purpose to corrupt our manners : " He considered it a consequence of the gross immoralities imported of late years into this kingdom from France, the Directory of which country, finding that they were not able to subdue us by their arms, appeared as if they were determined to gain their ends by destroying our morals,—they had sent over persons to this country, who made the most indecent exhibitions in our theatres." He added, that it was his intention to move, on some future day, that an address be presented to his Majesty, beseeching him to order all such dancers out of the kingdom, as people who were likely to destroy our morality and religion, and " who were very probably in the pay of France ! " This appeal, seems to have produced some interference of authority ; for on the very next night, Saturday, the 3rd of March, the ballet of Bacchus and Ariadne, which was to have been performed at the Opera House, was postponed, and another substituted, until other dresses could be prepared. The improvement, as we learn from the newspaper reports, consisted in substituting

less than four hundred divorces pending before the Parliament ; and eight hundred more before the Chatelet. A striking proof to what a height the corruption of morals is arrived in that kingdom." This must be set down as one of the true precursors of the revolution, which so soon followed.

white stockings for flesh-coloured silk, and in adding a certain
quantity of drapery above and below. The change made no
little noise abroad, and was the subject of abundance of ridicule;
the bishops and the opera-dancers figured together in numerous
caricatures. In one by Gillray, published on the 14th of March,
a group of *danseuses* are made to conceal a portion of their
personal charms by adopting the episcopal apron; it is entitled
"Operatical reform; or, *la Danse à l'Evêque*," and is accompanied with the following lines:—

> " 'Tis hard for such new-fangled orthodox rules,
> That our opera troop should be blamed;
> Since, like our first parents, they only (poor fools!)
> Danced naked and were not ashamed."

The figure to the right will be recognised as that of Miss

THE DANSE A L'EVEQUE.

Rose. Another ca-
ricature by Gillray,
published on the 19th
of March, and en-
titled "Ecclesiasti-
cal Scrutiny; or, the
Durham Inquest on
Duty," represents
the bishops attend-
ing at the dressing
of the opera girls,
where one is mea-
suring the length of
their petticoats with
a tailor's yard, an-
other is arranging
their stockings in
the least graceful
manner possible, and
a third is giving directions for the form of their stays. Amongst
others on the same subject, one of the best is entitled "Durham
Mustard too powerful for Italian capers; or the Opera in an
uproar," and represents the bishop armed with his pastoral
staff rushing on the stage to encounter the spirit of the evil one
embodied in bare legs and open bosoms. How long the episcopal censure kept the opera in order we are not told; but the
rage for opera dancing increased under the influence of Vestris.

The regular drama, in the meantime, continued to hold the
elevated position given to it by Garrick, and a number of actors

of first-rate talent drew constant audiences to the theatres. It would take too much room in a slight sketch like this even to allude to the various potty squabbles and rivalries of actors and managers during this long reign, or to the numerous pamphlets of different kinds to which they gave rise, and which deserve only to be forgotten. Drury Lane flourished under the proprietorship of Sheridan, and with the dramas which have given celebrity to his name, while it enabled him in more ways than one to support his position as a statesman, although his thoughtless extravagance often drained its resources, and sometimes clogged the regular movement of the company. In the September of 1788, John Kemble became the stage-manager, and gave strength to the company. On the extraordinary success of the tragedy of "Pizarro" in 1799, the Tory party seem to have attributed it in great part to Kemble's acting; and a caricature, published with the *Anti-Jacobin Review* on the 1st of October, represents Sheridan in the character of Pizarro borne

through upon Kemble's head. Gillray had published a caricature on the 4th of June, entitled "Pizarro contemplating over the product of his new Peruvian mine," which represents Sheridan exulting over his newly-acquired riches. The popularity of this play was so great, that it produced a number of pamphlets

SHERIDAN UPON KEMBLE.

relating to its hero, and made multitudes read the history of Peru who had never thought of it before. The performances at Drury Lane seem to have been falling in interest and in pecuniary productiveness, when, on the 5th of December, 1803, a "serio-comic romance" was brought out under the title of "The Caravan," the chief characteristic of which was the introduction on the stage of real water and of a large Newfoundland dog, which was made to rush into it and drag out the figure of a child. A contemporary criticism tells us that "the main object of the author seems to have been to produce novelty, and, through novelty to excite surprise. The introduction of real water

flowing across the stage, and a dog acting a principal part,
chiefly attracted attention, and seemed amply to gratify curiosity." This piece, in spite of the puerility of the idea, had
an extraordinary run, and, to use the words of the critic just
quoted, was "very productive to the treasury." The Tory
opponents of Sheridan as a politician represented this as a well-
timed and very necessary relief; and Sayer, in a large caricature
published on the 17th of December, represents the dog Carlo, in
his artificial pond on the stage, holding Sheridan's head above
water. It is inscribed, "The Manger and his Dog; or, a new
way to keep one's head above water, a Farce performed with
rapturous applause at Drury Lane Theatre. Motto for the
Farce,—'And Folly clapped his hands and Wisdom stared.'"
Thalia, on a pedestal, is represented weeping at the prostitution
of the drama.

The Drury Lane company appears to have been now under
the frequent necessity of having recourse to expedients of this
kind to catch popular favour. The year 1805 witnessed the
extraordinary sensation produced by the "infant Roscius,"
(Master Betty), who was brought on the stage at Drury Lane
when only twelve years of age. The extraordinary sums of
money which this child produced were an important assistance at this moment to Sheridan, who made the most of his
good fortune. His political op-
ponents were loud in their
declamations against "The Theatrical Bubble," a title under
which Gillray published a caricature on the 7th of January,
1805, in which he represented
Sheridan as Punch on the boards
of old Drury, with a few additional gems added to his ruby
nose from the profits of his theatrical treasury, blowing the
bubble which had replenished it,
and surrounded by some of his
friends who had been loudest in
their patronage of the prodigious
infant, among whom we easily
recognise Lord Derby, Lord
Carlisle, Mrs. Jordan, and her
admirer the Duke of Clarence.
Fox is expressing somewhat
boisterously his joy at the success of his political friend.

A PUNDLE.

This appears to have been the most prosperous period of Sheridan's finances. On the 24th of February, 1809, Drury Lane theatre was burnt to the ground, while Sheridan was at his post in the House of Commons. With it ended his theatrical and parliamentary prospects.

Covent Garden theatre had been involved in the same calamity only a few months before, on the morning of Tuesday the 19th of September, 1808, and was now in rapid progress of rebuilding. Its reopening led to the most extraordinary theatrical riots that this country has ever witnessed. John Kemble had left Drury Lane to become part proprietor and manager of Covent Garden, where he made his first appearance on the 24th of September, 1803. Kemble was unpopular with all but the aristocratic portion of his audience, to whom exclusively he was accused of paying his court. He is said to have been proud and authoritative in his bearing towards others, and to have given disgust by the affectation which was exhibited in his manners, language, and even in his acting. An amusing instance of this was shewn in the obstinacy with which he contended that the word *ache* should be pronounced as if written *aitche*, and in the pertinacity with which he held himself to that pronunciation. In a sketch of the history of Covent Garden in the same number of the *Examiner* which contains the account of the burning of the theatre, the writer expresses the popular sentiments in his concluding observation :—" From the general tenour of his management, I am sorry that instead of concluding this brief chronicle with the customary 'whom God long preserve!' it will be much more congenial to the wishes of the town to hope that, as a stage-manager, Mr. Kemble may be speedily removed."

Immediately after the destruction of the theatre by fire, Kemble solicited a subscription to rebuild it, which was speedily filled up, the Duke of Northumberland, to whose son he had given instruction in elocution, contributing the handsome donation of ten thousand pounds. Gillray has commemorated this circumstance in a caricature entitled, " Theatrical Mendicants relieved," in which the manager of Covent Garden theatre is represented in garments all tattered and torn, seeking charity at the door of Northumberland House. The first stone of the new building was laid with great ceremony by the Prince of Wales, (as grand master of the British free-masons,) on the last day of the year 1808, and it was completed with such rapidity, that on the 18th of September, 1809, it was opened with Macbeth, Kemble himself appearing in the character of Macbeth. In the new arrangement of the hall, a row of

private boxes formed the third tier under the gallery ; they were
twenty-six in number, with a private room behind each, and the
access was by a staircase exclusively appropriated to them, with
an exclusive lobby also, having no communication with the
other parts of the house. The furniture of each box and of the
adjoining room, was to be according to the taste of the several
occupants. To make these extraordinary accommodations
for the great, the comforts of the rest of the audience were
considerably diminished, especially in the other tiers of boxes, and
the gallery, and one part was reduced to a little better than a
row of pigeon-holes. To crown all, the theatre opened with an
increase of the prices, the pit being raised from three shillings
and sixpence to four shillings, and the boxes from six shillings
to seven shillings. The manager said that this was necessary to
cover the great expense of rebuilding the theatre; but the
public were not satisfied with this explanation ; they declared
that the old prices were sufficient, and that the new ones were a
mere exaction to contribute to Kemble's private extravagance,
to enable him to pay enormous salaries to foreigners, like
Madame Catalani, (who had been engaged at one hundred and
fifty pounds a week to perform two nights only,) and to pander
to the luxury of the rich. The popular belief in the extreme
profligacy of the higher classes, led people to figure to themselves that the rooms attached to the private boxes were to be
used for the most shameful purposes, and they accused the
manager of having built a bagnio instead of a theatre.

On the first night of representation, which was Monday, the
curtain drew up to a crowded theatre, and the audience seemed
to be lost in admiration at the beauty of the decorations, until
Kemble made his appearance on the stage in the character
of Macbeth ; a faint attempt at applause, got up by his own
friends, was in an instant drowned by an overpowering noise of
groans, hisses, yells, and every species of vocal power that
could be conjured up for the occasion, which drove him from the
stage, after two or three vain attempts to proceed, and which
was redoubled every time he made an attempt to return. Mrs.
Siddons then came forward, but met with no better reception
than her brother. The performance was, however, persevered
in, but the uproar continued through the whole of the evening,
and was continued to a late hour. It was understood that
Kemble had declared that he would not give in to the popular
clamour, and had anticipated that if it was allowed to take its
course, it would soon wear itself out. But the next night, and
the nights following, it was continued with greater fury than

ever, and to the voice were now added a multitude of cat-calls, horns, trumpets, rattles, and a variety of other instruments of discordant music. An attempt at intimidation served only to increase the exasperation of the audience. On Wednesday night, the manager came forward to address the audience, and attempted to make a justification of his conduct, which was not accepted; on Friday he presented himself again, and proposed that the decision of the dispute should be put to a committee composed of the governor of the Bank of England, the attorney general, and a few other great names. On Saturday night this was agreed to, and the theatre was shut up till the decision was obtained, the obnoxious Catalani having, in the meantime, agreed to cancel her engagement. On the following Wednesday the theatre was reopened, but the report of the committee being of a very unsatisfactory kind, for it was believed that the whole was a mere trick to gain time, in hopes that the excitement would subside, the uproar became greater than ever. The manager, who was determined to vanquish the popular feeling, is said to have hired a great number of boxers, and on the Friday night following the various pugilistic contests in the pit gave it the appearance of a regular boxing-school. Bow-street officers were also called in, but they appear to have acted indiscreetly, and the only effect of this appeal to violence was to fill the police-offices with cases of assault and riot, the result of which added fuel to the flame, which it appeared totally impossible to extinguish.

The rioters, who appear to have been acting under the guidance of people of education and talent, did not restrict themselves to mere noise. They said it was John Bull against John Kemble, and they were determined that John Bull should have the mastery. As no expression of sentiments could be heard amid the uproar, they stuck up placards, and raised banners all over the house, covered with proverbs, lampoons, and encouragements to persevere, written in large characters, and to these were soon added large painted caricatures. In the latter Kemble was figured hanging, or fixed in the pillory, or in some other ignominious position. The private boxes, and those who came to occupy them, were the especial objects of abuse, and the theatre was filled with placards, inscribed, " No private boxes for intrigues!"—" No private boxes with sofas!"—" No crim. con. boxes !" These were mixed with numerous others, of the most licentious description, and large pictures of such a character that it was impossible for any respectable woman to remain in the theatre a moment. The consequence of this

o o

was, that very few attended except those who took part in the riot, and the part of the theatre which contributed most to the treasury was nearly empty. Songs were also made for the occasion; and the following parody on the national anthem was especially popular :—

> "God save great Johnny Bull,
> Long live our noble Bull,
>   God save John Bull!
> Make him uproarious,
> With lungs like Boreas,
> Till he's victorious,
>   God save John Bull!
>
> "O Johnny Bull, be true,
> Oppose the prices new,
>   And make them fall!
> Curse Kemble's politics,
> Frustrate his knavish tricks,
> On thee our hopes we fix,
>   Confound them all!
>
> "No private boxes let
> Intriguing ladies get,—
>   Thy right, John Bull!
> From little pigeon-holes
> Defend us jolly souls,
> And we will sing, by Goles!
>   God save John Bull!"

There was much satire expended on Kemble, and his "*aitches*" were turned to ridicule in every possible manner. Many of the placards were extremely humorous, and these, with the jokes and squibs that passed thickly about, helped to keep up the spirit of the riot, while songs and caricatures circulated freely about the town. Badges, consisting of the letters O. P. (*old prices*), in large characters, were worn at the theatre, at first cut in pasteboard, but afterwards formed in metal, and some even in silver. Medals were also struck, and distributed

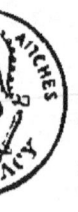

AN O. P. MEDAL.

about. One of these, now before me, represents on the obverse the head of Kemble, wearing a fool's cap, and accompanied with a penny-trumpet and a rattle; above it is the inscription, "Oh, my head *aitches!*" and below the word, "Obstinacy!" The reverse bears the letters O. P. in the centre, surrounded with the inscription, "John Bull's Jubilee—Clifford for ever!" The allusion is to the jubilee, to celebrate the completion of the fiftieth year of the King's reign, and to a barrister of the name of Clifford, who was understood to be the chief leader of the riot.

This profuse exhibition of placards was quite a novelty in theatrical rioting. One of the placards in the month of October was inscribed, " A row for our rights to be continued for *forty* nights," but the uproar seemed likely to be carried on for ever. It soon took a form quite regular and systematic : the play was heard with few interruptions till half-price ; the boxes, especially the private ones, were nearly empty, and even the pit was almost deserted. At half-price the rioters rushed in, the placards were raised, the uproar commenced, and all that passed on the stage afterwards was mere pantomime. At the conclusion, the audience rose and sang "God save the King !" had a dance in the pit, gave three groans for John Kemble, then three cheers for John Bull, and so dispersed. Sometimes the uproar was continued in the streets, and in more than one instance it was carried to Kemble's house, and he was himself mobbed and insulted. This was continued night after night, with scarcely any interruption, not for weeks only, but for more than three months. During this period everything distinguished by the epithet O. P. became fashionable. There was an "O. P. dance." The most active agent of the managers against the rioters, and, therefore, the most unpopular with them, was the box-keeper, Mr. Brandon. He had caused Clifford to be arrested on slight grounds, and the latter brought an action against him for damages, and obtained a verdict against him in the Court of Common Pleas on the 5th of December. Gillray on that day published a caricature entitled " Counsellor O. P.—defender of your theatric liberties," in which Clifford is represented holding a torch behind him, and looking on while Covent Garden Theatre is in flames. The verdict against Brandon gave new courage to the opponents of the new prices ; and finding it utterly impossible to appease them in any other way, Kemble at length gave up the contest. A public dinner of the more respectable of the O. P. agitators was held on the 14th of December at the Crown and Anchor, at which no less than five hundred persons are said to have attended, and Kemble came in person to make an apology for his conduct, and announce his willingness to accede to any compromise that should be agreeable to them. After dinner there was a crowded theatre, and amid considerable uproar, a humble apology was accepted from the manager, and it was agreed that the private boxes should be reduced to the same number which existed in 1802 ; that the pit should be reduced to its original price

of 3s. 6d., but that the price of admission to the boxes should
remain at 7s.; that the obnoxious Mr. Brandon should be
dismissed (at least he was compelled to resign his place); that
all prosecutions and actions on both sides should be abandoned;
and that Kemble should make a public apology for having
introduced improper persons into the theatre. The last article
referred to the boxers and police. After all these demands had
been complied with, a large placard was unfurled, containing the
words, " We are satisfied," and at the conclusion of the play the
pit gave three cheers for Clifford. Thus ended this extraordinary contest. A theatrical reconciliation dinner was given on
the 4th of January, 1810, at which both parties attended, and
at which Clifford was placed in the chair.

Drury Lane theatre was also rebuilt by subscription, under the
directions of Mr. Whitbread, who agreed that Sheridan should
receive £20,000 for his moiety of the property, with an additional £4000 for the property of the fruit-offices and reversion
of boxes and shares, in consideration of which he was to have
no connexion whatever with the new undertaking. Many complained of the manner in which Whitbread thus thrust Sheridan
out of the proprietorship which had so long supported him to be
an ornament of the legislative assembly of the nation, while

CLEARING AWAY RUBBISH.

others exulted in his
overthrow. A carica-
ture, published in the
October of 1811, when
the new theatre was
completed, and these
stipulations put in
force, is entitled,
" Clearing away the
rubbish of Old Drury,"
and represents Whit-
bread in the character
of a brewer's man
wheeling away Sheri-
dan in a barrow among
a heap of old bricks.
Sheridan is made to
exclaim (in allusion to his peculiarly persuasive eloquence),
" Hope told a flattering tale—d—n that brewer and his entire,
he has washed me out with only £20,000, but I know how to
palaver them over, and get in again."

The general taste for the drama had certainly increased

towards the end of the last century, and it was evinced in the new fashion for private performances among the aristocracy. The houses where this fashion was indulged in with greatest splendour, were Wynnstay, the seat of Sir W. W. Wynne; Wargrave, the seat of Lord Barrymore; and Crewe Hall, near Chester. The parties at Wynnstay were especially distinguished for their elegance. At the commencement of the century, a society of private, or, as they termed themselves, "dilettanti" actors, was formed in London, and assumed the name of the Pic-Nic Society, from the manner in which they were to contribute mutually to the general entertainment. That old meteor of London fashion, Lady Albina Buckinghamshire, is understood to have been the originator of this scheme, in which, besides the performance of farces and burlettas, there were to be feasts and ridottos, and a variety of other fashionable amusements, each member drawing from a silk bag a ticket which was to decide the portion of entertainment which he was expected to afford. The performances took place in rooms in Tottenham-street. This harmless piece of fashionable amusement produced a greater sensation than it is now possible to conceive. The populace had been so long accustomed to hear of aristocratic depravity, that they could understand nothing private in high life without attaching to it ideas of licentiousness, and there was a notion that the Pic-Nic Society implied some way or other an attack upon public morals. Complaints were made against it which led almost to a pamphlet war. The professional theatricals were angry and jealous, because they thought that the aristocratic love of theatrical amusements, which had supported them in their exertions, would evaporate in private parties.

Nearly the whole periodical press attacked the Pic-Nics without mercy, and the daily papers teemed with abuse and scandal. They were ridiculed and caricatured on every side. Gillray produced no less than three caricatures on the Pic-Nics. The first of these, published on the 2nd of April, 1802, soon after the society had been established, is entitled "Blowing up the Pic-Nics; or Harlequin Quixotte attacking the Puppets,—vide, Tottenham Street Pantomime." The Pic-Nic party are represented as puppets in the midst of their festivities, which are disturbed by the attack of the infuriated actors, among whom we recognise Kemble, Siddons, Billington, &c., led by Sheridan, who, dressed as harlequin, rushes to the assault, armed with the pen of the *Post*, *Chronicle*, *Herald*, *Evening Courier*, &c., whose attacks he is supposed to have directed against them. In another of Gillray's caricatures, entitled "The Pic-Nic Or

chestra," the noble and fashionable performers are represented
on duty. A third caricature, published on the 18th of February, 1803, is entitled "Dilettanti Theatricals,—vide Pic-Nic
Orgies;" it represents the motley group dressing for the stage,
and is full of humour, with a considerable sprinkling of licentiousness. At this latter date the society seems to have been
already sinking under the load of obloquy and ridicule to which
it was exposed, and before the year was out the regular theatricals
were relieved from any jealousy that such attempts might excite.

During the whole of our present period, the managers of the
two principal theatres continued to exert themselves in making
Shakspeare popular on the stage, and for some time with
success. Garrick had done most of any to bring the bard into
fashion, and the Stratford Jubilee in 1769 had raised an absolute Shakspeare mania. This new fashion had also exhibited
itself in the extensive study of Shakspeare's writings, and in
the extraordinary number of new editions that succeeded each
other. Annotator followed annotator, and the text of the poet
seemed in danger of being torn to pieces amid Shakspeare admirers and Shakspeare disputes. The following ballad, from
the *Westminster Magazine* for October, 1773, gives rather an
amusing and not an inaccurate enumeration of the Shakspeare
editors who had succeeded each other previous to that period:—

"SHAKSPEARE'S BEDSIDE.

" Old Shakspeare was sick ;—for a doctor he sent ;
    But 'twas long before any one came ;
Yet, at length, his assistance Nic Rowe* did present :
    Sure all men have heard of his name.

" As he found that the poet had tumbled his bed,
    He smooth'd it as well as he could ;
He gave him an anodyne, comb'd out his head,
    But did his complaint little good.

" Doctor Pope to incision at once did proceed,
    And the bard for the simples he cut ;
For his regular practice was always to bleed,
    Ere the fees in his pocket he put.

" Next Tibbald advanced,† who at best was a quack,
    And dealt but in old woman's stuff ;
Yet he ensured the physician of Twick'nham to pack,
    And the patient grew cheerful enough.

* Nicholas Rowe was the first *editor* of Shakspeare ; his edition appeared
in seven volumes in 1709-10.
† Theobald's edition of Shakspeare was first printed in 1733, and was
often reprinted. After all that has been done to the text since, it is one of
the best editions, in spite of the character our ballad-writer here gives him.

"Next Hanmer,* who sees ne'er descended to crave,
In gloves lily-white did advance;
To the poet the gentlest of purges he gave,
And, for exercise, taught him to dance.

"One Warburton then, though allied to the church,
Produced his alterative stores;
But his med'cines the case so oft left in the lurch,
That Edwards† kicked him out of doors.

"Next Johnson arrived to the patient's relief,
And ten years he had him in hand;
But, tired of his task, 'tis the general belief
He left him before he could stand.

"Now Capell drew near—not a quaker more prim—
And number'd each hair in his pate;
By styptics, called stops, he contracted each limb,
And crippled for ever his gait.

"From Gopsal then strutted a formal old goose,
And he'd cure him by inches, he swore;
But when the poor poet had taken one dose,
He vow'd he would swallow no more.

"But Johnson, determin'd to save him or kill,
A second prescription display'd;
And that none might find fault with his drop or his pill,
Fresh doctors he call'd to his aid.

"First, Steevens came loaded with black-letter books,
Of fame more desirous than pelf;
Such reading, observers might read in his looks,
As no one e'er read but himself.

"Then Warner, by Plautus and Glossary known,
And Hawkins, historian of sound;
Then Warton and Collins together came on,
For Greek and potatoes renown'd.

"With songs on his pontificalibus pinn'd,
Next Percy the great did appear;
And Farmer, who twice in a pamphlet had sinn'd,
Brought up the empirical rear.

"'The cooks the more numerous, the worse is the broth,'
Says a proverb I well can believe;
And yet to condemn them untried I am loth,
So at present shall laugh in my sleeve.'"

It was this rage for everything Shakspearian that brought
into existence those forgeries of William Henry Ireland, so well

* Sir Thomas Hanmer's *handsome* edition was published at Oxford in 1744.

† "One Edwards, an apothecary, who appears to have known more of the poet's case than some of the regular physicians who undertook to cure him." Thomas Edwards published, in 1748, what is described as a Supplement to Warburton's Shakspeare, under the title of "The Canons of Criticism and Glossary."

known as the Shakspeare manuscripts. The history of the pretended discovery of these papers was in substance closely similar to the story fabricated by Chatterton for his Rowley Papers, and indeed to that of all other literary frauds of the same description. A few documents were first produced, as having been found among old family deeds, and the success of these led to the production of others. These the inventor first shewed to his father, Samuel Ireland, so well known by his illustrations of Hogarth and other works, and by him they were communicated to others, and a number of men of high literary character, such as Dr. Parr, Dr. Warton (who had previously believed in the Rowley Papers), Boswell, Erskine, and others, declared their full belief in their authenticity. In 1796, a substantial folio was published, containing miscellaneous papers and legal instruments, under the hand and seal of William Shakspeare, with the tragedy of "Lear" and a fragment of "Hamlet," *from the original manuscript.* This work caused the most extraordinary sensation, and scarcely anything else was talked of, not only in the literary world, but among society in general. But Malone, Steevens, and others, who were more critically acquainted with the writings of the great poet, at once pronounced all these documents as forgeries, and Malone published a volume, addressed to Lord Charlemont, exposing the fraud. Before this exposure came out, young Ireland had proceeded another step in the plot, for he produced a play entitled "Vortigern," as an unknown work of Shakspeare, which had been found among the same papers, and he took it to Sheridan for representation at Drury Lane. Sheridan made no pretensions to antiquarian knowledge; he expressed some surprise at the mediocrity of many parts of the play, but he said that it was evidently an *ancient manuscript,* and he thought that the public excitement on the subject might justify his bringing it forward at Drury Lane.

The night fixed for the representation of "Vortigern" was the 2nd of April, 1796, and it was supported by all the talent of John and Charles Kemble, Mrs. Jordan, Mrs. Powell, and the other best actors of the company. Malone's critique on the printed papers had appeared before this performance, and, to counteract it, a declaration of their authenticity was produced, signed by a number of distinguished but credulous persons, with Dr. Parr at their head; and a handbill was distributed at the door and in the theatre, designating Malone's "Inquiry" as "a malevolent and impotent attack," and promising a prompt and satisfactory reply. A prologue had been written by Pye, the poet laureate, which seemed to insinuate a doubt of the fact of Shakspeare being the author, and this was therefore laid aside, to make place for one written by Sir James Illand Burges, which, read by Mr. Whitfield (who is said to have been too flurried to speak it), commenced with a bold assertion that the piece about to be acted was the work of Shakspeare, and demanded the attention of the audience to it as such :—

> " No common cause your verdict now demands,
> Before the Court immortal Shakspeare stands—
> That mighty master of the human soul,
> Who rules the passions, and, with strong control,
> Through every turning of the changeful heart
> Directs his course sublime, and leads his powerful art."

The theatre was crowded with an immense and anxious audience, who, after a few scenes, disgusted with the poverty of the play, began to express their dissatisfaction in no equivocal manner. About the beginning of the fourth act, Kemble came forward, and begged they would hear it through with candour; and it was then allowed to go on; but the proposal to give it for repetition was received with such loud and universal disapprobation, that it was not persevered in. An epilogue, delivered by Mrs. Jordan, spoke not of the piece which had been acted, but called upon the sympathy of the audience in general terms for Shakspeare, compared the characters of the old drama with those of the present day, and ended with a faint appeal to their indulgence :—

> " 'Tis true, there is some change, I must confess,
> Since Shakspeare's time, at least in point of dress.
> The ruffs are gone, and the long female waist
> Yields to the Grecian more voluptuous taste ;
> While circling braids the copious tresses bind,
> And the bare neck spreads beautiful behind.
> Our senators and peers no longer go,
> Like men in armour, glittering in a row ;
> But for the cloak and pointed beard we note
> The close-cropt head and little short great-coat.
> Yet is the modern Briton still the same,
> Eager to cherish, and averse to blame,
> *Foe to deception, ready to defend,*
> A kind protector, and a generous friend."

The result of the performance at Drury Lane sealed the fate of the Shakspeare manuscripts. Those who had stood forward in their defence, became objects of ridicule for their ready credulity, and at the end of the year the public indignation was moved by the effrontery of William Henry Ireland, who pub-

lished a full confession of the forgery, and joined in the ridicule
cast on Dr. Parr, Warton, and others. Samuel Ireland, the
father, now came forward, to disavow any complicity in the
affair, and declare that he had been a dupe equally with others.
The question continued to agitate the public during the whole
of the year 1797, and on the first of December, Gillray published
a portrait of the author of the fraud, under the title of "Notorious Characters,—No. 1," with the following lines, said there
to be written by Mason (but on better authority attributed to
Steevens), comparing the four great literary forgers of the age,
Lauder, Macpherson, Chatterton, and W. H. Ireland:—

> " Four forgers, born in one prolific age,
> Much critical acumen did engage.
> The first was soon by doughty Douglas scared,
> Though Johnson would have screen'd him, had he dared ;
> The next had all the cunning of a Scot ;
> The third, invention, genius,—nay, what not !
> Fraud, now exhausted, only could dispense
> To her fourth son their three-fold impudence."

The popularity of Shakspeare had, in another quarter, acted
in a very different manner, and produced an influence upon
native art which, whatever the jealousy of that age may have
said, must ever render the name of Alderman Boydell an object
of grateful remembrance to posterity. He had come to London
a young man at a time when engraving was at so low an ebb in
this country, that all our good prints were imported from abroad,
and, first as an engraver, and subsequently as a print-dealer, he
laboured with so much success, that at the end of his career the
exportation of English engravings far exceeded the number of
foreign ones imported. Not content with patronizing engraving,
Boydell conceived a plan for patronising native art in painting ;
and he aspired to raise an English school of historical painters
which should rival by its works the celebrity of the ancient
masters. Seizing on the popular object of adoration, he employed the first English artists of the age, at high prices, in
painting compositions illustrative of the works of the bard of
Avon. Sir Joshua Reynolds, as well as West, Barry, Fuseli,
Northcote, Opie, Smirk, and all the chief painters of the time,
contributed to the celebrated Shakspeare Gallery, which was
open for exhibition in 1789, and had for its professed object to
establish an English school of historical painting. Subscribers
were at the same time received for a splendid series of engravings
illustrative of Shakspeare's plays. Many, however, appear to
have been jealous of Boydell's efforts, which they represented as

the mere schemes of an avaricious man to gather money into his own private treasury. Gillray entered into this feeling in a truly magnificent caricature, entitled "Shakspeare Sacrificed; or, the Offering to Avarice," published on the 20th of June, 1789. The genius of Avarice, the object of Boydell's adoration, is seated aloft on a ponderous volume, entitled "List of Subscribers to the Sacrifice," which is supported on portfolios of the works of "Modern Masters;" he grasps in his arms two bags of money, and an imp on his shoulder, with peacock's feathers for hair, is blowing the bubble "immortality" with a pipe. Within the magic circle, surrounding the object of his worship, Boydell stands by a fire, into which he is casting the tattered fragments of Shakspeare's works, in the smoke of which, as it rises towards heaven, we see exaggerated sketches of some of the more remarkable designs which his gallery had brought together. Outside the circle, the portfolio of the "Ancient Masters" lies neglected on the ground, and a snail is seen crawling slowly over it. In the

THE GENIUS OF AVARICE.

distance, Fame is blowing away the great bubbles of former days, while he scatters around him a shower of puffs from the *Morning Herald* and other papers, as the only effectual instruments of fame in modern times.

Boydell's opponents, indeed, accused him not only of puffing, but of resorting to all kinds of expedients to call public attention to his Gallery. In the spring of 1791, it appears that an evil-minded person had gained admission for the purpose of damaging some of the pictures, and a malicious report was set abroad that Boydell himself was the perpetrator of this act of Vandalism. Gillray, who was no friend to the Shakspeare Gallery, published, on the 26th of April, a caricature portrait of the alderman in the act of mutilating his pictures; and, in allusion to a malefactor of the name of Renwick Williams, whose attacks upon helpless females by cutting them with a knife had a short time previously given him an extraordinary but unenviable notoriety under the epithet of "The Monster," he entitled it "*The Monster broke loose;*

*or,** a Peep into the Shakspeare Gallery." The accusation

AN AMATEUR OF THE FINE ARTS.

it is intended to convey, and the motives supposed to have led to it, will be understood by the soliloquy here put into Boydell's mouth:—" There, there! — there's a nice gash!—There!—ah! this will be a glorious subject for to make a fuss about in the newspapers; a hundred guineas reward will make a fine sound;—there! there! —O there will be fine talking about the Gallery; and it will bring in a rare sight of shillings for seeing of the *cut* pictures; there! and there again!—egad, there's nothing like having a good head-piece!—here! here!—there! there!—and then these *small* pictures won't cost a great deal of money replacing; indeed one would not like to cut a large one to pieces for the sake of making it look as if people envied us; no! that would cost rather too much, and my pocket begins—but, mum!—that's nothing to nobody—well, none can blame me for going the cheapest way to work, to keep up the reputation of the Gallery; there! there! there!—there! there!"

In his memorial to the House of Commons, at the beginning of the present century, praying for an act to enable him to dispose of his stock in trade of the fine arts by lottery, Boydell stated that he had expended more than four hundred thousand pounds in encouraging talent in this country. He had become reduced in circumstances, and the Gallery was dispersed by public sale. At a later period he was obliged to appeal to the law to oblige many of his subscribers to continue their subscriptions to his series of Shakspeare illustrations, which they refused to do on account of the length of time that had elapsed before the publication was completed.

With a few exceptions, our historical school of painting at first shewed no great symptoms of talent; it savoured too much of that general mediocrity which flourished under the equivocal kind of patronage which the third of the Georges had substituted for the scornful contempt shewn to art as well as literature by his two predecessors. West, with his coarse Scriptural pieces,

* The words in italics are crossed through in the engraving, as though to be erased.

and the foreign Loutherbourg with his gaudy landscapes, basked in the sun of royal favour, while Sir Joshua Reynolds and Wilson were treated with neglect. West was elected president of the newly-instituted Royal Academy, and received every kind of mark of royal attention; for the King was rather vain of passing for a connoisseur, and he liked to show it by his familiarity with the artist. Before Boydell came forward to offer encouragement to art, the academicians had been exposed to the bitter shafts of satire. The "Lyric Odes to the Royal Academicians," drawn forth by the exhibitions of the years 1782, 1783, 1785, and 1786, were the first productions that made known the name of Peter Pindar. The humorous but skilful critic of art, who made his debut under this pseudonym, shows no mercy to the academic president, the favourite of royalty, whom he accuses of painting the Saviour "like an old-clothes man" and the apostles like thieves, and of aspiring to cover "acres of canvas" rather than aiming at perfection in a few works. Still,—

> " To give the dev'l his due, thou dost inherit
> Some pigmy portion of the painting spirit ;
> But what is this, compared to loftier things !—
> Thine is the fortune (making rivals groan)
> Of wink and nod familiar from the throne,
> And sweetest whispers from the best of kings.
>
> " Nods, and winks-royal, since the world began,
> Are immortalities for *little* man."

Peter treats with as little ceremony the favoured portrait-painter Chamberlin, and the royal landscape-painter Loutherbourg,—

> " Thy portraits, Chamberlin, may be
> A likeness, far as I can see ;
> But, faith ! I cannot praise a single feature :
> Yet, when it so shall please the Lord
> To make his people out of board,
> Thy pictures will be tolerable nature !
>
> " And Loutherbourg, when heav'n so wills
> To make brass skies, and golden hills,
> With marble bullocks in glass pastures grazing ;—
> Thy reputation, too, will rise,
> And people, gaping with surprise,
> Cry, 'Monsieur Loutherbourg is most amazing !'
>
> " But thou must wait for that event—
> Perhaps the change is never meant—
> Till then, with me thy pencil will not shine—
> Till then, old red-nosed Wilson's art
> Will hold its empire o'er my heart,
> By Britain left in poverty to pine.

" But, honest Wilson, never mind ;
    Immortal praises thou shalt find,
And for a dinner have no cause to fear.—
    Thou start'st at my prophetic rhymes !
    Don't be impatient for those times—
    Wait till thou hast been dead a hundred year."*

Peter's predictions have been fulfilled sooner than he anticipated, for the works of Wilson are now bought up at high
prices, while those of the men who were most cried up in his
time are thrown aside with contempt. Among the latter was
Wright of Derby, an affected painter of moonlight scenes, which
the satirist describes as exhibiting

" Woollen hills, where gold and silver moons
    Now mount like sixpences, and now balloons ;
    Where sea-reflections nothing nat'ral tell ye,
    So much like fiddle-strings, or vermicelli ;
    Where ev'rything exclaimeth (how severe !)
    ' What are we !' and ' What business have we here !' "

Reynolds was one of those whose works had no charms for the
eyes of royalty, and the satirical critic exclaims, with an air of
satisfaction,—

" Thank God ! that monarchs cannot taste control,
    And make each subject's poor, submissive soul
    Admire the work that judgment oft cries fie on :
    Had things been so, poor Reynolds we had seen
    Painting a barber's pole—an alehouse queen—
    The cat-and-gridiron—or the old red lion !
    At Plympton, p'rhaps, for some grave Doctor Slop,
    Painting the pots and bottles of the shop ;
    Or in the drama, to get meat to munch,
    His brush divine had pictured scenes for Punch !

" Whilst West was whelping, 'midst his paints,
    Moses and Aaron, and all sorts of saints !
    Adams and Eves, and snakes and apples,
    And dev'ls, for beautifying certain chapels ;—
    But Reynolds is no favourite, that's the matter ;
    He has not learnt the noble art—to flatter.

" Thrice happy times ! when monarchs find them hard things
    To teach us what to view with admiration ;
    And, like their heads on halfpence and brass farthings,
    Make their opinions current through the nation !"

Public opinion eventually forced Sir Joshua Reynolds to royal

* We are informed in a note to this passage, that Wilson, who was certainly a great artist, was desired by his friend, Sir William Chambers, to
paint a picture for the King, on which occasion he produced one of his best
paintings. Yet, when this picture was shown to his majesty, it was laughed
at, and the King exhibited his knowledge of art in returning it with contempt.

attention. Peter Pindar closes his attacks on the academicians
with an expression of rather general censure,—

> " Ye royal sirs, before I bid adieu,
>   Let me inform you, some deserve my praise
> But trust me, gentle squires, they are but few
>   Whose names would not disgrace my lays.
> You'll say, with grinning, sharp, sarcastic face,
> ' We must be bad indeed, if that's the case.'
>   Why, if the truth I must declare,
>   So, gentle squires, you really are."

But a few years passed over from the time Peter Pindar thus
pointed out the empty pretensions of so many of the earlier
academicians, when a large portion of that eminent body became
the dupe of a piece of very remarkable quackery. In the year
1797, a young female pretender to art, a Miss Provis, professed
to have discovered the long-lost secret by which Titian and the
other great artists of the Venetian school produced their gor-
geous colouring, and, by dint of puffing and other tricks, she
succeeded in gaining the faith of a large portion of the Royal
Academy. Seven of the academicians are said more especially
to have been her dupes, Farringdon, Opie, Westall, Hopner,
Stothard, Smirk, and Rigaud. Until her discovery was exploded,
this lady sold it in great secret for a very high price. She would
now probably have been entirely forgotten, but for the pencil of
Gillray, who, on the 2nd of November, 1797, made her secret
the subject of a very large and remarkable caricature, entitled
"*Titianus redivivus; or, the Seven Wise Men consulting the
new Venetian Oracle.*" In the upper part of this bold picture,
the lady artist is dashing off a daring subject with extraordinary
effect of light and shade, her long ragged train ending in the
immense tail of a peacock. The three naked Graces behind her,
in the genuine coloured copies of this caricature, are painted of
the gayest hues. She is leading the crowd of academicians by
the nose over the gaudy rainbow to her study to behold her
specimen of Venetian art. On one side, the buildings appropriated to the Royal academy at Somerset House are falling
into ruin, while on the other the temple of Fame is undergoing
reparation. Below, we are introduced into the interior of the
Academy, where the luckless seven occupy the foremost seats,
deeply immersed in studying the merits of the new discovery.
The ghost of Sir Joshua Reynolds rises up from the floor, contemplates the scene with astonishment, and apostrophises the
groups in the words of Shakspeare,—

> " Black spirits and white, blue spirits and grey,
>   Mingle, mingle, mingle,—you that mingle may !"

On the opposite side are three persons making a hasty flight; they are West, the president of the Academy, who was not a believer; Boydell, whose fears are excited for the fate of his Gallery, if this new invention should succeed and destroy the value of what had been done while it was unknown; and Macklin, who experiences an equal alarm for his grand illustrations of the Bible, which were put up by lottery, the tickets five guineas each. These fears, as far as the " Venetian secret" was concerned, were not of long duration.

No class of literature was undergoing a greater change during the middle part of the reign of George III. than the periodical press, which was especially affected by the revolutions in political and moral feelings which characterised the age preceding, as well as that which followed the bursting out of the French revolution. The newspapers, which had varied but little in appearance from the beginning of the century to the earlier part of George's reign, now appear with new titles, and present themselves in a much enlarged and altered form. From an estimate given in the *European Magazine* for October, 1794, we learn that, while in 1724 only three daily, six weekly, and ten evening papers three times a week, were published in England, in 1792 there were published in London thirteen daily, twenty evening, and nine weekly papers, besides seventy country papers, and fourteen in Scotland. Among the London papers we recognise the names of the principal daily papers of modern times. The *Morning Chronicle* was established in the year 1770, the *Morning Post* in 1772, and the *Morning Herald* in 1780, and they were followed by the *Times* in 1788. They began, in accordance with the depraved taste as well as manners of that age, with courting popularity by detailing largely the most indelicate private scandal, and with coarse libels on public as well as private characters, things for which the *Post* enjoyed a special celebrity. The *Chronicle* was from the first the organ of the Whigs; the *Post* was at first a violent organ of Toryism, it subsequently became revolutionary in its principles, and then returned to its original politics; the *Herald* also has not been uniform in politics from its commencement. Of seven new magazines which were started from 1769 to 1771, the *Town and Country Magazine*, the *Covent Garden Magazine*, the *Matrimonial Magazine*, the *Macaroni Magazine*, the *Sentimental Magazine*, the *Westminster Magazine*, and the *Oxford Magazine*, two at least were obscene publications, and the feeling of the time allowed the titles of the licentious plates which illustrated them and of the articles they contained to be advertised

hly in the most respectable newspapers in words which left
)ubt of their character. The others gave insertion to a
of scandal that ought to have been offensive to public
lity. After a few years society seems to have resented the
ge, the newspapers became less libellous, and the offensive
zines disappeared.

e literary character of the magazines, which may always be
ι to a certain degree as an index of public taste, remained
very low. They consisted of extracts from common books
reprints of articles which had appeared before, of crude
s by unpaid correspondents, who were ambitious of seeing
.selves in print, and of reviews of new publications, which
.ituted the most original part of the mixture. The reviews
nued for a long time to be short and flippant, and in many
the writer seems to have read or seen only the title of the
he reviews.

ιus, in the *Westminster Magazine* for May, 1774, Jacob
.nt's well-known "New System of Ancient Mythology," in
large quarto volumes, is reviewed in four words,—"Learned,
:al, and ingenious;" and another quarto volume, "Science
ΓΟΥ God," by Thomas Harrington, is condemned with similar
ity—"Crude, obscure, and bombastic." In the same maga-
for September, 1774, that important work, Strutt's "Regal
quities," is dismissed with the observation,—"Curious,
ιl, and pleasing." The triad of epithets, which recurs per-
.ally, is amusing. It is an authoritative style of giving
ment that seems to come from the Johnsonian school.
c of the most remarkable examples are found in the *Town
Country Magazine*, which, in March, 1771, expresses its
:al judgment in the following elegant terms:—

The Exhibition in Hell; or, Moloch turned Painter. 8vo. price 1s.
A hellish bad painter, and a d—d bad writer!"

:w years later, the critical notices in the magazines became
ɔwhat more diffuse; the reviews endeavoured to give their
ers a little more information relating to the contents of new
lications; and sometimes, as in the *European Magazine*,
ɣ added a chapter at the end, under the title of "Anecdotes
he Author," in which they stated all they knew of his pri-
ɔ history. Towards the close of the century, professed
ews, in contradistinction to magazines, began to be more
mon.

'he reviewers of the last century were strongly tainted with
feelings which agitated and divided society, and they con-

P P

stantly overlooked that necessary qualification of a critic,—impartiality ; they too often punished the political opinions of the
writer by abusing his writings, however far they might be from
allusions to political subjects, or however meritorious in character: but they deserve praise for the constancy with which they
attacked that shoal of frivolous and often pernicious matter that
was daily sent into the world in the shape of novels and secret
memoirs, of the most nauseous and indelicate description.   The
influence of these was most extensive previous to the year 1790.
The violent intellectual agitation which followed the French
revolution gave a more manly vigour to the literature of the
following age.   It seemed for a moment to have raised the
burthen which had so long weighed heavily upon the mental
energies, and to promise them relief from that cold influence of
interested patronage which had so often blighted genius in the
bud.   The most distinguished literary characters of the last age,
the Wordsworths, Campbells, Southeys, Coleridges and Roscoes,
began their career in ardent admiration of the democratic
principles which were spreading from revolutionized France:
they imagined they had fallen upon the opening of a new and
brighter era, and they looked forwards in vain hopes to the
prospect of an age in which genius would no longer be the slave
of selfish or capricious patronage on the one hand, or of specula-
tive avarice on the other.   The illusion soon passed away, but
not without leaving an imprint which has effected a total
change in the literature of this country.

   The change which was taking place at the end of the century,
placed the two literatures of the past and the future for a while in
direct hostility to each other, and produced a number of satirical
writings of a new description, the types of which are found in
" The Pursuits of Literature," published anonymously, but now
understood to be the work of Mathias, and the " Baviad and
Mæviad" of Gifford.   These now appear dull enough, but they
applied the lash unsparingly to the crowd of fashionable writers
who constituted the literary legacy of the preceding age.   Perhaps, among the different shades of literary pretension which
were struggling for fame at the period when the influence of the
French revolution began to be felt, the least dignified was that
party of individuals who attempted to raise a reputation on the
fragments which had been scattered from the table of Johnson.
Boswell, and Madame Thrale, who had by a rather discreditable
marriage with a music teacher, taken the name of Piozzi, and
several others, long disputed over the remains of the " great

moralist," as he was termed, and afforded no small amusement to the public. This was one of the few public literary questions which, during the latter part of the century, became the subject of caricatures, and those possess nothing very striking in their character. Two of these, published in 1786 and 1788, were by Sayer. This dispute, which caused much sensation for several years, is better known by Peter Pindar's "Town Eclogue" of Bozzi and Piozzi.

The ungenial patronage of the court of George III. was as little successful in fostering literature and science, as it had shewn itself to be with respect to art. It was during this reign that societies began to be formed more generally to forward literary and scientific objects, but they in some instances seemed to share in the jealousy that was shewn towards political associations. The Society of Antiquaries, which had received its charter of incorporation from George II., was received into some degree of favour by his grandson, who, in 1780, placed it in apartments near his favourite "Academy" in Somerset House. Its labours had hitherto been little productive, and often puerile; it took no prominent part, even in the historical literature of the day, and is seldom mentioned in the popular literature, except in terms of ridicule. In 1772, the society was brought on the stage by Foote, deliberating on the history of Whittington and his cat. It appears that the honour shewn to it by royalty, did not protect it from becoming a dupe to practical jokes. In 1790, some wag produced a drawing of a stone pretended to have been discovered in Kennington Lane, on the site of an ancient palace of Hardicnut, bearing an inscription to that monarch's memory in Saxon characters and in Anglo-Saxon verse, which, literally translated, informed the world that "Here Hardyknute the king drank a wine-horn dry, and stared about him and died." It is said that this inscription and explanation were received and read at one of the meetings of the society of antiquaries as a *bond fide* communication, and the perpetrator of the joke immediately made it public for the amusement of the world, and to the discomfiture of the learned archæologists. This trifling incident made its noise at the time, and was taken up in a satirical vein by other humorists, who followed it up with mock dissertations and mock translations. Some of the latter exhibited the same vein of personal satire which had dictated the longer and more celebrated "probationary odes." Thus Sir Cecil Wray is made to contribute the following poetical version—

> " Here Hardyknute, with horn of wine,
>   Drank, died, and stared much ;
>   And at my last elec—ti—on
>   Too many there were such."

Another parliamentary and ministerial rhymer, Sir Joseph
Mawbey, was also introduced making a personal application of
the theme,

> " Here Hardyknute his *wast* (O brute !)
>   Did *swill* from Danish horn ;
>   So bursting wide his *harslet*, died,
>   And of his life was shorn.

> " As *pig* doth look, that's newly stuck,
>   And stare, so stared he ;—
>   And so, at my next canvass, I
>   May stare for company."

Among other versions, the joking editor cites the first line of
that by M. le Texier, who he says had, "with the levity peculiar
to his countrymen," given a gay turn to the epitaph, which he
made to open thus—

> "Aha! cher Monsieur Ardiknute !"

And he adds, "The last has the same defect as the two preceding ones, for it is rather a sportive paraphrase than a fair translation. As it comes, however, from a young poetical divine,
resident in the archiepiscopal palace at Lambeth (the very place
of Hardyknute's demise), it will possibly be received with indulgence, and especially by the gentleman who produced its
original to the Antiquary Society.

> " If Hardyknute at Lambeth feast,
>   Where *each* man made himself a beast,
>   On such a draught did venture ;
>   Though drink he did, and stare, and die,
>   'Tis clear to every mortal eye
>   That he was no dissenter."

However respectable their character as societies, and however
talented and well-intentioned some of their members, it must be
acknowledged that neither archæology nor science were at this
time receiving the benefits they might have done from the
labours of the society of Antiquaries and its neighbour the
Royal Society. The latter was rent to pieces by jealousies and
disputes. It had received a gleam from the sun of royal favour
in the person of its president, Sir Joseph Banks, who had pursued science in company with Captain Cook in the distant isles
of the Pacific, and whose adventures in the study of natural
history at home and the undue eminence which he was believed

to hold by the mere title of royal favouritism, made him the object of many a caricature and satire. In one of the latter, in the collection of Mr. Burke, the learned president of the Royal Society is represented under the character and title of "The great South-sea Catterpillar transformed into a Bath butterfly." His wings are adorned with figures of starfish, crabs, and other favourite objects of his attention. This print is dated on the 4th of July, 1795, soon after Sir Joseph had been chosen a knight of the Bath. Another caricature, also in the possession of Mr. Burke, represents the scene described in Peter Pindar's well-known tale of "Sir Joseph Banks and the Emperor of Morocco." The "president in butterflies profound," as he has termed him, was a subject of frequent satire from Peter's pen.

THE BUTTERFLY OF SCIENCE.

CHAPTER XV.

GEORGE III.

The Imperial Parliament—Change of Ministry—Peace with France—New Step in Buonaparte's Ambition—Renewal of Hostilities, and Threatened Invasion—Defensive Agitation; Volunteers; Caricatures and Songs—Return of Pitt to Power—Buonaparte Emperor—Trafalgar—Death of Pitt—The Broad-Bottom Ministry—Death of Fox—General Election—The War.

THE nineteenth century opened in this country with political prospects by no means of the most cheering description. With a burthen of taxation infinitely beyond anything that had ever been known before, England found herself in danger of being left single-handed in an interminable contest with a power which was now rapidly humbling at its feet the whole of the continent of Europe, and which had already adopted, with regard to us, the old motto of *delenda est Carthago*. We had no longer to contend with a democratic republic, as heretofore, but with a skilful and unscrupulous leader, who was already a sovereign in fact, and who was marching quickly towards a throne. The union with Ireland had been completed, and was put into effect; but the sister isle remained dissatisfied and turbulent, and but a few months passed over before a new rebellion broke out, of a serious character. The union itself had not passed without considerable opposition in this country, and the advantages which its advocates promised as the result, were ridiculed or disbelieved. Among the caricatures on this subject which appeared during the year 1800, one represented Pitt from the state pulpit publishing the banns of union between John Bull and Miss Hibernia. In another, under the title of "A Flight across the Herring-pool," the Irish gentry are seen quitting their country in crowds to share in the good things which Pitt is laying before them in England, thus setting the example of that evil of absenteeism which has been so much complained of in more recent times.

The first imperial parliament met on the 22nd of January, 1801, and was attended with two remarkable circumstances, the election of the Rev. John Horne Tooke for the borough of Old Sarum, and the reappearance of Fox at his post in the House of Commons. Fox reappeared in the house for the first time on the 2nd of March, and one of the earliest signs of his returning activity was his support of the right of Horne Tooke to a seat there. A caricature, published on the 14th of March, entitled "The Westminster Seceder on Fresh Duty," represents Fox bending his broad back to enable the reverend candidate to get into St. Stephen's chapel through the window, while Lord Temple is shutting the door against him. Tooke had been returned for Old Sarum by Lord Camelford. His admission was opposed on the ground of his clerical profession, and it led to a bill making clergymen incapable of sitting in parliament. Tooke held his seat for a very brief period, during which he did no act of importance. A caricature, by Gillray, published on the 15th of March, under the title of "Political Amusements for Young Gentlemen; or, the old Brentford Shuttlecock," represents the head of Tooke formed into a plaything, the feathers of which intimate sufficiently his character, tossed backwards and forwards between Lord Camelford, to whom he owed his election, and Lord Temple, who led the opposition to his admission.

Before this question came under discussion, Pitt had quitted the ministry. Having in his anxiety to procure the support of the Catholic body in Ireland for his grand project of union, made an implied promise to support the cause of Catholic emancipation, and finding the King obstinately opposed to it, he seized upon this as the occasion for retiring from office. The opposition ascribed to him different motives: they said that, alarmed at the difficulties into which he had plunged the country, he wished to withdraw from personal responsibility, and they prophesied that he would continue to be, in fact, as much minister as

A SHUTTLECOCK.

before. This seems to receive some confirmation from the fact that Henry Addington, the son of Doctor Addington, one of the physicians who had attended on the King in his derangement, and the special *protégé* of the Pitt family, was nominated for his successor. A caricature, published on the 20th of February, under the title of "The Family Party," represents Pitt, Dundas, Grenville, and Canning, seated round the card-table; Pitt gives his hand to Addington, saying, "Here, play my cards, Henry; I want to retire a little;" and the other players join him in the wish to remain a while behind the screen.

An unexpected event added to the embarrassments of this situation of public affairs. The King, in consequence of the agitation and uneasiness caused by Pitt's resignation, was suddenly attacked with his old malady, in the midst of the negotiations for a new ministry, and he remained in an uncertain state of health during three weeks. Although the public were kept in ignorance of the exact state of the King's health as long as possible, enough was known to create general uneasiness; and it was this, probably, which drew Fox to town, and restored him to the House of Commons, for it was still believed that the formation of a regency would be, under any circumstances, attended by the dismissal of the present ministry, to make place for one under Fox.

In the middle of March, immediately after the King's recovery, the new ministry was publicly announced; Addington was first lord of the Treasury and chancellor of the Exchequer; the Duke of Portland remained president of the Council; Lord Eldon was made Chancellor; Lord Pelham, Home Secretary; Lord Hawkesbury, secretary for Foreign Affairs; and Lord Hobart, secretary for the Colonies; the Hon. Charles Yorke, secretary at War; Lord Chatham, master of the Ordnance; and Lord Lewisham president of the Board of Control for the Affairs of India. Gillray, who, on the 24th of February, had represented Pitt and his colleagues marching out of the Treasury with conscious honesty on their features, while the Whigs were with difficulty hindered from rushing in to seize upon their places,* now (on the 28th of May) made a humorous comparison between the old ministers and their successors, in a caricature, entitled "Lilliputian substitutes;" a title which was not ill bestowed on the latter, for they were men of so little influence in politics,

A NEW MINISTER IN AN OLD BOOT.

that it was evident from the first they could only retain office by indulgence. Lord Loughborough's vast wig appears to hide

* The caricature alluded to is entitled "Integrity retiring from office."

entirely from view its new wearer. Next to it stands on the treasury bench "Mr. Pitt's jack-boot," in which Addington is plunged to the chin, yet he imagines that it, and the rest of Pitt's clothes, are made exactly to fit him—" Well, to be sure, these here clothes do fit me to an inch!—and now that I've got upon this bench, I think I may pass muster for a fine tall fellow, and do as well for a corporal as my old master Billy himself." Lord Hawkesbury, who had talked of marching to Paris, has his spare form enveloped in Lord Grenville's capacious breeches—" Mercy upon me! what a deficiency is here!—ah, poor Hawkie! what will be the consequence, if these d—d breeches should fall off in the march to Paris, and then should I be found out a sans-culotte!" Lord Hobart, a portly individual, is flourishing and swaggering with " Mr. Dundas's broad sword!" Another individual, with no less plumpness in his proportions, is quarrelling with " Mr. Canning's old slippers,"—" Ah! d—n his narrow pumps! I shall never be able to bear them long on my corns!—zounds! are these shoes fit for a man in present pay free quarters?"

At the beginning of the year, England had been again threatened with French invasion; but Addington's administration set out as a peace ministry, and it proceeded so resolutely in this course, that on the 1st of October, preliminaries had been agreed to and were signed, and Lord Cornwallis was soon afterwards sent over as minister plenipotentiary. Buonaparte him-

LARGE SHOES FOR LITTLE PEOPLE.

self was evidently desirous of a cessation of hostilities that he might be left for a while to pursue his ambitious designs at home. After many crosses and difficulties, and sufficient evidence of bad faith on the part of the French government, the definitive treaty of peace was signed at Amiens on the 27th of March, 1802.

There was still a strong war-party in England, and many with keen foresight looked at it as an unnecessary sacrifice of our own dignity, rendered futile by the certainty that no peace could be

of long duration with the then ruler of France, unless purchased with an unconditional submission to his will. The opposition was strong in parliament, and when the terms of peace
were known, there was a loud complaint at the yielding up of so
many of our recent conquests, while France was allowed to keep
her overwhelming influence on the continent. The peace was,
however, lauded by Fox and the Whigs, and approved by Pitt.
On the 6th of October, Gillray published a caricature, entitled
"Preliminaries of peace; or, John Bull and his little friend
marching to Paris." The little friend is Lord Hawkesbury,
who is leading the way across the channel, over a rotten and

BRITANNIA VICTIMIZED.

broken plank; John Bull, accompanied by Fox and all the
approvers of the negotiations, allows himself to be led by the

nose, while Britannia's shield
and a number of valuable conquests are thrown into the water
as useless. On the 9th of November appeared another caricature by
Gillray, entitled "Political dream-
ings; visions of peace!—perspective
horrors!" Windham had described
in strong language the evils which
the peace would draw down upon this
country, and, as embodied in this
picture, they are certainly fearful.
The preliminaries are endorsed as
"Britannia's death-warrant;" and
she herself is seen in the clouds
dragged off to the guillotine for

AN OMINOUS SERENADER.

execution by the Corsican depredator. Visions of headless bodies crowd around. Lord Hawkesbury's hand, as he signs the peace, is guided by Pitt. On one side justice has received a strong dose of physic. On another, we see St. Paul's in flames. And here the long gaunt form of death treading in stilts (two spears) on the roast beef and other good things of old England. At the foot of Windham's bed, Fox, as an imp of darkness, gives the serenade.

At first the new administration went on smoothly ; it escaped attack, in the eagerness of the old Whig opposition to attack its predecessors. They imagined that Pitt and his colleagues had been overthrown by the weight of their own iniquities, and they talked of visiting them with parliamentary censure, and even with impeachment. The leader in the projected attack was to be Sir Francis Burdett, and great threats were held out, which, however, had no serious result. A caricature by Gillray, entitled " Preparing for the grand attack," published on the 4th of December, 1801, represents Burdett rehearsing for his speech against ministers; Sheridan is instructing him in eloquence; Fox draws up the accusations; and Horne Tooke acts as scribe. The year 1802 produced few subjects of domestic excitement. The repeal of the income tax gave universal satisfaction; and people in general believed in the efficacy of Pitt's grand project of the sinking fund to relieve them from much of the burthen of the public debt. Some of the caricaturists ridiculed the popular credulity on this point. The mania for balloons had been revived, after the reconciliation with France, where they still remained fashionable, and were more caricatured than in England ; and in a caricature, entitled "The national parachute; or, John Bull conducted to plenty and emancipation," published on the 10th of July, Pitt is represented supporting John Bull in the air in a parachute, entitled " The sinking fund." While the new peace occupied everybody's attention, the Parliament was allowed, without much opposition, to vote a million sterling to pay off debts contracted on the civil list. On the other side, republicanism still appeared to have some advocates, and the close of the year witnessed the discovery of the mad conspiracy of Colonel Despard and his companions, who were executed early in 1803. A new parliament had been elected in autumn, in which Westminster was again contested with obstinacy. In France, on the 6th of August, 1802, Buonaparte advanced another step in his course of ambition, by obtaining the appointment of consul for life : it was but another name for a crown.

Peace was at first hailed with joy throughout the country. It produced, within a few weeks, illuminations, feasts, congratulatory addresses, sermons, poems, in great profusion. Englishmen went to visit Paris in hundreds and thousands, and this country was inundated with French fashions and inventions. Among the English visitors to France was Charles James Fox, who went to pay his respects to the future emperor, in company with his nephew, Lord Holland, and with Erskine, Grey, and some other members of the opposition in parliament. They were treated with marked attention by Buonaparte; and their admiration was carried to a degree of indiscretion which did not increase their popularity in England, where they were accused of obsequious flattery to the oppressor of Europe. On the 15th of November, Gillray published a caricature entitled, "Introduction of citizen Volpone and his suite at Paris," in which Fox and his wife, Lord and Lady Holland, and Grey, are stooping low to the new ruler of France. A few days before (on the 8th of November) an anonymous caricature on the same subject appeared under the title of "English patriots bowing at the shrine of despotism." Gillray published on the 4th of December, a caricature, entitled "The nursery, with Britannia reposing in peace," in which Britannia is represented as an overgrown baby, reposing in her cradle, and nursed in French principles by Addington, Lord Hawkesbury, and Fox. It was at this moment that Lord Whitworth was sent over as our ambassador to the French government, amid general doubts of the good faith of the latter, and dissatisfaction of Buonaparte's conduct. This dissatisfaction was most strongly expressed in the English newspapers, which is said to have given so much offence to the first consul, that he forbade their circulation in France.

Still, although the general dissatisfaction in England was increasing, the peace continued popular till the end of the year. On the 1st of January, 1803, Gillray satirized the posture of affairs in a humorous caricature, entitled "The first kiss this ten years; or, the meeting of Britannia and citizen François." Britannia, who has suddenly become corpulent, appears as a fine lady in full dress, her shield and spear leaning neglected against the wall. The citizen expresses his joy at the meeting in warm terms—"Madame, permittez me to pay my profound esteem to your engaging person; and to seal on your divine lips my ever-lasting attachment!!!" The lady, blushing deeply at the salute (in the coloured copies a strong tint of red is bestowed on her cheek), replies—"Monsieur, you are truly a well-bred gentleman'! —and though you make me blush, yet you kiss so delicately that I cannot refuse you, though I was sure you would deceive me again!" On the wall, just behind these two figures, are framed profiles of King George and Buonaparte scowling on each other. This caricature enjoyed an unusual degree of popularity; many copies were sent to France, and Buonaparte himself is said to have been highly amused by it.

THE FIRST KISS THESE TEN YEARS.

From this time, however, the communications between the two countries began to take a much less pacific character, and it was more and more evident that the peace could not be of long duration. The French consul was anxious to obtain possession of Malta, and while he accused England of breaking the faith of treaties, he acted in everything contrary to the spirit of the treaty which he had so recently concluded with her. He required that we should drive the royalist emigrants from our shores, demanded that the English press, which he looked upon as one of his most dangerous enemies, should be deprived of its liberty as far as regarded French affairs, and he actually asked for modifications in our constitution. At the same time he was actively employed in exciting a rebellion in Ireland, and distributing agents, under the character of consuls, along our coasts, with treacherous objects, which were accidentally discovered by the seizure of the secret instructions to the consul at Dublin, which contained, among other matters of the same character, the following passages:—"You are required to furnish a plan of the ports of your district, with a specification of the soundings for mooring vessels. If no plan of the ports can be procured, you are to point out with what wind vessels can come in and go out, and what is the greatest draught of water with which vessels can enter the river deeply laden." There began to appear other indications equally distinct of ulterior designs against this country, which it was of the utmost importance to anticipate. Even Fox and his party, while they advocated peace as long as it could be maintained, acknowledged that there was room for suspicion. A patriotic indignation was raised throughout the country in the March of 1803, by the publication of an official document, signed by the first consul, in which he declared that "England alone cannot now encounter France." It was now universally believed that Buonaparte only delayed open hostilities as long as he could gain anything from us by pretended negotiations, and that he was preparing to crush us by the magnitude of his attack. It was the misfortune of this country to have at such a moment an administration remarkable for its incapacity. Pitt is said to have made a secret attempt to return to power; but Addington began to love the sweets of office, and was not inclined to quit, and his submissive pliancy to the crown had gained him the King's favour. The Foxites were afraid that if they entered into opposition, they would only throw the Doctor, as they all styled him contemptuously, into the arms of Pitt; and Buonaparte declared publicly that if Pitt returned to power, France would lose all hopes of obtaining further concessions from England. A caricature by Gillray, published on the 9th of February, is entitled the "Evacuation of Malta." The French ruler is forcing Addington to evacuate one conquest after another, until he cries out, "Pray do not insist upon Malta! I shall certainly be turned out, and I have got a great many cousins, and uncles, and aunts to provide for yet." A French officer who is receiving what the minister gives up, expostulates with his commands, "My general, you had better not get him turned out, for we shall not be able to humbug them any more."

The statement officially made by the French government, that England was not able to contend with France single-handed, produced a violent outburst of indignation in the House of Lords on the 9th of March. The day before, a royal message had been laid before both Houses, stating that the King had received positive information that very considerable military preparations were carrying on in the ports of France and Holland, and that he had judged it expedient to adopt additional measures of precaution for the security of his dominions. At the same time proclamations were issued encouraging the en-

listing of seamen and landsmen, calling up the militia and
volunteers, and ordering the formation of encampments in the
maritime counties. The volunteer associations, which had been
formed two years before in anticipation of invasion, also began
to reassemble. On the debate upon the King's message, Fox
seemed to think the apprehensions were premature, and advised
caution ; Windham, who had violently opposed the peace, now
said that it had placed us in a position of weakness towards
France, which had rendered us less able to defend ourselves than
we should have been had the war continued ; but the most
patriotic of all patriotic speeches made in the House of Commons,
was that of Sheridan. He accused Windham of entertaining
the same sentiments on the weakness of this country which had
been expressed by Buonaparte, "Whatever sentiments both of
them may entertain," he said, "with respect to the incapability
of the country, I hope and trust, if unhappily war be unavoidable,
that we shall convince that right honourable gentleman, and
the first consul of France, that we have not incapacitated ourselves
by making peace, to renew the war with as much promptitude,
vigour, and perseverance, as we have already evinced. I trust,
sir, we shall succeed in convincing them, that we are able to
enter single-handed into war, notwithstanding the despondency
of the right honourable gentleman, and the confident assertion
of the first consul of France. . . . . By the exertions of a loyal,
united, and patriotic people, we can look with perfect confidence
to the issue ; and we are justified in entertaining a well-founded
hope, that we shall be able to convince not only the right
honourable member and the first consul of France, but all
Europe, of our capability, even single-handed, to meet and
triumph over the dangers, however great and imminent, which
threaten us from the renewal of hostilities."

This debate was made the subject of a clever caricature by
Gillray, published on the 14th of March, under the title of
"Physical aid; or, Britannia recovered from a trance; also the
patriotic courage of Sherry Andrew, and a peep through the
fog." The "peep" exhibits in the distance Buonaparte leading
on the French boats, which are to carry over the army of invasion. Britannia, waking suddenly from her trance of security,
is struck with the imminence of the danger, and implores
assistance in a parody of the words of Shakspeare, " Angels and
ministers of *dis*-grace defend me!" Her shield is cracked and
her spear blunted. Addington and Lord Hawkesbury stand by
her, giving encouragement ; the former applies a bottle of
gunpowder to her nose to revive her. Sheridan wields the

club, inscribed, "Dramatic loyalty," in threatening attitude against the invaders, and blusters out his menace, "Let 'em come, damme!—damme!!—where are the French buggaboos?—Single-handed I'd beat forty of 'em!! damme, I'll pay 'em like renter shares, sconce off their half crowns, mulct them out of their benefits, and come the Drury Lane slang over 'em!" A crowd of people are excited in dif-ferent ways. Fox, half con-cealing his face in his hat, cannot see the buggaboos, and wonders, "why the old lady has woke in such a fright."

A THEATRICAL HERO.

The negotiations were still persevered in, although it was daily more evident that they would fail to avert hostilities. Even as late as the 2nd of May, caricatures appeared ridiculing John Bull's submission to the continued demands made upon his forbearance. The date just mentioned is that of a cari-cature by Gillray entitled, "Doctor Sangrado curing John Bull of repletion." Lord Hawkesbury is holding up John Bull, sick

JOHN BULL IN BAD HANDS.

and emaciated, while Addington performs the operation; the blood which issues from the incision is inscribed with the names of Malta and the other conquests that were to be restored.

which Buonaparte is receiving in his hat; Fox and Sheridan are bringing warm water; and they all exhort the patient to have courage.

It was but a few days after this, that our ambassador, who had been personally insulted by Buonaparte, and who had long perceived that the latter had carried on the negotiations merely for the sake of gaining time, received final orders to leave Paris, and the French ambassador, Andréossi, was ordered to quit England. The declaration of war was received throughout England with enthusiastic joy;—the falsehoods and prevarications which Buonaparte had made use of throughout the negotiations, which now exposed his true character to the world; the infamous manner in which he had treated the countries that had fallen under his power; and the reckless contempt of the laws of nations with which he seized as prisoners of war the crowds of English visitors whom his peaceful declarations had allured into France; all made the ruler of France an object of such abhorrence and hatred that war seemed to every one preferable to peace, and the ministers were only rendering themselves unpopular by continuing the friendly relations between the two countries so long. Gillray has perpetuated the memory of this feeling in a clever caricature, published on the 18th of May, entitled "Armed Heroes." "Addington,"* the "doctor," is represented in a ridiculous dilemma, between assumed courage and real fears, anxious to preserve the roast beef threatened by the Corsican usurper. Lord Hawkesbury, seated behind him with an equally passive appearance of courage, calls to mind his old threat of marching to Paris.

Buonaparte commenced hostilities by seizing upon Hanover, and raising a rebellion in Ireland. The former was an inevitable evil; and the latter was soon subdued. But the immense preparations for invasion were a cause of more serious alarm, and called forth a unity of patriotic exertions such as had never been seen before. The volunteers, raised in the course of the summer and autumn, who were well armed and soon well trained, amounted to not less than three hundred thousand. Meanwhile France seemed for once earnest in her threats, and she was marching to the opposite coast her best troops in fearful masses. Buonaparte came in person to overlook the preparations, and to take the command of the invading forces when they were completed. He established his head-quarters at Boulogne, on the roads to which finger-posts were erected to remind all Frenchmen that it was the way to London. Every possible means was

* A copy of this caricature is given in the accompanying plate.

resorted to for exciting the people against the English, and attracting them to his standard. The soldiers were promised indiscriminate plunder, and they were reminded that the English women were the most beautiful in the world, and that no restriction should be placed on the gratification of their passions. Inflammatory addresses from the cities and towns to the first consul were followed by equally inflammatory answers. Atrocious falsehoods were published and placarded over the country to raise the national exasperation to the greatest height.

Equally efficacious means were resorted to in England to raise up an enthusiastic spirit of hatred of France and its ruler. People exerted themselves individually, as well as in associations, in printing and distributing what were known as "loyal papers" and "loyal tracts," which were bought up in immense numbers, and the proceeds often applied to the defence of the country. Some of these consisted of exaggerated and libellous biographies of Buonaparte and his family; accounts of the atrocities perpetrated by himself and his armies in the countries they had overrun; burlesques, in which he was treated with ridicule and contempt; parodies on his bulletins and proclamations; and accounts of his preparations for the invasion and conquest of England. Others contained words of encouragement; exhortations to bravery; directions for acting and disciplining; promises of reward; narratives of British bravery in former times; everything, in fact, that could stir up and support the national spirit. Every kind of wit and humour was brought into play to enliven these sallies of patriotism; sometimes they came forth in the shape of national playbills, such as the following :—

"THEATRE ROYAL, ENGLAND.

"In Rehearsal, and meant to be speedily *attempted*, a farce in one act called THE INVASION OF ENGLAND. Principal Buffo, Mr. Buonaparte, being his first (and most likely his last) appearance on this stage.

"*Anticipated Critique.* The structure of this Farce is very *loose*, and there is a *moral* and radical defect in the ground-work. It boasts however considerable novelty, for the characters are *all mad*. It is probable that it will *not* be played in the country, but will certainly never be *acted* in *town*; wherever it may be represented, we will do it the justice to say, it will be received with *thunders* of—CANNON!!! but we will venture to affirm will never equal the success of JOHN BULL. It is, however, likely that the piece may yet be put off on account of the *indisposition* of the principal performer, Mr. Buonaparte. We don't know exactly what this gentleman's merits may be on the tragic boards of France, but he will never succeed here; his figure is very diminutive, he struts a great deal, seems to have no conception of his *character*, and treads the stage very *bally*; notwithstanding which defects, we think if he comes here, he will get an *engagement*, though it is probable that he will shortly after be reduced to the situation of a *scene-shifter*.

" As for the Farce, we recommend it to be withdrawn, as it is the opinion of all good political critics, that if play'd it will certainly be damned.

" *Vivant rex et regina.*"

Sometimes they were coarse and laughable dialogues between the Corsican and John Bull, or some other worthy, who gave him small encouragement to persevere in his undertaking. Then we had laughable proclamations to his own soldiers, or to those he was threatening with invasion. Now the invader was compared to a wild beast, or some object of curiosity, for a promised exhibition. Such bills as the following were common :—

" *Most wonderful wonder of wonders!!*

"Just arrived, at Mr. Bull's Menagerie, in British Lane, the most renowned and sagacious *man tiger* or *ourang outang*, called Napoleon Buonaparte. He has been exhibited through the greatest part of Europe, particularly in *Holland*, *Switzerland*, and *Italy*, and lately in *Egypt*. He has a wonderful faculty of speech, and undertakes to reason with the most learned doctors in law, divinity, and physic. He proves incontrovertibly that the strongest poisons are the most sovereign remedies for wounds of all kinds ; and by a dose or two, made up in his own way, he cures his patients of all their ills by the gross. He *picks* the *pockets* of the company, and by a *rope* suspended near a *lantern*, shows them, as clear as day, that they are all richer than before. If any man in the room has empty pockets, or an empty stomach, by taking a dose or two of his *powder* of *hemp*, he finds them of a sudden full of guineas, and has no longer a craving for food : if he is rich, he gets rid of his *tædium vitæ ;* and if he is overgorged, finds a perfect cure for his indigestion. He proves, by unanswerable arguments, that *soup maigre* and *frogs* are a much more wholesome food than *beef* and *pudding*, and that it would be better for *Old England* if her inhabitants were all *monkeys* and *tigers*, as, in times of scarcity, one half of the nation might devour the other half. He strips the company of their clothes, and, when they are stark naked, presents a *paper* on the *point* of a *bayonet*, by reading which they are all perfectly convinced that it is very pleasant to be in a state of nature. By a kind of hocus-pocus trick, he breathes on a *crown*, and it changes suddenly into a guillotine. He deceives the eye most dexterously ; one moment he is in the garb of the *Mufti ;* the next of a *Jew ;* and the next moment you see him the *Pope*. He imitates all sounds ; bleats like a lamb; roars like a tiger ; cries like a crocodile; and brays most inimitably like an ass.

" Mr. Bull does not choose to exhibit his *monkey's* tricks in the puffing way, so inimitably p ayed off at most foreign courts ; as, in trying lately to puff himself up to the size of a *bull*, his monkey got a sprain, by which he was very near losing him.

" He used also to perform some wonderful tricks with *gunpowder ;* but his monkey was very sick in passing the channel, and has shown a great aversion to them ever since.

" Admittance, one shilling and sixpence.

" N.B.—If any gentleman of the corps diplomatique should wish to see his ourang outang, Mr. Bull begs a line or two first ; as, on such occasions, be finds it necessary to bleed him, or give him a dose or two of cooling physic, being apt to fly at them if they appear without such preparation."

In other papers, the conqueror of the greater part of Europe was ridiculed as a mere pigmy, when compared to King George and his valiant Britons :—

> "Come, I'll sing you a song, just for want of some other,
> About a *small* thing, that has made a *great* pother ;
> A mere *insect*, a *pigmy*,—I'll tell you, my hearty,
> 'Tis the Corsican hop-o'-my thumb Buonaparte.
>   Derry down, &c.

> "This *Lilliput* monster, with *Brobdignag* rage,
> Hath ventured with Britons in war to engage ;
> Our greatness he envies, and envy he must,
> If the *frog* apes the ox, he must swell till he burst.
>   Derry down," &c.

It was in this spirit that Gillray, on the 26th of June, represented King George as the king of Brobdignag, eyeing his diminutive assailant with contempt. Other caricatures represented

THE KING OF BROBDIGNAG AND GULLIVER.

the blustering invader in the same character. In a fine engraving by Gillray, bearing the same title as the one just mentioned, "The King of Brobdignag and Gulliver," the diminutive boaster is seen attempting to manœuvre his small boat in a basin of water, to the great amusement of King George and his court.

Songs innumerable, of encouragement and defiance, were distributed about the country in the same form of loyal broadsides, as well as in tracts and collections.* Of many of these, the following will furnish a good example:—

"SONG ON THE THREATENED INVASION.

"Arm, neighbours, at length,
And put forth your strength,
Perfidious bold France to resist ;
Ten Frenchmen will fly
To shun a black eye,
If one Englishman doubles his fist.

"But if they feel stout,
Why, let them turn out,
With their maws stuff'd with frogs, soups, and jollies ;
Brave Nelson's sea thunder
Shall strike them with wonder,
And make the frogs leap in their bellies.

"Their impudent boast
Of invading our coast,
Neptune swears they had better decline ;
For the rogues may be sure,
That their frenzy we'll cure,
And we'll pickle them all in his brine.

"And when they've been soak'd
Long enough to be smok'd,
To the regions below they'll be taken ;
And there hung up to dry,
Fit to boil or to fry,
When Old Nick wants a rasher of bacon."

The following song was sung in the theatres, and drew the most enthusiastic shouts of satisfaction :—

"THE ISLAND.

"If the French have a notion
Of crossing the ocean,
Their luck to be trying on dry land ;
They may come if they like,
But we'll soon make 'em strike
To the lads of the tight little Island,
Huzza for the boys of the Island !—
The brave volunteers of the Island !
The fraternal embrace
If foes want in this place,
We'll present all the arms in the Island.

"They say we keep shops
To vend broad-cloth and slops,
And of merchants they call us a sly land ;

---

* These loyal papers were almost the only broadsides for which purchasers could be found, and it is not improbable that this first gave the blow to the old English popular ballad literature, which had hitherto kept its ground almost undiminished.

But though war is their trade,
  What Briton's afraid
    To say he'll ne'er sell 'em the Island.
    They'll pay pretty dear for the Island !
    If fighting they want in the Island,
  We'll shew 'em a sample,
  Shall make an example
    Of all who dare bid for the Island.

"If met they should be
  By the Boys of the Sea,
    I warrant they'll never come nigh land ;
  If they do, those on land
  Will soon lend 'em a hand
    To foot it again from the Island !
    Huzza ! for the king of the Island !
    Shall our father he robbed of his Island ?
  While his children can fight,
  They'll stand up for his right,
    And their own, to the tight little Island."

In these papers, as well as in the caricatures, it was confidently prophesied that, if the enemy should escape our ships at
sea, it would only be to meet certain destruction on landing.
Gillray published several caricatures during the months of June
and July, setting forth the consequences of the landing of
Buonaparte. In one, our brave volunteers are driving him and
his army into the sea. In another, entitled "Buonaparte forty-
eight hours after landing," John Bull is represented bearing the
bleeding head of the invader in triumph on his pike. In a third,
the King, in his hunting garb, is holding up the Corsican fox,
which he has hunted down with his good hounds, Nelson, Vincent, &c.

It was our fleets, indeed, that offered our best guarantee
against the vengeance of France, for as long as our ships swept
the Channel, and insulted the French coasts, destroying towns
and shipping with impunity, there was little chance that our
enemies would be able to put their threats in execution. They
stood there manœuvring, and blustering, and threatening, while
Jack Tar was waiting very impatiently for their coming out.

"They've fram'd a plan
  (That's if they can)
To chain us two and two, sirs;
  And Gallia's cock,
  From Cherbourg rock,
Keeps crying Doodle doo, sir."

However, with the distinguished courage so much boasted of
in the proclamations and bulletins of their leader, it was said

that they waited for the first fog, that they might slip over
unseen.

> " It seems in a fog these great heroes confide,
> When unseen, o'er the sea they think safely to ride ;
> For taught by our sailors, they know to their shame,
> With Britons to see and to conquer's the same."

Jack Tar's impatience was set forth in a caricature by Gillray,
published on the 2nd of August, in which John Bull is represented as taking to the sea in person, to chant the serenade of
defiance. The head of Buonaparte is just seen over the battle-
ment, uttering the threat which he had now been repeating

JOHN BULL OFFERING LITTLE BONEY FAIR PLAY.

several weeks : "I'm a coming!—I'm a coming!" His boats
are safely stowed up under the triple fort in which he has
ensconced himself for personal security, and John Bull taunts
him with some ill humour :—

> " You're a coming !—
> If you mean to invade us, why make such a rout !
> I say, little Boney,—why don't you come out !
> Yes, d— you, why don't you come out !"

One of the songs distributed in the "loyal papers," which
seems to have been a very popular one, furnishes us with—

BUONAPARTE'S ANSWER TO JOHN BULL'S CARD.

"My dear Johnny Bull, the last mail
　Brought over your kind invitation,
And strongly it tempts us to sail
　In our boats to your flourishing nation.
But Prudence she whispers ' Beware,
　Don't you see that his fleets are in motion?
He'll play you some d—d *ruse de guerre*,
　If he catches you out on the ocean.'
　　Our fears they mount up, up, up,
　　　Our hopes they sink down-y, down-y,
　　Our hearts they beat backwards and forwards,
　　　Our heads they turn round-y, round-y.

" You say that pot-luck shall be mine :
　Je n'entend pas ces mots, Monsieur Bull ;
But I think I can guess your design,
　When you talk of a good belly-full.
I have promis'd my men, with rich food
　Their courage and faith to reward ;
I tell them your puddings are good,
　Though your dumplings are rather too hard.
　　Oh my Johnny, my Johnny,
　　　And O, my Johnny, my deary,
　　Do, let us good fellows come over,
　　　To taste your beef and beer-y.

" I've read and I've heard much of Wales,
　Its mines, its meadows, and fountains ;
Of black cattle fed in the vales,
　And goats skipping wild on the mountains.
Were I but safe landed there,
　What improvements I'd make in the place!
I'd prattle and kiss with the fair,
　Give the men the fraternal embrace.
　　O my Taffy, my Taffy,
　　　Soon I'll come, if it please ye,
　　To riot on delicate mutton,
　　　Good ale, and toasted cheese-y.

" Caledonia I long to see,
　And if the stout fleet in the north
Will let us go by quietly,
　Then I'll sail up the Frith of Forth.
Her sons, I must own, they are dashing ;
　Yet, Johnny, between me and you,
I owe them a grudge for the thrashing
　They gave that poor devil Menou.
　　O my Sawny, my Sawny,
　　　Your bagpipes will make us all frisky ;
　　We'll dance with your lasses so bonny,
　　　Eat haggis and tipple your whisky.

" Hibernia's another snug place,
　I hope to get there, too, some day,
Though our ships they got into disgrace
　With Warren near Donegall Bay.

Though my good friends at Vinegar Hill,
  They fail'd ; be assured, Jack, of this,
I'll give them *French liberty* still,
    As I have to the Dutch and the Swiss.
    O my Paddies, my Paddies,
      You are all of you honest good creatures ;
    And I long to be with you at Cork,
      To sup upon fish and potatoes.

"A fair wind and thirty-six hours,
  Would bring us all over from Brest ;
Tell your ships to let alone ours,
  And we'll manage all the rest.
Adieu, my dear boy, till we meet ;
  Take care of your gold, my honey ;
And when I reach Threadneedle Street,
  I'll help you to count out your money.
    But my fears they mount up, up, up,
      And my hopes they sink down-y, down-y ;
    My heart it beats backwards and forwards,
      And my head it runs round-y, round-y."

The House of Commons, which was not prorogued till late in the summer, added by its votes to the general patriotic spirit of the country. Sheridan was there the foremost in praising and encouraging the volunteers, and in calling attention to the important service done by the multitude of placards and songs that were thus distributed about the country. Those of his party who followed Fox in still wishing for friendship with France, and believing it possible, set him down for a confirmed alarmist ; and in a print, published on the 1st of September, Gillray has caricatured him as a bill-sticker, alarming John Bull with the announcements of peril and danger, which he is so busy scattering over the land. The print is explained by the following dialogue :—

AN ALARMIST.

"JOHN BULL AND THE ALARMIST.
"John Bull as he sat in his old easy chair,
  An alarmist came to him, and said in his ear,
  'A Corsican thief has just slipt from his quarters,
  And's coming to ravish your wives and your daughters

   " ' Let him come and be d—d f thus roar'd out John Bull,
   ' With my crabstick assur'd I will fracture his skull,
   Or I'll squeeze the vile reptile 'twixt my finger and thumb,
   Make him stink like a bug if he dares to presume.'

   " 'They say a full thousand of flat-bottom'd boats,
   Each a hundred and fifty have warriors of note,
   All fully determined to feast on your lands,
   So I fear you will find full enough on your hands.'

   "John smiling arose upright as a post,—
   ' I've a million of friends bravely guarding my coast;
   And my old ally Neptune will give them a dowsing,
   And prevent the mean rascals to come here a lousing !' "

The effect of the songs and papers was confined to home, but
the caricatures were carried abroad, and gave no little uneasiness
to Buonaparte, for they were often coarsely personal, and the
first consul was particularly sensitive to anything like ridicule
against himself or his family. The caricature which gave him
the greatest offence was a rather celebrated one by Gillray, published on the 24th of August, 1803, under the title of "The
Handwriting upon the Wall." It is a broad parody on Bel-
shazzar's feast. The first consul, his wife Josephine (to whom
the artist has given a figure of enormous bulk), and other members of his family and court, are seated at their dessert devouring the good things of old England. Buonaparte himself is
called off by the vision from the palace of St. James's, which is
seen in his plate with his fork stuck into it ; another worthy is
swallowing the Tower of London ; Josephine is drinking large
bumpers of wine. A plate, inscribed "Oh, de roast beef of Old
England !" bears the head of King George. The bottle labelled
"Maidstone" is understood to refer to some of the Irish conspirators, tried at the assizes in that town. A hand above holds
out the scales of Justice, in which the legitimate crown of
France weighs down the red cap with its attendant chain—
despotism under the name of liberty. Behind Josephine stand
the three princesses of the afterwards imperial family, the
Princess Borghese, the Princess Louise, and the Princess Joseph
Buonaparte. These ladies, who were the cause of some scandal
by their alleged irregularities, were bitterly satirized, not only
in caricatures, but even in medals and in other shapes, some of
which were not of a character to describe here. In Gillray's
large caricature of "The grand Coronation Procession," published on the 1st of January, 1805, on occasion of Napoleon's
assumption of the imperial dignity, the three princesses, clad in
very meretricious garb, walk at the head of the procession as

"the three imperial Graces," and scatter flowers in the way of the emperor and empress.

Most of the caricatures published during the latter part of the year 1803 were personal attacks on the ruler of France. In one, published in September, "The Butcher Buonaparte" is lifted on the shoulders of Talleyrand that he may spy over his battlements the English cannon destroying his navy of gunboats; he is made to exult over the slaughter of his own subjects, who began to be an embarrassment to him. It is said that Talleyrand always advised him against the invasion. In

THE GRACES.

another caricature, published on the 6th of October, the spirit of evil is represented roasting Buonaparte for his supper; it is the fulfilment of a wish expressed in one of the songs quoted above. A third, published on the 25th of October, represents a party of "French *volunteers* marching to the conquest of Great Britain." The miserable "volunteers," who have been dragged from their homes much against their will, and shew very little inclination for tho employment, are marched along chained and manacled.

Several of the "loyal papers" contain expressions which shew that there were still apprehensions that many people in this country were so discontented with King George's government that they would join the invaders, or, at least be very lukewarm in resisting them.   To counteract this feeling, the associations distributed strong appeals to the patriotism of all classes, shewing that the evils which they complained of at present were trifling in comparison with those that were threatened from abroad, placing before them the atrocious ravages committed in Holland, Switzerland, Germany, and Italy, and even in France itself, by the republican plunderers, and admonishing them that these were only to be avoided by uniting vigorously and heartily in the common defence.   English, Scot, and Irish, it was represented, had an equal interest at stake,—if they acted together, they were invincible.   One of the garlands (to use an expression of the olden time) of loyal songs introduces them discussing "the Invasion" in the following terms :—

"At the sign of the George, a national set
  (It fell out on a recent occasion),
A Briton, a Scot, and Hibernian, were met
  To discourse 'bout the threat'n'd invasion.

"The liquor went round, they joked and they laughed,
  Were quite pleasant, facetious, and hearty ;
To the health of their king flowing bumpers they quaff'd,
  With confusion to great Buonaparte.

"Quoth John, "Tis reported, that snug little strait,
  Which runs betwixt Calais and Dover,
With a hop, step, and jump, that the consul elate
  Intends in a trice to skip over.

" ' Let him try every cunning political stroke,
  And devise every scheme that he 's able ;
He 'll find us as firm and as hard to be broke,
  As the bundle of sticks in the fable.'

"The Scot and Hibernian replied—' You are right—
  Let him go the whole length of his tether ;
When England, and Scotland, and Ireland unite,
  They defy the whole world put together.' "

In spite, however, of all this courage and enthusiasm, and of the great measures taken for the defence of the country, it was a year of alarm and terror in England, such as it is to be hoped will not be experienced again.   It was but a gloomy Christmas which closed it, and ushered in a new year with little improve-

ment in our prospects. Every intelligence from abroad spoke
of the marching of troops from all parts of the French territory
to the coast from which the invasion was to be made. It was
known that Buonaparte had been at Boulogne just before Christmas, to visit and inspect the preparations. The general uneasiness was increased towards the end of February by the information which gradually spread abroad that the King was suffering
under a new attack of the dreadful disorder to which he was
constitutionally subject, and the country was thus in danger of
losing the active assistance of its monarch at the moment of
peril. Fortunately, however, the King's illness was not this
time of long duration, and as summer approached the fears of
invasion also began to wear away,* and public attention was
called off to political changes of another kind.

Pitt, who had previously supported the Addington ministry,
suddenly quarrelled with it in the spring of 1804, and placed
himself in the opposition. This defection was at first evinced
in frequent observations on the incapacity of the present government to help the country out of its difficulties, and in wishes
for the formation of a strong administration on a "broad
bottom" which should include "all the talents" of the different
parties. It was soon known that Temple and the Grenvilles
had joined Fox's party, but Pitt cautiously avoided compromis-
ing himself, although he spoke as much as anybody in favour of
a coalition of parties. On the 14th of March, Gillray published
a caricature entitled "The State Waggoner and John Bull; or,
the Waggon too much for the Donkeys,—together with a distant view of the new coalition among Johnny's old horses."
Addington, the state-driver, has run his waggon into a deep
slough, from which the donkeys that are harnessed to it are
unable to drag it. The unfortunate driver screams out—"Help,
Johnny Bull! help!—my waggon's stuck fast in the slough!—
help! help!" John Bull, dressed in the then fashionable
accoutrements of a volunteer, and attended by his faithful dog,
replies,—"Stuck fast in the slough?—ay, to be sure!—why
doesn't put better cattle to thy wain?—look at them there
horses doing o' nothing at all!—what signifies whether they
matches in colour, if they do but drag the waggon out of the mud?
—don't you see how the very thought o' being put into harness

---

* In July, 1804, the Paris papers, as quoted in our newspapers, said,—
"The invasion has been only deferred, to render it more terrible when the
whole strength of the French empire, destined to make the attack, shall be
collected."

makes 'em all love and nubble one another?" The horses to which
he points occupy a neighbouring bank, and present the well-known
faces of Pitt, the Marquis of Buckingham, Fox, who is courting the
friendship of Lords Temple and Grenville, Lords Holland, Grey,

Erskine, Lauderdale, Moira,
Castlereagh, Lord Carlisle,
Canning, Wilberforce, Windham, and Sheridan, the two
latter of whom are kicking at
each other. The day after the
date of this print, on the 15th
of March, Pitt made a direct
attack on the ministry in a
motion on the naval defence
of the country, which was supported by Fox, but opposed by
Sheridan, who seemed to have
deserted his old party to league
with Addington. After the

JOHN BULL TURNED VOLUNTEER.

Easter recess, the opposition took a much more decisive character. On the 23rd of April, Fox brought forward a motion
relating to the defence of the country (the subject now nearest
to everybody's heart); and he was opposed by Addington, who
insinuated that the mere object of the mover was to embarrass
and overthrow his ministry. Pitt then rose to support Fox;
he declared that he had no confidence in ministers, whom he
blamed severely for their want of intelligence and foresight. In
the course of the debate which followed the coalition was openly
spoken of; but it was denied by Fox and Pitt, who declared
that they were only united in a common opinion of the ineffi-
ciency of the men then in office. On a division, the usually
large ministerial majority was reduced to fifty-two. Two nights
afterwards this majority was further reduced to thirty-seven.
Before the end of the month Pitt was in communication with
the King for the formation of a new cabinet. A large caricature by Gillray, was published on the 1st of May, under the
title of the "Confederated Coalition; or, the giants storming
heaven, with the gods alarmed for their everlasting abodes;" in
which the discordant elements of the opposition are represented
under the character of the mythic giants following their chief
leaders, Pitt and Fox, to the assault of the heavenly abode
occupied by the ministerial triumvirate, Addington, Lord
Hawkesbury, and Lord St. Vincent.

On the 12th of May, the *Gazette* announced that William Pitt was restored to his old place of chancellor of the Exchequer. In forming his cabinet, Pitt neither coalesced with Addington nor took in Fox. His quarrel with the former had ripened into personal hostility. He appears to have wished to conciliate Fox, and to give him a place in his cabinet; but here he had to contend with the hostility of the King, who met this proposal with a flat refusal. Lord Temple and the Grenvilles, who had engaged that Fox should come in, refused to take office without him. In the new administration, the Duke of Portland was president of the Council; Lord Eldon, chancellor; the Earl of Westmoreland, lord privy seal; Lord Chatham, master-general of the ordnance; and Lord Castlereagh president of the board of control. These had all formed a part of the Addington ministry. Pitt's friend, Dundas, who had now been raised to the peerage under the title of Lord Melville, was appointed first lord of the Admiralty; Lord Harrowby succeeded Lord Hawkesbury as secretary for foreign affairs; Lord Camden was made secretary for the colonies; and Lord Mulgrave chancellor of the Duchy of Lancaster. Mr. Canning, who was now Pitt's main support in the House of Commons, was made treasurer of the Navy, without a place in the cabinet.

The change in the ministry produced a clever caricature from Gillray, published on the 20th of May, under the title of "Britannia between Death and the Doctors—Death may decide when Doctors disagree." Britannia is reclining on her bed of sickness, with abundance of nostrums scattered over the room, but evidently not much relieved by her physicians. One of them, Fox, who grasps in his hand a bottle of "republican balsam," lies on the floor, stretched beneath the foot of Pitt, who with the other foot is kicking Addington and his "composing draught" out of doors. The new doctor raises triumphantly in his hand a bottle of his "constitutional restorative." While the doctors are thus settling their dispute, death, in the personage of Buonaparte (who still kept his immense army on the opposite coast with the professed intention of invading us) steals from behind the curtains, and aims a blow with his spear at their patient.

The opposition, thus swelled by the accession of Addington and his friends, as well as the party of the Grenvilles, was very formidable, and Pitt actually came in with smaller majorities than those upon which Addington went out. The first trial of strength was on the 5th of June, when Pitt brought forward his plan for the military defence of the country. Sheridan attacked the new ministers with great bitterness, pointed out their weakness in the House of Commons, and expressed his opinion that they ought not to remain in office with such a strong feeling there against them. Pitt shewed more anger than it was usual for him to exhibit; he said, in reply to Sheridan, that, "as to the hint which had been so kindly given him to resign, it was not broad enough for him to take it; even if the bill were lost, he should not, for that, consider it his duty to resign—his Majesty had the prerogative of choosing his own servants;" and he complained much of the opposition of the Grenvilles. Other members of the opposition now rose in succession, and attacked the ministry; Fox declaimed against Pitt's indecent defiance of the opinion of the House; and the Grenvilles defended themselves.

Pitt, however, was evidently embarrassed by the hostility he had to encounter. It was clear that the old and compact party with which he had so long ruled the country, had been entirely broken up, and he seemed confused and irritated among the discordant materials that now lay before him. The singular position in which the little parties that had thus sprung up stood towards each other, and the personal intrigues they engendered, afforded subjects for the caricaturist on every side, and these were not overlooked. On the 18th of June Gillray caricatured the whole body of the opposition in a large print, entitled "L'Assemblée Nationale; or, grand co-operative meeting at St. Anne's Hill; respectfully dedicated to the admirers of a 'Broad-bottomed Administration.'" It was at this period that Sayer produced some of his latest efforts in the cause of his old patron, Pitt. Many believed that the statesman's influence was sensibly affected by the probability that a new reign was near at hand, when he would no longer enjoy the royal countenance; and on the 11th of July Sayer published a large caricature, in which the Prince of Wales was represented as the rising sun, the Grenville party are on their knees as "Persians (stowed together) worshipping the rising sun;" Sheridan, and Fox, and some of their followers, are there as "Greeks;" the former says to Lord Temple, "Lower, my lord," although the "Greeks" themselves remain upright; and a solitary individual on one side is described as "Achitophel; an old Jew Scribe, lately turned Greek." A paper, which protrudes from his pocket, exhibits the words, "Secret advice to his R.H.—No respecter of persons, to invite tag, rag, and bobtail to dine . . ."

The caricaturists attacked Pitt unsparingly. One of their

prints, the only copy of which that I have seen is in the possession of Mr. Hawkins, pub-
lished on the 1st of August,
the day of the prorogation of
parliament, represents the
minister in the character of a
Pierrot, playing on his puppet,
which is apparently intended
to represent Canning. The
performer addresses himself to
his audience,—" Here he is,
gentlemen, a chip of the old
block, one of my own manu-
factory,—

BILLY PIERROT AND HIS PUPPET.

" Here you go up, up, up,
    And there you go down, down, down-y !"

Fox had latterly assumed a much more moderate tone than
when Pitt's supreme influence left him no hopes of power; he
spoke with less bitterness of his political opponents, rested
his opposition on the necessity of joining all parties in the
support of the country and its constitution; he still shewed a
little partiality for France and its rulers, but he called for
vigorous exertions to carry on the war, now that wo were
irretrievably engaged in it. But there was another party now
gaining head, much more extreme in its political principles than
the Foxites, and which a little later assumed the name of
Radicals. The leader of this party in the House of Commons
was Sir Francis Burdett, who was taking the position in politics
which had been held by Wilkes at the beginning, and by Fox in
the middle of this reign; and it was supported out of doors by
Horne Tooke, still an active agitator,—by Cobbett, who had
already commenced his political writings,—and by a number
of other zealous partizans. Burdett triumphed over the
ministers in the Middlesex election in August, 1804, as Wilkes
had done on the same scene of action. This occurrence has
been commemorated in an elaborate caricature by Gillray, published on the 7th of August, and entitled, " Middlesex Election
—a long pull, a strong pull, and a pull all together." The scene
is laid in the neighbourhood of the hustings, to which Burdett
is carried in triumph in his barouche, with Horne Tooke, his
pocket full of speeches, as driver. Behind stand Sheridan,
Tierney, and Erskine, carrying flags and banners. That held up
by Sheridan bears the representation of Britannia fixed in the

R R

pillory, and scourged by Pitt, in allusion to the punishment

of political offenders in
the prison of Coldbath
Fields, the key of which
is carried by Tierney,
while Erskine hoists the
standard of the " good
old cause." In place of
horses, the carriage is
dragged along by the
chiefs of the Whig
party, consisting of Fox,
the Dukes of Norfolk
and Bedford, the Mar-
quis of Lansdowne,
Lords Derby, Carlisle,

BRITANNIA SCOURGED.

and St. Vincent, with Grey and Bosville. Lord Moira acts as
drummer. Tyrrell, Jones, Grattan, and Fitzpatrick are at the
hind wheels. In the distance we see the Radicals pelting with
mud the sign of Church, King, and Constitution.

With so many difficulties to face, Pitt seemed to lose his
wonted courage, and his health, impaired by his devotion to the
bottle, was rapidly breaking down. He did not venture to meet
parliament until the 15th of January, 1805, when, after vain
efforts to bring over the Grenvilles, he had at last succeeded in
detaching Addington from the opposition. The latter was
rewarded with a peerage, under the title of Viscount Sidmouth,
and the office of president of the council, vacated by Lord
Portland on account of his advanced age. Still Pitt was not
strong in his majorities, and the opposition he had to encounter
was remarkably pertinacious and annoying. His own friends
seemed to join in giving him uneasiness. At the beginning of
the session Wilberforce persisted in bringing forward the question of the abolition of slavery, in spite of the entreaties of the
minister; and he afterwards joined in promoting the impeachment of Pitt's old friend Lord Melville (Dundas) for whom he
had contracted a sort of puritanical dislike, because he was a
hard drinker and sometimes a rather profane joker. Wilberforce's conduct on this occasion, is said to have given great
annoyance to Pitt. Sayer has commemorated the attack upon
Lord Melville in two caricatures, in both of which Wilberforce
is represented as the puritan preacher, venting from his tub his
saintly spleen against the sinner. In one of these, Whitbread,
who had led the attack, is represented as a barrel of porter

bursting, and stinking the members out of the house; Wilberforce exclaims, from his tub, "'Tis the Lord's doing, and has
spoilt our brewery." In the other, Whitbread, a figure built up
of tubs and barrels, is aiming a blow at the Scotch thistle
(Melville) with his flail. This print is entitled, "The brewer
and the thistle," and is accompanied with an epigram on Whitbread:

> "Sansterre forsook his malt and grains,
> To mash and butter nobles' brains,
> By lev'lling rancour led;
> Our Brewer quits brown stout and washey,
> His malt, his mash-tub, and his quashes,
> To mash a Thistle's head."

In May, Pitt had to contend with the question of all others
most disagreeable to him at the present moment, from the part
he had already taken in it, that of Catholic Emancipation,
which, however, he opposed on the ground of the inexpediency
of bringing it forward under the circumstances of the time. On
the defeat of this attack from the opposition, Gillray published
a caricature, dated the 17th of May, and entitled "The end of
the Irish farce of Catholic Emancipation." The opposition,
under the guidance of Fox, seated on a bull (of Irish breed) with
a miniature of Buonaparte round its neck, after having reached
the very threshold of the treasury, are overthrown by three
blasts which come from the mouth of Pitt, Hawkesbury, and
Sidmouth. Lord Grenville, who was in advance of the attacking
party, and bears the crosier, is staggering backwards. Lord
Moira is rolling over Mrs. Fitzherbert, who is stretched on the
floor in a very undignified attitude. Lord Stanhope is incense
bearer, and Sheridan is about to elevate the host; but Lord
Lauderdale drops the bell in alarm. Horne Tooke carries the
cross, which is crowned with the *bonnet rouge*. Cobbett exhibits the *Weekly Register*, and carries a representation of an
auto da fé performed in Smithfield. Others are acting a variety
of parts. In the foreground stand the Duke of Clarence, who is
struck with astonishment; the Duke of Bedford, meditating on
transubstantiation; the Duke of Norfolk, preparing to toast the
host in a goblet of Whitbread's entire; and Lords Derby,
Carlisle, and Thanet, Sir Francis Burdett, and Mr. Grattan,
singing vespers.

Pitt's budget was not allowed to pass without severe remarks,
and a heavily increased duty on salt excited general dissatisfaction. People said that, when the grand contriver of taxes had
visited every corner of the house above stairs, he had now descended

into the kitchen; and one of the caricatures published at this

BILLY IN THE SALT-BOX.

period, represents the premier alarming the poor cook by popping his head out of the salt-box, with the unexpected salutation — "How do you do, cook-ey?" The person thus apostrophised cries out in consternation, "Curse the fellow, how he has frightened me! —I think, in my heart, he is getting in everywhere!—who the deuce would have thought of finding him in the salt-box?"

One only incident occurred to cheer the minister in his painful struggle to carry out his plans, and that was one of an unusual character in the political warfare of former days. When an attempt, in his absence, was made to implicate Pitt in the charges of malversation brought against Lord Melville, Fox generously stood forward in his defence, and bore testimony of his high opinion of the personal integrity of the premier. Some said that this indicated in Fox a wish to be allowed to share in the pleasures of office, a sentiment which is exhibited in a caricature published by Gillray on the 21st of June, under the title of "Political Candour; i. e. Coalition Resolutions of June 14, 1805."

In the midst of this parliamentary strife at home, our inveterate enemy Buonaparte had made the last grand step in his political ambition. He was proclaimed emperor of the French, under the title of Napoleon I., on the 20th of May, 1804, and crowned in Paris with extraordinary ceremonies on the 2nd of December following. A few days before this latter event, on the 26th of November, Gillray rejoiced all loyal volunteers, who hated the very name of the new sovereign, with a caricature, entitled "The Genius of France nursing her Darling," in which the genius is represented in the form of a veritable *poissarde*, her garments stained with blood, and her spear, dripping with gore, supported against the wall. A picture of the head of Louis XVI. is thrown on one side. The lady is tossing Napoleon, armed with his sceptre, as a child in one hand, and endeavouring to pacify his cries for a rattle surmounted with a crown, which she holds in the other. She sings a parody on the old nursery rhyme,—

"There 's a little King Pippin !
He shall have a rattle and crown !
Bless thy five wits, my baby !
Mind it don't throw itself down.
　　　Hey, my kitten, my kitten !"

The same caricaturist published, on the 1st of January, 1805, a large burlesque print of "The Grand Coronation Procession." From this time, during several months, caricatures on the new emperor and empress, some of them very libellous and coarse, abounded. One by Gillray, published on the 26th of February, entitled "The Plum-pudding in danger; or, State Epicures taking *un petit souper*," represents Napoleon and Pitt contending over the globe in the shape of a plum-pudding, from which Pitt is cutting off the ocean as his share, while his antagonist is helping himself to the whole of Europe. Measures, however, were now in active preparation for disputing with the new pretender to the insignia of sovereignty his claims to the share which he thus arrogated to himself. In the course of the summer a third coalition against France was completed, the chief parties to which were Great Britain, Russia, and Austria. One of the English caricatures on this new armament was published in the October of 1805, under the title of "Tom Thumb at bay ; or, the Sovereigns of the Forest roused at last ;" Napoleon, flying from the eagle of Austria, the Russian bear, and the Westphalian pig, and dropping his crown and sceptre in his flight, is rushing into the open jaws of the British lion. In the distance the Dutchman is throwing off his yoke, and advising Spain and Portugal to do the same, and still further off is seen the British fleet riding triumphant on the sea. The new war on the continent only led Napoleon to new victories ; after the Austrians had experienced several defeats, General Mack made a dishonourable surrender of Ulm to the French on the 17th of October, and thus laid open the Austrian empire to the invaders. Only four days after this disastrous event, on the 21st of October, the combined French and Spanish fleets were utterly destroyed in the memorable battle of Trafalgar. But the French army continued its victorious career ; on the 14th of November Napoleon made his entry into Vienna ; and the 2nd of December was fought the fatal battle of Austerlitz, which compelled the Russians to retreat and the Austrians to submit to a humiliating peace.

The caricatures on these momentous events have little merit, and are scarcely worth enumerating. On the 23rd of January, 1806, when Napoleon had begun his system of king-making with his kings of Wirtemberg and Bavaria, Gillray produced one of a

superior character, under the title of "Tiddy Doll, the great
gingerbread baker, drawing out a new batch of kings, his man,
hopping Talley, mixing up the dough." Talleyrand, who was
short of one leg, is employed as thus described, while his master,
Napoleon, as baker, is drawing from the oven a batch of gingerbread kings. A number of figures scattered over the bakehouse
represent the melancholy condition of Europe at this period.
On a board on one side stands a number of "little dough vice-
roys intended for the next new batch," on which we trace the
faces of Fox, Sheridan, Lord Derby, and others of the English
Whig leaders. The broomstick in Napoleon's hand is inscribed
as the "besom of destruction."

Pitt's health had been fast declining through the autumn and
winter, and parliament met on the 21st of January, 1806, only to
witness his death, which occurred on the 23rd. A new opening
was thus made for the intrigues of parties, and the task of forming
a ministry was not an easy one. The King still detested the
name of Fox; but after several persons had refused to take the
responsibility of forming a ministry, among whom were Lord
Hawkesbury, Lord Sidmouth, and, it is said, the Marquis Wellesley, he was at length obliged to throw himself on the Grenvilles and Foxites, and consented to the formation of the comprehensive coalition ministry, which became known by the title
of "All the Talents." In this ministry, the formation of which
was announced on the 4th of February, Lord Grenville was first
Lord of the Treasury ; Fox, Secretary for Foreign Affairs ; Lord
Sidmouth, Lord Privy Seal ; Earl Fitzwilliam, President of the
Council ; Grey, now Lord Howick, first Lord of the Admiralty ;
the Earl of Moira, Master-general of the Ordnance ; Earl
Spencer, Home Secretary ; Windham, Secretary for the Colo-
nies ; Lord Henry Petty, Chancellor of the Exchequer ; Erskine,
Lord Chancellor ; and Lord Minto, President of the Board of
Control. Among the minor places, Sheridan, who was noto-
riously unfit for business, obtained that of Treasurer of the
Navy.

This extraordinary cabinet contained far too many jarring
elements to be lasting, and it soon became universally unpopular.
The number of caricatures against this "broad-bottomed"
ministry was very great. An anonymous print, published on
the 20th of February, represents the King making a bowl of
punch from a number of bottles, each bearing the face of one or
other of the members of this strange coalition : he says,
"Though the ingredients, taken separately, may not be pleasing
to every palate, yet, when mixed together, they may go down

with a tolerable relish." On the same day, Gillray published a humorous caricature entitled, "Making decent; *i. e.* Broad Bottomites getting into the Grand Costume;" in which most of the new ministers, who had long been out of office, are represented as dressing themselves for presentation at court. On the 5th of March, the same artist published a caricature entitled, "More pigs than teats; or, the new litter of hungry grunters sucking John Bull's old sow to death ;" in fact, the numerous hungry claimants that were now brought in, promised small relief to John Bull's burthens, and he is here made to express the fear that there will soon be nothing left for "Boney," if he come. Another of Gillray's caricatures, published on the 14th of March, and entitled, "A tub for the whale," represents the crew of the "Broad-bottom packet," throwing out a tub to amuse the whale that pursues them, (public opinion,) which is spouting out "ridicule" and "contempt;" the sun of Whig government is setting, and a broom at the mast-head indicates that the vessel is for sale. Another, by the same artist, on the 5th of April, under the title of "Pacific overtures; or, a flight from St. Cloud's 'over the water to Charley,'" burlesques the attempt at negotiations for peace with France, provoked by Napoleon himself, but overthrown by his extravagant pretensions. It is described as "a new dramatic *peace*, now rehearsing," and implies a somewhat unmerited censure on the Whigs. Fox, as minister, showed no inclination to sacrifice the honour of his country, in these futile negotiations. On the 21st of April Gillray founded a caricature on a declaration by Fox that his place was not a bed of roses; which he entitled, "Comforts of a bed of roses; vide, Charles's elucidation of Lord Castlereagh's speech!—a nightly scene near Cleveland Row." Fox and his wife are asleep in bed, when Napoleon is attacking the minister in the midst of his slumber; the ghost of Pitt rouses him— "Awake! awake! or be for ever fallen!"

The moderation which had lately characterized Fox's sentiments, was accounted for by some by supposing that he had fallen under the influence of Lord Grenville; in fact, Lord Grenville, they thought, had tamed the bear. A caricature by Gillray, published on the 19th of May, was entitled "The bear and his leader," and represented Lord Grenville teaching Fox, as his bear, to dance; the leader holds in his hand a "cudgel for disobedient bears;" and in his pocket is seen a paper inscribed, "rewards for obedient bears." Lord Sidmouth, with a patch on one eye, acts as fiddler, and M. A. Taylor sustains the character of the monkey.

The necessity under which Fox, who had so severely criticised the acts of former ministers in this respect, found himself of

THE BEAR AND HIS LEADER.

increasing the burthen of taxation, completed the unpopularity of the new ministry. Two caricatures by Gillray, published on the 9th and 28th of May, have reference to this subject. The first is entitled, " A Great Stream from a Petty Fountain ; or, John Bull swamped in the flood of New Taxes; Cormorants fishing in the stream." The face of Lord Henry Petty, Fox's Chancellor of the Exchequer, adorns the fountain from which the flood of taxation issues; and a numerous herd of placemen, in the likeness of so many cormorants, are greedily snatching at the loaves and fishes.   In the second of these caricatures, which is entitled, " The ' Friend of the People' and his Petty new Tax-gatherer paying John Bull a visit," Fox and Lord Henry Petty, with a terrible book of new taxes, make their call on

TAX GATHERERS.

John Bull, who has shut up his shop (which is announced " to

let") and removed his family to the first floor, from motives of economy. Lord Henry Petty knocks, and raises the cry, " Taxes! taxes! taxes!" to which John Bull responds from the window above, " — Taxes! taxes! taxes!—why how am I to get money to pay them all? I shall very soon have neither a house nor hole to put my head in." The man of the people, little touched by this appeal, shouts to him, "A house to put your head in?—why what the devil should you want with a house?—haven't you got a first-floor room to live in?—and if that is too dear, can't you move into the garret or get into the cellar?—Taxes must be had, Johnny—come, down with your cash!—it's all for the good of your dear country!"

The proceedings on Lord Melville's impeachment drew other caricatures on the Foxites, and, of course, more especially on Whitbread, who is represented in one of them as taking refuge in a cask of his own entire. Fox's frail tenure of office was hinted at, on the 20th of June, in a caricature by Gillray, entitled, "Bruin in his boat, or the manager in distress." Even the signs of approaching dissolution did not shield the great leader of the Whigs from the shafts of satire. A caricature by Gillray, published on the 28th of July, under the title of "Visiting the Sick," represents Fox on his couch of death, insulted by some, mourned over by a few, while many are rejoicing at the prospect of getting rid of him. On the 1st of September, when every one was aware that the minister had but few days to live, Gillray ridiculed his attempts at negotiating for peace in a caricature entitled, "Westminster Conscripts under the training act," in which Fox appears as drummer to his awkward squad, and Lord Lauderdale, his ambassador, is a Scottish dove, bearing the insulting "terms of peace" for his olive branch. On the 13th of September, Charles James Fox followed his great rival to the grave, doubling the irretrievable void which had already been felt on the political stage. On the very day of his death, Gillray published a new caricature, in which his negotiations for peace were again incidentally turned to ridicule; it is entitled, "News from Calabria; capture of Buenos Ayres; *i. e.* the comforts of an imperial breakfast at St. Cloud's." Napoleon is represented, while at his breakfast-table, bursting into one of those petulant paroxysms of rage to which he is said to have been subject under contradiction or disappointment: the cause on this occasion is an accumulation of bad news from different parts of the world; the breakfast-table is kicked over; the hot water thrown on the empress, who is losing her crown in the first start of consternation.

The death of Fox produced no immediate change in the
ministry of any importance. He was succeeded as Foreign
secretary by Lord Howick (Grey), who was now the true
representative of Fox's principles. Mr. T. Grenville succeeded
Lord Howick as first lord of the Admiralty; Sidmouth became
president of the Council in place of Lord Fitzwilliam, who had
resigned, and was succeeded as keeper of the Privy Seal by Lord
Holland, the only new member introduced into the cabinet.
For reasons which are not very evident, an immediate dissolution
of Parliament was resolved upon, and the new elections were
not altogether favourable to ministers, who, moreover, had
never enjoyed the confidence of the King. The most remarkable
of the elections were those for Middlesex and Westminster,
which produced a considerable number of caricatures, besides
multitudes of political squibs of all descriptions. Gillray
published not less than half-a-dozen caricatures on this occasion.
Sir Francis Burdett figured prominently in both elections,—he
was beaten at Brentford by the Court candidate (for he was in
opposition), and at Covent Garden he supported his radical
friend, Paul, against Sheridan and Lord Hood, who had formed
a coalition against him. The first of Gillray's caricatures is
entitled the "Triumphant procession of little Paul the tailor
upon his new goose;" Burdett was usually caricatured by his
opponents under the form of a goose; he is here led in a noose
by Horne Tooke, and urged forwards with a kick from Cobbett
behind. His second, published on the 18th of November,
represented Sheridan and Hood tossing Paul in the coalition
blanket, and was entitled, "The high-flying candidate (*i.e.*,
little Paul Goose) mounting from a blanket." A third caricature by Gillray, is a very spirited sketch entitled "Posting to
the Election; a scene on the road to Brentford, Nov. 1806."
Each of the various parties interested, is hastening on in its own
way. Sheridan, who was supported by Whitbread, is dashing
through thick and thin on a brewer's horse, which looks as if it
had just broke loose from the dray. He carries Lord Hood
behind him; hung to the horse's side is a pannier of "Subscription malt and hops from the Whitbread brewery;" in his pocket
a manuscript entitled, "Neck or Nothing, a new coalition." A
kick of the horse behind is overthrowing Paul from his
donkey. On the other side, rapidly gaining ahead of them, is
Mr. Mellish, one of the victorious candidates for Middlesex,
driven by Lord Grenville in a coach and four, behind which, as
footmen, stand the Marquis of Buckingham, Lord Temple, and
Lord Castlereagh. They are followed close by Mr. Byng, in a

post-chaise drawn by two spirited hacks; he represents the old
Whig interest, and has a wooden bust of Fox on the box before
him. Last comes Burdett, in a cart slowly dragged through a
pool of muddy water by four donkeys; behind him in the cart

A COALITION OF CANDIDATES.

are Horne Tooke, Mr. Boeville (one of the very active
radicals of the day), and Cobbett, who is acting as drummer,
with his "Political Register" and "Inflammatory Letters," as
drumsticks; his drum has for its
badge the republican *bonnet rouge*.
A parcel of sweeps are pushing the
cart behind, to help it forwards.
A " View of the Hustings in Covent
Garden," published by Gillray on
the 15th of December, represents
Hood and Sheridan browbeaten by
the mob-eloquence of their opponent
Paul; Whitbread is encouraging
and consoling Sheridan with a pot
of porter. A fifth caricature on
this subject, published by Gillray
in December, is entitled, " Peter
and Paul expelled from Paradise;"
they are on their way to Wimble-
don, where Tooke resided, and their

A RADICAL DRUMMER.

condition is intimated by a parody on Milton,—

"The world was all before them, where to choose
Their place of rest, and Parson Tooke their guide."

No measures could now save the present ministry long, for
the King had already determined they should go out, and only
waited for an occasion for dismissing them. This was furnished
in March, 1807, by a bill proposed by Lord Grenville for the
relief of the Roman Catholics in Ireland. The King announced
his intention of changing his ministers about the middle of
March; he appears to have carried on private negotiations before that time, or even before the opportunity for the blow was
given; but it was not till the beginning of April that the new
ministry was definitely formed. It consisted of the Duke of
Portland, first lord of the treasury; Lord Hawkesbury, home
secretary; George Canning, secretary for foreign affairs; Lord
Castlereagh, secretary for war and the colonies; Spencer
Perceval, chancellor of the exchequer; Earl Camden, president
of the council; the Earl of Chatham, master of the ordnance;
the Earl of Westmoreland, keeper of the privy seal; Earl
Bathurst, president of the board of trade; Lord Eldon, chancellor; and Lord Mulgrave, first lord of the admiralty. Perceval, who was notorious for his opposition to the Catholic
claims, was considered as the chief.

The court, in making this change, adopted the tactics so
often used with success before, of raising an agitation against
the Whigs, by stirring up popular prejudices. The cry of "No
popery!" was raised again, and with good effect; and a host of
new caricatures came out to ridicule the broad-bottomed administration of "All the Talents." On the 23rd of March, Gillray
represented the King kicking out his old ministry very unccre-
moniously, in a caricature entitled "A kick at the broad
bottoms; i. e. emancipation of All the Talents." A caricature
by the elder Cruikshank, published on the 4th of April, under
the title of "The Protestant St. George too much for all the
Tallons; or, The beast with seven heads," represents the King
encountering his ministerial hydra, while Mrs. Fitzherbert is
seen behind lamenting over its defeat, and the prince is making
his escape to hide himself. A caricature published by Gillray,
on the 18th of April, represented King George as John Bull's
farmer, driving the herd of rapacious pigs out of his sty—it is
entitled "The pigs possessed; or, the broad-bottomed litter
running headlong into the sea of perdition." The artist had
already, on the 6th of April, celebrated the demise of the
ministry in a humorous caricature, entitled "The funeral procession of Broad-bottom." About the same time, Gillray published a clever caricature, entitled "Charon's boat; or, the

ghosts of All the Talents taking their last voyage." The boat, with Earl St. Vincent at the helm, is heavily laden with the principal members of the late administration. On the opposite shore an expectant group, consisting of the ghosts of Fox, Oliver Cromwell, Robespierre, Despard (who had been hung for treason in England), and Quidgley (an Irish rebel executed at Chelmsford), are prepared to welcome the new arrival. In the clouds are the three fatal sisters who had joined in cutting the thread of the broad-bottomed cabinet, bearing the figures of Lord Hawkesbury, Lord Castlereagh, and George Canning. In another caricature, published on the 28th of April, Gillray selects Lord Temple as the more especial object of his satire. It was spread abroad as a piece of scandal against Lord Temple, that he had provided himself, while in office, with a small per-quisite, to the amount of between one and two thousand pounds' worth of stationery. This story was the subject of many jokes and epigrams. Under the title of "The fall of Icarus," Gillray represents Lord Temple attempting to fly away with wings made of the quills he had thus appropriated to himself, but the wax being melted by the sun (exhibiting the face of King George), the adventurer is falling in a very perilous posture on "a stake from the public hedge."*

> " With plumes, and wax, and such like things,
> In quantities not small,
> He tries to make a pair of wings,
> To raise his sudden fall !"

When the " No popery !" cry was at the highest, and every effort had been made to decry the supporters of the late motley administration, Parliament was again dissolved. The elections, which took place in May, were, as might be expected, in favour of the new administration. Immense sums of money were expended on the elections, and the country was agitated in the most violent manner. Westminster was again the scene of a turbulent contest. Burdett, who had quarrelled with his old fellow-radical Paul, after the election of the year preceding, to such a degree that it ended in a duel in which both were wounded, now offered himself as a candidate against him at the election, and was placed at the head of the poll. He was again backed by Horne Tooke, and a caricature, published in May, represented the Brentford parson carrying the successful candi-

---

* This alludes to an incident in the debate on the right of Horne Tooke to sit in the House of Commons. Lord Temple, who was his great opponent, having stated that he had a stake in the country, Tooke re-sponded that he also had a stake, although it was a small one, but it was not taken out of " the public hedge."

date at the end of his *pole*, and exhibiting him to the crowd collected in Covent Garden;
it is entitled " The head of
the Poll; or, the Wimble-
don Showman and his Pup-
pet." Tooke exhibits him
as " the finest puppet in
the world, gentlemen, en-
tirely of my own forma-
tion. I have only to say
the word, and he'll do anything." Gillray adopted
the same pun in a carica-
ture published on the 20th
of May, under the title of
" Election Candidates; or,
the republican Goose at the
top of the *pole*." The four

AT THE HEAD OF THE POLL.

candidates, Burdett, Lord
Cochrane, Sheridan, and
Paul, are climbing the election pole; Burdett, as a goose, is
perched on the top, where he is held by the assistance of the
evil one; next below him is Lord Cochrane, then Sheridan, and,
finally, Paul, who, having missed his grasp, comes tumbling to
the ground.

The Tories, now in power, attacked the foreign policy of their
predecessors, and accused them of having paved the way for
Napoleon's successes. It was certainly the period at which the
imperial power was at its highest point. Gillray, on the 25th
of June, 1807, satirized the fallen " Talents" in a caricature
entitled " The new Dynasty; or, the little Corsican Gardener
planting a royal Pippin-tree," an allusion to the numerous new
kings lately raised into existence by Napoleon. The Marquis of
Buckingham, Lord Grenville, and Lord Lauderdale are demo-
lishing the royal oak, while Napoleon and Talleyrand are busy
planting new trees. A plantation of continental king-pippins
occupy the background, while in front lie, as grafts ready for
planting, Horne Tooke, Sir Francis Burdett, and Cobbett. On
the top of the royal pippin-tree in Napoleon's band is seen the
head of Lord Moira.

The war had not, however, been inglorious to England,
although alliance after alliance had been broken up, and all the
great powers of the continent had not only been separated from
us, but they had been obliged to turn against us. Nevertheless,
the battle of Maida, in the summer of 1806, had broken the

spell which had made people believe that the French armies were invincible; and victory continued to attend our fleets in every part of the world. It was in 1807 that Napoleon began to shew his designs upon Spain, and commenced the war which first brought him in direct contact with British armies, and contributed so much to his final overthrow. In England the terrors of "invasion" had given way to a feeling of triumph and exultation in our position in the war. On the first day of the year 1807 appeared a caricature representing John Bull grasping the "little Corsican" as a fiddle, and playing upon him with his sword, to the tune of "Britons, strike home!" it is entitled, "John Bull playing on the *base villain.*" Caricatures in this spirit began now to be frequent; and the numerous prizes brought in by our ships, during the very period at

JOHN BULL TURNED FIDDLER.

MASTER AND MAN.

which the French emperor expected to ruin us by setting the whole continent against us, animated the English people to new exertions and new sacrifices. Among the caricatures published at this period, was one by Woodward, which appeared on the 27th of November, 1807, soon after the British order of council placing all France under blockade, in answer to Napoleon's Berlin decree; it is entitled, "The continental dockyard." On one side of the Channel is "The Gallic storehouse for English shipping," which is empty and falling into ruin. In front stands Napoleon, angrily threatening his master shipwright,—" Begar, you must vork like de diable, ve must annihilate dis John Bull!" The shipwright, aghast, replies, " Please you, my

JOHN BULL AND HIS INDUSTRIOUS SERVANTS.

grand Empereur, tes no use vatever ; as fast as ve do build dem, he vas clap dem in his storehouse over de way."   On the other side of the water stands John Bull's storehouse full of captured ships, with John himself surrounded by his industrious tars, whom he addresses, " I say, my lads, if he goes on this way, we shall be overstock'd."   One of the sailors replies with the dry observation, " What a deal of pains some people take for nothing."

CHAPTER XVI.

GEORGE III. AND THE REGENCY.

New Prospects—Struggles of Parties; Sir Francis Burdett; John Bull in
Admiration—The Regency—The War; Elba; Waterloo; St. Helena
—England after the Peace; Taxation and Reform; The Dandies and
the Hobby-Horses.

THE prospects of England under the new ministry were,
indeed, far from encouraging. Napoleon was gradually
bringing the whole of Europe under his yoke, and turning it
against this country, and many looked forwards to the time
when we should have to prepare for an invasion under much
greater disadvantages than in 1803. Few months had passed
since the formation of the cabinet, when Russia, which declared
war against England on the 1st of December, leagued with
France, and was added to the list of our enemies. In the course
of 1808 the French occupied Spain, and invaded Portugal.
Austria rose up in indignation at the humiliating treatment she
received from the French emperor in the spring of 1809; but
within four months her territory was overrun by the victorious
armies of her enemy, and she was compelled to accept a still
more humiliating peace.

The nation in general, however, felt no discouragement, and
people indulged more than ever in coarse ridicule on the person
and pretensions of the Emperor of the French. The caricatures
became now so numerous, that in the course of a few years their
titles alone would fill a volume. Gillray's labours in this line
closed with the year 1809. On the 10th of April, 1808, this
celebrated artist satirized the sanguine promises of success held
out by the English ministers in a caricature, entitled " Delicious
dreams !—Castles in the air !—Glorious Prospects !" The ministers, full of wine and punch, are sunk in slumber, under the
shade of which splendid visions break in upon them. Britannia
and her lion occupy a triumphal car, formed of the hull of a
British ship, drawn by an Irish bull and led by an English tar.
She drags to the Tower the Corsican tyrant and the Russian
bear both in chains, and followed by a countless host of meaner
captives, while a crowd of English soldiers and sailors escort and
welcome her. On the 11th of July of the same year, when

S S

Napoleon, by the basest treachery, had plunged himself into the fatal Spanish war, he was represented by Gillray as a luckless "matador," engaged in a Spanish bull-fight; he has already broken his sword in the animal's flank, but with only partial effect, and his infuriated opponent is tossing him with his horns and goring him to death.   The spectators in the gallery are the

BRITANNIA TRIUMPHANT.

different sovereigns of Europe, among whom King George of England appears to take most interest in the combat.   Another caricature on foreign affairs was published by Gillray on the 24th of September, under the title of "The Valley of the Shadow of Death."   Napoleon is represented, with the Russian bear at his command, entering the fearful vale, where his progress is arrested by the British lion, the Sicilian terrier, and the Portuguese wolf, who are urged on by Death mounted on a horse of the "royal Spanish breed;" others of the European states appear as monsters ready to beset him in his path; even the Russian bear shews an inclination to get loose from his chain.   As Gillray was disappearing from the scene, a number of clever caricaturists supplied his place—the Rowlandsons, Woodwards, Cruikshanks, and their companions—under whom the taste for these productions was not allowed to diminish. From their hands our foreign enemies were assailed with numerous caricatures during this and the following year.   As the power of Napoleon seemed to become more firmly established, these became more insulting; and no event produced a greater number than his divorce and his marriage with the arch-duchess, but they are nearly all coarse and indelicate.

Although in appearance sufficiently occupied in Europe, Napoleon's secret desires were still supposed to be turned towards the East, in the hopes of getting at our Indian possessions.   He was known to have envoys intriguing at Constantinople, and in Syria and Egypt.   One of the best of the anonymous caricatures of the year 1808 was published on the 9th of July, under the title of "Boney bothered; or, an unexpected Meeting." The hero thinks that he has made his way through the globe unperceived, and suddenly starts forth and places his foot upon Bengal, but in his dismay at finding John Bull there before him, he drops

AN UNEXPECTED MEETING.

his sword and his "plan of operations in the East Indies," and exclaims, "Begar, Monsieur Jean Bull again!—Vat, you know I vas come here?" His sturdy opponent, who has his pocket full of letters of "secret intelligence," replies, "To be sure I did!—for all your humbug deceptions, I smoked your intentions, and have brought my oak twig with me, so now you may go back again."

The ministry of 1807 had other and greater difficulties to contend against than the embarrassments of foreign affairs. It had succeeded a ministry that was remarkable for the discordancy of its materials, and it was on that account ridiculed even by its successors, yet they were so far from being distinguished by their unanimity, that they are said to have disagreed almost as soon as they were brought together. The success of the cry of "no popery," which had been spread abroad with extraordinary zeal, and the fear of our enemies abroad, had ensured them a majority in Parliament; but the opposition was still strong, both from the questions it had to work upon, and from the number of small parties who, included in the proscription of the "broad bottoms," were willing to join in embarrassing those who kept them from office, on whatever question the attack might be based. Out of doors the dissatisfaction was increasing, people became more clamorous and more riotous, and the radical party was gaining ground rapidly. We can only briefly trace the struggle of parties in a few of the more striking of the caricatures to which it gave rise. The satire of Gillray was now invariably directed against the opposition. On the 22nd of March, 1808, in a caricature entitled "Phaeton alarmed," he represented Canning as the political Phaeton, setting the world on fire by driving too near "the sun of Anti-Jacobinism." The heavens are filled with threatening constellations,—here Leo Britannicus disturbs him by his roar; there the Duke of Norfolk, under the figure of Silenus, threatens him with his bottles; Napoleon is riding on Ursa Major; and in other parts of the firmament are seen the vast Scorpion of broad-bottomry, the Bull of Ireland, with the porridge-pot of Catholic emancipation attached to its tail, and the other "horrors of the heavens." Lord Lauderdale, Whitbread, Lord Sidmouth, and Erskine, are making a futile attempt to quench the burning rays of the sun. The chariot of Phaeton is drawn by four horses, representing Lord Hawkesbury (now Lord Liverpool), Mr. Perceval, Lord Castlereagh, and Lord Eldon. Neptune looks aghast on the scene of devastation. Pitt, in the character of Apollo, is rising to the rescue; and Fox, as Pluto, is taking a peep from the shades. On the 2nd of May, under the title of "Broad-bottom drones storming the hive; wasps, hornets, and humble bees joining in the attack," Gillray represented the Treasury as the royal hive, with its honey-pots filled with gold; the industrious bees who are in office rush out boldly to defend their pleasant quarters from the crowd of assailants, whose difference of colour and method of opposition is represented by their division into drones, wasps, hornets, and humble-bees. In April, he had published a caricature entitled, "The Constitutional squad (i. e. opposition) advancing to attack," in which the most formidable weapon of the assailants is an immense brass cannon, entitled "Revolutionary argument." The Tories still kept up the old accusation against their opponents of republicanism and Jacobinism, and they now declared that they aimed at the introduction of popery. Mrs. Fitzherbert was again brought on the stage; and it was intimated that, through her influence, the Prince of Wales, who still supported the Whigs, had been induced to favour the claims of the Catholics for relief. The suspicion of a tendency towards Rome, thus raised, remained years afterwards attached to the prince in the belief of a considerable portion of English society. Several caricatures, which appeared about this time, represented the opposition as led by the prince, Mrs. Fitzherbert, and the *pope*. On the 25th of June, 1808, appeared a bold and clever print by Gillray, entitled, "Disciples catching the mantle ; the spirit of darkness overshadowing the priests of Baal." On one side the ministers are seen standing round "The altar of the constitution," which is planted on "The rock of Ages." Pitt, as a political Elijah, is carried up to the heavens of immortality in a fiery chariot, and they are receiving his mantle. The opposition, on the other side, are scattered in confusion and dismay on the "broad-bottom dunghill," where the spirit of Fox, in the shape of a fiend, is hiding them under his cloak ; Lord Grenville is getting into "Charley's old breeches."

During the following year (1809) a number of unfortunate occurrences, the mismanagement of the Spanish war, the revelations of Mrs. Clarke, and above all the expedition to Walcheren, strengthened the opposition and embarrassed the court. The ministers were irritated at the pertinacity of the attacks to which they were exposed within doors and without, and they retaliated by more frequent prosecutions for political writings or speeches. This method of lacing the danger only made the evil worse, and the cry for reform soon took a form too threatening to be disregarded. The Tory party continued to tell people that reform was only another name for republicanism, but people would no longer believe it, now that they were relieved from the fears of French propagandism. Gillray published on the 14th of June, 1809, a caricature entitled, "True Reform of Parliament, *i.e.* Patriots lighting a revolutionary bonfire in New Palace Yard," in which the radical portion of the opposition, led by Burdett and his supporter Cobbett, are represented as so many incendiaries burning the records of the rights and privileges of Englishmen, while the mob are busily destroying Westminster Hall and the Parliament House. The moderate "broad bottoms," alarmed at these proceedings, turn their backs on their old comrades. This and a series of prints of the life of Cobbett, whose fortune the ministers were now making, by the notice they took of him, were the last political works of Gillray; and it is not an unimportant sign of the times, that most of the numerous caricaturists who sprang up to supply his place took the popular side of every question. Burdett and Cobbett were now the two great heroes of political agitation ; and the former was raised into especial importance by

an unwise persecution for what may fairly be termed a piece
of political coxcombry.   The enforcing the standing orders
against the admission of strangers during the inquiry concerning
the Walcheren expedition had given great offence to the liberal
party out of doors.   A debating society, entitled the " British
forum," presided over by a man named John Gale Jones, publicly announced as a subject for discussion, the conduct of the
House of Commons in excluding the public from its debates,
and the house angrily and very indiscreetly voted it a breach of
privilege and committed Jones to Newgate.   Sir Francis
Burdett, thinking it a good opportunity for making a noise,
delivered a very intemperate speech in the house, and afterwards
published it with an equally intemperate letter to his constituents in Cobbett's Weekly Register.   This was a much more
gross attack upon the House of Commons than anything that
had been said in the debating society, and seemed intended only
to stir up the most violent passions of the populace.   The
House of Commons voted Sir Francis into the Tower, and
the Speaker issued a warrant for his apprehension ; but he shut
himself up in his house in Piccadilly, and barricaded it for a

JOHN BULL ENJOYING THE SUNSHINE.

siege, and then set the Speaker and the House of Commons at
defiance.   Inflammatory placards were displayed in every part
of the town, an immense mob collected, it was found necessary
to bring out the military, and for several days the metropolis
presented scenes of riot and violence such as had rarely
been seen.   Some persons were killed, and the jury, under the
strong influence of party feeling, brought a verdict of guilty
against the military.   Burdett, however, was at last secured in
the Tower, where he remained till the close of the session
of parliament, when the House of Commons found that it had

only given itself much trouble to make Sir Francis Burdett a greater man in the eyes of the populace than he was before. One of the political squibs of the day announced that "on Thursday, June the 21st (the period for the prorogation of parliament), or near that time, the sun of patriotism will emerge from the region of darkness in the east, and again cheer the inhabitants of the west with the warmth of his rays, the malignant planets will, for some time at least, lose their baleful influence under the cloud which ought to obscure them for ever." A caricature, apparently by Woodward, entitled, "Genial rays; or, John Bull enjoying the sunshine," represents this "sun of patriotism" (Burdett) shining in its full glory, and John Bull reclining on a bed of roses, is basking joyously in its rays.

It would be an amusing task to trace John Bull through his varieties of figure and expression in the caricatures during half a century. This singular personification of Old England seems to have been brought into existence by the admirable political satire of Pope's friend, Dr. Arbuthnot. For a long time Britannia and her lion were the only national representatives in the caricatures, and John Bull hardly took a pictorial form before the time of Gillray. It was in his hands that he became the plump, sleek, good-humoured individual we are at present in the habit of beholding. In the first attempts at representing him, he had none of these characteristics. Different artists of a later period, while they gave him more

JOHN BULL A LA ROWLANDSON.

or less individuality, according to their own style and sentiments, still kept the general character which he had received from Gillray's pencil. Thus Rowlandson pictured him with that coarse and vulgar air which characterizes all his drawings, and for which that artist might not unaptly be termed the Reubens of Caricature. The type of John Bull, according to Rowlandson's idea of him, here given, is taken from a caricature of that artist, entitled "The Head of the Family in Good-humour." An amusing caricature, entitled "John Bull come to the Bone," perhaps by Woodward, and published at the time of the peninsular war, when John was suffering heavily from the burthen of taxation, represents him as reduced to poverty which is accompanied by a great reduction of his personal appearance. He still, however, retains his stick of good " Wellington oak." In this condition he is accosted by the Frenchman, who exults in the belief that his poverty has almost made him harmless:—" By gar, Monsieur Jean Bull, you var much alter,—should not know

you var Jean ; I vas as big as you now !" John is indignant at the insult : —" Why, look you, Mounseer Parleyvou, though I have got thinner myself, I have a little sprig of oak in my hand that 's as strong as ever ; and if you give me any of your palaver, I 'll be d—d if you shan't feel the weight of it."

The Walcheren expedition had the almost immediate effect of breaking up, or at least of dividing, the cabinet. Some of the ministers, among whom was Canning, had been from the first opposed to the expedition, which seems to have been a plan of the King's, and Canning and Castlereagh are said to have been personally jealous of each other

JOHN BULL RATHER THIN.   form the first.   The disagreement between them at length broke out into an open quarrel, and the two ministers fought a duel on Putney Heath, on the 21st of September, 1809, in which Canning was wounded. This was immediately followed by their resignation, as well as by that of the Duke of Portland, and other members of the administration. Mr. Perceval and Lord Liverpool remained, who made an ineffectual attempt to form a coalition with Lord Grenville and the Whigs. At length the Marquess of Wellesley agreed to take Canning's place of secretary of state for foreign affairs, Mr. Perceval took the Duke of Portland's place of president of the council along with his own, Lord Liverpool took the place of Lord Castlereagh as secretary of war, and the Hon. R. Ryder was appointed home secretary.

The disastrous results of the Walcheren expedition contributed towards an event of much greater moment than this change in the ministry. The King, whose measure it was, and at whose particular desire the appointment of the inefficient Lord Chatham as commander was made, is said never to have ceased brooding over it ; and this, with other political annoyances, added to domestic affliction, brought on, at the end of October, 1810, a

new attack of insanity, from which he never recovered. The
Parliament met on the 1st of November under the same embarrassing circumstances as in 1788, and a bill of regency was now
brought in and passed, modelled upon that brought forward by
William Pitt on the former occasion, except that, as the hopes of
the King's recovery were now much more faint, the restrictions
were made only temporary. On the 8th of February, 1811, the
Prince of Wales was formally installed as Prince Regent. This
event produced on the whole less sensation than might have been

A FALLEN HERO.

expected, certainly much less than it would have done when Pitt
and Fox were alive and in their vigour.
Contrary to people's expectations, the
regent retained the ministers whom
he found in office, and he afterwards
separated himself from the Whigs.

The successes of the peninsular
war were now filling the country
with exultation, and caricatures
against the French and against Napoleon were becoming more numerous
than ever. Burlesques on their defeats spared not the fallen foe, and
even a dead Frenchman had something about him to provoke a laugh.
The specimen here given is taken
from a caricature published on the
10th of July, 1813, under the title
of "A Scene after the battle of Vit-
toria; or, more Trophies for Whitehall." The Russian campaign, and
the disastrous retreat, were still more
fertile in subjects for satire and
burlesque. Jack Frost and his mer-

SNUFFING OUT.

ciless allies, the Cossacks, are represented taking their revenge on the invader in every possible manner. In one by George Cruikshank, published on the 1st of May, 1814, the commander of the latter is represented very unceremoniously "snuffing out Boney."—Cruikshank was the great caricaturist of this period.

The English had now fought their way through Spain, and entered the French territory on the south, while the allies advanced on all sides upon Paris from the north, and they entered the French capital in triumph on the last day of March. Among the numerous caricatures celebrating these events, one, published on the 9th of April, represents "Blucher the brave extracting the groan of abdication from the Corsican Bloodhound." The abdication and the departure for Elba, were celebrated with a mass of pictorial exultation. The caricatures of this period appear under such titles as "Bloody Boney the carcass-butcher left off trade

and retiring to Scarecrow Island;" "The Rogue's March," exhibiting the imperial culprit drummed out of his kingdom, while the kings of Europe are shewing their joy by dancing round a political May-pole; "A grand Manœuvre; or, the Rogue's March to the Island of Elba," in which the tyrant is represented as undergoing still greater indignities. One of these is an excellent specimen of Rowlandson's vulgarity of style. It was published on the 25th of April, 1814, and is entitled "Nap dreading his doleful doom; or, his grand entry into the Isle of Elba." The exile has just landed, and receives no great encouragement in the coarse physiognomy and manners of the inhabitants, who rush from the hills in crowds to welcome him. With anything but joy in his countenance, he exclaims, "Ah! woe is me! seeing what I have and seeing what I see!" A beauty of the island offers him consolation in the shape of a pipe—"Come, cheer up, my little Nicky, I'll be your empress." It was soon found that the deposed emperor had not yet laid aside his ambition. Little less than a year had elapsed, when he left the narrow limits of his island, reappeared in France, and entered Paris in triumph. Europe again resounded with the din of war;—but the end of Buonaparte's career was now fast approaching; for, after a short and uneasy reign of a hundred days, the great and decisive battle of Waterloo consigned him to the prison of St. Helena.

A DOG CAUGHT.

We will only allude briefly to the subsequent history. The Prince-Regent had already rendered himself extremely unpopular at home by his selfish love of indulgence, by his extravagance, and, above all, by his treatment of his wife. When

A RECEPTION AT ELBA.

tne Emperor of Russia and the King of Prussia visited this country, after the restoration of the Bourbons in 1814, numerous caricatures, songs, and squibs contrasted the soberness and activity of the foreign monarchs with the voluptuous life of the English prince :—

> "There be princes three,
> Two of them come from a far countrie,
> And for valour and prudence their names shall be
>   Enrol'd in the annals of glorie :—
> The third is said at a bottle to be
> More than a match for his whole armie,
> And fonder of fur caps and *fripperie*
>   Than any recorded in storie.
> Those from the North great Warriors be,
> And warriors they have in their companie,
> Who have humbled the pride of an enemie,
>   Their rival in valour and glorie :—
> But he of the South must stare to see
> Himself in such goodly companie ;
> For to say what his usual consorts be,
>   Would make but a pitiful storie."

People's minds were now left at liberty to contemplate the condition of the country at home, and they began to be more and more alarmed at the fearful weight of taxation with which it was burthened. Increasing dissatisfaction and distress produced louder cries, and the financial sins of ministers were visited with caricatures and satires, as well as with the severer comments of radical journals and pamphlets. The tax on soap in 1816, is celebrated in a caricature, published on the 21st of June, representing a scene in a wash-house, where the merry figure of

A MINISTER IN THE SUDS.

the minister, Vansittart, issues from a tub of suds, to the great astonishment of the washerwoman :—" Here am I, Betty ; how are you off for soap ?"—" Lord, Mr. Vansittart! who could have thought of seeing you in the washing-tub."

The English government persisted in the old traditional no-movement policy of William Pitt, when all the excitement which supported him in that policy had long died away ; and they went on increasing the general discontent by a still more rigorous system of resistance to popular complaints and by an increase of political prosecutions. The period of the regency was one of national distress and national troubles. It abounded in caricatures, and in political satires and libels ; indeed, it is enough to say that it was the age of William Hone. It was the age of Burdett and Cobbett, of Hunt and radical reformers and riots. Hunt, the hero of Manchester and Smithfield, was now taking the place in mob popularity which had before been held by Burdett. A caricature, published in July, 1819, entitled, " The Smithfield Parliament ; *i. e.* universal suffrage—the new speaker addressing the members," represents Hunt with the head of an ass, mounted on a cart, and addressing an immense assemblage of cattle, sheep, pigs, donkeys, and other equally sapient animals, " I shall be ambitious, indeed, if I thought my bray would be heard by the immense and respectable multitude I have the honour to address." The animals applaud with a mingled murmur of voices, " hear ! hear !—bravo !"

A RADICAL.

The peace commences a new era in English history. Within the few years immediately preceding and following it, English society went through a remarkably rapid change ; a change, as far as we can see, of a decidedly favourable kind. In social condition and character, public sentiment and public morals, literature, and science, were all improved. As the violent internal agitation of the country during the regency increased the number of political caricatures and satirical writings, so the succession of fashions, varying in extravagance, which characterized the same period, produced a greater number of caricatures on dress and on fashionable manners, than had been seen at any previous period. During the first twelve or fifteen years of the present century, the general character of the costume appears not to have undergone any great change. The two figures here given, which represent the mode in 1810, may be compared with those of 1803, given on a former page. The principal difference consists in the change of the wide cravat, for a very large shirt collar, in the gentleman ; and, in the lady, the excess of covering to her person. Between cap, bonnet, collar, and frill, even their faces are nearly concealed ; and it is probably for this reason that they are termed in the original print "invisibles."

INVISIBLES.

A few years later the fashionable costume furnished an extraordinary contrast with that just represented. The waist was again shortened, as well as the frock and petticoat, and, instead of concealment, it seemed to be the aim of the ladies to exhibit to view as much of the body as possible. The

fops of 1819 and 1820 received the name of dandies, the ladies that of dandizettes. The accompanying cut is from a rather broadly caricatured print of a dandizette of the year 1819. It must be considered only as a type of the general character of the foppish costume of the period ; for in no time was there ever such a variety of forms in the dresses of both sexes as at the period alluded to. I give, with the same reservation, a figure of a dandy, from a caricature of the same year. The number of caricatures on the dandies and dandizettes, and on their fopperies and follies, during the years 1819, 1820, and 1821, was perfectly astonishing.

A DANDIZETTE.

A new mania also came to take the place of the old rage for balloons—it was the mania for hobby-horses. For two or three years it might literally be said that every man had his hobby. Hobby-horses figured in the parks, and were to be seen in every road, not only round London, but near most large towns in the country, whither this fashion was carried. Dandies, or not dandies, all were infected with this strange mania, which furnished matter for caricature upon caricature in great abundance. In these, the hobby mania was often applied politically, and all colours, and parties, and ranks,—whether prince or minister, Tory or Radical—were made to ride their hobbies in one way or other. The cut with which we close the volume is taken from a caricature published on the 8th of April, 1819, and represents the military episcopal Duke of York—he was commander-in-chief and prince-bishop of Osnaburg—riding his hobby for economy, on the road to Windsor. It was a period at which the outcry against the extravagance of the civil list—in which the duke partook largely—was particularly loud and violent. John Bull, who is somewhat astonished at the figure cut by the royal hobby-rider, and his boasts of economy, exclaimt, "Dang it, mister bishop, thee art saving, indeed ; thee used so ride in a coach and six, now I pay thee £10,000 a-year more,

A DANDY.

thee art riding a wooden horse for all the world like a gate-post!"

A ROYAL DUKE AND HIS HOBBY.

Trivialities like these close one of the most extraordinary periods of our history.

THE END.

LONDON:

SAVILL, EDWARDS AND CO., PRINTERS, CHANDOS STREET,
COVENT GARDEN.

Crown 8vo, Coloured Frontispiece and Illustrations, cloth gilt, 7s. 6d.

Advertising, A History of.

From the Earliest Times. Illustrated by Anecdotes, Curious Specimens, and Notes of Successful Advertisers. By HENRY SAMPSON.

"We have here a book to be thankful for. We recommend the present volume, which takes us through antiquity, the middle ages, and the present time, illustrating all in turn by advertisement—serious, comic, roguish, or downright rascally. The volume is full of entertainment from the first page to the last."—ATHENÆUM.

Crown 8vo, cloth extra, with 639 Illustrations, 7s. 6d.

Architectural Styles, A Handbook of.

Translated from the German of A. ROSENGARTEN by W. COLLETT-SANDARS. With 639 Illustrations.

Crown 8vo, with Portrait and Facsimile, cloth extra, 7s. 6d.

Artemus Ward's Works:

The Works of CHARLES FARRER BROWNE, better known as ARTEMUS WARD. With Portrait, Facsimile of Handwriting, &c.

Second Edition, demy 8vo, cloth extra, with Map and Illustrations, 18s.

Baker's Clouds in the East:

Travels and Adventures on the Perso-Turcoman Frontier. By VALENTINE BAKER. Second Edition, revised and corrected.

Crown 8vo, cloth extra, 6s.

Balzac.—The Comédie Humaine and its

Author. With Translations from Balzac. By H. H. WALKER.

Crown 8vo, cloth extra, 7s. 6d.

Bankers, A Handbook of London;

With some Account of their Predecessors, the Early Goldsmiths; together with Lists of Bankers from 1677 to 1876. By F. G. HILTON PRICE.

Bardsley (Rev. C. W.), Works by:

English Surnames: Their Sources and Significations. By CHARLES WAREING BARDSLEY, M.A. Second Edition, revised throughout and considerably Enlarged. Crown 8vo, cloth extra, 7s. 6d.

"Mr. Bardsley has faithfully consulted the original mediæval documents and works from which the origin and development of surnames can alone be satisfactorily traced. He has furnished a valuable contribution to the literature of surnames, and we hope to hear more of him in this field."—TIMES.

Curiosities of Puritan Nomenclature. By CHARLES W. BARDSLEY. Crown 8vo, cloth extra, 7s. 6d.

"The book is full of interest; in fact, it is just the thorough and scholarly work we should expect from the author of 'English Surnames.'"—GRAPHIC.

Small 4to, green and gold, 6s. 6d.; gilt edges, 7s. 6d.

Bechstein's As Pretty as Seven,

And other German Stories. Collected by LUDWIG BECHSTEIN. Additional Tales by Brothers GRIMM, and 100 Illustrations by RICHTER.

ART HANDBOOKS—*continued.*

Pictures at South Kensington. (The Raphael Cartoons, Sheep-shanks Collection, &c.) With 70 Illustrations. 1*s.*

The English Pictures at the National Gallery. With 114 Illustrations. 1*s.*

The Old Masters at the National Gallery. 128 Illusts. 1*s. 6d.*

Academy Notes, 1875-79. Complete in One Volume, with nearly 600 Illustrations in Facsimile. Demy 8vo, cloth limp, 6*s.*

A Complete Illustrated Catalogue to the National Gallery. With Notes by HENRY BLACKBURN, and 242 Illustrations. Demy 8vo, cloth limp, 3*s.*

UNIFORM WITH "ACADEMY NOTES."

Royal Scottish Academy Notes, 1878. 117 Illustrations. 1*s.*
Royal Scottish Academy Notes, 1879. 125 Illustrations. 1*s.*
Royal Scottish Academy Notes, 1880. 114 Illustrations. 1*s.*
Glasgow Institute of Fine Arts Notes, 1878. 95 Illustrations. 1*s.*
Glasgow Institute of Fine Arts Notes, 1879. 100 Illusts. 1*s.*
Glasgow Institute of Fine Arts Notes, 1880. 120 Illusts. 1*s.*
Walker Art Gallery Notes, Liverpool, 1878. 112 Illusts. 1*s.*
Walker Art Gallery Notes, Liverpool, 1879. 100 Illusts. 1*s.*
Royal Manchester Institution Notes, 1878. 88 Illustrations. 1*s.*
Society of Artists Notes, Birmingham, 1878. 95 Illusts. 1*s.*
Children of the Great City. By F. W. LAWSON. With Fac-simile Sketches by the Artist. Demy 8vo, 1*s.*

Crown 8vo, cloth extra, 6s.

Beccaria on Crimes and Punishments.

A New Translation, with an Essay on the Theory of Punishments. By J. A. FARRER.

Folio, half-bound boards, India Proofs, 21s.

Blake (William):

Etchings from his Works. By W. B. SCOTT. With descriptive Text.

"*The best side of Blake's work is given here, and makes a really attractive volume, which all can enjoy. . . . The etching is of the best kind, more refined and delicate than the original work.*"—SATURDAY REVIEW.

Crown 8vo, cloth extra, gilt, with Illustrations, 7s. 6d.

Boccaccio's Decameron;

or, Ten Days' Entertainment. Translated into English, with an Intro-duction by THOMAS WRIGHT, Esq., M.A., F.S.A. With Portrait, and STOTHARD'S beautiful Copperplates.

Crown 8vo, cloth extra, gilt, 7s. 6d.

Brand's Observations on Popular Antiquities,

chiefly Illustrating the Origin of our Vulgar Customs, Ceremonies, and Superstitions. With the Additions of Sir HENRY ELLIS. An entirely New and Revised Edition, with fine full-page Illustrations.

Bowers' (Georgina) Hunting Sketches:

Canters in Crampshire. By G. BOWERS. I. Gallops from Gorseborough. II. Scrambles with Scratch Packs. III. Studies with Stag Hounds. Oblong 4to, half-bound boards, 21s.

Leaves from a Hunting Journal. By G. BOWERS Coloured in facsimile of the originals. Oblong 4to, half-bound, 21s.[*Nearly Ready.*

Bret Harte, Works by:

The Complete Collected Works of Bret Harte, arranged and revised by the Author. Vol. I. POEMS AND DRAMA, including a fine Steel-plate Portrait, and an Introduction by the Author; and Vol II. containing EARLY SKETCHES, SPANISH AND AMERICAN LEGENDS; TALES OF THE ARGONAUTS, &c., are now ready. The series will consist of Five handsome Library Volumes, to be issued at short intervals. Crown 8vo cloth extra, 6s. per volume.

The Select Works of Bret Harte, in Prose and Poetry. With Introductory Essay by J. M. BELLEW, Portrait of the Author, and 50 Illustrations. Crown 8vo, cloth extra, 7s. 6d.

An Heiress of Red Dog, and other Stories. By BRET HARTE. Post 8vo, illustrated boards, 2s.; cloth limp, 2s. 6d.

"*Few modern English-writing humourists have achieved the popularity of Mr. Bret Harte. He has passed, so to speak, beyond book-fame into talk-fame. People who may never perhaps have held one of his little volumes in their hands, are perfectly familiar with some at least of their contents . . . . Pictures of Californian camp-life, unapproached in their quaint picturesqueness and deep human interest.*"—DAILY NEWS.

The Twins of Table Mountain. By BRET HARTE. Fcap. 8vo, picture cover, 1s.; crown 8vo, cloth extra, 3s. 6d.

The Luck of Roaring Camp, and other Sketches. By BRET HARTE. Post 8vo, illustrated boards, 2s.

Jeff Briggs's Love Story. By BRET HARTE. Fcap. 8vo, picture cover, 1s.; cloth extra, 2s. 6d.

Small crown 8vo, cloth extra, gilt, with full-page Portraits, 4s. 6d.

Brewster's (Sir David) Martyrs of Science.

Small crown 8vo, cloth extra, gilt, with Astronomical Plates, 4s. 6d.

Brewster's (Sir D.) More Worlds than One,

the Creed of the Philosopher and the Hope of the Christian.

Demy 8vo, profusely Illustrated in Colours, 30s.

British Flora Medica:

A History of the Medicinal Plants of Great Britain. Illustrated by a Figure of each Plant, COLOURED BY HAND. By BENJAMIN H. BARTON, F.L.S., and THOMAS CASTLE, M.D., F.R.S. A New Edition, revised and partly re-written by JOHN R. JACKSON, A.L.S., Curator of the Museums of Economic Botany, Royal Gardens, Kew.

THE STOTHARD BUNYAN.—Crown 8vo, cloth extra, gilt, 7s. 6d.

Bunyan's Pilgrim's Progress.

Edited by Rev. T. SCOTT. With 17 beautiful Steel Plates by STOTHARD, engraved by GOODALL; and numerous Woodcuts.

Crown 8vo, cloth extra, gilt, with Illustrations, 7s. 6d.

Byron's Letters and Journals.

With Notices of his Life. By THOMAS MOORE. A Reprint of the Original Edition newly revised, with Twelve full-page Plates.

Demy 8vo, cloth extra, 14s.

Campbell's (Sir G.) White and Black:

The Outcome of a Visit to the United States. By Sir GEORGE CAMPBELL, M.P.

"*Few persons are likely to take it up without finishing it.*"—NONCONFORMIST.

Crown 8vo, cloth extra, 3s. 6d.

Carlyle (Thomas) On the Choice of Books.
With Portrait and Memoir.

Small 4to, cloth gilt, with Coloured Illustrations, 10s. 6d.

Chaucer for Children:
A Golden Key. By Mrs. H. R. HAWEIS. With Eight Coloured
Pictures and numerous Woodcuts by the Author.

"*It must not only take a high place among the Christmas and New Year books
of this season, but is also of permanent value as an introduction to the study of
Chaucer, whose works, in selections of great kind or other, are now text-books in
every school that aspires to give sound instruction in English.*"—ACADEMY.

Crown 8vo, cloth limp, with Map and Illustrations, 2s. 6d.

Cleopatra's Needle:
Its Acquisition and Removal to England Described. By Sir J. E.
ALEXANDER.

Crown 8vo, cloth extra, gilt, 7s. 6d.

Colman's Humorous Works:
"Broad Grins," "My Nightgown and Slippers," and other Humorous
Works, Prose and Poetical, of GEORGE COLMAN. With Life by G.
B. BUCKSTONE, and Frontispiece by HOGARTH.

Conway (Moncure D.), Works by:
Demonology and Devil-Lore. By MONCURE D. CONWAY,
M.A. Two Vols., royal 8vo, with 65 Illustrations, 28s.

"*A valuable contribution to mythological literature. . . . There is much
good writing among these disquisitions, a vast fund of humanity, undeniable
earnestness, and a delicate sense of humour, all set forth in pure English.*"
—CONTEMPORARY REVIEW.

A Necklace of Stories. By MONCURE D. CONWAY, M.A.
Illustrated by W. J. HENNESSY. Square 8vo, cloth extra, 6s.

"*This delightful 'Necklace of Stories' is inspired with lovely and lofty
sentiments. . . . It is a beautiful conception, and is designed to teach a
great moral lesson.*"—ILLUSTRATED LONDON NEWS.

Demy 8vo, cloth extra, with Coloured Illustrations and Maps, 24s.

Cope's History of the Rifle Brigade
(The Prince Consort's Own), formerly the 95th. By Sir WILLIAM
H. COPE, formerly Lieutenant, Rifle Brigade.

Crown 8vo, cloth extra, gilt, with 13 Portraits, 7s. 6d.

Creasy's Memoirs of Eminent Etonians;
with Notices of the Early History of Eton College. By Sir EDWARD
CREASY, Author of "The Fifteen Decisive Battles of the World."

"*A new edition of 'Creasy's Etonians' will be welcome. The book was a
favourite a quarter of a century ago, and it has maintained its reputation. The
value of this new edition is enhanced by the fact that Sir Edward Creasy has
added to it several memoirs of Etonians who have died since the first edition was
prepared. The work is eminently interesting.*"—SCOTSMAN.

Crown 8vo, cloth extra, with Coloured Frontispiece, 7s. 6d.

Credulities, Past and Present.
By WILLIAM JONES, F.S.A., Author of "Finger-Ring Lore," &c.
[*In the press.*]

Crown 8vo, cloth gilt, Two very thick Volumes, 7s. 6d. each.

Cruikshank's Comic Almanack.

Complete in TWO SERIES: The FIRST from 1835 to 1843; the SECOND from 1844 to 1853. A Gathering of the BEST HUMOUR of THACKERAY, HOOD, MAYHEW, ALBERT SMITH, A'BECKETT, ROBERT BROUGH, &c. With 2,000 Woodcuts and Steel Engravings by CRUIKSHANK, HINE, LANDELLS, &c.

Parts I. to XIV. now ready, 21s. each.

Cussans' History of Hertfordshire.

By JOHN E. CUSSANS. Illustrated with full-page Plates on Copper and Stone, and a profusion of small Woodcuts.

"*Mr. Cussans has, from sources not accessible to Clutterbuck, made most valuable additions to the manorial history of the county from the earliest period downwards, cleared up many doubtful points, and given original details concerning various subjects untouched or imperfectly treated by that writer. The pedigrees seem to have been constructed with great care, and are a valuable addition to the genealogical history of the county. Mr. Cussans appears to have done his work conscientiously, and to have spared neither time, labour, nor expense to render his volumes worthy of ranking in the highest class of County Histories.*" —ACADEMY.

Two Volumes, demy 4to, handsomely bound in half-morocco, gilt, profusely Illustrated with Coloured and Plain Plates and Woodcuts, price £7 7s.

Cyclopædia of Costume;

or, A Dictionary of Dress—Regal, Ecclesiastical, Civil, and Military— from the Earliest Period in England to the reign of George the Third. Including Notices of Contemporaneous Fashions on the Continent, and a General History of the Costumes of the Principal Countries of Europe. By J. R. PLANCHÉ, Somerset Herald.

The Volumes may also be had *separately* (each Complete in itself) at £3 13s. 6d. each:

VOL. I. THE DICTIONARY.

Vol. II. A GENERAL HISTORY OF COSTUME IN EUROPE.

Also in 25 Parts, at 5s. each. Cases for binding, 5s. each.

"*A comprehensive and highly valuable book of reference. . . . We have rarely failed to find in this book an account of an article of dress, while in most of the entries curious and instructive details are given. . . . Mr. Planché's enormous labour of love, the production of a text which, whether in its dictionary form or in that of the 'General History,' is within its intended scope immeasurably the best and richest work on Costume in English. . . . This book is not only one of the most readable works of the kind, but intrinsically attractive and amusing.*"—ATHENÆUM.

"*A most readable and interesting work—and it can scarcely be consulted in vain, whether the reader is in search for information as to military, court, ecclesiastical, legal, or professional costume. . . . All the chromo-lithographs, and most of the woodcut illustrations—the latter amounting to several thousands —are very elaborately executed; and the work forms a livre de luxe which renders it equally suited to the library and the ladies' drawing-room.*"—TIMES.

"*One of the most perfect works ever published upon the subject. The illustrations are numerous and excellent, and would, even without the letterpress, render the work an invaluable book of reference for information as to costumes for fancy balls and character quadrilles. . . . Beautifully printed and superbly illustrated.*"—STANDARD.

Second Edition, revised and enlarged, demy 8vo, cloth extra,
with Illustrations, 24s.

Dodge's (Colonel) The Hunting Grounds of

the Great West: A Description of the Plains, Game, and Indians of
the Great North American Desert. By RICHARD IRVING DODGE,
Lieutenant-Colonel of the United States Army. With an Introduction
by WILLIAM BLACKMORE; Map, and numerous Illustrations drawn
by ERNEST GRISET.

Demy 8vo, cloth extra, 12s. 6d.

Doran's Memories of our Great Towns.

With Anecdotic Gleanings concerning their Worthies and their
Oddities. By Dr. JOHN DORAN, F.S.A.

"*A greater genius for writing of the anecdotic kind few men have had. As
to giving any idea of the contents of the book, it is quite impossible. Those who
know how Dr. Doran used to write—it is sad to have to use the past tense of one of
the most cheerful of men—will understand what we mean; and those who do not
must take it on trust from us that this is a remarkably entertaining volume.*"—
SPECTATOR.

Second Edition, demy 8vo, cloth gilt, with Illustrations, 18s.

Dunraven's The Great Divide:

A Narrative of Travels in the Upper Yellowstone in the Summer of
1874. By the EARL of DUNRAVEN. With Maps and numerous
striking full-page Illustrations by VALENTINE W. BROMLEY.

"*There has not for a long time appeared a better book of travel than Lord
Dunraven's 'The Great Divide.' . . . The book is full of clever observation,
and both narrative and illustrations are thoroughly good.*"—ATHENÆUM.

Demy 8vo, cloth, 16s.

Dutt's India, Past and Present;

with Minor Essays on Cognate Subjects. By SHOSHEE CHUNDER
DUTT, Rái Báhádoor.

Crown 8vo, cloth extra, gilt, with Illustrations, 6s.

Emanuel On Diamonds and Precious

Stones; their History, Value, and Properties; with Simple Tests for
ascertaining their Reality. By HARRY EMANUEL, F.R.G.S. With
numerous Illustrations, Tinted and Plain.

Demy 4to, cloth extra, with Illustrations, 36s.

Emanuel and Grego.—A History of the Gold-

smith's and Jeweller's Art in all Ages and in all Countries. By E.
EMANUEL and JOSEPH GREGO. With numerous fine Engravings.
(In preparation.)

Crown 8vo, cloth extra, with Illustrations, 7s. 6d.

Englishman's House, The:

A Practical Guide to all Interested in Selecting or Building a House,
with full Estimates of Cost, Quantities, &c. By C. J. RICHARDSON.
Third Edition. With nearly 600 Illustrations.

Crown 8vo, cloth boards, 6s. per Volume.

Early English Poets.

Edited, with Introductions and Annotations, by Rev. A. B. GROSART.

"Mr. Grosart has spent the most laborious and the most enthusiastic care on the perfect restoration and preservation of the text; and it is very unlikely that any other edition of the poet can ever be called for. . . . From Mr. Grosart we always expect and always receive the final results of most patient and competent scholarship."—EXAMINER.

1. **Fletcher's (Giles, B.D.) Complete Poems:** Christ's Victorie in Heaven, Christ's Victorie on Earth, Christ's Triumph over Death, and Minor Poems. With Memorial-Introduction and Notes. One Vol.

2. **Davies' (Sir John) Complete Poetical Works,** including Psalms I. to L. in Verse, and other hitherto Unpublished MSS., for the first time Collected and Edited. Memorial-Introduction and Notes. Two Vols.

3. **Herrick's (Robert) Hesperides,** Noble Numbers, and Complete Collected Poems. With Memorial-Introduction and Notes, Steel Portrait, Index of First Lines, and Glossarial Index, &c. Three Vols.

4. **Sidney's (Sir Philip) Complete Poetical Works,** including all those in "Arcadia." With Portrait, Memorial-Introduction, Essay on the Poetry of Sidney, and Notes. Three Vols.

Folio, cloth extra, £1 11s. 6d.

Examples of Contemporary Art.

Etchings from Representative Works by living English and Foreign Artists. Edited, with Critical Notes, by J. COMYNS CARR.

"It would not be easy to meet with a more sumptuous, and at the same time a more tasteful and instructive drawing-room book."—NONCONFORMIST.

Crown 8vo, cloth extra, with Illustrations, 6s.

Fairholt's Tobacco :

Its History and Associations; with an Account of the Plant and its Manufacture, and its Modes of Use in all Ages and Countries. By F. W. FAIRHOLT, F.S.A. With Coloured Frontispiece and upwards of 100 Illustrations by the Author.

"A very pleasant and instructive history of tobacco and its associations, which we cordially recommend alike to the votaries and to the enemies of the much-maligned but certainly not neglected weed. . . . Full of interest and information."—DAILY NEWS.

Crown 8vo, cloth extra, with Illustrations, 4s. 6d.

Faraday's Chemical History of a Candle.

Lectures delivered to a Juvenile Audience. A New Edition. Edited by W. CROOKES, F.C.S. With numerous Illustrations.

Crown 8vo, cloth extra, with Illustrations. 4s. 6d.

Faraday's Various Forces of Nature.

New Edition. Edited by W. CROOKES, F.C.S. Numerous Illustrations.

Crown 8vo, cloth extra, with Illustrations, 7s. 6d.

Finger-Ring Lore :

Historical, Legendary, and Anecdotal. By WM. JONES, F.S.A. With Hundreds of Illustrations of Curious Rings of all Ages and Countries.

"One of those gossiping books which are as full of amusement as of instruction."—ATHENÆUM.

One Shilling Monthly, mostly Illustrated.

Gentleman's Magazine, The,

For January contained the First Chapters of a New Novel entitled QUEEN COPHETUA, by R. E. FRANCILLON: to be continued throughout the year.

. *Now ready, the Volume for* JANUARY *to* JUNE, *1880, cloth extra, price 8s. 6d.; and Cases for binding, price 2s. each.*

The Gentleman's Annual, containing one or more works of high-class fiction, is published every Christmas as an Extra Number of the Magazine, price 1s.

THE RUSKIN GRIMM.—Square 8vo, cloth extra, 6s. 6d.; gilt edges, 7s. 6d.

German Popular Stories.

Collected by the Brothers GRIMM, and Translated by EDGAR TAYLOR. Edited with an Introduction by JOHN RUSKIN. With 22 Illustrations after the inimitable designs of GEORGE CRUIKSHANK. Both Series Complete.

"*The Illustrations of this volume . . . are of quite sterling and admirable art, of a class precisely parallel in elevation to the character of the tales which they illustrate; and the original etchings, as I have before said in the Appendix to my 'Elements of Drawing,' were unrivalled in masterfulness of touch since Rembrandt (in some qualities of delineation, unrivalled even by him). . . . To make somewhat enlarged copies of them, looking at them through a magnifying glass, and never putting two lines where Cruikshank has put only one, would be an exercise in decision and accurate drawing which would leave afterwards little to be learned in schools.*"—*Extract from Introduction by* JOHN RUSKIN.

Post 8vo, cloth limp, 2s. 6d.

Glenny's A Year's Work in Garden and

Greenhouse: Practical Advice to Amateur Gardeners as to the Management of the Flower, Fruit, and Frame Garden. By GEORGE GLENNY.

"*A great deal of valuable information, conveyed in very simple language. The amateur need not wish for a better guide.*"—LEEDS MERCURY.

New and Cheaper Edition, demy 8vo, cloth extra, with Illustrations, 7s. 6d.

Greeks and Romans, The Life of the,

Described from Antique Monuments. By ERNST GUHL and W. KONER. Translated from the Third German Edition, and Edited by Dr. F. HUEFFER. With 545 Illustrations.

Crown 8vo, cloth extra, gilt, with Illustrations, 7s. 6d.

Greenwood's Low-Life Deeps:

An Account of the Strange Fish to be found there. By JAMES GREENWOOD. With Illustrations in tint by ALFRED CONCANEN.

Crown 8vo, cloth extra, gilt, with Illustrations, 7s. 6d.

Greenwood's Wilds of London:

Descriptive Sketches, from Personal Observations and Experience, of Remarkable Scenes, People, and Places in London. By JAMES GREENWOOD. With 12 Tinted Illustrations by ALFRED CONCANEN.

Square 16mo (Tauchnits size), cloth extra, 2s. per volume.

Golden Library, The:

Ballad History of England. By W. C. Bennett.

Bayard Taylor's Diversions of the Echo Club.

Byron's Don Juan.

Emerson's Letters and Social Aims.

Godwin's (William) Lives of the Necromancers.

Holmes's Autocrat of the Breakfast Table. With an Introduction by G. A. Sala.

Holmes's Professor at the Breakfast Table.

Hood's Whims and Oddities. Complete. With all the original Illustrations.

Irving's (Washington) Tales of a Traveller.

Irving's (Washington) Tales of the Alhambra.

Jesse's (Edward) Scenes and Occupations of Country Life.

Lamb's Essays of Elia. Both Series Complete in One Vol.

Leigh Hunt's Essays: A Tale for a Chimney Corner, and other Pieces. With Portrait, and Introduction by Edmund Ollier.

Mallory's (Sir Thomas) Mort d'Arthur: The Stories of King Arthur and of the Knights of the Round Table. Edited by B. Montgomerie Ranking.

Pascal's Provincial Letters. A New Translation, with Historical Introduction and Notes, by T. M'Crie, D.D.

Pope's Poetical Works. Complete.

Rochefoucauld's Maxims and Moral Reflections. With Notes, and an Introductory Essay by Sainte-Beuve.

St. Pierre's Paul and Virginia, and The Indian Cottage. Edited, with Life, by the Rev. E. Clarke.

Shelley's Early Poems, and Queen Mab, with Essay by Leigh Hunt.

Shelley's Later Poems: Laon and Cythna, &c.

Shelley's Posthumous Poems, the Shelley Papers, &c.

Shelley's Prose Works, including A Refutation of Deism, Zastrozzi, St. Irvyne, &c.

White's Natural History of Selborne. Edited, with additions, by Thomas Brown, F.L.S.

Crown 8vo, cloth gilt and gilt edges, 7s. 6d.

Golden Treasury of Thought, The:

An ENCYCLOPÆDIA OF QUOTATIONS from Writers of all Times and Countries. Selected and Edited by Theodore Taylor.

Large 4to, with 24 facsimile Plates, price ONE GUINEA.

Grosvenor Gallery Illustrated Catalogue.

Winter Exhibition (1877-78) of Drawings by the Old Masters and Water-Colour Drawings by Deceased Artists of the British School. With a Critical Introduction by J. Comyns Carr.

Crown 8vo, cloth extra, gilt, with Illustrations, 4s. 6d.

Guyot's Earth and Man;

or, Physical Geography in its Relation to the History of Mankind. With Additions by Professors Agassiz, Pierce, and Gray; 12 Maps and Engravings on Steel, some Coloured, and copious Index.

Hakel(Dr. Thomas Gordon), Poems by :

Maiden Ecstasy. Small 4to, cloth extra, 8s.

New Symbols. Crown 8vo, cloth extra, 6s.

Legends of the Morrow. Crown 8vo, cloth extra, 6s.

Medium 8vo, cloth extra, gilt, with Illustrations, 7s. 6d.

Hall's (Mrs. S. C.) Sketches of Irish Character.

With numerous Illustrations on Steel and Wood by MACLISE, GIL-BERT, HARVEY, and G. CRUIKSHANK.

"*The Irish Sketches of this lady resemble Miss Mitford's beautiful English sketches in 'Our Village,' but they are far more vigorous and picturesque and bright.*"—BLACKWOOD'S MAGAZINE.

Post 8vo, cloth extra, 4s. 6d.; a few large-paper copies, half-Roxb., 10s. 6d.

Handwriting, The Philosophy of.

By Don FELIX DE SALAMANCA. With 134 Facsimiles of Signatures.

Haweis (Mrs.), Works by :

The Art of Dress. By Mrs. H. R. HAWEIS, Author of "The Art of Beauty," &c. Illustrated by the Author. Small 8vo, illustrated cover, 1s.; cloth limp, 1s. 6d.

"*A well-considered attempt to apply canons of good taste to the costumes of ladies of our time. . . . Mrs. Haweis writes frankly and to the point, she does not mince matters, but boldly remonstrates with her own sex on the follies they indulge in. . . . We may recommend the book to the ladies whom it concerns.*"—ATHENÆUM.

The Art of Beauty. By Mrs. H. R. HAWEIS, Author of "Chaucer for Children." Square 8vo, cloth extra, gilt, gilt edges, with Coloured Frontispiece and nearly 100 Illustrations, 10s. 6d.

Vols. I. and II., demy 8vo, 12s. each.

History of Our Own Times, from the Accession

of Queen Victoria to the Berlin Congress. By JUSTIN MCCARTHY.

"*Criticism is disarmed before a composition which provokes little but approval. This is a really good book on a really interesting subject, and words piled on words could say no more for it. . . . Such is the effect of its general justice, its breadth of view, and its sparkling buoyancy, that very few of its readers will close these volumes without looking forward with interest to the two that are to follow.*"—SATURDAY REVIEW.

, Vols. III. and IV., completing the work, will be ready immediately.

Crown 8vo, cloth extra, 5s.

Hobhouse's The Dead Hand :

Addresses on the subject of Endowments and Settlements of Property. By Sir ARTHUR HOBHOUSE. Q.C., K.C.S.I.

Crown 8vo, cloth limp, with Illustrations, 2s. 6d.

Holmes's The Science of Voice Production

and Voice Preservation : A Popular Manual for the Use of Speakers and Singers. By GORDON HOLMES, L.R.C.P.E.

Crown 8vo, cloth extra, 4s. 6d.

Hollingshead's (John) Plain English.

"*I anticipate immense entertainment from the perusal of Mr. Hollingshead's 'Plain English,' which I imagined to be a philological work, but which I find to be a series of essays, in the Hollingsheadian or Sledge-Hammer style, on those matters theatrical with which he is so eminently conversant.*"—G. A. S. in the ILLUSTRATED LONDON NEWS.

Crown 8vo, cloth extra, gilt, 7s. 6d.

Hood's (Thomas) Choice Works,

In Prose and Verse. Including the CREAM OF THE COMIC ANNUALS. With Life of the Author, Portrait, and Two Hundred Illustrations.

Square crown 8vo, cloth extra, gilt edges, 6s.

Hood's (Tom) From Nowhere to the North

Pole : A Noah's Arkæological Narrative. With 25 Illustrations by W. BRUNTON and E. C. BARNES.

"*The amusing letterpress is profusely interspersed with the jingling rhymes which children love and learn so easily. Messrs. Brunton and Barnes do full justice to the writer's meaning, and a pleasanter result of the harmonious co-operation of author and artist could not be desired.*"—TIMES.

Crown 8vo, cloth extra, gilt, 7s. 6d.

Hook's (Theodore) Choice Humorous Works,

including his Ludicrous Adventures, Bons-mots, Puns, and Hoaxes. With a new Life of the Author, Portraits, Facsimiles, and Illustrations,

Crown 8vo, cloth extra, 7s.

Horne's Orion :

An Epic Poem in Three Books. By RICHARD HENGIST HORNE. With a brief Commentary by the Author. With Photographic Portrait from a Medallion by SUMMERS. Tenth Edition.

Crown 8vo, cloth extra, 7s. 6d.

Howell's Conflicts of Capital and Labour

Historically and Economically considered. Being a History and Review of the Trade Unions of Great Britain, showing their Origin, Progress, Constitution, and Objects, in their Political, Social, Economical, and Industrial Aspects. By GEORGE HOWELL.

"*This book is an attempt, and on the whole a successful attempt, to place the work of trade unions in the past, and their objects in the future, fairly before the public from the working man's point of view.*"—PALL MALL GAZETTE.

Demy 8vo, cloth extra, 12s. 6d.

Hueffer's The Troubadours :

A History of Provençal Life and Literature in the Middle Ages. By FRANCIS HUEFFER.

Two Vols. 8vo, with 52 Illustrations and Maps, cloth extra, gilt, 14s.

Josephus, The Complete Works of.

Translated by WHISTON. Containing both " The Antiquities of the Jews " and " The Wars of the Jews."

A NEW EDITION, Revised and partly Re-written, with several New Chapters and Illustrations, crown 8vo, cloth extra, *7s. 6d.*

Jennings' The Rosicrucians:

Their Rites and Mysteries. With Chapters on the Ancient Fire and Serpent Worshippers. By HARGRAVE JENNINGS. With Five full-page Plates and upwards of 300 Illustrations.

"*One of those volumes which may be taken up and dipped into at random for half-an-hour's reading, or, on the other hand, appealed to by the student as a source of valuable information on a system which has not only exercised for hundreds of years an extraordinary influence on the mental development of so shrewd a people as the Jews, but has captivated the minds of some of the greatest thinkers of Christendom in the sixteenth and seventeenth centuries.*"—LEEDS MERCURY.

Small 8vo, cloth, full gilt, gilt edges, with Illustrations, *6s.*

Kavanaghs' Pearl Fountain,

And other Fairy Stories. By BRIDGET and JULIA KAVANAGH. With Thirty Illustrations by J. MOYR SMITH.

"*Genuine new fairy stories of the old type, some of them as delightful as the best of Grimm's 'German Popular Stories.' . . . . For the most part the stories are downright, thorough-going fairy stories of the most admirable kind. . . . Mr. Moyr Smith's illustrations, too, are admirable.*"—SPECTATOR.

Crown 8vo, Illustrated boards, with numerous Plates, *2s. 6d.*

Lace (Old Point), and How to Copy and

Imitate it. By DAISY WATERHOUSE HAWKINS. With 17 Illustrations by the Author.

Crown 8vo, cloth extra, with numerous Illustrations, *10s. 6d.*

Lamb (Mary and Charles):

Their Poems, Letters, and Remains. With Reminiscences and Notes by W. CARRW HAZLITT. With HANCOCK'S Portrait of the Essayist. Facsimiles of the Title-pages of the rare First Editions of Lamb's and Coleridge's Works, and numerous Illustrations.

"*Very many passages will delight those fond of literary trifles; hardly any portion will fail in interest for lovers of Charles Lamb and his sister.*"—STANDARD.

Small 8vo, cloth extra, *5s.*

Lamb's Poetry for Children, and Prince

Dorus. Carefully Reprinted from unique copies.

"*The genial and delightful little book, over the recovery of which all the hearts of his lovers are yet warm with rejoicing.*"—A. C. SWINBURNE.

Crown 8vo, cloth extra, gilt, with Portraits, *7s. 6d.*

Lamb's Complete Works,

In Prose and Verse, reprinted from the Original Editions, with many Pieces hitherto unpublished. Edited, with Notes and Introduction, by R. H. SHEPHERD. With Two Portraits and Facsimile of a Page of the "Essay on Roast Pig."

"*A complete edition of Lamb's writings, in prose and verse, has long been wanted, and is now supplied. The editor appears to have taken great pains to bring together Lamb's scattered contributions, and his collection contains a number of pieces which are now reproduced for the first time since their original appearance in various old periodicals.*"—SATURDAY REVIEW.

Demy 8vo, cloth extra, with Maps and Illustrations, 18s.

Lamont's Yachting in the Arctic Seas;

or, Notes of Five Voyages of Sport and Discovery in the Neighbourhood of Spitzbergen and Novaya Zemlya. By JAMES LAMONT, F.R.G.S. With numerous full-page Illustrations by Dr. LIVESAY.

"*After reading through numberless volumes of icy fiction, concocted narratives, and spurious biography of Arctic voyagers, it is pleasant to meet with a real and genuine volume. . . . He shows much tact in recounting his adventures, and they are so interspersed with anecdotes and information as to make them anything but wearisome. . . . The book, as a whole, is the most important addition made to our Arctic literature for a long time.*"—ATHENÆUM.

Crown 8vo, cloth, full gilt, 7s. 6d.

Latter-Day Lyrics:

Poems of Sentiment and Reflection by Living Writers ; selected and arranged, with Notes, by W. DAVENPORT ADAMS. With a Note on some Foreign Forms of Verse, by AUSTIN DOBSON.

Crown 8vo, cloth, full gilt, 6s.

Leigh's A Town Garland.

By HENRY S. LEIGH, Author of "Carols of Cockayne."

"*If Mr. Leigh's verse survive to a future generation—and there is no reason why that honour should not be accorded productions so delicate, so finished, and so full of humour—their author will probably be remembered as the Poet of the Strand. . . . Very whimsically does Mr. Leigh treat the subjects which commend themselves to him. His verse is always admirable in rhythm, and his rhymes are happy enough to deserve a place by the best of Barham. . . . The entire contents of the volume are equally noteworthy for humour and for daintiness of workmanship.*"—ATHENÆUM.

SECOND EDITION.—Crown 8vo, cloth extra, with Illustrations, 10s. 6d.

Leisure-Time Studies, chiefly Biological.

By ANDREW WILSON, Ph.D., Lecturer on Zoology and Comparative Anatomy in the Edinburgh Medical School.

"*It is well when we can take up the work of a really qualified investigator, who in the intervals of his more serious professional labours sets himself to impart knowledge in such a simple and elementary form as may attract and instruct, with no danger of misleading the tyro in natural science. Such a work is this little volume, made up of essays and addresses written and delivered by Dr. Andrew Wilson, lecturer and examiner in science at Edinburgh and Glasgow, at leisure intervals in a busy professional life. . . . Dr. Wilson's pages teem with matter stimulating to a healthy love of science and a reverence for the truths of nature.*"—SATURDAY REVIEW.

Crown 8vo, cloth extra, with Illustrations, 7s. 6d.

Life in London;

or, The History of Jerry Hawthorn and Corinthian Tom. With the whole of CRUIKSHANK'S Illustrations, in Colours, after the Originals.

Crown 8vo, cloth extra, 6s.

Lights on the Way:

Some Tales within a Tale. By the late J. H. ALEXANDER, B.A. Edited, with an Explanatory Note, by H. A. PAGE, Author of "Thoreau: A Study."

Crown 8vo, cloth extra, with Illustrations, 7s. 6d.

Longfellow's Complete Prose Works.

Including "Outre Mer," "Hyperion," "Kavanagh," "The Poets and Poetry of Europe," and "Driftwood." With Portrait and Illustrations by VALENTINE BROMLEY.

Crown 8vo, cloth extra, gilt, with Illustrations, 7s. 6d.

Longfellow's Poetical Works.

Carefully Reprinted from the Original Editions. With numerous fine Illustrations on Steel and Wood.

Crown 8vo, cloth extra, 5s.

Lunatic Asylum, My Experiences in a.

By a SANE PATIENT.

"*The story is clever and interesting, sad beyond measure though the subject be. There is no personal bitterness, and no violence or anger. Whatever may have been the evidence for our author's madness when he was consigned to an asylum, nothing can be clearer than his sanity when he wrote this book; it is bright, calm, and to the point.*"—SPECTATOR.

Demy 8vo, with Fourteen full-page Plates, cloth boards, 18s.

Lusiad (The) of Camoens.

Translated into English Spenserian verse by ROBERT FFRENCH DUFF, Knight Commander of the Portuguese Royal Order of Christ.

Macquoid (Mrs.), Works by:

In the Ardennes. By KATHARINE S. MACQUOID. With numerous fine Illustrations by THOMAS R. MACQUOID. Uniform with "Pictures and Legends." Sq. 8vo, cloth extra, 10s. 6d. [*In preparation.*]

Pictures and Legends from Normandy and Brittany. By KATHARINE S. MACQUOID. With numerous Illustrations by THOMAS R. MACQUOID. Square 8vo, cloth gilt, 10s. 6d.

"*Mr. and Mrs. Macquoid have been strolling in Normandy and Brittany, and the result of their observations and researches in that picturesque land of romantic associations is an attractive volume, which is neither a work of travel nor a collection of stories, but a book partaking almost in equal degree of each of these characters. . . . The illustrations, which are numerous are drawn, as a rule, with remarkable delicacy as well as with true artistic feeling.*"—DAILY NEWS.

Through Normandy. By KATHARINE S. MACQUOID. With 90 Illustrations by T. R. MACQUOID. Square 8vo, cloth extra, 7s. 6d.

"*One of the few books which can be read as a piece of literature, whilst at the same time handy in the knapsack.*"—BRITISH QUARTERLY REVIEW.

Through Brittany. By KATHARINE S. MACQUOID. With numerous Illustrations by THOMAS R. MACQUOID. Square 8vo, cloth extra, 7s. 6d.

"*The pleasant companionship which Mrs. Macquoid offers, while wandering from one point of interest to another, seems to throw a renewed charm around each oft-depicted scene.*"—MORNING POST.

Crown 8vo, cloth extra, with Illustrations, 2s. 6d.

Madre Natura v. The Moloch of Fashion.

By LUKE LIMNER. With 32 Illustrations by the Author. FOURTH EDITION, revised and enlarged.

Handsomely printed in facsimile, price 5s.

Magna Charta.

An exact Facsimile of the Original Document in the British Museum, printed on fine plate paper, nearly 3 feet long by 2 feet wide, with the Arms and Seals emblazoned in Gold and Colours.

Small 8vo, 1s.; cloth extra, 1s. 6d.

Milton's The Hygiene of the Skin.

A Concise Set of Rules for the Management of the Skin; with Directions for Diet, Wines, Soaps, Baths, &c. By J. L. MILTON, Senior Surgeon to St. John's Hospital.

BY THE SAME AUTHOR.

The Bath in Diseases of the Skin. Sm. 8vo, 1s.; cl. extra, 1s. 6d.

Mallock's (W. H.) Works:

Is Life Worth Living? By WILLIAM HURRELL MALLOCK.
Demy 8vo, cloth extra, 12s. 6d.

"*This deeply interesting volume. . . . . It is the most powerful vindication of religion, both natural and revealed, that has appeared since Bishop Butler wrote, and is much more useful than either the Analogy or the Sermons of that great divine, as a refutation of the peculiar form assumed by the infidelity of the present day. . . . . Deeply philosophical as the book is, there is not a heavy page in it. The writer is 'possessed,' so to speak, with his great subject, has sounded its depths, surveyed it in all its extent, and brought to bear on it all the resources of a vivid, rich, and impassioned style, at well as an adequate acquaintance with the science, the philosophy, and the literature of the day.*"—IRISH DAILY NEWS.

The New Republic; or, Culture, Faith, and Philosophy in an English Country House. By WILLIAM HURRELL MALLOCK. Crown 8vo, cloth extra, 6s. Also a CHEAP EDITION, in the "Mayfair Library," at 2s. 6d.

The New Paul and Virginia; or, Positivism on an Island. By WILLIAM HURRELL MALLOCK. Crown 8vo, cloth extra, 3s. 6d. Also a CHEAP EDITION, in the "Mayfair Library," at 2s. 6d.

Poems. By W. H. MALLOCK. Small 4to, bound in parchment, 8s.

Mark Twain's Works:

The Choice Works of Mark Twain. Revised and Corrected throughout by the Author. With Life, Portrait, and numerous Illustrations. Crown 8vo, cloth extra, 7s. 6d.

The Adventures of Tom Sawyer. By MARK TWAIN. With One Hundred Illustrations. Small 8vo, cloth extra, 7s. 6d. CHEAP EDITION, Illustrated boards, 2s.

A Pleasure Trip on the Continent of Europe: The Innocents Abroad, and The New Pilgrim's Progress. By MARK TWAIN. Post 8vo, illustrated boards, 2s.

An Idle Excursion, and other Sketches. By MARK TWAIN. Post 8vo, illustrated boards, 2s.

A Tramp Abroad. By MARK TWAIN. With 314 Illustrations. Crown 8vo, cloth extra, 7s. 6d.

"*The fun and tenderness of the conception, of which no living man but Mark Twain is capable, its grace and fantasy and slyness, the wonderful feeling for animals that is manifest in every line, make of all this episode of Jim Baker and his jays a piece of work that is not only delightful at mere reading, but also of a high degree of merit as literature. . . . The book is full of good things, and contains passages and episodes that are equal to the funniest of those that have gone before.*"—ATHENÆUM.

Post 8vo, cloth limp, 2s. 6d. per vol.

Mayfair Library, The:

The New Republic. By W. H. MALLOCK.

The New Paul and Virginia. By W. H. MALLOCK.

The True History of Joshua Davidson. By E. LYNN LINTON.

Old Stories Re-told. By WALTER THORNBURY.

Thoreau: His Life and Aims. By H. A. PAGE.

By Stream and Sea. By WILLIAM SENIOR.

Jeux d'Esprit. Edited by HENRY S. LEIGH.

Puniana. By the Hon. HUGH ROWLEY.

More Puniana. By the Hon. HUGH ROWLEY.

Puck on Pegasus. By H. CHOLMONDELEY-PENNELL.

Muses of Mayfair. Edited by H. CHOLMONDELEY-PENNELL.

Gastronomy as a Fine Art. By BRILLAT-SAVARIN.

Original Plays. By W. S. GILBERT.

Carols of Cockayne. By HENRY S. LEIGH.

. *Other Volumes are in preparation.*

New Novels.

NEW NOVEL BY MRS. LYNN LINTON.

WITH A SILKEN THREAD, and other Stories. By E. LYNN LINTON. Three Vols., crown 8vo.

OUIDA'S NEW NOVEL.

PIPISTRELLO, and other Stories. By OUIDA. Crown 8vo, cloth extra, 10s. 6d.

CHARLES GIBBON'S NEW NOVEL.

IN PASTURES GREEN, and other Stories. By CHARLES GIBBON. Crown 8vo, cloth extra, 10s. 6d. [In the press.

NEW AND CHEAPER EDITION, crown 8vo, cloth extra, 3s. 6d.

UNDER ONE ROOF. By JAMES PAYN.

NEW AND CHEAPER EDITION, crown 8vo, cloth extra, 3s. 6d.

THE SEAMY SIDE. By the Authors of "The Golden Butterfly," "The Monks of Thelema," &c.

NEW NOVEL BY JULIAN HAWTHORNE.

ELLICE QUENTIN, and other Stories. By JULIAN HAWTHORNE. Two Vols., crown 8vo. [Nearly ready.

MR. FRANCILLON'S NEW NOVEL.

QUEEN COPHETUA. By R. E. FRANCILLON. Three Vols., crown 8vo. [In preparation.

JAMES PAYN'S NEW NOVEL.

A CONFIDENTIAL AGENT. By JAMES PAYN. With 12 Illustrations by ARTHUR HOPKINS. Three Vols., crown 8vo. [In preparation.

MRS. HUNT'S NEW NOVEL.

THE LEADEN CASKET. By Mrs. ALFRED W. HUNT. Three Vols., crown 8vo. [In preparation.

NEW NOVEL BY MRS. LINTON.

THE REBEL OF THE FAMILY. By E. LYNN LINTON. Three Vols., crown 8vo. [In preparation.

Small 8vo, cloth limp, with Illustrations, 2s. 6d.

Miller's Physiology for the Young;

Or, The House of Life: Human Physiology, with its Applications to the Preservation of Health. For use in Classes and Popular Reading. With numerous Illustrations. By Mrs. F. FENWICK MILLER.

"*An admirable introduction to a subject which all who value health and enjoy life should have at their fingers' ends.*"—ECHO.

Square 8vo, cloth extra, with numerous Illustrations, 9s.

North Italian Folk.

By Mrs. COMYNS CARR. Illustrated by RANDOLPH CALDECOTT.

"*A delightful book, of a kind which is far too rare. If anyone wants to really know the North Italian folk, we can honestly advise him to omit the journey, and sit down to read Mrs. Carr's pages instead. . . . Description with Mrs. Carr is a real gift. . . . It is rarely that a book is so happily illustrated.*"—CONTEMPORARY REVIEW.

Crown 8vo, cloth extra, with Vignette Portraits, price 6s. per Vol.

Old Dramatists, The:

Ben Jonson's Works.
With Notes, Critical and Explanatory, and a Biographical Memoir by WILLIAM GIFFORD. Edited by Colonel CUNNINGHAM. Three Vols.

Chapman's Works.
Now First Collected. Complete in Three Vols. Vol. I. contains the Plays complete, including the doubtful ones; Vol. II. the Poems and Minor Translations, with an Introductory Essay

by ALGERNON CHARLES SWINBURNE. Vol. III. the Translations of the Iliad and Odyssey.

Marlowe's Works.
Including his Translations. Edited, with Notes and Introduction, by Col. CUNNINGHAM. One Vol.

Massinger's Plays.
From the Text of WILLIAM GIFFORD. With the addition of the Tragedy of "Believe as you List." Edited by Col. CUNNINGHAM. One Vol.

Crown 8vo, red cloth extra, 5s. each.

Ouida's Novels.—Library Edition.

Held in Bondage.	By OUIDA.	Dog of Flanders.	By OUIDA.
Strathmore.	By OUIDA.	Pascarel.	By OUIDA.
Chandos.	By OUIDA.	Two Wooden Shoes.	By OUIDA.
Under Two Flags.	By OUIDA.	Signa.	By OUIDA.
Idalia.	By OUIDA.	In a Winter City.	By OUIDA.
Cecil Castlemaine.	By OUIDA.	Ariadne.	By OUIDA.
Tricotrin.	By OUIDA.	Friendship.	By OUIDA.
Puck.	By OUIDA.	Moths.	By OUIDA.
Folle Farine.	By OUIDA.		

, Also a Cheap Edition of all but the last, post 8vo, illustrated boards, at 2s. each.

Post 8vo, cloth limp, 1s. 6d.

Parliamentary Procedure, A Popular Handbook of. By HENRY W. LUCY.

Crown 8vo, cloth extra, with Portrait and Illustrations, 7s. 6d.

Poe's Choice Prose and Poetical Works.

With BAUDELAIRE'S "Essay."

Crown 8vo, carefully printed on creamy paper, and tastefully bound
in cloth for the Library, price 3*s*. 6*d*. each.

Piccadilly Novels, The.
Popular Stories by the Best Authors.

READY-MONEY MORTIBOY. By W. BESANT and JAMES RICE.

MY LITTLE GIRL. By W. BESANT and JAMES RICE.

THE CASE OF MR. LUCRAFT. By W. BESANT and JAMES RICE.

THIS SON OF VULCAN. By W. BESANT and JAMES RICE.

WITH HARP AND CROWN. By W. BESANT and JAMES RICE.

THE GOLDEN BUTTERFLY. By W. BESANT and JAMES RICE.
With a Frontispiece by F. S. WALKER.

BY CELIA'S ARBOUR. By W. BESANT and JAMES RICE.

THE MONKS OF THELEMA. By W. BESANT and JAMES RICE.

TWAS IN TRAFALGAR'S BAY. By W. BESANT & JAMES RICE.

THE SEAMY SIDE. By WALTER BESANT and JAMES RICE.

ANTONINA. By WILKIE COLLINS. Illustrated by Sir J. GILBERT
and ALFRED CONCANEN.

BASIL. By WILKIE COLLINS. Illustrated by Sir JOHN GILBERT
and J. MAHONEY.

HIDE AND SEEK. By WILKIE COLLINS. Illustrated by Sir
JOHN GILBERT and J. MAHONEY.

THE DEAD SECRET. By WILKIE COLLINS. Illustrated by Sir
JOHN GILBERT and H. FURNISS.

QUEEN OF HEARTS. By WILKIE COLLINS. Illustrated by Sir
JOHN GILBERT and A. CONCANEN.

MY MISCELLANIES. By WILKIE COLLINS. With Steel Portrait, and Illustrations by A. CONCANEN.

THE WOMAN IN WHITE. By WILKIE COLLINS. Illustrated
by Sir J. GILBERT and F. A. FRASER.

THE MOONSTONE. By WILKIE COLLINS. Illustrated by G.
DU MAURIER and F. A. FRASER.

MAN AND WIFE. By WILKIE COLLINS. Illust. by WM. SMALL.

POOR MISS FINCH. By WILKIE COLLINS. Illustrated by G.
DU MAURIER and EDWARD HUGHES.

MISS OR MRS. P By WILKIE COLLINS. Illustrated by S. L.
FILDES and HENRY WOODS.

THE NEW MAGDALEN. By WILKIE COLLINS. Illustrated by
G. DU MAURIER and C. S. REINHART.

THE FROZEN DEEP. By WILKIE COLLINS. Illustrated by G.
DU MAURIER and J. MAHONEY.

THE LAW AND THE LADY. By WILKIE COLLINS. Illustrated by S. L. FILDES and SYDNEY HALL.

PICCADILLY NOVELS—*continued.*

THE TWO DESTINIES. By WILKIE COLLINS.

THE HAUNTED HOTEL. By WILKIE COLLINS. Illustrated by ARTHUR HOPKINS.

THE FALLEN LEAVES. By WILKIE COLLINS.

DECEIVERS EVER. By Mrs. H. LOVETT CAMERON.

JULIET'S GUARDIAN. By Mrs. H. LOVETT CAMERON. Illustrated by VALENTINE BROMLEY.

FELICIA. By M. BETHAM-EDWARDS. Frontispiece by W. BOWLES.

OLYMPIA. By R. E. FRANCILLON.

GARTH. By JULIAN HAWTHORNE.

IN LOVE AND WAR. By CHARLES GIBBON.

WHAT WILL THE WORLD SAY? By CHARLES GIBBON.

FOR THE KING. By CHARLES GIBBON.

IN HONOUR BOUND. By CHARLES GIBBON.

UNDER THE GREENWOOD TREE. By THOMAS HARDY.

THORNICROFT'S MODEL. By Mrs. A. W. HUNT.

FATED TO BE FREE. By JEAN INGELOW.

THE QUEEN OF CONNAUGHT. By HARRIETT JAY.

THE DARK COLLEEN. By HARRIETT JAY.

NUMBER SEVENTEEN. By HENRY KINGSLEY.

OAKSHOTT CASTLE. By HENRY KINGSLEY. With a Frontispiece by SHIRLEY HODSON.

THE WORLD WELL LOST. By E. LYNN LINTON. Illustrated by J. LAWSON and HENRY FRENCH.

THE ATONEMENT OF LEAM DUNDAS. By E. LYNN LINTON. With a Frontispiece by HENRY WOODS.

PATRICIA KEMBALL. By E. LYNN LINTON. With a Frontispiece by G. DU MAURIER.

THE WATERDALE NEIGHBOURS. By JUSTIN McCARTHY.

MY ENEMY'S DAUGHTER. By JUSTIN McCARTHY.

LINLEY ROCHFORD. By JUSTIN McCARTHY.

A FAIR SAXON. By JUSTIN McCARTHY.

DEAR LADY DISDAIN. By JUSTIN McCARTHY.

MISS MISANTHROPE. By JUSTIN McCARTHY. Illustrated by ARTHUR HOPKINS.

LOST ROSE. By KATHARINE S. MACQUOID.

THE EVIL EYE, and other Stories. By KATHARINE S. MACQUOID. Illustrated by THOMAS R. MACQUOID and PERCY MACQUOID.

PICCADILLY NOVELS—*continued*.

OPEN! SESAME! By FLORENCE MARRYAT. Illustrated by F. A. FRASER.

TOUCH AND GO. By JEAN MIDDLEMASS.

WHITELADIES. By Mrs. OLIPHANT. With Illustrations by A. Hopkins and H. Woods.

THE BEST OF HUSBANDS. By JAMES PAYN. Illustrated by J. Moyr Smith.

FALLEN FORTUNES. By JAMES PAYN.

HALVES. By JAMES PAYN. With a Frontispiece by J. MAHONEY.

WALTER'S WORD. By JAMES PAYN. Illust. by J. MOYR SMITH.

WHAT HE COST HER. By JAMES PAYN.

LESS BLACK THAN WE'RE PAINTED. By JAMES PAYN.

BY PROXY. By JAMES PAYN. Illustrated by ARTHUR HOPKINS.

UNDER ONE ROOF. By JAMES PAYN.

HER MOTHER'S DARLING. By Mrs. J. H. RIDDELL.

BOUND TO THE WHEEL. By JOHN SAUNDERS.

GUY WATERMAN. By JOHN SAUNDERS.

ONE AGAINST THE WORLD. By JOHN SAUNDERS.

THE LION IN THE PATH. By JOHN SAUNDERS.

THE WAY WE LIVE NOW. By ANTHONY TROLLOPE. Illust.

THE AMERICAN SENATOR. By ANTHONY TROLLOPE.

DIAMOND CUT DIAMOND. By T. A. TROLLOPE.

Post 8vo, illustrated boards, 2s. each.

Popular Novels, Cheap Editions of

[WILKIE COLLINS' NOVELS and BESANT and RICE'S NOVELS may also be had in cloth limp at 2s. 6d. *See, too, the* PICCADILLY NOVELS, *for Library Editions*.]

Maid, Wife, or Widow? By Mrs. ALEXANDER.

Ready-Money Mortiboy. By WALTER BESANT and JAMES RICE.

The Golden Butterfly. By Authors of " Ready-Money Mortiboy."

This Son of Vulcan. By the same.

My Little Girl. By the same.

The Case of Mr. Lucraft. By Authors of "Ready-Money Mortiboy."

With Harp and Crown. By Authors of "Ready-Money Mortiboy."

The Monks of Thelema. By WALTER BESANT and JAMES RICE.

By Celia's Arbour. By WALTER BESANT and JAMES RICE.

'Twas in Trafalgar's Bay. By WALTER BESANT and JAMES RICE.

Juliet's Guardian. By Mrs. H. LOVETT CAMERON.

Surly Tim. By F. H. BURNETT.

The Cure of Souls. By MACLAREN COBBAN.

The Woman in White. By WILKIE COLLINS.

Antonina. By WILKIE COLLINS.

Basil. By WILKIE COLLINS.

Hide and Seek. By the same.

POPULAR NOVELS—*continued.*

The Queen of Hearts. By WILKIE COLLINS.

The Dead Secret. By the same.

My Miscellanies. By the same.

The Moonstone. By the same.

Man and Wife. By the same.

Poor Miss Finch. By the same.

Miss or Mrs. ? By the same.

The New Magdalen. By the same.

The Frozen Deep. By the same.

The Law and the Lady. By WILKIE COLLINS.

The Two Destinies. By WILKIE COLLINS.

The Haunted Hotel. By WILKIE COLLINS.

Roxy. By EDWARD EGGLESTON.

Felicia. M. DETHAM-EDWARDS.

Filthy Lucre. By ALBANY DE FONBLANQUE.

Olympia. By R. E. FRANCILLON.

Dick Temple. By JAMES GREENWOOD.

Under the Greenwood Tree. By THOMAS HARDY.

An Heiress of Red Dog. By BRET HARTE.

The Luck of Roaring Camp. By BRET HARTE.

Gabriel Conroy. BRET HARTE.

Fated to be Free. By JEAN INGELOW.

Confidence. By HENRY JAMES, Jun.

The Queen of Connaught. By HARRIETT JAY.

The Dark Colleen. By HARRIETT JAY.

Number Seventeen. By HENRY KINGSLEY.

Oakshott Castle. By the same.

Patricia Kemball. By E. LYNN LINTON.

The Atonement of Leam Dundas. By E. LYNN LINTON.

The World Well Lost. By E. LYNN LINTON.

The Waterdale Neighbours. By JUSTIN McCARTHY.

My Enemy's Daughter. By JUSTIN McCARTHY.

Linley Rochford. By the same.

A Fair Saxon. By the same.

Dear Lady Disdain. By the same.

Miss Misanthrope. By JUSTIN McCARTHY.

Lost Rose. By KATHARINE S. MACQUOID.

The Evil Eye. By KATHARINE S. MACQUOID.

Open! Sesame! By FLORENCE MARRYAT.

Whiteladies. Mrs. OLIPHANT.

Held in Bondage. By OUIDA.

Strathmore. By OUIDA.

Chandos. By OUIDA.

Under Two Flags. By OUIDA.

Idalia. By OUIDA.

Cecil Castlemaine. By OUIDA.

Tricotrin. By OUIDA.

Puck. By OUIDA.

Folle Farine. By OUIDA.

Dog of Flanders. By OUIDA.

Pascarel. By OUIDA.

Two Little Wooden Shoes. By OUIDA.

Signa. By OUIDA.

In a Winter City. By OUIDA.

Ariadne. By OUIDA.

Fallen Fortunes. By J. PAYN.

Halves. By JAMES PAYN.

What He Cost Her. By ditto.

By Proxy. By JAMES PAYN.

Less Black than We're Painted. By JAMES PAYN.

The Best of Husbands. By JAMES PAYN.

POPULAR NOVELS—*continued.*

Walter's Word. By J. PAYN.

The Mystery of Marie Roget. By EDGAR A. POE.

Her Mother's Darling. By Mrs. J. H. RIDDELL.

Gaslight and Daylight. By GEORGE AUGUSTUS SALA.

Bound to the Wheel. By JOHN SAUNDERS.

Guy Waterman. J. SAUNDERS.

One Against the World. By JOHN SAUNDERS.

The Lion in the Path. By JOHN and KATHERINE SAUNDERS.

Tales for the Marines. By WALTER THORNBURY.

The Way we Live Now. By ANTHONY TROLLOPE.

The American Senator. By ANTHONY TROLLOPE.

Diamond Cut Diamond. By T. A. TROLLOPE.

An Idle Excursion. By MARK TWAIN.

Adventures of Tom Sawyer. By MARK TWAIN.

A Pleasure Trip on the Continent of Europe. By MARK TWAIN.

Fcap. 8vo, picture covers, 1s. each.

Jeff Briggs's Love Story. By BRET HARTE.

The Twins of Table Mountain. By BRET HARTE.

Mrs. Gainsborough's Diamonds. By JULIAN HAWTHORNE.

Kathleen Mavourneen. By the Author of "That Lass o' Lowrie's."

Lindsay's Luck. By the Author of "That Lass o' Lowrie's."

Pretty Polly Pemberton. By Author of "That Lass o' Lowrie's."

Trooping with Crows. By Mrs. PIRKIS.

Two Vols. 8vo, cloth extra, with Illustrations, 10s. 6d.

Plutarch's Lives of Illustrious Men.

Translated from the Greek, with Notes, Critical and Historical, and a Life of Plutarch, by JOHN and WILLIAM LANGHORNE. New Edition, with Medallion Portraits.

Crown 8vo, cloth extra, 7s. 6d.

Primitive Manners and Customs.

By JAMES A. FARRER.

"A book which is really both instructive and amusing, and which will open a new field of thought to many readers."—ATHENÆUM.

"An admirable example of the application of the scientific method and the working of the truly scientific spirit."—SATURDAY REVIEW.

Small 8vo, cloth extra, with Illustrations, 3s. 6d.

Prince of Argolis, The:

A Story of the Old Greek Fairy Time. By J. MOYR SMITH. With 130 Illustrations by the Author.

Crown 8vo, cloth extra, with Portrait and Facsimile, 7s. 6d.

Prout (Father), The Final Reliques of.

Collected and Edited, from MSS. supplied by the family of the Rev. FRANCIS MAHONY, by BLANCHARD JERROLD.

Proctor's (R. A.) Works:

Easy Star Lessons for Young Learners. With Star Maps for Every Night in the Year, Drawings of the Constellations, &c. By RICHARD A. PROCTOR. Crown 8vo, cloth extra, 6s. *[In preparation.*

Myths and Marvels of Astronomy. By RICH. A. PROCTOR, Author of "Other Worlds than Ours," &c. Demy 8vo, cloth extra, 18s. 6d.

Pleasant Ways in Science. By RICHARD A. PROCTOR. Crown 8vo, cloth extra, 10s. 6d.

Rough Ways made Smooth: A Series of Familiar Essays on Scientific Subjects. By R. A. PROCTOR. Crown 8vo, cloth, 10s. 6d.

Our Place among Infinities: A Series of Essays contrasting our Little Abode in Space and Time with the Infinities Around us. By RICHARD A. PROCTOR. Crown 8vo, cloth extra, 6s.

The Expanse of Heaven: A Series of Essays on the Wonders of the Firmament. By RICHARD A. PROCTOR. Crown 8vo, cloth, 6s.

Wages and Wants of Science Workers. Showing the Resources of Science as a Vocation, and Discussing the Scheme for their Increase out of the National Exchequer. By RICHARD A. PROCTOR. Crown 8vo, 1s. 6d.

"Mr. Proctor, of all writers of our time, best conforms to Matthew Arnold's conception of a man of culture, in that he strives to humanise knowledge and divest it of whatever is harsh, crude, or technical, and so makes it a source of happiness and brightness for all."—WESTMINSTER REVIEW.

Crown 8vo, cloth extra, gilt, 7s. 6d.

Pursuivant of Arms, The;

or, Heraldry founded upon Facts. A Popular Guide to the Science of Heraldry. By J. R. PLANCHE, Somerset Herald. With Coloured Frontispiece, Plates, and 200 Illustrations.

Crown 8vo, cloth extra, with Illustrations, 7s. 6d.

Rabelais' Works.

Faithfully Translated from the French, with variorum Notes, and numerous characteristic Illustrations by GUSTAVE DORE.

" His buffoonery was not merely Brutus's rough skin, which contained a rod of gold: it was necessary as an amulet against the monks and legates; and he must be classed with the greatest creative minds in the world—with Shakespeare, with Dante, and with Cervantes."—S. T. COLERIDGE.

Crown 8vo, cloth gilt, with numerous Illustrations, and a beautifully executed Chart of the various Spectra, 7s. 6d.

Rambosson's Astronomy.

By J. RAMBOSSON, Laureate of the Institute of France. Translated by C. B. PITMAN. Profusely Illustrated.

Square 8vo, cloth extra, gilt, 10s. 6d.

Rimmer's Our Old Country Towns.

Described by Pen and Pencil. With over 50 Illustrations by ALFRED RIMMER. *[In preparation.*

Crown 8vo, cloth extra, 10s. 6d.

Richardson's (Dr.) A Ministry of Health,
and other Papers. By BENJAMIN WARD RICHARDSON, M.D., &c.

"This highly interesting volume contains upwards of nine addresses, written in the author's well-known style, and full of great and good thoughts. . . . The work is, like all those of the author, that of a man of genius, of great power, of experience, and noble independence of thought."—POPULAR SCIENCE REVIEW.

Handsomely printed, price 5s.

Roll of Battle Abbey, The;
or, A List of the Principal Warriors who came over from Normandy with William the Conqueror, and Settled in this Country, A.D. 1066-7. Printed on fine plate paper, nearly three feet by two, with the principal Arms emblasoned in Gold and Colours.

Two Vols., large 4to, profusely Illustrated, half-morocco, £2 16s.

Rowlandson, the Caricaturist.
A Selection from his Works, with Anecdotal Descriptions of his Famous Caricatures, and a Sketch of his Life, Times, and Contemporaries. With nearly 400 Illustrations, mostly in Facsimile of the Originals. By JOSEPH GREGO, Author of "James Gillray, the Caricaturist; his Life, Works, and Times."

"Mr. Grego's excellent account of the works of Thomas Rowlandson . . . illustrated with some 400 spirited, accurate, and clever transcripts from his designs. . . . The thanks of all who care for what is original and personal in art are due to Mr. Grego for the pains he has been at, and the time he has expended, in the preparation of this very pleasant, very careful, and adequate memorial."—PALL MALL GAZETTE.

Crown 8vo, cloth extra, profusely Illustrated, 4s. 6d. each.

"Secret Out" Series, The.

The Pyrotechnist's Treasury;
or, Complete Art of Making Fireworks. By THOMAS KENTISH. With numerous Illustrations.

The Art of Amusing:
A Collection of Graceful Arts, Games, Tricks, Puzzles, and Charades. By FRANK BELLEW. 300 Illustrations.

Hanky-Panky:
Very Easy Tricks, Very Difficult Tricks, White Magic, Sleight of Hand. Edited by W. H. CREMER. 200 Illustrations.

The Merry Circle:
A Book of New Intellectual Games and Amusements. By CLARA BELLEW. Many Illustrations.

Magician's Own Book:
Performances with Cups and Balls, Eggs, Hats, Handkerchiefs, &c. All from Actual Experience. Edited by W. H. CREMER. 200 Illustrations.

Magic No Mystery:
Tricks with Cards, Dice, Balls, &c., with fully descriptive Directions; the Art of Secret Writing: Training of Performing Animals, &c. Coloured Frontispiece and many Illustrations.

The Secret Out:
One Thousand Tricks with Cards, and other Recreations: with Entertaining Experiments in Drawing-room or "White Magic." By W. H. CREMER. 300 Engravings.

Crown 8vo, cloth extra, 6s.

Senior's Travel and Trout in the Antipodes.

An Angler's Sketches in Tasmania and New Zealand. By WILLIAM
SENIOR ("Red Spinner"), Author of "Stream and Sea."

"*In every way a happy production. . . . What Turner effected in colour on
canvas, Mr. Senior may be said to effect by the force of a practical mind, in language that is magnificently descriptive, on his subject. There is in both painter
and writer the same magical combination of idealism and realism, and the same
hearty appreciation for all that is sublime and pathetic in natural scenery. That
there is an undue share of travel to the number of trout caught is certainly not
Mr. Senior's fault; but the comparative scarcity of the prince of fishes is
adequately atoned for, in that the writer was led pretty well through all the
glorious scenery of the antipodes in quest of him. . . . So great is the charm and
the freshness and the ability of the book, that it is hard to put it down when once
taken up.*"—Home News.

Shakespeare and Shakespeareana :

Shakespeare. The First Folio. Mr. WILLIAM SHAKESPEARE'S
Comedies, Histories, and Tragedies. Published according to the true
Original Copies. London, Printed by ISAAC IAGGARD and ED. BLOUNT,
1623.—A Reproduction of the extremely rare original, in reduced facsimile
by a photographic process—ensuring the strictest accuracy in every detail.
Small 8vo, half-Roxburghe, 10s. 6d.

"*To Messrs. Chatto and Windus belongs the merit of having done more
to facilitate the critical study of the text of our great dramatist than all the
Shakspeare clubs and societies put together. A complete facsimile of the
celebrated First Folio edition of 1623 for half-a-guinea is at once a miracle of
cheapness and enterprise. Being in a reduced form, the type is necessarily
rather diminutive, but it is as distinct as in a genuine copy of the original,
and will be found to be as useful and far more handy to the student than the
latter.*"—ATHENÆUM.

Shakespeare, The Lansdowne. Beautifully printed in red
and black, in small but very clear type. With engraved facsimile of
DROESHOUT's Portrait. Post 8vo, cloth extra, 7s. 6d.

Shakespeare for Children: Tales from Shakespeare. By
CHARLES and MARY LAMB. With numerous Illustrations, coloured and
plain, by J. MOYR SMITH. Crown 4to, cloth gilt, 10s. 6d.

Shakespeare Music, The Handbook of. Being an Account of
Three Hundred and Fifty Pieces of Music, set to Words taken from the
Plays and Poems of Shakespeare, the compositions ranging from the Eliza-
bethan Age to the Present Time. By ALFRED ROFFE. 4to, half-Roxburghe, 7s.

Shakespeare, A Study of. By ALGERNON CHARLES SWIN-
BURNE. Crown 8vo, cloth extra, 8s.

Crown 8vo, cloth extra, gilt, with 10 full-page Tinted Illustrations, 7s. 6d.

Sheridan's Complete Works,

with Life and Anecdotes. Including his Dramatic Writings, printed
from the Original Editions, his Works in Prose and Poetry, Translations, Speeches, Jokes, Puns, &c. ; with a Collection of Sheridaniana.

Crown 8vo, cloth extra, with Illustrations, 7s. 6d.

Signboards:

Their History. With Anecdotes of Famous Taverns and Remarkable Characters. By JACOB LARWOOD and JOHN CAMDEN HOTTEN. With nearly 100 Illustrations.

"*Even if we were ever so maliciously inclined, we could not pick out all Messrs. Larwood and Hotten's plums, because the good things are so numerous as to defy the most wholesale depredation.*"—TIMES.

Crown 8vo, cloth extra, gilt, 6s. 6d.

Slang Dictionary, The:

Etymological, Historical, and Anecdotal. An ENTIRELY NEW EDITION, revised throughout, and considerably Enlarged.

"*We are glad to see the Slang Dictionary reprinted and enlarged. From a high scientific point of view this book is not to be despised. Of course it cannot fail to be amusing also. It contains the very vocabulary of unrestrained humour, and oddity, and grotesqueness. In a word, it provides valuable material both for the student of language and the student of human nature.*"—ACADEMY.

Exquisitely printed in miniature, cloth extra, gilt edges, 2s. 6d.

Smoker's Text-Book, The.

By J. HAMER, F.R.S.L.

Crown 8vo, cloth extra, 5s.

Spalding's Elizabethan Demonology:

An Essay in Illustration of the Belief in the Existence of Devils, and the Powers possessed by them, with Special Reference to Shakspere and his Works. By T. ALFRED SPALDING, LL.B.

"*A very thoughtful and weighty book, which cannot but be welcome to every earnest student.*"—ACADEMY.

Crown 4to, uniform with "Chaucer for Children," with Coloured Illustrations, cloth gilt, 10s. 6d.

Spenser for Children.

By M. H. TOWRY. With Illustrations in Colours by WALTER J. MORGAN.

"*Spenser has simply been transferred into plain prose, with here and there a line or stanza quoted, where the meaning and the diction are within a child's comprehension, and additional point is thus given to the narrative without the cost of obscurity. . . . Altogether the work has been well and carefully done.*"—THE TIMES.

Demy 8vo, cloth extra, Illustrated, 21s.

Sword, The Book of the:

Being a History of the Sword, and its Use, in all Times and in all Countries. By Captain RICHARD BURTON. With numerous Illustrations. [*In preparation.*

Crown 8vo, cloth extra, 9s.

Stedman's Victorian Poets:

Critical Essays. By EDMUND CLARENCE STEDMAN.

*"We ought to be thankful to those who do critical work with competent skill and understanding, with honesty of purpose, and with diligence and thoroughness of execution. And Mr. Stedman, having chosen to work in this line, deserves the thanks of English scholars by these qualities and by something more; . . . . he is faithful, studious, and discerning."—*SATURDAY REVIEW.

Crown 8vo, cloth extra, with Illustrations, 7s. 6d.

Strutt's Sports and Pastimes of the People

of England; Including the Rural and Domestic Recreations, May Games, Mummeries, Shows, Processions, Pageants, and Pompous Spectacles, from the Earliest Period to the Present Time. With 140 Illustrations. Edited by WILLIAM HONE.

Crown 8vo, cloth extra, with Illustrations, 7s. 6d.

Swift's Choice Works,

In Prose and Verse. With Memoir, Portrait, and Facsimiles of the Maps in the Original Edition of "Gulliver's Travels."

Swinburne's Works:

The Queen Mother and Rosamond. Fcap. 8vo, 5s.

Atalanta in Calydon.
A New Edition. Crown 8vo, 6s.

Chastelard.
A Tragedy. Crown 8vo, 7s.

Poems and Ballads.
FIRST SERIES. Fcap. 8vo, 9s. Also in crown 8vo, at same price.

Poems and Ballads.
SECOND SERIES. Fcap. 8vo, 9s. Also in crown 8vo, at same price.

Notes on "Poems and Ballads." 8vo, 1s.

William Blake:
A Critical Essay. With Facsimile Paintings. Demy 8vo, 16s.

Songs before Sunrise.
Crown 8vo, 10s. 6d.

Bothwell:
A Tragedy. Crown 8vo, 12s. 6d.

George Chapman:
An Essay. Crown 8vo, 7s.

Songs of Two Nations.
Crown 8vo, 6s.

Essays and Studies.
Crown 8vo, 12s.

Erechtheus:
A Tragedy. Crown 8vo, 6s.

Note of an English Republican on the Muscovite Crusade. 8vo, 1s.

A Note on Charlotte Brontë.
Crown 8vo, 6s.

A Study of Shakespeare.
Crown 8vo, 8s.

Songs of the Spring-Tides. By ALGERNON C. SWINBURNE. Crown 8vo, cloth extra, 6s.

Medium 8vo, cloth extra, with Illustrations, 7s.

Syntax's (Dr.) Three Tours,

In Search of the Picturesque, in Search of Consolation, and in Search of a Wife. With the whole of ROWLANDSON'S droll page Illustrations, in Colours, and Life of the Author by J. C. HOTTEN.

Four Vols. small 8vo, cloth boards, 30s.

Taine's History of English Literature.

Translated by HENRY VAN LAUN.

.*. Also a POPULAR EDITION, in Two Vols. crown 8vo, cloth extra, 15s.

Crown 8vo, cloth gilt, profusely Illustrated, 6s.

Tales of Old Thule.

Collected and Illustrated by J. MOYR SMITH.

"*It is not often that we meet with a volume of fairy tales possessing more fully the double recommendation of absorbing interest and purity of tone than does the one before us containing a collection of 'Tales of Old Thule. These come, to say the least, near fulfilling the idea of perfect works of the kind; and the illustrations with which the volume is embellished are equally excellent. . . . We commend the book to parents and teachers as an admirable gift to their children and pupils.*"—LITERARY WORLD.

One Vol. crown 8vo, cloth extra, 7s. 6d.

Taylor's (Tom) Historical Dramas:

"Clancarty," "Jeanne Darc," "Twixt Axe and Crown," "The Fool's Revenge," "Arkwright's Wife," "Anne Boleyn," "Plot and Passion."

.*. The Plays may also be had separately, at 1s. each.

Crown 8vo, cloth extra, with Coloured Frontispiece and numerous
Illustrations, 7s. 6d.

Thackerayana:

Notes and Anecdotes. Illustrated by a profusion of Sketches by WILLIAM MAKEPEACE THACKERAY, depicting Humorous Incidents in his School-life, and Favourite Characters in the books of his everyday reading. With Hundreds of Wood Engravings, facsimiled from Mr. Thackeray's Original Drawings.

"*It would have been a real loss to bibliographical literature had copyright difficulties deprived the general public of this very amusing collection. One of Thackeray's habits, from his schoolboy days, was to ornament the margins and blank pages of the books he had in use with caricature illustrations of their contents. This gave special value to the sale of his library, and is almost cause for regret that it could not have been preserved in its integrity. Thackeray's place in literature is eminent enough to have made this an interest to future generations. The anonymous editor has done the best that he could to compensate for the lack of this. It is an admirable addendum, not only to his collected works, but also to any memoir of him that has been, or that is likely to be, written.*"—BRITISH QUARTERLY REVIEW.

Crown 8vo, cloth extra, with numerous Illustrations, 7s. 6d.

Thornbury's (Walter) Haunted London.

A New Edition, edited by EDWARD WALFORD, M.A., with numerous Illustrations by F. W. FAIRHOLT, F.S.A.

"*Mr. Thornbury knew and loved his London. . . . He had read much history, and every by-lane and every court had associations for him. His memory and his note-books were stored with anecdote, and, as he had singular skill in the matter of narration, it will be readily believed that when he took to writing a set book about the places he knew and cared for, the said book would be charming. Charming the volume before us certainly is. It may be begun in the beginning, or middle, or end, it is all one: wherever one lights, there is some pleasant and curious bit of gossip, some amusing fragment of allusion or quotation.*"—VANITY FAIR.

Crown 8vo, cloth extra, gilt edges, with Illustrations, 7s. 6d.

Thomson's Seasons and Castle of Indolence.

With a Biographical and Critical Introduction by ALLAN CUNNING-
HAM, and over 50 fine Illustrations on Steel and Wood.

Crown 8vo, cloth extra, with Illustrations, 7s. 6d.

Timbs' Clubs and Club Life in London.

With Anecdotes of its famous Coffee-houses, Hostelries, and Taverns.
By JOHN TIMBS, F.S.A. With numerous Illustrations.

Crown 8vo, cloth extra, with Illustrations, 7s. 6d.

Timbs' English Eccentrics and Eccentrici-

ties: Stories of Wealth and Fashion, Delusions, Impostures, and
Fanatic Missions, Strange Sights and Sporting Scenes, Eccentric
Artists, Theatrical Folks, Men of Letters, &c. By JOHN TIMBS,
F.S.A. With nearly 50 Illustrations.

Demy 8vo, cloth extra, 14s.

Torrens' The Marquess Wellesley,

Architect of Empire. An Historic Portrait. *Forming Vol. I. of* PRO-
CONSUL and TRIBUNE: WELLESLEY and O'CONNELL: Historic
Portraits. By W. M. TORRENS, M.P. In Two Vols.

Crown 8vo, cloth extra, with Coloured Illustrations, 7s. 6d.

Turner's (J. M. W.) Life and Correspondence.

Founded upon Letters and Papers furnished by his Friends and fellow-
Academicians. By WALTER THORNBURY. A New Edition, considerably Enlarged. With numerous Illustrations in Colours, facsimiled
from Turner's original Drawings.

Two Vols., crown 8vo, cloth extra, with Map and Ground Plans, 14s.

Walcott's Church Work and Life in English

Minsters; and the English Student's Monasticon. By the Rev.
MACKENZIE E. C. WALCOTT, B.D.

Large crown 8vo, cloth antique, with Illustrations, 7s. 6d.

Walton and Cotton's Complete Angler;

or, The Contemplative Man's Recreation; being a Discourse of Rivers,
Fishponds, Fish and Fishing, written by IZAAK WALTON; and In-
structions how to Angle for a Trout or Grayling in a clear Stream, by
CHARLES COTTON. With Original Memoirs and Notes by Sir HARRIS
NICOLAS, and 61 Copperplate Illustrations.

Carefully printed on paper to imitate the Original, 22 in. by 14 in., 2s.

Warrant to Execute Charles I.

An exact Facsimile of this important Document, with the Fifty-nine
Signatures of the Regicides, and corresponding Seals,

20th Annual Edition, for 1880, cloth, full gilt, 50s.

Walford's County Families of the United

Kingdom. A Royal Manual of the Titled and Untitled Aristocracy of Great Britain and Ireland. By EDWARD WALFORD, M.A., late Scholar of Balliol College, Oxford. Containing Notices of the Descent, Birth, Marriage, Education, &c., of more than 12,000 distinguished Heads of Families in the United Kingdom, their Heirs Apparent or Presumptive, together with a Record of the Patronage at their disposal, the Offices which they hold or have held, their Town Addresses, Country Residences, Clubs, &c.

Beautifully printed on paper to imitate the Original MS., price 2s.

Warrant to Execute Mary Queen of Scots.

An exact Facsimile, including the Signature of Queen Elizabeth, and a Facsimile of the Great Seal.

Crown 8vo, cloth limp, with numerous Illustrations, 4s. 6d.

Westropp's Handbook of Pottery and Porce-

lain; or, History of those Arts from the Earliest Period. By HODDER M. WESTROPP, Author of "Handbook of Archaeology," &c. With numerous beautiful Illustrations, and a List of Marks.

SEVENTH EDITION. Square 8vo, 1s.

Whistler v. Ruskin: Art and Art Critics.

By J. A. MACNEILL WHISTLER.

Crown 8vo, cloth extra, with Illustrations, 4s. 6d.

Williams' A Simple Treatise on Heat.

By W. MATTIEU WILLIAMS, F.R.A.S., F.C.S., Author of "The Fuel of the Sun, &c. With numerous Illustrations.   [*In the press.*

Crown 8vo, cloth extra, with Illustrations, 7s. 6d.

Wright's Caricature History of the Georges.

(The House of Hanover.) With 400 Pictures, Caricatures, Squibs, Broadsides, Window Pictures, &c. By THOMAS WRIGHT, M.A., F.S.A.

Large post 8vo, cloth extra, gilt, with Illustrations, 7s. 6d.

Wright's History of Caricature and of the

Grotesque in Art, Literature, Sculpture, and Painting, from the Earliest Times to the Present Day. By THOMAS WRIGHT, M.A., F.S.A. Profusely Illustrated by F. W. FAIRHOLT, F.S.A.

J. OGDEN AND CO., PRINTERS, 172, ST. JOHN STREET, E.C.

www.ingramcontent.com/pod-product-compliance
Lightning Source LLC
Chambersburg PA
CBHW021927110726
47901CB00003B/747